Ekaterina Sedia is the author of *The House of Discarded Dreams*, *The Secret History of Moscow*, and *The Alchemy of Stone*. She is also the editor of such anthologies as *Paper Cities: An Anthology of Urban Fantasy*, *Running with the Pack*, *Bewere the Night*, and *Bloody Fabulous*. Sedia was born and raised in Moscow, and currently lives in New Jersey with her family. You can visit her online at www.ekaterinasedia.com.

The Mammoth Book of

Gaslit Romance

Edited by Ekaterina Sedia

ROBINSON

RUNNING PRESS
PHILADELPHIA · LONDON

ROBINSON

First published in Great Britain in 2014 by Robinson

A CIP catalogue record for this book
is available from the British Library.

ISBN 978-1-47211-164-7 (paperback)
ISBN 978-1-47211-169-2 (ebook)

Typeset in Plantin Light by Hewer Text UK Ltd, Edinburgh
Printed and bound by CPI Group (UK) Ltd, Croydon, CR0 4YY

Robinson
is an imprint of
Constable & Robinson Ltd
100 Victoria Embankment
London EC4Y 0DY

An Hachette UK Company
www.hachette.co.uk

www.constablerobinson.com

First published in the United States in 2014 by Running Press Book Publishers,
A Member of the Perseus Books Group

Books published by Running Press are available at special discounts for bulk
purchases in the United States by corporations, institutions and other organizations.
For more information, please contact the Special Markets Department at the
Perseus Books Group, 2300 Chestnut Street, Suite 200, Philadelphia, PA 19103,
or call (800) 810-4145, ext. 5000, or email special.markets@perseusbooks.com.

US ISBN: 978-0-7624-5467-9
US Library of Congress Control Number: 2013953115

9 8 7 6 5 4 3 2 1
Digit on the right indicates the number of this printing
Running Press Book Publishers
2300 Chestnut Street
Philadelphia, PA 19103-4371

Visit us on the web!
www.runningpress.com

ACKNOWLEDGEMENTS

Born in England, **Mary Elizabeth Braddon** was a prolific writer, producing more than eighty novels with very inventive plots. The most famous one is *Lady Audley's Secret* (1862), which won her recognition as well as fortune. The novel has been in print ever since its publication, and has been dramatized and filmed several times. Braddon also founded *Belgravia* magazine (1866), which presented readers with serialized sensation novels, poems, travel narratives and biographies, as well as essays on fashion, history and science. In addition to this she edited *Temple Bar* magazine.

Richard Bowes has won two World Fantasy Awards, an International Horror Guild and a Million Writer Award. He has published six novels, four short story collections and seventy short stories, and 2013 saw the republication of his Lambda Award-winning 1999 novel *Minions of the Moon* and his new novel *Dust Devil on a Quiet Street*, both from Lethe Press. Also in 2013, his collection *The Queen, the Cambion and Seven Others* was published by Aqueduct Press and his *If Angels Fight* by Fairwood Press.

Maurice Broaddus has written hundreds of short stories, essays, novellas and articles. His dark fiction has been published in numerous magazines and anthologies, including *Asimov's Science Fiction*, *Cemetery Dance*, *Apex Magazine*, and *Weird Tales Magazine*. He is the co-editor of the *Dark Faith* anthology series (Apex Books) and the author of the urban fantasy trilogy, *Knights of Breton Court* (Angry Robot

Books). He has been a teaching artist for over five years, teaching creative writing to students of all ages. Visit his website at www.mauricebroaddus.com.

Vivian Caethe's short stories and novellas have appeared in a variety of magazines and anthologies. Her most recent novella, *The Diamond City,* is published by Bold Strokes Books. While writing, thinking and breathing in general, she drinks tea in the constant search for the perfect cup. She lives in Colorado with her husband, his dog who think he's a human with hypertrichosis, and a supervillan cat.

Seth Cadin is a mammal who lives on Earth. He has one daughter and many pet mice. His favourite colour word is 'periwinkle'.

Mae Empson has a Master's degree in English literature from Indiana University at Bloomington, and graduated with honours in English and in Creative Writing from the University of North Carolina at Chapel Hill. She lives in Seattle, Washington. Recent publications appear in print in anthologies from Prime Books, Innsmouth Free Press, Chaosium and Dagan Books, and online in *The Pedestal Magazine* and *Cabinet des Fées*. Recently, two of her stories were nominated for Ellen Datlow's long list of Honorable Mentions for Best Horror of the Year, Volume 5. Follow Mae on twitter at www.twitter.com/maeempson and read her blog at www.maeempson.wordpress.com.

Nestled in the mountains of northern California, **Olivia M. Grey** lives in the cobwebbed corners of her mind writing paranormal romance with a steampunk twist. She dreams of the dark streets of London and the decadent deeds that occur after sunset. As an author of steamy steampunk, as well as a poet, blogger, podcaster and speaker, Olivia focuses both her poetry and prose on alternative relationship lifestyles, and deliciously dark matters of the heart and soul. Her work has been published in various anthologies and magazines like *Stories in the Ether, Steampunk Adventures, SNM Horror Magazine* and *How the West Was Wicked.*

Ella D'Arcy (Constance Eleanor Mary Byrne D'Arcy) (c.1857–1937) was a short fiction writer in the late nineteenth and early twentieth centuries. D'Arcy is mostly known for her short stories in the *Yellow Book*. D'Arcy also published in *Argosy*, *Blackwood's Magazine* and *Temple Bar*. Her work on the *Yellow Book* bought her into contact with the publisher John Lane, who initially published her collection of short stories, *Monochromes* (1895), and went on to publish her further works, *Modern Instances* (1898) and *The Bishop's Dilemma* (1898). As well as writing fiction, D'Arcy also translated into English André Maurois's biography of Percy Bysshe Shelley, *Ariel* (1924).

Sara M. Harvey hails from the San Francisco Bay Area and really wants them to name the Bay Bridge after Emperor Norton. Her *Blood of Angels* trilogy (*The Convent of the Pure*, *The Labyrinth of the Dead* and *The Tower of the Forgotten*) from Apex Publications blends fantasy, horror and steampunk with lesbian protagonists. She has an amazing husband, an awesome daughter and too many terrible dogs. She can be found on Facebook, Twitter (@saraphina_marie) and at www.saramharvey.com.

Actress, playwright and author **Leanna Renee Hieber** is the award-winning, bestselling author of Gothic Victorian fantasy novels for adults and teens. Her *Strangely Beautiful* saga won three Prism awards for excellence in the genre of Fantasy Romance, hit Barnes & Noble's and Borders' bestseller lists and garnered numerous regional genre awards. The *Strangely Beautiful* saga is also being adapted into a musical theatre production. Leanna's *Magic Most Foul* saga began with *Darker Still*, an Indie Next List pick and a Scholastic Book Club 'Highly Recommended' title. The trilogy is now complete. Her new gaslamp fantasy saga, *The Eternal Files* begins early 2015. Her short fiction has appeared in numerous anthologies, including *Queen Victoria's Book of Spells*, and *Willful Impropriety*. A proud member of performers' unions Actors Equity and SAG-AFTRA, she works often in film and television on shows such as *Boardwalk Empire*. A perky Goth girl with more corsets than is reasonable, Leanna enjoys ghost stories, long walks through graveyards in full Victorian regalia, playing

Malfoy and visiting family in Salem. She lives in New York City with her husband and their beloved rescued lab rabbit. More at leannareneehieber.com, twitter.com/leannarenee and facebook.com/lrhieber.

N(ora). K. Jemisin is an author of speculative fiction short stories and novels who lives and writes in Brooklyn, NY. Her work has been nominated for the Hugo (three times), the Nebula (four times), and the World Fantasy Award (twice); shortlisted for the Crawford, the Gemmell Morningstar, and the Tiptree; and she has won a Locus Award for Best First Novel as well as the Romantic Times Reviewer's Choice Award (three times). Her short fiction has been published in *Clarkesworld*, *Postscripts*, *Strange Horizons*, and *Baen's Universe*, as well as podcast markets and print anthologies. Her first five novels, *The Inheritance Trilogy* and *The Dreamblood* (duology), are out now from Orbit Books. Her novels are represented by Lucienne Diver of the Knight Agency.

Eliza Knight is the multi-published, award-winning, best-selling author of sizzling historical romance and erotic romance. While not reading, writing or researching for her latest book, she chases after her three children. In her spare time – if there is such a thing – she likes daydreaming, wine tasting, travelling, hiking, staring at the stars, watching movies, shopping, and visiting family and friends. She lives atop a small mountain, and enjoys cold winter nights when she can curl up in front of a roaring fire with her own knight in shining armour. Visit Eliza at www.elizaknight.com or her historical blog History Undressed: www.historyundressed.com.

Sarah Prineas has published a bunch of SF/fantasy stories for adults, but now writes mostly fantasy novels for kids. *The Magic Thief* series and *Winterling* trilogy were published by HarperCollins in the U.S.; *The Magic Thief* books were published in nineteen other languages around the world. Sarah lives in rural Iowa with her husband and kids, two dogs, a cat and three adorable goats.

Tansy Rayner Roberts is the author of the *Mocklore Chronicles*, *The Creature Court* trilogy, and the short-story collection *Love and Romanpunk*. She is the co-host of two all-women pop-culture podcasts, *Galactic Suburbia* and *Verity*. Tansy writes about *Doctor Who*, superheroes and feminism on her blog, for which she received the Hugo for Best Fan Writer in 2013.

Barbara Roden was born in Vancouver, British Columbia, and is the author of the World Fantasy Award-nominated collection *Northwest Passages*. Although she grew up a long way from the expansive prairies of 'The Wide Wide Sea', that region of the country, and the toll it took on early settlers, has always fascinated her. Of the story she writes, 'Several years ago, an article in the Canadian news magazine *Maclean's* talked about the women who made the trek across the Atlantic to start a new life in Canada, and mentioned that some of them were so overwhelmed by the vastness and emptiness of the prairies that they literally ran mad with terror. I was fascinated with this idea, especially when I combined it with a young woman marrying for what seemed to her like the right reasons – or at least good ones – and then realizing, too late, that she might have made a terrible mistake. How can you share someone else's dream when everything about it terrifies you?'

Nisi Shawl's collection *Filter House* was a 2009 Tiptree winner; her stories have been published in *Strange Horizons*, *Asimov's Science Fiction*, and in several anthologies, including *Mojo: Conjure Stories* and both volumes of *Dark Matter*. Shawl was WisCon 35's Guest of Honor. She co-edited *Strange Matings: Science Fiction, Feminism, African American Voices and Octavia E. Butler*. She edited *The WisCon Chronicles, Volume 5: Writing and Racial Identity* and *Bloodchildren: Stories by the Octavia E. Butler Scholars*, and currently edits reviews for *The Cascadia Subduction Zone*. Shawl co-authored *Writing the Other: A Practical Approach*. She co-founded the Carl Brandon Society and serves on the board of directors for Clarion West. Her website is www.nisishawl.com.

Delia Sherman's most recent short stories have appeared in the young-adult anthologies *Steampunk!* and *Teeth*, and in Ellen Datlow's urban-fantasy anthology *Naked City*. Her adult novels are *Through a Brazen Mirror*, *The Porcelain Dove* and (with Ellen Kushner) *The Fall of the Kings*. Novels for younger readers include *Changeling* and *The Magic Mirror of the Mermaid Queen*. Her most recent novel, *The Freedom Maze*, a time-travel historical about antebellum Louisiana, received the Andre Norton Award, the Mythopoeic Award, and the Prometheus Award. When Delia is not writing, she's teaching, editing, knitting and travelling. She lives in New York City with Ellen Kushner, piles of books, some nice Arts and Crafts wallpaper, and a very Victorian rock collection.

Caroline Stevermer, originally from a dairy farm in south-eastern Minnesota, lives in Minneapolis. She has written *A College of Magics* and *River Rats*, among other novels, and in collaboration with Patricia C. Wrede, *Sorcery & Cecelia* and its two sequels. She likes baseball, steamboats, trains and bookstores.

E. Catherine Tobler is a Sturgeon Award finalist and the senior editor at *Shimmer* magazine. Her first novel, *Gold & Glass*, is now available.

Tiffany Trent is the award-winning author of *The Unnaturalists* and *The Tinker King* (Simon & Schuster Books for Young Readers). She has published in several anthologies and magazines, including Willful Impropriety, *Magic in the Mirrorstone*, *Corsets & Clockwork*, *Subterranean* and many others. When not writing, she's out playing with bees or chickens.

Genevieve Valentine's first novel, *Mechanique*, won the 2012 Crawford Award and was nominated for the Nebula. Her second novel, *The Girls at the Kingfisher Club*, is forthcoming from Atria. Her short fiction has appeared in *Clarkesworld*, *Strange Horizons*, *Journal of Mythic Arts* and others, and anthologies *Federations*, *After*, *Teeth* and more. Her non-fiction has appeared at NPR.org, io9, *The A.V. Club* and *Weird Tales*. Her appetite for bad movies is insatiable, a tragedy she tracks on her blog, www.genevievevalentine.com.

'Seeking Asylum' by Vivian Caethe © 2013. Printed by permission of the author.

'A Christmas Carroll' by Leanna Renee Hieber © 2010. Originally published in *A Midwinter Fantasy*, Dorchester Publishing, 2010. Reprinted by permission of the author.

'Outside the Absolute' by Seth Cadin © 2012. Originally published in *Willful Impropriety*, 2012. Reprinted by permission of the author.

'The Emperor's Man' by Tiffany Trent © 2010. Originally published in *Corsets & Clockwork: 13 Steampunk Romances*, 2011. Reprinted by permission of the author. (This story has been significantly expanded for this anthology.)

'Lady in Red' by Eliza Knight © 2013. Printed by permission of the author.

'Where the Ocean Meets the Sky' by Sara M. Harvey © 2011. Originally published in *Steam-Powered: Lesbian Steampunk Stories*, 2011. Reprinted by permission of the author.

'The Queen and the Cambion' by Richard Bowes © 2012. Originally published in *The magazine of Fantasy & Science Fiction*, March/April 2012.

'The Dancing Master' by Genevieve Valentine © 2012. Originally published in *Willful Impropriety*, 2012.

'The Tawny Bitch' by Nisi Shawl © 2002. Originally published in *Mojo: Conjure Stories*, 2003. Reprinted by permission of the author. 'The Problem of Trystan' by Maurice Broaddus © 2011. Originally published in *Hot & Steamy: Tales of Steampunk Romance*, 2011.

'Irremediable' by Ella D'Arcy. Originally published in *Yellow Book,* Vol 1.

'Item 317: Horn Fragment w/Illus' by Elise C. Tobler © 2013. Originally published in *Daughters of Icarus*, 2013. Reprinted by permission of the author.

'Jane' by Sarah Prineas © 2006. Originally published in *Realms of Fantasy*, April 2006. Reprinted by permission of the author.

'The Wide Wide Sea' by Barbara Roden © 2007. Originally published in *Exotic Gothic*, 2007. Reprinted by permission of the author.

'Her last Appearance' by Mary Braddon. Originally published in *Weavers and Weft and Other Tales*, 1877. John Maxwell.

'The Cordwainer's Daintiest Lasts' by Mae Empson © 2012. Originally published in *Cucurbital 3,* edited by Lawrence M. Schoen © 2012 by Paper Golem LLC. Reprinted by permission of the author.

'Waiting for Harry' by Caroline Stevermer © 1992. Originally published in *All Hallows' Eve*, 1992. Reprinted by permission of the author.

'Queen Victoria's Book of Spells' by Delia Sherman © 2013. Originally published in *Queen Victoria's Book of Spells*, 2013. Reprinted by permission of the author.

'Lamia Victoriana' by Tansy Rayner Roberts © 2011. Originally published in *Love and Romanpunk,* 2011. Reprinted by permission of the author.

'The Effluent Engine' by N. K. Jemisin © 2011. Originally published in *Steam Powered: Lesbian Steampunk Stories*, 2011. Reprinted by permission of the author.

'A Kiss in the Rain' by O. M. Grey © 2011. Originally published in *Caught in the Cogs: An Eclectic Collection, 2011*. Reprinted by permission of the author.

CONTENTS

SEEKING ASYLUM

Vivian Caethe

As the wheels of Mr Fowler's carriage rattled down the macadam driveway of the Minerva House Asylum, Astrid Fowler stared out the window, clutching her arms against her stomach. Mr Fowler sat next to her in stony silence. She had inadvertently embarrassed him in front of the servants by near-fainting on the front steps of his house, and he had yet to forgive her.

Even the slightest motion of the wheels over the rough surface jarred her, and she bit back a moan. The pain had lessened over the months since her husband had taken her from Colney Hatch Asylum, but it had grown again with her increasing dread at being returned to such an inimical environment. Mr Fowler's silence deepened.

The March rain had not ceased for two days, and it obscured her view of the approaching buildings, increasing her sense of unease. They had called it a disease, her condition, a mental disease. She had not felt at ease for years.

She risked a glance at her husband and saw his expression furrowed with anger. It was always furrowed, but she had learned over the duration of their marriage to decipher the signs of his displeasure. It had become a means of survival when she had been in his house. When she had been at Colney Hatch, she had been given greater concerns than her husband's shifting moods.

The carriage rolled to a stop and Mr Fowler got out. She heard the crunch of his footsteps as he rounded the carriage. As the driver descended to open her door, the motion jostled the carriage, nauseating her further. The driver opened the door and she tried to smile as he handed her down, the scars on her abdomen throbbing with her pounding heartbeat. He thought she was too pretty to be here. She shuddered.

Three women waited at the top of the stairs leading to the asylum's main entrance. Astrid squinted up into the rain to see the three-storey building loom above her. The brick walls and arched windows did nothing to reassure her. Colney Hatch had been cast from the same mould.

Mr Fowler took her elbow and led her towards the stairs. Resigned, she looked down at the macadam under her feet, watching as it led to red sandstone stairs. Her shoes made dull thudding sounds on the rain-soaked stone.

'Mr Fowler, I presume.' The tall woman at the centre spoke first. The other two women arranged on either side of her were dressed as nurses, so she presumed the woman in the middle must be Dr Amherst.

'Of course,' replied Mr Fowler. 'My wife, Astrid.'

He pushed Astrid forward. All his resignation, determination and drive rushed through her, bringing with it a wave of nausea.

After a brief glance up at the women, Astrid looked down, watching the concentric circles in the small puddles that filled the dents in the stone. Raindrops dripped from the brim of her hat on to the steps, shaking the puddles with their impact.

'It's a pleasure to meet you, Mrs Fowler.' Dr Amherst spoke in the tone of someone repeating herself. Astrid glanced up to see if she was angry. The doctor smiled at her kindly. 'Would you care to come in?'

'Please.' Astrid remembered her manners and smiled around the lie. 'It would be my pleasure.'

'If you would get her bags?' Dr Amherst asked the nurses bracketing her. One of them, the taller one, frowned as the shorter, thinner one nodded.

'I will take my leave then,' Mr Fowler said. 'I trust that she is in good hands.'

'Only the best, Mr Fowler,' the doctor replied. 'I don't suppose I could invite you in for some tea before your journey home?'

'I would rather not tarry.' The disgust in his voice leaked into his expression. Astrid swallowed nervously. He would not tarry at the asylum, but he would condemn her to its custody?

She watched dismally as her husband abandoned her without a word at the steps of an asylum for the second time. Jostling past her with her luggage, the nurses ignored her. The doctor reached for her arm and gently guided her to the door. 'Let's get you out of the rain.'

The rain pelted the expansive grounds outside, transforming the carefully manicured lawns and extensive foliage into muted shades of blue and grey. With an effort, Astrid pulled her attention back to Dr Amherst. The doctor waited patiently for her to come back. That was new. Mostly they shouted at her, dragging, roughly yanking her to the here and now.

'I know your experience with such places in has been . . .' the doctor paused, compassion imbuing her expression, 'less than peaceful. But our goal here is not to force you into a state of socially approved sanity, but rather to assist you in finding your own means to find peace in your condition.'

Astrid's attention wandered again. She tried to focus back on this room, light and airy, comfortably feminine, with gaslights burning cheerily in the wall sconces. Pastels, whites and fresh flowers decorated the room, instead of dark wood and menacing masculinity. 'Peace?'

'Function, if nothing else. Control to the degree you feel you need. Hopefully more, but that is entirely up to you. Healing comes from the inside, not imposed through machines and treatments meant to console men who are, at best, guessing and, at worst, experimenting.' The doctor's expression grew dark for a moment before returning to placid calm. 'We employ different methods here from the ones you may be used to.'

Astrid folded her arms across her belly, the scars rough under the comforting weight of her dress and stays. It was the first real dress she had been allowed in years, a costume of normalcy and dignity. The doctor's demeanour gave her more comfort than she would have dreamed possible. The wounds on her soul, still raw through the rough sutures of uncaring cures, throbbed once, twice. The loss as strong as the betrayal. If this woman could . . . Astrid nodded slightly, unused to even the implication of consent.

'Let's get you settled in then.' Dr Amherst smiled and gestured towards the door.

Astrid turned to see a woman there, the taller of the two nurses who had greeted her. She held open the door, her face neutral. 'Whenever you are ready.'

Standing, Astrid glanced at the doctor, then at the nurse again. Dr Amherst smiled kindly, patiently. The smile reached her eyes.

She allowed herself to be escorted from the doctor's office. The nurse led the way down the hall and into the parlour. The nurse's shoes thudded while Astrid's made quiet whispers on the deep rugs that lined the wood-floored hallway. The nurse glanced at her, frowning for a moment.

'Wait here.'

Astrid sat on one of the davenports tastefully arranged in the parlour and watched the rain stream down the windows. She blinked rapidly, afraid to lose herself in the patterns of water on the glass. Despite the doctor's words, she doubted she was safe enough to lose herself. She would, despite herself, but she always tried to delay it for as long as possible. Instead, she glanced at the other woman in the room.

The other woman sat on the couch across the room from the floor-to-ceiling windows, her gaze on her feet. Astrid glanced away, not wanting to be caught staring. The carpet whorled beneath her, a cascade of brilliant blues and reds winding around green and gold. It reminded her of water, streams and rivers, churning the colour of the rocks beneath into a white, milky foam. Foam like water and blood—

A woman's scream tore her back to reality. She flinched and gripped the arm of the couch. The woman across the room from her writhed in pain. As Astrid watched in horror, she stood and walked toward Astrid, her gaze down on the floor.

'I see you two have met.' The nurse returned, wiping her

hands on her apron. Astrid stood and stepped around the back of the couch.

'I'm afraid . . .' The woman spoke without raising her head. Her wide-brimmed hat obscured her features as she addressed her shoes. 'We haven't . . . I mean . . .'

'Oh, of course not.' The nurse smiled sourly. 'Miss Inga Ryan, please let me introduce to you Mrs Astrid Fowler.'

'It's a pleasure,' Miss Ryan told her shoes.

'Indeed.' Astrid addressed her shoes as well. It seemed the thing to do. Her black shoes melted into the shadows under her dress.

'Well.' The nurse clapped her hands, making Astrid jump. 'If you ladies would come with me, supper is not for several hours yet and Dr Amherst has requested that all inmates be sent to their rooms.'

Astrid glanced at Miss Ryan and caught a glimpse of her profile. The woman's features glowed with beauty. In fact . . . Astrid shook her head. No. It was her mother's curse, not hers. Never hers. They had cured her of that. She put her hand to her abdomen.

But she was not safe. Not yet. Maybe not ever. Not here.

The nurse showed her to her room. 'Supper is at eight.'

Turning, the nurse slammed the door and Astrid heard the click of the lock in its place. The sound of the door's closing resonated through her like a slap, and it took Astrid several moments to catch her breath.

Her three suitcases lay opened on the small bed, taking up the entire space. From their appearance, her dresses and belongings had been rifled through, searched, she presumed, for dangerous items. She had hoped, no matter how pointlessly, that Minerva House would be different from Colney Hatch.

Astrid supposed she should unpack her belongings and place them in the small wardrobe which, along with a small armchair, comprised the room's other sole furnishings. But the door . . . the nurse had locked the door, trapping her inside.

Seating herself in the small armchair by the high window, she tried to breathe, tried to control the shaking in her hands. Closing her eyes, she could hear the patter of rain on the roof tiles. The sound reassured her, reminding her of her parents' manor on the moors, of a time before asylums and doctors. She leaned her head back and listened to the rain.

'Your husband tells me that you often succumb to hysteria.' Dr Amherst steepled her fingers and tapped them together as she thought. Astrid waited patiently. This was the part she had dreaded: the questions. She had believed Dr Amherst yesterday, but a sleepless night locked in a small room while the rain continued had only exacerbated her doubts. Certainly if her husband approved of this place, it could not be trusted. The doctor's statement confirmed her fears. If Dr Amherst believed him, then what was this but yet another prison?

'My husband makes many diagnoses.' Her attention wandered to the window. Outside, the damp grass sparkled in the morning sunlight, cheerful points of light that drew her eye. If she could hide in one of those drops of light, then no one would come for her, no one would hurt her and tell her she was mad.

'I personally don't believe in hysteria.' Dr Amherst's voice gently drew her back.

Astrid blinked. Hysteria was real. That was why they had cut her open, they told her. It had to be real. Why else would they do such a thing? 'But they said . . .'

'I know what they say,' the doctor said gently. 'They always say that. But I have never seen a case of hysteria that could not be explained by another condition or cause, or simply by the female condition in our world. For example, if I was married to your husband, I would take refuge in the symptoms of hysteria.'

Inhaling, Astrid felt a defence come to her lips. She swallowed it down. She had defended Mr Fowler for too long. He was the reason she was here, after all. The reason she had been sent to Colney Hatch. She exhaled.

After a moment, Dr Amherst spoke again: 'Why do you think you are still alive?'

'I'm sorry?' Astrid had drifted off again, this time caught up in the patterns in the light-wood desk in front of her. She gripped the arms of her chair to keep from touching her scars, a habit she had grown all too aware of in the past two days.

'Why do you think you are still alive?' Dr Amherst asked patiently. 'Many women who have suffered as you do die from the shock. You fade, yet you remain. Why do you think that is?'

Astrid glanced out the window again, blinking against the brilliance of the morning. The windows faced north, but still the summer sun glimmered through the trees as it rose, weaving patterns of light and dark to capture her eyes. 'My mother would have said that it was because God still had a purpose for me.'

'Do you believe in God, Astrid?' Dr Amherst leaned in, her expression intent.

Memories of prayers screamed throughout the past years echoed through her mind. She blinked and shook her head. She had thought once that God was cruel, but now she wondered if He had merely gone deaf from all the cries for mercy.

'I didn't expect so.' Dr Amherst sighed. 'Faith can often buoy the downtrodden spirit.'

'Do I require faith to be healed?' Surprised at her own temerity, Astrid clamped her lips shut. Perhaps it was not the sort of question one asked.

'No.' The doctor shook her head. 'And in some cases I have found it to be actively detrimental to my treatments.'

'Is that why . . .' Despite her husband's coddling, she had still heard the rumours in the week he had tolerated her presence in his home. The servants whispered about Minerva House, whispers she had heard while lying awake in bed, unable to move beyond the occasional blink. But it was the only solely women's asylum in the country, the only place where he was sure no man would touch her again. Perhaps he thought that he was protecting her. It had come too late.

'Among many reasons.' Dr Amherst nodded, reading her intent. 'Any time that a woman seeks a place in professions held only by men, her intentions will always be suspect and labelled deviant and mad, as it were.'

Astrid nodded, thinking of her mother and of her own aspirations before her father married her off to 'settle her down'. She looked at the carpet, seeing how the pile crushed under her shoe, like tiny blades of grass beneath the feet of a giant.

'So tell me, why do you think you are still alive?'

Looking up, Astrid's gaze caught on the rows of books on the doctor's shelves. 'I honestly don't know.'

Miss Ryan was painfully beautiful. Astrid had never thought that phrase to be particularly apt, but with Inga . . . She dared to use the woman's first name in the quietness of her mind, in the space before she faded, as Dr Amherst had taken to calling it.

Her initial session with Dr Amherst had occupied most of the morning. Afterwards, she had found her way to the garden, where one of the servants offered to bring her some tea. She had discovered Miss Ryan there, tea already served. It would have been rude to turn and leave. Instead she swallowed and asked, 'May I join you, Miss Ryan?'

'Mrs Fowler.' The woman looked up, surprised. 'Of course. Please.'

Now her hands shook as she rested the cup and saucer in her lap and tried hard not to look at the other woman. But she couldn't help but glance from time to time.

Inga had flame-coloured hair that cascaded in curls from a simple chignon. An effortless beauty suffused her face, transforming her pale skin to ivory luminescence. Her startlingly blue eyes flicked towards Astrid and then away, a delicate flush becoming her cheeks.

Astrid glanced away, embarrassed to have been caught staring. She took a sip of her cooling tea and stared at the hedge-maze that rested on the lower terrace of the manor's grounds. Her scars ached, punishment for her thoughts, she supposed. She placed the cup back on the saucer with a rattle. Heat flared through her face at the *faux pas* and she swallowed. She should say something. The silence grew intolerable.

'Are you mad?' she blurted out.

Miss Ryan started, and then turned towards her slightly. She addressed her shoes. 'As mad as mad may be, I'm afraid. Or that is what my brother says to place me here.'

'Ah,' Astrid said, at a loss for words. As intrusive as her original question had been, she found herself less than inclined to continue her line of thought. 'I'm sorry . . . I didn't mean—'

'It passes the time.' Miss Ryan smiled.

'Do you often find yourself in possession of much time to pass?' As she said it, Astrid wasn't sure if she made any sense, or if she was being presumptuous again. Her tongue had disconnected from her mind, taking its own way through the conversation.

'Only when I am at peace.' The smile that crossed Inga's face reminded Astrid of . . . she swallowed, trying to clear her dry throat. She went to take a sip of tea and found her cup empty. She placed it on the table between them, trying to ignore how her hand shook.

'The weather is lovely.' Miss Ryan said, after the pause became uncomfortable.

'I love it when it rains,' Astrid commented. 'And after it rains, when the world feels cleansed.'

'Does the world often appear sullied to you?'

'You sound like Dr Amherst.' Astrid smiled to take the sting from her words.

'I suppose it is through long acquaintance with those in her profession.'

Astrid found herself at a loss for words again. Every time their conversation began, it spiralled back to the topic they both knew they should avoid. The scars were too raw, even now, for her to be comfortable discussing it with a stranger.

The hedge-maze drew her attention, giving her relief from the discomfort of small talk. She had never been skilled at it. Too blunt for her own good, her father had said. As his everlasting shame, he had hurried to marry her to the first man who would take her. Fortunately for him, her large dowry attracted more men than her looks did. She had never been fond of the idea that a man's heart could be bought, but she also knew that love only existed between the pages of novels.

Her eyes traced the lines of the maze, the whorls and dead ends drawing her gaze even as she knew she should speak. Miss Ryan and she were not good enough friends to warrant a companionable silence.

She heard an intake of air and then a muffled shriek. Startled, Astrid turned to Inga and saw that she had her hands clasped over her mouth, a look of unspeakable horror in her eyes. Following the other woman's gaze, she saw the nurse who had locked her away approaching.

'Run. Run away.' The words slipped past Miss Ryan's hands. 'Run away.'

Startled into standing, Astrid turned to see if Miss Ryan addressed her. But the woman fixed her unblinking blue gaze on the nurse, her mouth still covered by her gloved hands.

Before she could determine whether to leave or stay, the nurse arrived, descending upon them as if they were recalcitrant children. 'Dr Amherst wants to see you, Miss Ryan.'

The nurse took Miss Ryan's arm and, before Astrid could cry out in her defence, dragged the suddenly sobbing woman back to the asylum. In the silence that followed, she realized she had forgotten the most important lesson of all. She had forgotten that she was in an asylum, and that Miss Ryan was as mad as she was.

'The first step to a cure, if you will, is to accept that you might, perhaps, not be mad.' Dr Amherst said, addressing the salon of patients. Astrid looked around curiously, trying to see if there was any trace of madness in the women gathered there. There were fourteen patients, built from almost every mould imaginable. The only thing they had in common was their presence here. From an outsider's perspective, it could be any salon in any house, genteel women gathered for thoughtful discussion. Only they knew that they were all insane.

She had not been permitted to the salons in the first months of her staying here, but as the May flowers began to bloom, she had been given permission to attend one a week. At first, Dr Amherst thought they might be too stressful for her fragile mind, but now that she was stronger, the doctor said, she could begin reintegrating with company. The door was still locked on her room every night, though.

Dr Amherst looked at each of them before continuing: 'Society has told you that you are mad and treated you as they say madwomen should be treated. Many of those who have given you such a disservice have truly meant well, but in their ignorance, they have done more damage than they intended.'

Astrid's scars ached and she pursed her lips at Dr Amherst's understatement. The doctor knew about her scars; perhaps she spoke for all the women there. Did they also have scars? She glanced around, but there was no way to tell under the tea gowns that were *de rigueur* for the doctor's salons. The absence of stays pressing against her scars gave her a strange floating sensation, as if she was not entirely there, firmly fixed into the world through the bones. Perhaps without the bones, she was merely a soul, set to wander the world.

'Are you quite all right, Mrs Fowler?' Miss Ryan's soft voice drew her back. The woman had arranged herself on the window seat next to Astrid's armchair. She still addressed her shoes, but there was a quick uptilt of her eyes, which took in Astrid's condition.

Astrid turned at her murmur and Inga's sky-blue eyes caught her own. Pausing for a moment, she tried to catch her breath before answering, 'Quite all right, thank you.'

'You just looked so pale.' Miss Ryan raised her gaze to meet Astrid's and smiled shyly.

'Thank you for your concern,' Astrid said, then flushed at her abruptness.

'After accepting that you might not be mad,' Dr Amherst's voice drew her attention back to the lecture, 'the second step is to determine why society thinks you mad, and what you will do about this accusation.'

Grateful for the distraction, Astrid applied herself to listening, trying to ignore the sensation of Miss Ryan's gaze upon her. It had been better when she'd addressed her shoes. She could barely stand the full strength of the other woman's regard.

'In societies like ours, and as enlightened as we consider ourselves to be, there is still no place for the female psyche, except in the corners to which male considerations consign it. Those corners may grow, but it would take an enlightened civilization indeed to put the female mind on the same plane as that of the male consciousness.' Dr Amherst smiled wryly. 'And since we can only hope for the future, it behoves us to find practical means to deal with the present.'

Astrid's gaze caught on the lace curtains as she tried to imagine a present where she was not mad. Certainly she was mad, for her husband thought so, and the doctors would not have cut her open had something not been wrong with her. But what if she were sane?

Nothing would change, she decided. Madness applied to sanity was still madness; the infection had taken hold. She could never go back to the way she had been, not after all they had done to her. If she had not started out mad, then surely she was now.

She glanced at Miss Ryan. Perhaps madness did not stick to everyone. Certainly Miss Ryan was mad in name only. She lacked the distance that Astrid knew she herself possessed, or the wildness she had seen in the eyes of the women of Colney Hatch. Especially after they came back from the special rooms the doctors did not allow visitors to see.

The lace curtains shifted in the breeze, freeing her from her reminiscences. She blinked, turning her attention back to the salon. Everyone stared at her. Dr Amherst paused with a concerned expression on her face.

'I'm sorry,' she said, sweating with embarrassment.

'Are you sure you are quite all right?' Miss Ryan asked. 'You are as white as a sheet.'

'Of course.' She felt herself flush. 'I just need some air. If you would all excuse me?'

'Let me accompany you.' Miss Ryan offered. Astrid could think of no way to gracefully refuse. She stood unsteadily and walked from the room, Miss Ryan next to her, close enough to touch. Knees shaking, she walked with Miss Ryan towards the courtyard in the centre of the mansion. Part of her pondered the irony that half the cause of her trepidation was because of her condition, and the other half her companion.

'If we could sit, perhaps,' Astrid said.

'Of course, Mrs Fowler.' Inga glanced up and smiled that quiet smile of hers. Astrid seated herself on the bench by the fountain and folded her hands in her lap, trying not to clench her skirt. The fountain burbled to itself, partly disguising the soft sound of Inga's skirts as she settled herself next to Astrid.

Astrid swallowed and concentrated on the play of light through the water. Rainbows of colour arced through the afternoon sunlight, cascading down to the pool of water below. She tried to lose herself in the colours and texture of the water in the air, but Miss Ryan's presence distracted her. She placed her arms across her scars.

'Are you troubled?' Miss Ryan asked.

Smiling at the implication that she was not always troubled, Astrid shook her head. 'I just needed some air, that is all. Thank you for your consideration.'

'Of course. We are all sisters here, as Dr Amherst said.'

Astrid shook her head. She hadn't been listening to the doctor's lecture. 'I'm sorry, but please, I just need . . .'

'Some air, of course.' Miss Ryan's gaze returned to her shoes. 'I'll let you be.'

'Please stay.' The words dropped from Astrid's lips before she could consider them.

'I . . .' Miss Ryan half stood. 'I should get back. The others . . .'

'Of course.' Astrid flushed. 'I'm sorry, I shouldn't have.'

'No. It's quite all right.' Inga's cheeks reddened and her beauty struck Astrid again. She quickly looked away, not wanting to embarrass the woman or herself further. She fixed her gaze on her hands.

'If you really want . . .' Miss Ryan stepped closer. 'I mean, I can stay.'

Astrid forced herself to relax. Miss Ryan meant well. 'If you would like.'

Miss Ryan sat down again, and for a moment they gazed at the fountain together. The moment passed and Astrid dared to glance at the other woman. 'Can you tell me what I missed?'

'You truly were suffering so much that you didn't hear? I had wondered what was amiss,' Miss Ryan said, her voice almost too soft to hear over the fountain. 'I don't know if I could explain well. I understood less than half of it myself and agree with even less.'

'Then why are you here?' Astrid closed her eyes at her own stupidity. She kept asking questions she had no right to ask.

'Why are you here?' Miss Ryan asked pertly.

Startled at her transition from a shy violet, Astrid glanced at her and saw a mischievous smile play across her features. Her heart ached. 'I am mad. Aren't you?'

'Only as mad as men will make me. On that I do agree with the good doctor.' Inga's smile grew. 'For men will always claim madness to cover their own faults.'

'Then what fault your brother?'

'You remembered my little indiscretion, then?' Miss Ryan smiled. 'I had thought you would not. I have been forbidden to speak of him, nor of his position. Even my name is a shame.'

'You are not Inga Ryan, then?'

'I am Inga, true and true, but a Ryan I am not, nor shall I ever be.' Now that she had disregarded her obsession for conversing with her shoes, Inga's voice lilted. Despite her light tone, darkness lurked in the space between the words, a darkness Astrid thought she recognized all too well.

'Then if I am to be allowed another impertinent question.' Astrid waited for a slight nod from her companion to continue. 'What other asylum's accommodations have you enjoyed?'

'You know well the secrets that I carry in my heart, and can read my words as they should be said,' Inga replied. 'And yet I suspect your tale may be darker than mine.'

'You would ask me to tell my tale?' Astrid swallowed. This woman threatened with mere words to undo the protections she had woven around her heart.

'Only if it is a story you can tell,' Inga said gently. 'If not, then my story will have to suffice to pass the time until we are recalled to our devotions.'

Astrid smiled at the allusion to the doctor's schedule for their days. Every morning there was breakfast, then the salon or quiet contemplation, journal-writing or reading, then tea, followed by time for quiet activities and personal sessions with the doctor. Enough to occupy their time, but not enough to keep Astrid from fading away. The nurses would come too soon to summon them for tea.

'If you wouldn't mind, your story please,' Astrid said. 'We do have an hour yet.'

Inga's demeanour transformed from that of a wilting flower to full-blown rose. 'My brother, who for the sake of this tale shall be Mr Ryan, and I are born from the same womb on the same day. Despite our shared date of birth, we could not be more different. He was born with the rough good looks of my father, while I was cursed with the devilish facade of our maternal grandmother.' She touched her red hair ruefully and smiled.

Astrid didn't think there was anything devilish about her, but dared not disagree as Inga continued with her story. 'With my devilish cast came my obstinate nature. I was, as they said, a hellion of a child, and I grew up into an opinionated woman.'

She gave Astrid a significant glance and Astrid nodded. Had her own father been less loving of her mother, more than one woman in their lineage would have spent time in the asylum for disease of the feminine kind. As it was, he barely tolerated Astrid in the years after her birth, hoping, perhaps, for a male to continue the line. Her mother had died in childbirth when Astrid was only thirteen, leaving her in her father's care.

Blinking, she realized she had become lost in her own reminiscences. Inga waited patiently, until Astrid looked at her again, then continued her story, a slight smile playing on her lips. 'As a twin, and the evil twin at that, my brother was taught not to tolerate my excesses of opinion.'

'Would he have otherwise?'

'I doubt it. He does not tolerate much that does not come from obedience.'

'Ah.' Astrid understood. 'Pray, go on.'

'Upon the untimely passing of our parents, my brother determined that, if he was to gain control of our inheritance, the best way to do so would be to declare me mad and thus wrest what little I was granted from me. He was, of course, loath to pay a large enough dowry to attract suitors of quality sufficient to provide him the prestige he craved. It was better, in his estimation, to have a sister who had retired from public life than one married to a pauper.'

'Did you love him?' Astrid asked. 'The pauper, I mean.'

Emotion flushed Inga's face and Astrid realized she had asked another indelicate question. Before she could apologize, Inga's smile was back. 'It doesn't matter now. My brother, on the other hand, would never forgive me for even entertaining the thought. It must have been, in his estimation, near enough to madness that he had me committed to Bethlehem Royal Hospital.'

Horrified, Astrid sucked in a breath. Even she had not been so mad as to justify being sent to the infamous Bedlam. Inga shrugged and continued. 'He had to realize that a sister in Bedlam was no better than a sister wed to a pauper. However, it took him six months to come to this realization.'

In the painful pause that followed, a thousand questions came to Astrid and were quickly discarded. She prayed, for both their sakes, that Inga had been spared.

'Six months in Bedlam.' Inga took a breath. 'It was not as it has been described. Or at least not a horrific madhouse filled with the gibbering lunatics of days gone by. But for the female patient . . . well, you understand from Dr Amherst's opinion the expectations of the male doctor from the female patient.'

'And from experience.' Astrid tried to smile ruefully, but the expression failed in its commencement. A thought occurred to her. 'Why then do you say that you do not agree with the doctor?'

'Ah.' Inga's smile withered. 'We come to the crux of the story. For, you see, Dr Amherst's belief is that madness is a state of mind and the surrounding culture. I believe, however, that madness is real, immediate, and in the cases of many unfortunates, very serious.'

'Are you mad, then?'

'Not in the slightest,' Inga said. 'But I have witnessed such madness as to be a true believer. For who would countenance such behaviour from their own person were they not mad?'

'You mean the catatonics and the gibbering lunatics.' Astrid felt a sinking in her stomach.

Inga was not mad, and she would judge Astrid for her madness.

'Those and more, for all kinds resided in Bedlam, next to the civility of the modern institution,' Inga explained. 'And so it should be, for they were taken care of in a manner as their madness necessitated.'

'And those who were not mad, like yourself?'

'We were driven to distraction by the environment, and perhaps some of the madness was catching, for I found in myself a growing sentiment that might be described as . . . inappropriate for a woman of my status.'

'You became a suffragist?' Astrid smiled at her own joke. It was better than the alternative: hope could be treacherous in places like this.

Inga nodded seriously. 'Among other things.'

Astrid opened her mouth to ask, then didn't dare, for fear of making a fool of herself. Or worse, of proving herself to be as mad as Mr Fowler claimed. Instead she asked, 'How did you get out?'

'I threatened my brother with letters.' Inga smiled. 'I told him I would write to his peers and neighbours, inviting them to visit me in the madhouse, and considering that perhaps they only neglected to do so out of ignorance of my current address. He reconsidered, but persisted in believing that I was well and truly mad, and that my madness had only been exacerbated by my treatment in Bedlam. We reached a compromise he and I: I was to select the place of my incarceration and he was to entertain the concept of my eventual cure. I bide my time here while the good doctor affects my cure.'

'I see.' Astrid glanced at the fountain, surprised to see that the sundial had moved an hour in the interval. It occurred to her that only the mad would claim sanity in an asylum.

Inga surmised her train of thought. 'Of course, we are all mad here.'

She smiled at Astrid, as if sharing a joke. Astrid shook her head, embarrassed to be confused. 'I'm sorry?'

'Never mind.' Inga glanced up and moved her hand from where it had strayed towards Astrid's. 'Our keeper approaches.'

The bravado in Inga's voice did nothing to reassure

Astrid. The tall nurse that had greeted her on arrival walked down the path towards them, her expression sour. In the intervening months, she had experienced only the coldest treatment from this nurse, reminiscent of the treatment she had received at Colney Hatch. The cold menace of the sane against the insane.

Astrid stood, and with her Inga, who whispered. 'Are you feeling better?'

'I am, thanks to your care and distraction.' Astrid dared a smile before the nurse was on them.

'You are expected at tea, Mrs Fowler, Miss Ryan.' The tall nurse frowned, emphasizing their titles. Astrid had not had an opportunity to learn the woman's name, but from her continued demeanour she doubted she would want to. She shivered and looked down at the stone path. The varicoloured stones drew her gaze until she found herself lost in the occasional glimmer of mica or quartz. Her attention jumped from one to the next.

'Come with me.' The nurse stepped forward, reaching out for Inga, who stepped back. Astrid flinched on her behalf.

'Of course, Nurse Harriet.' Inga addressed her shoes. Astrid thought she could see her shaking, but whether from fear or anger, she did not know. 'We were just readying ourselves to join the others. I do believe Mrs Fowler has recovered sufficiently.'

Astrid bit her tongue at the rebuke in her companion's voice. The nurse stiffened, and Astrid was reminded of Inga's horrified response to the nurse's presence the other day. For a moment, she thought the nurse would strike Inga. Astrid inhaled, remembering where she was. No one could stop her if Nurse Harriet tried to harm her friend. No one but Dr Amherst, though Astrid could still not bring herself to trust her.

'I want you to close your eyes and think of the most peaceful scene you can imagine.' Dr Amherst's voice spoke soothingly from behind her. 'And tell me when you can see it fully.'

Astrid closed her eyes, but all she could see was the fountain in the courtyard and hear Inga's voice instead of the doctor's.

It had been days and still she could not stop thinking about their conversation. She opened her eyes again. 'I'm not sure . . .'

'Take your time,' Dr Amherst said. 'The mind in your condition is unused to the rigours of relaxation. It will take time and patience to achieve our goal here. All I ask is that you try.'

'Very well.' Astrid closed her eyes again and exhaled, trying to see something other than the fountain, or Inga's red hair in the sunlight.

Inhaling, she settled on the cool mist over the moors of her childhood, before her father had moved them to London and demanded his daughter be what her mother never would.

The fog enveloped her, covering her scars, dissolving her until she was solely a creature of mist and spirit. She floated above the moor, cut off from the world, apart from the things that hurt her. She barely remembered to speak. 'I'm on the moors.'

'While you are there, do your thoughts plague you?' Dr Amherst's voice floated nebulously across the moor. She turned her attention away from it; if she listened to the doctor, then she would be drawn back, away from the safety of the fog, the calmness of the morning of her childhood.

If she could only stay here, she could float along the moor for ever, free of pain, free of desire, free of her nature, which demanded so much and gave so little. Free—

'Come back, Astrid.' The doctor's voice broke through, startling her.

Astrid blinked and sat up. No comforting mist remained, shattered by the doctor's voice. She turned to look at Dr Amherst. The woman had a rueful expression on her face. 'I should have known better than to try hypnosis with you. You fade too quickly; you're too strongly tied to the spirit world.'

'Then what do I do?' Astrid asked. 'How am I cured?'

'We will try another method,' the doctor said confidently. 'And if that doesn't work, there are many more paths you can take to finding your function. There is no cure, but there is peace.'

'No cure?' Astrid knew that she would say that, but it still hurt to hear it.

'How can there be a cure when you are not physically ill? Insanity is a disease, yes, but not one that can be cured like the common cold. There is no miasma, no taint that can be erased or extracted from a person who is mad. You know that very well.'

Astrid nodded. They had tried their cures on her for two years, and none of them had worked. Lightheaded, she leaned back on the couch and tried to concentrate. 'Then what do you propose?'

'That you learn to live with it, to control it. You may still fade, yes, but perhaps you will learn to control it and manage it. Perhaps one day it will not take you away for ever.'

'One day I will be safe?' Her heart beat fast enough to all but burst from her chest. She sat up again and clenched her hands together over her abdomen. 'Can I be safe?'

'If we can manage it, then yes.' Dr Amherst nodded. 'But first you have to trust me. You don't yet, do you?'

'My husband trusts you.'

'Your husband only trusts me because I'm not a man touching his property,' Dr Amherst said acerbically. 'Do you trust me to treat you?'

Astrid took a breath and let it out slowly. 'Not really.'

'You trust me enough to tell the truth. Some can't even go that far. Do you feel safe when you fade, or do you fade when you're not safe?'

'I try not to fade if I'm not safe. I know . . . it . . .' She lost the words.

'You know people will hurt you when you fade.' Dr Amherst spoke softly. 'You have to learn to trust, but perhaps not yet.'

Astrid nodded. She gripped her skirts with her hands, wrinkling the fabric.

'I want to try something,' Dr Amherst said, 'but it means you must trust me, if only a little bit. It might help with your fading and it will be a good practice. Will you?'

Swallowing against a suddenly dry throat, Astrid paused a long moment before nodding. Consent, if given, could not be rescinded as easily. But Dr Amherst didn't trust her husband any more than she did. Surely that meant she could be trusted, even a little?

Too late to take her nod back, Astrid watched nervously as the doctor noted her assent and stood. 'It's all right. I want you to inhale, then exhale. Slowly and regularly. Close your eyes.'

Astrid obeyed, but her breath came out ragged.

The doctor's cool hands touched either side of her head. She flinched away. No. No one would touch her here. The doctor's cool hands remained. Tears welled in Astrid's eyes, running free from under her eyelids. She had given consent. She had trusted. She had been foolish to trust.

'Relax.' Dr Amherst was close enough that Astrid felt her breath on her forehead. 'You are safe.'

A light grew in Astrid's mind, soft and gentle, like the sunrise on a misty spring morning. She heard Dr Amherst's voice in her head. *You are safe, you are calm. You don't fade while the sun is shining.*

She shook her head, trying to find the peace of the moor, trying to escape. But she couldn't escape Dr Amherst's voice: *You are safe, you are calm.*

Astrid screamed.

The doctor left her mind with a gasp. In the silence that followed, Astrid opened her eyes. Dr Amherst watched her warily, assessing her like a woman encountering a strange dog.

Gasping, Astrid couldn't catch her breath. She leaned over, feeling her stays creak. For a horrible moment she thought she was going to throw up.

'I never suspected you would be able to feel that,' Dr Amherst said after a moment. 'No wonder the procedure affected you so badly. You could sense what they were thinking.'

Astrid blinked, seeing the men in front of her, their voices commingling in her head, their depravity and curiosity. They had tied her down and drugged her. She couldn't struggle. If they killed her, then her husband would know. The great and fearsome Mr Fowler would find out. As they cut into her, as they took her apart to see how she ticked, she felt their thoughts in her mind. Dark and horrible, their avarice and lasciviousness washed over her. Her husband had been right to distrust them.

Astrid shuddered back to reality. She felt raw, as if the memory had been torn from her. The doctor watched her carefully as she stood slowly. 'I think I would like to take a walk.'

'Of course.' Dr Amherst smiled gently. 'It gets easier, now that we've released it.'

'So I shall live in a waking nightmare?' Astrid shook, but whether from fear or anger, she could not tell. She had trusted the doctor.

'We must release it so it may dissipate.' Dr Amherst's voice comforted her. 'It might not feel like it now, but this is progress.'

Astrid nodded and turned away, not caring if she was rude. She needed air . . . she needed . . . no. She just needed air.

She walked through the house, her footsteps silent on the rugs. An early summer rain pressed against the windows, the chill seeping through to rub against her skin. She folded her arm and tried not to fade. If she kept moving, she wouldn't fade.

Walking brought her to the conservatory and she opened the door. The smooth metal of the knob on her hand grounded her. Her thoughts returned, but they were no comfort. The conservatory air surrounded her, redolent with growing things, of life and energy and all the things Dr Amherst said were good for the healing mind. The hot weight settled on her like a blanket, warming her chilled skin. Comforted, she walked further on to the path that wound through the large space, finding her way to one of the benches.

Arranging her skirts around her, Astrid let her thoughts roam free. They gambolled inside her, tumbling and confused. Was the doctor right? Had she made progress? She hadn't faded as badly since the memories came back. In the months past, the direct memories had made her catatonic for hours.

But about Inga . . .

The implication troubled her. She knew she was fixated on the one person here who had comforted her, but there was something else, something deeper and more dangerous. Something that had caused her husband to send her to the asylum in the first place.

She finally allowed herself to say the name. Regina.

Regina had been her first love, her forbidden secret. She had been Mr Fowler's spinster sister. Every time she saw her husband, she would see Regina in the cut of his jaw, in the colour of his eyes. It made it tolerable to be married to him, if only barely.

When Regina had moved in with them . . . it had been Astrid's downfall. Incapable of resisting Regina's charm, she had fallen in love with the green-eyed brunette.

Inevitably, her husband had caught them. Little escaped his hawk-eyed notice. He had been enraged, not because of the nature of the act, but that someone had touched his wife. He had always been possessive, and this possession had been promised to him in sickness and in health, to do with as he willed.

For her sins against him, he condemned her to Colney Hatch and the mercies of the doctors. In truth, she doubted he knew the practices there, although it would take the most hardened of hearts to condemn her to what he had witnessed there, even while incarcerating her. But the doctors had assured him that she would be given the best of care, as a personal favour.

The best of care . . . she shuddered away from the memory.

'Astrid!' Inga's voice came from behind her and she turned to see the woman approaching on the path from the asylum. 'I heard . . . did you . . . are you all right?'

'I am now.' The words slipped, unbidden, from her lips. She clamped them shut.

Why was she still alive? The question came back to her. There was no reason for it. She faded every day, and it grew worse as she spent time at Minerva House and succumbed to Dr Amherst's treatments. She had no reason to live and yet . . . she glanced at Inga.

The woman sat next to her and took a breath. After a moment, she reached out and touched Astrid's hand. The shock of the touch thrilled through Astrid, along with the soft sensation of the woman's thoughts. She almost pulled her hand away, but took a breath and let it stay.

As if sensing her thoughts, Inga smiled gently at her, then turned her attention to the flowers. 'My mother used to have flowers like this.'

Astrid sensed the lie. Inga's mother had died in childbirth. How could she know this? How *did* she know this? She sensed a connection through her hand, which Inga still retained in her grasp. She rarely sensed others' thoughts, perhaps it was because she rarely touched other people.

The touch of the doctors' hands on her skin, the cold, sickening, piercing sensation of their surgery. She stared at the roses that grew across the path from her. The shadows between the petals called to her, wending their spiral way through the petals. Shadows like the ones in her cell, which had crawled across the wall with the movement of the moon.

'Astrid.' Inga's voice intruded. She tried to focus, but there were more shadows, shadows within shadows, shadows behind shadows, shadows upon shadows.

'Astrid!' Inga said. 'Wake up.'

Blinking slowly, Astrid looked at Inga. There were even shadows there on her face, where her nose met her cheek, where her ears curled.

Inga took both her hands in hers; there was something there, something in the contact. She wanted to go back, she didn't want to fade.

Regina had died. It had all started after Regina's death. But it wasn't Regina here. It was Inga. And it was Astrid.

She was Astrid.

Astrid inhaled, for what felt like the first time in minutes. Inga leaned close to her, a concerned expression on her face. 'Are you quite all right?'

'I will be.' Astrid smiled weakly. She hadn't wanted to fade. She hadn't meant to.

'I want to learn to stop fading,' Astrid said, sitting in Dr Amherst's office several days later.

Dr Amherst looked at her for a moment before speaking. 'Why?'

For a moment, Astrid was flabbergasted. 'What do you mean, why?'

'This is a sudden change for you, a deviation from what you have been doing for years. Why the change?'

Astrid looked down at her skirt, seeing the weave of the fabric. One thread folded over the other. No. She inhaled. 'I want to live.'

'Then we have answered the first question.' Dr Amherst smiled. 'What, then, makes you want to live?'

Shaking her head, Astrid dared not say.

Dr Amherst nodded to herself. After several moments, she spoke. 'Do you know why this asylum is for women only, Astrid?'

Astrid shook her head again. 'No, doctor.'

'It's because relationships in an asylum can be treacherous.'

Her heart dropping, Astrid nodded. She knew what the doctor was going to say, but she didn't know what Dr Amherst would do about it. Would she forbid them to converse? Or would one of them have to leave Minerva House?

The thought had become incomprehensible to her. She had been here since March, a mere four months, and yet it had already become a safe place for her. Here she was free of her husband, here she was safe to fade, and here she was safe to heal. Her scars had stopped bothering her. And she had possibly ruined her chances to remain. All for a woman. She blinked back tears.

'However, if managed appropriately, they can heal scars long since forgotten,' Dr Amherst said and then smiled. 'I have a suspicion that it will help you heal, if managed well.'

'Then . . .' Astrid couldn't bear to say it. Saying it out loud made it real. She wasn't sure if it was supposed to be real yet.

Astrid walked to the garden, still thinking about what Dr Amherst had said. She hadn't been consciously thinking of finding Inga, but she found herself unsurprised when she saw the woman walking towards her.

'I thought I'd find you here,' Astrid said when they met.

Inexplicably, the woman flushed a pretty pink and looked down at her shoes again. Astrid gathered her courage and spoke again: 'Thank you, Inga, for your assistance the other day. I don't think I properly thanked you.'

'So formal.' Inga looked up and met her eyes. 'Are you always this way with friends?'

'So we are friends?' Hope blossomed in her chest and she swallowed it down.

'Of course.' The woman entwined her arm in Astrid's. Astrid caught her breath, thrilled at the casual touch. She sensed . . . trust.

'I have never had a friend with a pseudonym before,' she teased, unsure of what else to say.

'I don't have a pseudonym,' Inga said.

'But you said . . .'

'Dr Amherst says I need to work on my lying.' Inga flushed and looked down at her feet.

Astrid had no idea how to respond to that. After a long pause, Inga released her arm. 'You hate me now, don't you?'

'Of course not.' Astrid took her arm again. 'We all have our madnesses, our ways.'

'Dr Amherst says we are not mad.'

'And yet we are here. Mad together.' Her words caught in her throat. There was no chance that Inga felt . . . and yet there were signs attributed to excessive shyness, or . . . 'Mad enough to . . .'

'Yes?' Inga looked up at her. When Astrid didn't answer, she asked, 'What are we mad enough for?'

'Perhaps . . .' Astrid swallowed. 'Perhaps we are not mad enough for the bravery required.'

They walked to the maze in silence. Pausing at the entrance, Inga turned to Astrid. 'Do you know the way of these things?'

'Of hedge-mazes? No,' Astrid admitted, not speaking what she thought about losing herself.

'You turn right to find the centre, and return left to find the entrance.' Inga smiled up at her. 'Do you trust me?'

Astrid almost shook her head, but she found that she trusted Inga. Perhaps it was only because of her growing attraction, but there was something so honest and true about the woman beneath the lies she wove. After a moment Astrid said, 'Yes.'

Inga grinned and took her hand. A burst of happiness surged through Astrid, warm like the summer sun. 'Follow me.'

Astrid allowed Inga to lead her into the maze, her hand gripping Astrid's tightly. She felt a laugh come to her lips. She had not felt like this since the sunny days in Regina's arms while Mr Fowler was away. The treacherous feeling returned, the one that told her she was doing something wrong, something she would be punished for. She didn't care. *Why are you still alive?*

Right, right and then right again. Astrid followed Inga

through the hedge-maze, holding in the giggle that threatened to come out. This was permission, this was safe. This was secret.

No. She stopped suddenly. Secrets weren't safe. Regina had been a secret. Regina had jumped off a bridge when Mr Fowler found out. Secrets killed.

'What is wrong?' Inga turned with a concerned look on her face.

'What do you mean by this?' Astrid asked.

'Nothing, merely something to pass the time.'

Astrid's chest hurt as she nodded. 'I suppose I should get back then. Nurse Harriet will be looking for us.'

'Please stay,' Inga implored. 'I so wanted to show you the centre of the maze.'

Pausing for a moment, Astrid wondered if she was lying again, and whether it mattered if she was. Looking back, she could see only the roof of the asylum from the greater height of the structure. She turned back to Inga. 'Are we allowed?'

'They wouldn't have it here if we weren't.' Inga grinned.

'Do many get lost here?'

'Most of the patients don't venture beyond the walls of the asylum.'

'And yet it is permitted?'

Inga gave her a mischievous grin. 'No one has told me not to.'

Astrid wondered if she had been told not to. Nothing about Inga steadied her sense of the world, and yet Astrid trusted her. Perhaps it was foolish to trust her, but nevertheless she did. It was possible, she supposed, that she only found her folly in attraction. 'Show me the centre of the maze.'

Dragging her onwards, Inga led her around the right corners, one after another after another until Astrid would have lost all sense of direction but for the sun above. And then the maze opened into the centre of the garden. Astrid gasped.

Trees arched over the hedges, shading the bench that sat at the far end under a covered bower. Lavender, yarrow and daisies accompanied violets and other flowers in a profusion of colour that carpeted either side of the gravel path leading to the bench.

Inga led Astrid to the seat and guided her to sit next to her. Looking up, Astrid saw clouds looming on the horizon. 'We should go back. It may rain.'

'What if it rains?' Inga asked. 'And what if we die tomorrow? We have this moment in the sun.'

Astrid glanced at her out of the corner of her eyes, but Inga had her face turned to the sunlight that trickled through the leaves of the elm shading them. On an ill-considered impulse, she took Inga's hand.

When Inga didn't draw away, Astrid's breath caught in her throat. Perhaps . . . perhaps it was safe. She heard the echoes of the doctor's voice in her head: *You will not fade in the sunlight.*

Inga squeezed her hand, drawing her back from her thoughts. 'Are you truly mad then, or, as Dr Amherst says, are you merely . . . different?'

'I . . .' Astrid braced herself, but the memories came more softly this time, the men around her accusing her, her husband's irate expression. 'I used to be merely different, but I fear my experiences have driven me mad.'

'Then perhaps new experiences . . .' Inga glanced away. Astrid found that she enjoyed how quickly the woman blushed; how her pale skin hid no emotion. 'Perhaps . . .'

Barely countenancing her bravery, Astrid raised Inga's hand to her lips and kissed it softly. The woman folded her fingers around Astrid's. Daring to look up, Astrid saw a shy smile cross her face.

She placed Inga's hand in her lap and held it as she willed her heart to stop beating so quickly. Glancing at Inga, she wondered if the other woman could feel the pulse of her heart through her palm. She looked down and studied her shoes, wondering if she dared to . . .

Gently turning her face toward hers, Inga pulled her closer. Astrid's heart thudded in her chest like a rough staccato. Emotions, hers perhaps, or maybe Inga's, flowed through her, coursing between the two of them. Astrid blinked, surprised. Could she be like Astrid, could she also sense—

Inga kissed her.

Her breath catching, Astrid leaned in to return the kiss, feeling her lips soft against Inga's. They parted after a moment, and Astrid could feel the flush rise to her cheeks as well. She felt no shame, though, none of the emotions Mr Fowler would have her feel for her 'unnatural attractions'. Instead she felt . . . release.

'Are you . . . are you all right?' Inga asked as the silence between them stretched.

She trusted Inga, despite everything. And if Dr Amherst was correct, then she needed to know. 'I . . . I can see the truth, Inga.'

'What do you mean?' Inga gave her a confused look.

'I can . . . I trust you. Despite your condition. I can sense . . . I can sense thoughts.'

'So you are different . . . in more ways than one.' Inga pulled her hand away.

A cold knot formed in Astrid's stomach and she folded her hands on her skirt. 'I suppose I am.'

'Then you . . .' Inga paused, although whether out of confusion or a need to gather her thoughts, Astrid couldn't say.

Astrid clenched her hands together and looked away. She had made a mistake, this was all a mistake. *Cure the body, cure the mind,* the doctors had said it. But there had been no cure, not for her, not for her 'differences'.

'You can really tell when I'm lying?' Inga said finally.

'I can,' Astrid said.

'Then you are truly like me, you are . . . sensitive. You can help me.' Inga smiled. 'But how can I help you?'

'Prove to me that I am not mad.'

Inga kissed her again.

Nurse Harriet caught them coming out of the hedge-maze. Astrid let Inga's hand drop as a cold chill went through both of them. The nurse glared. 'It's time for tea.'

'Of course, Nurse Harriet.' Inga looked down at her shoes.

'And don't think I won't be telling the doctor that you were in there.' The nurse's lips pursed impossibly thin.

'The doctor has yet to forbid us the use of the gardens.' Inga spoke softly, taking Astrid's hand again. Astrid sensed a burning rage in her, born from the same flames that burned in Astrid's scars. She had forgotten about her scars there, in that one small moment in the sun. Now the pain returned tenfold, as if to punish her for the one illicit moment of happiness. She gasped and folded her arms over her stomach.

A deep frown crossed Nurse Harriet's sour expression. The frown looked like the nurse who had dragged her from her cell at Colney Hatch, along the long corridor from her cell to the room; the room where they—

Nurse Harriet reached forward and grabbed Astrid's arm. Astrid gasped at the contact. Fear and hate churned through her, nauseating her on top of the pain of her scars. 'Come with me. You are going to explain yourself to the doctor.'

'Don't touch her!' Inga followed them, but the nurse rounded on her, pulling Astrid's arm painfully. 'You stay here. We'll have no more of your lies.'

The nurse dragged Astrid towards the asylum. Nurse Harriet would take her to the room. They would hurt her again. She would— Pain like she had not felt in years surged through Astrid, coming in waves and making her lightheaded. She clutched at her stays with her free arm, praying that the bones would hold her here, make her . . .

She found herself falling; the sickly sweet sensation of losing all control of her body came over her. Nurse Harriet clutched at her, trying to keep her on her feet.

A popping sensation presaged the loosening of Astrid's mind from her body. She watched her body fall in a crumpled heap on the ground, the dead weight pulling the nurse down with her.

Inga rushed forward, and Nurse Harriet pushed her away with a curse. She crouched over Astrid's body. Astrid felt a strange tugging sensation, as if a thousand fingers pinched her skin, then there was nothing. She remained tethered to her body, or rather, she was not sent floating when the wind kicked up. Her only sense of the wind was in how Inga's hair blew and how her dress flapped as Nurse Harriet picked up her body.

She looked around herself and found the world fogged, as if on the moor. Immediately comforted, she watched as her body was wrenched from her, sensing the ties pull and stretch. She supposed she could follow, but the fog comforted her. The sun shone too brightly on her body. It was easier to stay here, stay safe, stay hidden.

Part of her knew she had been here before like this; she remembered the floating feeling, the lack of pain, the lack of sensation altogether. Pain had sent her here and pain had returned her here.

She blinked, remembering the scalpels and knives shining in the gaslight. She turned away further into the fog.

A flash of red caught her vision and she turned despite herself. They had put her in her bed and Inga threw herself over Astrid's motionless body, refusing to leave despite Nurse Harriet's strident demands. For a moment, Astrid felt a pang. Surely she should go back, surely she should comfort Inga?

The fog comforted her, muffled her concerns. Safety came from the fog, no one could touch her here. No one could hurt her. They couldn't drag her back to the asylum, they couldn't hurt her ever again.

No. She didn't want to fade any more. She wanted to be free. She wanted . . .

All she had to do was turn away, walk away into the fog. She turned away.

'Astrid.'

She shook her head and took one step into the fog. She did not want to confront her feelings or memories. Safer instead to fade, to lose herself.

But . . . Inga.

'Astrid. Astrid, come back.' The doctor's voice echoed through the fog, weak and far away.

'No,' she mouthed the word, finding her voice gone. She wanted to say yes, but the fog muffled even that.

'Astrid.' Dr Amherst stood next to her in the fog and Astrid flinched away.

'Go away.'

'Please listen to me.' Dr Amherst spoke calmly; she didn't shout like the men had shouted in her head, their avarice and sickness driving her farther into the fog. Astrid hesitated. 'The body cannot be long divorced from the spirit. You must return.'

Astrid shook her head and took another step. She wouldn't return. Not if life was like this. Not if there was no end to the pain. Not if she couldn't stop fading.

But she had Inga; she could love as she willed. Inga wasn't Regina. Mr Fowler wouldn't know.

She took a third step and Dr Amherst's voice came to her more softly. 'What about Inga?'

Startled, Astrid turned back. Dr Amherst appeared in the fog, an understanding smile on her face. The doctor spoke again: 'What about Inga?'

Astrid remained silent, despite the fact that her entire being yearned to return, to be with Inga.

Dr Amherst sensed what she did not say. 'Minerva House is an asylum, a safe place. You will never be forced to leave.'

'I'm here, Astrid.' Inga's voice joined Dr Amherst's. Astrid sensed a connection between the two women stretching to her, a lifeline to save her from herself.

Astrid's heart soared. 'Inga.'

Astrid opened her eyes and saw Inga's face close to hers. The woman smelled of roses. Reaching out her hand, Astrid touched her cheek.

Inga placed her hands over Astrid's and smiled with tears in her eyes. 'Nurse Harriet said you were not waking up; she told me I wouldn't be allowed to see you.'

Dreading what she would find, Astrid looked around for the nurse. When she saw Dr Amherst instead, the dread unknotted. The doctor smiled. 'I have other nurses who treat my patients like human beings, not animals who must be caged. There was no longer a place for her here.'

She took Inga's hand and held it as a question occurred to her. 'And what if Mr Fowler comes to reclaim his property?'

'Surely he will not want a raving lunatic as a wife?' Dr Amherst smiled. 'If you truly want to remain here, then you shall also remain mad.'

'But . . .'

'Not truly mad, but with your differences, you will never be truly sane. Not in the way our society defines sanity,' Dr Amherst clarified. 'Perhaps one day rational minds will prevail, but for now, we must remain insane in an irrational world.'

'And my madness? Is it safe? Can I learn to control it?'

'I learned to, and Inga has made some progress. Yet I have not had the experiences you have, nor the suffering.' Dr Amherst became solemn for a moment. 'But you show resilience few women in your situation have shown. Perhaps one day you will not fade, perhaps one day you will not sense quite as strongly. But first, you must heal from your scars and your pain.'

Astrid reflexively put her hand to her stomach, but for the first time in years the scars did not flare at their mention. 'And what do you want, Inga?'

Inga glanced at Dr Amherst, who nodded reassuringly. Inga looked down at Astrid. 'I want . . . I want you to stay.'

Astrid sat up and took both of Inga's hands in hers. Where their hands met, thoughts and feelings moved between them like flowing water around two rocks. Gasping at the sensation, Astrid looked up at Inga. Before she saw it, she sensed the smile on the woman's lips.

She was safe. She would not fade.

A CHRISTMAS CARROLL: A STRANGELY BEAUTIFUL NOVELLA

Leanna Renee Hieber

Prologue: December 1888, at the edge of London's reality

Three spirits murmured to each other, standing in the luminous Liminal that separated the waiting Whisper-world from the dazzling, drawing light of the Great Beyond. The Whisper-world was quite the grey purgatory, while the Great Beyond, well . . . who possesses the words to describe Paradise?

The Liminal is a place where magic is discussed and made, from whence spirits receive duties and inspiration, where dreams are both created and abandoned. Where those who are worthy might become angels. It is a place where time is porous and malleable; it keeps its own clock. Here pasts are recaptured and futures glimpsed; here spirits from every walk of death – those still invested in parties on Earth – discuss their current designs on the living, for better or for worse.

The present trio at the Liminal edge was shrouded in shadow, and they contemplated parties in London, England, under the reign of Queen Victoria. Their clothing, too, represented various decades within Her Highness's extensive reign, long may she live. The spirits stood before a living portrait, rendered by exquisite hands: the vast proscenium of an elaborate stage dwarfed their spirit trio. The set scene laid wide before them was a stately school on a moonlit night, dim, eerie, engaging . . . and awaiting its players.

The eldest of the three spirits stepped forward, as if to touch this threshold upon which the past would play, a tall woman, appearing nearly forty and garbed in a plain dress. Her long, waving tresses – in life, they would have been a dark blonde – hung gamesomely down around her shoulders. Though she wore the greyscale of death, the palette of the Whisper-world, her eyes were kind and her face very much alive.

She addressed the two spirits before her – a fair young woman and a raggedy little boy – in a boisterous Irish accent, as if she were presenting a vaudeville act, a mischievous light in her grey hazel eyes. 'Lady and gentleman, our forces of divine intervention present to you one of several scenes rather recently acted, starring our charges Headmistress Rebecca Thompson and Vicar Michael Carroll, members of that honourable spectral patrol known as the Guard. Because we all have a history with them, we are charged now to help them.'

She took the hands of her fellow spirits, and the Liminal clock set high above the stage frame – a device consisting simply of two vast floating metal hands above shifting metal barrels of numbers, arranged to display a calendar date – started to turn. The scene began to play, memory cast wide, as if upon a photography plate, sounds emanating forth quite like magic.

'We must view key past moments, my fellow spirits,' the eldest instructed, 'and understand the hearts that are at stake. Watch and learn, so we may bring about answers to these issues.'

The spirits did . . .

In the scene, distant music and laughter lured a tall, willowy woman with silver-streaked auburn hair from her book-filled office into the tenebrous hall of the stately, Romanesque fortress that was Athens Academy. She wore a dark woollen dress, buttoned primly and proper as befitted her station as headmistress, yet sewn with just enough elegance to keep her from looking entirely the spinster. Up a grand staircase to a shadowy landing she crept, a wide, colonnaded foyer lit only by great swathes of moonlight and several low-trimmed gas lamps. Hanging back out of sight, she took in the antics of her longtime compatriots, this motley family fate had provided in her youth, the spectre-policing Guard.

A foppish blonde man stood arm in arm with a gorgeous brunette, both swaying beside a broad-shouldered woman playing a waltz on a fiddle, her face mirrored the greyscale woman at the Liminal . . . At this, the spirit watching her living past grimaced.

Nearby stood a distinguished figure in clergyman's garb, singing a soft and tender verse in accompaniment to the strings. From the shadows, the headmistress stared at him as if she'd never known or paid attention to his voice, and for a fleeting moment she appeared enchanted. But it was the centre of the scene that clearly struck her a blow, the black-clad man and his ghost-pale partner, who danced slowly through a wide shaft of moonlight.

The waltzing pair was clearly enraptured. Languorous steps, their bodies partaking in the close confidence only marriage could fashion . . . The girl in the moonlight was nothing short of an angel, graceful and blinding white, radiating love as pure as her skin, her eyes and hair colourless. Her partner stared down at her as if she were salvation incarnate, his otherwise stoic manner entirely transformed.

The headmistress donned pain like a mask. She retreated from the tableau, letting tears come as they would. Keeping to the shadows, she slipped down the stairs and to the corner of the foyer below, looking out over the courtyard. Pressing her forehead to the window, she sighed and did not hear the soft tread behind her.

His voice made her whirl: 'I know that certain things do not unfold according to our desires.'

It was the clergyman. He stood partly in shadow, his bushy, grey-peppered hair smoothed down from its usual chaos, and his blue eyes danced with an unusually bright light. 'I know we cannot always choose who we love. And I know how it hurts to see the one we love look adoringly at someone else. I know; I have been watching you watch Alexi for years.'

The headmistress registered his words, gaped, flushed and then returned to staring out the window, as if by turning away she might hide her transparent heart from his unmatched scrutiny.

'I cannot replace him,' the clergyman began again, and waited patiently for her to turn. He continued with a bravery that seemed to surprise them both. 'And I do not fault you your emotions, though I must admit a certain jealousy as to their bent. I do not expect to change anything with these words. I know I am bold and perhaps a fool, but I can remain silent no longer. Should you desire closer company . . .' His fortitude wavered and he could not continue the invitation.

He dropped his gaze and said, 'I shall now return to a glass of wine. Or two. But as we're too old to play games and deny our hearts, I felt it my duty to speak. At long last. At long, long last.' He then offered her his signature winning smile, which could warm the most inhuman heart, bowed slightly and retreated, leaving the headmistress clearly thunderstruck, standing alone once more in the glare of the moonlight through the window.

The scene paused in its inexorable march of a now-past event, and the voyeur spirits in the Liminal turned to one another.

'What is to be done of it?' the younger female asked in her London accent, staring at the subject before her with both pity and recognition.

'And what stands between them?' said the little boy in urchin's clothes, his voice a Scots brogue.

'They stand between themselves. And they stand grieving,' the Irishwoman's spirit replied. 'They need a good shaking, the both of them. Twenty years of nonsense, which shall end with us. If we do all we can, if we do what I wish, we'll end up with *this.*' She murmured a brief Catholic prayer for intercession – all she could think to offer – and opened her hands in supplication.

The Liminal responded, recognizing the tongues of all faiths, and the great scene shifted.

The Liminal clock turned, the numbers trembling, the long hands quivering, as this outcome was not certain. But this possible future scene revealed a warm hearth and home, a blazing fire backlighting two silhouetted forms, the subjects in question, bending close as only lovers would. The trio of spirits gave sighs of appreciation, felt a gruesome weight of melancholy lifted.

The Liminal felt the change in their hearts and the corners of its proscenium reacted: sparkling, vibrant, humming. The relieving of melancholy wielded great power. So, conversely, did the creation of it.

'But it's dangerous, the tasks they must be taken through,' the little boy protested, knowing her intent. He shifted his feet on the glassy stone of the Liminal. 'We could lose them to time and shadow. We could lose *ourselves,* be trapped for ever if we're not careful. I do love hangin' from the Athens chandelier, but a nice rest might make a lovely Christmas present . . .' The loving scene before the fire faded to darkness with a slow hiss.

The second female nodded. 'Even if it weren't nigh impossible . . . it's dangerous to weave souls through memories and time. Dark moments can rewrite themselves even darker. To take them through time, to risk changes? To change only the necessary moments of their particular history for the correct outcome? And, doing so with members of the Guard? Why, doesn't that make it even more perilous? Especially considering Darkness?'

The Irishwoman pursed her lips, undeterred. 'True, we only vanquished the lord of this realm in form, not in spirit. We broke the cycle of the vendetta, but human misery will build him again. If we bring the headmistress into his world and she cannot overcome the poison inside her, if she's captured by the shadows, we'll have lost. I'll have died for nothing, the Guard toiled for nothing and the darkness that presses in around us even now will win her. But I'm willing to risk another sacrifice, to threaten my own eternal love and rest. For I believe in many things, but I believe most heartily in Rebecca and Michael.'

'You'll dare bring them here?' asked the young woman in awe.

'I assure you we've been up against far worse,' said the Irishwoman. 'I warred against the worst of the Whisper-world, remember! I tell you, I'll make a sacrifice.' She called to the Liminal, announcing herself like a prophet. 'Liminal edge, you tell those who beg your aid that you'll not change the course of lives without barter. But be clear, I make my deal with you, not the devil, and I expect generous justice. Thus I place my soul on the line. I agree to remain trapped here in this uncomfortable between, unable to appear to my beloved, my friends, unable to gain the Great Beyond, until our two charges make the first honest step unto the lessons we must teach.'

The Liminal stage had gone dark, a wall of black before them, the occasional tendril of Whisper-world mist curling across its surface.

'How . . . does one make a . . . deal?' the little boy murmured, breathless.

'Aodhan told me. My love travelled between worlds for ages and learned many things.' The Irishwoman did not hesitate. She pressed her palms against the Liminal wall and hissed in pain, as if there were needles in that barrier. A deep black fluid oozed from her palms, phantom blood, sipping a bit of her life force before her wounds closed, her compact sealed. The Liminal sparked across its dark threshold like a fork of lightning, the air was charged and the portal was open. Clearly, it was ready to begin.

She turned to her fellows with hope upon her grey face. 'Sometimes a good haunting is just what a soul needs, even the most heroic. And we shall surely give them that. Come, we've not long before Christmas. It is the time of miracles.'

'And the Liminal well knows it,' said the boy, peering warily at the portal of infinite possibility. The edges of the frame sparked again, as if in assent.

The Irishwoman nodded. 'Go, let us begin. Call upon them, the both of you. I daresay *one* of them will be thrilled to see you.'

They all three closed their eyes in concentration.

The Liminal clock hands and numbers shifted to the hour and date concurrent with the mortal present, just days beyond the memory they had viewed. A new scene was born, and the living portrait now displayed a modest apartment filled with the same lively Guard characters, all save the headmistress and she who was lost.

The little boy spirit was the first to descend through the now-porous Liminal membrane, to pass through that proscenium portal and into the room. Immediately inside, there was great tumult regarding him.

The spirit of the Irishwoman chuckled at this, her greyscale eyes filling with fond tears. The other spirit placed a hand upon her shoulder, but the Irishwoman shrugged it off. 'Go on, Miss Peterson.' She gestured her forward, grinning. 'I trust that I will eventually be able to follow you.

Her voice was hopeful but her mood anxious.

As Ms Peterson descended, the Irishwoman remained in the Liminal, watching the familiar, tumultuous melee of spectral and human interaction. 'I'll forever miss that. You,' she murmured to the friends who could not see her.

After a moment, she moved into the thicker shadows. There she drew back a drape on another picture, made manifest by the powers of the Liminal edge, a further masterwork in the museum of the cosmos, and murmured, 'On a separate stage, the curtain now rises on Headmistress Thompson. Alone.'

Indeed, just beyond sat Ms Thompson, isolated in her academy apartments, her knees folded awkwardly upon bedclothes that showed no signs of having been slept in. Usually a model of efficiency, hard work and propriety, the headmistress was uncharacteristically undone.

The Irishwoman clucked her tongue. 'Rebecca. Why aren't you with our friends? We scored a victory against Darkness. All of us. Why can't you make use of it?'

The headmistress's eyes were red with tears, her blouse askew. A white cat lay curled at her feet, and her thin hand stroked it almost mechanically, as if she dared not stop.

'I've no regrets, Rebecca. Not a single one,' the voyeur spirit murmured. 'It's time you felt the same.' She turned back to the great stage opposite, inside of which her friends had resettled. Her two ghostly companions had disappeared, and so she addressed the former Guard, those she considered family. 'It's time *all* of you felt the same.'

In the living painting that showcased her cohorts, the sturdy man who had confessed his heart in the earlier scene still sported distinguished age lines, unruly salt-and-pepper hair and clergyman's clothes. His blue eyes were wide and sparkling with an incomparable quality of compassion, but somewhere deep behind those oceanic orbs, somewhere deep behind the wide and contagious smile and armour of good humour, lay the same private, keening pain that had just been on display.

'Twenty years of nonsense, Michael Carroll. Upon my dead body, I swear to you, you'll have a very Merry Christmas if it's the last thing I do.'

Chapter One

Vicar Michael Carroll turned the ladle in his pot of mulled wine and let the scented steam rise to his nostrils, unlocking emotion, memory and all those forces that such smells do around the Christmas holiday. He glanced out the window of the kitchen in his small Bloomsbury flat, which looked unflatteringly down upon an alley, and was pleased to witness a solitary flake of snow brush the thick, uneven glass before vanishing. It would be the first of many firsts this season, if the fates allowed.

Drawing himself a heaping tankard of Josephine's favourite cabernet, procured from the stores of her café and heated with bobbing chunks of cinnamon, fruit and cloves, he moved into his small dining room. The corners of the chamber were plastered at uneven angles, having settled awkwardly at the beginning of the century when the building was new. The window here only gave half a view of the avenue beyond, but he could see lamplighters plying their trade and nearing his street. It was not yet dark, and a purple sky reigned over parapets and smokestacks that grew ever higher and higher, the churning wheels of industry cranking them upward to challenge twilight's celestial throne.

He sat at a rough-hewn wooden table, worn smooth by use, company and the press of his own hands. Sliding his palms forward onto it, he eased into his chair, bracing himself and his heart, connecting with something solid and simple. The odd powers that had coursed through his body had once made his fingers twitch. Those powers were no more. Nonetheless, holding his palms firmly down, rooting himself to the table and to humanity, was one of his usual exercises. It brought him peace.

Michael, unlike his five compatriots in the Guard, who until very recently had been charged with the Grand Work, had never cursed it. Theirs was a strenuous and at times lonely responsibility, though it didn't have to be, but it was ultimately rewarding. The Guard had been the law of the land, spectrally speaking. Though they'd left benign spirits well enough alone, each of their coterie had been granted a specific, beautiful power to arraign evil spirits and keep them from harassing the unwitting mortal populace. The Guard had controlled traffic of the unfettered and malignant dead all throughout London for near twenty years. They'd done the world a great super-natural deal of what Michael would consider Christian charity. But he had to admit that his role in the Grand Work had held some irony.

Literally the Heart of the group, he could open locked doors, touch a breastbone and flood someone's veins with joy, change the emotional contents of a room, shifting energy and intent like metals processed by alchemy. And yet he'd never gained happiness of his own, or the heart of the woman he'd loved for near twenty years.

In the beginning they'd been simple teenaged youths, arraigned by a goddess-like force and called to duty. They'd been universally awkward and unlikely companions from disparate backgrounds and classes; they'd suspected little of their lives ahead. Michael hadn't known anything when he began seeing ghosts and learning how his respective gift augmented their group. He hadn't known how long it would take for their prophesied seventh member to join their ranks, or that one of their beloved number would fall in recent battle. What he did know was that, from the very first moment he laid eyes on her, he loved the young and spindly brunette who would be their second-in-command. He'd loved Rebecca Thompson since Westminster Bridge in the summer of 1867.

She, in turn, likely from that very same moment, had loved the young man who would become their leader: Alexi. The battle with the Darkness and the Whisper-world, in retrospect, seemed the easy part.

Michael pressed his hands harder against the table and slid them farther from his body, stretching his taut muscles and wrestling with his nerves, like Jacob did the angel. He'd not seen Rebecca since they laid Jane in the tomb three days prior; she had gone to her apartments and locked herself in. She blamed herself, he could tell, wished God had taken her instead. Michael thought the sentiment might kill him. Nothing felt familiar. He'd lost his powers, Jane, and now he was losing Rebecca. His heart, so full of joy and love, was suffering a tumbling withdrawal from its preternaturally augmented height. It was a terrifying, dizzying fall.

'Pull yourself together, man,' he murmured. 'It's nearly Christmas.'

His front door burst open, making him jump and splash warm wine on to his hand. Pursing his lips, knowing just who it was without even a glance, he finally looked up to behold the stern and striking figure upon his threshold. All in black stood his dear friend and unintentional rival, Alexi Rychman, former leader of the London Guard.

'Dear God, Professor. I truly thought, now that the weight of the known world is no longer entirely on your shoulders, that you might at least allow yourself the more socially preferred custom of knocking upon a friend's door before entering.'

'Old habits,' Alexi intoned, his voice rich, low and commanding. It would always be thus, even though he had no group to lead any longer.

Behind Alexi, a moonbeam of a young woman stood with an apologetic look on her face. Michael grinned and forgot his irritation. 'Ah, well, Mrs Rychman . . . with you at his side, all debts are erased.'

Alexi turned proudly to his entering bride. She was certainly the youth among them, Alexi not quite twice her age, but then again, where ancient prophecies were concerned, when gods were fiddling with mortal lives and taking their bodies as their own, age hardly mattered. Her fine taffeta skirts, in her favourite shade of rich blue, brushed the coarse wood of the door and rustled as she closed it.

She received Michael's warm expression with a radiant smile that transformed her death-white face into a ray of magical starlight. There was nothing about her that was ordinary. The whole of Mrs Persephone Rychman remained white as a spectre, even the hair piled atop her head in an elegant coif. But the light here was diffuse enough that she did not have to wear the dark blue tinted glasses that shielded her eerie, breathtaking, ice-blue eyes from any harshness.

'My husband never allows me to get to a door first, Vicar Carroll, otherwise I might abate his most startling tradition,' she said sweetly.

'Since we've lost so many traditions, I suppose we'd best keep the ones remaining,' Michael chuckled in reply.

While he had wanted an evening alone – to plan, ruminate and dream – he could not deny that Persephone made all disappointments bearable. She had saved them all from spectral Armageddon, and her mere presence reminded him of hope. Even her husband, a cold and fearsome man, eased into something more handsome around his strangely beautiful wife.

'Come then, you must sit down, now that you've come calling and disturbed my quiet. I see your nostrils flaring at the smell of it, Professor, so I know you'll want a cup of your favourite brew.'

Alexi nodded and drew out a chair for his wife. She looked up at him with fond eyes, her hand unconsciously grazing her abdomen where her corset stays were bound more loosely these days. Having almost lost what she'd hardly known she had, under horrific circumstances that Michael didn't wish to relive, he noticed her hand now rested there often, cradling the invisible life their beloved Jane had died to save.

Ducking into his small kitchen, he returned with a glass of wine for Alexi and a cup of steaming tea for Percy: as a parochial vicar for the Church of England, he always had a kettle of water at the ready, for he never knew when a parishioner might need guidance. It was more often that the Guard came calling. Would they still, now that they had lost their gifts?

The pair accepted their drinks, and Alexi wasted no time in admitting the reason for his visit.

'Michael, dear chap, now that we're no longer arbiters of escapees from the spectral realm, I feel it necessary that Percy and I take the genuine, lengthy honeymoon we were so rudely denied by the onslaught of spectral warfare. However, I think it ill-advised to leave Athens Chapel unattended, should there be . . . spiritual backlash or any other such nonsense. I'll need your assistance to keep an eye open in case something flares up. Not that we could band together again without our powers, without our healer . . .' Alexi's usually firm voice faltered, and everyone looked at the table. He cleared his throat. 'I assume this is not a problem?'

Michael opened and closed his mouth. He didn't want more responsibility; he wanted time now to be a suitor.

Alexi read the conflict upon his face. 'You've something better to do?'

'The good vicar does have a job, Alexi,' Percy murmured.

Alexi looked unimpressed. 'Be that as it may, I might need him to step in and assist Rebecca with goings-on at the school, too. I'm not officially an administrator, but I might as well have been; the headmistress deferred to my judgement in many things.'

True, Rebecca often listened to him, but Alexi didn't have to be so smug about it. His unwavering air of confidence rode Michael far rougher than usual.

About to open his mouth and chide his friend, he stopped and considered the impulse. What was this overwhelming irritation he felt for his dear comrade? He had always suffered notions of fleeting jealousy or resignation, like any mortal, but never with such a sudden sense of petty anger. His great heart had indeed withered with the loss of his gift. He wondered if his inner foundation of faith, too, his touchstone of assurance, would prove similarly shaken.

Percy's voice roused him from his worried reverie. 'How are you faring, Michael, in our new retirement?' She spoke softly, brushing her hand over his. Looking into her eyes, he fancied he could see her thoughts. Curious, empathizing, she was so intuitive despite her innocence, such an old soul in such a young, inexperienced body.

He shrugged. 'Good, good. I spend more time at the church – never a bad place to be when one faces such a dramatic shift in life. There's more chance to think, to pray . . .

I've plans, you know. You two are not the only ones trying to make up for lost time.' Percy took a breath, but Michael continued before she could interject. 'And how is *he* faring?' He indicated Alexi.

'I'm not sure he quite knows what to do with himself,' Percy replied, allowing herself a little grin.

Alexi turned. 'Please don't *you* go calling me insufferable, as the Guard has always done.'

At that moment, the door was thrown wide and a nasal voice was quick to comment, 'Did I hear the word "insufferable"?' Lord Elijah Withersby entered, a lean, flaxen-haired man in foppish satin sleeves, and he opened his arms to the assembled company. 'Why, you must be talking about His Royal Eerieness, Minister of the Constant Sneer!' He bounded forward and clapped the grimacing Alexi on the arm.

Percy bit back a giggle, ever entertained by Lord Withersby's outlandish titles for her imperious, black-clad husband. Michael was glad she was so good-humoured about the teasing, the Guard's eldest tradition of all.

'Alexi, my dear man,' Elijah exclaimed, 'I know you simply cannot be away for long without missing me terribly, so I thought I'd oblige you. Rebecca said you were here on business.

Hullo, Vicar! Wine, please!'

'Rebecca spoke with you?' Michael asked, on edge. 'Did you see her?'

Elijah shrugged. 'She barked at me from the other side of her door.'

Alexi nodded. 'Have we all called upon her then, and she has admitted no one?'

'So it would seem.' Michael wasn't sure if his clenched fists were noticed, but he couldn't be bothered if they were. He sighed, rose and went for more wine. The instinct of hospitality ran deep.

A beautiful and impeccably dressed woman appeared through the front door. Rolling her eyes, she closed it behind her with the same consideration as Percy had done, and moved to Lord Withersby's side. 'Neither of you knock,' she complained, offering fond, French-accented derision to both Elijah and Alexi. She looked at Percy with empathy, a twinkle in her eye. 'We trail behind well-dressed animals, my dear.'

Josephine Belledoux, the Artist of London's onetime Guard, and Lord Withersby, its Memory, had been lovers for longer than they'd cared to reveal. Not wanting to conflict with the delicate, pathetic love triangles already scoring the group, they'd thought it best to keep their happy pairing away from their cohorts. The truth of their relationship had been only recently admitted.

Michael returned with more mulled wine and pulled spare, rickety chairs from what could hardly be called a sitting room into the dining area.

'Yes, *I* am here on business, Withersby.' Alexi eyed the turquoise fabric of Elijah's sleeve, which was splayed upon the table. Reaching out to finger the starched gilt lace upon the cuff, he withdrew in distaste. 'What are *you* doing?'

'I don't know what to do!' Elijah cried, collapsing dramatically upon the table. 'How on earth can I traipse about London as I wish, commandeer auntie's house as I please, if I cannot bend anyone's mind to my bidding? If I cannot make them forget, if I cannot become invisible in their presence . . . Oh, the horror of living the *real* life of a gentleman!'

'Oh, Withersby, you're hardly a gentleman. You'll make do just fine,' Alexi replied.

'He's maddening,' Josephine muttered. 'I'm painting more beautiful canvases than I've ever painted in my life, finally, subjects besides angels and death, and he won't leave me alone for a minute. *Mon Dieu.* I told him he should take up a sport, use all this excess energy of his—'

'You know, Withersby, I shudder to think what would have happened to you without our Grand Work to set your life's early course,' Alexi remarked. 'That said, you might enjoy what leisure your class offers you, now that you're free to fully take part.'

Elijah stared as if his friend were daft. 'You'll never understand the finer points of high society. Why, if I've taught you nothing, I'd have thought you'd realize it's a requirement of my class never to be content!'

Everyone turned, eyeing Josephine with pity. 'I know, I know, I'm a fool,' she said, her French accent making her words drip with drama. 'I tell him he needs a hobby, a new club, something. But no, he goes careening about the estate or pacing madly about our flat—'

'You've a flat?' Michael asked.

'We've always had a flat,' Elijah replied. 'But with the upcoming nuptials—'

Josephine interrupted. 'That's truly the reason why we're here, Vicar, we need to set a date for the wedding.'

Alexi turned to her. 'You know, you don't have to do this.'

Josephine chuckled. 'Our fates were sealed long ago,' she said with mock weariness, touching her fiancé's face with such obvious adoration that no sarcasm in the world could have countered it. 'I accept as best I can and suffer onward. Right, Madame Rychman?'

Percy shrugged. 'Alexi's not nearly the handful that Lord Withersby is. I find myself resigned to no fate but happiness.' She smirked at Elijah, a sparkle in her eerie eyes. Alexi grinned triumphantly and snuggled his wife close.

It was still uncanny, Michael thought, to see Alexi smile. Twenty years he'd known the man and all Alexi had done was scowl. The transformation was truly remarkable. But some things would never change, particularly such endless verbal fencing.

'Alexi,' Elijah whined, 'how*ever* will I have the upper hand now that you have this sweet young thing to take your part?'

Alexi shrugged. 'Your fiancé will have to put on a better act of being your champion.'

Josephine lifted her hands in mock chagrin. Elijah grabbed her fingers and kissed them.

Further discourse was ended as the room suddenly lit with a strange and shifting light, as if the air were a curtain blown in a breeze. A spirit burst through the wall – a young boy – and the temperature plummeted. Alexi jumped up and lifted his palms. The Guard all stood and reached for one another, ready for action. Percy rose from respect, having been brought late into their circle. She was not quick on the defensive, having rarely been ambushed by ghosts of the villainous variety, and she stared at the boy in recognition.

Alexi opened his mouth to say a benediction in a foreign tongue never meant for mortal ears, bequeathed only to the Guard. He anticipated the bursts of an angelic choir, braced himself for a charged and ancient wind that would whip up around them, magnifying their powers against the restless dead . . . but he could say nothing. He could hear nothing. There was no familiar blue fire crackling from his hand, no celestial music hanging glorious on the air. He was a demigod no more. None of them retained such honours. They had earned this retirement, but clearly none of them had grown accustomed to it.

The spirit bobbed before them, a ghostly urchin, unperturbed. Michael recognized him, too, he haunted the ceiling of the foyer of Athens Academy, circling the chandelier, always watching the headmistress with interest.

Alexi's upraised arm slowly sank, defeated. Michael watched his former leader and felt for him; the general was back from the war, with nothing to command after spending more than half his life in service. No, it was not an easy shift – for any of them.

Percy instinctively took her husband's hand. 'It's all right, Alexi. Billy means no harm, he comes bearing tidings,' she murmured. Her beloved sank into a chair, crestfallen, and Percy gave him one last empathetic glance before turning her attention to the spirit. 'Yes? What have you come to tell me, Billy?'

The boy only had eyes for Percy, with an occasional glance at Michael. The one-sided conversation continued as the boy rapidly gesticulated. Percy nodded, clearly still translator to the dead, their medium, the only member of the Guard who had ever been able to hear spirits speak, and the only one still apparently in possession of any of her powers. Translating had been part of her duty as the Guard's prophesied seventh member, if only one of her many gifts.

A second spirit bobbed through the wall, a once-lovely girl now cast in a ghostly greyscale, her clothing dated a half-century prior, her spectral curls weightless in a phantom breeze. Percy's eerie eyes widened. 'Oh, Constance!' she cried, rushing forward joyfully. The ghost moved to embrace her with a cold gust of air. Percy closed her eyes and waited out the chill, as if this were a perfectly normal greeting – for a girl who was born seeing spirits and calling them friends, it likely was.

'How I've missed you, Constance,' she said. 'Are you well and at peace?'

The female spirit spoke as animatedly as the boy, but she seemed to be offering reassurances. She turned to the urchin and they both nodded, glancing again, Michael noted uncomfortably, at him.

'I think it's a lovely idea!' Percy exclaimed.

'What is?' the ex-Guard chorused.

Percy turned to them with a mysterious smile, her eyes lingering on Michael in a way that made him even more uneasy. 'Oh nothing, just a bit of a Christmas present these spirits have in mind.' She looked demurely at the company. 'Pardon me, Michael, but might the spirits and I discuss matters in the adjoining sitting room? I feel it is rude for me to carry on a conversation none of you is privy to and' – excitement played across her lips – 'that I'm not at liberty to relay, it being private business.'

Her husband scowled in clear displeasure at being left out. Percy dotingly stroked his black hair but offered no apology.

Michael gestured to the next room. Percy moved into it, the spectral boy close on her heels. Constance wafted to follow, offering Alexi a curtsey on the way out. Michael recalled having seen her at Athens Academy, too.

Alexi addressed her. 'It is good to see you, Constance,' he called as the spirit moved to pursue Percy. She stopped at the sound of her name. His scowl eased, though his schoolmaster tone remained. 'I owe you a bit of credit for making it quite clear, despite my inability to hear you, that I should teach my then-pupil to waltz. That thrilling lesson began our downfall; your friend is now my wife. As I didn't see you haunting our wedding, I assume the news might please you.'

Constance's gaunt face brightened into a delighted smile that lit her whole transparent being, and she clapped her hands soundlessly in delight.

Percy poked her head out from the next room. 'Constance, are—?'

The ghost said something, grinning, bobbing in the air.

Percy blushed. 'Oh, yes, the professor and I are married. Isn't it wonderful?' She stared at her husband with renewed excitement, as if she could still hardly believe her good fortune, and Alexi's scowl was again vanquished by his earnest wife. A moment later, the spirits and Percy also disappeared to discuss their mysterious business.

Percy – they'd found her so late in the course of their Grand Work. She'd been with them for such a short time before their powers were taken back that Michael wondered what more they might have accomplished had she spent her entire life with them. Then again, she was only nineteen, and had he known her as a child it would have been awkward for Alexi to up and marry her. But true love overcame all obstacles, despite needing to await its time. Michael supposed if an immortal incarnation of Rebecca had taken up residence in one of his young parishioners and sought him out at an appropriate juncture, he'd think about her age a bit differently, too. As for its time . . . he had certainly awaited love long enough.

Elijah and Alexi fell to quarreling, filling up the silence with familiar chatter. Withersby demanded Alexi be present for his and Josephine's imminent wedding, but Alexi was set upon taking immediate time away. Each demanded theirs was the more important event, and neither budged. The debate then progressed to who, in truth, was the more difficult man in the realm of cohabitation. Josephine steered clear of a vote.

The two men whirled on Michael at the same time, both clearly expecting his acquiescence.

'You'll take care of the Athens particulars I delineate?' Alexi barked.

'You'll arrange the wedding?' Elijah insisted.

Michael took a breath and called upon the one gift that thankfully had not left him: his patience. He took a sip of mulled wine and examined his anxious compatriots. 'Professor, you'd be hard-pressed to find anywhere I'd rather be than at Athens Academy to help the headmistress,' he said. 'And Withersby, anything to get you into a church – may the Lord forgive me or bless my efforts.' He smiled. 'Perhaps it's best if Alexi and you aren't both under one sacred roof, though. I fear other guests might be harmed by chastising lightning bolts from Heaven should you quarrel in His house.'

Percy breezed back into the room. The spirits were gone. Alexi stared at her expectantly. She kissed her husband on the head, beaming. 'I love Christmas!' she exclaimed, and took her empty teacup into the kitchen. If any of the former Guard were waiting for an explanation, they received none.

Michael picked up his tankard and followed her. As they both set their cups down upon a side table near the washbasin, the two turned to look at each other. 'Truly, how are you?' they both asked at once. Percy smiled. Michael chuckled.

'You first,' Michael prompted. 'As I'm not sure I want to know what those spirits said, do tell me of your recent life. Be honest.'

Percy's moonbeam eyes sparkled. 'I'm very well . . . though I'm often reminding Alexi that he's just as impressive as he's always been, that he's just as important. The world needs mathematicians as much as it needs ghost hunters. More perhaps.' She chuckled. 'My, how he does like being in charge.'

'Just think, my dear Percy, how long he's been in relative control of everything. He was tasked with directing our little group from the start. That control first slipped when we fumbled over Prophecy, when we met you, and it's been sorely tried ever since. He's had little opportunity to impress you, to show you our work when it was humming with maximum efficiency under his leadership. There was a time that we were like machines in a divine factory,' Michael promised her with a smile. 'And he does so love to impress you.'

Percy blushed. 'But he already did, long before I ever knew about the Grand Work or the Guard. I'm waiting for him to trust me that I fell in love with him as a professor, not as leader of a force against the supernatural.'

'It will take time for him to adjust,' Michael said. 'In the meantime, I assume he'd like to orchestrate your every move? Though I must say, you handle him brilliantly.'

Percy shared his half smirk. 'Alexi's restrained himself from giving me direct orders, but takes great care to make sure I'm always comfortable, always provided for and always supported. I cannot say I mind. It's rather sweet to have a man like him doting. Especially in my condition,' she said, brushing her abdomen. 'Now, your turn. You'll not play the counsellor and avoid being counselled.'

Michael clenched his jaw, not wanting to speak of it. 'I don't even know where to begin.'

Percy knowingly shook her head. 'But you two have already begun.' She'd been the one to encourage him to confess his feelings to Rebecca in the first place, there in that darkened Athens foyer. Percy had been directly invested in this matter since she first became aware of it.

'Have we? Begun, I mean? It was a desperate time. We've not seen one another since we laid Jane to rest, all of us fiddling and making uncomfortable small talk, stifled by grief . . . It's been as though none of us knows one another any more.'

'Alexi and Elijah were at each other again. I'd say life's returning to normal.'

Michael bit his lip and gave in to temptation. 'All right, I can't bear it. What did the spirits say about me?'

Percy smiled. 'Are you a fan of Dickens?'

Michael blinked. 'Of course. I'd have liked to have recruited him for the Guard, were we around forty-odd years ago. Who isn't a fan of Dickens?'

'Oh, Alexi, for one.' Percy laughed. 'He claims the man a consummate fraud in ghostly matters, but I think dear Charles is rather to the point. I suppose the poor man could have used a Guard to relieve him of his three plaguing spirits, but then we'd never have such a wonderful story.'

Michael nodded, then paused, eyeing her. 'But wait . . . what are you aiming at?' Dickens? Christmas? Ghosts? His uneasiness mounted.

Percy continued. 'It would seem that spirits are interested in turning the tide. Reversing the roles. Rather than corralling spirits, as you used to do, they'll corral you. For a time.'

Michael furrowed his brow. 'Turn the tide? Whose tide?'

'Why, yours, of course. They want to see you happy.'

'Do they?'

'Oh, yes. My friend Constance, she understands this situation all too well. I've missed her desperately.' Percy offered a tiny, sad laugh. 'The danger of having spirits for friends. You wish them peace but then, when they find it, you're terribly lonely without them.'

Michael's heart swelled. It wasn't the first time he'd wondered if she was a guardian angel as well as a mortal young woman; kindness and goodness incarnate.

She took his hand and returned his fond expression, her white face all the more radiant. 'There's a journey ahead. Await its coming.'

Michael raised an eyebrow. 'Expect three spirits? Before the bell tolls one?'

Percy shrugged. 'Alas, while I maintain I deem Master Dickens insightful, I doubt this will play out just like his *Carol*, Mr Carroll, so I can't be sure of the time.'

A thought occurred to him, and Michael felt his smile fade. 'Percy . . . will it be dangerous? Will I be the only one—'

She shook her head. 'Oh, no, it's really more for the head-mistress than for you.'

'Is it dangerous?' he pressed, even more forcefully.

A shadow crossed Percy's face. 'While your experience has taught you not to trust every spirit, I do trust *these*,' she replied. Her voice was too careful for him to feel reassured. 'And . . . I shall be on guard,' she added.

'But your husband wants to whisk you away.'

'Your long-overdue Merry Christmas is more important,' Percy stated, stretching up to kiss him softly on the cheek. 'I will find a way to remain. For safety's sake.'

Without another word she returned to the dining table. Michael followed, puzzling over this new development.

Elijah was insisting that Alexi would look much better in a verdant green than in his constant black, and Alexi was regarding him – and the notion – with disgust.

'Yes, yes,' Michael interrupted. 'All your bickering must be attended in good time, and your various requests. But for now, leave a vicar in peace, will you?'

His friends made their farewells, some of them eyeing him with surprise. Michael shut the door Elijah couldn't manage to shut for himself, returned to his table and sat. The tumult was out of his house. 'Good riddance,' he murmured, then he stood back up. He went for his wine cup. It needed refilling.

He stared at his empty home. It was too bare. While never the lavish sort, he wanted something just a bit grander, as he could never imagine Rebecca Thompson in anything less than a well-appointed town house with windows and fireplaces in every room. It embarrassed him to dream of making a home with her here; how could he even presume? It was terribly hard to entertain guests in so small a space, and he enjoyed nothing so much as guests.

His grumbling was a show; he'd delighted in company. Always a social creature, he was, after all, the Heart of the group. Or at least he had been. Yet for all the activity, the one person he wanted present was off somewhere else, likely tucked away at the top of Athens Academy in her cosy attic apartments, possibly pondering the same questions as he: Could they start anew? What would come next?

Pouring the last of his batch of mulled wine into his tankard, he sat with a common book of prayer, hoping a bit of gospel could set his soul at ease. Tomorrow he would call upon her, right after his rounds. It was a man's duty to call upon a woman. They'd indulged for years in behaviours hardly common, excusing themselves each breach of etiquette, always allowing the Grand Work to take precedence over custom, but it was high time they began acting like the upstanding citizens of the Queen's great England that he wondered if they could ever become.

His hands shook slightly, so he set down the book of prayer and placed them on the table. The fleshy edges of his palms vibrated against the wood. He was a man in his late thirties, and he wasn't any surer of how to address a woman than he'd been at fifteen, when he'd first wanted to tell Rebecca Thompson how lovely and interesting she was. His tongue had been shackled then, and two decades had done nothing to unlock it. What opportunity would there be? It wasn't as though the Guard had seen one another every day, back when they'd had their powers, but Rebecca's recent absence worried him. There was no pull to bring them all together, no spiritual call to arms that would assure him of seeing his beloved and thus being fed on her presence for yet another day.

Her presence. He'd subsisted on that meagre portion for just over twenty years, so how could he now ask for more? What was to be done about it, and what if he did something wrong? She was so tender, so raw, and so utterly not in love with him. He was paralysed with fear, and the feeling was unprecedented. For years he'd been the great Heart, so named by the goddess on that first day the Grand Work brought them together. Now he was a mortal man, a simple vicar. And a doubting one, at that.

He did not believe that heaven would cater precisely to his whims, so he prayed that whatever Percy and the spirits intended would indeed help. He could no longer open locked doors and one heart had always remained shut to him, even when he could. Thus, though it went against years of instinct, Michael would accept a bit of ghostly intervention.

Chapter Two

Headmistress Rebecca Thompson sat curled upon her bed, hugging her long and slight frame and stroking Marlowe, Jane's familiar, a white cat as sullen as she. She peered into the beast's green eyes, hoping to see the luminous quality that once resided there, a sign of an otherworldly power. But that luminosity had vanished when the cat's mistress breathed her last, when the possessing spirits of the Guard vacated them all in a rush of wind, leaving only a searing emptiness. The result-ant vacuum felt wrong, and Rebecca regretted that she'd ever taken the Grand Work for granted.

She'd had a familiar as well: Frederic, a raven. He was nowhere to be seen, and Rebecca ached for him. She'd had no idea how comforting it was simply to have that black bird outside on a windowsill; something that was hers, an ever-present companion. Poe had been ungrateful in his prose. Now that her bird had quit her chamber, Rebecca Thompson had never felt so alone.

Lit dimly in gaslight, a dark London night passed her drawn window, she was caught between utter terror, incapacitating grief and a slight *frisson* of possibility. She had supped upon bland soup, tried to read, considered rearranging Athens

Academy curriculum for the new year, reorganized her small pantry, changed the direction of her Persian rugs and nearly paced holes in them before at last curling up with Marlowe, her trembling hands gliding haphazardly over his fur, staring at her apartment, bewildered.

When the board of Athens Academy sent her a letter asking her to apprentice as headmistress at the tender age of sixteen, an act she assumed came from Prophecy rather than from her proficiency, she didn't dare say no. Their sacred space and the heart of the Grand Work centred around Athens, and so it was fate that had placed her in this building. But she'd wanted, as had the rest of them, her own space not so tied to the Grand Work. She had wanted to retire separately, to a neutral place. But alas, she had been, and perhaps would always be, defined by the academy in her waking and sleeping hours.

Craning her head towards the window, she watched snow-flakes begin to fall. As much as she may have wished to be elsewhere, she hadn't gained the courage to leave the apartment for days. Her thoughts were murky as she contemplated her broken state. She should have been the one to die, not Jane. For all her mistakes, Rebecca mused with sullen surety, it should have been she.

As early as she could remember, she had striven to be a woman both accomplished and reliable, gifted and strong. Once, she had been all those things. For years she had performed her duty to the Guard with aplomb, had been their Intuition. Then she'd nearly caused Prophecy to fail.

She was a Judas. She was weak. She should never have been spared. Even saving the lives of her students and helping to prevent warring spirits from tearing up London brick by brick could not diminish her guilt.

She had no idea where her friends were on this cool winter night. Usually she could sense them, but since the forces previously driving their destinies had gone, the group had become disconnected. She spared a moment of pity for the world at large, people who'd never known what it was like to be tethered in some direct way to loved ones, but then that passed. Her bond was now sundered. Perhaps the rest of the world was better off ignorant of such a thing.

Because she did not know where to find her friends, she was
hesitant to go out into the night and search for them. Her
melancholy did her the disservice of supposing them assembled and having a grand time without her. Not that the party
could ever again be complete. Not without Jane, their modest
Healer, their keen judge of character and quiet recluse, the
Guard's steadfast hope and Rebecca's dearest friend.

'What is wrong with you, Headmistress?' she chided herself.
'Pull yourself together; you've an institution to run. You've
never been unable to perform that venerable duty. Oh, but for
the grief and these nerves . . .'

There was just so much to *feel* – something she'd attempted
for years to avoid. She needed help sorting out the guilt-ridden,
lonely, excitable and confused mess that was her present state
of mind. But to this end she had no idea where to turn. She
would once have gone to Jane, to sensible, stalwart Jane, since
she most certainly couldn't have turned to Alexi, both her
friend and her greatest agony. But Jane had gone to the angels,
to be eternally by the side of the man she loved; she had no
further time for the sorry human lots of those back in London.

Rebecca allowed herself a moment of supposition: What if
Vicar Michael Carroll came and called upon her? What if he
roused her from melancholy as had been his job for twenty
years, confessing again the new shock of his love to her? Yet
she'd ignored everyone who had knocked upon her door, even
Michael. She simply couldn't talk, exist or relate. She did not
feel, after everything she had done and what was left of her
soul, that she deserved such adoration. Not by such a kind and
wonderful man. Surely there was something better for him
than her tired, misguided self.

Tucking herself beneath her covers, shifting but not daring
to let go of Marlowe, she shuddered. The air was full of
murmuring whispers, like the voices of angels, or of ghosts.
After years of dealing with spirits in silence, the whispering did
nothing for her nerves. She had faced down demons and was
weary from the toil, so if there were indeed supernatural forces
breathing down her home, she prayed that these were angels.

Christmas. The holiday was all about angels. On every street
corner were carollers; Christmas trees – all the rage since

Prince Albert's use of them – sparkled in windows. Candles adorned sills, welcoming wassailing and friendly company; glitter and firelight beckoned angels to tend the lost shepherds and sheep of London and tell them of miracles.

She'd seen many unbelievable sights over the course of the Grand Work, but she wasn't sure if any of them had been angels. Sure, she'd seen winged things, and the godlike forces that drove the Grand Work had their angelic qualities, though they remained more of a myth and legend. None of them called themselves angels and they didn't quite act as she'd expect an angel to. So she couldn't say she believed in the creatures – being a practical woman despite how little she found strange – as she couldn't vouch that she'd encountered any.

Nonetheless, Rebecca had long held a secret hope every Christmas tide that an angel would come to her, just like in the stories, and point to a star of reassurance. It would be a private prophecy, just for her, and one that promised she might one day be able to unlock herself, to feel the sort of warmth, joy and celebration that the rest of London so effortlessly benefitted from during this holiday.

Thus, this year, as she had for many previous, though she felt her betraying, tortured heart unworthy, she allowed herself a desperate prayer that a miracle of this season might save her from herself.

Chapter Three

'Alexi, darling . . . we cannot go on holiday just yet,' Percy said as her husband took great care to settle her next to him before the fire in his study. As she'd told Michael, he had been achingly tender with her since they'd found out about the pregnancy.

Her husband frowned. 'What do you mean? What on earth could possibly be more pressing than spending a quiet week lounging about with me, indulging me, loving me . . .' He traced a finger down her cheek and neck, towards her bosom, following the line of her dress and sliding it aside.

Percy sighed in delight. 'Nothing at all, husband, could be more pressing,' she murmured, taking his fingers and bringing them to her lips. 'And we shall go, I promise, but I'm needed here for a bit. Not for long, but I must help Michael have a Merry Christmas.' Alexi opened his mouth to protest, but she stopped him. 'You and I will go away, as we have planned. We'll spend Christmas just the two of us, but there's work to be done.'

'Christmas is not even a week hence!' Alexi said with a slight whine.

Percy smiled. 'Have you learned nothing from Master Dickens? Spirits can work wonders in just one night.'

Alexi raised an eyebrow. 'Dickens? Claptrap. Is that what you and they were discussing?'

'It's their idea.'

'Well, you and the spirits had best wrap up your salvation by Christmas Eve day, when I'll have you to myself for as long as I please,' he stated, then rose and moved to the door. His eyes narrowed, flashing darkly. 'And if there's any thought of you going again into the Whisper-world, I swear to you I will open Hell with my bare hands to come collect you.'

'I don't doubt it.' She laughed, used to his zealous protection and knowing just how to defuse it. 'But that's hardly the plan, my love. I'll be a mere bystander. Someone who can hear spirits should be on hand. Trust me.'

Her husband took a breath. Despite his domineering nature, he was adapting admirably to keeping his voice and mood tolerably level. 'I trust you, Percy, with all my life. In fact, I've learned to trust you more than myself . . .' Percy opened her mouth to thank him for the hard-fought praise she well deserved, but he continued, 'But I don't trust ghosts. I can't. You wouldn't either if you'd seen the same sights and performed the Grand Work for the years the rest of us did. It's one thing to help a spirit find peace. It's another to allow one to meddle with your life.'

'Alexi, please.' Her voice was calm and sure. She artfully managed to hold the rose of his love without grasping the thorns. 'You must support me in this. You and I have such love between us. It's possible for all the world to have such passion, and if we are given the opportunity to help soul mates finally come together—'

'You cannot force them to love one another.'

'But they do already!' she argued. 'Michael has *always* loved Rebecca, and she's only just now realized it. They simply have to trust it, and themselves. As we shall have to trust Constance, a spirit friend I would trust with any noble life. The pair will also need to procure a hearth of their own; the spirits insist on it. We'll employ our and Withersby's fortunes to that end, I suppose, and make it look like it came from Athens. Oh, Alexi, I want to see those two happy so badly it hurts!'

A lump rose in her throat. 'In addition, maybe this can alleviate my guilt. Maybe this can be my penance for . . .'

Realizing what she could not bring herself to say, Alexi moved to her side and bent a knee. 'Darling, Jane's death was not your fault!'

Tears fell from her eyes. 'I'm not sure I'll ever believe that. Nor will you ever overcome your own sense of responsibility. I know you.' Her expression brightened suddenly, a hopeful look in her eye. 'Oh! Perhaps Jane could help! Do you think she could? If Constance could return . . .'

Alexi only shrugged. They hadn't seen Jane's spirit since the night of the final confrontation with Darkness. 'Though I'd love to see her, she went towards peace, to the arms of her ghostly love. How could we wish her to linger with us instead?'

'Of course,' Percy murmured. 'Perhaps seeing ghosts has spoiled us to the precious fragility of mortal life.'

'Ah, I've had too many reminders of the precious fragility of life,' Alexi murmured, kissing her cheek, then bending to kiss her abdomen; the living miracle within. 'Having nearly lost all that I'd begun to live for.'

Not wanting to lose himself to sentiment, the stern professor rose and cleared his throat. 'Yes, indeed. Do make our friends' Christmases merry, Percy; do. You've such magic about you and I suppose it's only right that you should share it.' He softly kissed her atop the head and rose, turned on his heel and strolled towards the other room. 'Come to bed, though,' he called. 'Where magic assuredly awaits.'

It was an irresistible command.

Chapter Four

Michael went to the orphanage infirmary in the morning, as was his weekly custom and the duty he'd long ago requested.

As a child, he'd had no idea which vocation would call him. He'd been a strapping lad, strong and energetic, with a zeal for life that family and friends envied and admired. He had supposed he'd be a woodworker like his father, but then came the Guard. As their Heart, there was suddenly too much love, goodness and wonder within him to possibly contain; he'd had to give it to others – as many others as he possibly could – or it would overcome him with its intensity.

The church had been the obvious choice, and he'd pursued a level within the hierarchy that maintained autonomy and a bit of flexibility, so as not to conflict with outside work, his *Grand* Work. The vicar duties of guest preaching, visits to shut-ins, infirmary patients and children of orphanages had quite served his need. Now, however, the Grand Work was gone and Michael feared for his faith. They'd been inextricably tied.

Of course, duty was duty, and he could hardly explain to his superiors that he was suddenly unfit for his position; the guiding force he'd lost had been an ancient power that in the church's eyes might appear more than a bit pagan. He doubted the children would care even if he was pagan, and he hoped they wouldn't notice any difference. He still loved them.

Little Charlie's condition had worsened overnight, and the nurse who ushered Michael into his tiny room looked grim. Wan light and a worn screen separated the boy from a comatose girl opposite who was wasting away. Michael was ever surprised the girl stayed dreaming, and he prayed those fluttering eyelids housed glorious visions: angels, beauty and joy, all the things little girls ought to be imagining in their blessed young lives.

Charlie's sickly face brightened. 'Hello, Father!' The children all called him 'Father' here, rather than Vicar, and Michael let them use the more Catholic term. He rather liked the familiarity of it, as hearing the word eased the ache of not having children of his own.

'Hello, Sir Charles. I was told you've been fiercely battling a most vile dragon, and I am here to commend you for your bravery!' He looked down at the fine buttons on the lower cuffs of his coat and surreptitiously plucked one free, placing it in the palm of the child. 'Your medal of honour, sir. The Queen herself has heard of your service to the Crown, and she declares that even the great St George holds you in highest esteem.'

Charlie's grin took up his entire face, and his shaking yellow hands clutched the proffered button. He gave a salute. 'Thank you, my lord Carroll. I accept this honour with a grateful heart and pledge my life to more such battles.' He spoke cheerfully, as if the wheeze in his lungs were no trouble at all, nor the cough that rattled his frame. Michael always found it hard to keep tears at bay here in the sickroom of the orphanage, and it was never so hard as now. He steeled himself to remain strong.

Not that Charlie was frightened, as were many of the other wards; the boy was shockingly insightful, uncannily intelligent and calm. He cocked his head to one side, and Michael suddenly felt himself being examined in much the same way as Mrs Rychman had examined him the day prior. It was disconcerting.

His discomfiture was interrupted. The air around him grew frigid, and one by one ghosts wafted through the modest brick walls and hovered behind Charlie's head. Michael's heart sank and tears welled up. Surely these spirits came to collect the boy. How God could take such a gifted soul escaped him, unless he was covetous and wanted such dearness closer . . .

Charlie eyed him with a dawning realization. 'Oh! You can see them, too, then.'

Michael hesitated. It wasn't something he admitted in public, his ability to see ghosts; it was a Guard's pledge to keep his skills secret. Though their power over spirits was revoked, the ability to see them was not. He could see no harm in admitting so with this child. It would even be a point of commiseration. He nodded, a tear spilling on to his cheek.

'Don't cry, Father, it's not for me that they've come. It's for you. It seems *you're* the one in need of caretaking this day. That's what they said.'

Michael's tears vanished and his heart quickened. 'You can *hear* them, child?'

The boy shrugged. 'Those of us who live in the shadow of death can often hear the whispers of those who have gone before us. Yes, we've been conversing, sometimes about them, sometimes about me. But today they've been talking about you. About your doubt.' Charlie screwed up his face and continued. 'How can *you* doubt, Father? You're the kindest man I know. You're what I imagine angels to be like. Archangels, even. Like your namesake. Doubting does not suit you, Father. I beg you, be done with it.'

Michael fought off shame. 'Would it were that easy, my child, to slay my dragons.'

Charlie smiled sadly. 'I wish I could give you the peace the spirits say you crave. But they'll help you. Do let them, Father. They mean no harm.'

The boy shuddered violently, the ghosts' cool draft was having an effect, and Michael rushed to stoke the fire in the meagre hearth. Turning to address the spectres, he said, 'Leave the child be. Come to me alone, if and when you will,' he commanded sternly.

The spirits vanished, nodding.

Charlie was looking at him strangely. 'That story you always tell,' the boy breathed, narrowing his eyes in thoughtful concentration, 'about the princess and her devoted knight. In every adventure they battle the devil himself, and then the knight returns the princess to her attic loft, where she sits alone. You've told me the moral of these adventures is perseverance against forces that would take us under, and that I must be such a knight and must struggle onward to find my own princess to cherish, as all good men should. But . . . it's you who's the knight in these stories, isn't it? Who's the princess, Father? Why doesn't she accept you? And must you always part ways? How can that be a happy ending?'

The two of them stared at each other for a moment.

'Those are questions for which I have no answers,' Michael said thickly, breaking the long silence.

The nurse came with ointments and gruel, and so Michael was spared telling that familiar story. He kissed Charlie's feverish head before leaving, heavy hearted. His powers had once kept anxiety at bay. Powerless, he was becoming its slave.

But there was a duty to be done. Likely the spirits would chastise him for cowardice. He must anticipate their demands and begin to try and prove himself before their harrowing journey began. Perhaps he could avoid it entirely. Even better, perhaps he could save Rebecca the trial to come. This, above all, strengthened his resolve.

He ascended the grand staircase of Athens Academy and up to the third-floor apartments, where his princess lived, again taking up his knightly quest. 'It will do no good to cloister ourselves away,' he murmured, trying to rally his courage – after all, he was the suitor. He had to call – but his hand trembled as he lifted his fist to knock upon the door. Behind his back he tightly clutched two bouquets, and thorns dug into his palm.

'Yes . . . ?'

'Hullo, Headmistress! May I have a moment of your time?' Michael's voice jarred him as it was reflected back, loud and forcedly jovial, by the wooden door. 'It's been . . . days.'

Her booted footsteps grew nearer but hesitated. 'Hullo, Vicar,' he heard. After a long moment Rebecca opened the door. 'I suppose.'

Michael smiled – a reflex – and took in the sight of her. She seemed taller somehow, there against the door frame in her usual choice of prim dress, which was blue-grey like her eyes. As it was winter she wore pressed wool, and a cameo brooch at her throat. She was always appointed with quiet elegance, and her face was, as ever, stoic, but those eyes betrayed tides of emotion. As for her hands, one was pressed tightly against the door frame, one was behind her back. He doubted they shook the way his did.

Not to be deterred, Michael reminded himself of the fact that generally when he smiled at her she could not help but smile back. He lifted one of the two bouquets from behind his back, roses of an exquisite deep burgundy, and his cheeks reddened as he presented them. 'For you.'

'Oh, Michael, how lovely! Thank you,' Rebecca said, blushing as well. 'Come in, let me put them in water.' She gestured him into her small rooms, filled with carved wooden doors and fine rugs, countless books and scattered pieces of art. 'Sit, I won't be but a moment.'

As she disappeared, Michael withdrew the second bouquet, a cluster of yellow posies, made his way to his favourite chair in the corner of the sitting room, a Queen Anne partly facing the window, and sat. Staring at the Athens courtyard below, snow-covered, with its fountain angel lifting up wings, a book and flowers towards heaven, he silently asked the statue for her benediction.

There was rustling in the pantry. Michael shifted the flowers upon his knees, unsure what to say when Rebecca emerged. *Good God, this could not be more difficult if I were sixteen,* he thought wearily. *Why I didn't press my claim then I'll never know.*

Rebecca returned with the flowers in a vase and set them on a carved wooden table. Turning to Michael, she raised an eyebrow at the second bouquet.

'For Jane,' he murmured. 'It isn't as if we can ignore our grief. It rules our hearts at the moment.'

Rebecca blinked back tears. 'Indeed. It would be nice to lay them on her tomb.' She paused, then said, 'I would offer you tea, but I simply must get out of these rooms. I've entirely shut myself away here—'

'I know.'

She looked at the ground. 'Yes, I suppose you do. I am sorry if not admitting you before seemed rude. I was – I *am* – unfit for company.'

'I've never thought so.'

If anyone had ever seen her truly vulnerable and unfit for company, it had been he. He'd always made himself available at times of her need. He wondered if she resented that – or feared it.

She glanced at him. There was an uncomfortable silence.

Michael rose and brandished the flowers, moving to the door. 'Jane always would exclaim about yellow flowers whenever we passed them in the street, even en route to an exorcism or poltergeist. I bought her some for her birthday once, and now I'm ashamed I didn't buy them for her all the time.' He opened the door and gestured Rebecca into the hall.

'I'm ashamed of a great deal,' she replied, following his lead. Her voice was thick. Starting down the stairs, they descended to floor level.

'You mustn't be. Not about Prophecy, not about Jane, none of it. Whatever you fear, none of us has ever been perfect.'

'My gift failed, Michael. It failed because of my frailty. Would you tell Judas Iscariot not to be ashamed?'

They crossed the foyer, devoid of students, all gone on holiday, and rounded the corner towards Athens Chapel. Michael shrugged. 'We've all of us parts to play. And you hardly sent a messiah to his death. Are you *still* grieving over choosing Miss Linden as Prophecy over Percy? Haven't we moved on?'

Rebecca looked sharply at him. 'The part of the betrayer was never a part I wanted.'

'I daresay Judas wasn't fond of it either, but it was necessary.' He wagged a finger at her.

'But don't go equating yourself to scripture, Headmistress; our dramas are not played on so grand a stage. And remember, that same gift went on to save Percy's life.'

Rebecca sighed. 'I suspect you'll be taking my ongoing confessions for some time. The past months weigh upon me so.'

'It will be my pleasure,' he replied.

She offered him a slight smile and looked away. He wanted so desperately to touch her, but the chasm between their bodies seemed impossible to cross.

The chapel of Athens Academy was white and modest, with a plain table draped in white linen for an altar and windows with golden stained-glass angels lining the walls beside unornamented pews. A painted dove of peace floated on the back wall.

'So strange to come here and not have it open to our sacred space, eh?' Michael asked. 'Strange to have this simply be a chapel. So strange to be *normal*.'

There were two alcoves at the back, like those that would house baptismal fonts but less elaborate; this was built a Quaker institution and thus there was no great pomp in the style. The founder of Athens had his tomb here and had left space for another. Rebecca had long ago abdicated her natural claim to it, not wishing to live floors above her imminent grave. None of the Guard had ever dreamed it would eventually be the resting place of their dear friend Jane, but it gave them some small comfort to know that she was close, that her mortal coil was interred here in this space that had been the doorway to so many incredible things, so near the raw power that had once driven their lives together.

Michael and Rebecca approached the tomb bedecked in fresh bouquets – other Guard had paid their respects. Rebecca stared at the flowers, her hand to her lips.

'They're all those yellow favourites of hers . . .'

'For as self-involved as our group has been, we listened to small yet important details,' Michael said with quiet pride. He offered his bouquet for Rebecca to do the honours.

Her blush had returned. 'And some remain oblivious . . .'

Michael was unsure what exactly she meant.

'Pray over her, Vicar. Please,' Rebecca insisted, closing her eyes.

Michael searched his mind for appropriate scripture and found it in Corinthians, an adulation suitable to the Grand Work that in recognizing separate gifts had created their family for life: Some people God has designated in the church to be, first, apostles; second, prophets; third, teachers; then, mighty deeds; then, gifts of healing, assistance, administration and varieties of tongues. We miss you, Jane, you and your gift. All of our designated gifts left with you. We hope somehow to honour your name as we live on without you. We . . . we wish to see you again, but not if that would cost you your peace. Be our angel, Jane. You always were.' Michael looked up. 'Oh, Heavenly Father, I hope you recognize what gold you've collected unto your bosom.'

He felt a cold draft and glanced around in anticipation. But there was nothing. Perhaps he'd imagined it. Surely Jane was at peace; gone to the arms of a long-lost love. He could not begrudge her that. What more could they wish for her than love and peace? It was selfish, wanting to see her again. He forced back tears.

Rebecca's face was unreadable. She moved to a pew and sat. Michael joined her, keeping a decorous distance, though he yearned to slide close and put his arm around her. Just for support, for commiseration, for contact. He yearned for simple contact. How could it be too much to ask?

The silence continued. Perhaps it was the sanctity of the church setting that was keeping them quiet, but Michael felt a riptide roiling deep within him, struggling and churning. *Please. Say something. I don't know how to begin, Rebecca. You know how I feel; I've already confessed. Your silence makes me believe it was all in vain. I admitted my love, but what are you going to do with it? Insist you still that you were the one God should have taken? Can you possibly know how that pains me?*

The quiet continued. Michael felt himself drowning in it. They were too old. They were too broken. It was too late for them. Any relationship they could cobble together would be a joke. He was second best and always would be. Knowing what they knew about the afterlife, even death wouldn't change that. He felt a heretofore uncharted depth of melancholy, and speaking his love aloud now seemed its own death sentence.

The room grew frigid, and a harrowing wind burst through, though there were no open windows or doors. A darkness came over Michael. He and Rebecca cried out in unison, and then there was a new silence; deathly empty.

'Oh, no, the spirits,' Michael murmured. He'd thought he had time, that the ghosts would come at night, that he might prepare her. 'I should have warned you! Rebecca, can you hear me?'

On his feet, he reached out his hands but found nothing; no pews, no Rebecca, only darkness. He'd failed. His cowardice had doomed them both to what surely would be a harrowing ghostly course. Would she be ready for it? Or would it at last break her?

What in the Whisper-world were they in for?

Chapter Five

Percy was startled by Billy bursting through the wall, his torn clothes flapping about him where he floated in the air of the Rychman estate parlour. 'It's begun, Miss Percy! They're at the academy. Are you comin' to be the guardian angel for the headmistress, then, like Miss Constance said?'

Percy rose to her feet. 'Oh, yes, Billy, but I wasn't expecting it so soon.'

The ghostly urchin shrugged. 'It's one.'

One in the *afternoon*. Perhaps it was a ghostly joke. This wasn't Dickens's story, this was their reality, so either way Percy could not expect it to play out in the grand tradition of famous literature.

'Do be careful, Percy. It's a danger, bringin' the Liminal threshold down on the living. Might trap us all if we're not careful. We'll need that light of yours to keep us from turnin' Whisper for ever . . .'

Percy nodded. The spirits had explained the Liminal to her, and she knew she could not control it like she did other portals to the Whisper-world. But she was undeterred, despite her aversion to the Whisper-world and its contents.

The bell of the grand clock down the hall tolled, and she rushed into her husband's study. 'Alexi, it has begun. I must go to Athens. What horse shall I take?'

He rose and closed the distance between them. 'You think to go alone, that I'll not be by your side? Danger may come in an instant. The headmistress is my friend, too, you know. My best friend. I wish to help. I'll be on hand,' he declared in a tone that clearly brooked no argument.

'Darling,' Percy said in a soft murmur, her hands on his shoulders. 'Don't you see you may do more harm than good? All I ask is that you leave me to my task.'

Alexi's stern brow furrowed in confusion.

Percy explained what she felt was obvious. 'If the head-mistress were to see you during this vulnerable time . . . well, it wouldn't be without its complications. Considering her feelings for you, it would likely set the task back. Come with me if you must, but please remain in your office. I'll run to you the moment the spirits are done. Though I've every faith in the couple of the hour, it's just best . . .' Her eyes glittered with sudden tears. 'Oh, my dear, don't you see? I cannot imagine how difficult it would be to fall out of love with you. Thank God I don't have to,' she murmured, cupping his chin and kissing him.

Alexi's cheeks coloured slightly, and Percy found it the greatest treasure in the world that she could make such a man blush. Fate be damned, true love was the only power she craved – and it was her own. She hoped the spirits would help grant it now to her friends.

'Come,' she said excitedly. 'While I keep watch, you must send Withersby and Josephine to the property, and you must plant the letter—'

'It will all be done according to plan, my dear,' Alexi stated, and went out to ready the carriage.

Despite the delay in their trip, he seemed to have taken to the plan they'd discussed, and to leading part of the charge. She didn't doubt for a minute that he wished his friends the very best and would do whatever he could to assure it. Percy had not mentioned the specific dangers the spirits discussed, lest Alexi worry maddeningly over her in ways that would not be helpful. But where the Whisper-world was concerned, one could never be entirely sure.

She bit her lip. So much of her life had been throwing herself towards things she did not entirely understand or trust, events where she was fearfully unsure of the outcome. She shuddered and offered a prayer that it would not come to what the spirits had warned her about, the grim possibility of an *extraction*. The Whisper-world fed on melancholy, provender of which the headmistress was keen; it might not wish to let her go. Percy might have to step in – perhaps literally – and there was no conceivable place she wanted to revisit less.

She ran to her room and opened a jewellery box, plucking out a beautiful pearl rosary that had been a gift from the convent where she was raised. Before their recent battle, Michael had blessed these beads with the additional power of his gift. They were resonant with peace and love, and when Percy squeezed them in her hand, her heart was fortified, her own gift at the ready.

'Come now, Vicar, Headmistress . . . Let there be light.'

Chapter Six

Michael was alone in the foyer of Athens Academy. He whirled. 'Rebecca?'

'She'll be all right. You're on separate journeys. Parallel, but separate. Billy, the boy from the chandelier, has asked me to help.'

Michael looked down to behold the small voice's owner. The ghost of a little girl reached up and tried to take his hand, but her own passed through it. She stared for a moment, then up at him.

'Hello, Father.'

Michael blinked, processing this new development. 'I can *hear* you.'

'For now,' she said.

'This is what was foretold to me?' he clarified.

She nodded.

Michael recognized the girl. He'd just seen her at Charlie's bedside, at the orphanage, whispering and murmuring about him. Little Mary, he recalled. She'd been in the orphanage all her life, quite ill for most of it. He'd always regretted that he wasn't there when she died. He'd been out saving another little girl from malevolent spectral possession. Would that doctors had such skills to cast out influenza.

Little Mary, in her drab orphanage dress, smiled. 'It's all right, Father, you always blame yourself. It isn't *your* fault when we die. I knew you were with me, in *spirit.*' She grinned at her little joke.

Michael reached out to touch her cheek, but met only cold mist. The girl was right: he did always feel responsible, wishing there was some part of the Grand Work that extended to healing sick children. He'd assuaged his need by offering Jane the key to the orphanage, and every now and then she'd worked a few healing wonders inconspicuous enough to avoid arousing suspicion.

It also kept the children believing in angels, which he felt was an invaluable service to the church. He believed in angels, though he couldn't recall ever meeting one. He didn't figure Percy counted, being flesh and blood and all.

'Come,' the little girl said, 'we must have you take a look at things.'

There was a crushing darkness as all light was expunged from the chapel, followed by a fierce wind and strange noises whispering, so much *whispering*. But then everything went silent, slowly brightened, and Rebecca again found herself in the dim afternoon haze of the chapel.

Michael was gone.

'Michael?' She gasped, whirling to find herself alone with a ghost. A young woman floated before her, in slightly dated fashion and ringlet curls about her lovely, hollowed face.

'Hello, Headmistress,' the haunt said with an eager expression.

Rebecca blinked. They weren't supposed to hear spirits! Only Percy had been able to do that. Was she going mad?

The ghost anticipated her. 'You've spent your life in service to this world and the next. Your entire group has earned a good rest, though I daresay none of you are prepared to enjoy it. Now it's *our* turn. Your powers have retired. Now we have power over you.'

Rebecca's blood ran cold. 'Where's Michael?'

'Safe.'

'But where have you taken him?' Rebecca insisted. 'If you—'

The ghost held up a hand. 'Only the good of our kind have power over you at present, so do not fear. But you've separate journeys this night, ere you again stand side by side. And be careful of the bent of your heart, for shadows are close at hand.'

Rebecca shuddered, unsure what the woman meant.

The spirit smiled. 'Your safety shall be monitored.'

It was a small comfort. Rebecca pursed her lips. 'I know you, don't I?'

'Indeed. Constance Peterson, haunt of the science library, at your service, Headmistress.' The ghost bobbed a curtsey.

'And . . . why is it that you're going to help me?'

'Because I was called upon to help you. Because I understand.'

'Who called upon you?'

'A friend. And . . .' Constance pointed upwards with a sheepish smile.

Rebecca was silent. Perhaps her secret Christmas prayer was being answered? Perhaps this was divine intervention after all, though she'd never thought it would come like *this*. This was much too dramatic, the stuff of Gothic fiction, suitable for Alexi and Percy, not her.

'We're all worthy of an opportunity like this, Headmistress.' The ghost's eyes sparkled knowingly. 'Even if few of us are so fortunate. You've never lived a normal life, Headmistress. You should not expect one.'

Rebecca stared at her, ever trying to see sense in the fantastical. 'You. How did you . . . see the light?' Did you see errors in your mortal ways and thusly have evolved? For a spirit, I trust you are well and fully at peaceable understanding to be able to lead me now?'

The ghost nodded. 'I am indeed at peace, enlightened, free to do what I will, after help from Miss Persephone Parker. She found what I'd been looking for, just as she's now found her own heart's desire and taken his name. We're all looking for something, you know.'

Rebecca nodded, her jaw clenching involuntarily. She felt an icy cold weight press down upon her.

The ghost scowled. 'I can feel that, Headmistress: melancholy's dread march. You must stop. You must not hear the girl's name and cringe.'

Rebecca looked away so that Constance would not see her shame. 'It is a curse,' she admitted. 'My heart is cursed and I want to remove it.'

'That, Headmistress,' said the ghost, 'is our task: to cure the accursed. Come. We've much to do and I dare not tax you. While you've a most stalwart mind for a mortal, too much talk with spirits threatens sanity.'

The young woman held up a hand, closed her eyes and murmured, invoking power. 'Liminal; the journey, I pray.'

In response, the air rippled like thin fabric and their surroundings melted away. In an instant they were back in time, in the science library of the academy, when it was fresh and new and all the chandeliers still sparkled like diamonds, before dust settled permanently into their crystalline grooves.

'Before you point out that it is indulgent of me to show you my past,' Constance spoke up, 'let me remind you that we recognize problems in others before we recognize them in ourselves. I humbly offer myself as an example.'

The ghost pointed to a table, to herself. She had been quite beautiful while alive, full of health and vigour if the countenance she wore appeared hard, unrelenting, annoyed. She sat poring over a stack of books, adjusted quite pointedly to block her from the view of a young man who sat unobtrusively studying different work at an angle opposite. The young man's face was gentle and kind. He slid a book between them.

The ghost gestured Rebecca closer. The memory did not come without pain for her, Rebecca saw, and she felt humbled that Constance should torture herself for the sake of helping her.

The living Constance was staring at the biological reference book that had been shifted towards her; not at the scientific content, but at the scribblings in the margin.

> Constant is my care for you, sweet girl, my Constancy.
> All I ask is that you, for one blissful moment, put aside
> your obsession long enough to look into my eyes.
> —P

The young Constance scowled and slid the book back across the table, moving it around the fortress of tomes she'd stacked to buffer herself against his simple request. She was careful that their fingertips did not connect as he received the book. Rebecca noted this with a bit of pride; even under her own rule, students were not allowed to touch members of the opposite sex.

And yet, if the girl had taken this boy's hand, she couldn't have said she would mind. She'd likely not punish them; it seemed innocent enough. In fact, she found herself wishing Constance would brush his hand, for it would clearly mean so much to him.

Undeterred by her rejection, the young man turned pages and found a new illustration, one that spoke to him, and he began to write. Rebecca opened her mouth to admonish him for defacing school property when she read what he'd scripted so carefully next to a diagram of the human heart:

> Can science explain everything, my Constancy,
> when my heart beats only for you?

Constance returned the book, writing a shaky reply on the opposite margin:

> Dear P, though you share my library table, I cannot commit any part of my heart, for I fear I do not have one to divide. The course of my blood flows towards science alone.
> —C

She looked up at the boy and peered over their books, her voice a whisper: 'Science is a man's profession, Mr Clarke. I am a woman, and I must make a choice: whether to live as my sex or to deny it and take the man's profession I crave. The demands of our age unfairly divide us. I'm sorry I cannot choose you.'

Mr Clarke appeared crestfallen.

Constance turned to Rebecca, tears in her phantom eyes, her greyscale face taut with sorrow. Rebecca recalled all the young women to whom she'd boasted of choosing to run an institution rather than a household, justifying her life choice. But it had been a damned lonely choice, especially when secretly pining for a chance to run the Rychman estate.

'I realized my mistake too late,' the ghost said. 'My greatest folly was to deny a lovely soul who asked nothing more than to remain by my side. Of all the places I could have been a scientist *and* a woman, it was here at Athens. These blessed bricks never asked me to choose. I never gave him – *us* – a chance, despite having no true objection. I pushed him away for three years before the fever took me.' The spirit's eyes narrowed and her voice was cool. 'You've pushed someone else away for twenty. Why?'

'I don't know,' Rebecca replied.

'Is there any more beautiful a calling in life than love?'

'I have *loved*,' Rebecca hissed. 'Desperately.'

The ghost nodded. 'So did I. I loved science – something that couldn't love me back. There's safety in that solitude. Do you understand?'

Rebecca could only nod.

'Safety, but no solace. I haunted this Earth until Miss Percy found that book, revealing the one critical experience I denied. There come many callings on Earth, and Heaven allows us them all.

You'd do well to realize the same, and to do it before you're dead.'

'But that's just it!' Rebecca began, her eyes wide. 'I . . . I don't think I merit being alive right now. I think the heavens made a mistake.'

Constance's eyes glittered threateningly. The deceased had an uncanny ability to make one shiver, it was certain. 'Ah. Indeed,' the ghost replied. 'And this is not the only time you've wished yourself dead.' These were condemning words and they chartered their next course. Rebecca didn't know what the Liminal was, this force Constance wielded, but it responded.

Rebecca had no time to protest. The environment whirled, spun and shifted, and suddenly she stood in a darkened foyer of Athens Academy. There was the distant sound of an argument. Rebecca turned, wringing her hands. 'Oh not this. Please, not this. It is my penance, I am sure, for my failures, but please . . .'

Constance gazed upon her with pity. 'We've not much time, and I'm not the only visitation. There's something you didn't see, then, that you must see now. And through your pain you may yet make it right.' The ghost sighed. 'And I beg you, do so while you yet *live*. Come.'

Rebecca gulped, trying to prepare herself. She knew exactly what she was about to see, and her body felt colder than if a horde of spirits was accosting her.

Constance led her toward her office, where the door was shut. The ghost gestured her forward. Rebecca fumbled at the door but passed through, as if she too were a spirit. These were chimerical things, past memories, thinner than paper; visions, illusions . . . yet potent and all too real.

Rebecca's throat constricted. A younger Professor Alexi Rychman paced in her office, his dark robes billowing about him as he moved, his face set in characteristic consternation. She herself sat stoic, though she remembered her pain.

She looked at herself, in this moment fifteen years or so younger, and noticed the lines of worry already beginning to form, the thin mouth, so prim and composed, those blue-grey eyes that stared at the imperious man before her, secretly drinking in his striking, stifling presence.

'Damn it, Rebecca,' Alexi hissed. 'I am no closer to telling you when Prophecy might come than I was years ago when the Goddess heralded our destiny and pronounced us the Guard. How should I know how long it will take?'

'It isn't about when Prophecy might come, Alexi, but how you're thinking of it. Tonight at the exorcism, when we stumbled at the force of that devilish blow, when you buckled at the strain, I heard you mutter, "My bride shall make it well."'

Alexi stopped pacing and turned. 'And?'

'Alexi, Prophecy won't be your bride. She'll come as a companion to all of us, not some predestined lover of yours.'

Young Alexi's features went slack. 'What do you mean?'

'The prophesied seventh member was never specified as *yours.*'

'Yes she was,' he replied.

'Tell me the precise words the Goddess said that make you think so.'

'Why, *everything* she said.' But Alexi thought back, clearly trying to latch onto a specific phrase.

'Nothing more than insinuations.' Rebecca closed her eyes, using her gift of texts, the library of her mind, and plucking free an exact transcript of the Goddess's words: '"I hope you will know her when she comes, Alexi, my love. And I hope she will know you, too. Await her, but beware. She will not come with answers but be lost, confused. I have put protections in place, but she will be threatened and seeking refuge. There shall be tricks, betrayals and many second guesses. Caution, beloved. Mortal hearts make mistakes.

Choose your seventh carefully, for if you choose the false prophet, the end of your world shall follow."' Rebecca stared hard at Alexi. 'What in that promises you a lover?'

'Everything,' he replied. 'When she comes, I will love her. You may be the Intuition of the group, but your belief does not therefore supersede mine. On this point I am sure, and that's final. Good night, Headmistress.' The young Alexi exited in a rustle of black fabric, and the room expanded; breathing was easier.

It was the first time this particular argument was voiced, the elder and wiser Rebecca recalled, and most certainly not the last. They argued these precise points for the next fifteen years, until Prophecy finally did show up, a snow-white girl unlike anything the Guard expected, and Rebecca would grow blinded by jealousy and make dangerous mistakes in an effort to disprove an undesirable fate.

Yet it was not this failure that Constance wanted her to see; it was the next torturous few moments. Rebecca watched herself sit stiffly in her chair, watched her eyes cloud, watched her shoulders tense against the thick wool of her jacket. Such pain, Rebecca felt and saw, shocked by its magnitude. Such pain, all to love a man who was saving himself for some future stranger, when she was yet so close and could grasp those black robes and pull him near . . . Even looking back, knowing all she knew, she could not think herself wrong for urging caution in the matter of Prophecy, or for loving him. She had never been able to help it. But then, as now, such love was futile. Empty. Hopeless.

A sound came from the windowsill. Frederic, her raven, a single blue breast feather indicating his service to the Guard, had alighted upon the ledge outside. He rapped again upon the casement.

'He'll never love me,' her younger self said. 'I do not want this fate. I do not want to patrol the dead if I *feel* dead, and this shall surely kill my heart. I don't want this destiny, for I am ill-suited to it.' Her face held no expression, though Rebecca recalled all too well how her body had shuddered against her corset bones, how her heart lurched in agony. She'd never been fond of emotions, and they'd certainly never been more useless or cruel.

Her young self rose, went to the window and dragged a finger across the glass, absently mollifying the bird. Then she walked out of the office, her elder self and Constance in silent pursuit.

The younger Rebecca descended and burst from the school into the cool London night. A host of spirits followed, curious, worried by her air of misery, and they turned to one another in consultation. Frederic was immediately upon her, squawking and swooping to get her attention, but she paid him no heed. The bird went so far as to pull on a lock of her hair, but this only caused her to whirl, batting at him and hissing in the language of the Guard, 'Leave me be!' The bird offered one more gruff call before flying off.

Frederic, her stalwart companion. One couldn't know how such a creature might be missed until he was gone. Rebecca suffered a pang watching the raven fly off. She wished to run forward and chide her younger self: how foolish it was to go out into the night unaccompanied, how it was begging for trouble. She remembered how this had crossed her mind and how she hadn't cared. In that moment she'd cared for nothing but finding a drastic solution to the unnecessary complication that was her heart.

Out into the dark London night she glided, in and out of the pooled light of gas lamps, as if she were already a wraith, past clattering carriages, avoiding puddles of filth and ignoring the occasional inappropriate comment hurled from the safety of shadows, likely by gentlemen with wives awaiting them at home. Rebecca remembered how sickened she'd been by humanity as a whole, how she'd wondered why they even deserved any protection.

'To Hell with them,' she heard her younger self hiss. 'To Hell with all of it. There is nothing here worth saving, not even myself.'

The hazy night held the buildings in a wet fog that rose from the riverbank, and young Rebecca moved through it to the crest of Westminster Bridge. She stared down at the deep black Thames, at the cargo ships and ferries so far below, and at countless manner of traffic, all ringing bells and making noise. She stepped on to the ledge, grasping the parapet beside her. She pulled up her skirts as if preparing to climb, intending to pitch herself into the air, to hurl herself to freedom, to end it all.

Constance touched Rebecca's sleeve. 'You may think, Headmistress, that this is just a recollection, and that it will unfold just as you remember. But the Liminal is far greater than mere memory. It can change. So I beg you, beware your heart, right at this moment, lest it alter the outcome before you.'

Rebecca turned back to watch herself, her heart pounding in fear, terrified to speak lest the wrong words send her tumbling . . .

Her younger self trailed death in her wake, literally. The spirits that had followed her from the academy rushed close, trying to save her from her sorrow. They bobbed before her, making a barrier, though they knew full well she could slip past and through their transparent bodies to her death if she tried. Still they attempted to make her see, tried to make her pause and think. Rebecca remembered this scene as if it had happened yesterday. But this time she could hear what the spirits were saying.

'Headmistress, don't!' the spirits cried. 'Don't you understand the balance hinges on *all* of you? It affects the whole city, everyone we love. Don't you see you can't just break rank, walk away and kill yourself? You mustn't! And Athens; what about Athens? And the Guard? Michael. What of poor Michael?'

As the spirits exclaimed, phantom images began to float through the air like reflections upon water. A shimmering picture of a dusty Athens came into view, its fine Romanesque windows shuttered and boarded. The scene included Rebecca's friends, all in black, flowers hanging limply from their hands. They descended those formidable academy steps to never again enter its now-locked doors. Spirits were everywhere. Too many of them. The Work was faltering.

Michael stood at the rear of the procession, his once jolly and engaging face entirely devoid of colour, life or anything recognizable. His luminous heart was doused. It was the most terrifying sight Rebecca had ever beheld, watching this unfold in the mist before her eyes, her hand to her mouth, tears in her eyes.

Constance spoke gently, but gravely. 'In this delicate space between time and memory, any one of these phantom reflections could become reality. If you accept it, down you go into the cold, deadly kiss of the Thames. What say you?'

'No,' was all Rebecca could manage, in a desperate murmur.

In a panic she rejected those images. She did not want to see or to bring about this future. Yet her younger self still stood precarious.

Constance gestured behind her. 'See here what you missed.'

From a dark alley, a figure broke from shadow. He wore a dark, modest coat, his hair was dishevelled, and his cheeks glowed bright with a blush, even in the dim lamplight. His beautiful blue eyes were wide with panic, and he was prepared to run forward and save her. But he was far enough away that, even if he ran full tilt, he might not cross the distance before she fell.

'Michael,' Rebecca gasped into her hand. 'Oh, Michael, I did not want *you* to see this.'

'He was the Heart,' Constance murmured. 'He felt it before he saw it. Before Frederic summoned him, he was already on his way.'

'He was there,' Rebecca choked.

'He always has been.'

It was a solid truth that turned Rebecca's stomach.

'Now you must watch and accept,' Constance added.

As Michael ran forward, she saw that he held something large and black in his hands, something surprisingly docile for a wild creature. It was Frederic. Michael held the raven in his palms, its blue breast feather aglow. He released the bird with a soft prayer, and it flew to the younger version of Rebecca on the bridge.

Rebecca watched herself pause. She remembered how she'd reflected in that instant, seeing the swarm of spirits wishing to block her. They did not want her to join them, she'd realized. Not yet. And when she'd felt Frederic alight on her shoulder, she'd reached a trembling hand up to his talons and her heart had grown less heavy upon contact.

The blue glow of the bird's breast feather faded. Rebecca saw now that Michael had used Frederic as his gift's conduit, to impart what his hands were too far away to bequeath. Her younger self's foot shifted and slid back off the ledge.

'What am I doing?' she heard herself mutter. Tears were pouring down her younger cheeks. Frederic rubbed his head against her and she stroked his feathers. 'I'm so sorry, Frederic. I love you. Thank you.'

Michael had saved her. His talent for leavening the heart had bridged the gap until her gifts could regain control. Instinct now reassured her younger self, but Michael's gift had pulled her back from the edge. The bleak alternate future dissipated like fog in a breeze.

Rebecca glanced over at him and absorbed the intense relief on his face. It was beautiful and poignant, his tears tiny glimmers in the gaslight. He stepped back into partial shadow but did not leave.

A spirit approached her younger, shaking self, and though silent, she'd understood as the ghost, a young woman in century-old clothes, who had, perhaps, thrown herself off that same bridge, carefully mouthed the words, 'Thank you.'

The elder Rebecca heard the words this time, and she was moved to reply, 'No. Thank you.

Thank all of you.'

Constance, who had stood as still and impassive as a statue, smiled.

'That simple exchange, that thank-you,' Rebecca murmured, 'fed my lonely soul for years I knew that while I wouldn't receive the love I craved from Alexi, that crowd of spectres alone was evidence that I did have a purpose.'

Her focus shifted to Michael, still standing in the shadows. 'Why didn't he say anything?'

'You know him,' Constance replied. 'You know why.'

'Because he knew the shame and horror I felt,' Rebecca said, watching those sentiments so evident on her younger incarnation's face. 'He was not worried I would try again, and he felt my embarrassment would overshadow any benefit. This was a private moment so unlike me, something I'd never share – that was why he said nothing.'

She turned to Michael's shadow and said words she'd never been known to utter. 'Thank you for being there, Michael

Carroll. It's not the last time you and Frederic would prove my valorous knights, but thank you for being my champion *here,* when no other living person was.' She faltered as she recollected the grim images presented as an alternate future. 'And I don't want to ever see that heart of yours broken. That was a sight more terrible than the face of Darkness itself.'

Little Mary floated at Michael's side. He was forced to watch the scene on Westminster Bridge, and wondered if Rebecca was watching it, too, from elsewhere. What would she see? Were each of them trapped in their own memories, the events once again unfolding? Was this what the ghosts had in mind? If so, to what purpose?

The scene grieved him now, as it had then. Worse, even, for his love for Rebecca had only grown. Again he wanted to run forward, to take her in his arms and ask her what on earth she was thinking; she the strong and stalwart second-in-command; she to whom they all looked for strength, guidance and sensibility. He yearned to kiss her madly and wipe all thoughts of Alexi Rychman from her consciousness, just as he'd wanted to do then and hadn't.

He turned to the ghost and said, 'I am a coward.'

'Are you? Or did you surmise that it would have been worse if you'd shamed her by your appearance? Didn't you really know that strong silence, your secret guardianship, was a better choice at that moment?'

'I maintain that I am a coward.' Michael set his jaw, unwilling to be praised.

The little girl smirked. 'It is true that it is safer to love someone unattainable than to love someone in reality. This moment could have changed everything. You were as scared for yourself as you were for her, weren't you?'

He stared at the ghost. 'You're wise for a child.'

'Death expands the mind,' she said airily, then grinned. She touched his hand, and suddenly they were at a dance.

Rebecca threw her hands up at the bright light. Everyone was dressed in finery, and there was music. It was the same autumn as the scene on the bridge, though some weeks afterward. The academy ball. The glorious ballroom of Athens was thrown open for one day, its gilded and glittering interior packed with guests bedecked in jewels and garbed in fine dresses and frock coats accessorized with buttons, bows, lace, silk and perfume. In addition, there were ubiquitous floral bouquets, confections and the finest in modern music played by a string quartet. The students relished this day of freedom to stand close, to chat, to *touch,* and even the chaperones were not fully averse to camaraderie and flirtation. Rebecca herself remembered hoping to find an opportunity.

It was her year to chaperone, and she remembered thinking that while she was headmistress, it was still a chance to look stunning. She'd put Alexi's name on the chaperone list as well, praying that perhaps he'd notice her this time. He hated such frivolities, and she knew he'd likely stand in the corner and scowl, looking every bit the brooding, Gothic hero of sensationalist novels, a trait that garnered him endless teasing from the Guard. But if Alexi dreaded the event, all the better if she looked stunning. He might be discomfited in the very best of ways.

She saw herself in a corner sipping the champagne reserved for the faculty, looking lovely indeed in a rich-red gown that matched the colour of Alexi's favourite accessory, his crimson cravats. Complemented by all the staff, she chuckled at the raised eyebrows of every student who had never dreamed to see their headmistress's uncovered collarbones. Her younger self didn't yet know that Alexi would never come. That he would claim family business with his sister. That she would soon feel the bitter sting of rejection.

The room brightened just a bit. 'Ho-ho, Headmistress! Why . . . My God!' came a voice through the open side doors. Michael strode in, wearing a fine navy suit coat over a charcoal vest and lighter cravat that enhanced the oceanic blue of his eyes. His usually haphazard hair was combed neatly, his side-burns trimmed to accentuate a firm jaw, his dark brown moustache shaved away to reveal a firm mouth. The only wrinkles on his kind face were laughter lines.

Had she seen then how handsome he looked, how engaging and endearing? Had she felt the breeze of fresh air that was his constant good cheer? Watching how his smile drew out that of her younger self, Rebecca remembered being glad to see him. She remembered thinking what a good husband he would make for some kind and uncomplicated woman, for some soul as devout as he, someone saintly and flawless, some angel. She still felt he deserved that, but her older self gasped at the way he looked at her. The desire and appreciation she saw in his eyes made her realize his intentions were anything but saintly.

He *wanted* her. She'd grown used to the idea that she was not the type of woman a man would crave, but this . . . Something shifted in her body and Rebecca moved forward into the scene, yearning to be closer to Michael, to warm herself at the fires in his eyes.

'I hope you don't mind my stealing into the party,' he said to her younger incarnation, his hungry appreciation curtained by winking camaraderie. 'You know I cannot resist social engagements.'

'Oh, *please,*' the young Rebecca said with exaggerated weariness, raising her hand to her head. 'My students' shock at seeing their headmistress in her finery has palled. Do save me.'

'I'd save you from anything,' he replied, 'even yourself.' He must have realized how that sounded, for he offered a gracious explanation: 'And by that I mean how dangerously fetching you are in this dress, Headmistress. You ought to be warned!'

Her younger self blushed, ignorant, but the older Rebecca saw exactly what he meant. Suddenly she knew how very truly he spoke, and how he had striven to save her, to rally her, to care for her, each and every time they were together. When they hunted as the Guard, when they sat at their favourite café, when they commiserated as friends – he was always there for her. More memories flooded forth, countless scenes flashing before her eyes: grim confrontations of malevolent spirits, glad conversations at La Belle et La Bête. Dining at the Withersby estate. Strolling about Regent's Park. Running off to intercept violent poltergeists. There had been so many moments where this man had made her smile and laugh and forget that there was such a thing as pain and spectral horror in the world.

So many times he'd saved her, with tiny, life-affirming gestures. No one else had such power over her, she realized. And no one else had ever looked at her like this. She recognized his look – she'd aimed it for years at someone unattainable – but had she shown this same fire? For there was a *fire* in Michael's eyes, and that was a thrilling concept: the *fire* of love, not just the cold emptiness of unrequited adoration. What a silly game they'd played! How stupid she was not to have taken each of these small moments and made sense of them.

Something must have been writ upon her face, for Constance looked pleased and the flickering ball vanished. Rebecca swayed upon her feet.

'A good beginning to your journey,' the ghost said. 'Everything you need to know you already do. Here, somewhere' – her transparent finger poked at her temple – 'and on its way here.' She pointed toward Rebecca's heart. 'Trust the journey. You'll be a lovelier woman if you choose happiness.'

The ghost flickered and, reeling, Rebecca found herself at the entrance to the Athens foyer.

'Farewell, Headmistress, do find your peace, for it shall aid in securing mine for ever. We rest happier in heaven if we've helped those on Earth.' Constance's gaze darkened. 'But if you falter . . . you might bring us all down with you. And now the next guide shall take you onwards.'

Chapter Seven

Students twirled past Michael, where he stood oblivious within memory. Little Mary seemed just as captivated. The headmistress was stunning in her crimson gown; it brought out a bloom in her cheeks, accentuated her every feature and highlighted the pallor of her smooth skin.

'Is this just to torture me?' he choked out, overtaken by fresh desire.

'No, no,' Mary said. 'It is to remind you, to embolden you. You called yourself a coward and that cannot be. But, come. Billy's got you next.'

She took his hand and warned, 'You'll feel seasick. The Liminal presses hard against this academy to drag the two of you through the veil of time like this. But thankfully these mysterious stones can take whatever's thrown at them, can't they? I heard your recent battle here was rather brilliant. Now close your eyes.'

Michael did not hesitate; he closed his eyes and felt the world change again.

Rebecca glanced around, wanting to bid Constance a final farewell. Instead, a familiar spirit floated at face level: the young boy from the chandelier, a spirit she'd made a fond habit of greeting.

He grinned. 'My turn, Mum.' He had a Scots accent.

'Well, hello there, young man,' Rebecca said, finally able to talk to the boy and glad of it, but the world was suddenly a dizzying blur in front of her, and her question was lost in her throat. Years whirled by. She, Alexi, the Guard and students came and went, appearing and disappearing, moving in hurried motion through this hall and foyer of Athens, and all the while the young man from the chandelier watched and smiled. Each day, a wink was offered up to him by an ageing Rebecca. And suddenly she understood: he was showing her everything he'd seen in two decades.

She found her voice. 'I don't know your story, young man.'

He shrugged. 'Street urchin. Ran away from an orphanage up north. Bad lot, that. Not much better in London. Fell ill. Nurse who worked at Athens took me in, died up there.' He gestured towards the wing with the infirmary. 'But this was home, as much as I ever had one, while I was here. Didn't feel like leavin'. Liked it when you winked at me. Only mum I've had, really,' the lad admitted.

Rebecca turned away. She had wanted to be a mother once, as she supposed most women did.

'But enough o' that,' the boy said gently. 'This is about you. Keep watchin'.'

Rebecca cleared her throat and watched the whirlwind of images. Alexi stalked across the foyer and back again, like some great, swooping raven. Rebecca saw herself pace to and fro, realizing how unnecessarily stern she looked. 'Most certainly, unnecessarily stern,' she muttered.

But then Michael would enter. He would make no pause, see no other sights, just make his way surely and directly across the foyer to her office. Each and every time, there on business or as a friend, her door was his only destination. His hesitation outside struck her. He would stride confidently forward, then stop and stuff his hand in a pocket. Did he tremble slightly? He'd close his eyes, loose a prayer, perhaps, and finally, after that less-than-confident pause, knock. It happened over and over.

Rebecca shook her head. 'Good God, Michael, you're not *nervous*, are you?'

'Always,' Billy replied. 'Every time, he was. Reminded of it now, too, as he's living this right now. Or reliving it.'

'Why is Michael enduring this trial?'

'To learn.'

'What on earth does *he* need to learn? He's always been the perfect one, the one that never needed any help.' Rebecca's breath gave out. 'I'm the broken one.'

The ghostly boy's hand touched hers. It was a freezing connection, but Rebecca subdued her shiver. The contact was fond, however uncomfortable, and she appreciated the gesture.

'He needs to trust his heart. Especially now. He fears he's worthless since his power is gone.'

'Why, that's ridiculous! His heart was always beyond capacity. Just because our Guard spirits went and—'

'Have you ever told him so?'

Rebecca looked at her feet. 'No.'

'Do so. But first he must believe it himself. You need not be separately broken to make a whole together, but separately whole to remain unbreakable. Only that makes a healthy home.'

Was it as easy as the ghost intimated, just to say yes and make a home together? Perhaps it was. She eyed the boy. 'You're wise for a child.'

'Staring down eternity will make one so,' he replied, but he bobbed his head and she could tell he was greatly pleased.

Despite herself, Rebecca chuckled. 'I imagine so.'

'So,' the young ghost continued, 'while you may think you've a thousand things keepin' you from happiness, a

thousand flaws and mistakes, here's a man who thinks himself
a coward. He wonders if he has enough to give you. He's nervous every time he's alone with you. All for love.' The ghost's
eyes grew a bit cold and his face ominous. 'You both live in
fear, and I tell you, the whole of the spirit world fears you
cannot overcome it. You've given much of your life to these
blessed bricks. Do you want to give your eternity to hauntin'
them? There are two paths here. Now from the darkness,
choose.'

And then Billy gave her a small but decisive push and everything went black.

'Percy, come closer!'

Constance appeared at her side and Percy started. She had
maintained her perch overlooking the foyer, rosary in hand,
sitting on a bench on the second floor of Athens, remaining
inconspicuous but on guard. Constance and Billy had been
told to call upon her if something needed attention. Nothing
had raised an alarm until now.

'The Liminal presses in, right into the heart of us, she's in
the Whisper-world now,' the ghost warned. 'The shadows will
be close and they'll not want to let the headmistress go. She's a
perfect candidate for a state like mine, forever haunting these
bricks.'

Percy moved to the edge of the landing. She'd been mesmerized by visions below, all done in a misty, giant picture frame,
the hazy clouds of shifting images filling the foyer and then
vanishing as the memories moved elsewhere. She'd never seen
anything like it; hundreds of images superimposed upon one
another, shifting in and over and across in curling tendrils of
smoke, like ink bleeding into water to form ever-changing
shapes, all of them individually poignant. These were private
matters played out in mist, and so Percy did not strain to make
out the particulars; all she heard were murmurs, and all she
saw were greyscale silhouettes.

But, then, Percy wasn't exactly sure what she was looking
for. The precise nature of angels, demons, ghosts, guardians
and the worlds between wasn't something any of them would
ever master. But Percy chose to believe in angels. While she'd

never seen them during the course of the Grand Work, she was *sure* she'd heard them. She hoped they heard her now and could sing at her side.

Constance grimaced. 'The Liminal can change many ways. Let's make sure it twists the way we hope. I've seen two possible futures, one I like a great deal better than the other! Come to the threshold edge. Fate cuts along a razor-thin line.'

Chapter Eight

All was darkness. The chill went to the bone and Rebecca shuddered. She might appear as stoic and fearless as their leader, Alexi, but she knew her frailty all too well.

'Mortal hearts make many mistakes,' she murmured, ruminating on her various failures. The longer she stood in the dark, the more the chill of death itself began to seep in. She wondered if she'd been abandoned in some corner of the dark netherworld.

'And what is this, then?' she asked, feeling nothing on her skin but cold, seeing nothing in her gaze but blackness. There was no echo of her voice; it sounded flat, enclosed, like a coffin.

She stretched out her hands in a panic, wondering if she was indeed entombed, but she was free to move. She was standing upright.

There was nothing at her back; nothing before her. But considering the extent of the darkness, she dared not take a step. 'This must be the "yet to come" part, Master Dickens? Did you have any idea what you were toying with, sir? I maintain your tale was overwrought,' Rebecca murmured. 'Tell me, is this where I see my headstone and repent my every sin? Where I pray for a second chance? I *do* regret. Repent. But what if there's no second chance? Is darkness to be my final judgement? Is there to be no spirit guide through this last, harrowing phase?'

There was a long silence. Rebecca had held a glimmer of hope, had begun to feel the lightness of a heart opening to its true call; she had begun to truly see the man who loved her as she is and always was. But all was precarious. In vain. Too late. There was no one to guide her.

'Oh, no! Don't ye dare let go of that glimmer, Rebecca Thompson, or I can't do my duty and we'll all be bound to these damned stones! And who would want to see ye happier than I?' came a familiar, chiding Irish brogue, an accent always heightened by anxiety. Suddenly there was a grey light, a silver halo around a solid woman who wore the greyscale of the dead.

'Jane!' Rebecca cried, and threw her arms around her. 'Oh, how we miss you! Wait. Am I dead?' In this existence, in this time and place, Jane was solid.

'No, you're not . . . yet. But the spirits are all in agreement—'

'That it should have been me!' Rebecca cried.

'No!' Jane hissed. 'That's not the answer.'

There was a rumble of thunder. Lightning illuminated the shadows and Rebecca screamed as pillars of human skulls were revealed marching off into the endless distance. Shadows lurked behind those pillars and Rebecca squeezed her eyes shut, not wanting any further illumination.

Jane shook her head and whispered, 'None of that nonsense, now. Watch your words in these parts.'

'Where are we, exactly?'

'This is the Whisper-world, Rebecca.'

'Here? *Me?* I'm not supposed to be here, am I?'

'No, it's dangerous while you're alive. You're on the edge of a dark realm. Ahead of us sits the Liminal threshold. A powerful place not to be trifled with. It's what allows us this final examination.'

She led Rebecca forward. As they moved, the darkness lightened; the air became a luminous silver and her muffled footfalls over the wet stone sounded across something more like glass. The air was less dank in her nostrils, the breath of sadness less oppressive.

'Are you happy, Jane?' Rebecca asked. 'Where is your ghostly love, your Aodhan? I've prayed so dearly for your peace.'

Jane spoke carefully. 'I chose my path. Aodhan awaits me in the Great Beyond, but I can't go to him till I see you choose *your* path. No matter what happens, I regret nothing. But if you fail . . .'

'What . . . what will happen?'

'I'll be trapped here for ever. It's the price the Liminal asks. But I love and believe in you that much.'

'Oh, Jane—'

'Hush your mouth, we've work to do.'

A great proscenium of a stage was gleaming before her. Both females looked onto a scene that Rebecca recognized from her very recent past. The scene was still, frozen, waiting to leap to life. Rebecca's heart raced. It was a darkened Athens, right before the spirit war.

Hearing music from the upstairs foyer, she anxiously turned to Jane. 'In Dickens, the past was the purview of the first spirit alone. How are *you* showing me this?'

Jane pursed grey lips. 'I thought you didn't like Dickens.'

Rebecca paused. 'Well . . . I suppose he's my only reference here.'

Jane smirked. 'You're an infinitely more complicated creature than Ebenezer Scrooge, Headmistress, and so the same methods of salvation cannot apply.'

Rebecca sniffed, straightening her shoulders. 'I didn't think he got it exactly right. Too dramatic.'

Jane laughed. 'Oh, but he got it exactly right. Yet while we're not following his script, we *must* teach you and repeat until you really see.'

'I see—'

'Do you?' Jane insisted, placing an icy hand upon her chest. 'No. You're not free. Not yet.'

'No,' Rebecca agreed, looking down. 'I don't know that I'll ever be free.'

Suddenly, she emitted a torrent of confession. 'All I've hoped for in life is to valiantly serve those who depend upon me, to be an efficient, respected headmistress, a member of the Guard, an upstanding citizen. Of course I wanted to be loved in return by Alexi! I wanted a home and a family with him. But our Grand Work had its own agenda, his heart its own call. So now, as I stare down at my life, I find my past ruled by cowardice and second-guessing. What could I have done differently? I'm nothing of what I wish to be.'

So satisfyingly low, the words felt good the moment they dripped from her lips. But their effect was anything but. As they escaped, Rebecca's guilt only magnified. Sorrow crested in her blood, and the darkness around her intensified, pressing in, urging her to simply wallow in a deep well of never-ending self-pity. She could drink from this bubbling font of misery, as she had every night for twenty years, from now unto eternity. The better air she had begun to breathe again went rancorous, the shadows around them lengthened.

'Rebecca,' her friend warned, 'this is a deadly place to go melancholy. Do not ingest such a drug—'

'But I've so much pain—'

'Well *mitigate* it before it's too late!' Jane exclaimed. The Liminal stage of possibility went black. Shadow pressed in upon Rebecca's heart and she recognized the sensation. While the Guard had briefly halted Darkness, its ruler, the Whisper-world was its own entity and lived on, attuned to misery and fear, an ethereal, subtle and dangerous predator. That predator was hungry for a restless soul. Her misery was just the sort of food the Whisper-world craved.

Suddenly, in the distance, far outside the now-black picture frame through which she gazed, in the thick shadows becoming recognizable as Athens, there came a bright white gleam, like a star, widening. It was a beautiful light, a familiar light, and there was a petite figure within, drawing inexorably closer.

'What's that?' Rebecca breathed.

Jane offered a partial smile. 'A guardian angel, watching out for us beyond the Liminal edge. But we mustn't test her. This realm wants her for its own more than any of us, and if she had to come in for you' – Jane shuddered – 'who knows what it might do to her again. Look what surrounds you in the Whisper-world. Do you want to join them?' She gestured to the shadows, to figures Rebecca saw there that moved listlessly, shapeless, aimless.

Jane continued, 'These souls are here because of second-guessing themselves, because of mortal frailty or selfishness. You're hardly the first to come. What keeps them here is their inability to let go, which is their greatest crime. To err is mortal. To not forgive is the stuff of the Whisper-world. Who knows why events needed to unfold as they did, to press, madden or even kill' – she gave Rebecca a meaningful glance – 'some of us as they did? Who are we to question? We must forgive.'

Rebecca could not meet her gaze. She gave a sob and the air thickened further.

Her friend sighed. 'You're a powerful woman, Rebecca, but stop thinking you have power over everything. You can't make someone love you who doesn't, and you can't change what fate has already wrought. You cannot live well if you're unable to discard regrets! In the end, this isn't about me, or Alexi, or Percy. It's about you – and the man who's always loved you. The man who was meant for you, though you never let yourself believe it. You hid from the reality of his love in the dream of Alexi's. Try, for once, to be unselfish. Be *grateful*.'

Rebecca bit her lip, helpless. 'Show me the scene,' she gasped, turning to the Liminal stage. 'Help me see what I must . . .'

The Liminal agreed, and the bright guardian star remained visible, a soft glow in the corner of the stage frame as the past began to play its chosen scene: the Guard were all assembled on the dark third-floor foyer of Athens Academy, where Jane played the fiddle for the waltzing Percy and Alexi. Elijah and Josephine were arm in arm, and Michael was . . . staring at Rebecca. She had been too focused on the waltzing couple to notice before, always too preoccupied.

She wasn't much to look at here, having already given herself over to an identity built around efficient administration. And yet there Michael was, staring at her with the same desire he'd worn on his face when she'd done herself up for the ball years earlier. Here she was drawn and shadowed, her face a grimace, so sure she could never be loved – some part of her was still certain of that – and yet . . .

'He must see something I cannot,' Rebecca murmured, baffled to see that he not only desired her but cared for her, ached for and knew her – truly *knew* her, knew all the complications of her life like no one else possibly could – and here he was, likely as scared as she to reach out and take what he wanted by the hand.

'After all you've seen and been through, he still looks at you that way. He always will. You must trust it,' Jane said.

'I . . . don't understand how. I don't know that I—'

'What? You don't deserve love? That's the talk of a person who jumps off bridges, who does terrible things, or lets terrible things be done to her. You are not she. You must not fear that look, and you must not fear what it means. You must open your eyes to what shines in him and embrace it.' Jane pressed her hand to Rebecca's heart again. 'But there's a catch here, a hiccup. Thinking you understand and *feeling* that you understand are two different beasts. Stare what you fear in the face.'

'I've stared down death,' Rebecca said.

'But what about *love?* Because that, Headmistress, is your greatest fear. Look at it,' Jane insisted, guiding Rebecca towards the frame.

Rebecca stared. She watched Michael Carroll and let herself entertain the idea of what it would be like to receive, accept and possibly return his look of adoration and everything it contained. It was true, she was afraid. Pining, unrequited love was indeed of one dimension. This look, this heart, this love of Michael's was all-encompassing. Yet it was not desperate, cloying or imbalanced; it was simply solid. It could be her foundation.

She'd never conceived of anything quite like this. Her heart began to expand from its tiny, huddled, clutched position and allowed for something new to take its place. She felt like a phoenix being reborn. But she was not a woman who liked earth-shattering change. She was fond of routine, not the unknown. The unknown was terrifying. Her heart huddled close again, clutching at its familiar loneliness, a reflexive contraction. An interior door somewhere slammed closed.

The shadows were ready for her this time, lurching close. A distant beat of horse hooves, a cacophony of whispers, hisses and deadly threats filled the air. The rushing river of restless souls again gurgled in the distance, its currents churning upward, beckoning her to drown herself at last, in waters worse than the Thames.

'Rebecca,' Jane chided.

An inward chill spread inside her, the sort of dread she'd felt when facing demons and the stuff of eternally damning horror. The cold had hooks into her, a fluid invasion and perversion such as blood into a pure spring. It was as if a possessing spirit had slipped cold, wet fingers around her heart and was digging a hole. That unwelcome guest found her melancholy and made a nest within, birthing a wasting madness and inescapable loathing. Rebecca cried out in physical, mental and spiritual pain.

But then there was that bright angel's light again, coming closer, as if from across a long room, as if from across Athens's foyer. Brighter, brighter ... The shadows sliding inside Rebecca seemed to jump back, scalded, no longer as bold, if still nipping at the hem of her skirts. She felt her body warm; the forces that wished to keep her prisoner were for the nonce held at bay. That light was no match for this shadow and Rebecca longed to warm herself in it.

Jane glanced from the light to Rebecca, gauging her progress. 'I've told you before, you and Alexi would never have been a good fit. All you'd have done was scowl at each other. You loved him because he was safe, because he felt familiar. Because you didn't trust anyone else, didn't trust that anyone could love you, hardly even yourself. But at some point you have to let go and be loved, for there are people who love you.'

She pointed. 'Look at Michael Carroll. Imagine turning the tide from the first moment you know him, *from the very first moment.* This should be a good trick,' she added in a mutter. 'Please, God, let it work. Maestro, from the top . . .'

Jane snapped her fingers, and the world whirled into something entirely different but familiar. Suddenly Rebecca was a youth on Westminster Bridge. It was a grey day in autumn, and six unlikely children had been called to police spirits throughout London. It was the first day of the Grand Work. It was the first day she fell in love with Alexi Rychman. The very first day.

Rebecca watched her spindly, awkward, confused self, waiting and shifting upon her heels, not knowing what trials and tribulations lay before her. Alexi hadn't arrived yet. Instead, she and Michael were alone. Why hadn't she remembered that they were the first to arrive? He was staring at her with such kindness and admiration, *from the very first.* And his smile . . .

This, she realized, was destiny. She'd cursed a fate that hadn't provided for her, but fate had provided and she had turned away. She was destined for Michael from the first, but she'd been intimidated even then.

'Can you see?' Jane murmured.

'Yes.' Rebecca breathed. Honestly. She did. 'I see that it's right.'

She stared at Michael, at her young self and her current self, and she truly saw him, completely, for the first time. With clarion focus she knew that he would never be second best. He was, simply, *best*. For her, he always had been.

Her huddled heart exploded with joy. Her body shifted, expanded; her every muscle, so tightly clenched in quivering fists, finally let go. The transformation was whole and glorious, a revelation that could never be undone, á knowledge so sure that it put all other pain in distant shadow. Her love of Alexi had no power here. She was broken free from the unwitting spell he'd never intended to cast. The gentle heart before her, fiercely passionate for nothing but her, had overcome all. It was the greatest power yet seen in all manner of strange in her life of spectral mayhem.

She turned to Jane in wonder, and the friends shared a beautiful, moved silence. Rebecca saw the new light in her eyes reflected in Jane's.

'Now,' her friend pressed, 'the last question. Do you forgive yourself for the past?'

Rebecca faltered, the word 'forgive' an impossible obstacle. She felt the chill of shadow pierce her again, finding that hollow, tender place and ripping the fresh stitches. She groaned, a terrible swinging pendulum in the pit of her heart, bloodied and razor sharp. Oh, to feel such joy, only to regress again and feel it ripped away . . . The scene on Westminster faded, and she was once more in grey shadow.

Jane was talking again, giving words of reassurance to turn the tide. Rebecca couldn't hear her. The shadows encircled them both and they seemed too powerful. These shadows didn't think she deserved a second chance; they wanted her a wasting form, unable to pass on, doomed for eternal regrets. Why had she made so many mistakes? Why had she wasted all the time she'd been given with Michael? What was left for her when so much time had passed and the Grand Work was done? She began to weep.

Her shoulders felt a gentle pressure. Jane held her. But Rebecca still could not hear her. She saw the hideous form of the defeated Whisper-world lord, Darkness, a form of bones and rot, a force comprised of everything one wished humanity could just leave behind. Rebecca saw him in her mind's eye, in that serpents' nest within her, reassembling. Digit by digit, vertebrae by vertebrae. Eyes of hellfire and a tongue of damnation.

She recalled that she had life yet to live. She had the power to retaliate, just as when her feet were on the bridge's edge. She did not want Darkness, so recently torn apart, to so easily be put back together. Not by the mere regrets of her weak, mortal heart. She did not want Darkness to win her as a bride. She would not *let* Darkness win her.

'I reject thee,' she murmured to shadow.

She wanted the bright hearth of Michael's heart. She would be lured, fooled and seduced by misery no longer. Jane was right: the heavens had made no mistakes. Darkness only wanted her to think so.

'And now I see,' Rebecca murmured. 'Forgiveness.'

Suddenly everything was light.

Chapter Nine

Percy maintained her position in the Athens foyer and watched how the shadow shapes responded to her light through the portal before her, how she curbed them. This was her power, her gift, and it had saved them all once before. While it hurt dearly to let it burn, it was worth the discomfort to know that she could turn tides, that so long as she focused, she could strike back and declaw misery's talons.

'Oh, Percy, look how it worsens,' Constance murmured, bobbing in the air beside her. 'The headmistress chose correctly at least, I think, but it's not over.'

The whole vast room had grown dark over the course of the journey. There were terrible murmurs and whispers through the portal, hung like a curtain in the middle of the foyer, seeping out into their mortal reality, and the blood chilled in Percy's veins. She rushed forward to its very edge, staring in, straining to see the dim figures beyond. A dark mist rose inside, and Percy could hear its familiar hissing, trying to invite her in, insidious and eerily seductive. This edge of shadow was a dangerous place for coming and going. And it wanted her, like it had before.

As if through a veil, Percy recognized the headmistress, unsteady on her feet, surrounded by flickering shadows. The headmistress was in the midst of a battle.

'This is the Liminal?' Percy asked.

'Yes,' Constance murmured. 'It's here that the greatest change of a soul can take effect. The danger is necessary because the transformation can be the richest. The Liminal can be a beautiful place, but it edges the Whisper-world, and with any darkness present . . . Well, it amplifies *all* things.'

The mists of the Whisper-world swirled up around the edge of Rebecca's skirts, clearly trying to hold her like shackles. But Rebecca fought – and who was the spirit beside her?

Percy's heart swelled in sudden recognition. 'Jane!' she breathed. Close enough to touch her friends if she reached through the portal, Percy kept to the side, a bright candle at the base of a vast altar. She dared not step inside, not because she feared for herself, but for the child she carried.

Jane looked out from the portal and smiled. 'Hello, Percy. Could you spare us just a bit more of your light? Rebecca's done what she must, but we're still precarious. You're just the one to tip the scales.'

Rebecca didn't seem able to hear past her internal fight.

Percy squeezed in her hand the rosary Michael had blessed, staring deep into the offending, greedy shadows that wanted to make sadness a forever state throughout Creation. The burning in her breast intensified, searing. The unfortunate effect of a divine power using her mortal body was that there were limits, but as Percy had herself once lived a life domineered by melancholy, she was more than ready to give what she could for this battle. She'd be damned if such melancholy was going to hold Rebecca and feed the beast they'd already bested.

'Headmistress, go on. Release your tears,' Jane was saying. 'Don't hold them in or give them power. Shed your tears upon the stones and leave them. When all is done, step into the light.

The headmistress looked up. She seemed to hear. Her cheeks were wet, but her face was more open than Percy had ever seen it.

'Let that caged heart of yours free,' Jane urged. 'I love you, Rebecca. I always have and I always will. You're right about forgiveness. It's time to begin again.'

The friends embraced, and Rebecca's healing tears flowed faster. Seeming to realize what came next, the two said good-bye – and Merry Christmas.

Jane stepped from the portal. She appeared at Percy's side, floating, changing from her solid form in the Whisper-world to her transparent, spectral buoyancy upon Earth. Inside the portal, Rebecca looked around, squinted out at them, apparently seeing only light and feeling that she was alone. More tears had to drain before she could start life anew.

Placing a cool draft of a hand on Percy's shoulder, Jane murmured, 'Let her have a good cry; she needs it. Let sorrow drain into the river. When she's done, carefully help her off the ledge.

Now that the headmistress's change of heart has freed me, I must be off to shake final sense into a vicar.'

When Jane grinned, Percy returned the expression. 'Sense? Indeed.' But her heart was heavy; they'd have to say goodbye again.

'I'll be back to spook you and your beloved,' Jane promised, anticipating her. 'I know Alexi will be insulted if I don't give him his fair haunting. He'll never forgive me.'

'Thank you. It's so good to see you,' Percy murmured. 'But, I am – we all are – so sorry to have lost you. Grateful for your sacrifice, but sorry.'

Percy's inner light, that otherworldly beacon of hope, flickered. Jane rolled her eyes. 'Not you, too! All of you with your regrets,' the Irishwoman scoffed. 'My fate was what was meant to be. Now, tend your light.' Jane turned to Constance, floating patiently at Percy's side. 'Good work, my lass. Stay here with

Percy till the last, and then I daresay we've all earned our blessed peace, and then some!'

Constance nodded, and placed her ghostly hand on Percy's shoulder. Percy's light burned brighter for friendship. Being a beacon was exhausting and painful, and she wondered if her skin would bear the mark of a burn.

Graceful, dark movement from the floor above caught Percy's eye. Alexi stared down at the scene from the floor above; down at the roiling portal, the headmistress's vague form within, at the ghosts of Jane and Constance, and then at his luminous wife. Tears stood in his dark eyes. He made no move to stop Percy, or to move her away from the perilous edge where she stood guard; he only stared at her with awestruck pride. Jane smiled and waved up at him.

'Merry Christmas!' Jane whispered and vanished.

Alexi blew Percy a kiss and turned away, leaving her to her miracles as she had requested.

Percy's light was sustained anew.

Rebecca looked up. The light yet blinded her, but she was done; her tears had run their course. Everything was different.

She stood. 'What do I do?' she murmured, seeing only the light, unsure.

'Come,' said a sweet voice. 'Give me your hand.'

Rebecca reached out towards the light. A soft, small hand met hers and pulled. There came a whirling sensation and she found herself stepping down on to firm ground in the foyer of Athens Academy. A small pop sounded behind her, and the portal, shadows, mists and encroaching danger were no more.

It was indeed the sturdy marble floor of her academy; she was in the school she had run with strength and aplomb, the place that had given so many opportunities otherwise absent to its students and staff. God, she loved this building.

Her eyes found those of the guardian angel, whose light had helped her fight the greedy Whisper-world: they were the eerie, ice-blue irises of Persephone Rychman. The young woman's inner light, as white as her skin, faded as Rebecca moved to safety. She was breathing heavily, as if from great pain and exertion, but save for a bit of sweat on her brow she seemed otherwise composed. Her faintly rouged lips curved into a small smile just as radiant as her spirit.

'Welcome back, Headmistress!'

Rebecca swallowed hard, at a loss for words. 'Indeed. Th– thank you, Percy.'

There was a short pause.

'Merry Christmas!' Alexi's young wife cried, and she threw her arms around Rebecca.

Rebecca took a moment to take stock. There was no jealousy. There was no pining. There was only possibility. The spirits had granted her new life. She felt entirely, wholly, utterly *new*. She returned the girl's embrace, no longer tentative.

Percy pulled back and grinned again.

Curtseying before either of them could say another word, the young woman trotted off up the staircase . . . and the vast room seemed suddenly all the more empty for the lack of her. There was no remaining bitterness as Rebecca's unwitting rival disappeared. This girl had never wished to be her rival; she had only embraced fate – something the headmistress intended to do from now on.

'They did it all in one night,' she murmured, wandering to her office, a grin on her face. 'Spirits. Good spirits. Of course they did it all in one night. Of course they can.' Dickens was to the point after all, damn him. She realized she didn't mind being proven wrong.

It seemed her surprises weren't done. There was an envelope on her desk bearing the official seal of Athens. From the board of directors. Rebecca's heart was in her throat, for she feared something had finally snapped. Perhaps closing the school to battle Darkness had brought about repercussions? Perhaps the board had heard that she'd been acting odd of late, which she most certainly had. But her tension vanished as she read, and a grin again spread across her face.

In recognition of your exemplary work as headmistress, the board of Athens Academy has voted to secure you more spacious housing near but not on the grounds of the academy. We will convert your existing apartments into space for visiting faculty, there being a number who

wish to learn from and champion Athens's impressive
and progressive model as their own. Enclosed, please
find the keys for 6, Athens Row.

Merry Christmas.

It looked like Alexi's handwriting, but she couldn't be bothered
to verify it.

A home. A real home, just down the block. Of course she
wouldn't want to be far, but . . . a home! Not some attic perch
or cloistered closet filled with memories of loneliness. She'd
now have a hearth. She had someplace to begin her new life,
someplace to invite the some*one* she wanted to be part of it.
Now that she was whole, now that she knew the heavens
wanted something of her – demanded it, in fact – a glorious
future awaited.

She nearly ran out the door.

Chapter Ten

Considering all the spiritual upheaval the school had seen, it was
lucky Athens was tucked into an area of Bloomsbury and placed
at such an odd angle: the red sandstone fortress was surrounded
on all sides by alleys and the backs of other buildings. Billy and
Mary floated at face level, their arms crossed, and they were just
outside the front doors of the academy, in the cold. The breeze
felt good on Michael's flushed face; bracing.

He was still reeling from admitting his constant nerves
when coming to call upon Rebecca.

Surely that made him seem less of a man. But Michael had
done as the ghosts wished, moved in his own footsteps through
years and years, all seen from the spinning temporal axis of
Billy's chandelier vantage. The boy and Mary had taken turns
urging him on, and now he was certain he could knock upon
the headmistress's door without trembling. He wanted her and
loved her more than any fear could obstruct.

'So ye see,' Billy said, taking a paternal tone, 'it isn't that you
fear for your Guard gifts being gone. You fear for the very
human gift of love being accepted. You fear havin' what you
desire. You've feared it all along.'

Michael nodded, dizzy.

'So now what are you waitin' for? You, of all people! We'd have thought you'd seen plenty to give you perspective. Do ye need to be frightened by something far more terrifying? Do you want to go back and fight Darkness again? He could live again, could take your bones as his own . . .' Billy threatened. He made a motion and there was a tearing sound. Where the front door of Athens stood, a dark maw of a portal opened to the Whisper-world. A rushing river of bones gurgled by.

Michael gulped. 'No, thank you. I'm grateful to battle the heart, instead.'

'And are ye going to win the battle this time, Vicar?' cried a voice in an Irish brogue. Stepping from the portal, a woman floated down to hover over the Athens stoop.

'Jane!' Michael cried as he rushed forward.

Jane wafted close, giving his cheek a phantom kiss of cold condensation.

'I . . . I can *hear* you, too!' He was amazed and pleased.

She grinned. 'You're still under my spell.'

'*Your* spell? Are you all right? Is Rebecca all right? Where is she?'

'Oh, yes, I'm grand. She's grand. She's still inside, working a few things out. Percy's watching her, the dear heart. Time's a bit funny here and there, especially crossing in and out like we've been doing, toying with the past. It doesn't all add up, exactly . . . but then again, that's the Whisper-world for you, full of baffling wonders and terrors. When has it ever added up?'

Michael's face darkened. 'What do you mean, she's "inside"?'

'Inside the Whisper-world. The Liminal, to be exact. It's dangerous, but that's where a soul best gets changed. Would you like to go? Do you *need* to go? Or might we move on to the next phase of this ridiculous and beautiful production?'

Michael shook his head and his fists clenched. 'The Whisper-world? We're not meant to go in there. That was the whole point of the war of the spirits – that we couldn't go in, that Alexi couldn't run in after Percy, that we'll go mad if we go in. What do you mean you've taken her in? I'll go in after her and get her out!' He prepared to run inside the gaping portal.

Jane made a motion and the portal snapped closed behind her. 'Why, Vicar Carroll, such spirit,' she said.

Michael eyed her with desperation. 'You know I'd do anything for Rebecca. Always would have.'

'Except say that you love her,' Jane accused.

'I did! Much too late, but I did! Can't that count for something? Where is she? Promise me she's not in danger.'

'Michael, my dear, if anyone was suited for the mental rigours of the Whisper-world, it's our headmistress. You, dear heart, would be destroyed by the sadness of that place. You'd be unable to break free; it would cripple and scar you for ever. Let this moment be. Let *her* be. Focus on yourself.'

'When can I see her?'

'Momentarily. I promise.'

The tension in Michael's shoulders eased and his fists uncurled. Jane would never leave Rebecca without recourse. He stared at the greyscale spirit, noting how only colour and transparency differentiated her from when she lived.

'Oh, goodness, what is it now?' she said, smiling as his eyes welled with tears. She'd always loved his sentimentalism but teased him for it.

'It's so very good to see you,' he explained. 'I think the idea of the Grand Work made us take for granted how much we care for one another. Are you well? Are you at peace? It's so frightfully good to see you. But I didn't mean to rouse you as we prayed at your—'

Jane drew her cold fingers across his eyes, and the draft dried them. 'I happily chose to linger on, to help make this right. And there's only one thing I've left to do. Tell me, Vicar, are you ready to start again? It's my favourite trick, this.'

She didn't wait for a response when she snapped her fingers. In a blink, Michael was suddenly fourteen years old again, standing on a street corner and staring. He'd been summoned from his home as if by a great bell, knocked to the ground by a great wind, and his heart exploded with new sensations. His eyes were full of ghosts. It was the first day of the Grand Work, and he was living it.

Living it, indeed. He was no longer watching himself, as he'd done in Athens; he was *in* this memory. He stared down at his hands and flexed them, felt the vigour of youth pounding in his veins. His consciousness was fully aware, though these events happened years long past. With a little giggle he ran full tilt until he reached the crest of Westminster Bridge. If time and memory were both flexible, perhaps there were ways of making things right.

She was waiting, young and spindly legged, the most beautiful thing he had ever seen. Strands of her brown hair were caressed by the wind, and she glanced around nervously, clutching her skirts and shifting from foot to foot. She'd been the first to arrive, the first of them anxiously awaiting destiny.

'Hello. I'm Rebecca,' she said. She opened her mouth to say something else but stopped, staring at him intently. Something on his face had stilled her.

Michael took a step forward. He reached for her hand and she gave it willingly.

'Hello, Rebecca, I'm Michael,' he heard his young voice say. But his old heart shaped new words, released the thunderbolt of knowledge he felt but had once feared to utter. 'And I will always love you.'

The young Rebecca gasped. She blushed furiously and smiled a welcoming smile.

History changed.

Chapter Eleven

Released from time, from memory, from the magic of the past, or perhaps caught in some sweet mixture of the three, Vicar Michael Carroll stood at the back door of a building he did not recognize. He felt a new man. He wasn't sure what he was suddenly doing on the steps of this lovely town house, or how he'd got there.

He looked around for Jane. She was nowhere to be seen, but his heart pounded with the same vigour he had just felt. He wasn't sure if what he'd seen had truly happened, or if it had been a dream, but either way he yearned to find

Rebecca, to walk up to her right now, again, a lifetime later. He would approach her with that same surety and change history again.

A sound on the street made him turn: a slowly approaching carriage. The curtain on the window was flung aside, the glass opened and a snow-white face beamed an expression of joy up at him where he stood on the steps. She waved.

Mrs Rychman's eerie eyes were shaded from the winter glare by dark-tinted glasses, and she turned to someone behind her and uttered a sort of admonition. 'I have to tell him something,' she insisted, and soon the door was flung open and a firm male voice barked for the driver to stop.

Before her husband could help her out of the carriage, Percy had lifted up her skirts, disembarked and trotted up the stairs to Michael's side. Professor Rychman exited behind her, standing tall and imperious, his black hair, frock coat and carriage a stark contrast to the white of his wife and the snow on the street.

'Hullo, dear girl,' Michael said, squeezing her hand, 'I'm not sure what has happened, but Jane told me you were at hand, so I'm sure I owe you some sort of—'

'The town house is unlocked,' Percy blurted over him. 'Your key on the table. The headmistress's key is in her office, with a letter from the academy board explaining the change in quarters. You *must* have a home, Vicar,' she added earnestly. 'A fresh new start, with no memories but those you two now make. The spirits told me so; they insisted upon it. You must have a home free from the haunting of memories gone by, and you shall make new memories to inhabit *these* bricks. Spirits understand the need of such things: hearths and homes, it's why they haunt them. There is very little more important.'

'Indeed,' Michael said, having never thought about such a detail. 'Most sensible.'

'Merry Christmas!' Percy cried, throwing her arms around him. She released him, lifted her skirts and scurried back towards her husband, who awaited her with a small smile tugging at his mouth.

'But . . . where did this home come from? To whom do I owe . . . ?' He stopped short.

Percy waved her hand as if it didn't matter.

'This building is the property of Athens Academy. How it was paid for is none of your concern,' Alexi said, his tone businesslike, though Michael knew there was warmth beneath. 'As Percy said, the board voted to give the headmistress better lodging. Go on, Vicar, we've all got Christmas merrymaking to do. We're hosting a New Year's celebration at the Rychman estate, don't you know. Do come with your fiancée.'

'My fiancée . . . ?' Michael registered the words, processed them and stepped back a pace. Then he grinned and nearly jumped in the air.

'Go on, she'll be here any minute!' Percy squealed, and dragged Alexi back to the carriage.

He gladly helped her up, and they started off.

Michael entered the front hall of the town house. There were spicy scents and warm, alluring lights. Ignoring the stairs that ascended, surely, to bedrooms and studies, he entered the main room to find it well furnished and decorated, with a blazing hearth.

'My God,' he murmured, staring at the painting above the mantel. Josephine was right: she was painting more beautifully than ever. Her distinct style was no longer limited to guardian angels, as required by the Grand Work, now her subjects were free and entirely her own. Tumbling masses of sumptuous flowers, bursting with colour and life, threatened to spill directly onto the mantel below.

He heard a hiss from the rearmost room – a kitchen, likely – from which warm and intoxicating odours flowed. Someone was mulling wine, a fine cabernet. 'Go, go out the side. One of them is here!' hissed a voice with a French accent.

Michael rushed forward. He was in time. In the kitchen he found Josephine, who had prepared a feast that overflowed from tables and countertops. Lord Withersby was lighting candles, careful to keep his absurdly excessive mauve sleeves from catching fire.

'Hullo, friends.' Michael grinned.

Josephine and Elijah turned, sheepish. 'Sorry, old chap,' Elijah murmured. 'We wanted to have this all done and ready before you got here, but the spirits sure were quick about it, weren't they?'

Michael didn't know what to say.

Seeming to understand, Josephine took his hands. 'Have you lived a whole life over? For us it's only been a day. You must promise to tell us all about it!'

'Josie, it's private,' Elijah scoffed. 'If the spirits went rooting around in our pasts, do you think we'd want to share?'

Josephine raised an eyebrow, shocked at her fiancé's unusual moment of discretion. *'C'est vrai.* I suppose for once you are right.'

'Listen,' Michael said, grabbing Elijah, 'who do I have to thank—?'

Elijah waved at him to be silent. 'I've a message from the orphanage. Little Charlie's health has turned a corner. He said an angel came and commended him for his help. You should have him over for a nice dinner, he said he'd like that – and "God bless us" and all that nonsense.' Withersby grinned. Michael pressed his hands to his face in a prayer of thanksgiving.

Josephine removed her apron, showing herself in a far fancier gown than anyone should have been found cooking in, and threw one last handful of cinnamon sticks into the wine. *'Fini.'* She turned to Elijah. *'Allons-y, ma chère.'* She turned to Michael. *'Joyeux Noël!'* Kissing him on both cheeks, she darted into the main hall and out the front door.

Elijah plucked a piece of paper from his vest pocket and pressed it into Michael's hands. 'Get done with this quickly and stop us all from living in sin. I love you!' He kissed Michael's forehead and darted out the door.

Michael opened the paper. Stunned by his good fortune and his even better friends, he entered the sitting room and sat before the hearth, tears of joy in his eyes. While the Guard couldn't be more different as individuals, Michael doubted there'd ever been such care between other humans. He held a certificate for two rings, courtesy of Lord Withersby's favour-ite jeweller.

He felt as though his heart might burst from the magnitude of his blessings. It was hard to imagine that just yesterday he'd been feeling as though his world was collapsing, that he'd lost everything. His heart was as full as the first day he joined the Guard. He'd lost nothing. He had everything yet to gain.

Heedless of the falling snow, flakes melting immediately against her flushed cheeks, Rebecca was down the block before she knew it, at the address specified in the letter. She went to turn the key in the lock and found it already open. The interior was lit and it smelled like heaven.

She did not take the stairs to the upper landings because a crackling warmth drew her towards the parlour. Inside sat a dapper man upon a divan, his hair more kempt than Rebecca was used to seeing, and his oceanic blue eyes wide and brimming with promise. In what surely must be firelight, it seemed as though a great aura hung about him, as if he were channelling an angel. Or perhaps they were illuminating him for her. Lighting the way.

Michael Carroll. This was the man she'd been meant to love all along, the dear friend whom she *had* loved all along. And now she understood the truth. He was her past, her present, her . . .

'My Christmas yet to come,' she murmured from the doorway.

Michael's eyes snapped up to behold her, and his face, somehow joyous even without expression, shone like a sun when he bestowed upon her his magnificent smile. The light was, in fact, his own. Jumping to his feet, he rushed to the threshold and took her hands. From there he escorted her into the parlour, where surely a hundred candles were lit. The pungent smell of spice wafted from a back kitchen. The walls were bare save for the most gorgeous canvas she'd ever seen: Josephine's rich style, uninhibited, the voluptuous beauty of flowers that had Rebecca feeling as fresh and untouched as those blooms.

'Welcome home, Headmistress,' Michael murmured, drawing close. He lifted a key. 'I assume you've been given one, too. It would seem this is our home, Rebecca. If you'll—'

She silenced him with a kiss.

It was a soft but deepening kiss, one that began as a mere taste and appreciation of the press of lips but progressed towards a hunger unquenchable, a release of tension, a discarding of years gone by, a desperate need to savour the present and a promise of what was to come.

She pulled back. Michael gasped and touched his lip. 'Am I dreaming?'

Rebecca chuckled and shook her head. 'No. But . . . are you all right?' she asked, wondering if he felt as oddly drained yet vibrant as she. 'Did the spirits put you through quite the tasks?'

'Oh, indeed. I'd much to learn. To trust, mostly. I've been so scared. I'd lost heart, though that seems impossible. I feared that in losing our Grand Work I'd lost what little I had to give you.'

Rebecca placed her hand on his cheek. 'You have the greatest heart of any man who ever lived, with or without the power of the Guard. I know this. I truly *know* this. I am new. I am reborn, like the phoenix, our incarnate patron. Now, please, please, show me how to love like you.

Teach me, for the headmistress is ready to learn – and to love you in return, from now until the end of our days, if you will have it so.'

The joy upon Michael's face outshone the fire in the hearth. 'Amen!' he cried.

Taking her in his arms, he kissed her reverently. Achingly slowly, he kissed her in a progression of passion, demonstrating all the courses of his epic emotions, all he was capable of feeling. In caresses and presses and torturous promises of expanding passion, he showed her who he was and who they would yet become.

Their clasping embrace sent them to the divan, their limbs wrapping tightly, no caress or gasp or devouring kiss enough to express the pent-up passion of twenty unrequited years. Yet there were no regrets. Only possibility.

Soft carols played on church bells nearby, the bells of Michael's parish, songs promising a child was to be born who would bring love to the world. For two lovers reborn in a second chance, it seemed oddly fitting.

Epilogue

As their carriage travelled away from the town house of the soon-to-be Carrolls, Percy removed her glasses and gazed at her husband. The force of her dramatic, ice-blue eyes was as mesmerizing as ever.

'Oh, Alexi. Thank you for postponing our proper honeymoon. Won't it be glorious to attend the two weddings of our most beloved friends? Isn't it wondrous how the world is full of ghosts and angels, muses and magic?'

He placed an arm around her. 'Tell me, Percy, how, if spirits can do all this to humans, did we not know it possible? How could the Guard, arbiters of ghosts in this great city, not be privy to these cataclysmic shifts spirits can wreak?'

'Dickens knew about them,' Percy teased. 'Hardly claptrap.'

Alexi opened his mouth to retort but she continued. 'Because, Alexi, what happened here was done with love. Your job was to halt malevolence from penetrating this world, not goodness, these sorts of miracles weren't in your purview. But love conquers all, especially in this season. My dear.' She breathed. 'There is so much good in this world, and in the next, and even in the world between. Such incredible opportunities! Jane took hers to become an angel, and now the world of the Great Beyond will open to her. Perhaps that's the difference between spirits and angels; it's in the *becoming*.'

Alexi's furrowed brow eased, dazzled. 'You are one of the angels of *this* world,' he murmured.

Percy blushed, nuzzled against him and denied it.

The carriage jostled on. Snow again began to fall on the cobblestones, kissing London crystalline pure, dusting its sooty eaves with the white of renewal. The city was reborn, too. There *were* angels on the streets, or those who might be angels. There were angels in the hearts of all those who worked wonders, in all who do, and in all who will.

Of course they can.

OUTSIDE THE ABSOLUTE

Seth Cadin

Looking down the narrow street, more usually identical to several twisting others like it in Manchester, Sam felt amazed at how completely they had, in less than a fortnight, transformed it from its usual dreary sulk of a state into this marvel of vibrancy, thrillingly full of colours, with joyfully defiant banners and flags. The soot-caked bricks and half-crumbling walls of its tightly packed buildings were still there; the cobblestones in the street itself were still cracked, and missing entirely in a few treacherous places, tripping around which had left more than one careless drunken wanderer battered and bruised. Yet the grime and decay itself now seemed somehow enlivened, as if it were a wildly blooming industrial garden, instead of a place for poor people to sleep badly between hard shifts of work.

Or at least Sam had to assume most of the cobblestones were still there, because every inch of them was now covered by some boisterous activity, until they were blocked from view by the sheer size of the crowd. Being of a less idealistic mindset than certain of her comrades, she paused to wonder whether the count of cobblestones might indeed have changed from the night before, with a few of the looser ones prised up and piled neatly somewhere not too far from reach.

Her thoughts were interrupted by the passing of one of the very people to whom she might ascribe the possibility of such forward-thinking activity – Tristan, jubilant that his treasured but previously hidden contraptions would soon make their debut, who half yelled above the growing din of the throng, 'Can't imagine the Institution's ever had a queue quite like this, eh?'

'Nor would they care to,' Sam said absently, still watching the narrow street and thinking about the different ways in which a cobblestone could do damage to a human form. 'They'd sooner face the shame of having to whistle for Peeler's lads than have their royal associated with this lot.'

Merchants of the right mannerisms and acquisitions were welcome. Yes, Sam thought, a suitable fortune could now sway the otherwise disdainful heads of the aristocracy, who lately had begun to find themselves rather longer on titles than they were deep in purse. But the men and women working to make those merchants rich were not as welcome in the city's small answer to London's assumption that the North was without culture, or indeed perhaps even without civilization itself.

These mere labourers, as now surrounded her, though there were so many more of them – and more every day as Manchester boomed around them, thanks to the work of their rugged, sooty hands – were not yet expected or understood by the ruling class to have any interest in, or ability to understand, the world of art, let alone to harbour suspiciously political thoughts about making some of their own. Most especially not in ways that defied the entrenched hierarchies of London's Royal Academy, or its highly specific views on what constituted art worthy of critique, let alone display.

'Oh, but it's open to the public, don't you know that, Sam?' Tristan called over his shoulder, with a laugh they shared, knowing that to the patrons of the Institution, 'the public' was a very different entity than 'the people'.

'No, but not like this!' Sam yelled at Tristan's departing back. 'We've hours yet to open and already I'm not trusting the place won't burst at the seams!'

The fact that the merchants and workers had already begun to collect – in woodcuts and engravings, whatever pieces of art they could afford – almost at the very moment they were available, was hardly considered worth noting to the members of the Royal Manchester Institution. After all, the minions of merchants were known to have their own unpleasant little ways of passing their time, not to mention their money, along.

The tiny street already contained more people than Sam, or any of them, except perhaps Antoine, had imagined would rise to the occasion. Yet the Frenchman had not only imagined it, but believed it with such fervour that his passion opened up a way for even those who could not envision it or hope for it.

Hope for it enough to work for it, separately and together, in each of their unique ways, shaping both the fact and the way it had been brought about. As Sam surveyed what had once been a familiar landscape, and was now somehow both more and less itself than it had ever been before, she realized that nothing fundamental about it had been altered, and yet it was a new place nevertheless.

Sam looked down at the carefully hand-sewn frock she had worn that morning, touched her stolen wig, and understood, though still without knowing exactly what it was she was understanding, that she had some deep and essential connection to the almost occult process they had all worked so hard to bring about here.

Even as Antoine ascended to his old crate and attempted to catch the attention of a crowd whom he had not yet realized had no further need of him, Sam felt this had become a place not just refreshed and reformed, but somehow transmuted into a fragment of a different world entirely.

She found herself tracing all the paths that led from the old world to this new one. All the while, she wondered at whether each step taken had been essential to the destination, or whether instead they would have been propelled to this strange and wonderful place regardless of the choices they had made, pulled there by forces beyond their understanding or control.

She felt as though she had been fated to come to this moment, standing and watching as the crowd somehow swelled, with even more bodies attracted to the commotion and spectacle – not to mention the rumours that had been running wild as they'd quickly taken all the complicated steps necessary to prepare for this display, especially when the details of what people (or creatures to some minds) were behind its production.

Later, with the long chestnut-coloured hair – donated by a kind friend who'd decided she preferred her own short-cropped to go with her suspenders – unpinned and returned to its tattered hatbox, and the plain but precious dress hanging neatly once again beside the ragged trousers and workman's rough shirt, which together were all to be found hanging in the room's excuse for a wardrobe – Sam thought it must have been Uncle Andrew and his Shop of Wonders, rather than fate, who set it all in motion, for purposes that would remain for ever unknown.

When he saw it for the first time, all Sam could think was that it would have to do. The carefully hand-lettered sign in its window declared that within were 'wonders to behold' – though apparently not, he thought wryly, to be dusted now and then. 'Wonder' might be less dear than its reputation suggested, his cynical mind continued, as he stood there in his trousers, beholding it as instructed by the sign, as it was assembled there, in a jumble of creaking shelves and upturned crates, with only the occasional panel of glass to betray the late shop-keeper's thoughts about worth, in terms of finance rather than fascination.

Yet it would do; there was nothing for it but to be done – this dusty shed of junked down marvels consisted of all the valuable worldly goods Sam had ever owned, as of the previous morning, which had been far more surprising than most of those that had come before.

Firstly, news of an uncle – thus also once a brother – previously unmentioned by a sister – also a mother – though admittedly not much of one, Sam thought with more forgiveness than was due to the woman, who'd briskly left him on the steps of the City Hall without a word at the age of seven, as if to declare he was now Manchester's problem to resolve.

Most everyone's ship is anchored eventually, and few of them find the best ports. Just the closest, he'd thought upon occasion, whenever he happened to think of her. Just the ones in reach before we crash.

Now he was in possession of a small new shard of knowledge about her: the youngest brother of Sam's absent mother had been called Andrew, and Uncle Andrew would never exist in the present tense for Sam.

The first surprising morning of the week was delivered by a man unexpected in himself, in his carefully tailored suit, with his impeccable hat, the smell of London overpowering even the lasting tang that hung around him from the effects of sitting backwind of horses on the move. The appearance of his carriage had seen the disappearance of several clutches of vagabonds and rag children, who scattered like mice when a cat stalks down the cellar stairs. He was a barrister, this vision of a hundred hungry nights woven tightly into just one vest, appearing in Sam's row like the demon of money itself.

Surely, Sam had thought before, there would be demons for the evils of the world, just as there were saints and angels for the better aspects, though he'd found himself dubious of a few of those. He'd not previously, however, thought of it the other way around. He had not considered that what was demonic might, at least, play the part of an angel now and then.

The papers were surely official, and Sam found himself thinking of bread and soup again as he looked over the gilt-covered seals. Yet he said nothing, and the barrister said much, though none of it was anything, because the papers said it all, and Sam could, at the cost of his own great effort over many years, read rather well, and knew better than to let himself listen instead, on a morning such as this was becoming.

The verbose papers could easily have been reduced to one simple word: property. A piece of land, pre-occupied by a building, for lack of a better word, and all that was contained therein. An unknown Uncle Andrew, for reasons of his now eternally mysterious own, had in a flourish of papers transformed Sam from a peasant to an owner of property – not property such as the rough bed he slept fitfully in, or the table he'd made himself out of discarded pine scraps, carefully hinging together each piece like a puzzle – but property with value, enough to call for the signing of papers worth more than the shack in which Sam silently regarded them.

Finally, the rich man stopped speaking in the language of his kind and Sam said, 'Yes. I understand. Only show me where to affix my signature, and give me the keys to this' – he peered at one of the papers again, hardly able to believe what was plainly stated – 'collection of antiquities and wonders' that have made a merchant out of me.'

Sam spent the rest of that first day in trousers, because he knew even the strange and forgiving company he kept would take him more seriously when he approached them as 'the boy'.

He thought of it that way, himself: not so much that he was the boy, or that, when so attired, she was the girl, but rather that Sam was always Sam, and which side emerged to be worn on the outside of Sam when the day began was an enigmatic matter with its own capricious agenda.

Although not so much that Sam could not, when necessary, decide upon which was best to wear, rather than waiting until it felt clear.

Having been called forth and given directions, the companions he'd gathered met him at the address that he could now rightfully call his own the following afternoon – few of them were gainfully, or at least legally, employed, and they were therefore lucky if they rose before teatime, let alone ventured forth into the harsh light of day. It was unlikely they'd have arrived before dusk if not for the fact that a pub quite dear to most of them happened to be just across the way, though none of them, Sam included, had ever taken notice of the shop before, so quietly did it keep to itself.

Each had their own reasons for avoiding the daylight – drink, or sloth, for some – but neither of these vices had ever much appealed to Sam, whose own difficulty with mornings came mostly in the form of lying awake for hours before deciding what to wear that day; which door of the wardrobe to open. In this twilight of self, Sam would sit, feeling not so much indecisive as impossibly decided. The problem was not which sex to emulate, but that occasionally, in the centre of Sam there was a feeling that, impossible as it seemed, both at once would be most appropriate.

Of the thirteen quick visits he had made the day before – speedily delivering a speech that ended with a dramatic and pleasingly bell-like jangle of keys – somehow seventeen hopeful young faces appeared. This was likely due to the part of the speech that had included the promise that anyone who arrived to help Sam empty the place in order to sell its contents as quickly as possible would have some part of the profits thereof distributed back to them.

Sam had been vague on this point, not yet knowing how big the pie he was promising to divide might turn out to be. Yet as he surveyed them, gathered and eager for paying work that involved dust instead of soot, he became keenly aware that any size slice at all would do for this ragged assemblage.

Packed neatly away, the wonders of the shop were somehow even more desolate than they had been in their jumbled time on display. It was how one thing fitted against another, though neither had a regular shape to it – a broken cuckoo clock, hand-carved, tucked sideways against an old shaving mirror, its tarnished brass frame warped, its still-intact glass nestled carefully by a stack of worn rag dolls. And so on, until all the wonder had been taken away and what remained was just a room, smaller than before, as if the resident inanimate had created a way of folding space over time, until a single shelf came to feel as though whole infinite rows of shelves would pull out from behind it if it were removed. Only dust and cobwebs were there instead, and so the room was smaller now. Sam wondered how the trick was done, then let it be, with an easy flick of his mind.

There was a fascinating presence to the walls themselves. Once exposed, they made Sam a little ashamed of his own prior cynicism towards the place. There was treasure here, and not the flimsy tin kind men in linen suits sold along the docks in any city with a port.

The tired but satisfied haulers of wonder had, on finishing, found themselves surrounded by panels, five to each wall, and two more in the drop ceiling Sam hadn't even glanced at until now. Each panel fitted into the other like a puzzle, with metallic protrusions and eclipses intertwining so delicately and yet so precisely that it became difficult to determine where one panel ended and the next began.

The skirting boards revealed the answer to this visual conundrum – brass bolts, somehow kept to a perfect shine while the faux wonders were left to decay, held each panel in place along strips of varnished wood – from some tree that was dark and surely exotic, from how it seemed to hint at a bigger, deeper world. Sam's collection of workers stood at the centre of them, their chatter slowly falling into silence as they contemplated what they had uncovered, and then immediately began a lively debate over what should be done with it.

Sam surveyed them again and found he only knew a few of them well, though the stowaways attached to the core were familiar for their habit of following wherever their centre wandered.

There was Antoine and Tristan, at the moment inseparable despite their frequent fallings-out, the racket of which would echo down the whole row as they cursed and tussled in their rooms on the ground floor of the building at the corner of the street. With them as always was an ever-shifting collection of lads, always just a shade younger than themselves, who seemed to regard them as beyond reproach and correct in all their oft-expressed opinions, which of late had been unsettlingly Chartist for Sam's nervous disposition.

If ever there were men who had no sense to keep their heads down and their names out of the mouths of the rich, it was those two and their pretty young denizens – still, they were also the most talented, devoted and unusual artists he knew, and more passionate on the subject of defying the traditional techniques and accepted subjects of the Royal Academy than Sam could find it in himself to be.

Certainly he felt art should be, and indeed necessarily was by its nature, an exploration in progress at all times, but he'd never in his own painting paid much attention to why he was going about it entirely wrong, whereas Antoine had come from France and therefore had much stronger feelings on the subject. Tristan was by nature a contrarian for whom defiance was less a political or artistic philosophy and more a way of life.

They and their hangers-on made strange company with the rest, who were mostly young women, since Sam had found that those who wore skirts and bonnets as a matter of habit were more inclined to be of an open mind towards keeping company with someone who did so seemingly at random. They were, like Sam, all artists – some painters, some sculptors, a few, like Tristan, who did a bit of both and also found fascination in the possibilities of mechanized display – but all united in their determination to keep on scrabbling at the edges of a world that had thus far found them insignificant, regardless of its judgement of their work.

Joyti was the most colourful, in the long skirts she stitched together herself from what appeared to be pieces of old curtains, in different textures and patterns, creating a strange patchwork in which, for example, a scrap of lush purple velvet was sewn neatly aside a thinly green-striped strip of cotton. Sam imagined she scrounged them when the aristocracy felt it was time for a bit of a freshening up around what they surely called a 'cottage', despite its dozens of rooms and staff of willingly cooperative workers when it came to passing on odd bits and pieces.

Joyti would have been colourful even in white, though. Like a diamond, she seemed to fracture light around and through herself as she moved, so that from one angle she looked shadowed by some perilous mystery, and from another bright with inspiration.

She spoke quietly, but there were times when she spoke firmly as well – not insistent, but with certainty, as if the discussion were a chess match she'd already calculated herself winning.

She had that tone now: 'There is another way, a balancing.'

Antoine, who had been holding forth on the subject of how the panels might be removed and reassembled for display, halted at once, as part of the charm he had, which induced forgiveness of his arrogance in others, was his ability to know when it was wise to let them speak instead.

Joyti went on: 'What we must do foremost is honour these walls. They are a gift from our greatest patron, the Holy Spirit, who has given us, through an unknown artist, a way to become ourselves as God wills us to be. Yes, it is true that any gift, once given, is then the domain of the grateful recipient, who may display or alter or even discard it at will and according to his wisdom. So let us use our wisdom, as guided by the spirit within us.'

'We make it part of the show,' Sam said. 'We use it somehow, not just tear it down and mix it up. She's saying, "We found it; it's something we found incomplete, so we have to complete it."'

There was silence in the room, for once – not even fabric shifting, as each by each they were struck by a vision and lived in it for a moment – before beginning to argue again, but this time in much more specific and useful ways.

Sam slipped away and aside, to stand with one hand resting on one of the exquisite panels, tracing the lines with his finger-tips and wondering if Uncle Andrew himself had created this marvel, or merely discovered it and found it an appropriate encasement for his wares. He was so lost in its complexity that he only knew he had company at the last moment, when the delicate scent of powder reached his senses.

Ingrid, unlike Joyti, rarely wore colours at all, though her paintings were full of them, so explosively vivid and unusual that more than one viewer had felt they must surely be some-how offensive, despite any obvious display of crudity. Her dresses were sombre, and even the rows of buttons she'd patiently sewn on, one by one, were small, carefully polished fragments of dark shells she had collected, so that they blended into the solemn fabrics almost entirely.

When she spoke, it was with a seriousness matching her attire, but also with a bluntness that seemed to echo her paint-ings, so that the whole picture of her somehow emerged between the two seemingly opposite poles.

'Are you entirely sure of what you're about with this?' She was speaking low and almost directly in his ear, and for a moment he could hardly breathe for wanting to turn and touch her face to find her expression reflected what his heart had, through their years of friendship, never found the courage to convey.

'Not a bit,' he answered cheerfully, turning indeed, but only smiling, forcing his hands to return from the panels to his sides rather than her cheek. 'All I know is that there's no reason we shouldn't have a permanent exhibition of our own, for our kind of work. They have theirs, so let us have ours as well.'

He'd meant to speak quietly, but as he finished he found the crowd had fallen silent and turned its attention to him. He spread his hands at them – what more was there to say? And almost in one slow synchronized motion, their regard turned towards Antoine, who was already clearing his throat in prepa-ration to say it at some length.

Eventually, the endless talking descended into general agreement that the debate should be moved to the pub across the way, which they had all nicknamed 'the Absolute' so long ago they could no longer remember what amusing absolute they had decided it was on the night they'd so christened it.

Sam could have reminded them that the property was emphatically and officially his own, which they seemed to be forgetting by the moment, but found himself unable to care – unable to really think of it as not belonging to all of them already, despite his distance from their heated discussion over how they ought to shape its destiny. Half their earnings for the work would go directly to the Absolute tonight, he knew, and the rest would slip through their fingers in hardly any time at all.

And so, instead of joining them, and knowing she would refrain as well, Sam followed Ingrid when she slipped away, despite feeling all the while that he should instead turn down every path that branched away from her. Any small alley or dung-riddled crossing would do, and he'd be a free man again, making choices that were his and not some miserable form of destiny pressing his body forwards, like a strong wind on the deck of a ship at sea.

Though he had more than a bit of experience trailing a person without being noticed, he could see the moment on her face when Ingrid knew first that someone was following her. Sam imagined that, given the secret she had to protect, her senses had long ago become habitually keen in this way.

And so he also saw when she made herself ready, shifting in a way he knew meant she was gripping the handle of her dagger firmly and letting the flat of its blade rest gently under her sleeve. He watched as her other hand gripped a less grace-ful satchet of herbs with a handful of small rocks nestled inside them, ready in her jacket, so either hand could answer what-ever danger might approach her.

At this point, he felt it might be best to make himself known, and coughed quietly before he approached and reached her side.

'Ah,' she said, 'only Sam.' She let her hands release their hidden weaponry, seemingly ignorant of the expression of dismay that passed quickly over him at this pronouncement. She might at least have been a bit pleased, he thought, though on reflection he realized that perhaps relief and trust were the same for her.

'I knew where you'd be going,' he said. 'If you'd rather go alone—'

'No,' she said, perhaps just a bit quickly, and his heart lifted again. 'Come along, you can help me with the boards. They are always trying to keep us out.'

The abandoned chapel, set far back in the wilder parts of the dismal cemetery, had indeed been boarded over once again, but not with much enthusiasm, as if the labourers felt unsure about their task. It was one matter to miss a sermon now and then, but another one entirely to box up a house of God like an oversized wooden rocking horse, bound for the shelves of a private gallery in some posh mother's attic – besides which, they'd been sent out to do it enough times now that it had become a kind of game, which Sam suspected they had reasons of their own for playing.

And so, some distantly heard call to grace summoned from the workers' hearts, or perhaps just a packet of wages too late too often, made it easy for Sam and Ingrid to prise out a loose or rusted nail or three and make a spot big enough to clamber through. He went through first, because it was a trousers day – otherwise, Ingrid would have done so, though Sam suspected neither of them would ever be able to define the terms of this silent agreement between them.

As he expected, first there was an imminence of bats disturbed from their slumber – Sam could think of them no other way but that, as some fabulous single creature with many parts looming up above them, all around them, and then departing through the rough window they had made. All in a tidy column, Sam thought, each knowing where the other was, like humans in a queue, only with wings.

Together in the mouldy chapel, which had been stripped bare of pews and altar until the only signs remaining of its holy purpose were crumbling saints painted on stone in lurid tones, having all this while been falling slowly down the walls in pebbles and chunks. Sam couldn't tell the Marys from the Margarets, but he recognized an icon of St Lucy, because of

the eyes, or rather the absence of eyes, or rather the presence
of eyes, but held out on a tray just as neatly as they had once
been set into a face.

'Horrible,' Ingrid remarked, following Sam's gaze. 'And
they say we are the deviant ones.'

'Joyti would see it differently,' he said loyally, or perhaps
charitably, or both.

'Yes, but she sees everything differently.' Ingrid stepped
over fallen boards and rocks until she stood at the chapel's
centre, and looked at him as if expecting something, though
nothing else in her eyes told him what it might be.

Sam followed and stood beside her, then moved a little
closer and found she did not move away. They shared a long
moment of silence, enjoying it together after the day's hard
work and noisy evening, and then . . . a beam of the drifting
evening light happened to bounce upon a remaining shard of
glass in a high broken window at the very moment he was
reaching to touch her hand, bare of its glove, which she'd torn
on a nail and then stripped and dropped outside into the
bracken, like trash in the gutter. Thoughtlessly, horribly waste-
ful, he told himself, and wanted her regardless, or even more,
and let his hand keep moving towards hers. Then the sun
intervened, and her attention was brought back to the moment
and caught – her hand drew back as if he'd been pressing a
viper or hot coal towards it.

'I . . . I apologize,' he stammered, but before he could make
even more of a fool of himself, she reached out with her own
hands and took both of his, then pulled him as close as he'd
longed to be to her for so many years.

'You should,' she whispered in his ear, even as she drew him
closer still, even though pressing their bodies together meant
that if he hadn't already known her secret, he would surely
have guessed it then. 'You certainly left me wondering long
enough.'

He would have laughed, but quickly found his lips were
otherwise occupied by an even more pleasurable activity, as he
needed no more encouragement than that to lean up and let
them brush against hers, at last.

★   ★   ★

The unnamed committee of outcasts and undesirables who fancied themselves renegade artists met again the next day, and again the numbers had somehow swelled to what seemed like twenty or so people milling through the former shop. In Sam's mind it was theirs, though each one of them called it 'ours' – *our* command post, *our* hideout, *our* gallery. They said it as often as they could in as many ways, delighting themselves each time, though Sam found it totemic, a kind of witchery. They wanted the truth to emerge by collective insistence.

Arguing happily in little crowds, which shifted and reformed with each passing resolution, none of them seemed aware of their own futility. Theirs, thought Sam, who felt she'd had enough of the trousers and could trust the group now to allow her the frock and wig for this evening's increasingly organized session of planning. Theirs, but not hers at all any more, though certainly ours, if she stayed.

She knew that she would stay. She saw Ingrid, as unattached to any of their clumps as herself, drifting through the space, not as if it were empty, but full instead of different people in different kinds of clothes.

As Sam watched her, she could almost see them herself – up close, as she never had, rather than from a distance in the street, or as a portrait on a wall. Glittering, hands and throats heavy with the weight of priceless jewels – the women would be graceful and the men resolute, standing just as stiffly in one place as their wives would flow dynamically through the room, one distant day.

Then Ingrid saw Sam, too, saw that she was seeing both near her and through her eyes, and this was almost as extraordinary as the moment itself. They shared, across a field of ragged backs – huddled in now quieter, more conspiratorial and above all else more sectarian groups than before – a look that Sam knew meant the same to each of them, a thought unspoken: They will rise. This wretched lot will rise. We will pull them up and drag the other ones down, until the reckoning.

They met their third personal conspirator after the third night's debate – moving together to meet her just at the street's corner, at the edge of the light cast by the tall gas street lamp on its twisting iron column. They met her there as if they had arranged to, though no mention of it had passed between any of them.

Ingrid, Sam and Joyti. Two women, one boy – again today, through the cheap stage magic of trousers and hairpins and putting his shoulders back more. Ingrid had remarked once upon how Sam walked differently as a girl than as a boy; how Sam's body seemed to have two separate rhythms, side by side, into which it could, or perhaps simply did, without Sam's willing it, slip on any given morning.

Joyti, for her part, seemed not indifferent but perhaps entirely unnoticing of how Sam changed sometimes from she to he or back again. She spoke to him now the same as she had yesterday when they met, when Sam's magic trick was a hand-sewn frock instead. In her regard there was not the slightest flicker of confusion or awareness that anything about Sam had changed.

She sees differently, just as you said, Sam thought, looking at Ingrid and knowing he could convey this meaning with his eyes. All the time.

Sam watched as Ingrid, forgetting to guard her face, seemed to wonder at her own mind, decoding such messages in a glance as quick as the shadows flickering through curtains in the windows above them. He knew that Ingrid considered herself more rational than to have such strange thoughts, share such moments with . . .

'You don't mind when I'm a girl,' Sam observed mildly.

'Do you have the gift?' Joyti responded before Ingrid could, rounding upon Sam with an affect almost like anger. 'You've done that, speaking to thoughts before. You've done it with Antoine, only he—'

'Didn't notice,' said Sam. 'Wouldn't.'

'But we do,' Ingrid said, and felt their unity again where, she now reflected, Sam had been building a wall. 'So is she right? Can you . . . see people's minds?'

There was a precarious moment, a sense that Sam might turn and flee, or even attack them; that he was on the cusp between these impulses and did not himself know which one would tip him. Yet balance returned when he laughed, instead, girlishly but with a rattle that went with the trousers.

'I can pretend to all right,' he said, twinkling all over with some delightful secret, and the growing confidence that he could share it. 'Have done, it's good for a bit of push. But no, Lady Joyti, I've just a knack for seeing people's faces, and that can be quite like seeing their minds, if you know the way of it.'

Both women spoke at once:

'The way of—' started Joyti just a moment before Ingrid said, 'Lady?'

The second surprising morning of the week contained rather more pillows than Sam was accustomed to, and indeed than he could recall laying his head down on the night before. Those had been two flat rags on the floor of what had been a shop and was now an impending exhibition, whereas these were plush with down and coated in some impossibly soft fabric which, he decided after a moment's cautious thought, was the same colour as a young salmon seen through the water of a muddy river.

The bed too was surely not the one Sam had occupied for all the nights and early mornings of seven years – that one was also flat, and so familiar that every piece of straw stuffed inside seemed like an old friend saying hello when it poked him in his slumber.

Then he remembered – Joyti laughing, Ingrid scowling, himself wanting to flee again but instead letting himself be led, at Joyti's insistence, to the grand old house he had only suspected was real when he'd let slip the guess of a title. It was the way she carried herself – she was surely one of them, but she hadn't started life that way.

And so, as she assured them her parents were away at one of their other houses, attending to their busy social season, he and Ingrid had found themselves just outside the city, after walking for what felt like hours, and probably was, which explained the exhaustion with which Sam fell into what must surely be the most comfortable bed in the world. And from which he was too soon pulled by the clanging of a bell, a summons he followed outside, until he found, standing next to a squinting and dishevelled Ingrid, a beamingly radiant Joyti, who told him she'd been sent a wonderful vision in the night by God, and that she'd like very much to introduce them to her horses.

Ingrid seemed to choose not to see it, and Sam wished he didn't, but it was too starkly clear for his mind to reject: around Joyti, the horses were soothed in some uncanny way, and when she left them, they looked after her and shifted restlessly in their stalls. Of course she must visit them often, he thought, but still – the way she glided through the barn and touched them all and said their names – it felt like a sacrament, a ritual with more power than its components should have the capacity to produce.

When they had been suitably introduced to what must, Sam slowly realized, be Joyti's closest friends, she led them behind the barn to show them the seed of her idea. It was a carriage, with a quality to it much like her family's house had – so carefully maintained over so much time that for all its glorious worth it seemed nearly ramshackle, a patchwork of aristocratic frugality and the work of some craftsman who cared for his trade in the same way Joyti cared for her horses.

'Yes,' Ingrid said instantly, before Sam could see what was meant by this presentation. 'We can adorn it, transform it – for the opening.'

Sam felt uneasy, sure that as permissive as Joyti's family might be about their wayward daughter's wanderings through life, they would draw the line at the use of their property for this particular endeavour. They must know it, too, he thought, looking at his companions, but nevertheless both women looked back at him fiercely, as if defying him to disagree. He wished he'd brought the frock, because he sensed it would somehow have given him better ground to stand on with them in this moment.

As it was, he was outnumbered, and only let himself sigh as he said, 'Very well. Then I believe it's time we paid a visit to Tristan and Antoine.'

The rough little room was a pick-pocket in its wedged corner, with its ramshackle walls built straight up alongside the brick and mortar of the buildings around it, like ivy made of crate slats and bits of tin. The roof was proper thatch, as even artists needed a trade when lacking in patrons, or more precisely, when lacking the necessary traits of character to acquire patronage, such as the ability to regard property as defined in terms of ownership rather than possession. So two trades might be more accurate, Sam thought, as in addition to being notorious degenerates and occasional thatchers, the men who resided here were accomplished thieves, with Tristan's mechanical handiness in particular giving him a reputation as a fine cracksman.

Let inside by Antoine, who seemed to be expecting them somehow, Sam fell behind as he was overwhelmed by the many works of art and strange contraptions in various states of completion surrounding them. In green and golden tones, spanning more than half the long wall at the back of the studio, one huge canvas seemed almost to glow with an inner light, as if the artist had somehow imbued the oils with a living spirit.

'Everyone's off working,' Tristan said by way of greeting. 'And somehow word has gotten round that we're taking all comers. It's astonishing but it seems to have inspired rather lot of—'

'Of course,' Ingrid said, cutting off his rush of words. She sat primly upon a small chair as Antoine lounged luxuriously on a threadbare loveseat in the corner opposite from her.

'Many are called to the arts, to make beauty and create joy,' Joyti started to add.

Ingrid finished for her, 'They're just not normally allowed.'

'Nothing's stopping them,' Sam started to point out, but when he saw Antoine's head rise in response, he waved a hand as if to dismiss his own words. 'Never mind. The art will be there. Probably more than we can fit, so it's a good thing we have a carriage to display the rest on outside, and the Absolute will probably let us use its walls, too.'

Sam fell quiet as Joyti explained her vision, and then as Antoine did more than just lift his head, but rose and began to pace in circles. Tristan seemed to be ignoring them all, working at a canvas with his back to them, but Sam knew he was listening by the way his shoulders tightened when he heard Antoine speak.

'Not just space. We need to get the most attention we can, or they'll just ignore us. We need to throw an opening so spectacular they'll want woodcuts done of the day itself . . .'

He went on, listing his ideas, but all the while Sam kept his eyes on the tension in Tristan's spine, and the way Ingrid kept sending him sideways glances. He resolved, since he was stuck with the trousers anyway, to take Antoine aside and make clear his reservations.

This proved, once they had slipped away from what had descended into Joyti's dreamlike proclamations of the fuller details of the vision she felt sure had been sent by the Holy Spirit, to be an even more irritating task than Sam had anticipated.

No violence, Sam had insisted firmly, with a note that indicated he was aware that very different visions of just how newsworthy their little event would become if a riot ensued were already forming in Antoine's mind.

After that, the conversation had become a tangle of misdirection, until he heard Antoine saying, 'Still, it might be, or come to be, that one or another of us, perhaps a few in tandem . . .'

Sam was amazed to find there were yet more tones of voice in the Frenchman's repertoire to distinguish shades of condescension than he had encountered already. 'Tandem means two, Antoine, not a few, which doesn't mean anything,' he said after a moment of stillness.

'Yet your diversion means everything, because it's how you tell me to stop, and when *what is* becomes *what is not*, everything is one thing and nothing is everything.'

'Words aren't sport—'

'And you are not sporting, my dear. In my own defence, I seem to recall someone other than myself bringing us on to the subject of words.'

'And meaning. Yes. Aside from your usual drivel, you seem to have understood me quite well.'

'You want no part of it.'

'I couldn't begin to imagine what you mean, but I will note, on general principle, that I would agree with any vague suggestion of that undefined significance.' It was amazing the lasting effect just a few hours spent in a small room with a barrister flourishing papers could have on a person, Sam thought as he heard himself speaking.

'Ingrid will be in with it,' he said. 'She knows we need a spectacle to establish *ours* right from the start.'

Around them, the market was folding inwards on itself, tarps rolling down and workers retreating behind their sheds. After a moment, Sam pretended he hadn't heard and walked away – but it was a moment, and if he'd noticed, Antoine would have, too, and would have known that once Sam had spent a bit of time alone with this last, undeniable fact, then Sam would be in with it too.

The days that followed were a blur – each morning, Sam woke and rushed to the former shop to put a hand in the work that needed doing to prepare, and every afternoon and evening that followed was mostly comprised of the faces of old friends and new acquaintances appearing hopefully over a canvas or around the edge of a sculpture, none of which would ever be accepted to hang in any city's proudly traditional galleries, and almost all of which were accepted for display at theirs.

Yet the work was done and time passed until, with all the pieces in place, Sam found herself pausing to gather the other contents of her wardrobe before accepting Joyti's invitation to spend the final night before the opening with herself and Ingrid at her family's otherwise unoccupied estate. Uncomfortable as Sam felt intruding there, the call of the soft bed – and the thought of Ingrid in another room nearby– made her too weak to resist.

And indeed, once the horses had again been greeted and tended, and each of them settled into a different bedroom for the night, Sam found herself, still in the frock, sneaking down the carpeted hallway and slipping into Ingrid's room, where she found her beloved awake and sitting up, half-covered, in the bed.

Within a moment they were entwined, only their clothes between them – only fabric, with no room for air, or even time, which stopped for their embrace. Under it, the sense of untouched skin, hidden away but giving off from it a heat that was unmistakably fierce nevertheless.

That Ingrid would let Sam feel the true shape of her body, the secrets she concealed under her long, stern dresses, made

Sam feel more privileged than all the deeds of property in the world could ever do.

She whispered her name, and Ingrid gripped her shoulders as if she might suddenly fly away, drawn through the window into space by the same cosmic magnet that had brought her here

'Only a little while more,' Ingrid whispered back eventually, when the kiss that had seemed to start nowhere ended abruptly as she rolled away. Mentioning time, she summoned it again, and they both looked towards the dark window.

'We'd best . . .' Sam started to say, but Ingrid was already rolling back to push her away, out of the bed and on to her feet.

'Yes,' she said firmly. 'We need our rest, and this is no way to get any.' And so Sam headed back to her room, burning but waiting, which was not an unfamiliar sensation.

And then, hours indeed after Sam's last exchange with Tristan, our gallery was officially open. In the street outside, there were puppeteers and ribbon-twirlers, and at least thirty kites in the air at one moment, though several quickly dropped as they entangled. Antoine had carried on with his cryptic book-keeping of favours owed from exotic characters, and produced what Sam had to admit was an impressive display of a man's living trophies, the fellow humans he had met somehow along his various ways.

Joyti's two fine horses standing patiently outside the gallery, attached to a carriage with its sides entirely covered by some of the more unusual works their call for art had attracted, became the centrepiece of what began to feel more like a carnival than an opening.

There was even a lady Sam spied in the crowd who, upon careful inspection, seemed a bit uncomfortable in her dress, and who Sam caught several times slumping her shoulders inward, as if remembering suddenly to conceal their width. Another spy in the house of renegades, Sam thought, but left her to her business. Having had no problem deciding upon keeping with the wig and frock herself this morning, she sensed the stranger might prefer her privacy than a moment of flimsy camaraderie.

Joyti's ragtag collection of boys from the park had appeared as well, materializing around her in a cloud of grime and eagerness; they must each have loved her in some burning, unique way, Sam imagined, but she was entirely unaware, and treated them as if they were her personal coterie of angels, and kept them on their best behaviour by doing so. They stayed far away from the kinds of young men who tended to surround Antoine and Tristan instead, though an uneasy truce existed between them, thanks to the influence of Joyti's acceptance of each.

If she looked at you as if you were clean, Sam had noticed, you felt clean, even if you'd last bathed on a day you didn't know the name of, let alone its distance in time away from the one you were currently also at a loss to identify. Sam and time had never got on well, and she suspected this was one reason she and Joyti did, when they achieved similar orbits, at any rate.

'Have you imagined it, in yourself?'

Inside the gallery, pressed on all sides by the throng, which had waited all morning for this opening, Ingrid's voice brought Sam out of her reverie and into another one.

They stood there at the painting's edge, looking down into the convex in the floor onto which it had been painted. Sam dimly recalled a selection of irregular globes on crumbling stands, a shadow of Uncle Andrew's wonders overlaid upon the creation before her eyes. There now instead was Jean, the French saint, Antoine's muse – burning alive, eyes contorted towards an opening in the clouds, hinted at but not seen.

Ingrid and Sam watched as each viewer did what they had each first done: turned their heads upwards to follow the line of the martyr's gaze, where they found only colourful chalked stars on the ceiling, itself painted in shades of blue so perfect they had to be real. That was Joyti's work, of course – her memory of some sky she'd once prayed under and then brought here with her, to translate from her spirit to their eyes.

Around them, all the works hung from the drop ceiling, rather than against the panels, so that the visitors had to follow a spiralling pathway leading them between the extraordinary metalwork and many unusual and varied works of art facing them from the other side, into a central area around the painting on the floor.

But even before the first circuit of visitors had completed the route, the sound of a commotion outside reversed their direction. Whilst the general crowd went towards the noise, Sam and Ingrid followed a more direct route, to what they both knew was its most likely source.

They pushed past the crowds, now all mindlessly moving towards the approaching sound of boots on the march, which echoed down the lane, even over the noise of the mob, and went straight for the crowded room on the corner, where they found, as they knew they would, Antoine poised at his window, bottles and cobblestones stacked upon the table beside him, ready to be flung. Despite Sam's earlier suspicions, Tristan was nowhere to be seen, though she knew that didn't mean he wasn't off poised to make trouble elsewhere.

'Someone seems to have alerted the authorities,' Antoine said blithely, without turning, eyes focused sharply on the street outside. 'Theft of property, causing a public nuisance and general deviance on display – it's a shame, really, but it seems we'll be faced with the inevitable violence of the ruling class and forced to respond in kind.'

Sam took a step back as she saw Ingrid step forward, just as Antoine's hand reached past the pile beside him and closed around a thin glass bottle. He stood, turned and tapped it menacingly against the edge of the table.

'I should make you aware', Antoine said, layers of oily charm falling away by the moment, 'that my compunctions about cutting you rather badly are few, and much less compelling than the alternative, you . . . you creatures—'

Use his anger, Sam thought. Yet already she realized that Ingrid knew everything Sam did about a moment like this, and certainly much more than Antoine, who, for all his bravado, was of the mistaken belief that a fight was a civil engagement with rules, as if performed on a stage. The idea that Sam might be stealthily approaching from one side with a hefty chunk of cobblestone in her hand would simply never appear in his mind, for despite his arrogance and ambition, and his apparent inability to regard human life as important on an individual level, he was, to the bone, one of the world's truly naive men.

Ingrid was neither naive nor a man, and so, in response to his warning, she kicked him directly in the most delicately measured scrap of his tailored trousers, the proceeds of his felonious activities always having gone dually toward artistic supplies and his own preening vanity.

When he staggered back, she kicked again, this time low and at the knees, and when he hit the floor, she stomped his wrist with her boot until his writhing hand let free the bottle, which Sam snatched up and handed to her with a henchman's loyal reflex, this same quality leading her to keep a grip on the rock with her other hand, until the tussle had been decided.

'Joyti wouldn't care for the mess,' Ingrid said after a moment's reflection, during which she regarded the bottle as if it were a brush she was considering applying to a canvas, though she didn't sound entirely sure of what she might do next.

Then the moment instead of the bottle was broken, as Tristan finally appeared, rushing in with his toolbox clutched to his chest.

'They're coming,' he said. 'Antoine, we can't. We mustn't. What we've made happen out there – it's better. It's enough. No,' he finished, holding up a hand as Antoine started to protest. 'We're just having an exhibition to open our gallery, that's all. Sam said it – why shouldn't we? I know what to do. It's not too late, and we don't need you, but if you don't come with us, then I don't need you either.'

For all the times they'd hollered similar threats at one another, perhaps it was the simple, flat way in which Tristan delivered this one that made Antoine sag in defeat and leave his little pile of inanimate troublemakers behind, to follow where his man led them all.

Outside, between our gallery and the Absolute, the massive crowd was waiting, shuffling down the cobblestones in groups of three, five and ten. The word had gone round quickly, and an angry tone was buzzing through them now, as their delight in the festivities turned sour in the knowledge that the law was approaching, with all the weight of the elite behind it.

Sam followed, with Antoine between herself and Ingrid, and realized at some point that Joyti had appeared, trailing behind them as well, until they were standing at her carriage just outside the gallery. Tristan ascended, pulling himself up on its step to rise just a bit above the crowd, cupped his hands, and yelled, 'Barricade! Barricade now, do you hear me? Anyone with strong arms, follow me, and the rest of you, stay back out of our way!'

For a moment, Sam didn't understand. But then she saw Joyti smiling, and rushed after Tristan, whose toolkit was again clutched protectively to his chest, feeling Ingrid beside her and at least thirty pairs of strong arms pushing behind them.

Disassembling and removing the panels took less time than she'd thought it would, and Sam quickly realized this was because Tristan must have been at work on them already, loosening bolts here and there in the night, having seen even farther ahead than Sam had given him credit for. It still took all the might of what seemed like half the crowd, but working together, they pulled the panels free and manoeuvred them down the street, each born up by several shoulders, until they were arranged in an arc, cutting off the intersection neatly in a glistening crescent of magnificently shining metalwork – brass, silver and gold, all entwined and alive in the sunlight, as if it had meant to be brought here all along.

They propped each panel up, until it leaned on crates and overturned tables and stacks of broken cobblestones, some freshly freed from the street and others retrieved from Antoine's various stashes, which turned out to be tucked away in at least five different places, along with more bottles and other projectiles for the riot he'd so desperately wanted. They finished just as what looked like the full police force of the city of Manchester reached them, marching in form with truncheons in hand.

Then stopped, finding their progress blocked by the fantastic barricade, and all the people standing fiercely behind it, transformed by their united effort from a milling crowd of spectators to a silent force of human bodies as impassable as the barricade itself.

One of the officers seemed to be attempting to read out a list of charges, but every time he spoke the crowd hissed and booed, drowning out his attempt, to his clear frustration and confusion.

At this moment, Joyti broke free of their huddle, and Sam watched in blinking wonder as she walked calmly to the barricade and stood just a little bit back from it, hands at her sides. 'I'm sure there has been some misunderstanding,' she said calmly to the man who appeared to be leading the collection of Peelies. 'There's no trouble here, sir, just a little celebration of the gifts which God Himself has bestowed upon us.' She smiled in her special way, and though most of the crowd couldn't hear what she was saying, they rose up a great cheer regardless. When it had died down, she called to the men who had clearly been sent to shut all this nonsense down, 'Why don't you come and join us?'

A laugh rippled through them, and the crowd became lively again, splitting from its unified state once more into increasingly separate conversations, though for once, most followed the same general theme: somehow they had triumphed without fighting the battle, and somehow, in ways they were only beginning to understand, this meant they were more free than they had ever been before.

It was perhaps the strangest standoff in the history of riots that never happened, Sam thought later, as slowly the festivities got back under way and the gallery began to refill, slightly bigger now inside. People rotated in and out of it, and all around the carriage, as the police fell back in an attempt to determine exactly what procedure to follow against what appeared to be, not an armed resistance or general strike, but simply some strange kind of street fair.

After a few hours of waiting on further orders and seeming to receive none, whilst knowing they could remove the barricade themselves, but able to see that what lay behind it would only become a serious criminal situation if they actually did so, they slowly evaporated. Some time later, Sam was sure she saw Joyti helping a few sneak over the far side of the barricade to join the fun, their truncheons and helmets left tucked out of sight on the other side.

Distracted by this, standing beside Ingrid with their hands secretly entwined, Sam didn't notice Antoine's approach, and only knew he was there when Ingrid's hand dropped from her own.

'You've always turned my stomach, you know, *Samantha*,' Antoine hissed and spat. 'Whatever it is you think you are, parading around however you please, all you do is make life harder for good, *real* men like Tristan and myself, who have no need of your circus freakery, cluttering up people's minds even more than they already are.'

Sam looked at Ingrid, whose mouth was set firmly. Her dress felt heavy and useless, and all at once she knew she would still be Sam in this moment without it or with trousers, or perhaps, unthinkable as it was, wearing nothing at all.

There was no word for Sam, because Sam couldn't be confined by a dictionary or placed neatly on a map. As Joyti had seemed to understand, Sam was a dynamic force – all woman when she was woman, all man when he was man.

She *knew* it now, believed it now, and yet still needed this woman she loved, her beautiful friend Ingrid – who'd chosen the name because the one her parents had picked could never suit her – still needed the only one who could understand to hold her up by asserting it; to stand with her and unmake the secret binding them both with the hands of the truth.

Tell them your secret too, she thought at her beloved, meeting her eyes. Stand with me.

For a moment, it seemed as if Ingrid heard Sam's mental pleas, and was about to meet them with mercy. Instead, she turned on one perfect heel and walked away, leaving Sam and Antoine watching, to see if she would look back before she vanished out of sight. And she did, but only at the last, and then the happy masses closed over her like a curtain, hiding her expression from their view.

THE EMPEROR'S MAN

Tiffany Trent

For a long time, I could not remember how I came to be in the Imperial House Guard. There was a vague sense of shame, a sense that I was possessed of a dark past. I felt that if anyone knew what I'd been, I would be ejected from my position, and it was all the more troubling because I myself could not remember. The fear that someone would discover my past to be every bit as horrible and incriminating as I imagined was great indeed.

The only thing that banished these fears was the Imperial tonic I took daily, along with the rest of my regiment. The Emperor, who was a great inventor, had developed it to protect us from magical incursion. And while we soldiers jested with one another about sylph sickness and pixie infestations, we all knew that as long as we took the Imperial tonic daily and adhered to the Scriptures of Science, we were safe.

It was not so in the Forest that reached its knotted fingers towards our walls. In its depths hid all manner of Unnatural beings, and the depravity and danger they posed to us mortals was a constant threat to New London's safety. It had been this way since the Arrival, when St Tesla's Grand Experiment accidentally transported so many of us from Old London.

Though we could never return to the place from whence we came, His Most Scientific Majesty reminded us that we were at the vanguard of a glorious new Age of Enlightenment for this benighted land, that we alone had been given a grand opportunity to force magic and all its irrational power into the service of progress.

And if I woke in the night from vivid dreams of the Forest beyond New London's walls, dreams of a life wild and howling under the tangled branches, I fervently whispered the Boolean Doctrine or the Litany of Evolution, as revealed by St Darwin, until I became calm. I was the Emperor's man, after all.

What, then, did I have to fear?

Athena would teach me soon enough.

I knew of the Princess Royal, of course. I saw her often at a distance, sitting in a window seat, her nose deep in a book while the other nobles played bridge or gossiped. I saw her at various functions, speaking at length with Scholars of the newly founded University of New London. Her father's courtiers looked on with barely concealed sneers. While they fluttered about like perfumed, bejewelled peacocks, she stood apart, a drab peahen proud of her drabness. I felt a grudging kinship with her at those times. She was the only person I had ever seen besides myself who could be surrounded by people and yet still be so terribly alone.

When I was assigned to her during the Imperial Manticore Hunt, I wasn't overjoyed, but neither was I indignant, as many of my regiment would have been. We waited in the Tower courtyard for the Huntsman and his hounds to arrive. I was mesmerized by the leashed werehounds as they came – their knowing, malevolent eyes; the white brushes of their tails; the way they crouched when their master passed them. Something about them made me shudder and turn away.

And then I was looking straight into the Princess Royal's eyes. She regarded me steadily, gravely, her grey gaze more piercing than any pike or bayonet in the Imperial arsenal. She rode astride, much to everyone's horror, and was dressed in a plain but perfectly serviceable habit, devoid of lace or jewels or the plumed tricorns those around her favoured. Her dark gold hair was pulled back severely and bound up in a white snood. Despite her unfashionableness, she looked every inch the Empress she was destined to be. And then I realized why: she knew who and what she was. She had no need to compete or dissemble. And I envied her for it sorely.

'This is Corporal Garrett Reed, Your Highness,' my captain said, gesturing me forward. 'He will serve as your escort on the Hunt.'

'Corporal.' She nodded.

'Your Highness,' I said. I lowered my eyes so as not to meet her gaze. There was something unnerving in the way she looked at me, as if she knew things about me that even I didn't know. As if she knew my worst fear. My stomach tied itself in intricate knots.

The captain left us then to introduce the other nobles to their escorts.

'I expect you to stay as far from me as your duty will in good conscience permit,' she said.

Her gloved hands tightened on the reins. 'I have no need of escorts, and no desire for them, either.

I intend to continue my studies of the denizens of this Forest. You may find it dreary in comparison to the excitement of the Hunt you will surely miss.'

'I am at your service, Highness,' I murmured.

'Hmph.' She turned her mount away from me then, and rode out behind the others.

I followed at what I hoped was a respectful distance, far enough to honour her request; close enough should danger arise. I would be lying if I said her disregard didn't sting, but it was no more than I expected.

We passed down through the winding streets of New London, and the greenish cloud drifting from the newly built Refinery dulled the glitter of our cavalcade. The Emperor's Refiners had recently developed a new energy source called *myth* that was mined far to the north and brought here for refining. Using *myth* to heat homes and keep everlanterns lit throughout the city would save many from the madness and enchantment suffered so often by those who gathered wood in the magic-laden Forest. The refinery had also spawned a multitude of new inventions, among them the *myth*-powered, iron-clad Wyvern the Emperor rode. People lined the streets, and the women threw hothouse roses or embroidered kerchiefs, which were soon shredded beneath the Wyvern's claws.

I ignored those thrown to me.

In the Fey Market, grey sylphs flitted back and forth in their cages, careful of touching the nevered bars that kept their destructive magic from infecting their human captors. I swallowed the sudden, strange feeling that rose in my throat when one sylph shivered mournfully into dust, and I whispered a prayer to St Newton instead. I saw something in Athena's face sag. I could have sworn a tear glittered at the corner of her eye, but she dashed at it with a gloved hand, then her face became stone.

Apothecary shop assistants distributed broadsheets advertising sirensong syrup to aid with coughs, or nulling powders to extricate parasitic pixies. Over the River Vaunting, the Night Emporium spanned the entire bridge, its brothels, gin palaces and gambling establishments crouching between haberdasheries, millineries and antiquities shops. I glanced at her through it all, trying to gauge her reaction to the silk bolts spun from shadowspider webs, the fascinators and hair combs bedecked with the plumes of feathered serpents. But after that one moment, her expression never wavered.

My comrade-in-arms, Bastian, rode in close, nodding his head in her direction. 'Minding the mad witch, are we?' he asked. His round face was open and empty as the moon.

'You ought to show a little more respect,' I said. I sat taller, using my height as yet another way of embarrassing him into silence.

'It's only what everyone thinks, Garrett,' he said. 'Besides, she can't hear us anyway.' He gestured towards the Princess. We had passed through the City gates, and the Forest raised its thick, twisted tangle against us. Princess Athena had sent her horse ambling under its eaves, off the main track and away from the rest of the party.

'St Darwin and all his apes,' I muttered under my breath. The Forest was filled with evil, irrational, mind-corrupting magic. Anything could happen to her and I would be held responsible. And yet I felt a twinge of uncertainty. Should I do as she bid and leave her to her studies? The Emperor expected us to stay on the track, to let the Huntsman do his work. But if something happened to the Princess Royal on my watch . . .

Bastian laughed.

I spurred my horse forward as Athena disappeared through the trees, trying to ignore the crash of the iron wyvern's claws, or the feeling that I was somehow betraying my orders by following the Princess.

'Your Highness!' I called after her. The Forest swallowed my voice, yet it opened before me, leading me down its over-grown avenues. I glimpsed her ahead – here, the feathered fetlock of her mare; there, the white curve of her snood against a dark-clad shoulder. She passed through light and shade like a dream, a ghost of herself. And where she passed, the Unnaturals of the Forest followed. Filled with light, the sylphs came, dancing through the summer leaves, dayborn fireflies. Their wings whispered and chimed like little silver bells, so very different to their caged cousins in the market. When I looked up, white faces peered at me from the mottled trunks of sycamores and dark faces frowned from the hemlocks and pines. I whispered St Darwin's Litany of Evolution as a dryad peeled herself away from the bark of her tree and followed the Princess.

They were all around me – sylphs and sprites, gnomes and hobs, and many others for which I had no name. I tried to remember that the Imperial tonic protected me, that I wouldn't be enchanted by anything, but I couldn't help my uneasiness. Just when I realized I'd become more engrossed in looking at the sylphs than seeking my charge, I saw the Princess's mare wandering riderless, grazing along a tiny stream. I spurred my gelding towards the clearing ahead, my heart crowding my throat.

I found the Princess seated on a mossy stump, surrounded by toadstools and Unnaturals of every kind and description.

'Princess!' I shouted.

Some of the Unnaturals slunk away, but others hissed and bristled, their colours changing from soft pastels to angry vibrancy.

She looked up at me with eyes like ice. 'Stop,' she said.

'But, Your Highness, you're in great danger! You must . . .'

She transferred the quill and book she held to one hand, while holding up the other for silence.

'On the contrary, Corporal,' she said at last. 'It is you who are in grave danger. Now go back the way you came and let us be.'

I stared at her for a moment, trying to discern if the worst had already happened, if she had already been bespelled, and wondering how it could be. Did she not also drink the tonic her father had developed to protect us? Then my gaze wandered, drawn by the rustle of a leaf, and I saw what she meant. Little, taunting faces thrust out of the vines and branches. Little hands held darts that glimmered with poison in the morning light. If I so much as moved, I had no doubt the pixie army would turn me into a human pincushion in short order. I also had no doubt their darts were deadly.

I straightened my spine. 'You know I cannot do that, Your Highness. Your father, the Emperor . . .'

She laughed then. She looked me full in the face and laughed. The sound of it caused the angry colours of the sylphs to fade, and soon all the Unnaturals were giggling with her, too. She laughed so hard that the book fell to the ground next to her foot and tears streamed down her face. I thought for a moment she would fall off the stump.

'The Emperor,' she said finally, when she could catch her breath. 'You know, every time someone addresses him that way, it's all I can do not to burst into laughter. And right now, I can't be bothered to care!'

I could do nothing but stare. Perhaps Bastian was right, after all. Perhaps she was a mad witch.

'Oh, I am most certainly a witch,' she said, as if I'd spoken aloud. 'But I'm not mad.'

I gaped at her.

She pulled the book she'd dropped back up into her lap. 'Truthfully, I think I'm the only sane person left in this world. Aside from you all, of course,' she said to the Unnaturals at her feet. The Scriptures of Science dictated that I should be repulsed by the Unnaturals and the threat to rationality they represented, but here I was, fascinated by the colour chasing over their faces and through their wings. And their expressions! So rich, so varied, so full of life in ways I'd never imagined in that dull Tower . . .

I shook my head. I shouldn't be thinking these thoughts. The Unnatural magic was corroding my logic. How was that possible?

I focused on the Princess. 'I don't know what you mean,' I said coldly.

'Let me ask you this, Corporal. What do you remember before coming to the Tower?'

I blanched and looked down at my gloves. How had she been able to pinpoint the one worry that gnawed most constantly at my heart? I wished that I had just obeyed her and gone back the way I'd come. I didn't want to know where this was leading.

'That's about what I thought.'

I glanced at her. 'Your Highness, I hardly think my past . . .'

But she cut me short with something she held up in her hand. It glimmered darkly, a tiny, all-too-familiar vial held between her thumb and forefinger. The Unnaturals around her drew back, muttering.

'What is this, Corporal Reed?' she asked.

'Imperial tonic, Your Highness. But I fail to see—'

She glared me into silence. 'And you take this every day, yes?'

'Yes, Your Highness.'

She sighed. 'Oh, stop that nonsense. My name is Athena.'

I'm sure my eyes went as round as dinner plates at that. What royal in her right mind would permit – nay, demand – a lowly guard like me to use her familiar name? But I swallowed and nodded.

'I stopped taking this eight years ago,' she said. 'And when I did, I realized a few things.

Or remembered them, I should say. First, I remembered where we came from – the *real* London.

Remembered that my father was nothing more than an astonishingly well-read butcher from Cheapside, who liked to invent things when he wasn't killing them. He had always fancied himself a Man of Science, and he seized power in the chaos that ensued after the Arrival. I don't know entirely how he did it, though I have my theories, but the main point is that my father's power comes at a great price: the lives of the Elementals whose world we've stolen.'

Sylphs, pixies and dryads all nodded around her.

My lower jaw very nearly hit my pommel.

'You *are* mad,' I gasped.

'Oh yes?' she asked. She got up from her stump and stalked towards me, stepping over the toadstool ring as if it had no power at all. 'Who are you really, Corporal Reed? Why are you so afraid of your past and yet you can remember none of it? And if these beings, these Unnaturals as you so rudely call them, are so evil, why are we both still alive?'

She stood by my mount's shoulder, weaving her fingers into his mane. I looked down into her furious face. Her eyes flashed like icy lightning and a hectic glow spread across her cheek-bones. Little sylphs flitted to and fro around her head in a chiming halo. She was, in that moment, the most beautiful woman I'd ever seen. I forgot everything but that, lost in amazement at just how much could change in the span of a few hours. She was absolutely bewitching, but not at all in the way I'd been taught to expect.

'Corporal Reed?' I finally heard her say. 'Are you even listening to me?'

I could see quite clearly that she knew what I'd been thinking. I coughed, feeling suddenly constricted by my uniform. 'Ahem. Yes. You were saying, Your Highness?'

'Stop taking the tonic,' she said. 'It's a potion meant to make you biddable and forgetful. When you do, you'll see who is truly mad, I promise you.'

I opened my mouth in what I was sure would be a weak retort, but the only sound that came was that of a distant braying.

The horns of the Hunt.

The werehounds bayed, a ghostly howl that set my spine shivering. They had cornered their quarry.

Athena's face changed instantly. It was as though someone had slammed the shutter over her inner light. Panic was all I saw in her face as she called to her mare.

'The Manticore is in danger!' she said over her shoulder. 'We must hurry!'

'But Your Highness . . . Athena,' I said, 'isn't that why we're here? To kill the Manticore?'

'I didn't truly think he'd be able to find her!' she said as she climbed into the saddle. 'She's very powerful – she should have been able to hide. Something is very wrong!'

The lights in the trees dimmed all around me. The sylphs, colourful and laughing only a moment ago, dimmed to dusty browns and greys. Dryads slunk away like slices of shadow. There was a restless fear and sorrow that I inhaled with each breath.

'What will happen if she's killed?' I shouted at Athena's back, as she urged the mare forward. If the angry mutters and gestures were any indication, none of us would fare well.

'Without her magic, they will all ultimately die. Her power feeds theirs, from what I understand. If they can, they will try to stop that from happening. That's why we must go!' she called over her shoulder, slowing her mare enough so that I could hear.

She spurred her mount onward, and I was racing just to keep up. As she galloped, ducking branches, her snood came unbound and fluttered to the ground like a wounded dove, her hair uncoiling in a long curl behind her. I followed it like a golden semaphore through the trees, avoiding the Unnaturals – Elementals, she'd called them – that flowed alongside through the undergrowth and between the trees above.

The Emperor's *myth*-powered wyvern had cornered the Manticore. The monster shrank from the Emperor's mechanical mount, weeping tears of blood. The Huntsman affixed a strange gauntlet to his hand, a weapon so powerful its numbing chill froze everyone around it. The Elementals fell back from the miasma of icy horror, but it slowed many of the smaller ones, which were then unfortunate enough to be snatched up by observant courtiers and stuffed hurriedly into their saddle panniers. A new pet, a little extra money at market, didn't hurt.

I caught myself feeling sorry for them and gritted my teeth. I shouldn't be sorry for them at all. I vowed silently to drink another vial of tonic as soon as we returned to the Tower . . . If we returned.

The Manticore begged for mercy in her silver voice, even as the Huntsman advanced on her. The Emperor ignored her and gestured that the Huntsman should finish the job. 'Bring me its heart, if you can,' he said.

The Huntsman, eerily hooded like an executioner, nodded.

I watched the Emperor on his wyvern and couldn't help but wonder. Much about him suggested what his daughter had said. He had a craggy nose that looked as though it had been broken, and his eyes were narrow and hard. He was not a big man; in fact, he seemed pinched somehow at the edges, as though something ate at him from the inside out. Still, he had the charisma of a leader, the sharp command of someone destined to rule. Was he really only a butcher, as his daughter had claimed? Was everything I'd been taught a lie?

Then Athena edged her mare forward, her unbound hair causing the ladies-in-waiting to chatter and giggle. Some looked sidelong at me in amazement, and it occurred to me that they assumed we had been engaged in some sort of dalliance. I sat as tall as possible, looking neither right nor left and hoping my face was stone.

'Father!' Athena called as the Huntsman readied his knife. 'I beg you to spare this creature's life.'

A hush so deep descended that a single falling leaf seemed to crash into the Forest floor. Even the Manticore dared not breathe as she waited on the Emperor's reply.

He looked at his daughter with the shrewd glance of a man who believes everyone schemes against him, even his own flesh and blood.

'And why would you have me do that, Princess?' he asked.

Disdain was etched on the faces of all his courtiers. I will never forget how we all sat there, like statues in the vortex of the horrid weapon in the Huntsman's hands while the trees wept leaves around us. I will never forget the battle of wills, of calculation, that passed between the Emperor and his daughter as we all waited for her reply.

'A matter of scientific study, Father.' She looked at the Manticore, and the flash of her eyes belied the cold facts of her words. 'We know so little about the Greater Unnaturals; this is a perfect opportunity to understand them better. I'm sure the University would . . .'

'For what reason need we understand them?' the Emperor cut in.

'Surely,' she said, ever so calmly, 'His Most Scientific Majesty does not question the Doctrine of Logic to which we all ascribe?'

I couldn't help but smile. Well played, Princess, I thought.

She looked at me then and her small smile hooked me straight in the heart. All she had to do was tug. If I had felt the first stirrings of admiration when she flashed her anger at me in the clearing, it was nothing compared to now, when her gaze stripped me bare to the bone. I cast my eyes down to my pommel, certain she had bespelled me in that moment.

Through the ringing in my ears, I barely heard the Emperor reply, 'Take this Unnatural thing to the dungeons. It is very nearly my daughter's birthday; I shall acquiesce to her desires as a gift to her.'

The Huntsman bowed his head and sheathed his knife, then he unlooped a coil of silver chain that hung across his saddle.

Athena dismounted. 'Let me,' she said.

She went to the beast, who had ceased weeping, and whispered something I couldn't quite catch, then the Manticore bowed her head and allowed the Princess to slip the chain lightly over her neck. I thought I saw Athena's hands tremble, but when she turned and led the Manticore towards her mount, her face was as impassive as always.

There was murmuring. The Emperor seldom gave gifts, especially not in public and certainly not to his eldest daughter. What was he thinking? Were the winds of favour shifting? I could see suitors who had given a lacklustre performance rethink their strategies. Others mumbled that she had now gone beyond the barriers of good sense and enchanted her own father. All the while, I wrestled with the knowledge she'd given me, wondering what to do with it and why she'd trusted me – and whether I could believe her.

There were no easy answers, and I followed the procession as it wound back to the city, with the Manticore at its heart, trying to ignore the trees that wept at her passing or the dirges of mourning that followed us on the suddenly chill wind.

The Manticore was taken deep into the Emperor's dungeons. I refused to think about it, or anything else I'd experienced in the Forest. I resumed my duties, as usual, ignoring the whispers of witchery, fending off the jibes of my regiment about my involvement with the mad witch. I drank and diced, did my drills like any soldier, and hoped for the promotion that never came. Every morning, despite the Princess's admonition, I drank the Imperial tonic. I was the Emperor's man, after all.

And if I fancied that I heard the Manticore's silver voice raised on the border between waking and sleep, if I dreamed of running through the Forest on four feet instead of two, what of it? What soldier didn't wake in the night, hearing the croaking of the Tower ravens on the sill, and wish he'd chosen another path every now and then?

Every fortnight, we rotated through a night watch. I was grateful when my turn came, hoping it would banish my increasingly frequent night terrors. If I wasn't meant to sleep, at least I could be doing something useful.

Again, it seemed that fate, if the saints aren't to be believed, had a hand in my assignment.

I was to patrol the throne room and main halls. I cursed myself for wishing that I'd been assigned to the Imperial suite. I still saw Athena's face as it had been in the Forest – open, alive, full of light – and I wanted that back, but did I really think I would see her this late at night? It wasn't as if I had access to her bedchamber. At most, I might glimpse a shadow of her behind her bed curtains or in her easy chair by the fire. I would certainly not see or speak to her. And even if I did, what then?

I tried to banish the flutter in my stomach at the mere thought of her name as I paced up and down the echoing marble halls. This was ridiculous, and I knew it.

Clocks lined the walls, squatted on little tables and loomed in cabinets everywhere. The Emperor was deeply curious about time, so it was said, and he had made it part of his personal study to explore the Horological Arts. Why he needed so many clocks to do so was a mystery to me, but their numbered faces glared at me as I passed with my everlantern and pike. Their ticking measured out my worries in discrete units of consternation.

I had just returned for the sixth time that night to the notion that I should request a transfer to some outpost on the edge of the Copernican Wildlands, when something whispered across the stones at the edge of my light.

'Halt!' I said.

Click. Creak. Whoever it was refused to heed me.

The hallway was lined with doors, and the few everlanterns that circulated in the high ceiling made pools of light and shadow as they passed.

A whisper of white, the edge of a bare foot. A ghost? I ignored the tingling on the back of my neck, but raced forward and slid my pike between door and frame before the door could be shut and locked.

'I said: Halt!'

I thrust my lantern into the unlit room.

It would have all been much easier if I'd seen who I expected to see, instead of who I'd hoped for. I'd expected a petty thief – perhaps some member of the household staff pilfering candlesticks, that sort of thing – and I'd foolishly hoped for Athena, even though I couldn't imagine why she'd be roaming the halls at this hour and didn't know what I would say to her. Why should she even remember me?

Athena glared at me from the circle of light. She was in her nightgown, a darker dressing-gown wrapped loosely around her. Her feet were bare, and I couldn't help noticing the fine arches, the perfect fan of her toes against the marble.

'Are you going to stand there gawking at my feet or help me?' she asked.

I think I must have blinked before I found my voice. And even then, I couldn't think of a single thing to say beyond, 'Eh?'

'Just . . . get in here,' she said.

I stepped inside the room, trying to muster what was left of my dignity. 'Princess, you shouldn't be here. I'll escort you to your chamber now, and we'll pretend none of this ever happened . . .'

'We will do no such thing,' she said.

I opened my mouth, but that piercing stare shut it for me.

'I could *make* you go with me,' she said, 'but I don't think I've misjudged you that badly. Will you help me?'

I swallowed all my questions, except one. 'What are we doing?'

'Why freeing the Manticore, of course,' she said. 'You truly aren't that thick are you, Garrett?'

Then she did something completely odd. She leaned forward and sniffed me.

I frowned. 'Does something offend you, Highness?'

'You're still taking that blasted tonic, aren't you? I can smell its stench on your breath.' She sighed.

I wanted to cover my mouth, but my hands were full. Flushed with shame, I nodded.

'Look around you', she said, 'and tell me that I've played you false.'

The Emperor's Cabinet of Curiosities was generally kept locked. I had never seen inside it, though there was much speculation about its contents. It was the sort of room you'd find tucked under a staircase or in the eaves of an attic; the sort of room I'd never been in, I suddenly realized.

The floor yawned beneath my feet. It was as if I was standing here and running across the Forest floor – fleet, four-footed, furred – all at the same time.

'Garrett.' She bit the end of my name so hard it brought me back into the lantern-light.

I blinked.

Portraits, newspaper clippings, books, cases of strange insects – all were scattered willy-nilly. There was nothing especially out of the ordinary about any of it at first glance, but as I looked closer, the marble floor tilted under me again. A portrait entitled *Butcher Vaunt*, of the Emperor in his bloody apron, holding up a freshly killed goose, with a little girl who might have been Athena beside him. A picture of St Darwin, looking terribly ordinary in a suit and bowler hat, rather than the green, vine-covered robes held up by apes in the stained glass of the church chapel. Newspaper clippings with the wrong dates, mentioning places and people I'd never heard of. A globe with countries I'd never seen, and on the wall a battered map of an unfamiliar city also called London. A book under glass that said only *Holy Bible*, rather than *Holy Scientific Bible*, as all bibles did.

'What is all this?' I said.

'These are things from the real London. Things my father doesn't want anyone else to see. Things he can't bear to get rid of, even though they incriminate him as the fraud he is.'

My eyes wandered the chaos of the long, narrow room, trying to take it all in. One piece drew my gaze and wouldn't let go, a softly glowing thing that throbbed like a beating heart in its case. I went to it, spreading my fingers on the glass. Its power seeped through to my fingertips, buzzing up my arms and into my skull. It looked very like a heart, but none that I had ever seen, comprised of metal and light and whirring parts I had no names for.

'And that is how we got here,' Athena said over my shoulder. 'The Heart of All Matter.'

'How?' I said. I couldn't take my eyes off of it, even to look at her face.

'Tesla used it to power a secret experiment to create wireless electricity,' she said. 'He never realized that the Heart is much more powerful than mere electricity. It ripped a hole in space and time and brought us, along with buildings and artefacts from London's history, here. Our ancestors from the real London called this place Fairyland, Arcadia, Elysium, Shangri-La, Tir Na Nog – any number of names. Apparently they weren't sure it existed. But it does, and now we're trapped here.'

'But . . . surely . . .' I was so mesmerized by the Heart's pulsing light that I could barely think to form words.

'No,' she said. 'No one knows how to use it. My father, of course, has tried. That's why he founded the University: he thinks his scientists will find us a way home.'

I tore my gaze from the Heart. 'And you don't?'

She shook her head. And then came that sardonic smile that made my insides flutter. 'I surely hope not. Leave all this to become a lowly butcher's daughter again?'

With those few words she reminded me of her station, and of how far below her I was. 'I suppose not. You will be an Empress, after all,' I said stiffly.

She swatted at me then, and I looked her in the eyes.

'I was joking, you ninny!' she said. 'You know I don't care a fig for being an Empress. But it's true I don't want to go back. This world is so fascinating, so thrilling, so very beautiful. I want to explore it. I want to find out everything about it. Don't you?'

Truthfully, I had never thought about it. I had done my duty every day, and the Forest beyond the city walls was something strange and awful I seldom contemplated, except in my nightmares. All I could think about now was that if there was anything beautiful or thrilling or fascinating about this world, she was standing right in front of me. And as much as I wanted to find out everything about her, I knew that it could never be so. I also knew that she knew exactly what I was thinking. Her lips parted, soft and shining in the light of the pulsing Heart.

She reached, as if she would touch my cheek, as if she was trying to decide if I was real.

But then her face hardened and her hand fell back to her side. That icy resolve returned to her eyes and she said, 'Fetch your lantern and pike and follow me.'

She opened the case that held the Heart and gently lifted the thing into her hands. Instantly, its pulsing grew faster, its light stronger.

'What are you doing with that?' I asked, unable to take my eyes off its light, unable to take my mind off what had just happened between us. What had occurred to alter it?

'You'll see.'

She led me to the end of the room. A portrait hung there of a woman I didn't recognize but felt I should: a young queen, sashed and crowned with white roses. The plaque beneath the portrait read, 'Victoria Regina'.

Athena slipped her hand along the edge of the portrait and the wall slid away seamlessly and very nearly soundlessly.

Marble stairs curved down into darkness.

'Leave the lantern here,' she said.

I was about to protest that we would surely need light, but as her foot touched the first stair, Athena's hand blossomed with the Heart's light. She smiled at me then, and that swift hook tugged me after her down the stairs.

I wasn't surprised that the Emperor had his own secret access to the dungeons, but the fact that the passage saw frequent use definitely made me wonder. There were no cobwebs, no signs of disuse. The doors were well-oiled; the marble treads well-worn. The possibilities of what he did here were unnerving in the extreme.

Athena had no caution about her whatsoever. She hurried ahead of me, pushing through doors and rooms as if an invisible string drew her deeper into the labyrinthine prison. Any good soldier worth his salt knows that you don't go charging headlong into an operation like the one she was undertaking. I tried to hang back, but she urged me onward, with a raised brow and a gesture of her flame-ridden fingers.

At last she came to a door that required a bit more muscle to open; it was a sealed hatch with great gears and pressure valves, and it reminded me of the entrance to a boiler. I approached it with foreboding.

'Help me,' she said, setting the Heart down nearby. Its light went out of her hands and danced in little currents through the still air as she tugged on the door.

'Where does this lead?' I said. 'Shouldn't we consider what might be on the other side? Do you know if your father keeps guards stationed down here?'

'I thought you would know that,' she said. 'Clearly, my plan to use you for ill-gain has failed.'

I stared at her, then realized she jested again. I had never expected her to have a sense of humour.

'I can feel the Manticore beyond this door,' she said. 'I hope we're not too late.'

I dared not think about what the Elementals in the Forest might do if we were, or what would happen after we helped the Manticore escape. Instead, I put my hands near hers and turned.

Her arms curved under mine; her shoulders pushed against

my chest. The top of her head was just at my chin, and her hair smelled of cloves and oranges, of holidays long forgotten. We fitted so perfectly, like pieces of a puzzle finally coming together, that I just wanted to put my arms around her and stay there.

She coughed delicately. 'Corporal Reed, you'll recall that I can hear your thoughts.'

I pulled hard on the wheel and stepped away. 'Yes. Sorry.' The heat in my face was from exertion, I told myself.

I saw an amused flash in her eyes as the door swung open and she retrieved the Heart.

The deep well of the chamber echoed with laboured breathing. Something below, I knew, was in terrible pain. I put a hand out to warn Athena, but she had already begun creeping down the curved stairs. A glow rose from the floor, and then the stairs turned enough that I could see. In the shadows, things glinted – the silver body of an automaton, the clicking legs and arms of some nameless horror.

The Manticore lay across a long slab of table. A great machine squatted over her, its hoses and needles like the searching tentacles of some oceanic horror. Though the beast was secured at various places by silver chains, it was the machine that really kept her bound, its needles nosing into her flesh and drawing out her shining blood, replacing it with viscous ichor. The machine throbbed and hummed like the demonic twin of the Heart in Athena's hand. Steam escaped from its joints with each pulse.

Behind the machine stood the Emperor, working its levers and checking its dials, while the Manticore struggled to breathe.

Athena stood staring for approximately two seconds, a trembling hand raised to her mouth, the Heart's light abruptly doused. Then she raced down the remaining stairs, her bare feet slapping on the stones.

'Athena!' I hissed. But she ran on, heedless of my warning.

'What are you doing to her?' she cried. 'Stop this at once!'

The Manticore tried and failed to raise her head: 'Child, you must not.' Pain tarnished her voice.

I saw only half of the smile that sliced the Emperor's face, until he stepped from around the machine to face his daughter. He hadn't yet seen me, and I hoped he hadn't heard my warning. I slid slowly down the stairs, keeping as close to the wall as possible, praying my pike didn't rattle and give me away, but my hands shook almost uncontrollably. I couldn't bear to contemplate what I might have to do to protect Athena. Was I not the Emperor's man?

'Whatever do you mean?' the Emperor asked. 'Was it not you who said we should use her for scientific experiments?' His smile was the ugliest, most self-satisfied smirk I'd ever seen.

'I only meant . . . I didn't mean . . .' I could hear the tears in her voice.

'I know,' the Emperor said. 'You thought you would buy her enough time until you could figure out some way to help her escape. Look well upon what you've wrought, daughter. There will be no escape from this.'

I could see the Manticore's head and chest. Where there should have been red velvet fur and muscles over ribcage, there was a gaping hole of darkness.

The Emperor had taken her heart.

Athena ignored him. 'We're getting you out of here,' Athena said to the Manticore.

'Leave me,' the beast said.

'And just how do you think you'll do that?' the Emperor sneered at Athena. 'If you unhook her from my machine, she shall surely die, and we will have lost valuable understanding of the Unnaturals. You were correct, daughter. They are well worth our investigation – the properties I have discovered in her blood alone! They are worth so much more alive than dead. I shall bring all I can here into the dungeons. We shall create a world more rich than any we could possibly have imagined before, and when the time is right, we shall force the gate back to the old world open, and London, Britain, the Earth itself will be ours.'

I gaped. So what Athena had said was true. I crept down onto the floor, every muscle shaking so hard I wondered how I could stay standing. Anger, bitterness and grief chased one another in a vicious circle through my chest.

'Not without this,' Athena said. She raised the Heart in her hands then and it burst into eerie flame.

'No,' the Emperor said. His voice had an edge keen as my pike. 'Foolish girl, to think you can handle such power!'

He moved towards her, and a dagger coalesced in the shadows of his hand.

I scarcely dared breathe and certainly didn't think as I crept up behind him. Athena, wise witch, gave no sign that she knew I was there. I prayed the Emperor couldn't hear my thoughts as she could.

I dug the tip of my pike into his lower back. He wore no armour, no protection whatsoever.

I could slice him in half as easily as look at him. 'How do you dare, Sire,' I said, 'to threaten the one who might save us all? Or shall I call you Butcher Vaunt instead?'

He stiffened.

'Drop your weapon,' I said.

He laughed, half-turning to look at me. 'You shall regret this deeply one day, Corporal,' he spat, and then he disappeared in a thread of stinking smoke.

I cursed. 'Hurry,' I said to Athena. 'I'm quite certain he'll be back.'

Athena set the Heart down, and her hands roamed over the wires and tubes snaking in and out of the Manticore. She looked over her shoulder at me as I came nearer.

'Help me,' she hissed.

She started unhooking and pulling things, but the Manticore cried out in pain. I reached for Athena's hands. Her fingers were cold and shaking.

'You cannot release me,' the Manticore said. 'I shall die for certain.'

'Why?' Athena whispered. She had always seemed so much older than her years, so sure of herself, but now she was little more than a child. I longed to comfort her, but there was no soothing away this hurt.

'My heart is gone,' the Manticore said. 'This machine keeps me alive.'

It was then that the tears came. Her shoulders shook with them and she kneaded her finger through the Manticore's belly fur, for all the world like a nursing kitten, save for her howling grief. I took her in my arms without a word, and she folded herself there against my heart.

'Children,' the Manticore sighed at last. 'You should go while you still can. He will return. I am content with my fate.'

At that, Athena turned from my arms, wiping her face with the edge of her robe. 'I'm not,' she said. 'I won't let him win. All those afternoons . . . all you taught me . . . I proposed this to save you, not torment you!'

She heard my unspoken question, for she looked at me and said, 'I used to sneak out of the tower and ride to the Forest to meet her. She taught me all I know about magic, about how everything I'd been brought up to believe is not true. She taught me so much. I can't just leave her to die.'

'Forgive me,' I said to them both, 'but you may have to. Your father will return soon. Do you have magic enough to fend off his entire guard?' I glanced down at the Heart, glowing softly on the floor.

'There must be some way to undo this . . .' She paced up and down, glancing occasionally at the devilish machine. I tried to listen beyond the sounds of her pacing and the Manticore's laboured breathing. Was that the turn of a key in a door? A shift in the movement of an everlantern? I was about to urge her to hurry again when she stopped and stood so still that I wondered if the Emperor had secreted a Basilisk in the chamber. Athena was like stone. Then she grinned.

'What?' I said.

In her hands she held the Heart of All Matter.

'What will you do with it?' I asked, though I was fairly certain I already knew.

'Put down that pike and help,' she said.

I set my pike carefully on the stone floor and put my hands on the Heart, alongside hers, to lift it up. It had grown strangely heavy, and seemed to grow weightier the closer we got to the Manticore. The rhythm of its pulsing grew faster, like a heart waking into action after a long sleep.

'Child,' the Manticore said to Athena. 'You mustn't. Your father . . .'

'We both know my father will use this for evil someday,' Athena said. 'I'd rather he didn't have the chance. I'd rather you were able to live free.'

'But, it isn't mine to possess . . .'

The Manticore's protests were subsumed in a field of glittering light as together we placed the Heart in the beast's chest. A flash and a low concussion knocked us back from the table, and when I could see again, the Manticore stood on top of the table, her spiked tail twitching. With one swipe of her red paw, she sent the Emperor's horrid machine flying across the room. The Heart in her chest clicked and purred as it knitted itself between muscle and bone. Then the great beast's eyes met mine.

'Come here, child,' the Manticore said.

The inexorable pull of her voice sent shivers across my scalp. I went.

'Kneel.'

She loomed above me. The great, smiling mouth with its three rows of teeth was just above my head. I wondered for a moment if she would take me as her first free meal, and she must have heard that thought, for she laughed, a sound like deep silver bells ringing.

'I am going to give you something,' she said.

She bent her head and breathed on me.

'Remember,' she said.

The curtain over my mind shredded. It was as though someone had pulled a shroud from over me and I could at last breathe in the light. I remembered who I had been in the Forest. I remembered that I'd run away to become a guard because I was ashamed. I remembered that I was a wolf.

'I am . . .' I couldn't quite form the words. The idea was so strange, so forbidden, that I hardly knew how to comprehend it, except that I knew with every bone and muscle of my body that it was true.

'One of the Were, yes,' the Manticore said. 'Welcome, little brother.'

Then it was my turn to weep: for the pack I'd lost; for the wolf-brethren I'd forgotten; for all I'd never known.

'If you're done blubbering,' Athena said, 'I could use some help. This door is heavy!'

I gathered my pike up and turned to see her pulling frantically at the door to the chamber.

'Figured it out finally?' she asked as I approached. She was in complete control again; the vulnerable child I'd held in my arms had vanished.

'You knew?' I asked. 'You knew and you didn't tell me?'

She looked at me sidelong. 'Would you have believed me if I had? We barely knew one another. I hardly think one should tell one he's a werewolf, do you?'

I couldn't help but laugh. 'No, I suppose not.'

I rested my pike against the wall as we heaved the great iron door open together. There was no one on the other side, but I knew the Emperor would return soon. Every moment wasted was a moment we might lose for ever.

'Now let's get her out,' Athena said.

I had no idea how we would sneak a Manticore out of the Tower and down through the city in the middle of the night with the entire Imperial Guard after us.

'Use all your senses,' the Manticore encouraged.

I hated the thought that we might have saved her life only to botch up her escape. I stood in the doorway and sensed with all of my being. It had been a long time since I'd done anything like that, and I was amazed I still knew how. Worms and other insects crept through the foundation of the Tower all around us. Guards murmured in a distant dicing game. I smelled mould, stone, the remnants of torture. And then a thread of river air, a ribbon of freedom twining underneath all the rest.

'This way,' I said, nodding towards the ground-level door.

Athena stopped me. 'I doubt I can hide all of us with magic. But we may be able to hide in plain sight.'

'How so?'

'We'll just pretend we're transferring her elsewhere. I'll be the handler and you'll be the guard. Hopefully we'll get out before my father returns.'

The Manticore nodded her approval and Athena slipped a length of silver chain over her neck, murmuring an apology.

I watched as Athena magically altered her dressing-gown into a hooded robe that hid her face and most of her body. I shifted my pike into position, glad of its familiar weight in my hands.

Together the three of us entered the corridor. I prayed to every saint I could think of that the Emperor had not yet put the entire dungeon on alert, and hoped that no one would look too closely at my house uniform.

As it happened, there was no one on our corridor. We wended our way past prisons packed with hopeless victims, past torture rooms that my rediscovered senses told me I didn't want to explore. Then at last we came out into a great hall of sorts, a cavernous room hollowed from the living rock. There were cages there, mostly empty, but the Manticore paced past them sadly nonetheless.

'This place should not be,' she said. 'Great harm will come of it.'

'We must get you out of here,' I said. I didn't want to think about anything beyond seeing her to freedom.

We were nearly under the eave of the cavern wall and into a corridor that would lead us to the river when the word I'd dreaded came.

'Halt!'

A regiment of dungeon guards hurried across the shadowed floor, their pikes gleaming as they came.

I could think of nothing else to do. The guards were already aware of the devastation in the Emperor's laboratory.

'Run!' I shouted.

Athena and the Manticore ran past me, the silver chains slipping from the monster's body, while I took up the rear-guard. I had no idea how long I could hold the soldiers while the Princess and the beast worked at the door to our freedom.

And then I felt him – the Emperor – and with him a power so terrible I nearly dropped the pike I held. I gripped it tighter. If my death could delay him long enough for Athena and the Manticore to get free, then so be it.

The soldiers fell back as the Emperor approached. On his hand, the nulling gauntlet his Huntsman had worn in the Forest gleamed darkly.

'I told you that you would regret your insolence, Corporal,' he said.

'I regret nothing,' I said through gritted teeth, 'except that I ever bent the knee to you.'

'Is that so?' he asked.

He stepped forward and I nearly swooned under the influence of his fell magic.

'Then you shall die at my feet,' he said, his smile as sharp as a knife.

I lifted my pike, but he shattered it with a word. I waited until he came closer. One step. Another. My regulation dagger was in my boot, and perhaps at the last moment I could draw it and buy them time. Then I heard the sound I longed for: the door behind me scraping open. The light of the full moon poured in, turning the Emperor and his guard to skeletal shadows.

'Garrett!' Athena screamed. 'Come, now!'

I half turned. The river gleamed under the moon; its voice was deep and loud and I understood every word of its song. And in that moment, as the cold light touched my face, I was no longer human but wolf. The Manticore roared behind me. Several spikes from its tail felled guards in the mouth of the tunnel, and several lodged in the left side of the Emperor's body – his face, his shoulder and knee.

He fell, bellowing in agony, curses leaking from his paralysed lips.

I leaped to Athena and crouched before her. 'Climb up,' I said, my voice rough as the stone on which I stood. She climbed onto my back, digging her small hands into my ruff.

'Go!' Athena cried as the guard advanced. 'Go!'

I went. And the sound of my claws on stone was music. And the feel of her body against mine was delight. And the moon was nearly as bright as the Heart that burned in the Manticore's chest. I followed the Manticore into the river, the Emperor's man no longer.

We were foolish to think the Emperor would ever allow his daughter to escape him. We went to the Forest, where we were received with open arms by all the sylphs who had once threatened to curse us. My brethren had not forgotten me, though I had long forgotten them, and they welcomed me back with a grace that made me ashamed I had ever left.

We lived as happily as it was possible to live and Athena dreamed great dreams of a different world, where magic was free to all and human and Elemental lived side by side in peace. She taught me what I could learn of her magic, and though I was not as adept as she, she admonished me that with practice one day I might be.

The only shadow was cast by her father, and it was a long one indeed.

'If we called him out and showed him the good of what happens when magic is free,' she said to me one night, 'I know he'd have to see reason. He created an entire religion based on Logic. If we showed him that magic has a Logic all its own, and that it must be shared rather than hoarded, how could he refuse?'

I stared at her in the starlight, but I could only make out the barest outline of her face. 'Have you gone mad?'

'No,' she said. 'But you must think I have.'

'Yes!' Her arms slipped from my neck as I rose from where I lay beside her.

I paced. It was the way of the Were when they were troubled.

'What would you have us do, Garrett? Raise an army against him?' she said from the bower the sylphs had woven for us.

'Well . . . yes. That is the only way you will ever defeat him. He is drunk with power. You of all people know this.'

She raised herself on her elbows. I could feel her eyes, even though I couldn't see more than glints in the darkness. 'But that's the beauty of it, Garrett. When we show him how much more power can be gained when it is shared . . .'

'He doesn't care,' I interrupted. 'Look what he does to every Elemental he seizes. Look how he fed us all tonic to keep us ignorant. His way is the only way. There is no other.'

'I think once he is no longer angry about what I did, he will listen to me,' she said. 'I am the one thing that ties him to his past. I remember a time before he became a butcher, a time when he was kinder and gentler, before the world made him hard. Perhaps the magic has destroyed his sanity, but I feel I should at least try. He is my father, Garrett. I cannot consign him to the darkness.'

I had only heard such compassion in her voice when she spoke of the Manticore. I supposed it was because she thought she'd escaped the Emperor that she could afford such kindness towards him. Perhaps she even felt guilty for escaping him. I didn't learn more because that very night, they came to take her.

We set sentries, of course, but he overwhelmed them. He had many horrors at his disposal, and one of them was a new automaton – some sort of animated armour that could not be destroyed by regular magic. How he managed this I was uncertain, but his soldiers surrounded us quite quickly. The Emperor rode his *myth*-powered Wyvern, and it breathed a poisonous fog that either killed my brethren outright or caused them to fall into a dark sleep.

The black mist of the Wyvern's breath was like pitch. I tried to keep hold of Athena's hand and we ran as far as we could, but we never escaped the circle of darkness. I slipped into wolf shape so that she could climb aboard and we could escape as we had before. I was much faster and my senses were better as a wolf. I felt her fingers slide into my ruff and her weight settle just behind my shoulders, but before I could move ten paces, I felt her plucked from me. I looked over my shoulder to see the moon breaking the black fog. Athena was slumped in the mechanical Wyvern's jaws.

I did the only thing I could, then. I ran. 'I will deal with you later, coward!' he shouted after me, his laughter chasing me through the Forest.

I knew I could not rescue Athena from the Tower again. Though many of the Forest would have gladly helped me, I would not risk them. And I knew the Emperor was expecting me to do something foolish.

Instead I stayed in the Forest and bided my time. Emperor Vaunt was cruel, but he also liked spectacle. He would make an example of his daughter in public, I was certain of it. And when he did, I would be there to save her.

Word finally came that Athena was to be taken to the Euclidean Waste and publicly executed. There was a great outpouring of grief on the Emperor's behalf, that he should be forced by his daughter to lose her in this way. There was never any talk of mercy; the city folk had all hated her from the moment she'd shown herself different to them.

A carnival atmosphere pervaded the site the Emperor had chosen for his daughter's execution. People travelled from far and wide – by the newly developed *myth*-powered carriages, by train, even by airship – to a ghost town called Paradise that had nearly been swallowed up by the Waste. Only one old woman and her husband still lived there in the train station, selling cordials and fig cakes made from the tree that grew by the station building. But when word spread that the Emperor would bring his daughter to justice in Paradise, the place mushroomed into a tent city overnight.

I left the Manticore and my pack behind in the Forest. They had given me their blessing, but said they feared nothing could alter the outcome. The course was set. They all knew, though, that nothing would deter me from trying.

I took with me my new familiar, a raven named Malina. Nearly every Were has a familiar, usually something associated with his animal self. Ravens and crows often associate with wolves. Foxes and weasels may den with bears. Only the tiger walks entirely alone.

It was relatively easy to keep hidden in the carnival tents of Paradise, even to pretend to fortune telling like a Tinker, with Malina on my shoulder. I saw many others of my kind weaving through the tents, all disguised, pretending their familiars were pets or curiosities; but with my rediscovered senses, they were as obvious as the summer sun.

I wished there was time for us to speak, for there to be more than the flash of recognition, the flare of nostrils. I wished somehow that I could stand against the Emperor with an army of Were behind me. But we are solitary folk, not easily united, and not a one of them, I was sure, would be willing to fight alongside a Were who'd become tangled up with the Emperor's human daughter, witch or no.

If I was going to spring Athena from the jaws of death, I would have to do it alone. I had hired an airship that would take us to Scientia, no questions asked, when the ordeal was done. I hoped that Athena, once free of her father's nulling powers, would be able to cloak herself as she had before. Malina could fly free, rejoining us in Scientia if needs be. And though we would no longer be near the Manticore Athena loved, it was a small price to pay for our freedom.

It was all perfectly planned. The one thing I didn't count on was that Athena wouldn't want to go.

A wolf may slip through where men may not. In all the drunken revelry, most saw me as a dog, and those who did not were ridiculed for being too deeply in their cups.

The scent of Athena was a lure I couldn't resist. I tracked her to an inconspicuous-looking tent on the outskirts of the makeshift midway. I listened for a long time in the shadows, but there was no sound of torture or interrogation. A modest guard of two nodded at the tent flap, their pikes crossed. No one worried that anyone would come to the Princess's rescue. Who cared to free a witch?

I was able to force my way under the tent wall, though I was immediately hit by a magical jolt that nearly made me yelp in pain. It shook me so hard that it forced me back into man shape. I crouched, naked, wishing I could find a way to transform with weapons in hand.

'Garrett,' she whispered.

She sat on a strange chair in the middle of the tent. The chair looked a bit like a silver throne, but the wicked curves of its armrests and feet made me sure it was more than simply decorative. Though she wasn't bound in any way, the odd, constricted angle of her head and limbs made me think that somehow the chair held her tight.

There were hollows under her eyes and her lips were cracked. I sensed they'd barely fed her since her capture, and outrage filled me.

'It's a binding chair,' she said, ignoring my anger. 'My father has developed it specially for witches and Were. It holds magic to it like a powerful magnet, unless the one in control of the chair uses a reversal stone.'

'And I gather your father alone can reverse the field?' I said.

She would have nodded, but since she couldn't move her head, she said, 'Yes.'

'Then, I need to find him and take the reversal stone so I can free you.' I scented the air, trying to catch the horrid odour of the Emperor above the iron smell of the binding chair.

'I like the new uniform,' she said.

I looked down at myself and blushed. I started pacing the narrow confines of the tent to avoid her gaze, hoping to pick up the Emperor's scent.

She stiffened. 'Garrett, you must leave,' she said. 'They know you're here. My father will be here any moment. He'll not rest until he has you, too.'

'And I'll not rest until I've freed you,' I said. 'Let him come.'

'Garrett.' The way she said my name made me stop and turn. 'You must not free me.'

'Nonsense!' I very nearly shouted. 'If I don't, you'll . . .'

'Be executed. Yes. And you must let that happen.'

'What?'

She struggled to meet my eyes, but the chair made it difficult.

'As a witch, I have some little power. As a princess, I have even less, certainly not enough to sway the hearts and minds of the people. But as a martyr? If my name becomes a rallying cry for justice in the future? If my story becomes the antidote to the poison my father has fed everyone? Then I shall be power-ful indeed.'

'Athena, you can't mean . . .'

'I do mean it. And as your princess, I command you to let me go. And when this has been done, you will be my Architect. You will found a society of witches, warlocks, Were, and any others who wish to fight tyranny and reveal the truth.'

I stalked towards her, my entire body vibrating with anger. 'You can't mean this! Of all the stubborn, pig-headed . . . I won't let you do this!'

She gazed at me steadily, her eyes like ice. 'Leave me now, Garrett.'

I bowed my head, shaking so hard with despair and rage that I felt I might shiver apart. Despite her warnings about the chair, I leaned forward and kissed her on the forehead. A dark bolt of pain blossomed in my lips and skull. 'Athena, I . . .'

Her cool fingertips grazed my thigh as she said, 'He's here. Go.'

I have never stopped regretting that I did not kiss her on the lips one last time.

I did not sleep at all that night; I wandered the alleys of Paradise. The wolf in me wanted to rip out the Emperor's throat while he slept and free his daughter. The man in me, the one who served Athena, knew she had not given me that choice. For those of us who serve, it is never an easy burden to bear. But when our masters or mistresses ask us to step aside and leave them to their fates, that I think is worse than our own death – especially if we love them as I loved her.

As the sun rose, though, I knew that she was right. As an exiled princess, and a witch, she would have no power. She would, in fact, be a rallying point for those who believed witches and Were should be hunted down throughout the realm and killed. As a martyr, though, she might gain a following. If I could keep the truth alive, those like us might live on, too.

There was just one last thing I had to do.

It was not long after dawn when a commotion arose from near the Emperor's tents. I soon saw why. They had put Athena in a cage and were drawing her down the midway towards the Waste in a final spectacle. People jeered at her, threw rotten fruit and eggs and even the contents of their chamberpots at her. Through it all, she sat stiffly in the chair, bound to her suffering by its magical silver.

I noticed as I followed alongside, though, that not all ridiculed or rebuked her. There were some like me, who had come to pay their respects. They bowed their heads or mumbled prayers, and I noted their faces for the aftermath.

At last, we came to the edge of the Waste. Jesters and clowns joked with the crowd by pushing them towards it or pretending to fall and vanish into oblivion, then popping back up several lengths from where they had been, almost as if by magic. I ignored them as I crept closer to the wagon. The cage was unlocked; the reversal stone activated. She stood, moving past the guards who would have dragged her, preserving her final dignity. For just a moment, she stood at the edge of the wooden stairs, staring out over all the crowd. They had put a grey sackcloth robe over her tattered nightdress, which was emblazoned with a scarlet letter 'W' – no doubt some churlish final jab devised by the Emperor's execution staff.

The Emperor himself sat under a billowing awning some yards away, close enough that he could see the work done, but far enough, of course, that the black sands would not turn him into a pillar of salt.

She didn't say anything, didn't ask for mercy or make useless apologies. She walked down the steps one at a time, and if she seemed to tremble, it could only be the fault of the rickety wood.

I got near enough at the bottom of the stairs to slip the wooden heart I'd carved during the night into her palm. Her eyes, focused on the black distance, found my face. That little hook of her half smile caught in my heart. She looked down at the letters I'd carved and smiled.

'I have nothing more to give you in return, except what I have already taught you. Write it down. Spread it far and wide.'

'There is no need for more,' I said. 'Thy will be done.'

She closed her eyes and bowed her head, and I saw a little sigh catch in her chest. It was then I understood that she regretted all this, that she was only playing at being brave.

'Athena, there's still time,' I said. 'We can still . . .'

She shook her head as the guard, one of my old brethren, prodded her in the back with his pike; then, clutching my heart in her hand, she lifted her head and walked forward.

The Emperor rose. I looked at his face for a moment. He could have been a statue. Even his hands where he clutched the railing seemed made of stone. And yet, I thought I saw a faint glow around them, the barest hint of magic that none but those like me or Athena would see.

I watched Athena through to the end, until the very last step. She turned and her face shone with love and defiance, like a second sun. Then her toes touched the black sand and her smile, her hair, her eyes all unravelled and blew away in a cloud of salt on the sudden wind.

I may have gone mad for a time after that, but I'm not entirely certain. I ran under many moons through many towns and hamlets as a wolf, howling my anguish and rage. But those times are not part of this story. What is germane is that I did as Athena bade me. I have worked to bring Were and witch together, to defend the Elementals and found a new society. I have written down her commandments and sent them far and wide. But I have added a commandment of my own to the Oath of the Architects, which all who follow Athena must swear:

'Thou shalt not love a witch, for to love a witch is death.'

THE LADY IN RED

Eliza Knight

There was nothing unusual about the grey of the morning sky, nor in the hustle and bustle of those walking the streets of London. Even so, Terrence, Earl of Shaftesbury, stared hard out the window, his eyes riveted by the vibrant red of a certain hat.

Not just any hat, a hat fit for Queen Victoria herself. Bedecked with a several plumes of black feathers and ribbons, 'twas the same hat he'd seen fly by the windows of his study the past two mornings. Beneath the hat was the face of an angel – certainly a trick that helped her along her mischievous ways – eyes as blue as the non-existent London sky; creamy, flawless skin, and ruby-red lips that made a man lose his sense.

Terrence was not accustomed to losing his sense. In fact, he'd only ever lost it once – gazing into the eyes of an angel.

He'd sworn the first day the hat sailed past that it couldn't be her. That was Monday. Tuesday he'd risen well before dawn and stood before his study window, watching the gas lights until the sun rose and the lantern boys came to extinguish them. Still he didn't move. He'd examined each and every person that happened to walk in front of his London townhouse, and just when he'd been about to turn away, a flash of crimson caught his eyes, which widened as he stepped closer to the window, forehead practically pressing against the cool glass. The morning before, he'd doubted himself, but not today. It was her.

How bloody dare she? What was she about? The hat was a gift. A gift he'd given her as a token of his affection. Before she'd made him out for a fool.

Tuesday, he'd run out the front door, sailed down the brick front steps and through the iron gate. But by the time he'd reached the busy pavement, she was gone. No flash of red in the midst of black and grey hats.

Now here he was on Wednesday, prepared.

He grinned as he observed James, his valet, step from behind the row of tall shrubs positioned before his iron fence in front of his London townhouse. James gently pressed his fingers to the lady's elbow. She stared at the valet, startled, wide-eyed. As instructed, James tugged her through the gate and up the stairs.

Terrence's heart kicked up its pace. If it weren't seven in the morning he might like a glass of brandy. To hell with it. He poured himself two fingers into a tumbler and downed it before a tap sounded at his library door.

'Enter,' he said, surprised at the sturdiness in his voice. Setting down his glass, he went to stand casually beside the fireplace, his elbow resting on the mantle.

He hadn't seen Elizabeth in two years. A bead of sweat trickled from his temple.

The door swung open, revealing James and Elizabeth. Good God, she was still just as enchanting. Her hair was swept up, no doubt a pile of riotous golden curls beneath the fated hat. Eyes wide and bluer than he remembered: the colour of sapphires and excitement.

'My lord,' James said.

Elizabeth dipped into a curtsy, lowering her gaze. The gown she wore was plain, worn. He frowned at the coarseness of the fabric of her skirts and the out-of-date bodice. She should be wearing clothes that made women in the height of fashion swoon with jealousy.

'That will be all, James,' Terrence said, his voice gruff.

The valet crept from the room, closing the door silently behind him. Elizabeth stood not six feet away. She didn't look at him, her eyes still lowered to the floor. Two years. He should be full of rage, ranting at her, but instead, he could barely find his voice.

'You've had quite a lengthy trip to the mantua's shop.' Terrence thought he sounded rather clever for that one.

The morning she'd disappeared, Elizabeth had told him she was going to see the hat maker about commissioning an equally charming hat in blue. She'd never returned.

'Husband,' she murmured.

The title was not one he'd forgotten, and hearing it on her lips only left him bereft. 'Is that all the greeting I deserve?'

Her gaze flashed up, anger, raw and potent in her startling blues. 'What did you expect?'

More than she was willing to give, he supposed. 'An explanation.'

'That I cannot give you.'

Terrence kept his face empty of emotion, though inside his stomach twisted as if he'd been gutted. He'd been in love with her. Ever since he'd nearly run her over in Hyde Park with his horse. It didn't matter to him that she wasn't a noble-born lady, or that she had no family. Her smile and charm had swept through him, creating a hailstorm of emotion he'd never felt before. Feelings he'd thought she'd returned all through their courtship. But the morning after they wed, she'd disappeared.

'Where have you been?' he demanded.

Elizabeth's hands fisted at her sides. 'I was told you were in the country.'

Terrence smiled bitterly. 'A rumour I started myself.'

'Why?'

''Tis I who gets to ask the questions, not you, *wife.*'

Elizabeth startled, the anger still visible in her eyes. He couldn't decipher if she was angry that he'd found her or that he wouldn't let her go. Perhaps it was a bit of both.

He pushed away from the mantle and stepped closer to her, so that only a few feet separated them. 'Why did you keep the hat?'

Slim fingers reached up to touch the brim, and her plush lips turned down in a frown. 'I . . .'

Terrence closed the distance, the tips of his boots touching the toe of her rather feminine-looking leather ones. 'I'll ask you once more, Lady Shaftesbury. What's kept you?' He hated the hint of vulnerability in his voice.

Elizabeth's throat bobbed and for a moment he swore she'd run. But she squared her shoulders, lifted her chin and stared him straight in the eye. 'My husband and daughter.'

*　　*　　*

The believability of those words escaping her lips were just as inconceivable as they'd been two years earlier when Elizabeth had said, 'I do.'

Within seconds of being returned to Terrence's magnanimous presence, she'd given him the two darkest secrets she'd struggled with confessing to him before. Leaving had been the only option. Marrying him had been insanity. She'd had a job to perform and she'd failed. Agreeing to be his wife for life and beyond the grave when Linden was . . . Elizabeth shook her head. She wasn't going to think about either of her husbands – or her daughter, Sarah. Memories and thoughts only brought her pain and misery. Right now, she needed her wits about her. Without her faculties, she wouldn't be able to resist Terrence's charm – a potent and powerful wine she wanted to guzzle.

'What do you mean your husband and daughter?' Terrence's voice was calm. Too calm.

A shiver of fear raced along her spine, sending gooseflesh to cover her limbs. Her stomach cramped and she was close to losing the meagre breakfast she'd consumed.

Elizabeth forced herself to look him in the eye and said the first thing she could think of: 'I don't know what you're talking about.'

Not really a valid cluster of words, but enough, hopefully, to buy her some time. Time to think this through and figure out a way to once more escape the appealing man who should be her mortal enemy.

Terrence's eyes flashed anger for a moment. His lips pressed into a thin line. He stepped even closer, filling the space between them with his masculine, intoxicating scent: spicy, wood and all male. It was so hard to hate him.

'You know bloody well what I mean.' His tone wasn't menacing, but it left no room for argument all the same.

Elizabeth swallowed. And swallowed again. Her voice wouldn't work, her tongue felt twisted and swollen, but even worse, her mind did not seem to be within her full control either. She couldn't think, couldn't breathe. With him so close, all she could do was stare into his gorgeous, smoky-blue eyes and remember the last time he'd kissed her. It had been the morning she'd escaped. They'd made love the entire night through. She could still feel the tingle in her thighs – or was that renewed desire for him?

She'd kissed him goodbye, putting every ounce of herself into that last kiss, knowing she wasn't coming back, praying she'd never see him again, and then she'd made herself disappear. She had cried days for her broken heart. The sickening truth of it was that Elizabeth hadn't wanted to leave Terrence. She'd *had* to leave him. Despite *who* the Earl of Shaftesbury was, she actually loved him.

'Elizabeth . . .' His tone thickened, sounding more threatening.

'I can't, my lord,' she said, using his proper form of address rather than his name, in an attempt to put some distance between them.

Terrence growled and whirled around. He stalked towards the window, his stylish boots making a thunking noise against the polished wood floors with each step he took. She watched him retreat, watched the play of muscles on his backside as a burning shame came to flame in her cheeks. Was there really any harm in admiring a man with a most auspicious physique?

Bloody hell! There absolutely was harm in it.

Taking advantage of his turned back, Elizabeth, too, whirled around and headed for the door. She'd got her fingers wrapped around the handle when his larger, more callused ones closed over hers. Hands that worked side by side with his employees rather than taking the high-and-mighty overlord position. Linden admired Terrence for that very real and honest part of him. The only part. She had to remember that, to harden her heart and guard her soul. Betraying someone when they were at their lowest was a most horrid offence, one that cancelled out all precious good deeds.

'You're not going anywhere,' he growled into her ear. 'Not yet anyway.'

His breath cascaded over her neck, making her shiver with need, but also fear. He couldn't keep her here, could he? Sarah . . .

'You have to let me go.' Elizabeth searched for the words she needed to say, but came up empty. There didn't seem to be a right way. 'I can't stay here. I can't stay with you.'

'You betrayed me.' Beneath his words lay a sharp-edged sword.

What would Terrence do when cornered? When he felt he'd been wronged? She already knew what he would do to someone in need who didn't offer him any offence. He'd let them die for his own gain.

'I am not the one with blood on my hands,' Elizabeth said, wrenching away from Terrence's nearness. With him blocking the door, that meant sinking back into his office.

Escape was futile at the moment.

Elizabeth glanced around, her eyes catching on the lovely pair of blue and white imperial Chinese porcelain vases that she knew Terrence prized. Cracking one of those over his head might give her a few minutes to run away. But she wasn't the violent sort, and Terrence's valet was most likely lurking just beyond the library door. Besides, breaking a priceless vase had to be some sort of sin.

Seeming to have gained his composure after the shock of her insinuation, Terrence crossed his muscled arms over his chest and glowered at her. 'What the bloody hell does that mean? I've never killed anyone.'

Elizabeth sniffed, turning her nose up at him. He'd never see it her way. Terrence might be a charming man, a good kisser and one hell of a love-maker, but when it came to money, weren't all businessmen unscrupulous? Uncaring about who they harmed?

''Tis expected, though disappointing, that a man like you would see it that way.' Her nails dug into her palms, remembering Linden's words, the pain etched into his forehead. Then poor Sarah, growing up without the benefit of a father. Anger fuelled Elizabeth to step forward, her brows furrowed in a frown.

'At last a spark of life. Don't hold in the passion I know you have inside you,' Terrence goaded. 'Tell me what you mean by your vile words.'

Elizabeth was about to let him have it and tell him exactly what she thought of him, but that would defeat the purpose, and she had somewhere to be. A job to do. Survive or die.

'You don't deserve that much,' she said under her breath, forcing herself to envision Linden and Sarah, even though her anger was starting to seem superficial and forced.

'Elizabeth . . . ' Terrence met her gaze, his eyes stricken.

She couldn't look away. Couldn't force herself to turn around. Her belly twisted and she wished she could run into his arms, to tell him she was sorry for the pain she'd caused him. But doing that would make her untrue to Linden. Which was worse? Being untrue to herself seemed worse. Elizabeth bit her lip and glanced at the ground. What did she want? In a perfect world . . . There was no such thing as perfect.

'You have to let me go, Terrence.' This time she used his given name, hoping that the familiarity would give him a reason to let her out the door. She wasn't sure she'd make it there on her own. 'If you love me at all . . . let me go.'

And he did. Holding up his hands, he backed slowly away. His eyes never left her, dark in their intensity, and her heart skipped a beat.

'Thank you,' she whispered, forcing herself to stop thinking about him letting her go without question – he loved her that much?

Elizabeth was surprised when he didn't stop her from opening the door. Was surprised when he didn't pull her back in as she walked through it. Her heart hammered against her ribs and she felt nauseous leaving this place – her home for less than twelve hours – leaving the man she knew deep down in her heart she loved, though she should hate him for ruining everything.

Just as she entered the foyer, only a few feet from escape, his voice consumed her, stopping her in her tracks.

'Elizabeth, don't leave like this. Tell me why. I deserve that much, don't I?'

He did. She turned around slowly, her skirts twirling lightly at her ankles. When she raised her eyes to meet his, it was a feat of willpower not to sink to the floor and just give in. Giving in would have been far easier than this.

After he heard the truth, he would let her go. He wouldn't want her then. Not like he did when she'd walked into his library after two years. Desire had burned in his gaze, and she felt it reciprocated in her own veins. This was the best way to get him to let her go, even if it hurt like hell. Maybe the reason she'd fought it was that she hoped he would come after her, that somehow she could make him part of her life. But there was Sarah. And she would never abandon her.

'I married young,' Elizabeth started. She glanced to one side, then the other. There were no servants in sight, though she was sure they were listening from somewhere.

Pain flickered over Terrence's features. She guessed it was because he'd hoped to be her first. Whatever his feelings, he seemed to bottle them up quickly, his face clearing like a slate being wiped clean.

'My husband was an employee of yours.'

Terrence's facial features did not show his reaction, but when he spoke, his voice was low and too controlled. 'In my house?'

Elizabeth shook her head. 'No. He worked for Shaftesbury Luxury Steamships. We lived in East London.'

At that detail, Terrence's eye twitched. East London was notorious for its crime and slums.

Dark London. A place she'd grown up and somehow beaten.

'Linden worked at the docks, loading and unloading ships. That's where he met you.'

'I remember Linden.' Terrence's voice was softer somehow. 'Where is he now?'

Elizabeth's mouth fell open, shock permeating her body so much that she took a step back. 'How dare you.' She breathed out. Her hands came to her throat, as though she might be able to force her breath to release.

'Pardon?' Terrence said, confusion furrowing his brows. 'What happened to him?'

'You . . .' She couldn't speak. After all they'd shared – months of courtship and wooing and sweet bliss – he would play her for a fool. There was nothing for it. Elizabeth could not continue this conversation, not knowing whether Terrence would simply lie to her or feel compelled to tell the truth.

She whirled on her heel and lunged for the door. Terrence's fancy boots clicked quickly behind her, but not fast enough. Down the perfectly appointed brick steps she went. She sailed through the gate, lurching away from the place where James, the valet, had hidden earlier, though no one jumped out at her this time. Escape was the only thing on her mind. When her red hat flew from atop her head with a gust of sultry wind, she didn't stop to grapple for it, but let it go. Something she should have done long before now.

'Elizabeth!' Terrence's calls for her to stop and turn around went unheeded.

She raced away, jumping when carriage drivers shouted at her, and nearly colliding with many a heavily laden wagon. Her heels clipped against the cobblestones of Shaftesbury Avenue on to Charing Cross Road, sloshing in muck and stamping on spilled rubbish; dodging hawkers touting their wares – matchsticks, oysters, apples, flowers.

Elizabeth had been fully aware of the risk she took by working for another wealthy nobleman near Hyde Park – after all, she had to walk by Terrence's manse every morning; the man's family had a blasted road named after them – but for nearly a week he hadn't noticed her, and the job was not a choice. She needed it.

The hat. The blasted hat. It was the only reason she'd been caught, and now poor Sarah would suffer for it. What a fool she'd been to think she could marry such an influential, powerful man and come away from it unscathed.

She was so lost in her head, she didn't see an oncoming carriage until the horse's breath swooshed against her forehead. Elizabeth leapt out of the way less than a second before she would have been trampled.

'Get out o' the way, ye Judy,' the driver called, passing her by with a rude hand signal.

Elizabeth swallowed her shock at being publicly branded a prostitute. She might not be wearing a hat, and her shoes and the hem of her gown were covered in muck, but she . . . she probably did look like one. Her throat tightened, forming a lump she could hardly swallow.

Without a word of reply at the offensive man, she slipped into a narrow alleyway and slumped down onto someone's stoop, her back leaning against the saggy wood panels, and there she prayed they wouldn't open the door until she'd had her cry and gone.

*   *   *

Linden's wife?

Terrence was still reeling from what Elizabeth had told him. He'd not heard from Linden in over two years. The bloke had taken a pouch of silver to deliver to a supplier and never returned. Terrence had sent out men to look for him, but Linden had never turned up. He'd figured the man had taken the silver and run. It wasn't like Linden to do such a thing, but desperate men did desperate things, and Terrence had no real idea of the man's social life.

He'd never thought to look in the East End. Linden had always told him he lived near St Giles. What he didn't understand was how he had ended up marrying Linden's wife!

A staggering pain seized his chest. He wasn't truly married to her. Not if Linden was still alive.

Where the hell was the blighter?

'James!' Terrence shouted.

His valet slipped from the hallway leading towards the kitchen. The man was always near, his job including many more duties than that of a simple valet. 'Yes, my lord?'

'Go down to Bond Street and speak with Smith. Tell him to help you pick up his search of Linden in the East End.'

James nodded and left the house.

When Elizabeth had left him, she'd taken the hat and several banknotes, but other than that, nothing. What had she hoped to gain by reeling him in? There'd been nothing else missing. She hadn't stolen from him. Only broken his heart. What had her ultimate plan been?

Good God, the questions skittering through his brain set him on edge. He stormed into his library and poured another finger of liquid fire, then another, forgetting to measure and pouring at least three times what he needed. Walking towards the window, he looked out at the bustling streets, now fully alive.

Another ten minutes this morning and he would have missed her, the city swallowing her whole.

'My lord,' his housekeeper, Mrs Ball, interrupted.

'What is it?' Terrence said, without bothering to turn away from the window.

'A Lord Ainsley is here to see you.'

'Ainsley?' Though he'd heard of the man, he was not an associate of his, and he had never conversed with him. What could he want?

Mrs Ball stood patiently waiting.

'Send him in.' With a glower at not being able to drown his confusion and bruised ego, Terrence set the tumbler on the mantle and turned, prepared to greet his unwanted guest.

Lord Ainsley burst into the library in a cloud of bluster. 'I say, Lord Shaftesbury, what have you done with my new housekeeper?'

'Pardon me, my lord, I've not the faintest clue what you're talking about.'

Ainsley railed his fist in the air, the man's white hair waving with force in time with his loose jowls. 'Mrs Markum. I saw your man pull her in here on my way home from the park, and she never did arrive at my house. What did you do with her?'

Markum. Linden's surname. A bitter envy scorched its way up his throat.

'I did nothing with her. Mistaken identity, 'tis all.'

'I know what I saw.'

'I'm not doubting you, Lord Ainsley. Now if you please.' He had some drinking to do. Terrence picked up the tumbler, feeling the effects of the brandy.

'Are you dismissing me, my lord?' Ainsley asked.

Terrence imagined the older man's ruddy face growing three shades darker and spittle flying from his lips.

'Indeed, Lord Ainsley. It's been a pleasure getting to know you this morning, and if I should happen to see Mrs Markum, I will be certain to send her to her post.'

Housekeeper? His wife, a servant.

Not his wife, and a fact he'd known before.

When she'd leapt in front of his horse, cheeks rosy against the cream of her skin, blue eyes wide and frightened, her flowing hair, silky and shiny, hypnotized him. Mesmerized him. He'd yanked on the reins, terrified as his horse reared, front paws clawing at the air only inches from her face. Her voice had been soft music to his ears and, despite her ratty clothes and the baulking society would give them, he'd known then that she was the one for him.

Terrence had never been one to follow society edicts. He didn't spend his days in gentlemen's clubs. He did his duties for the House of Lords, maintained his properties as he should, but his true passion lay in his business: steamships. Not just any old steamships, though. Terrence built luxury steamships. And it was a very lucrative business, one he'd built from the ground up, and he loved every aspect of it, making sure he was involved in all parts.

At the dock that cold wintry morning three years earlier, when snow had fallen and men's breath looked like the steam coming from the ship's pipes, Terrence had spotted Linden stacking crates. The man was diligent, productive and, despite the chill of the morning, he worked as though it was a perfectly pleasant spring day, his eyes filled with determination. Terrence offered him a job on the spot. He needed someone like Linden Markum to work for him, to put that fiery spirit inside his other employees.

Terrence hadn't known the darker side of Linden, or that the man would swindle him. Worst still, he hadn't known the man to be so conniving that he'd involve his wife in the scam.

More fool, Terrence.

Forgetting Elizabeth would be difficult, but necessary.

The stairs to the little tenant apartment in Charing Cross that Elizabeth rented for her and Sarah with the last coins to her name, smelled of overcooked cabbage and spilled whisky. She climbed up the four flights, her head heavy and her eyes still stinging with the tears that hadn't ceased since she'd seen Terrence the day before. Her fingers were clutched by her young daughter, who'd spent the day helping the building owner and his wife clean. It wasn't at all what a five-year-old child should be doing, but it was necessary to get by.

'Momma, I'm hungry,' Sarah murmured, her voice tired.

'I'll fix you supper, then we both need to go to bed.'

Sarah nodded, stifling a too-large yawn. Since when did her daughter agree to go to bed early? The poor girl had probably been worked to the point of exhaustion.

'How were Mr and Mrs Crum today?'

Sarah shrugged.

They reached the door, and just as Elizabeth inserted the key, someone spoke from behind her.

'Mrs Markum.'

Elizabeth jumped and Sarah cried out in surprise. Terrence's valet, James, lurked in the shadowy corner several feet from her doorway. No wonder she hadn't seen him.

'What do you want?' she asked, holding tighter to Sarah, who sank closer to her mother's hip.

'Lord Shaftesbury sent me out to find Mr Markum. My findings led me here, to you. Would you kindly let me speak with him?' James's words were soft, even polite, but the way his eyes were dark and narrowed showed her he meant business. This was not a social call.

'I'm afraid you won't find him here,' she said, her spine stiffening.

'And where might he be?' James rolled his feet, his body bobbing like a pigeon on the flat of the ocean.

'He resides in Kensal Green on Harlow Road, but he's not accepting visitors.'

'I'll be the judge of that.' James tipped his hat. 'Good day to you, Madam.'

'Best of luck,' Elizabeth said, trying to keep the sarcasm from her voice. She turned towards her door, opened it and shuffled Sarah inside.

'Momma, why didn't you tell the man Papa is with the angels?' Sarah's voice was filled with innocent confusion.

Elizabeth cringed. 'He'll find out for himself soon enough, love.' Kensal Green was a borough of London, but it also housed the public cemetery: Linden's permanent address. 'Come now, let us get some supper.'

And forget about Terrence.

The opened window did little to stifle the heat of the room, nor air the smell of rotting floorboards and mildew that permeated the whole building. In fact, the scents of the city wafted through the window, mingling and creating air that was almost impossible to breathe.

Elizabeth flopped her arm over her eyes, willing sleep to come to her. Curled up beside her in the tiny bed was a sleeping Sarah, her breaths coming out in soft puffs.

A slight tapping started. *Tap tap. Tap tap tap. Tap tap*

tap tap tap. At first, Elizabeth ignored the noise, believing it to be something outside – a bird, or a loose cord hitting something with the wind propelling it to do so – but the more forceful it became, the more she realized it wasn't random.

She sat up and stared around the darkened room. *Tap tap tap tap tap*. Someone was knocking at her door. It wasn't that late yet, but it was certainly past visiting hours. She hoped it wasn't Mr or Mrs Crum telling her Sarah could no longer stay with them during the day. She'd only been able to obtain the position with Lord Ainsley because she didn't have to worry about Sarah, and he didn't want his house-keeper to live in the home. None of his female servants did, and as for the males – well, Lord Ainsley had a propensity towards that gender.

Panic made her tremble and sweat. As nimbly as she could, so as not to wake her child, Elizabeth climbed from the bed. The worn floor creaked beneath her feet. If the Crums couldn't work with Sarah, then Elizabeth would have to find employment elsewhere. They had a couple of weeks left until the rent was due again, and without another job, they'd be on the streets. Again.

The door rattled as someone knocked hard instead of tapping.

'Shh,' Elizabeth hissed, not sure if the person on the other side would even hear her. She cracked the door enough to see that it wasn't Mr and Mrs Crum, but James again.

Promptly, she slammed the door shut and locked it. 'Go away,' she said in a sharp whisper.

'I wanted to thank you for pointing me in the right direction,' James said, his voice coming muffled through the door.

'I did.'

'Indeed.' There was a thunk, as though James had dropped something, and then silence.

Curiosity ate away at Elizabeth's insides. Was he still there? What did he want?

No sound came from the other side of the door. After waiting for several nail-biting moments, Elizabeth eased open the door. James was gone, and on the floor was a brown-paper package.

Looking down the hall and into the darkened corners to make sure she wasn't being watched, she bent to pick it up. Shutting the door behind her, she rushed over to the rickety table and two unsteady chairs and lit the single candle. There were no gas lanterns in her tiny room; she couldn't afford one.

Elizabeth stared for a long moment at the paper. The package was held together with loosely tied twine. Whatever was inside felt like it would change her. She was scared. Why had James left it for her? Was it a threat? Money? Goosebumps stole over her flesh, and anxiety built a heated fire in her belly.

She glanced over at Sarah, sleeping like an angel, and wished with every ounce of her being that she could give her daughter the life she deserved. Wishful thinking.

Using her thumb and index finger, she pulled at the twine until it came undone, then she opened the paper, smoothing it flat and revealing in its centre her red hat, a stack of crisp bills and an envelope with her name scrawled on it in long, elegant strokes – handwriting she did not recognize.

She opened the envelope and pulled out the letter with an 'S' inked in a voluminous scroll at the top.

'My Dear Elizabeth . . .'

This was Terrence's writing. She stroked her fingers over it, never having seen it before.

'First, I want to offer my condolences to you on the death of Linden. I had no idea he'd passed away. The last I saw of him, he was taking a payment to one of our suppliers. I never saw him again. I mistakenly assumed he'd run off with my money, however, James's investigations seem to lead to another conclusion.'

Indeed. Linden had been mugged on his way home from work and left to die in the middle of the road. It was only because someone was kind enough to come and find Elizabeth at the baker's shop she'd been working in that she knew he was hurt. He confessed to her then that he'd been on an errand for Terrence. But he'd wanted to find her first, to show her something. What it was, she still had no clue, only that he kept muttering Terrence's name, and when she asked who was responsible, he'd said Terrence.

How could Terrence deny any knowledge of this?

Elizabeth picked up the red hat and threw it across the room, the soft fabric barely making a sound as it fell peacefully to the floor.

She wanted to burn the bills one by one beneath the candle's flame, but she knew that was out of the question. The money would, without doubt, help her and Sarah to live comfortably for another year. But why had he sent it to her?

I understand that Linden's untimely death left you with-out a penny to your name, and a child to take care of. I've included in this package enough money to help you get by for a time. When it runs out, do not hesitate to contact me. I want you to know, I love you, Elizabeth. I still do. I'd have you for myself if you'd allow it. Even your little child – an extension of you. I would not have cast you out. As much as I want to forget you, to be angry at you for lying to me, to never forgive you for leaving me and disappearing for over two years, I can't. You're a part of me. I've felt empty without you.

You're still my wife.

With all my love,

Terrence

Oh, dear God. She was still his wife.

What would society think of the great Earl of Shaftesbury now? Married to street trash and raising her dead husband's child . . .

Elizabeth frowned down at the letter, glowing orange in the candlelight. Terrence had never cared about the upper crust and what they thought. He lived for doing what felt right in his heart. It was the reason he built his luxury steamers. The reason behind hiring Linden to run his errands and supervise his employees. The reason why he'd stopped his horse, climbed down and taken Elizabeth by the hand, never looking back. It was one of the many reasons she'd fallen in love with him.

Her heart told her to scoop up little Sarah and run towards Shaftesbury Avenue; her head told her to take the money and run in the opposite direction, hoping for a better life for Sarah in the country.

She'd followed her head before, and ended up miserable for the last two years. Maybe this time, she should go with her heart and hear what Terrence had to say; make him explain why Linden might think Terrence was to blame for him being jumped by a crew of street thugs.

The morning seemed too far away.

But though she was out of the East End, Charing Cross was still dangerous at night, and she wouldn't risk the safety of her child. It would have to wait till morning.

Terrence reclined in the wing-backed leather chair in his study, sleeves rolled up, cravat tossed somewhere and his shirt unbuttoned halfway. He ran his hands through his hair and watched the sun try to break through the grey morning clouds. Sleep had been non-existent. After James returned from finding Linden's grave and speaking with many in the East End who knew of him, his valet found out that his loyal employee had been murdered while attending Terrence's directives. Was that why Elizabeth thought he had blood on his hands?

A flash of red caused his muddled brain to come fully alert. Elizabeth?

Terrence pushed out of his chair and pressed his hands to the glass of the window. Sure enough, her beautiful face taunted him. And this time, she brought with her a miniature version of herself: her daughter.

He didn't wait for her to knock as he didn't want the door to be answered by one of his staff. He rushed out of his library towards the front door, flinging it open before she could raise the knocker. Elizabeth stared up at him wide-eyed, mouth open in shock, hand stuck in mid-air.

'You're here,' he said, stating the obvious, mostly to convince himself he wasn't dreaming.

She nodded. 'I . . .' Her voice was small, nervous.

'Come in.' Terrence opened the door wider, taking a moment to stare down at the little cherub who looked up at him with innocent curiosity.

'Mama, what are we doing here?' she said, looking at Elizabeth.

'Would you like a hot chocolate?' Terrence asked the child.

'Hot chocolate?' she asked, her nose wrinkling.

His throat tightened, and he couldn't swallow past the ball that suddenly lodged there.

'It's a sweet drink, Sarah,' Elizabeth said, pressing her hand gently to the little girl's shoulder. 'You'll like it.'

'Come with me, dear child.'

Terrence tore his eyes away from Elizabeth and the girl to see his housekeeper standing a few feet away. Sarah looked up at her mother, and when Elizabeth nodded, she scurried down the hall with Mrs Ball.

'Terrence, I . . .' Elizabeth bit her lip, cutting off her own words.

He wanted to reach out to her, to hold her hands in his and tell her not to say anything, that if she wanted to come home to him he was willing to forgive and forget everything that had happened. But she held her own hands tight in front of her, and he didn't want to push her if she came for some other reason.

Patience was not a virtue he normally possessed, but it seemed in this case, he was blessed with an infinite amount.

'Can I offer you a drink?' he asked. 'Tea?'

She shook her head.

'Would you like to sit in the drawing room?'

This time she nodded. Terrence offered his arm and she slid hers through it, a spark of delicious memory firing from his brain to his middle. Her touch was warm, familiar, even though it had been fleeting years earlier. He pushed open the door to the drawing room and escorted her to the settee, begrudgingly leaving her to shut the door.

Elizabeth perched on the end of her seat, her fingers once more entwined and wringing. She lifted her eyes towards his, the edges rimmed with tears. Without thinking, Terrence sat beside her and swiped at the tears with the pads of his thumbs.

'Don't cry, sweeting,' he whispered.

'I'm so confused,' she said, her eyes searching his.

He couldn't stand to see her cry. Her lower lip trembled and he wiped his thumb over it, remembering every kiss, every whispered word.

'Was it all a lie?' Though he asked the question, he prayed she wouldn't answer. He wasn't sure he could bear it if she said it was.

'No.' Elizabeth licked her lips, the tip of her tongue touching his thumb before he could pull away. Her touch seared him, awakening in him a desire he'd laid to rest.

He blinked longer than necessary and pulled his hands away from her. He had to focus. He couldn't push her back on the settee, even if he wanted to.

'I loved you, Terrence. Despite my reason for finding you, for making you pay for the death of my husband, for wanting answers, I fell in love. But I couldn't stay. Not with Sarah counting on me.'

Loved. That was past tense.

'Why didn't you just tell me?'

Elizabeth shook her head, took off the red hat and set it on the seat beside her. Glorious blonde curls fell around her shoulders. 'I wasn't sure I could trust you. Linden said his death was your responsibility.'

Terrence sighed. 'It was. If I hadn't sent him out to our supplier that day, he never would have been jumped.'

'See, that's just it. You weren't behind it. I think, in his way, Linden was trying to tell me to find you; not that you were the one who took his life.' Her voice was soft, gone quiet with reflection. 'I'm sorry.'

'No, Elizabeth. You don't have to apologize.'

'Yes, I do.'

Terrence shook his head. 'You were doing what you thought was right.'

'But I still hurt you. I was still stubborn.'

'You didn't know if I would accept you and your child.' Terrence took a chance and slid his hands up her arms. 'I would have. I will now.' He wanted desperately to take her into his arms and kiss away the years of pain.

'Oh, Terrence.' Elizabeth sagged into him, her forehead pressed to his shoulder, her warm breath on his neck. Her shoulders shook as she let her tears release.

Terrence held his breath and stroked her back tenderly, threading his fingers into her hair. They'd barely begun their lives together when she'd disappeared and now he had a second chance.

'Elizabeth, my darling, I never want to see you hurt, and I know you've been through so much. I just want to take away your pain and see you smile. See the way your joy lights up the blue in your eyes. Say you'll let me try.'

'What will everyone say?' she said, a hiccup on the end. Tilting her head back, she stared up at him, tears streaking her cheeks.

He wiped at the tear tracks. 'I don't give a fig what they say. As long as we're happy, they can all go rot.'

'And Sarah?'

'A daughter to me.' He stroked his fingers over her face, turning her chin up so she looked at him. 'Give me a chance to prove I can be the man you need.'

'You already proved that years ago.' Elizabeth leaned up, her lips a hair's breadth from his.

'I was such a fool to run out on you, to not see the truth for what it was. You're a good man Lord Shaftesbury, and I love you.'

'I love you, too.' Terrence ended his declaration with a kiss, pressing his lips to her warm, plush mouth. He'd missed the pleasure of her kiss, the tenderness, the raw passion and excitement of it. Desire thrilled through his veins. He wrapped his arms around her, pulling her on to his lap so that he could devour her mouth all the more. Elizabeth answered his kiss with the fiery passion he remembered. The years of space and fear melted away, replaced with renewed energy and yearning.

'I'm so sorry,' she murmured again.

Terrence shook his head, opening his eyes to stare into hers. 'No, I'm sorry. I should have delved deeper, looked harder.'

'I didn't want to be found.' She kissed his chin.

Terrence pulled her closer. 'I never gave up hope you'd return.'

'I'm here now.'

'To stay.' He wouldn't let her leave again.

Elizabeth nodded, her eyes looking intently into his. 'For ever.'

'I want to make love to you.' He pressed her hands to his beating heart.

'Oh, Terrence, so do I.'

He claimed her mouth once more, passion and heat rising between them. She trembled in his embrace.

'Are you certain?' he asked.

'I've never been more certain in my life.'

Terrence laid her back on the settee and Elizabeth wrapped one leg around his hip, surrounding him in her warmth. Making love to her had been glorious, the best he'd ever experienced, and here she was again, his completely and for ever. Deepening the kiss, he stroked along her ribcage, down over her hip and thigh.

'You're more beautiful than I remember,' he murmured, kissing a path from her chin, down her neck to the valley of her breasts.

Elizabeth skimmed her hands up and down his back, sending shivers racing over his skin.

Blood roared through his ears in a desperate rush to reach his loins. He tried to go slow, to stroke her centre until she quivered, and lave her plush breasts until her nipples puckered like ripe cherries.

'Please, Terrence, I can't wait any longer.' Her desperate cry pushed him over the edge of control.

Terrence tore open his breeches, hiked up her skirts and pushed towards home. They both cried out at the joining of their bodies. Hands stroked, limbs entwined, mouths collided. They rode the waves of ecstasy in time with the beat of their racing hearts, until both could no longer move and pleasure soaked them in sweat.

Sated for the moment, they lay in each other's arms, hearts pounding, breath heaving. They were together again, the earl and his lady in red.

WHERE THE OCEAN
MEETS THE SKY

Sara M. Harvey

The city of San Francisco, although known for freedom and individuality, had some pretty restrictive rules about how her airspace should be used. Joshua Norton I, who had risen through the ranks of businessman and madman, finally becoming the great and benevolent lord of the sovereign city state, ruled with a parental attitude: spare the rod and spoil the city. Dirigibles were strictly forbidden, by order of the Emperor, who hated their growling motors and had a paranoia of one catching fire above the city streets, or perhaps snagging on a lightning rod or flagpole perched atop one of the many tall buildings, or at the very least dropping some cargo on to the unsuspecting citizens below. So, by Imperial decree, all airships must dock in the bay.

Ordinarily this wasn't a problem, but as an unusually severe spring storm buffeted the *Madame Barbary*, Captain Matilda Romero wished she had a more stable place to land. The cargo freighter blinked out its open mooring space in Morse code, or at least it looked like code in the driving wind and rain, though it could have just been a faulty wire. She headed for it anyway, having precious few other options. Across the bay from San Francisco, Oakland allowed land docking, but the bayside moorings were already full and Matilda didn't relish the thought of fighting the crosswinds that formed at the foothills as she searched for someplace inland to dock. Although the ship below her was positively storm-tossed, it was in sight and in range. And in her ship's hold rested the hard-won spoils of a very long and hazardous series of quests, something that was specifically dear to the Emperor.

She pulled down the ship's address horn with a sure hand and tucked a sweat-curled lock of black hair behind her ear. She took a deep breath to steady her voice before she spoke. 'All hands, prepare for a hard landing. If you're not needed, get the hell out of the way and hang on to something.'

The *Madame Barbary* lurched to starboard and Matilda corrected it, swearing. This was going to be her last run. There seemed no end to her tribulations, not to mention the fact that she was damned lonely, with none but her all-male crew for company. She was tired of this game.

Of course she had said that the last time, and the time before that, going back about six years. And yet here she was again, descending into danger once more. And with another dozen or so grey strands standing brightly in her dark hair to prove it.

The ship's lashings groaned against the strain and Matilda crossed her toes inside her boots. 'Come on, darlin', just a little further. You can make it, I know you can.'

A white canvas tarp tore free of the outer cargo hold below the main deck and went flapping past the window like a great, ghostly bat. It slapped up against the aft port side and threatened the altitude rudder.

'Oh for fuck's sake.' She grabbed the horn. 'Draw straws, boys, someone's got to get that blasted tarp off the rudders.'

Below decks, Matilda had amassed a spirited, if slightly felonious, crew of uprooted Indians, escaped slaves and ex-pirates. Well, they were all pirates now, technically, but since they flew under the Imperial flag, that made them privateers under the questionable authority of Joshua Norton I's rule.

Many years ago, when the dear man still walked among sane people, Norton had taken particular grievance to the Union forces building a fort in his fair city. No one knew why the government had thought that a sea fort was required to guard against Confederate forces – none of them seemed likely to circumnavigate South America nor trek across Mexico or Panama, nor was it likely that they would bypass the prosperous ports of San Diego, Los Angeles and Monterey to come and harass San Francisco – but there it was. In all honesty, it had been grandly designed, with a spare elegance and entirely made from blood-coloured bricks, but that was by the by as it was something done wholly without permission or proper justification. Never mind that it occurred twenty years before his Majesty's reign – things like that were irrelevant to the Emperor. The outright mockery he had received from the newly reunited nation when he had made his displeasure public resulted in the current tensions between his Imperial Majesty and the rest of the country. Furious, the Emperor seceded San Francisco from the Republic (in name only) of California and decreed that any sailing vessel or airship bearing the Union flag and entering San Francisco's sovereign territory would be seized. Vessels flying the Confederate flag would be seen as ballsy and indomitable and would be allowed to pass, after paying a small fee.

Matilda had never met his Imperial Majesty, but she liked him quite a bit and had written for her privateer's charter the moment she had read the ad in the newspaper. And now, her ship had a bellyful of Yukon gold, Black Hills gold, Sierra silver and a goodly supply of Tupelo honey, and she was not about to let a freak rainstorm keep her from delivering her share for the crown.

'Joachim is on his way,' came a crackling reply that sounded like Raul.

'Tell him to watch himself, the wind keeps changing.'

'I'll let him know.'

Matilda liked Joachim, although she teased him mercilessly. A small, stout Portuguese fellow, she knew that he'd contrived to lose the draw so as to be sure he was the one to crawl out into danger for his beloved captain.

She aimed the ship's nose down at the floating steel island, feeling every muscle in her body tense as the winds tried to push her on to another course. The altitude rudder was indeed good and stuck now and the *Madame Barbary* listed a little uncertainly.

Raul came into the wheelhouse, his black hair plastered to his face and neck and his shirt rain-splattered. He claimed to be Creole, of some nebulous royal lineage, but that didn't change the fact that she'd picked him up hitchhiking outside

Baton Rouge when the Feds were after him. She'd kept him on because he could cook, and that talent wasn't limited to his gumbo; he could make the most spectacular incendiary devices, often with only basic household goods. Raul was a godsend.

He also had a habit of knowing when he was needed, coming to her aid and never mentioning it to anyone else. This made him an ideal first mate.

Without a word, he came up behind Matilda and braced his left leg around her right, locking their bodies together at the hip. He took one half of the wheel and she the other. They could feel the tightening of one another's muscles and knew without speaking what needed to be done and when. It was an intimacy they shared – the only one, as Raul was about as interested in her as she was in him.

The wheel became manageable quite suddenly and nearly pulled them off balance as it tilted forward. Leaning back into their heels, they brought the nose back in line with the barge below.

'Joachim is back inside,' Michael, the youngest and newest member of the crew, reported over the address system.

The freighter-cum-airship mooring grew by slow increments in their vision. The ship swung to one side of it, then the other, leaving both Matilda and Raul to overcorrect and cause the cabin to sway wildly. A gale buoyed them up then let them drop a dozen or so yards. Swearing, Matilda pushed the engines hard, gunning them for short bursts to compensate for the rogue weather patterns. Had there been any sort of rhythm to the winds, she would have been happy, but the gusts came at random and drove the rain into their windows, first in one direction, then another.

She felt blisters rising beneath the calluses on her hands. Whatever pain Raul felt, he too buried it behind a mask of resolve as he worked in concert with his captain to deliver them to safety.

The deck came up fast as another downdraft knocked them towards the big boat below.

Matilda pulled down the address horn. 'This is gonna be bumpy, everyone hold on to something!'

Before she had even released the horn, the cabin impacted the deck of the carrier. They bounced, and both she and Raul desperately clutched the wheel. The second bounce was harder as the *Madame Barbary* came in slightly to one side and skidded. Somewhere below a lashing cord gave way with a sound like a gunshot. Although the crates held their fortune, Matilda hoped it was a cargo line and not one that held the airbag.

They scraped across the bleached wood deck as Matilda threw the engines into reverse.

'Easy, easy, Cap!' A shout came through the address, the whine of the engine nearly obliterating Birch the mechanic's voice. 'You're gonna burn us out!'

She eased the throttle closed just a bit. 'Happy now?'

He didn't answer and she suspected he hadn't heard. She rarely saw Birch out of the engine room, and when she did, it was usually the back of his head disappearing into a swap meet or a bar. He'd been the one who turned them on to the heist in the Dakota Territory, nabbing the prized multi-hued Black Hills Gold. The Black Hills were supposed to be sacred, but that didn't stop the government types from selling shares in their mining concern to dig the place up and bleed it dry of its precious metals. Birch could think of several dozen better uses of that gold than lining Union pockets, and he said as much, which was all that needed to be said. In fact, by dint of his having an opinion at all they sprang into action.

Matilda cursed the ease of that damned caper, when something that was so ripe for failure went off without a hitch, she knew there would be trouble further down the line. And so here it was and the blisters cracked and bled and she gripped the wheel even tighter, determined not to lose her ship or her crew. And would it be too much to ask that the cargo mostly make it through, as well?

'Cast the tie line!'

'Are you nuts?' Michael called back.

'You know how to swim?'

'Casting the tie line,' he muttered and clicked off.

The ship came to an all-too-abrupt halt, swinging it to starboard and knocking Matilda off her feet. Raul righted her with one arm while keeping his other hand on the wheel.

'Take it,' she gasped and went for the throttle. 'Hold on, Birch, you aren't gonna like this!' She dampened the port engine and opened the starboard, rocking the *Madame Barbary* into an uneasy equilibrium before clamping both engines shut.

The *Madame Barbary* slid a few more yards before grinding to a noisy halt. 'On your feet crew, we've got to inspect that cargo. This barge's people will be all over us in nothing flat. Now go!'

She followed her own orders, pushing open the now warped stair-plank and dashing out into the rain. Crates lay strewn everywhere and billows of steam poured from the engines. Joachim and Michael had scurried out and were assembling the ship's crane. Raul was on her heels, following up behind the two and picking up the pieces of metal and ore that fanned out around them. If the freighter's crew knew what cargo they carried, they'd be robbed blind by morning, and that's if they were lucky. Matilda heard tell of airship crews found on drifting dirigibles, throats cut and cargoes long gone, and she didn't fancy herself as a statistic.

She scanned the decks, nodding with satisfaction as her crew heaved crates on to the sturdiest dolly they had, and then turned back to the ship. The airbag had lost two of its lashings but the rest looked intact; it was nothing Birch couldn't fix given ample time and supplies. The engines were another story, however, and she hoped they only looked the worse for wear. She joined Raul in scrap collection and counted the crates.

'We're missing a couple,' she said.

He nodded. 'Down in the drink, I'm sure. Must have come lose in that first hit.'

'Or when we lost the tarp.'

He agreed. 'No telling.'

'You know which ones are gone?'

'Not the crates with the Black Hills, those are strapped to the underdeck and still safe. Most likely the silver, some of it anyway. Two out of twenty-six ain't bad.'

She sighed. 'Yeah, I just hate when it goes completely to waste, y'know? None but mermaids are going to be enjoying that now.'

'Maybe Birch has some trick to get us down there, a diving bell or something.'

Matilda shrugged and glanced up at the still steaming engine room. 'Perhaps, but I won't be asking him until tomorrow at least. Why don't you go and see if you can get some chow started. I'll finish up out here. Everyone could use a hot meal and a good night's rest after this.'

'Yes'm.' He dropped the handful of nuggets into her waiting hands and jogged back up the banged-up stairs.

A steaming bowl of jambalaya and brown rice waited for her in the mess hall. She volunteered for KP duty and sent Raul on first watch and the others to their racks. The dish water stung her torn-up hands, but it gave her time to decompress from a long night that was just getting started. Even though the others would take the shifts through the night, Matilda knew she wouldn't sleep. It wasn't that she didn't trust her crew, because she did, with her life; it was that she knew how incredibly clever and resourceful they were and how that trait was shared amongst many airship crews – and they weren't the only dirigible docked that night.

She must have dozed off at some point, though, because Raul had to shake her shoulders hard to wake her.

'The registrar is here,' he said. 'She wants you to sign.'

Matilda yawned, trying to remember how she'd got back to her quarters. A vague memory of an exhausted shamble from the kitchen surfaced and she found the dish towel on the pillow. 'She couldn't take yours?'

'Nope. She was real specific. She needs to see you and *just you.*'

'I see.' That couldn't bode well. 'OK, then, I'll take care of it.' She stretched and made her way casually down the stairs, expecting she didn't know what, but it wasn't a slim redhead in cargo pants and a shirtwaist. 'Can I help you?'

'Are you Captain Romero?' The woman had a faint trace of an Irish accent as she asked a question to which she already seemed to know the answer. Her blue eyes caught the dim morning's light and shone.

Matilda composed herself. 'Sure am.' She reached for the proffered clipboard.

'You did a number on the *Alma de Bretteville* decks, here, y'know.' The young woman nearly pouted. Matilda's heart raced, and not just from anxiety.

'Well, the storm last night ... I'm sure you have insurance ...' She put her hand into one of the deep pockets of her coat, feeling for a small bag of gold nuggets she kept on hand for just such a bribe emergency. 'Are you the one in charge of deck maintenance?'

'No.'

'Ah, well then, perhaps I could speak to the individual in charge of that and, um, work it out with them?' Matilda plucked a single nugget the size of an almond out of the bag.

The registrar's ginger brows crinkled with confusion. 'I'll send someone along. I'll still need your signature, though. And your docking fee.'

'But of course!' Matilda got her hands on the clipboard and signed her name. She passed the nugget over when she returned the pen and dug into her pants pocket for the docking fee. 'Which currency are you accepting? Union or Imperial?'

'Imperial.'

'Very good.' Matilda took out fifty cents and laid the four coins into the registrar's narrow palm, letting her fingertips graze her skin. 'That should be right, don't you think?'

The registrar pressed her lips together and looked confused. 'Fifty cents is the fee, yes. And, uh ...' She looked helplessly at the nugget still in her other hand.

'Are you new here?'

Sighing, the registrar dropped the nugget into her pocket and dumped the coins into the small box fixed to the bottom of the clipboard.

'I guess not.'

'Thanks,' she replied.

Silence came down on them, heavy and immovable. Matilda's mouth went dry and she was suddenly at a total loss for what to say. The redhead made a great show of checking over the paperwork, lingering there, one hip jutted out as she rested the clipboard against it.

Matilda's heart raced.

Finally the young woman straightened up and nodded her head. 'That'll do, I suppose.'

'Yeah. And . . . you know . . . if you need anything else, um, any other information or anything at all, really, I'll be right here. Because, you know, with the damages to the engines, we're going to be here a while. A little while anyway.' She rambled to a halt and shut her mouth with an audible click.

The registrar nodded again. 'I'll make a note of it.' She turned quickly on her heel and hustled back to the office at the far end of the old freighter.

Matilda shivered.

'Don't get in over your head, Captain,' Raul said, coming up behind her in time to watch her watch the registrar walk away.

'I won't,' she promised, but without much sincerity.

Over lunch, Birch figured it would take at least a week for him to fix the ship on his own. 'But if I could get some help, some decent, qualified help, I can have us off again in two days.'

Matilda nodded. 'I'll see what I can do. There should be a tea for the captains this afternoon, if this bucket is holding to Imperial traditions.'

The *Alma de Bretteville* did, indeed, hold with Imperial tradition and Matilda found herself in the company of the captains from the other four docked dirigibles. The winsome redhead was also there, making small talk and generally playing hostess.

Matilda tried to ignore her as she chit-chatted with the other captains, arranging some help for the wounded *Madame Barbary*. It wouldn't cost much; she downplayed their cargo, avoided promising favours and passed out a few of the smaller nuggets in her pocket. She was well-liked among the captains and it was days like this that she appreciated it.

As she went back for a second scone, the redhead hovered by the clotted cream.

'I'm sorry, we weren't properly introduced,' Matilda offered her hand. 'And we may not have got off to the best start. I'm Matilda.'

'Yes, I know.'

'Well, yeah. And you?'

'Deirdre O'Rourke.' She shook hands slightly hesitantly. 'A pleasure.'

Oh, yes, it is, thought Matilda dreamily. You have such soft hands. And they were, too, slender and smooth with neatly trimmed nails and nary a callous or ragged cuticle to be seen. She was immediately and ridiculously jealous. Not to mention, simultaneously imagining what fun such soft fingers might be.

Sweat broke out across her brow and her palm and she delicately extricated herself from the embarrassingly overlong handshake. 'Excuse me.'

Deirdre blushed, and instead of wiping her palm against her pants leg, she clasped her hands together as if they were lonely for companionship already.

When they spoke, they ran over one another's words.

'I'm sorry,' Matilda said, 'you were saying?'

'Oh, it was nothing, just that I ought to call the kitchen staff, it's time to clean up.'

'Ah. Yes, it is, isn't it?'

'And that it was so good to meet you, Matilda. After having heard so much about you, I mean. You're quite famous. I hope you enjoyed your tea.' She ducked her head in something that was part nod, part bow and part total discomfiture, and left the small galley in a hurry.

'Yeah,' Matilda murmured to Deirdre's receding form. 'I did, and I was going to ask you if you wanted to do it again sometime, only with just us . . .'

But there was no one to hear her.

When she returned to the *Madame Barbary*, Matilda found that a motley band of engineers had already descended on the engine room and were under the whip of Birch. Michael, Joachim, and even Raul had also been mobilized to help.

Matilda invited the whole work crew and their captains for dinner and Raul fed them well with gumbo and fresh bread. Although they began with ruthless teasing, especially on the subject of the halting, failed flirtation the other captains had witnessed over tea, they took to telling less embarrassing stories, as these types of gatherings always do. A small knock on the main door roused Matilda from her chair, and she bid Michael to finish the tale of the time they'd been nearly killed by geese during a *foie gras* heist.

'Lucky for us,' he said, settling into the tone reserved for only the most epic of stories, 'the bastards were stuffed to the gills with corn. They managed to corner us, but . . .'

Outside on the scarred dock, Deirdre waited, looking sheepish and likely to turn around and walk away at any moment.

'Well, hello there. Can I interest you in some supper?'

'Me?'

Matilda leaned out, looked right and looked left. 'Yup, you'd be the only one on my porch.'

'Oh. Yes. I suppose I am.' She blushed and it brought out her freckles.

Matilda steadied herself. 'Is this an official visit or a social call?'

'Did you say something, earlier? Um . . . about maybe having some dinner, or something . . . together?'

'I might have. We've got company presently, but there are an awful lot of quiet corners on my ship where a couple of bodies could just have a nice dinner and chat.'

'So long as I wouldn't be imposing, especially if you're engaged in . . . *captainly* things.'

'Come on in, before the boys drink all the beer.'

'You've got beer?'

'Captain Shelby of the *Siren Song*,' Matilda pointed at the next airship, flying a flag of a scantily clad mermaid. 'He's got a connection over at Anchor Steam.'

Deirdre followed, head lowered, shyly. 'As long as it isn't any trouble.'

'Bah, no trouble at all. A treat, actually. I was thinking you didn't like me.'

'What? I . . . no, I mean, yes, I mean . . . I didn't mean to give you that impression.'

In the crowded galley, the others gave a cheer at Matilda's return.

'I was just getting to the good part, Cap,' Michael told her. 'Where Raul leaps in with that fillet knife.'

'You go ahead and finish the tale; I like the way you tell it.'

She set Deirdre down with her in the corner at a tiny tin table that folded out from the wall.

It was a cosy fit.

'So,' Matilda said.

'So,' Deirdre replied and sipped her beer from a porcelain-enamelled cup.

They sat watching one another over the steaming bowls of gumbo that slowly cooled as the revelry continued around them.

'So, I'm famous?'

Deirdre took a big spoonful of her neglected gumbo and nodded. 'There aren't that many airship captains with your . . . specific qualifications.'

'You mean, being a woman?'

'Yes, that or . . . your daring, either. Did you really manage to take a Union goldship?'

'Oh, no. Not one. Three.'

'Three?'

Matilda grinned. 'Three.'

'And they also say . . .' She trailed off and blushed to her toes.

'What do they say?' Matilda purred teasingly.

Deirdre opened her mouth, but no words came out of it. She sputtered and turned away, tugging on a lock of hair and digging furiously into her bowl.

'Oh, I see. That explains that, doesn't it?'

'I have no idea what you mean.'

'Don't you? Would you like a tour of the ship?'

Deirdre seemed to relish the change of subject. 'That would be lovely.'

They began in the wheelhouse.

'How did you come by her? The ship, I mean?'

'Same way every captain does, I suspect; I won her in a poker game.'

'You did?'

'Actually, no. I'm kidding. I bought her title at a pawn shop and the rest is history. The title was probably lost in a poker game, though.'

Deirdre laughed and wandered around the helm, looking at the controls.

'Deirdre,' Matilda touched her shoulder. 'You, uh . . . You seemed a bit intrigued by some certain rumours about me.'

She feigned disinterest. 'Rumours? Nah, I never listen to those.' She avoided Matilda's earnest gaze. 'I think I should go.'

'Please don't.' Matilda gently planted a kiss on her freckled cheek. 'It's true. I like girls. And I particularly like *you*.'

'Ah.' Deirdre stared at her boots.

'Is that OK?'

She frowned. 'I don't know. This isn't going at all like I thought it might.'

'And how did you imagine it going?'

'Without so much muddling through. I thought maybe you'd catch on and just sort of sweep me off my feet and into your bed . . .' Her eyes widened and she clapped her hand over her mouth.

Matilda laughed. 'Throw one milkmaid down in the straw and everyone thinks you're the female Casanova!'

'I should probably get back, then. Good night.'

'Not so fast! I hate to rob a girl of a hard-won fantasy.'

Deirdre shook her head. 'No, it's not necessary, I'm quite all right. I don't need to be a conquest just for the sake of—'

Matilda stopped her with a kiss. 'I was talking about *me*.'

'Oh. You were? About . . . me?'

She nodded. 'You leave quite a first impression.'

'I'm no fearsome privateer, I'm just a clerk on a mooring ship.'

'It is my understanding that mooring-ship clerks make the best lovers.' Matilda breathed against her ear, licking the lobe gently. 'It's all that *attention to detail*.'

Deirdre stiffened but did not step away; she looked up through her ginger lashes. 'We've only just met.'

'So true. Lovemaking in the wheelhouse needs to be reserved for the second date at least. Let's go to my quarters.'

When they found themselves in the captain's quarters, Deirdre began to chatter nervously.

'This is a very nice ship, wonderfully laid out and so cosy.'

Matilda brushed the backs of her fingers against Deirdre's cheek. 'Thanks. I've worked hard on it.'

'It's quite nice.'

'Thank you,' she stepped closer. Matilda pressed her lips against Deirdre's forehead. 'A much better place to start, don't you think? Lots of privacy. Lots of pillows.'

Deirdre tilted her face upwards to meet Matilda's mouth, sharing a kiss that surprised them both with its heat. They stepped back from one another, hearts racing.

'Well, now.' Matilda laughed and toyed with the delicate curls around Deirdre's face. 'That was delightful. We must do it again sometime. Perhaps lying down?'

Deirdre swallowed audibly. 'I've been away too long, I have to get back to the office. I'm on duty tonight,' she stammered, trembling. 'You know, with the clipboard.'

'Yes, of course. Let me walk you out.'

They strolled together through the rest of the ship and down the battered stairs. It was a damp evening, but clear, with a brisk wind whipping up the waves in the bay. The lights of San Francisco glimmered on one side and Oakland shone on the other.

'Have a good night, Deirdre,' Matilda said, lingering at the foot of the stairs.

'Thank you – you, too.' She didn't move right away, either.

They stood there in foot-shuffling embarrassment, studiously not looking at one another. Matilda put her hand on Deirdre's forearm. 'Will I see you tomorrow?'

'I hope so.'

'So, I haven't frightened you off. Excellent. Goodnight, Deirdre.' Matilda kissed her good night, gently, but with a sea of passion walled up behind it.

'Yeah.' And when Deirdre walked away from the *Madame Barbary*, Matilda didn't think her feet were touching the deck.

Back in the mess, the other captains and engineers hooted and cheered. She raised her hands for silence and bid them good night without saying a thing about Deirdre.

In the morning, Matilda sauntered into the wheelhouse and took Raul aside. 'I am going to see about renting a boat to bring the goods over to the city.'

He nodded. 'Let me know when. I'll come along.'

'Only if Birch can spare you.' She wagged a finger at him.

'I'm not going to leave you to a bunch of hired goons; not with our score of the century.'

'When you've finished picking lentils out of the fireplace, then you can go to the ball, Cinderella.'

He laughed. 'I'll go help Birch. Just holler before you go, I'm sure by then he can spare me.'

She waved and went back to the main building, enjoying the sunlight breaking through the silvery clouds.

A slender Asian fellow sipped tea and lounged at the counter.

'I need to rent a boat.'

He glanced up, swirled his tea, took another long drink and finally dragged out a scarred leather ledger. 'What needs transport?'

'Crates. Several. Heavy.'

'What's in the crates?'

'Lead,' she answered.

'How many?'

'About a dozen, I'd say.'

'A dozen crates of lead?'

'Factory.' She shrugged. 'I don't ask; I just bring the goods.'

'Fair enough.' He flipped through the ledger. 'I can rent you the *Sutro*, it's a converted trawler.'

'Sounds good. Can two people manage it?'

'Oh yes.'

'What's the deposit?'

'Two dollars. Plus a babysitter.'

'A what?'

He smacked a brass table bell with the palm of his hand. Deirdre climbed up the spiral staircase from the level below and they both stared in mute surprise.

'Good morning,' Matilda said, recovering her voice with a smile.

Deirdre's blue eyes widened. 'Hello, Captain.'

'So glad you'll be my escort this morning.'

Deirdre flushed. 'I'm glad that you're glad.' She looked away quickly. 'I'll have the crane guys meet us at your vessel in ten minutes, that should be ample time for you, yes?'

'Plenty, yes. See you then.' Matilda smiled and strolled back to the *Madame Barbary*.

Birch had indeed finished with Raul, and the First Mate was already counting out the Imperial share and crating it to be moved off the *Madame Barbary*.

'We're getting a boat in just a few minutes.'

'Good,' Raul replied, 'a few more minutes are all I need.' He hammered the last lid tightly shut and shoved it aside with the others. 'Including all the honey, which was His Maj's special request, we have eleven crates in total.'

'Perfect. Here come the fellows with the moving truck.'

The six bulky men that came over to them could have been plucked from any dock on the Mediterranean at any time in history with their thick, dark hair and deeply tanned complexions. They said nothing as they shoved, lifted and hauled the wooden crates by way of a large, rolling crane from the deck of the *Alma de Bretteville* and on to the *Sutro*. They sang out a chant to accompany their work. More than once the big machine looked like it would slip its chucks and careen off the barge's deck and into the bay, but the crane held firm until the last of the crates was safely deposited on to the boat.

Matilda and Deirdre supervised from the *Sutro*'s deck and Raul kept tabs up top. Satisfied, he tipped the six men and they rolled the heavy crane away. Raul deftly climbed down the ladder and made for the wheelhouse to take the helm, but Matilda stopped him.

'I think I can handle this on my own.'

'But, Captain!'

'Nothing is going to happen to me, or to the loot. Trust me.'

'I do, but . . .' His hazel eyes wandered from her to Deirdre. 'Are you sure this is a good idea?'

She said nothing, but gave him a glance that silenced him.

'Yes, ma'am.' He saluted her and left the wheelhouse. At her signal, Raul released the fat knot in the rope that lashed the *Sutro* to the *Alma de Bretteville*. The little boat's engines protested at first, but Matilda prevailed in coaxing them to life and they were away.

The main bayside harbour of San Francisco was but a quick jaunt from the freighter, but even a quick jaunt over choppy water left both of them wet and a little woozy. Matilda turned the collar of her thick coat up over her ears and gathered Deirdre close by. The *Sutro*'s windows apparently didn't close all the way and left the wheelhouse nearly as wet as the deck. Matilda didn't exactly dislike the water, she just wasn't a fan of the bone-chilling damp of the wind-driven spray. Deirdre said nothing, but leaned appreciatively against Matilda and wrapped her knitted scarf around her face.

They came up on the harbour in less than fifteen minutes and made their much slower way along the quay that led to the Imperial Palace. They docked at a pleasant loading area in the presence of two sturdy-looking Chinese guards. The guards inspected the boat and the crates briefly. Matilda gave them each a tiny nugget and asked for their help in offloading. One swung the free-arm crane in their direction and the other went to fetch a flatbed cart. Deirdre watched and waited, saying nothing but staying close.

A third guard arrived to help with the offload. He then turned to escort them as the other two heaved the creaking cart. A light drizzle crept up on them and made the march to the palace – a converted hotel – a soggy one. In the courtyard, two trumpets announced them with a thrilling fanfare while a buxom matron, who looked more like a beer wench than a lady-in-waiting, escorted them into the reception salon itself.

'Have you ever been in here before,' Matilda asked Deirdre.

'No,' she answered. 'Just seen pictures.'

'Same here. Have you ever met the Emperor?'

'No. Have you?'

Matilda shook her head. 'Nah, I mailed away for this.' She took out her letter of marque.

'Then I suppose this will be an adventure for us both, won't it?'

The palace still looked very much like a hotel, with a grand lobby sprouting clusters of chairs, low tables like tuffets in a meadow, and a staff of heralds idling at what used to be the front desk. The matron waved one over, whispered in his ear and sent him off ahead, where he ducked into what used to be a small function space.

They heard their names clearly and accurately announced. Deirdre looked impressed.

Matilda had seen many photographs of the Emperor, but she was quite shocked to see how small he was, barely five foot five. As he stood and addressed them, though, his short stature was entirely forgotten.

'Citizens.' His voice carried through the salon. 'I bid you fair welcome!'

Matilda bowed and Deirdre curtsied, an interesting task in cargo pants.

'Your Imperial Majesty,' Matilda began, 'we have come from all corners of the country and brought you a tribute worthy of your magnificence.' She snapped her fingers at the guard with the cart.

Behind her, she heard Deirdre's whisper, 'You're good!'

Matilda came forward and bowed, holding out a box that contained samples of what she'd brought: the various sorts of gold, the silver and the honey.

From between her eyelashes, she saw Norton's bearded face brighten.

'You've done it!' He cried, coming forward more like an excited child than a man of majesty. 'I mean, lots of folk said they were going to, and I signed lots of those letters, but you're the first one who has returned with tribute. Brilliant!' He clapped his small, square hands together and reached into the box. He did not put a finger on any of the precious metals, but instead brought forth the jar of honey. The warm light made it glow perfectly amber in the glass, and the courtiers made appreciative noises. 'I can tell just by the look of it that it's real Tupelo. The finest honey in the world.' He turned the jar over in his hands and watched the air bubble slowly morph and move. 'My mother used to serve this on sourdough.' He spoke in strange tones, like one remembering a dream.

Matilda set the box down with a grin and, flashing a wink at Deirdre, took one last thing from her pocket: a small, oblong, linen-wrapped parcel. She untied the purple silk ribbon that held it, and the linen fell away to reveal an elegant, golden soup spoon. Kneeling, she offered it up on the palms of her hands.

The Emperor smiled and took the spoon, and an attendant opened the jar with a flourish. He stabbed the spoon into the jar and popped it into his mouth with gusto. When his eyes shut with delight, Matilda knew she had succeeded.

'Madame Privateer,' he said, with words garbled by honey, 'we give you the highest commendation a courtier can receive, a commendation begun by the great Emperor Napoleon, a Knighthood in the Order of the Honeybee.' He waved the dripping spoon as if it was a sceptre and bestowed a sticky glob on each of her shoulders. 'Rise, Dame Tupelo.'

Matilda did as she was bid and, although she stood on the step below him, looked the Emperor right in the eye. 'I accept with gratitude, my liege.'

'Excellent!' He set the honey aside and rifled through the rest of the box. 'Well now! Would you get a load of this!' He let the nuggets and coins pass through his fingers and then counted the crates behind them. 'So how much is honey?'

'Five out of the eleven,' she said. 'Two crates each of Yukon gold, Black Hills gold and Sierra silver.'

'All raided from Union ships?'

'Aye.'

'Brilliant! Where's your ship?'

'Docked at the *Alma de Bretteville*.' Matilda nodded at Deirdre, who curtsied once more.

Norton's smile was sly. 'I tell you what, we shall make a proclamation that your ship . . . what's it called?'

'The *Madame Barbary*.'

'Yes, yes, we proclaim that the *Madame Barbary* shall have free space to dock and free leave to fly over my fair city. And the next time you come – tomorrow, what say you? – you must leave her with my engineers for a proper Imperial paint job. She'll be an auxiliary member of the corps, that way, you know.' He winked and laughed. 'I do so love having another person around to rely on.'

It was a mixed blessing, Matilda realized, but one with which she could live. In fact, she'd have flown into battle to aid the Emperor already, regardless of any commendations or knighthoods. She just liked him too much not to want to fight for him. She suspected she was a lot like Joachim in that regard.

He called for the medal that went with the honour and raised a toast as the thing was brought – a red striped ribbon from which hung a brass gear affixed with a gilded honeybee charm.

He pinned it to Matilda's coat himself, smearing the fine wool with even more honey.

'There, now you look like a proper knight.' The Emperor retreated with his jar of honey, dismissing Matilda and her companions as he did so. The two palace dogs, Boomer and Lazarus, woke from their slumber at the commotion and went begging at Norton's feet.

Matilda and Deirdre bowed and backed out of the presence chamber.

Out in the drizzly courtyard, Deirdre swore good-naturedly. 'Honey? It was about *honey*?'

'I'm sure he was very interested in the gold and silver as well,' Matilda said, 'but mostly it was the honey. He's a funny little man, but he's the Imperial Majesty.' She touched the medal on her sticky lapel with pride.

'I had no idea you were such an Imperial supporter. I mean, I suspected, seeing as how you're a registered privateer, but I didn't know the sentiment ran so deep.'

'When a man loses his life savings and becomes destitute, but he doesn't go lie in the gutter and feel sorry for himself, and instead declares himself Emperor, that's worth a little respect. And the beauty of San Francisco is that they believe him and worship him.'

Deirdre nodded. 'And coincidently, it works in California's favour, seeing as how they never wanted to stay in the Union, what with the state being on the far side of society and the richest state on this continent. She's all on her own out here and making the best of it. That's why I came here.' She said the last like a confession. 'I'm a deserter. Left the Union airship corps for this place.'

'If you aren't pleased with your digs on the *Alma de Bretteville*, I am sure we could find you a bunk on the *Madame Barbary*, especially seeing as you're a Union deserter and Imperial supporter. You'll fit right in.'

Deirdre demurred as she let Matilda step into the boat. 'I'm not too sure about airships. I track them, I don't fly them.'

'Nonsense! It isn't any harder than boating.'

She raised an eyebrow. 'You've got up and down in an airship!'

'Details.'

About halfway back to the barge, Matilda cut the engines and let them drift. The rocky outcrop of Alcatraz vanished behind the undulating hills of Angel Island, while fog squeezed through the narrow channel of the Golden Gate. Matilda stepped out on to the deck as the *Sutro* bobbed in the misty rain.

Deirdre waited a moment in the wheelhouse doorway before joining her out in the damp air. 'So, you'll be taking off after you've got your ship fixed up, then?'

Matilda nodded. 'They should be finished in the morning. The boys will want a chance to spend their money, so we were thinking of docking over in the East Bay, but since we've got a fly-over pass, we might stay in the City.'

'I could arrange for you to stay on at the *Alma de Bretteville* as long as you like, you know, I have enough clout. And I'd make sure you have access to a boat to get you across the bay, in either direction.'

'You sound like you want me to stay on a bit longer.'

'Well, we've only just met. And I thought that we might . . .' Deirdre grew shy again suddenly.

'Might what?'

She swore under her breath, took Matilda's face between her palms and kissed her meaningfully on the mouth. Matilda wrapped her arms around Deirdre's lithe body, and pulled her close as Deirdre relaxed into the embrace. For a long moment, they stayed that way, lips pressed together and oblivious to all else.

'What now?' There was a fragile note of hope in Deirdre's voice. She stood easily on the deck, moving with the pitch of the water, perfectly balanced from many years aboard boats.

Matilda watched Deirdre's smile and her heart sank just a bit. She was a soul who belonged to the water, just as she belonged to the sky.

Matilda sighed. 'I don't know. I won't know until we get back to the *Alma de Bretteville*. But until then . . .'

She pulled Deirdre close once more and her cold fingers unclasped the belt at the woman's waist. The buttons of the cargo pants gave her some trouble. 'A little help?'

Laughing, Deirdre said, 'I'm going to make you work for this.' And she busied herself reaching inside Matilda's coat for the waistband lacings she knew kept the captain's breeches on. The boat dipped and rose, knocking Matilda off balance more than once or twice. The wet fabrics clung to them both, and when finally they had given way, the chill air made them both tremble.

They were soon warm enough, though.

On the *Alma de Bretteville*, Matilda helped Deirdre out of the boat and walked her to the office to sign the *Sutro* back in. Her nerves sang like violins and she was remarkably wired for someone who'd just had her ashes hauled. All she could imagine was more of Deirdre, of stripping her naked on a soft bed – one that wasn't moving – and doing every last little trick she'd ever learned to her. But at the door, Deirdre gave her only a chaste kiss and bid her goodnight.

'But, darling!'

'Don't. This isn't going to work and you damn well know it,' she'd said shortly. 'I can't. You can't. *We* can't. You said it yourself, we're from different worlds.'

'I didn't say that.'

'No? Well you thought it awfully loud, then. It's true. You belong to the air, I belong to the water.'

'But there is a place where the ocean and the sky always meet.'

'The horizon. But it's a place we can never go. Every time you think you're there, it's always that much farther away. No matter how you chase it, it runs from you.'

'Do you plan on running?'

'Only if you plan on chasing.' And she closed the door between them, leaving Matilda on the doorstep in the darkening afternoon.

Raul had been busy. He'd broken out their ration of honey and made glazed chicken, sweetcorn bread and baklava. The crew revelled late into the night and made round after round of cheers in Matilda's honour. She wished she could share their merriment, but her memory hung on to the sensations of Deirdre's body, and each bite she ate tasted of the registrar's sweetness.

Come morning, as the patchy sun scattered gleaming shapes on the grey water, the *Madame Barbary* prepared to take her leave and fulfill her Imperial command.

Matilda stood on the dock of the *Alma de Bretteville* in her bare feet, feeling the wet wind rake through her hair. As they prepared to lift off, there was no darling redhead to be seen. Finally, she stepped up on to the bent stair, wondering if the Imperial Airship Works might be able to fix up the hatch – even before the crash it hadn't worked properly. She realized, as she stood there, imagining the railing new and whole, what she was really doing: waiting for Deirdre.

Matilda radioed in to the bridge of the *Alma de Bretteville*. 'The *Madame Barbary* is taking her leave.'

'Roger,' replied a familiar voice. 'The *Alma de Bretteville* bids you fair winds and safe travel and a sincere wish to see you back again. And I mean that.'

'Good, because I seem to have misplaced my heart, would you be so kind as to keep a lookout for it?'

A long pause followed. 'Aye,' Deirdre said finally, and the connection ended.

'Well, Captain?' Raul said.

'Set course for the Imperial Airship Works and let's get going.'

'Not bringing the redhead?'

'Not this time.'

He glanced out the window. 'Next time, perhaps?'

'I hope so.'

They lifted away from the scratched and battered deck. Matilda wanted to feel guilty about the damage she had done, but she had left a nice tip, not to mention the prize that lay at the bottom of the bay for any soul clever enough to retrieve it. As they drifted over the ferry building, Matilda looked back. There on the freighter in the bay, a tiny figure stood at the edge of the deck, waving.

Raul brought over some biscuits, smothered in honey. He saluted and took the wheel.

Matilda waved back, not sure if Deirdre could see her. But she was already plotting a reason to return to the *Alma de Bretteville*, because as she watched, the bay seemed to rise and the sky seemed to lower, catching the old freighter between the two and leaving it sitting just on the horizon.

THE QUEEN AND THE CAMBION

Rick Bowes

'Silly Billy, the Sailor King,' some called King William IV of
Great Britain. But never, of course, to his royal face. Then it
was always, 'Yes, sire,' and, 'As Your Majesty wishes!'

Because certain adults responsible for her care didn't watch
their words in front of a child, the king's young niece, and heir
to his throne, heard such things said, and it angered her.
Princess Victoria liked her uncle and knew that King William
IV always treated her as nicely as a boozy, confused, former
sea captain of a monarch could be expected to, and much of
the time rather better.

Often when she greeted him he would lean forward, slip a
secret gift into her hands and whisper something like,
'Discovered this in the late King your grandfather's desk at
Windsor.'

These, generally, were small items – trinkets, jewels, memen-
tos, long-ago tributes from minor potentates that he'd found in
the huge half-used royal palaces, stuck in his pocket and as
often as not remembered to give to his niece.

The one she found most fascinating was a piece of very
ancient parchment that someone had pressed under glass
hundreds of years earlier. This came into her possession one
day when she was twelve, as King William passed Victoria and
her governess on his way to the royal coach.

His Britannic Majesty paused and said in her ear, 'It's a
spell, little cub. Put your paw in mine.'

Victoria felt something in her hand and slipped it into a
pouch under her cloak while the Sailor King lurched by as
though he was walking the quarterdeck of a ship in rough

water. 'Every ruler of this island has had it and many of us have invoked it,' he mumbled while climbing the carriage steps.

She followed him. 'To use in times of great danger to Britain?' she whispered.

He leaned out the window. 'Or on a day of doldrums and no wind in the sails,' he roared, as if she was up in a crow's nest, his face as red as semi-rare roast beef. 'You'll be the monarch and damn all who'd say you no.'

Victoria didn't take the gift from under her cloak until she was quite alone in the library of the dark and dreary palace at Kensington. It's where she lived under the intense care of her mother, the widowed Duchess of Kent, a German lady, and Sir John Conroy, a handsome enough Irish army officer of good family.

The Duchess had appointed Conroy comptroller of her household, and between them they tried to make sure the princess had no independence at all. Victoria really only got out of their sight when King Billy summoned her to the Royal Court.

Nobody at Kensington ever used the library. She went to the far end of that long room, lined with portraits of the obscure daughters and younger sons of various British kings, many with their plump consorts and empty-eyed children. Victoria pushed aside a full-length curtain, and in the waning daylight looked at the page. She deciphered a bit of the script and discovered words in Latin that she knew. She saw the name Arturus, which made her gasp. Other words just seemed to be a collection of letters.

Then, for fear that someone was coming, she hid it away behind a shelf full of books of sermons by long-dead clergymen. It's where she kept some other secret possessions, for she was allowed very little privacy.

She knew the pronunciation for the Latin, and by copying several of the other words and showing them to her language tutor, she discovered they were Welsh. Her music teacher, born in Wales, taught her some pronunciation, but became too curious about a few of the words she showed him. Victoria then sought out the old stable master, who spoke the language, including some of the ancient tongue, and could read and write a bit, too. He was honoured and kept her secret when the princess practised with him.

One evening, when she had learned all the words and her guardians were busy, Victoria went to the library, took out the page and slowly read it aloud.

She wasn't quite finished when a silver light shone on the dusty shelves and paintings. Before her was a mountaintop with the sun shining through clouds. In the air, heading her way, sailed a man who rode the wind as another might a horse.

In his hand was the black staff topped with a dragon's head. His grey cloak and robes showed the golden moon in all its phases. His white hair and beard whipped about as the wind brought him to the mountaintop. At the moment he alighted, he noticed Victoria, and a look of such vexation came over his face that she stumbled on the words and couldn't immediately repeat them. He and the mountaintop faded from her sight. She, however, remembered what she'd seen.

Victoria was no scholar, but the library at Kensington Palace did contain certain old volumes, and she read all she could find about Arthur, and especially about Merlin.

An observant child like Victoria knew John Conroy was more than the Duchess's comptroller. She understood that it was his idea to keep her isolated and to have her every move watched, and from an early age she knew why.

She heard her uncle tell someone in confidence, but with a voice that could carry over wind, waves and cannon fire, 'The mad old man, my father, King George that was, had a coach load and more of us sons. But in the event, only my brother Kent produced an heir, fair, square and legitimate before he died. So the little girl over there stands to inherit the crown when I go under.'

If the King did 'go under' before she was eighteen, Victoria knew, her mother would be Regent. The Duchess of Kent would control her daughter and the Royal Court, and Conroy would control the Duchess.

In the winter before her eighteenth birthday, five years after he gave her the spell, King William became very ill. But even in sickness, he remembered what the Duchess and Conroy were up to, and though his condition was grave, he resolutely refused to die.

On 24 May 1837, Victoria would become eighteen. On 22 May, the king was in a coma, and the Duchess and her comptroller had a plan.

From a window of the library at Kensington Palace, Victoria saw carriages drive up through a mid-spring drizzle and saw figures in black emerge. She recognized men that Conroy knew: several hungry attorneys, a minor cabinet minister, a rural justice and the secretary of a bishop who believed he should have been an archbishop. They gathered in Conroy's offices downstairs.

Because the servants were loyal, the princess knew that a document had been prepared in which Victoria would cite her own youth and foolishness and beg that her mother (and her mother's 'wise advisor') be regent until she was twenty-one.

Even those who admired Victoria would not have said the Princess was brilliant, but neither was she dull or naive. She knew how much damage the conspirators would be able to do in three years of regency. She might never become free. All they needed was her signature.

Understanding what was afoot, Victoria went to the shelf where the manuscript page was hidden. She wondered if she was entitled to do this before she was actually the monarch, and if the old wizard would be as angry like the last time.

Victoria heard footsteps on the stairs. She looked at the pictures of her obscure and forgotten ancestors, all exiled to the library, and made her choice.

The door at the other end of the library opened, and the Duchess and Conroy entered with half a dozen very solemn men.

'My dearest daughter, we have been trying to decide how best to protect you,' said her mother.

By the light of three candles, Victoria stood firm and recited the Latin, rolling out the Welsh syllables the way she'd been taught.

The Duchess and her accomplice exchanged glances – madness was commonplace in the British dynasty; George III had been so mad that a regent had been appointed. They started towards Victoria, then stopped and stared. She turned and saw what they did: a great stone hall lit by shafts of sun through tall windows. The light fell on figures, including a big man crowned and sitting on a throne. Victoria saw again the tall figure in robes adorned with golden moons in all their phases. In his hand was the black staff topped with a dragon's head. This time his hair and beard were iron grey not white. He shot the king a look of intense irritation. The king avoided his stare and seemed a bit amused.

Merlin strode out of the court at Camelot and the royal hall vanished behind him. Under his breath he muttered, 'A curse upon the day I was so addled as to make any oath to serve at the beck and call of every halfwit or lunatic who planted a royal behind on the throne of Britain.' Then he realized who had summoned him to this dim and dusty place, and his face softened just a bit. Not a monarch yet, to judge by her attire. But she would be soon enough.

Victoria gestured towards the people gaping at him. Merlin was accustomed to those who tried to seize power using bloody axes, not pieces of paper. But a wizard understands the cooing of the dove, the howl of the wolf and the usurper's greed. He levelled his staff and blue flames leaped forth.

The documents Conroy held caught fire and he dropped them. The red wig on one attorney and the ruffled cuffs of the bishop's secretary also ignited. Since none of them would ever admit to having been there, none would ever have to describe how they fled, the men snuffing out flames, barely pausing to let the Duchess go first.

When they were gone, Merlin erased the fire with a casual wave. Easy enough, he thought. Nothing like Hastings or the Battle of Britain. Shortly he'd be back in Camelot giving the king a piece of his mind.

'Lord Merlin,' the young princess began. 'We thank you.'

A wizard understands a bee and a queen equally, and both can understand a wizard. Merlin spoke and she heard the word 'Majesty' in her head. He dropped to one knee and kissed her hand. For young Victoria, this was their first meeting. For Merlin it was not.

Time was a path that crossed itself again and again, and memory could be prophecy. Later in her life, and earlier in his, this queen would summon him.

He had a certain affection for her, but in his lifetime he'd already served all four of the Richards, five or six of the Henrys, the first Elizabeth, the ever-tiresome Ethelred, Saxon Harold, Norman William and a dozen others.

He waited for her to dismiss him. But Victoria said in a rush of words, 'I read that you are a cambion, born of Princess Gwenddydd by the incubus Albercanix. She became a nun after your birth.' The princess was enthralled.

Merlin met her gaze, gave the quick smile a busy adult has for a child – one trick that always distracted monarchs was to show how they came to have power over such a one as he. The wizard waved his hand and Victoria saw the scene after Mount Badon, the great victory that made Arthur king of Britain. That day Merlin ensorcelled seven Saxon wizards, while Arthur slew seven Saxon kings, and may well have saved his sorcerer's life.

For this princess Merlin mostly hid the gore. He showed her Arthur and himself, younger, flushed with victory and many cups of celebratory mead, as in gratitude the wizard granted the king any wish within his power to give.

'Neither of us knew much law, so it wasn't well thought out,' he explained, and showed himself swearing an oath to come forever more to the aid of any monarch of Britain who summoned him. 'But my time is precious and must not be wasted,' he told her.

Even this mild version left Victoria round-eyed with wonder, as was Merlin's intent. For certain monarchs his message could be so clear and terrifying that Richard III had gone to his death on Bosworth Field and Charles I had let his head be whacked off without trying to summon him.

For a moment wizard and princess listened and smiled at the sounds downstairs of carriages fleeing into the night.

He bowed and asked if there was anything more she desired. When she could think of nothing, he bowed once more and stepped backwards through the bookshelves and the wall of Kensington Palace.

She watched as the great hall of the castle with its knights and king appeared and swallowed Merlin up.

'I am ruled by our young queen and happily so, as is every man of fair mind in this land,' said Lord Melbourne, Queen Victoria's first Prime Minister. And for a brief time that was true.

Melbourne could be a bit of a wizard, producing parliamentary majorities out of nothing, or making them disappear without a trace. A few years into young Victoria's reign, gossip held she was in the palm of his hand.

In fact, she found him charming, but with her mother left behind at Kensington Palace and John Conroy exiled to the Continent, the headstrong young queen was led by no one. The dusty castles and palaces in London and Windsor were lately the haunts of drunken and sometimes deranged kings. She opened them up and gathered visiting European princes and her own young equerries and ladies-in-waiting for late-night feasts and dances.

Then Lord Melbourne explained to her that the people of Britain were unhappy with their monarch. 'The time has come', he said, 'for you to find a husband, produce an heir and ensure stability. The choice of a groom will be yours, an opportunity and a peril, like every marriage.'

Victoria's first reaction was anger. But she knew that few women of any rank got to choose their husbands. Her choices were wide, and the eligible princes of Europe paraded through Buckingham Palace and Windsor Castle.

Victoria and the Grand Duke Alexander of Russia danced the wild mazurka. Young equerries of her staff had her picture on lockets next to their hearts in the hope that she might decide to marry into her nobility and select one of them.

The nation was fascinated with its legendary past, and so was its queen. She dreamed of sending the candidates on quests, having them do great deeds. But she knew that wasn't possible. Victoria's resentment of the task made her unable to decide among the candidates And, naturally, everyone grew impatient – the potential grooms, the government and the people of England.

As the situation worsened, the Queen considered invoking Merlin, but she felt intimidated.

Then Melbourne himself said the future of Britain hung on her decision. She thought this surely was a moment to summon the wizard?

One evening in her private chambers, she drew out the parchment and ran through the invocation. Immediately the light of the oil lamps in her room was drowned by sunlight shining on ocean waves, pouring through windows of clearest glass into a room as blue as the sea around it.

Despite his robes with the golden moon in all its phases, it took her a few moments to recognize the tall figure with dark hair and a beard standing over a giant tortoise that rested on an oaken table.

Victoria watched fascinated as he stopped what he was doing and said goodbye effusively but quickly to a figure with liquid green eyes and saucy silver back flippers. The sea king's daughter and her palace disappeared as he strode into Victoria's private drawing room.

Merlin, in the full flush of his wizardry, had just murmured, 'Gryphons and Guilfoils, marjoram and unicorn mange, the heart of Diana's own rabbit soaked in the blood of humming birds from the Emperor's gardens in far Cathay . . .' Then he'd felt the summons, turned, seen Victoria and lost track of the spell he was working. A summons when it came had to be obeyed. It could originate at any point in the long history of Britain's monarchy, from the battle of Badon onwards. And each caught him at a moment in his life when he was deep into weaving magic and casting spells. At his most powerful, he was at his most vulnerable.

He stepped out of a place where each drinking cup had a name and every chair an ancestry, into a room with walls covered by images of flowers and pictures of bloodless people. The floor was choked with furniture and every single surface was covered with myriad small objects.

Merlin had encountered Victoria when he was just a youth and she was middle-aged. That meeting would, of course, not have happened to her yet. Now, in her private apartments at Windsor Palace, he knelt before Victoria, whose expression was full of curiosity about the tortoise, the palace, the creature with the flippers and him. But what she said was, 'I brought you here because my prime minister and my people have decided I must marry for the good of Britain. I need your help to make the right decision.'

And he told her as patiently as he could, 'In the palace of the sea king's daughter, as an act of charity, I was working a spell to restore the zest of life to an ancient tortoise. It houses within itself the soul of Archimedes, the great mage of legendary times. This is the sort of favour I hope someone might some-day perform if I ever needed it.

'It was all about to come together: ingredients at hand, incantation memorized, pentagrams and quarter circles drawn, the tortoise staring up with hope in its eyes.'

She sat amazed by this and by the man, dark bearded and thirty years younger than when she'd seen him a few years earlier.

Victoria dreamed of turning her kingdom into a kind of Camelot, a land of castles, enchanted woods, knights in armour and maidens under sleeping spells floating down rivers. She looked at Merlin now and thought how perfectly he would fit into such a world.

Merlin understood. He was young, vain and used to being wanted. He found himself liking her, but memories of the complications and quarrels after an extended tumble with Elizabeth I reminded him of how unwise such liaisons could be. His interest at the moment was getting back as quickly as possible to the life he'd had to leave.

Victoria watched him stand at the floor-length windows and stare out into the night. When he gestured, one window blew open.

Any wizard is a performer and Merlin intended to bedazzle her. He held out his right arm, candlelight danced and a bird appeared. The shadow of a raptor rested on his wrist and seemed to flicker like a flame. Merlin had summoned a questing spirit, the ghost of the Lord of Hawks. He whistled a single note and it became solid, all angry, unblinking eyes and savage beak.

The wizard filled a clear crystal bowl with water and said, 'Your Majesty, give me the name of a suitor.'

She named the Grand Duke Alexander of Russia.

Merlin held the hawk near the bowl, which was so clear that the water seemed to float in air. He whispered the grand duke's name and looked at the surface of the water. On it he saw Alexander's fate, a winter scene with blood on the snow. An anarchist had hurled the bomb that tore the Tsar apart.

Merlin knew Victoria was not a vicious soul. If she saw this particular piece of the future it would be hard for her to keep it a secret from the Tsar-to-be, and it was best not to upset the balance of the world. Undoing that would require more magic than he had, so he looked at the young queen and shook his head – this one was not suitable. She looked but he had already cleared away the image.

'Who is Your Majesty's next suitor?'

Victoria spoke the name, Merlin relayed it to his medium and the image of a mildly retarded prince of Savoy floated in the bowl. He shook his head; she looked relieved and they ran through some more European royalty.

Merlin knew the man he was looking for, the one she had actually married. He'd seen pictures galore at the time in her future and his past when he'd been summoned by this queen.

She stared at Merlin as she smiled and said, 'Lord Alfred Paget.' This was the most dashing of her young courtiers. A royal equerry of excellent family, he made no secret of his romantic love for the Queen. She in turn was charmed and more than a bit taken with Paget. He would be her choice if she decided to marry one not of royal birth.

But Merlin knew that wasn't the name he was looking for. When an image floated on the water, it actually made Merlin grin. He let Victoria see the once dashing Paget fat, self-satisfied and seventy years old.

'Oh dear. This will not do!' she said with a horrified expression. Then she and the wizard laughed. This search for a husband was far more pleasant than much of what he did in service to the Baden oath. Merlin had seen an unfaithful royal princess killed in Paris by flashing lights and a wilful, runaway machine. He had visited a distant time when the king of Britain was not much more than a picture that moved.

Victoria gave the name and title of Albert Prince of Saxe-Coburg and Gotha. A glance at the face floating on the water was all Merlin needed. This was the one he'd been waiting for. Albert would die long before Victoria, and she would mourn him for the rest of her life. A hardier husband might be in order, but Albert was the one she was destined to marry and that's how it would be.

The image floating in the bowl was flattering. Merlin invited the queen to look, indicated his approval and congratulated her.

His task done, Merlin prepared to leave. Victoria realized this and looked stricken. Anyone, be they human or cambion, enjoys being found attractive. And to have won the heart of a queen was better still. Merlin bowed deeply to the monarch and wished her great happiness in her marriage.

As he strode out of her presence, Victoria saw the tortoise that contained the soul of Archimedes and the sun dancing on the waves outside the palace and the lovely daughter of the one who rules the tides. The queen noted every detail and wondered if her kingdom could ever contain anything so beautiful.

She wrote a letter to Prince Albert of Saxe-Coburg and Gotha, as she thought of Merlin.

'Twenty-five years into her reign, Her Majesty has abandoned her responsibilities.'

'Since poor Prince Albert died, I hear she wears nothing but mourning clothes . . .'

'The processes of government demand the public presence of a monarch.'

'. . . and talks to the trees at Windsor Palace, like her daft grandfather did . . .'

'No one in her royal household, her government and especially her family dares to broach the subject with her.'

'. . . curtsies to them trees as well, I got told.'

Isolated as a monarch is, Victoria heard the nonsense her people were saying. She knew they said she talked to her late husband as she walked the halls of Buckingham Palace and Windsor Castle, of Balmoral in Scotland and Osborne House on the Isle of Wight. And here they were right, sometimes she did. More than anything else, what she had lost with the death of the man to whom she'd been married for twenty years was the one person in Britain who could speak to her as an equal. She still spoke to him, but there was no reply. She felt utterly alone.

At Osborne House, after a day with little warmth in the sun, she stood at a window with a wind coming in from the sea and thought of Merlin. Indeed, with its graceful Italianate lines, fountains and views of the water, Osborne was Victoria's attempt to evoke the glimpses she'd caught of the palace of the sea king's daughter. She envied that royal family as she did no other.

In the years of her marriage, she sometimes remembered the handsome wizard of their last meeting and always with a pang of guilt. It almost felt as if she had betrayed the marriage. In her widowhood, though, she thought about him more often.

That evening at Osborne, Victoria demanded she be completely alone in her private apartments. The queen debated with herself as to whether this was a time of danger to the crown or, as her uncle had said, a day of doldrums and no wind in the sails. Finally Victoria decided it was a good deal of both. She took the glass-bound page out of its hiding place and read the summons aloud. Immediately she saw half-naked people in savage garb looking up at a huge picture that moved. It showed some kind of carriage without horses racing down a dark, smooth road.

As monarch of a forward-looking nation, the queen had been shown zoetropes and magic lanterns. This appeared far more like real life, except that it moved too fast. Her royal train was always an express and its engine could attain speeds of almost fifty miles an hour, but that was as nothing to what this machine seemed to do.

A man, who looked familiar, like a distant cousin perhaps, sat in it smiling. 'In this driver's seat everyone is a king,' he said.

The queen couldn't know that she'd just glimpsed a distant successor. In the year 2159, King Henry X had on a permanent loop in his offices what he called 'My Agincourt'. The great triumph of his reign was being named spokesperson for Chang'an/Ford/Honda, the world's mightiest automaker.

Victoria saw that the people who had been looking up at the image were now frozen, staring at a figure running straight towards her. This one had long dark hair but no sign of a beard; he was tall, but not quite as tall as the Merlin she remembered. He looked very young. Instead of robes he wore what Victoria identified as some abbreviated form of men's underclothes, a thing about which she made a point of knowing nothing. As he stepped into her room, she saw emblazoned on his shirt the lion and the unicorn – the royal crest – directly over his heart.

Victoria had sons and she placed this boy as fifteen at most. She stared at him and said, 'You're just a child. Who are you? Where are your proper clothes? And how did you get here?'

After a moment of surprise, Merlin looked this small woman in black directly in the eyes, which none had done since Albert. Victoria heard him say, 'I am Merlin, the cambion of Albercanix and Gwenddydd. I was apprenticed to Galapas, the Hermit of the Crystal Cave, a disagreeable old tyrant.

'One morning, running through my spells, I found myself summoned by Henry X, King of Britain. I was working a great magic on his courtiers when you called me here.' He glanced down at the soft clothes and shoes that still puzzled him, 'And this is the livery of that king.' He seemed confused.

When the young wizard first arrived in 2159, King Henry peered at him over a glass and said, 'Not what I expected. Just curious as to whether this old piece of parchment actually worked – needed something to remind myself and others of the old mystique of royalty. Perhaps you could turn a few advertising people into mice. It'll teach them to respect me and the monarchy in its last days.'

Victoria saw in this somewhat lost and gangling lad the man she'd encountered. The Queen realized that King Arthur and the Baden Oath were well in his future and that he didn't understand what had happened to him. It occurred to her that the child of a demon and a princess who became a nun might be as separate and alone as she was.

'Your attire simply won't do,' she said.

Merlin discovered that unlike King Henry, this monarch was greatly respected. All the servants deferred to her and some courtiers were even afraid of her. The queen had a trusted footman and pageboy dress the stranger in clothes her sons had outgrown. Merlin hated the infinite buttons and hooks, the itching flannel and stiff boots. Then Victoria passed him off as a young visiting kinsman 'from the Anhalt-Latvia cousins'.

Merlin remembered King Henry, so full of strange potions and drinks he sometimes had trouble standing and often couldn't remember who Merlin was. The young wizard had tried not to show how bedazzled he was by the magic of that court, lights that came and went with the wave of a hand, cold air that seeped out of walls to cool a kingdom where it was always hot outdoors, unseen musicians who beat drums, sang, played harps of incredible variety through the day and night without tiring.

The king's entourage was so amazed by Merlin's spells of invisibility and the way he could turn them into frogs and then back into courtiers that they lost any interest in their monarch and flocked around him. They persuaded Merlin to surrender his own rough robes and gave him shorts, T-shirts and soft shoes, like everyone else in the kingdom. He had never worn clothes with legs or felt fabric as light before.

All he knew for certain was that he didn't want to return to the Crystal Cave and the Hermit. He spent some amazing days and light-filled nights in the court of 2159.

Victoria, everyone agreed, seemed more cheerful since the appearance of her strange relative. The two of them took walks together and he showed her nixies riding in on the morning waves and sprites dancing by moonlight. He turned her pug dog into a trained bear and turned it back again.

Merlin didn't understand this world in which palaces and castles all looked utterly indefensible, ruins had been built just to be ruins and the queen's knights seemed an unlikely band of warriors, without a missing eye or gouged-out nose among them.

On their walks, Victoria sometimes ran on about wanting to create a court full of art and poetry, like King Arthur at Camelot. It amazed her that he understood none of this. So she told him the bits and pieces she had learned over the years about the Baden Oath and Arthur's kingdom. The young mage was fascinated.

Once she made Merlin sit through a chamber music concert and talked afterwards about 'the melodies of the wonderful Herr Mendelssohn, to whom I could listen for ever'. He told her about the court of her descendent Henry X, where invisible musicians played all day and all night. He could have told her more about the future of her kingdom, but out of respect, and even affection, he never much mentioned her descendant. Never described seeing King Henry in a false crown, armour and broadsword quaffing 'Royal English Ale' from a horn cup and signifying his approval. Never said how he'd sampled the ale and found it so vile he'd spat it out.

When he finished that endorsement, the king had turned and seen the shocked expression on young Merlin's face. He said, 'I'm the last, you know. I'm preserved in so many formats that they'll never need another king for their ads. I've no children that I know of and no one is interested in succeeding me. I'm sorry I let you see all this.' Then he started to cry great drunken tears.

Merlin walked away as quickly as he could. He strode into the room where His Majesty's greatest promotional moments played on a screen. He didn't know where he was going, but he headed for a door and the blazing hot outdoors.

When some of His Majesty's courtiers tried to stop him, he froze them in place with a spell. At that moment of his magic, Victoria's summons rescued him. For that and her stories he would always be grateful. But he was young, male and a wizard, and this was a queen's court with many young women without much to do.

Merlin knew little about such things, but others did. There was a fine rumpus of a rendezvous in a linen closet with an apprentice maid of the wardrobe, and another more leisurely meeting with a young lady-in-waiting in her chamber.

Spells to blank the memories of passers-by didn't quite dispel the stories. The queen found out about it and knew it was her fault. Even Albert, as good a man as any that has ever lived, had more animal in him than was reasonable or necessary. Keeping Merlin here was as unnatural as imprisoning a wild beast. And now there would be anxious months spent waiting to find out if the grandchild of an incubus had been spawned at the royal court.

She ordered certain clothing to be made. One day Merlin returned to his rooms and found on the bed, robes and a cloak with the moon in all its phases and fine leather boots like the ones Her Majesty had noticed the older Merlins wearing. The youth had never seen anything so splendid. He changed and went to her private rooms, where she was waiting.

'Sir Merlin, you have fulfilled and more the tasks for which you were summoned,' she said, and he saw how hard this was for her. 'You are dismissed with our thanks and the certainty that we will meet again.'

Merlin bowed low. And before the royal tears came, or his own could start, he found himself hurtling backwards through the centuries to the hermit Galapas and the Crystal Cave.

Merlin didn't linger there, but immediately set out across Wales, finding within himself the magic to cover miles in minutes. One story Victoria had told was of a king trying to build a castle before his enemies were upon him. Each day the walls would be raised and each night they would be thrown down. All were in despair until a bold youth in a cloak of moons appeared. He tamed two dragons that fought every night in the caves below the castle and made the walls collapse. Merlin knew he was that youth.

'Queen Victoria,' a commentator said at her Golden Jubilee, 'inherited a Britain linked by stagecoach and reigned in a Britain that ran on rails. She rules over a quarter of the globe and a quarter of its people.'

At Balmoral Castle in the Highlands, late in her reign, the queen went into high mourning because a gamekeeper, John Brown, had died. 'Mrs Brown mourns dead husband,' was how a scurrilous underground London newspaper put it. In fact, Brown – belligerent, hard drinking and rude to every person at court except Her Majesty – was the only person on earth who spoke to her as one human being to another.

He died unmourned by anyone but the queen, but she mourned him extravagantly. Memorial plaques were installed; statuettes were manufactured. He was gone but the court's relief was short-lived. To commemorate becoming Empress of India, Victoria imported servants from the subcontinent.

Among them was Abdul Karim who taught her a few words of Hindu. For this the queen called him 'the Munshi' or teacher and appointed him her private secretary.

Soon the Munshi was brought along to state occasions, allowed to handle secret government reports and introduced to foreign dignitaries. He engaged in minor intrigue and told Her Majesty nasty stories about his fellow servants.

The entire court wished the simple, straightforward Mr Brown could come back. Victoria's children, many well into middle-age, found the Munshi appalling. The government worried about its state secrets.

'Indian cobra in Queen's parlour,' the slanderous press proclaimed.

The queen would hear nothing against him. But she knew he wasn't what she wanted.

'Oh the cruelty of young women and the folly of old men,' Merlin cried as he paced the floor in the tower of glass that was his prison cell. Nimue, the enchantress who beguiled his declining years, had turned against him, using the skills he'd taught her to imprison him.

As a boy, Queen Victoria had told him about King Uther Pendragon, whose castle walls collapsed each night. Solving that, young Merlin won the confidence of Pendragon. The birth of the king's son, Arthur; hiding the infant from usurpers; the sword in the stone; the kingdom of Britain and all the rest had followed on from that. But Victoria never told Merlin about Nimue. She thought it too sad.

'Sired by an incubus, baptized in church, tamer of dragons, advisor to kings, I am a cambion turned into a cuckold,' he wailed.

Most of his magic had deserted him. He hadn't even enough to free himself. Still he did little spells, turned visiting moths into butterflies, made his slippers disappear and reappear. Merlin knew he had a reason for doing this, but he couldn't always remember what it was.

Then one morning, while making magic, he found himself whisked from the tower and summoned to a room crammed full of tartan pillows, with claymore swords hung on the walls as decoration. Music played in the next room and an old lady in black looked at him kindly.

The slump of his shoulders and unsteadiness of his stance led the Queen of England, Empress of India, to rise and lead him over to sit on the divan next to her.

'That music you hear is a string quartet playing a reduction of Herr Mendelssohn's Scottish Symphony,' she said. Musicians are on call throughout my waking hours. You told me long ago that this was how things were arranged at the Royal Court in 2159.'

It was a brisk day and they drank mulled wine. 'The sovereign of Britain requires a wizard to attend her,' she said, 'for a period of time which she shall determine.'

Merlin realized he was rescued, and when 'the Munshi' walked into the room unannounced, the Wizard stood to his full height. Seeing a white bearded man with flashing eyes and sparks darting from his hands, the Munshi fled.

Everyone at Balmoral marvelled at the day her Majesty put aside her secretary and gave orders that he was not to approach her. They all wondered if someone else had taken his place, but no evidence of that could ever be found. People talked about the eccentricities of Queen Victoria's last years: the seat next to hers that she insisted always be kept empty in carriages, railroad cars and at state dinners; the rooms next to hers that must never be entered. At times the queen would send all the ladies and servants away from her chambers and not let them in until next morning.

Some at court hinted that all this had shaded over into madness, and attributed it to heredity. Most thought it was just old age, harmless and in its way charmingly human. In fact, a few members of her court did see things out of the corners of their eyes. Merlin could conjure invisibility, but his concentration was no longer perfect.

Her majesty walking over the gorse at Balmoral in twilight, on the shore on a misty day at Osborne, or in the corridors of Windsor Castle, would suddenly be accompanied by a cloaked figure with a white beard and long white hair. When the viewer looked again he would have disappeared. Those who saw thought it best not to mention it to anyone.

Victoria talked to Merlin about their prior meetings and how she cherished each of them. The wizard would once have sneered at the picturesque ruins and undefendable faux castles that dotted the landscape near any royal residence. Now he understood they had been built in tribute to the sage who'd saved the young princess, the handsome magician who had helped choose her husband, the quicksilver youth of her widowhood.

When she finally became very ill at Windsor, Queen Victoria had ruled for over sixty years. Merlin remembered that this was the time when she would die, and he stayed with her, put in her mind the things he knew she found pleasing and summoned up music only she could hear. He wondered if, when she was gone, he would be returned to Nimue and the tower.

'She assumed the throne in the era of Sir Walter Scott and her reign has lasted into the century of Mr H.G. Wells,' *The Times* of London said.

In the last days, when her family came to see her, Victoria had the glass with the parchment inside it under her covers. Merlin stood in a corner and was visible only to the Queen. When her son, who would be Edward VII, appeared, Merlin shook his head. This man would never summon him. It was the same with her grandson, who would be George V. A great grandchild, a younger son who stammered, was brought in with his brothers. Merlin nodded: this one would summon him to London decades later when hellfire fell from the skies.

The boy was called back after he and his brothers had left, was given the parchment and shown how to hide it.

'You are my last and only friend,' Victoria told Merlin. He held her hands when she died and felt grief for the first time in his life. But he wasn't returned to his glass prison.

Uninvited, invisible and utterly alone at the funeral, he followed the caisson that bore the coffin through the streets of Windsor, carrying the only friend he'd ever had to the Royal Mausoleum at Frogmore.

'We say of certain people, "She was a woman of her time",' an orator proclaimed. 'But of how many can it be said that the span of their years, the time in which they lived, will be named for them?'

'A bit of her is inside each one of us,' said a woman watching the cortege. 'And that I suppose is what a legend is.'

In the winter twilight, with snow on the ground, Merlin stood outside the mausoleum. 'I don't want to transfer my mind and soul to another human or beast, and I won't risk using that magic and getting summoned. There's no other monarch I wish to serve.'

He remembered the Hermit of the Crystal Cave. Old Galapas hadn't been much of a teacher, but Merlin had learned the wizard's last spell from him. It was simple enough and he hadn't forgotten.

Merlin invoked it, and those who had lingered in the winter dusk saw for a moment a figure with white hair and beard, wearing robes with the moon in all its phases. The old wizard waved a wand, shimmered for a moment, then appeared to shatter. In the growing dark, what seemed like tiny stars flew over the mausoleum, over Windsor, over Britain and all the world.

THE DANCING MASTER

Genevieve Valentine

'Compliance with, and deference to, the wishes of others
is the finest breeding.'
  Routledge's Manual of Etiquette, 1875

'No person who has not a good ear for time and tune
need hope to dance well.'
  Routledge's

The dancing master was summoned to Evering Park before
the last of the winter frost had burned off the lawn, so that
Leah could polish herself before the London Season began in
the summer.

'Are you sure that's enough time to keep Leah from making
a spectacle of herself?' asked Reg at supper.

Leah lowered her fork out of sight of the table and debated
her chances of landing a successful blow on his leg if she tried.

Their mother, however, was the sort who kept a firm eye on
which piece of cutlery was in use, and what for, and she
cleared her throat and glanced at Leah over the bridge of her
nose. 'I hope both my children might keep from making spectacles of themselves,' she said, with warning looks at each of
them in turn.

Leah set down her fork. Reg smoothed his dark hair and
shot her a triumphant look.

Her father added vaguely between bites, 'I'm sure all will be
well. And Reg, naturally, as Leah's brother, you will use your
superior knowledge of all our upcoming society to assist her.'
He said it with a sigh; he wasn't fond of London. Leah was

already seventeen, and her mother had yet to prevail upon him to take them.

Reg, who had already spent three summers in London, doing whatever it was young men did when they went to London in the summer all alone, looked Leah up and down for a moment with a look of mild horror at the realization that she would be linked to him in public.

'You needn't act as if I'm Medusa just because I can't waltz,' Leah snapped.

'Leah,' said Mother, 'don't be peevish. Everything is settled; do let's all try to be settled, too.'

Leah stared at her fork without blinking until the next course came.

Miss Hammond had been another of her mother's clever ideas, and had replaced Leah's governess two years earlier as a genteel companion, in preparation for the inevitable Season.

'She had a good family,' Mama had told her with a sigh, two years ago, as they sat in the morning parlour and waited for Miss Hammond to appear and throw her vocation on their mercy. 'And some prospects, once.'

That was when Leah began to worry about London.

Of all her mother's schemes, however, Miss Hammond had been by far the best. She was only nine years older than Leah, and had a way of looking at Reg as if she wished she could light him on fire, which kept Leah from being peevish more often than anything else could.

As Leah knocked on Miss Hammond's door, she could feel a weight already falling off her shoulders. Miss Hammond would know what to do – the thing that frightened her most about going to London was that she was still so often foolish about little childish things.

Miss Hammond was dressed for the evening – occasionally she was summoned to provide music in the evenings, if Reg was out and they could enjoy music without him groaning about it – and Leah was comforted just to see the familiar deep-grey bombazine in the candlelight.

Miss Hammond had been reading; the book still sat open on her little table, next to her lamp. She read essays and histories and love stories, one after another, making a little chain of pockmarks around Father's library.

'I can't bear to go to London,' Leah said without preamble. 'I'm going to throw myself from the attic window. Shall you come?'

Miss Hammond smiled and stepped aside.

'Why don't you come in first,' she said, 'and tell me what's happened.'

> 'To attempt to dance without a knowledge of dancing is not only to make one's self ridiculous, but one's partner also. No lady has a right to place a partner in this absurd position. Never forget a ballroom engagement. To do so is to commit an unpardonable offence against good breeding.'
>
> *Routledge's*

Mr Martin came highly recommended by the Ladislaws – 'Their oldest girl married a duke,' said Mama, with a significant look at Leah – and if one was to welcome a dancing master for as long as Leah required one, then he was the only sensible choice in the matter.

And he was going to come, and Leah was going to learn everything she could from him.

'Your mother is only trying to make sure you don't have any worries when you're there,' Miss Hammond had said, tucking some stray hair behind her ear and looking as young as Leah. 'Suffer a little now, so that when you have your Season you are secure in yourself, and then you'll be free to enjoy the evening when you're in the ballroom. I'll be there if you have any worries, but it's much better to study before one recites, no?'

Leah thought about that. A moment too late, she said, 'All right.'

Back in her own room, she had looked at her round, ordinary face in the mirror for a long time, her mousey hair and strong nose, two small dark eyes that flickered and shook until she blew the candle out.

★   ★   ★

Reg had gone into town for the morning on some pretence, and Father had declared he wasn't in to visitors, so it was only Leah and Miss Hammond and Mama to greet him when he came.

'Reg should have to study with Mr Martin, too,' Leah said. 'He promised not to make a spectacle of himself in London.'

'He learned his manners at school,' said Mama, as if that was an endorsement.

Leah would have been more than happy to learn dancing if it could have been part of an education in London. It would be worth suffering a mazurka every so often if you were also learning mathematics and history and articles of law.

'Mr Charles Martin,' announced Stevens, and Leah pushed the thought aside and stood to greet the guest.

Mr Martin was tall and handsome and had blonde hair carefully curled; he wore yellow gloves, and his blue coat was almost too sharp for the fashion, and he entered with a smile that felt larger than it was, so Leah had an impression of white teeth, though she had seen none.

'Lady Clement,' he greeted, with a bow one degree more formal than necessary.

Mother stepped forward with her arm held out just so. 'Mr Martin, a pleasure to meet you. This, of course, is my daughter Leah.'

Mr Martin bowed and lifted one hand slightly, palm up, to take her hand. But Leah had laced her fingers together, and though she thought she might extend a hand and have him take it, somehow her fingers wouldn't move, and so she just stared at him.

He blinked, adjusted his expression back to a polite smile and slid his eyes past her.

'And this is Ms Hammond,' Mother said. 'My daughter's companion.'

'Charmed,' said Mr Martin, turning his face to catch up with his eyes.

Miss Hammond curtseyed, and Leah watched her, for a moment, turn into a lady – the smooth dip of the motion, the lowered eyes, the glance back up to him, smoothing the skirt in a discreet sweep of the palm as she stood.

It was exactly the way a lady should look when meeting a gentleman, and Leah's heart sank just looking at it.

'If I might suggest Miss Clement might change into a low bodice for our lesson,' Mr Martin turned to Mama and explained. 'It's a common request among the dance instructors most familiar with the Season. One might learn the correct form straight away, and it is an extra source of ease, I find, to practice on the instrument on which one intends to perform.'

The idea of wearing her low bodice in front of Mr Martin, a stranger who hadn't even looked at her when he suggested it, made Leah's hands go cold. But Mama nodded at her, which meant the decision had been made, and there was nothing left for Leah to do but obey.

Miss Hammond moved to follow, but Leah snapped, 'Don't trouble yourself,' and kept walking.

As she turned for the stairs, Leah could hear Mama saying, 'She can be clever, Mr Martin, but she's always been a bit peevish. My apologies. Too long in the country, I suspect.'

The lesson took place in the ballroom. Evering Park was an estate landed enough to have a true ballroom, even though they hadn't hosted anything grander than a dinner party since Leah could remember. 'Your father isn't fond of a fuss,' Mama had said once or twice, when Leah had asked. Then she had closed the doors of the ballroom with a sigh and moved to the little drawing rooms where they spent their evenings.

As Leah walked in, Mr Martin was examining the room with the air of a tenant. Miss Hammond hung back near the doorway, watching him.

'Excellent room,' he said, and tossed a grin over his shoulder at Miss Hammond, then at Leah, as he caught sight of her. 'It's a bit of a trick trying to teach the new dances with nothing but a morning parlour at one's disposal. One should see how a dance moves over a room in order to be able to dance it with grace.'

'This might not be big enough,' said Leah.

Miss Hammond squeezed her hand for a moment. 'Leah, don't underestimate yourself. Many girls with less to recommend them have managed to muddle through a Season or two and come out the other side all right.'

'All right' meant 'married,' but it couldn't be true – Miss Hammond had had her Seasons and now here she was. If Miss Hammond couldn't 'manage', Leah couldn't imagine how she would. But that was an unkind thing to think – for one of them, or both of them. It was hard to say.

'Right,' said Mr Martin, who was hanging his greatcoat carefully across one of the chairs.

'Now, Miss Clement, your mother didn't mention to me how much you already knew about dancing.'

Leah remembered vaguely that her cousins, the Fosters, had thrown a family party at the Hall when she was thirteen or fourteen. She had practiced beforehand with Lily Foster, and then shuffled her way through some dance where you met and parted with strangers all the way down the line, and sometimes met up in quarters so that your right arms joined in a star, and throughout the whole affair Lily had tried valiantly to give her silent reminders as to what was coming next.

'I think it's safest to assume nothing,' Leah said.

Mr Martin checked a laugh. 'Right. I see. And Miss Hammond, you strike me as a young woman of the world – do I have the pleasure of an assistant in this endeavour?'

Miss Hammond inclined her head. 'I'm a little out of fashion,' she said, 'but happy to help if I can.'

Mr Martin was quiet a moment, looking at her, and then turned to Leah.

'Why don't we begin with making an entrance,' he said, and turned to indicate the open doors. 'I'll be your escort, and Miss Hammond will provide the sage advice that only a lady can communicate to another of her kind.'

Leah looked at Miss Hammond, who was smiling at her and nodding for her to go on.

'A young lady,' began Mr Martin, 'always enters a ballroom quietly, so as not to draw attention to herself by causing any disturbance to others at the party. She should, rather, be noticed because of the refinement of her carriage, her manner and her grace. Her first dance happens before she ever takes the floor.'

He held out his hand, palm down. 'So, Miss Clement?'

Leah took a breath (her ribs strained against her corset), rested her palm on his hand. His kid gloves were fitted tight, thin as skin, and he was watching her with sharp blue eyes. He smiled; she had the impression of teeth.

'Let us begin,' he said.

They walked nearly the length of the ballroom as he said, 'No weight on the joined hand,' and, 'Hold the chin slightly lower, so people don't think you're displeased,' and once, 'There's no hurry, Miss Clement.'

'Yes,' said Miss Hammond with a grin, 'perhaps let's not gallop,' and Leah flushed to her temples and forced herself to walk so that the toe of one shoe touched the heel of the other.

'Well done,' he said, and for a moment his thumb brushed the edges of her fingers. It startled her; it was like skin, just like. She looked up at him, at his bright blue eyes and his quarter of a smile and his shoulders held with more ease than any gentleman she'd ever met.

As they turned to walk back up the room, Leah glimpsed her mother in the doorway, passing out of sight.

'A lady cannot refuse the invitation of a gentleman to dance, unless she has already accepted that of another, for she would be guilty of an incivility which might occasion trouble.'

   Manners, Culture and Dress of the Best American Society, Richard Wells (1891)

'I'm thinking of inviting your cousin William to come and stay, Reg,' said their mother at supper, three days later. 'You know there's hardly any sport worth having on his grounds at this time of year.'

Cousin William Foster was the heir to the Foster estate in Surrey, and only a few years older than Leah, and she set down her spoon in the soup so suddenly it splashed.

From the look on Reg's face, he wasn't any keener to have cousin William come and stay, which made Leah wonder why mother would think to invite him. But Mama was pointedly not looking at Leah, and Leah began to worry.

'I'm sure that's not necessary,' Leah said. She wished Miss Hammond took supper with them – she would know what to say that was roundabout and polite and that could put the invitation out of the question – but Leah was here alone, and her face hurt from practising a smile that showed no teeth, and now she knew her mother had been watching her with Mr Martin, and looking at his smile and making plans.

Her mother glanced at their father. 'It might not be strictly necessary, but won't it be nice for Reg and Leah to spend a little time with their cousin before the crush of the Season, Father?'

Leah stared at her father, willing him to look at her and take her side – he had to know what was happening when an eligible cousin was invited to stay; it was what had happened with him and Mother.

But Father only glanced up from his soup and said, 'Quite right,' with a smile.

Nothing was quite right, Leah thought, though there was no saying why.

There was no saying anything at all.

('A lady can never go wrong by being economical in conversation and avoiding strong opinions,' Mr Martin had said. 'In the dance, it's a distraction from your fine form, and in company, it can be seen as an attempt to distinguish oneself.'

'But I'm supposed to distinguish myself,' Leah had pointed out. 'There are dukes in London, and my mother has expectations.'

Mr Martin had tilted his head like a bird. Then he looked at Miss Hammond and said, 'I see we might want to have some lessons in conversation.'

'If you like,' Miss Hammond had replied with that coquette smile, and when Mr Martin had turned his back she'd given a smaller, real smile to Leah.)

Leah sat in silence through the rest of supper, and waved aside the beef and pudding with custard; her appetite had gone.

'Very good, Leah,' said her mother, as if she really was proud. 'I'll make some enquiries about a modiste of repute, and we'll see what's to be done with your figure, how's that?'

Leah didn't answer; under her fingers, her knife turned over and over.

'You know why, don't you?' Reg asked.

They were on their way upstairs to retire, after two hours in the drawing room, where Leah had flipped nervously through a manual of etiquette Mr Martin had recommended, not paying any mind to what she saw and not even wondering that there was so much.

Usually Reg smoked with Father in the dining room and stayed up later than Leah was allowed. It was rare that he left with her; now Leah knew why.

'I suspect it's because Mr Martin is handsome.'

'I knew it,' said Reg, curling his lip. 'You're in a fancy.'

'Hardly.' Leah flinched at the speed of her answer and amended, 'On the contrary, there's something about him I truly do not like. He's a fine instructor, but really, don't imagine I need cousin William to come and shame me out of something.'

Reg raised an eyebrow. 'That's not what Mother thinks, clearly.'

'Well, then she should spare our cousin and just send you to watch over me,' Leah said.

Reg barked a laugh. 'God, no! Bad enough to suffer through ten balls a Season looking into a sea of gormless faces from which you have to pluck a wife trained never to think anything of matter. I'm not about to be lectured through the mazurka with my own sister by our Mr Martin on top of it all.'

He took the stairs two at a time and vanished into his room.

Reg had never talked to her before about how he spent his time in London. Given what their mother hinted about his finances, she had imagined him at gaming tables and horse races.

She wasn't sure if this was better or worse.

At their next lesson, Leah walked with Mr Martin until both he and Miss Hammond were content with her carriage, the incline of her head, the lightness of her expression and the length of her step – 'Please, let's not gallop,' said Miss Hammond once, with just enough of a smile that Leah obeyed.

Mr Martin stopped; she kept her hand hovering a hair's breadth above his, and he smiled. 'Well done, Miss Clement. Now, might I interest you in taking refreshment?'

Leah glanced down and up through her lashes, slid her fan half open to indicate mild fatigue but not disinterest, and smiled without showing any teeth. 'Yes, thank you, Mr Martin.'

'No, Leah,' said Miss Hammond softly from her chair with a quick shake of her head. 'You can't accept. He is not a close enough friend of the family.'

Leah wondered why it sounded like such general custom to bring young ladies into society, loose them into a sea of strange men, and then starve them.

'I've accepted refreshments from men at parties,' she protested.

Mr Martin gave her a long-suffering look. 'At family parties, or among your neighbours, of course you may, but London is a different creature.'

For one wistful moment, Leah pictured the streets threaded through with dragons.

'And how close is close enough?' she asked. 'Would cousin William be able to fetch me some refreshment at an assembly, or would I have to hope Reginald is within shouting distance before I expire?'

'Your cousin would be an excellent choice,' Miss Hammond said, as if refreshments at a ball were the only thing being discussed. Maybe it was; Miss Hammond didn't employ the same style of hints as Mama did.

(Still, it felt like being thrown away, somehow, and Leah scowled.)

Mr Martin added, all kindness, 'These rules, Miss Clement, are in the interests of your comfort, that you needn't worry about your reputation in the slightest respect by making some unwitting error.'

Leah wondered who would be so anxious to ruin her reputation that she had to constantly be on guard for offers of punch, but looking at Miss Hammond, she saw this was something to be taken very seriously. It might be serious enough to explain why she had seen so little outside this county, and why she had never before been taken to London.

Her busk cut into the top of her right thigh, right through her skirts. She'd have a bruise tonight when it came off.

'All right,' she said. 'Then when he comes, I'll ask him.'

'Engagements for one dance should not be made while the present dance is yet in progress.

Never attempt to take a place in a dance which has been previously engaged.'

Routledge

Cousin William arrived four evenings later, punctual to the minute, and Leah nearly slipped on the stairs in her hurry to get into her place in the parlour before he could get out of the carriage and be announced.

(She had visited Miss Hammond's room to let her give the final word over her dress. The pearl earrings, with no cameo necklace, were deemed most suitable – a young lady of taste, apparently, needed no other adornment.

'Won't you come with me?' she'd asked Miss Hammond. 'You're my companion, I should have you with me.'

Miss Hammond had tried a smile and pinned closed the wire of Leah's left earring before she handed it back.

'That's not the sort of thing for which I'm required,' she said. The pearls were heavy, somehow; they ached in Leah's ears.)

She skittered for her place in as ladylike a manner as she could, under her mother's glare.

'Sir William Foster,' Stevens announced, as soon as Leah was settled.

Leah smoothed her skirt for an excuse to wipe the dampness off her palms. Reg shifted his weight back on to his heels, with one creak of the floorboards and sighed.

William came in with his hat still tucked under his arm and his shoulders pushed so far back that he seemed about to tip over.

She remembered him from the Christmas her family had been invited to celebrate in Surrey. He was taller now, and seemed slightly underfed; he had sharp features in a face that would probably grow to be respectable.

(They had the same nose, she thought.)

He bowed stiffly, then stood up and looked at Mama, as if unsure how formal to be. 'It's a pleasure to see you . . . Aunt?' he ventured finally.

He flinched as he spoke. Maybe he'd been suffering under a dancing master, too.

'William,' said Mama, coming forward and taking his hands. 'It's such a pleasure to see you. I trust you had a pleasant journey?'

'Of course, thank you.'

'Reg has been so looking forward to seeing you,' she said, without looking at Reg, 'and, of course, Leah has been hoping all day for a glimpse of her cousin. You know how fond of you she's always been.'

So they weren't even waiting a full day before the hints began. Leah held her breath and worked on her smallest, blankest smile. It fell apart; her lips were dry and sticking to her teeth.

It seemed to take a moment to sink in – Mama was still going on about refreshment and Stevens taking his things and wouldn't he care for a seat – but then William looked over at Leah, his expression too polite to be disgusted, but trying its hardest.

Leah's stomach sank.

In the drawing room, cousin William had to be refreshed and given a brandy, and had to relate to Father and Reg the quality of hunting back at home, and to Mama the quality of company, which meant that for nearly an hour Leah could get away with sitting silently on the sofa beside Mama, twisting her hands in her lap and trying to determine the best moment for escape.

(She had picked up her manual of etiquette on her way in, and it sat on her lap, in case she dared to ignore the guest.)

'And what entertainments are to be had at the Hall this time of year?' Mama was asking.

'Not many,' said William, looking into his brandy.

He didn't elaborate, and Leah nearly laughed at Mama's face as she struggled for a response.

'That must be unfortunate for your mother and sister. I know how fond they are of good company.'

'Mother and Lily are, yes,' he said finally.

'And we look forward to seeing all of you,' said Mama. 'How do you find the Season?'

'I don't,' he said. 'Indifferent health has kept me at home the last two springs.'

If nothing else came of this, Leah could at least take some comfort in the fact that peevishness ran in the family.

'I see,' said Mama.

It was cool enough that William glanced up and seemed to cast about for a way to save the sentiment. 'They pass their best wishes to Leah,' he said, 'and look forward to seeing her during the Season.'

'Oh, so do we,' said Reg. 'She's getting all the training of a diplomat headed for another continent. It's great fun to watch her trying.'

William's mouth thinned, and he glanced at Leah and then at Reg. 'Charming.'

Leah's cheeks blazed.

She opened the book, just for something else to look at besides his disapproving face. It had been nearly an hour; family honour had to be satisfied by now. Even being lectured by the manual had to be better than this.

Three pages later, she closed the book again. 'Please excuse me,' she said, standing up. 'I have a headache.'

Mama followed her and caught her at the doorway. 'Leah,' she said, 'this is extremely rude. I expected better of you.'

'Oh, don't worry, Mama,' said Leah, 'you've made it very clear exactly what you expect. Good night.'

On her way upstairs, she told Annabelle to send for Miss Hammond on an urgent matter.

As soon as Miss Hammond arrived, Leah dropped the open book on her bed and pointed at it. 'It says here that I can't decline an invitation to dance,' Leah said, her voice shaking.

Miss Hammond picked up the book (she always examined facts; she never got carried away). 'You mean at a private ball,' she said, closing the book. 'That's correct.'

Leah planted her hands on her hips. 'But if he's a stranger, can't I make some excuse? Strangers can't feed me; surely, then, they're not allowed to put their hand on my waist or just . . . impose that way.'

She was shaking with anger.

'Unfortunately, that's not the case.' Miss Hammond sighed. 'At a private ball, the hostess has chosen all present; it goes without saying that everyone is of impeccable character and equal to your time in a dance.'

She made a face that mirrored Leah's feelings on the matter. Leah wondered how many men Miss Hammond didn't care for had put their hands on her waist.

It was a terrible thought.

Leah shook her head, made fists at her sides. 'I don't understand it. First cousin William is lured in, and then I'm told I have to be pleasant and accommodating to strangers all Season long! It should be one way or the other – either I should be allowed to make my own choices, or William and Mama should just settle arrangements, and then at least I wouldn't have to pay attention to Mr Martin any more.' She sank on to the bed, tried to catch her breath.

Miss Hammond sat beside Leah. 'What's wrong with Mr Martin?'

His smile worries me, Leah wanted to say, but it sounded foolish, and she didn't want Miss Hammond to think she was inventing in her anger.

'Nothing,' said Leah. 'Except that he keeps asking me to do what I cannot do.'

Miss Hammond smiled, the candlelight flickering across her face. 'You'll learn, Leah, I'm sure – you have the potential to be a very passionate dancer, if you apply yourself, quite good enough for your cousin or anyone else.'

'My pins are too tight,' said Leah.

For a moment, Miss Hammond lifted her fingers, as if to reach out and touch Leah's hair herself. Leah sat perfectly still, held her breath. Then Miss Hammond got up and rang for Annabelle.

'The good news', said Miss Hammond, 'is that at private balls, if any man is worth having, you have filled twenty

minutes, and can beg off afterwards and never have to acknowledge him again. That's a lady's right.'

It seemed an awfully small one, but Leah supposed she
would have to make use of what she had.

'And at public assemblies, you can refer any unseemly gentleman to me,' said Miss Hammond, then smiled so that her nose
wrinkled slightly. 'I am not afraid to play the dragon for you.'

Leah closed her eyes as the door shut, to hold on to the
smile a little longer before night sank in.

> 'Never lower the intellectual standard of your conversa-
> tion in addressing ladies. Pay them the compliment of
> seeming to consider them capable of an equal under-
> standing with gentlemen.'
> 　*Wells*

When Leah arrived in the ballroom for her next lesson, William
was waiting. He stood at one of the windows, with his hands
clasped behind his back like a parson, and a furrow between
his eyes where he was squinting against the sun. Why did it
make Leah so low just to look at him this way?

'Good morning,' he said, without moving.

She said, 'Apologies if my mother sent you.'

From behind her, Stevens announced, 'Mr Martin for Miss
Clement,' (Leah jumped), and a moment later Mr Martin was
swanning into the room with a grin for them both.

'Excellent,' he said. 'Furnishing your own partners, even!'

'William Foster,' William said, frowning, and Mr Martin
grinned and bowed and finished the introduction, and then
without a pause he said, 'With both of you here we can practice some of the round dances after we attempt the waltz. Miss
Clement applies herself,' he told William, 'but round dances
can get the best of any lady unless she has a mind for figures.'

Leah flinched.

'I see,' said William.

Leah said, 'I'm sure cousin William doesn't intend to stay.'

William turned to look at her. The furrow was still there.
'I'm more than happy to be of service.'

'Wouldn't Reg come looking for you?'

His lips thinned. 'I expect so.'

(It was said in the same way he had said, 'Charming,' when Reg had crowed about her tutelage.

Interesting, thought Leah.) But just as William glanced at her and moved to leave, Miss Hammond appeared at the doorway. She smiled and nodded to Mr Martin, glanced at Leah and turned at last to William.

'Miss Hammond, I presume,' said William. 'It's a pleasure to meet you.'

She curtseyed. 'I wish you a pleasant lesson,' he said.

Miss Hammond's eyes went wide, and she said in that tone she reserved for company, 'Oh, can't you stay?'

'My cousin would rather not, I think,' said Leah.

'It's no trouble,' William said.

Leah scowled.

Mr Martin cleared his throat. 'Well, if someone must break this stalemate, I would treasure a fourth. If we may begin?'

Miss Hammond gave Leah a reproving look.

Leah folded her hands, gave the smile Mama had taught her was neither rude nor enthusiastic. 'Of course, Mr Martin.'

Reg passed by the doorway; he was dressed for riding, and as he crossed the open space he made a face at Mr Martin's back and fled.

'Truly, you may go with him if you'd rather,' said Leah under her breath. 'It will be no offence.'

'It is no offence to stay,' William said. 'I'm not particularly fond of hunting.'

It was an unusual thing for a gentleman to admit. (Father was very clear that a gentleman who didn't care for hunting was a gentleman deficient, though perhaps cousin William was rich enough that he could afford whatever pastime he chose.)

Mr Martin had taken his place in the centre of the room, and he turned to face them, grinning.

'Right. Let us begin the waltz!'

(The waltz – the dance that put a young lady full in the arms of some young man she could not refuse. Leah pressed her hands closer together.)

Mr Martin held out his arm with a bow, and Miss Hammond, blushing, and with a glance over her shoulder to Leah, took it.

She was embarrassed, Leah thought; her cheeks were pink, just at the place they disappeared under the plaits of her hair.

'Though it may seem stylish,' he said, and on 'stylish' his voice was a warning against drawing attention, 'it is still better to hold up one's skirt than to try to mend a rip in between the waltz and the quadrille. So, Miss Clement, if fashion dictates a train, please care for it. A gentleman will understand.'

Miss Hammond obligingly removed her right hand from Mr Martin's and caught up her skirt in the pressed-together flat of her hand, held with her thumb. An inch of grey flannel petticoat appeared above her right boot.

William blinked. 'And what would the man do with his hand then?'

(Leah remembered that this Season would be his first, too.)

'Behind his back, of course,' said Mr Martin, and demonstrated. 'A gentleman never questions the desires of a lady.'

It looked quite dashing when he did it, maybe even more than it did when their hands were joined. Not that Leah would ever say so; she guessed that the last thing Mama would want was for her to distinguish herself by being stylish, or any other thing.

'The man steps backward,' Mr Martin said, 'so that the lady may step forward and preserve her hem.' He demonstrated and, after a tiny hesitation, Miss Hammond followed him, her hand tightening a little on the edge of Mr Martin's shoulder as she tried for balance.

'From there, it's a simple pair of steps, and then into the next turn,' Mr Martin said. As he spoke, he was already moving faster, too quickly for Leah to understand what was required of her, though Miss Hammond followed with no trouble.

(Of course she would have no trouble with dancing, Leah remembered; Miss Hammond had had prospects, once.)

Mr Martin was humming now, and his golden hair caught the light every time he came in line with one of the windows, where the afternoon was going.

'It's really no trouble,' Mr Martin said as they passed, his smile flashing, his hand on Miss Hammond's back.

Leah curled her fingers around the edge of the chair.

William shifted beside Leah, glancing from them to her and

back again. She suspected he was wishing he had accepted Reg's invitation before an even speedier exercise was introduced.

Leah hardly cared; she was fixed, watching Mr Martin and Miss Hammond.

They turned circles within circles in the little empty ballroom, Mr Martin's smile growing as he hummed a song for them to keep time to, that one inch of Miss Hammond's grey petticoat flashing in and out of sight like a dove's wings.

That afternoon was the waltz.

Tuesday was the polka.

Wednesday was the quadrille.

'It's a simple enough dance as regards steps,' said Mr Martin, 'but an ease of carriage is what makes it a pleasure to watch, and to dance. Let us practice, then, and think of effortless grace.'

'Oh Lord,' Leah said under her breath, 'we'll be here until Sunday, then.'

William covered a laugh in a cough. Leah wasn't sure if it was compliment or mockery.

Two hours of practice later, she still was sure of nothing, except that grace should never be counted among the things in life on which she could rely.

'You look perfectly all right,' William said, with a narrowed glance at Mr Martin. 'He's just trying to be worth his fee, I suspect. You didn't tread on me once.'

'Comforting,' said Leah, and he almost smiled.

It must have been a comfort, though; the next round her hands weren't even shaking.

Thursday was mazurka.

'The trick to mazurka,' Mr Martin advised, 'is the sharp, clear action of the feet, and the easy movement from figure to figure.'

He was demonstrating, counting off the steps as he and Miss Hammond skipped this way and that. When he sank on to one knee, she held his upstretched hand in the tips of her fingers and moved around him like a bright ribbon around a maypole.

Leah and William stood side by side, watching the dance

unfold. Leah felt almost calm about it; the dance made so little sense that it seemed any mistakes could be covered up by swiftly changing direction, flinging out an arm and hopping in a circle.

'Leah,' said William, 'I hope your shoes are sturdy.'

Miss Hammond looked over, smiling. 'I'm sure it will be second nature, Mr Foster.'

He inclined his head. 'Then I might ask for your guidance, Miss Hammond.'

Miss Hammond glanced at Mr Martin; he frowned, barely, and then a moment later he was smiling at Leah, holding out a hand, saying, 'Let us begin!'

As it happened, Leah could acquit herself quite well at mazurka. The same could not be said of her cousin.

Finally, even Miss Hammond was required to sit out to recover herself. William bowed her into a seat, and seemed on the verge of retreating, until Mr Martin said, 'Now, let us see how well the students learn from one another!'

(He spoke to William, but watched Leah all the while.)

With the look of a martyr, William took hold; his hands were cold, and Leah felt a flash of sympathy.

'Don't worry,' she said. 'I'll make a fool of myself before you do.'

'We'll see about that, I suppose,' he said, but there was a ghost of a smile on his face, and his fingers were a little steadier as Mr Martin counted off the beat, and with Leah holding him back from a wrong move twice, they muddled through.

(He stepped on her toe once, but when he moved to apologize, she made a little warning face, and the corners of his eyes folded up when he smiled.)

When they finished, Miss Hammond applauded.

'Well done, Leah,' she said. 'Lovely!'

Leah flushed and pulled her hands from William's.

'We'll see how long it holds,' she said. 'Miss Hammond, you must promise to practice with me in London, so it's fresh when I venture out.'

Some little shadow crossed Miss Hammond's face, but she only said, 'Of course, my dear.'

William was looking at her – too solemnly, she thought; there was no hope for him with a dance like this – and she had already started to ask him what he saw to make him so grave when the dressing bell rang, and it was time to change one low bodice for another.

Friday, William did not come.

Leah promenaded and quadrilled with Mr Martin until her whole vision was filled with golden curls, bright smiles, and two blue eyes that Leah did not like.

'So,' said Mama at dinner on Saturday, all smiles, 'Reg tells me that you've been spending some of your afternoons with Leah during her dance lessons, William? That's very kind.'

'It's certainly something,' said Reg, and took a punctuating sip of soup.

'Leah and Mr Martin are very kind to let me join,' William said. 'I have much to learn before the Season, I think.'

'I'm sure Leah enjoys your company,' she said.

'You might ask her,' William said.

It was just calm enough to sound polite, and just pointed enough that Leah looked up from her plate.

Mama blinked and turned to Leah.

'Leah? How was today's lesson?'

They had practiced round dances again, until Leah was relatively certain she wouldn't cause a knot in the figure; then they had turned to waltzing, for quite a while after the steps had been learned and for a purpose Leah couldn't guess.

('I suppose it's just as well,' she had said. 'I should get used to it now. There's no good in going to London just to get seasick from it in someone's ballroom.'

'That would make a banner night,' William said, and she'd been so startled she'd laughed.)

'Thorough,' she said. Then, struck by something a little perverse, she added, 'William is a very steady partner.'

That got his attention. He looked up at her with a strange expression, seeming on the verge of speaking, until Mama turned her praises on him; then he was trapped in polite nothings for a while longer, and by that time it was Father's turn to rouse himself and talk about all the sport William had missed, and so they didn't say another word.

(She placed it more quickly than she wanted to admit; it was the same expression he'd had when she'd laughed at his joke and she had stopped worrying about her feet, and for a moment they had been comfortable together.

But then she had glanced at Miss Hammond – she didn't know why – and when she looked back, he had looked as solemn as before, and Leah was back to feeling as though all the manuals in the world were useless.

Miss Hammond had been waltzing with Mr Martin, smiling as if she had stumbled on another Season, and Leah had wondered what sort of prospects could ever have passed her by.)

The lady who gives a ball should endeavour to secure an equal number of dancers of both sexes. Many private parties are spoiled by the preponderance of young ladies, some of whom never get partners at all, unless they dance with each other.
Routledge

After dinner, Father must have been in high spirits, because when he led Reg and William into the drawing room, he was already looking for Leah, and even though she only caught '. . . little demonstration,' meant over his shoulder for William, she could guess what was coming.

'Oh, yes,' said Mama, turning to her. 'A splendid idea. And Miss Hammond can accompany. Stevens, please ask Miss Hammond and Mr Martin to come down.'

'Good heavens,' said Reg, 'this is like watching someone being sent to the gallows.'

'That's enough of that,' said Father, and Reg finished his brandy with a sour face and said nothing more.

William finished his as well, and then stood holding the glass as if looking for a way out.

Leah's sleeves cut into her shoulders, and she felt as though the waist of her skirt had gone suddenly too loose and would fall as soon as she stood. She concentrated on the tips of her fingers. It was no worse here than in the afternoon; this was much better than some great ballroom in London with everyone watching her, waiting to criticize. Why was she so anxious?

'Lady Clement,' Miss Hammond said from the doorway. 'Thank you so much for the invitation to join you.'

Leah glanced up sidelong at Miss Hammond in her deep grey dress, who didn't seem at all disconcerted that she was being summoned to be of use.

(She'd had prospects, Leah thought fiercely, that's what made it all so terrible – she deserved better than Leah ever would.)

Mr Martin came in a moment later, still fixing the last of the knot in his cravat. He glanced at Miss Hammond, who had already seated herself at the piano.

'I see there's to be dancing,' he said a moment later, giving the room a bow.

Mother smiled. 'If you would oblige us,' she said, 'we would dearly love some entertainment this evening.'

'With greatest pleasure!' He held out a hand. 'Would you care to quadrille with me, Lady Clement?'

And so it began. Leah partnered with William for the quadrille, and then through a mazurka, for which Mama herself played the music, so that Miss Hammond could make a fourth. For the waltz, Miss Hammond was invited back to her seat, and as Mama and Father partnered up, Mr Martin held out his hand to Leah.

'Miss Clement,' he said, and when he smiled she had the impression of teeth where there were none.

(A lady couldn't refuse an invitation at a private party; all men there were of impeccable character.)

'Of course,' she said, picked up her skirt in her right hand.

They made circles around the evening parlour, William frowning at them from a corner, and Miss Hammond at the piano in glimpses no longer than a blink, watching Mr Martin and Leah as if there were tears in her eyes.

Something about that look – something about it all – was overwhelming, so that long after Leah was safe back in her seat, her heart was pounding.

Leah couldn't settle, the whole time she was preparing for bed. Miss Hammond's face at the piano was haunting – a sign of something dreadful.

(It was as if she were jealous, Leah thought – she didn't know why – and for a moment her heart turned over.)

Alone in her room, she clutched her dressing gown closed and looked at herself in the mirror.

She looked older.

Courage, she thought over and over – courage, courage, until she could walk up the stairs and knock gently on Miss Hammond's door.

Miss Hammond was still dressed, and when she opened the door she seemed startled to see Leah.

'I'm so sorry,' said Leah, 'but I had to see you. Is it all right?'

Miss Hammond blinked, and something sad and fleeting moved over her face.

'Of course,' she said and stepped aside.

Her desk was cluttered with books in neat stacks and some abandoned writing, and Leah smiled at it as she sat on the bed.

Miss Hammond took a seat beside her. 'What's the matter, Leah? You look as if you've seen a ghost.'

Leah's neck was burning; her ears were on fire.

'I don't want you to worry,' Leah said. 'About William, I mean.' She looked up, fixed her eyes on Miss Hammond's green eyes, willed her purpose to be clear. 'I don't care for him.'

There was a moment of quiet; Miss Hammond blinked, looked down at a spot on her skirt before brushing it away.

'You'd do well to marry him, I think,' said Miss Hammond. 'He's a clever young man, and I waited five Seasons for a man half as kind as he is.'

Courage, Leah thought, courage.

'What if I don't wish to marry?'

Miss Hammond half smiled. 'Then you have doomed yourself to disappointment one way or the other, and I am sorry for you.'

'But surely you can understand,' Leah pressed.

Miss Hammond's mouth thinned. 'Leah, I could not be more fond of you, but rare is the woman who dreams of growing old in the servant's quarters of someone else's house. If a good man offers, I advise you to take him.'

Leah shook her head so hard that her pins stung her scalp.

'But that's not—' She couldn't breathe, had to struggle to speak. 'That isn't where my heart lies.'

Miss Hammond looked at her for a long time. The candle-light carved her face into a pool of dark, two wide green eyes, a slice of light along her jaw.

Leah's hands were fists in the bedspread.

Finally, Miss Hammond cleared her throat.

'Leah,' she said, as if her own voice pained her. 'Leah, there's no happiness in it, if you follow your heart and ignore the world.'

No, Leah thought wildly, that can't be true, that can't be true.

(Not always, she amended, her heart beating against her stays. Miss Hammond read romances – sometimes, if you loved someone enough and weren't afraid, maybe the world could be ignored.)

Miss Hammond reached out for Leah's hand, pulled it back, folded it under the one in her lap, like a dove's wings.

Leah's eyes stung; her fingers stung; her tongue was going dry.

'Leah,' she said. 'I'm sorry.'

Oh God, Leah thought, Oh God, pity!

Her heartbeat nearly knocked her over, and when Miss Hammond opened her mouth to speak again, Leah croaked out, 'Please, don't,' scrambled down from the bed, stumbled out (her stockings snagged on the floorboards).

If Miss Hammond called after her, she didn't hear; her breathing drowned out any other sound.

Leah was too embarrassed even for tears when she got back to her own room.

She could only close the door and turn the key with shaking hands, and pull the blankets nearly over her head, as if she could keep out her own folly. Her heart was pounding; she felt ill, she was going to faint at any moment.

Her fingertips stung as if singed where she had touched Miss Hammond's blanket.

She was the very greatest fool! What had she done to be so forward?

(Miss Hammond's little look of pity – oh, God, she was ill, she was ill.)

The grandfather clock in the front hall struck one, then two, and still Leah lay half awake, half dreaming of some way to draw back from the door before she knocked, and walk back into her own room, and never to see such a terrible look from Miss Hammond again.

Leah woke from a fitful sleep while it was still dark, with enough purpose to know she had to try to make amends. She took the stairs in stocking feet to wake Miss Hammond with apologies, and beg her to stay on for the Season, and to promise never to speak of it again.

That was how she became the first in the house to discover that Miss Hammond was gone.

> Withdraw from a private ballroom as quietly as possible, so your departure may not be observed by others and cause the party to break up. If you meet the lady of the house on your way out, take your leave of her in such a manner that her other guests may not suppose you are doing so.
> *Routledge*

Her parents met her in the breakfast room to look over the note Miss Hammond had left and discuss what was to be done.

'It seems to be in hand,' Father pointed out. 'They have dismissed themselves with all possible speed and can hardly expect references. I'm not sure what's left to be done.'

Leah's mother had more feeling on the subject; she re-read the note several times, as if it was of great import, instead of just a polite rescinding of a post and a wish for general goodwill, and even when she spoke she couldn't look away from it.

'We must do something,' she said. 'We have been taken greatest advantage of! We must put an announcement in the paper condemning them. This is despicable licentiousness, and under our roof! If word gets out, imagine what they'll say about us!'

'They'll say you dismissed two troublesome servants as soon as you suspected anything amiss,' said Father.

'They'll say we allowed unspeakable liberties under our roof,' Mother snapped. 'We must expose them.'

'No,' said Leah, 'you won't.'

'But they might well be married by now! They might this minute be on their way to some other county, to try to present themselves as a respectable couple!'

'Then let them,' snapped Leah. 'They're no concern of ours, now.'

'Leah, what on earth has come over you that you speak to me this way?'

Leah gritted her teeth. 'It is only that I was the person principally injured by this deception,' she said as calmly as she could. 'I feel that no goodwill can come to me from bringing this matter to other eyes.'

'Well, I see what good they have done your manners.' She turned to Father. 'What do you think of all this?'

Father sighed, rubbed his jaw and considered. Finally he said, 'The Ladislaws had nothing but praise for him, which is how he came to our notice. If we say no good of him, then he will not come to the knowledge of our acquaintance and that will handle the matter.'

He didn't mention Miss Hammond at all; she had, of course, already vanished from consideration. Either she was now Mrs Martin, or she would fall even farther than she had already.

Mama looked from Father to Leah; her hand holding the letter still trembled.

'Very well,' she said at last. 'I may mention what has happened to the Ladislaws, when we see them in London, so they do not recommend him to any other families. Then, perhaps, that will be an end of it. For the moment, I must try to compose myself and decide what should be done about preparations for the Season.'

After she had gone, Father nodded and said, 'I'll be in my library, I think,' and vanished likewise.

Leah doubted that Mother would keep the matter wholly quiet, but a small victory was still a victory, and at least, for once, her thoughts had been heard by her mother. She would have to take her comforts where she could find them, for a while, or she would go to pieces.

(There was another note that Mama hadn't seen. It was

even shorter, and by now was blurred with tears, and Leah had memorized it after reading it only once:

> Dear Leah,
>
> I have taken a chance at happiness. I know you will understand me; I pray you will give me your blessing. I wish nothing but the best for you.
>
> With great fondness, Marie.

If you loved someone enough and weren't afraid, the world could be ignored.)

Someone rapped gleefully on the doorjamb.

'Well,' said Reg, 'it's a wonder how fast word travels when there's any real news.'

Leah pinched the bridge of her nose. 'Reg, go back upstairs.'

'And miss this? Hardly.' Reg grinned. 'This is the first good bit of gossip we've had in ages. And you should be proud of trying to keep Mr Martin from coming – for once, you had the right idea about someone.'

'Leave it alone, Reg.'

He shrugged. 'I'm only saying, it's just as well you never thought much of him. Mother thought you very vexing about it, but events have borne you out, I'd say, and now we're well rid of two troublemakers.'

'Reg,' she said, and the word snapped against her teeth.

'Take a compliment when it's offered,' said Reg, all astonishment that she might take offence. 'You had more sense than that Hammond woman, at least, not that it's saying much.'

Leah's throat burned. Her fingernails cut into her palms. 'You're just being hateful because you're too idle to know anything. You don't know anything. Leave it alone!'

'I know that Miss Hammond had you wrapped around her little finger, sure enough. I was beginning to worry you'd pick up some terrible habits—'

'That's enough.'

It was William.

Leah turned; he was indistinct – her vision was blurred; she was going to cry any moment – but there he was, framed in the doorway, his posture betraying his anger.

(How did she know what his posture meant? Everything was strange, impossible and strange.)

William took another step into the morning parlour, his arms crossed over his chest. 'I suspect Mr Martin wasn't the only one under this roof who has no care for his reputation, Reg,' he said, with a pointed inflection on her brother's name. 'And Leah has made it clear that the last thing anyone needs is your half-formed opinions on the matter, so I suggest you leave off.'

Reg pulled a face. 'Christ, Foster, you're not married to her yet.'

'I haven't yet read where you need to be married to someone to note them when they speak,' said William.

Reg groaned theatrically, but a moment later he left, his footsteps exaggerated all the way back upstairs.

William moved no closer. Quietly, he asked, 'Are you all right?'

'Oh, quite,' Leah tried, but her throat had closed – her collar was too tight – and she could only manage to shake her head and pinch her mouth closed.

'I see,' said William. Then he bowed and said, 'You'll excuse me, I've recollected some business.'

After he'd gone, it was easier to breathe; she could breathe enough to go out into the garden, turn some corners and make sure she was alone before she sat down and wept.

William was sitting alone in the morning room when she came back. Though he looked up as she passed, he didn't call out for her, and she debated going upstairs to wash her face before she met him. But she was slowing down; she was stepping inside.

(His face had dropped all its politeness; he looked a little ill. Somehow it helped.)

He half rose, then sat back down, placed his hands at his sides, then on his knees and back again.

She took a seat in the chair beside him.

'That was kind of you,' she said.

He shook his head. 'Your brother is no better than some. I think he knows it.'

'I think he is beyond caring,' Leah admitted. 'My parents are not so intractable, but some things are just lost causes.'

He looked at her (the furrow in his brow, his nose that was just like hers).

'I'm sorry she left,' he said finally.

There was nothing in the words that sounded like triumph – it sounded like sympathy, and for a moment she struggled to breathe.

'Thank you,' she managed.

There was a little quiet.

It struck her, suddenly and too late, that her parents might have schemed for William to be alone with her like this.

Her mother would be scrambling for any good news that might overshadow the terrible inconvenience of the dancing master running off with the governess; an engagement would be just the thing to crow over in London.

He cleared his throat. 'Leah, I have something I'd like to say to you.'

Leah closed her eyes, steeled herself, looked at him with her polite smile at the ready.

('I waited five Seasons for a man half as kind,' Miss Hammond had said, before she ran away.)

His gaze was fixed on the floor at the other side of the room. 'I know that . . . I know your heart is not inclined to me,' he said. 'But I have nothing to look forward to in London. I know hardly anyone, and I am not at ease among strangers. I feel you understand me in this.'

She thought of their afternoon lessons, where he had walked through his round dances with the look of a man being led to the gallows, casting long-suffering looks at her when Mr Martin couldn't see.

'There was a reason they hired me a dancing master,' she said.

A shadow of a smile crossed his face. 'Quite so.'

But the thought of Mr Martin only made her think of Miss Hammond, sneaking out the back way in the dead of night, just under Leah's window, and vanishing into the dark.

She took two or three careful breaths, her busk pressing back against her ribs. 'My heart is broken, you know,' she said.

Her voice was quiet and sounded somehow far away, and for a moment she was afraid of how it must seem, to sound so sad about some governess (she was still so often foolish, about little childish things).

But he didn't laugh at her. He laced his hands together, looked at the ridge of his folded knuckles. He was flushed, just at the tips of his temples.

'But a broken heart can mend,' he said. 'I am sure that someday, you will find someone for whom you care.'

She tried to imagine that day. She tried to imagine walking into a ballroom in London and seeing William and her heart turning over; she tried to imagine seeing some sparkling countess laughing and glittering with diamonds, as in one of Miss Hammond's novels. But it was only Miss Hammond she thought about; Miss Hammond waltzing across the empty room, one inch of her petticoat showing, where she had picked up her skirt to pretend the glory days had come again.

'William,' she said, stopped. She was trying to put words to something that still ached too much to name. She tried again. 'You are very kind, but my heart is a contrary creature, and I dare not give you any expectation.'

He nodded, as if there were worse things, and took a breath or two, and then he looked over at her. 'With no expectation,' he said, 'I would be honoured to be your friend, if you need one, in London or anywhere else.'

The tips of her fingers went a little warm as she looked at him, as if they had been singed and were coming to life.

'You're just saying that because you don't know how to dance the mazurka unless I keep time for you,' she said.

'Quite so,' he said, solemn.

After a moment, he smiled.

After a moment more, so did she.

THE TAWNY BITCH

Nisi Shawl

My Dearest Friend,

This letter may never reach you, for how or where to send it is beyond me. I write you for the solace of holding you in my thoughts, as I would that I could hold you in my arms. So rudely was I torn from the happy groves of Winnywood Academy, I can only conjecture that you also have been sent to some similarly uncongenial spot. Oh, my dear, how I hope it is a better one, even in some small measure, than the imprisonment forced upon me here. I inhabit a high garret: bare of wall, low of ceiling, dirty-windowed. Through the bleary panes creeps a grey light; round their fast-barred frames whistles a restless wind. Some former inmate has tried to stop up the draughts with folded sheets of paper, and these provide the material platform on which stands my fanciful correspondence with you.

My pen is that which you awarded me, my prize for mastering the geometric truths of Euclid. Sentiment made me carry it always with me, next my heart. How glad I am! It is now doubly dear to me, doubly significant of our deep bond. As for the ink, I must apologize for its uneven quality, due entirely to its composition. In fact, I have rescued it from my chamber pot.

Yes, love, these words are set down, to put the matter quite plainly, in my own urine, a method imparted to me by my old African nurse, Yeyetunde. It has the advantage, in addition to its accessibility, of being illegible, almost invisible, till warmed above a flame. As I am allowed no fire of any sort, I may not see to edit my words to you. I hope my grammar and construction may not shame me, nor you, as my preceptress in their finer points. But I believe I will soon cease to trouble myself about such things.

Whom do you suppose to have betrayed us? I am inclined to suspect Madame, as she was the only one, probably, who knew of our attachment. Certainly none of the other pupils was in a position to do so. Though Kitty was most definitely set against me on account of my race, and pretended not to understand the difference between mulattoes and quadroons such as myself, she had no real opportunity to do us harm.

It vexes me that I made no attempt to buy Madame's silence when I had plenty of gold at my disposal. She dropped the most enormous hints on the subject, which I see quite clearly now, in hindsight.

I must school myself not to fret about these matters, over which I have no control. There is enough with which to concern myself in my immediate surroundings. If I spend my days fussing and fidgeting, I will wear out my strength, both physical and mental. My first concern is to preserve all my faculties intact.

When I came to myself in this place, I did doubt my senses. I had lain down to rest on a bed of ease, confined, it is true, as a consequence of our discovery, but still with my own familiar toys and bibelots ranged round me. I awoke with dull eyes, a throbbing head and a fluttering heart, in these utterly cheerless surroundings.

Well, some evil drug, perhaps, subdued me to my captor's power. He has yet to reveal himself to me, and my two gaolers say not a word in answer to my inquiries, but I have no doubt as to who it is: my Cousin John. When informed of our behaviour, he must have once more assented to be burdened with my maintenance. Certainly he could not have hoped to have kept me in school much longer, the backwardness ascribed to my race and colonial upbringing having by now vanished under your tender tutelage. I have thought much of these things during the two days I have spent here, there being little else to occupy my time, and I believe it must be so.

But now I have the comfort of writing. To hold intercourse with you, even through so attenuated a medium as this, will give me strength to endure whatever trials lie ahead.

I continue with the description of my prison. I believe I neglected to mention that the walls are washed a stark white: harsh, yet tainted, soiled with the careless print of unclean hands. The floor is a mere collection of loose boards. It is there that I shall hide this letter, and any other secrets my time in this place vouchsafes to me. Gloomy pillars rise at intervals to the rough rafters above, and a brick chimney, from which proceeds all the warmth afforded me. The windows, barred and begrimed, afford an ill view of the countryside.

That I am in the country I deduce from the silence surrounding me, unbroken save for the moaning wind and the monotonous nightly barking of a solitary dog. The glass is so befouled as to disguise all distinguishing visual characteristics of the neighbourhood. I have just formed the project of cleaning it, when left on my own as now, that I may perhaps ascertain my whereabouts. There, you see how good you are for me, what a salutary effect so slight a contact with you even as this can have upon me? Then do not chide yourself for the predicament in which I now find myself, love. The danger may yet be won through, and the rewards have been so richly sweet as to defy description. No need; you know them. Back, then, to the present.

One door only serves my prison, and it is a heavy barrier, much bolted. It opens twice a day to a brutish pair, whom for a while I thought to be deaf-mutes, so little did they respond to my pleadings for release. But just this morning— Stay! I hear

I have been honoured by such a visit, such attentions as would surely drive me to destroy myself were adequate means within my reach! No, I remember my promise to you, and there shall be no more attempts of that sort, whatever the goad, however easily the weapons were to come to my grasp. But oh, the insult of his touch! The vileness of the man, the ghastly glare as of his rotting soul, shining through the bloodshot eyes with which he raked me up and down, the moment he stepped into the room.

'Ho,' said Cousin John (for it was he), 'the little pickaninny loses what small comeliness she had. Martha, Orson, does she not receive good victuals? Remember, I pay all expenses and shall have a thorough accounting made.'

The shorter of my gaolers, a man (presumably Orson), replied that I consumed but a small portion of my meals. This is true, for who could be tempted by a nasty mess of cold beans and bloody sausages, or a bowl of lumpy gruel?

My cousin then turned back to me and said, 'So you would starve yourself, would you, my black beauty? Well, that's no good, for then your fortune will revert to that b_____ Royal Society, and though I am your guardian until you come of age, your father made no testamentary provision for me upon your death.' These last words were almost murmured, and seemed to be addressed to himself. He sank into a silent revery, which lasted a few moments, then roused himself to his surroundings.

'Now Martha! Orson! You must bring up some refreshment, and the means with which to partake of it. And a chair or two would not be amiss.' (For the lack of any furniture in my description of this room is not owing to your correspondent's negligence.) 'I dine with the young lady. What! Why stand you gawping there? Be off about your business!' Orson muttered something about the danger in which his master stood should I try to escape.

'Nonsense! This twig of a thing harm me?' And he laughed aloud at the idea, a heavy, bloated laugh. And indeed, he is much larger than me, and stronger, too, as he had occasion to prove at the conclusion of our interview.

For the moment, however, my cousin was all affability. He surveyed the sparseness of my accommodation and shook his head, saying, 'Well, 'tis a sad comedown from Winnywood. But you have been a very naughty puss, and must learn to repent your errors before you can be allowed anything like the liberality with which you have been used to be treated. I must not throw away money on the cosseting of a spoiled, sulky, ungrateful schoolgirl.'

Why should I be grateful? I thought to myself. The money is mine, though you seem inclined to forget this.

As though he had heard my unspoken words, my cousin showed himself somewhat abashed. He crimsoned, strode away, and hemmed and hawed for a moment before trying a new tack. The gist of this was that by my shameless behaviour with you, I had ruined for myself all hope of any respectable alliance with a man. He veered from this presently by way of allusions to the unacceptableness of my 'mulatto' features, the ugliness of which also unfitted me as a bride.

He paused, as if for breath, and I spoke the first words I had dared to utter in his presence: 'Love, affection of any sort, then, is quite out of the question? My fortune forms my sole—'

'Love! Affection!' interrupted Cousin John. He seemed astonished that I should dare to feel their want, let alone speak of it. 'After giving way to the unnatural perversions which have reported themselves to my ears, Belle, you ought to be grateful for common civility.'

He went on in this vein for some time. I confess that after a while I paid his lecturing scant heed. It put me in mind of my father's scolds to me when, as a child, I showed myself too prone to adopt the quaint customs of Yeyetunde and the other blacks about our place. As Cousin John prated away, I seemed almost to see my parent stand before me in his linen stock and shirtsleeves, urging rationalistic empiricism upon a child of ten. Of course, I was eventually brought to Reason's worship. But well I remember the attraction to me of the island's cult of magic, with its grandiose claims to control the forces of nature which my father sought only to understand. The brightly coloured masks and fans and other ceremonial regalia, surrounded by highly scented flowers; the glitter of candles in dark, mysterious grottoes; hypnotic chants and sweetly chiming bells; all clamoured at my senses and bade me admit in their train the fantastic beliefs with which they were associated. Then, too, I felt these practices to be connected somehow with my mother, of whom, as I told you, I have no true, clear, conscious recollection. Yet her presence seemed near when I was surrounded by these islanders, to whom the barrier between life and death was but a thin and permeable membrane.

Indeed, I can still dimly picture the altar which Yeyetunde instructed me to build in my mother's honour. It was a humble affair of undressed stone, with a wooden cup and a mossy hollow, wherein I laid offerings of meat, fruit and bread, and poured childishly innocent libations to her spirit.

My thoughts had wandered thus far afield when I was roused to my senses by the sudden seizure of my hand. Cousin John knelt, actually knelt on one knee at my feet, and held me in a grip firmer than was pleasant. Ere I had time to discover what he meant to be about, there came a knock on the door, and the sound of its several bolts and chains being shifted about in preparation for someone's entry.

My cousin with difficulty regained his feet, and the man Orson entered the room, bearing with him two chairs, followed by Martha, who carried a collapsed, brass-topped table.

I have not yet made you see these two, I think, fixtures though they are in my prison. Both are tall, stout, loose-fleshed and grim of countenance. Did they for some reason of devilry trade clothes, one would be hard pressed to note the change, for they are distinguishable otherwise only by the female's slightly greater height, Orson's face being smooth shaven.

In bringing in their burdens, this pair left open the door. I stepped round as noiselessly as I could to obtain a view through it, that I might determine what chance I had of making off. None, it appeared, for the door's whole frame was filled by a large, bony, yellow dog, a bitch. She eyed me suspiciously, and her hackles rose, and a low growl rose from some deeper region, it seemed, than her throat. Martha heard it. 'Come away from that!' she ordered harshly, whether speaking to me or the bitch, I could not tell. I backed away anyhow, and the bitch held her place.

I realized that in this apparition I had an explanation of the tiresome barking which plagues my dark hours here, and bids fair to keep me from ever obtaining a full night's sleep.

But my light and my ink both fail me, and I must postpone the telling of my thoughts and the rest of the day's events till morning.

I cannot recall exactly where I left off in my account. The door was open, I believe, and I had discovered it defended by the tawny bitch . . . yes, and I had just remarked how I believed her the source of the irksome barking which, together with the poorness of the pallet provided (Martha or Orson brings it in the evening, and it is removed on the arrival of my dish of gruel), and the uncomfortably chilly atmosphere, conspires to ruin my nightly rest. The barking goes on literally for hours: low, monotonous as the drop of water from some unseen, uncontrollable source. It is tireless, hopeless almost in its lack of change in tone, pitch, or volume; in frequency just irregular enough that one cannot cease to remark its presence. With daylight it ends, but so soon as I am able to fall into a broken slumber, my gaolers appear, remove the pallet, and the miserable day commences. No wonder, then, that this animal and I viewed each other in instant and seemingly mutual detestation.

'Come away from that,' cried Martha (have I already said?), and not knowing to which of us she referred, I retreated anyway. The two servants dropped their burdens and took turns in bringing in the food and other necessities, then shut the door and proceeded to set before us our dinner. This was much nicer than I usually get, consisting of a baked chicken, boiled potatoes, a side dish of green peas and a steaming hot pie, fragrant of fruit and cinnamon. I could not but imagine that Martha and Orson had designed this for *their* meal, and my mouth fair watered at the sight and smell of such good things. But Cousin John would have none of it at first and raised a fit, asking for soup and fish, jellies, cakes and such, and demanding that all be taken away and replaced with something better. However, there was nothing else, Orson told him, be it better or worse, so he was forced to make do with what was before him. But he did demand wine to drink, and two bottles were brought, and the servants then dismissed.

I made quick enough work of the portions on my plate, and surprised and pleased my cousin by requesting more. He helped me to it, refreshing himself with great draughts of wine between his labours. 'That's the dandy!' he said, spooning forth a quantity of gravy. 'Mustn't have you wasting away, merely because you are under a punishment.'

Well fed, I felt an increase of courage. How long, I asked him, must my punishment continue?

'Why, till you repent your sins, little Belle, and show that you are truly sorry for them.' As he said this he gave a heavy wink. Then he bellowed for Martha and Orson, who cleared the dirty dishes and broken meats, close-watched once more by the bitch, which confined itself, nonetheless, to the passage-way. Orson would have taken the wine with the other things, but his master bade him leave it.

Then we were alone, without hope of interruption. I had not drunk my wine, but lifted my glass now as cover for an inspection of my cousin's face. I hoped to reassure myself by tracing in his blurred, reddened outlines some coarse resem-blance to the beloved features of my father. I saw puzzlement there, and thick, unaccustomed lines bent the brow in frown-ing thought. I lowered my eyes, and when I looked up again upon setting down my glass, his expression had shifted to a false grin.

'Come, Belle,' said he, 'you are not so unseemly to look at when you smile a little, and let down your guard. Black but comely, a regular Sheba, one would say. As for your schoolgirl episodes, I could bring myself to set all that aside. Many a man would not have you, but for myself I say you're as good as a virgin, and a blood relative besides. Thicker than water, eh? You want no more than a proper bedding, which your little adventure proves you anxious to receive. I'm not proud, I'll take you to wife, let the world say its worst.'

'No more you will,' I muttered through hard-clenched teeth. In the next instant the table top was swept aside with a crash, and my cousin on his feet, dragging me to mine.

He seized me in a horrid, suffocating embrace, mauled me about with two fat, hairy paws and breathed into my shrinking face a thick, wheezing lungful of tobacco-scented, wine-soaked breath.

Half-swooning, I yet fought with ineffectual fists for my release. The monster loosened his grip, but only to change the angle at which he held me, leaving more of my frame subject to his inspection. And not with his eyes alone did he examine me! But with eager hands he sought to undo my bodice and gain sight of what its strictures denied him. Busied thus, he failed to notice my slow recovery, until I made him know it! He stooped to bestow upon my bosom a noxious kiss and received a sharp bite on the nose! Alas, not sharp enough, for no blood flowed, but a torrent of curses and ugly expres-sions of wrath.

I took advantage of my attacker's pain and distraction to extricate myself from his hold, and with trembling hands tried to restore somewhat of my customary appearance. When he saw this, he laughed. 'Don't bother yourself with that business,' he sneered. 'I've not finished yet.' In a most sinister manner he advanced, and I retreated to the utmost corner of my prison, protesting uselessly. A bully and a tyrant I called him, and other fine epithets, but it must have gone hardly with me, if not for intervention of a most unexpected sort. A great noise arose at the door, a confusion of banging, barking, scratching, scraping, howling and I know not what else. Though loud enough to herald the arrival of a pack of hell hounds, it proved, upon Orson's opening the door, to proceed solely from the tawny bitch. The beast rushed past him to a position which would have forced my cousin to engage with her in order to come at me. Though she is an ill-favoured brute, I admit an obligation to her for this timely interruption. A few blows quieted her, and gave vent to most of my cousin's spleen. This was further relieved by cursing Orson, and demanding to know what he was about to keep such an unruly animal. And why had he not better control of it, and what meant he by unlocking the door to it and exposing my cousin to its attack?

As he restrained the barely subdued dog, Orson seemed somewhat puzzled to defend himself, and made out that the bitch was not his own, but his master's. Hadn't he seen it trotting up behind my cousin's carriage as he arrived that afternoon?

'Mine?' cried Cousin John. 'Why should I saddle myself with such a wretched-looking animal as that? Put it out, have it whipped from the grounds!' And that he might supervise the execution of these orders, he left me to soothe my disordered nerves and recover from his attack as best I could on my own. No apology or inquiry as to my well-being came either that day or the next, today. Only I cannot think he was successful in barring the tawny bitch from the property, for again last night I heard her constant, irritating bark.

But perhaps it is not the same dog. These disturbances have gone on ever since my arrival here, and according to Orson, the bitch came with my cousin.

* * *

It is now afternoon, I think. Cousin John has not approached me all the day. Perhaps he may be gone away again. If not, if he should once more assault me, what shall I do? How can I defend myself? Should I agree to marry him in order to gain some measure of freedom? I do not think that in a case of coercion, the contract would be valid. Yet, I hesitate to take such a step, uninformed as I am of my rights here in England. Who could tell them to me? Who would deign to defend them? Escape is a better tack to try.

I contrived this morning to retain a damp cloth from amongst the meagre provision for my ablutions. With this I have been rubbing at the window panes, at least, as much as I could reach of them through the iron bars. Of course, a great deal of the dirt is on the outside, but I do think I have made an improvement. In one corner I can see a bit of the landscape. From this I judge that the house in which I am confined is in a hollow, for a dingy lawn sweeps up almost to a level with this window, topped by a row of dreary firs. A road – very rough, little more than a cart track – falls gradually along this declivity, till it disappears from sight around the house's corner. All is grey and forbidding, and altogether northern in its aspect.

Forgive me, my friend, I know you love this land, even its rural solitudes. You, in your turn, are as sensitive to my longing for the smiling skies of St Cecilia, for the loss of which you comforted me so sweetly. But now, separated alike from my home and my dear solacer, and ignorant as to how long this separation lasts – oh, my spirits are abominably low. I cannot go on writing in this vein. Besides, it grows too dark.

Very low. No plan as yet. My situation seems very bad, though still without sign of Cousin John. Left alone to brood on my wrongs. The food is as inedible as formerly. If it continues so, I shall not have to weigh my promise to you. Starvation will put a period to my troubles.

I try to think on happier times. It is now five days since I have been here. Allowing time for travel, and for the effects of the drugs I believe to have been administered upon me, it is perhaps not much more than a week ago that we were together.

Do you remember the delight with which you caressed my hair, likening it to rain clouds and the weightless fluff of dandelions? How you loved to twist and smooth and braid the dark masses, remarking on their softness and compactability! And how I loved your touch there, so gentle yet so thrillingly luxurious . . . I had not known such tender attentions since the sale of my nurse, on my father's death and the breaking up of our household. It frightened me sometimes, your tenderness; it seemed but a fragile insulator for the energy of your passion. As if, the more delicate its outer expression, the deeper and more primordial its final essence. Exactly so did I find this essence, when at last it was unveiled to me. And in its echoing through the sad hollowness of my orphaned heart I heard, I felt, music, rapture, bliss! To hold with all my might this joy, and to enfold my own within it, to wrap myself around you and your fierce love, to feel you yield it to me with such voluptuous uncontrol, and in your pleasure afford me mine, oh my dearest, it was right, it was good and inevitable. My maiden hesitancies melted all away in these heated storms, as a summer downpour annihilates the hard pellets of hail strewn before it.

I know that you believe our separation to be a judgement upon us. So much I was able to divine from your hasty note, though I read it only a few times the night I received it, and could not find it on waking here. I understand your assertion, but I deny it. We have harmed no one, have behaved only according to our natures. This time of trial is troublous, but hold fast and it, too, shall pass. My cousin may confine, he may persecute me, but over the passage of time he can have no control. In a few short months I shall be twenty-one, and mistress of my fortune. Better if I spent those months free from this confinement, but however slowly they may slip away, whatever horrors or privations I may have to endure, I will live to come of age. Nothing, then, can divide us.

I will find you; I will

A carriage has come up along the road. A sound so unusual stood in need of investigation, so I ceased my writing for a moment, to see if I could catch a glimpse of the equipage. I just made out the closed top of a smart brougham, giving no hint of its occupant as it wheeled swiftly by.

I cannot contain my hope and curiosity. The sound of the carriage's movement ceased abruptly. Has it brought rescue? Another prisoner, perhaps? Perhaps – my love, could it be you?

I am agitated; I think I hear signs of an approach—

So very wretched a turn things have taken that I cannot bring myself to write for long. Dr Martin Hesselius is the name of this new visitor; a proud, sparely fleshed man with a Continental accent, a cold eye and an even colder heart. My entreaties for release engrossed him but as symptoms. He has been persuaded of my insanity, and sees in me a rare opportunity to exercise his theories on the causes of, and effective treatments for, mental disorders.

Upon examining me he was greatly surprised that I spoke the Queen's English, and never seemed quite possessed of the idea that I could understand it. He made many offensive remarks on my physiognomy and physique, as of their primitive nature, and was deeply derogatory of my mother, hardly less so of my father, citing his 'degenerate lust' and her 'cunning animality'. Any protest I uttered against his infuriating statements was made to stand at no account, except that of proving my madness.

And then, my friend, Cousin John brought in his report of our doings. It was sickening to witness the happiness with which he made sordid-seeming all that I hold in my memory as sacred. And much worse was the light in which Dr Hesselius received these tidings. I take it now that for a woman to love a woman is more than just a crime, it is the very definition of insanity . . . How shall I ever, ever win my way from here?

Distracted. Bitch barking throughout the entire night. Early in the morning, just at dawn, I detected the sound of a carriage leaving, but I take no heart from that. By something I overheard Martha say to Orson, I believe Dr Hesselius has left, but only temporarily, in order to procure some 'medicines' and 'instruments' for my torture – he would have it, for my cure.

★   ★   ★

Somewhat better now. I have had a meal, the menu of which was decided by the good doctor: boiled lamb, finely minced, and asparagus. I had some difficulty in eating this, as I am no longer entrusted with cutlery, nor any implement more dangerous than a wooden spoon, even under the watchful eyes of my guards. The meal was not ill-prepared, though, and I did it some justice. The whole washed down with great lashings of green tea, of which, I am told, I am to have any quantity I like, this dietary regimen being a part of Dr Hesselius's recommended course of treatment.

Three other changes are to be instituted as a result of his prescription. I learned of them through indirect means, as neither of the servants will answer my questions, even now that I can call them by their names. But Orson complained to Martha of having to draw and haul the water for my baths, which I gather I am to be given daily from now on. Martha retorted that she was just as much put upon by the order to accompany me on my airings in the garden. Then there are 'salts' to be administered, which I hope will prove harmless when they arrive. I believe there are other points in the doctor's programme, with which I must wait to acquaint myself till his return.

The idea of being able to walk out of doors fills me with an almost unhealthy excitement! At last, I shall be able to look about me and form some estimate of possible means of escape. To abide in my cousin's power any longer than necessary, even though he makes no further advances upon me, is an uncountenanceable thought. I am not mad to be so confined, nor a naughty, impetuous little girl. I have full and clear possession of all my faculties.

Just returned from my first, highly anticipated airing. It was not much in the way of what I had expected. Martha wrapped me round with a rough, woollen shawl and hurried me out to a dull little plot of grass divided by a gravel walk. Along this she proceeded to lead me back and forth, under skies in that irritating state of not-quite-rain, and between thick, tall hedges which retained just enough of last year's leaves as to make it impossible to spy out any significant features of the landscape barely glimpsed between their branches.

Still, I managed to obtain some intelligence from this outing. From the general air of dirt and neglect visible on my quick trip through the house, I am strengthened in my belief that it has probably no other inhabitants than myself, Martha, Orson, and (if he yet remains) my cousin. There is no one else, then, whose sympathies might be won to aid me in my plight. However, one may also say that there is no one else to hinder any efforts I am able to make on my own behalf.

My evening walk and meal differed slightly from those of earlier in the day. Celery stalks substituted for the asparagus, and a muffler made an addition to my walking ensemble.

As we stepped rapidly along the gravel, I noted a peculiar effect occasioned by the stems of the hedges which we passed. Lit now by the pale, watery yellow of the declining sun, they alternated with their shadows in such a manner as to produce the illusion of *something* – some animal, perhaps – keeping pace with us on the hedge's further side. It was most marked. My eyes were able to discern that the effect rose to a height somewhat equal to my waist, in a blurry, irregularly shifting mass. That it was an illusion, and not an actual animal, was proved by the precision with which it matched our speed and direction; pausing where we paused, hesitating, turning and recommencing along with us in an exactitude not to be explained otherwise.

I amused myself by imagining to which natural laws my father would ascribe this curious phenomenon, from the wisdom accumulated through his naturalistic inquiries. He had studied thoroughly many occurrences which our islanders saw in a supernatural light, always assuring me, when I became frightened at one of old Yeyetunde's tales, that there was a rational explanation for everything to be encountered in

Such an uproar as there was last night! No one thought to inform me as to the cause of the hubbub, and I wracked my brains in sorting out its details, trying to see how they might be made to fit together to accompany a reasonable sequence of events.

First came the sound of an approaching carriage. Or was the noise sufficient for two? I got up and strained my eyes to look through the dark, dirty windows. There were lights, as of coach lanterns, but briefly glimpsed and not steady enough for me to count their number.

The horses halted. Muffled shouts and cries for assistance came in coarse workmen's voices. Then a furious gabble of frightened screams, heavy crashes, and ferocious barks. Now canine, now human tongue predominated, till at length came a lull, followed by the sounds of a carriage in movement again. This soon ceased as well, so presumably the vehicle was just led round to the stables. Then came a long silence. Then the sharp report of a pistol.

Nothing further disturbed the night's calm, not even the customary plaint of the tawny bitch. I am left to surmise that she attacked the arriving carriage, or its occupants, perhaps dislodging some heavy piece of luggage, and for her sins was shot. The sadness with which I greet this conclusion surprises me. Dogs are lowly animals, as my father taught me, unworthy of their fame as faithful, noble creatures. 'A wolf,' he would often say, 'is somewhat noble. A dog is a debased wolf; an eater of human waste and carrion; fawning, half-civilized, wholly unreliable.'

The islanders, too, hold dogs in very slight esteem. Their use in the tracking of runaway slaves, perhaps, has led to their general abhorrence. I am not sure whether any were sent after my mother. She was not a slave, because of being married to my father. Somehow she wandered away from the plantation and became lost. The exact circumstances leading to her death were never spoken of.

Yeyetunde, with that patient obstinance so typical of the African, said only that my mother had met her fate deep in the forest, after being missed at home for more than a day. What was she doing there? Who found her? And how came they to know where to look? I could not induce her to answer me, save with the stricture that such things were for my father to tell me, if he would.

He would not.

Oh, he spoke of my mother, and that frequently enough. Almost, I could believe his memories my own. Her beauty; her skin described in a multitude of hues, such as amber, honey, and the pure light of dawn; her genius for discovering rogues and ill-wishers amongst his pretended friends; the portside hostelry where first they met; the speed and ease of her confinement and my delivery; with these I am more than familiar. They only serve to make the blankness following the less bearable.

In time I grew so used to my father's evasions and silences on the subject of my mother's death, I began to conclude that the occurrence had been excruciatingly painful, and that he omitted to recount it, not from any conscious design, but from his positive inability to do so.

Still, I learned to note one peculiarity in his responses, which, however, I am yet uncertain as to how I might interpret it. For hard upon his silences, or at the heart of any irrelevancies with which my father might choose to distract me, came the subject of dogs: their viciousness, their unruliness, and their unpredictability, especially when dealt with as a pack.

I grow weary of lamb. Asked of Martha if there were no other provision to be had. She answered me with stony and insolent silence. The tea is good, though, and very warming after my cold immersion baths.

If last night's arrival was the doctor, or my cousin, I have not heard from them, nor received any word of their coming. How annoying to be dependent on the doings of servants for my augury of what goes on around me! Orson has been absent, all my needs being met this morning by Martha, even the toilsome task of hauling up and filling the tub for my bath. Was he injured in last night's fracas? Or perhaps another was hurt and requires his attendance. That would make of the present an opportune moment for my escape. I wish I knew.

Gathered no further intelligence from my morning's excursion, save that the odd phenomenon of the shadow beyond the hedge seems not to confine itself to evening hours. Mentioned this to Martha, who took it just as she takes all I say: with no further notice than an evil, impertinent look. But I noted her eyes trained nervously on the blur as it accompanied us, and I believe our exercise was curtailed as a result of its effect upon her. I shall not mention it aloud again, for I grudge every step denied me. I must keep up my strength. It would not do to come upon a chance to flee and be physically incapable of taking advantage.

Languid all the day. This must be the consequence of my perpetually disturbed rest. The bitch is back. That expressionless bark, as of a monotonous lesson learned by rote. I cannot sleep, but I begin to think that nonetheless I dream, for words fit themselves to its untiring, evenly accented rhythms. Admonishments, warnings, injunctions to take up unclear duties, the neglect of which foreshadows danger, yet the accomplishment of which is impossible because ineluctable. The whole effect is one of unbearable tension. I rise and pace, barely able to keep myself from rattling the barred windows, the bolted door – I dare not give way as I should like to do. I must remain in possession of my faculties, that I may engage the belief and sympathies of whomever I first come across on breaking free of my captivity. It may be the keeper of a nearby inn, or some pious and upright local divine; for their sakes, I must retain a rational appearance.

I must escape while I have the wit to do so.

Violation! Oh, foul and unwarrantable assault! To live and endure such a burden of shame, oh, my friend, how? How can I? My hand shakes; I have not the strength to write. But if I do not, I may be moved to relieve my outraged feeling on myself, and I have sworn to you—

I have a further thought that these words, so poorly penned, will yet stand witness to my sobriety. In order that I might give the lie to my cousin's claims as guardian of an unhinged mind, I will recount here all I recall. The sickening details . . .

The bed – I cannot bring myself to rest there. It is a symbol of my humiliation, with its awkward headboard and thick, stiff straps. When it arrived in my prison this afternoon, I thought I might perhaps be able to recoup some of my lost sleep, and so fight off the half-dreaming state that recently has plagued me. The straps repelled, but the thick mattress was more welcoming than my poor, vanished pallet. I had just lain down to test its softness when my gaolers made an unexpected return, wheeling with them a strange apparatus. A large, inverted glass bottle hung suspended from a tall rack. At its neck dangled a long, flexible tube, and on the end of this – oh, it is of no use, I cannot . . . yet, I will go on – a hard, slick nozzle, fashioned of some substance such as porcelain: white, cold; horribly cold . . . I fought, but Martha and Orson together managed to restrain me to the bed, strapped in so that I lay stretched out on my side. Beneath me they tucked a piece of thick, yellow oilcloth. As they did this they lifted and disarranged my skirts and draped sheets over my head and shoulders, and also about my knees. Thus I lay with my fundament exposed, while I had no way to see anything further of what passed.

Imagine my sense of shame, then, when I heard voices approaching and recognized the tones of Dr Hesselius and Cousin John! They entered the room, discussing my case as though I had not been there. Far from protesting this rudeness, I maintained a foolish, cowardly silence. A child with her head hidden beneath the counterpane, avoiding nightmares; that is how you must picture me.

Dr Hesselius spoke of how a host of substances he termed 'mortificacious' had deposited themselves throughout my inner workings. 'I deduce that they have chiefly attached themselves to the lower end of the patient's digestive system.'

My cousin cleared his throat. 'Mmm. Er, how did you arrive at this conclusion, sir?' He sounded a great deal embarrassed.

'You intimated that the patient's studies progressed well, exceedingly well, in fact, for one of her primitive origins. This indicates that the head's involvement is only a partial one. As the mortificacious material tends to gravitate to its victim's polar extremities . . .' So much I am sure he said, and a quantity of other quackish nonsense besides. My attention was distracted by a clatter nearby, as of glass and metal rattling together. Then came a liquid sound, like water running into a narrow container. I cannot convey to you the sense of unreasoning dread these noises aroused in me.

Suddenly, gloved hands seized me upon – no. Seized me, I say, and I was forced – forced to accept the nozzle. My shame and confusion were such that not for several moments did I realize another's howls of pain and outrage were mingled with my own. As this was borne in upon my suffering consciousness, I subsided into sobs, listening. The other sounds quickly died down as well, though a low, near-constant menacing growl made evident their author's continued presence.

The good doctor had ceased his ministrations at the clamour's height. He now ventured to ask my cousin why he had not done as requested and shot the damned bitch?

Cousin John replied that he had done so, 'and at pretty near point-blank range. But the revolver must have misfired, for the beast got up and ran away. I suppose it was only wounded.'

'A wounded animal is all the more dangerous,' Dr Hesselius informed him. 'I have already paid to your hell hound my tithe of flesh. Better take care of the problem at once.'

Only my cousin did not chance to have any weapon handy, so that these two brave, bold gentlemen were required to cringe in my prison with me while Orson was sent forth into the now silent passage, armed with a board torn from the floor. Meanwhile, I lay in my sodden clothes, half-naked, half-suffocating in a cooling puddle of noxious liquids. After some moments, the quiet continuing, Martha was ordered to unbolt the door again and go in search of the other servant. From her hallooing and the remarks subsequent upon her return, I deduced that the house appeared empty.

This filthy, *soi-disant* treatment is to be inflicted weekly. I do not intend to remain a captive here for long.

The hedge-haunter is no spectre, but live flesh and blood. It is the tawny bitch who has followed me on my daily walks. I saw her outline quite clearly through the hedge this morning, despite the rain. Orson accompanied me; I fancy Martha has taken a dislike to her duties, or to my other escort. I know not why, for the poor beast cannot help her looks. As for temper, the only signs she has shown of that have come upon threats to my well-being. I could almost love her.

*   *   *

Walked again with Orson this evening. I made sure he noticed how marvellously close the tawny bitch was able to follow our various paces. He liked it not.

Barking commenced earlier, at sunset, long before dark. Text: 'How sharper than a serpent's tooth it is, to have an ungrateful child,' etc., etc. Well-laid arguments, but I cannot see anything apposite in the quotation. Does it contain some hint as to how I may make my escape? I must reflect on this.

Oh, my friend, my best and most beloved friend, soon now I shall be able to confide my heart unto your very bosom! I have quite a clear presentiment that it will be so.

This evening I was let out to accomplish my walk on my own. Martha's eyes were ever on me, it is true, as she stood in the entrance to the kitchen garden, with all the long gravel walk in her plain sight, but she could do nothing to prevent my plan.

It came to me because they would give me so much lamb, and the poor thing looked so thin, gliding along outside the hedge. And indeed, she must have been quite wasted away to have slipped through those tight-packed branches and come to me. I coaxed her to take the meat straight from my hand. Such a pet! I called her my honey and kissed her cool, wet nose, and collared my arms about her soft, smooth-furred neck. Goat's meat would have been preferable. I remember that from Yeyetunde's teachings. It was goat's meat I placed upon her altar as a child. But the lamb was quite acceptable.

Twice more shall I make my offerings. I can hardly contain my great joy, but soon the barking will begin, so steadying to my nerves. So reassuring to know that she is there.

Afternoon. This morning I have given unto her the portion brought to me to break my fast, and she has shown me the passage, preparing for my escape. Thin as I am, the hole will yet need widening. My feeble hands have not been of much help. I am to leave this evening. She says she can dig all the day and that it will be ready. Of course I shall have to crawl and become fearfully dirty. So much the better if my light clothes are thereby darkened, as they will not so easily betray me to my pursuers.

Pursuers I shall have, but she says she can distract them. I do know that she can set up an awful cacophony at will. But would she actually turn back to attack them? If so, she shall no longer fight alone. Together we will tear, we will savage.

The preceding text has been assembled from a collection of fragmentary writings discovered during the demolition of an old country house. Their presentation is as complete and chronologically correct as my efforts could make it. The veracity of their contents, however, has proven somewhat difficult to determine.

Penmanship and internal references (Dr Hesselius drives a brougham; oilcloth rather than a sheet of India rubber is used during the enema's application) lead to the conclusion that the events narrated took place between 1830 and 1850. This very rough estimate I narrowed a bit further by deeds and entitlements pertaining to the purchase of the property, in 1833, by a Mr John Forrest Welkin, presumably the narrator's 'Cousin John'. Parish records show his death as occurring in 1844. He would, at this time, have attained forty-eight years; he was not young, but certainly he fell far short of the age at which one dies suddenly and without apparent cause, as seems to have been the case. He was single and had no heirs of the body.

Of the locations described by the author, only this house's 'high garret' is of unquestionable provenance. The papers were found secreted beneath the loose flooring of just such a bare, comfortless room. The house itself had been uninhabited for half a century, commencing early in the reign of our Queen. The place has a bad reputation in the district as being haunted, and reports of various canine apparitions are easily obtainable at the hearths of all the neighbouring alehouses. Of course, such superstitious folklore can scarcely be credited. No two 'witnesses' can agree as to the size or number of the pack, though as to colouring there seems a fair consistency. To the rational mind, however, the house's situation down in Exmoor, halfway between South Molton and Lynmouth, and its less than luxurious appointments, ought to be enough to account for its long state of tenantlessness.

Turning to those proper names revealed by the text, often so fruitful of information for the careful investigator, my researches became more and more problematic. Winnywood Academy may possibly have been located in Witney, near Oxford. A relevant document, a six-year lease, apparently one in a series of such contracts, has been uncovered. It stipulates an agreement between one Madame Ardhuis and the fifth Viscount Bevercorne for the use of Winny Hall. Contemporary records also indicate a pattern of purchases by this Madame Ardhuis at stationers, chandlers, coal merchants, and the like. Quantities and frequency are sufficient for the type of establishment sought.

Though the narrator writes of the 'smiling skies of St Cecilia,' there is no trace of such an island in any atlas. Santa Cecilia is a small village in the mountains of Brazil (26 .56' S, 50 .27' W) and there is also a Mount Cecilia in Northwest Australia (20 .45' S, 120 .55' E). Neither of these satisfactorily answers the description. We are left to make do with the uncomfortable knowledge that place names do change with time and that local usage varies.

In reference to most of the persons depicted above, none but Christian names are used: Belle; John; Martha; Kitty; Belle's old nurse, Yeyetunde. Four others are referred to only by title: Father, Mother, Madame and the document's intended reader, 'my friend'. The research involved in matching all these references with actual historical personages is beyond the scope of a lone amateur. Belle may have sprung from the loins of the irresponsible Hugh Farchurch, a connection of Welkin's on the distaff side. In postulating this, equating 'Madame' with Madame Ardhuis, as seems reasonable, and achieving the identification of 'Cousin John' with Welkin, I have done that of which I am capable.

In the case of Dr Martin Hesselius, we have a surname and corresponding historical linkages. The doctor was well known during his professional career (1835–71), and his presence would seem to vouch for the text's authenticity. But Hesselius's character as represented here is quite at odds with his reputation. He was known as a layer of mental disturbances, not as one who raised them into existence. Moreover, the few details of his personal appearance given us do not tally. We are left with the distinct impression that in this matter someone has been imposed upon.

THE PROBLEM OF TRYSTAN

Maurice Broaddus

The Tejas Express was a monstrosity of gleaming metal, though in its own way, beautiful to behold. A large cumbersome carriage with steam curling around the machine like caressing tendrils as it rumbled along on an intricate system of toothed tracks. It moved with a great thrumming sound, much like a racing heart attempting to be restrained. Winston Jefferson jostled about in the car, one eye on the group of soldiers milling about as if they were not on duty. Part of him resented the scarlet bleed of their red soldier uniforms – the antithesis of camouflage by design, as the object was to let the enemy know who was coming for them in the name of Her Majesty Queen Diana. His other eye rested on his charge, whom the soldiers amiably chatted up. Winston's hand tightened its grip on the handle of his cane as she sauntered towards him.

Olive complexioned, with long brown hair framing aristocratic features from her piercing brown eyes to her aquiline nose, Lady Trystan stood at a formidable six feet tall. He couldn't quite place her origin, but he didn't care enough to ask. He simply appreciated the view and thanked God for whatever country could produce such a resplendent specimen. Lips glossed to an exaggerated redness, pursed tightly, not betraying a hint of her feelings. She had a regal presence in her green gown with blue accent in a kente cloth pattern, and a crinoline supported her dress with its slight train. It had a high neck with a tatted collar and soutache trim. She gambolled towards the bench. His eyes wandered. For a moment they met hers. She held the gaze.

'Mr Jefferson,' she said in her demure drawl, pretending she didn't know him. One of the little games she liked to play.

'Colonel.' He tipped his top hat.

'My . . . Colonel. We are proud of our titles.'

'Only the ones "we" have earned.'

Winston still wore a grey sack coat, copper buttons running up each side, left open in order to display a four-in-hand neck tie and collared shirt – the veneer of respectability. He began his career as a soldier when he was seventeen, and for ten years he served Queen and country, earning a battlefield promotion to colonel during the Five Civilized Nations uprising. Not that the title was anything more than honorific, as one of his station couldn't hope to command men. A moot point; wounded as he was, he was soon discharged for his troubles. A lacquered black rod with copper fittings beginning midway up its shank to its hilt, which was an open-mouthed copper dragon's head, his walking cane allowed him to hide the slightest of limps.

'Lady Trystan.' He nodded towards the wrought-iron table bedecked with a silver tray set with tea and cream in matching pots, next to a plate of strawberries. 'A magnificent name.'

'LaDashia Rachel Brown Willoughby of the Virginia Willoughbys.' She dipped a strawberry into the cream, then rolled it in the sugar – a slow, deliberate action – before popping it into her mouth.

'A family of noble bearing. Your father, Sir Anthony Willoughby, must be proud.'

'Adopted father. My mother was widowed soon after I was born.'

'Still, he's a member of the Royal Academy of Sciences. A rare honour.'

'We both took his name when they married. I took Rachel as my confirmation name.'

'So where does the name Trystan come from?'

'Are we the sum of our names, or can we choose to own some of them but not others?'

'You tell me.'

'I had no say in my birth name, no say in my mother's remarriage, and my religion was thrust upon me. Trystan is what I choose to call myself.'

'To my ear, it almost sounds like Trickster.'

'We all could use some of Br'er Nanci's spirit sometimes.' She chatted to mask her unease, perhaps discomfited by the weight of his scrutiny. Her over-creamed coffee complexion allowed those who wanted to turn a convenient blind eye and let her pass for a white woman. However, despite being hidden by make-up and the distraction of her peculiar framed glasses, her features favoured the Negro. Her face rendered elegant by inquisitive eyes and the mischievous humour hinted about in her lips; a keen intelligence laid in wait behind the beguiling playfulness in her hazel eyes.

'My mother was Caucasian. My natural father was African. He passed away soon after my birth. But I was so fair, none were the wiser when we relocated to Virginia, where mother met Sir Anthony. My heritage would be an embarrassment to him, my mother impressed upon me.'

'So why entrust your secret to me?'

'You have one of those faces.'

'What kind of face is that?'

'Handsome, intelligent and something just short of trust-worthy.' She smiled – a terribly enticing thing.

He never imagined his oval-shaped face, with low-cropped hair matching the length of his closely shorn beard but little longer than a week's stubble, as a particularly pleasant countenance. At best, he tried to carry himself as a noble man, a proud oak of a man with a complexion to match.

She differed from most of the ladies of society he had encountered, with their full bombazine skirts or elegant dresses or the insipidity and air of self-importance that accompanied most of the people of high society. They reeked of privilege and uselessness, and he listened to their chatter with perfect indifference. Inane white noise that heavied his eyelids. Lady Trystan was cautious in her praise of any man, he imagined, and with her insouciant demeanour – both flippant and wry – she would make a poor wife by most men's standards. Not used to so bold a woman – sarcastic humour without reserve, with a keen mind and no care for other's thoughts on her manner – she intrigued him.

'Men are such foolish creatures, unsure of what you feel or

if you should feel it. It was good for you that God chose to create women to help you along.'

'I can sort my own feelings just fine, miss.'

'Oh, I hardly believe that. You don't even realize how much attraction you feel for me right now.'

Winston found it difficult to disengage from her commanding gaze. Suddenly he straightened in his seat, conscious of where he was and what he was supposed to be doing. He was a man with a job to do, and it wasn't to be caught up in the spell of this slip of a woman.

'You look as if you've swallowed a turnip,' Lady Trystan said.

'Merely reminded of my duty.'

'Sorry if I distracted you.'

'Your father entrusted me to guarantee your safe passage.'

'Are your coterie of soldiers not enough?'

'They serve their function.'

'Which is?'

'To distract.'

Winston studied the faces of the people who shared their car, searching for anything or anyone that looked out of place. He read their eyes. A gaunt, swarthy gentleman buried his face in a newspaper. On the short side of average, in his brown suit and bowler hat, he had the ill-build of a rodent dressed as a dandy. The newspaper's headlines declared the beginnings of the Troubles – how everyone referred to the Jamaican uprising – as well as the Queen's preparation to appoint Viceroy Reagan to rule the American colony in the name of Albion and carry the banner for the Empire. A former actor as puppet sounded about right to him, but he didn't have the benefit of an A-level education.

A young boy quavered as his father scolded him. The tone rose in volume and the tenor in harshness, a critical barrage fuelled by anger and maybe a little drink. The rest of the passengers turned away in polite deference. The man's contempt erupted as he drew back to beat the boy right there when Winston rose and, heedless of the pain that caused him to limp, sprang to the boy's side. His cane may have stayed the father's blow, but it was the steel of his gaze that stilled the man.

'There's no need to take so stern a hand to the boy,' Winston said.

'The boy,' the man started, swallowed hard, and then found his voice again. 'The boy needed a lesson in quieting his manner.'

'A lesson already delivered. Do not let me find this boy bruised.'

'What business is it of yours to interfere with a father doing his duty?'

Winston came from a family of five children, and the responsibility of the older siblings was to protect the younger ones. Funny, the number of his family was six actually, but his brother, Auldwyn, died when he was two. Though Winston was barely old enough to know him when he died, the thought of Auldwyn, more than the actual memory of his loss, continued to pain him. 'I can't abide bullies. They . . . vex me. You don't want to vex me.'

Trystan looked at him in a special way, as if seeing him for the first time. She was a frightfully insufferable woman who had a predilection for revealing all of her teeth when she smiled, which she brandished like a dagger she was too quick to stab with. She quickly turned away, her long hair curled up into a tight coif, and fanned herself as she stared out the window.

'As I was saying, my duty was to deliver you into the hands of Sir Melbourne.'

'Such was my father's wish.'

'He is a powerful man, your father, with many enemies.'

'And he sought to mollify some of them with this ill-conceived arrangement. My parents are quite cross with me at the moment.'

'I couldn't hazard a guess why.'

'I was to marry Sir Melbourne, the Archduke of Georgia. A noble man of noble family.'

'And?'

'He bored me.'

'And a husband's duty is to entertain his wife.'

'Your sarcasm has been duly noted. He wanted a wife who was interested in keeping a home and organizing social events, to be a trophy attached to his arm when at a party and placed on the mantle when at home.'

'And such is not the calling for your life.' Winston had no use for a wife. Marriage was a kind of ownership, one person belonging to another. Freedom was too precious a commodity for him to forfeit any measure of it.

'No, it most certainly is not. However, I have more to be about than just finding a husband. The problem is that it is unseemly to have your daughters marry out of order.'

'I trust that your younger sisters are vexed with you also?'

'All four of them.'

'You broke off all marriage talk with Sir Melbourne?'

'Sir, my heart is my own. And it tarries . . . elsewhere.'

'You still have time to change your mind.'

'I know. A lot can happen in a fortnight.

The dynamo of Albion, the American colony was a proud beacon that stretched from the Atlantic to the Pacific, between the Five Civilized Nations of the northwest territories and the Tejas Free Republic of the southwest territories. The Tejas Express was a product of American revolutionary design. A luxurious vehicle, with an interior of lacquered mahogany, polished brass and brushed velvet. A luridly painted car, like a brothel decorated with a decadent designer's eye – well, to Winston's mind anyway, as his tastes ran to the simple. Cast of bronze, the engine snorted a continuous billow of steam as it bustled forward toward Indianapolis on its way to Chicago. For every burgeoning overcity like Indianapolis, there was a burgeoning undercity, in Indianapolis's case, the residents referred to theirs as Atlantis.

Winston imagined himself starting over in a place like Indianapolis. Nondescript, a blank slate of a city where he could disappear and redefine himself. As of this moment, he was a forcibly retired – as forcibly as he was conscripted – soldier. His station was enough to spare him toiling away in the undercities, shovelling coal or assembling small machines in the industrial shops, the clockwork gears biting into scabbed fingertips for hours on end. He might be able to find a low-ranking position in the overcity, something he was overqualified for, but it'd be a place to start. Winston wondered why he couldn't just be content with his lot in life. No, the nagging fear that he ought to be doing something other than his father's profession dogged him. He'd inherited an estate of 750,000-dollar credits from his father, but he had made his fortune in trafficking – money made selling their own people into indenturetude – and the weight of the shame was not worth his soul. He would make his own way. He used some of the money to free others from indenture, then gave the rest away. He was meant for greater things, to have it all, and he wanted to be beholden to no one. Perhaps his destiny awaited him as a businessman. If he could grow a business to the point where he wasn't needed to run it day to day, then he could expand into other ventures. To dabble in airships was his dream, but it all began with starting a business. Only then could he hope to be with someone like Lady Trystan.

'Mr Jefferson.' She leaned on her frilly parasol in tacit imitation of him and his cane.

'Colonel.'

'Where are you from? Kentucky perhaps?'

'Why do you ask?'

'Your manner and speech betray you. Too affected.' A furtive glance. A less attentive gentleman may have missed it, but she tracked the movements of the soldiers. 'There's a hint of accent to your words. It doesn't slip out often, but it's there. You've worked hard to hide your roots.

'Your impertinence begins to irritate me.' By nature he eluded any attempts by others to get to know him, and he hated the way she saw through him, knowing him with a glance.

'There's no shame in it. Or you.'

She locked on to his eyes, as if her very being depended upon maintaining the intensity of their gaze. More powerful than the gravity of lust, it was magic. Their world was the train. Here they could pretend they had no outside responsibilities. Distance meant nothing, time meant nothing, even though he was across the table from her, she was probably unaware that he had slipped his fingers between hers.

Winston turned away and sought to master the emotions threatening to distract him from his appointed task. He noticed a gentleman in his early fifties, with an athletic build, silver hair and beard. A silver and blue eye patch matched not only the pocket handkerchief tucked into the left breast pocket of his black suit, but also his elegant silk tie. Finely tailored, pinstriped along the jacket, which stretched down to his knees, he cut a striking figure, though wearing perhaps too liberal use of toilet waters. The man took a moment to saunter over to them. Winston stood and allowed the occasion to compose his demeanour.

'Allow me to introduce myself, my name is Richard St Ives.' He had a queer, lilting resonance to his voice, as if he was speaking through his nose at high altitude.

'Pleased to make your acquaintance, Mr St Ives.' Lady Trystan offered her hand.

'Oh, I very much doubt that. You see, I'm an agent of Sir Melbourne.'

'Then whatever business you have is between you and he.'

'Would that it were so, but often the prevarications of family tread all over our well-intentioned designs.'

'The lady says she has no business with you.' Winston rested both of his palms on his cane. Not even the juddering of the train's movement budged him.

St Ives snugged his gloves, the corresponding gesture in their voiceless dance of intimidation and veiled threat. 'But I fear I've business with her, as I have been retained to sort out matters. That is what I do.'

'You sort out things. You should know that I am under the employ of Sir Anthony. I, too, sort out things.'

It was a bold manoeuvre to approach Lady Trystan so openly, especially with the occasional soldier wandering about. Winston scanned the car on the hunch that St Ives didn't work alone. The swarthy gentleman feigned attention to his newspaper, making too much effort to appear inconspicuous.

'What is it you want, Mr St Ives?' Lady Trystan asked.

'Your father has all manner of secret contraptions, not all of them built through his own ingenuity. Sir Melbourne's demands are simple: either go through with the proposed marriage so the two families can be enjoined . . .'

'Or?' Winston asked.

'Or, turn over all patents pertaining to his microclockwork project.'

'My father would never agree to that.'

'Your father finds himself in a precarious position – at odds with his government, at odds with his business and at odds with his religion. He is in need of allies, not further enemies.' St Ives' eyes grew flat and cold. 'Your father should not have meddled with the inventions of others. Only Sir Anthony's resources could keep the kabbalists from pursuing your family.'

'None of this has anything to do with me,' Lady Trystan protested.

'But it does, I fear. For the sins of the father shall pass on to the next generation – and the next and the next.' St Ives turned to Winston. 'Tell your man he has a day.'

'What was that about?' Winston asked as he watched St Ives depart the car. He gave no acknowledgement of knowing the man who pressed his nose back into the newspaper.

'I don't know.'

'I know a few things about the business of fathers, the secrets they keep in the name of building a family's fortune, and how much children can know – no matter how well their parents guard against their learning . . .'

'. . . secrets win out,' Trystan finished.

'As you say.'

She worried the 'kerchief in her lap. 'I fear Albion rots from its own wealth and bloat. The sun never sets on the Albion empire, yet its very strength is its weakness.'

'How so?'

'Intellectual laziness comes with a lifestyle of ease. We don't advance as fast as we should.'

'You sound like an insurrectionist. A Jamaican sympathizer.'

'Keep your voice down. You do me an injustice, sir.'

'My apologies, m'lady. Then the rumours about your father—'

'Do you traffic in rumours now, Mr Jefferson? My father is loyal to the crown.'

'I would hope, should I ever become the object of unwarranted speculation, that I have so staunch a defender.'

'Do you mock me?'

'I do not.'

'I always speak what I think.'

'That can be a dangerous trait in a lady.'

'Good, because I have dangerous thoughts. All I am saying is that America is the heart that pumps the lifeblood of resources and invention to Albion. It is they who should fear us breaking away.'

Lady Trystan cowed, as if another cage wall had been erected in her life. She reminded him of a prized flower kept under glass, to be viewed and kept as a piece of living art, but cut off from the world. Never touched. He was careful not to let their hands brush against one another.

'We are both playing to the roles expected of us.'

'Trapped by them, you mean.'

Winston slept for a few hours. His dreams, though unremembered, left him unsettled, his clothes damp with perspiration, and he, curiously, in a state of mild arousal. The pungent scent of bodily exudations filled the air, yet the thought that something was amiss lingered. He dressed hurriedly in order to check on his charge. He slipped out of his car, hand steady on his cane as he ambled towards Lady Trystan's compartment. Once the sight of the crumpled bodies of the two unconscious soldiers stationed outside it greeted him, he knew what he would find inside: her suite, filled with embroidered sofas, an armoire and stacked trunks of memorabilia, greatly dishevelled; her bed asunder.

Winston ducked out of the car and passed through the other passenger cars as he made his way through the train. His heart raced, pained with anxiety. Winston surveyed each car as he strode through, inspecting them for any sign of his charge. He cursed himself for not doubling the guard after their encounter with Mr St Ives. He closed his eyes and forced himself to remain calm. Not wanting to alarm the other passengers, nor create greater chaos, he did not rouse his soldiers. Affection clouded his judgement; he had to be the one to find her.

The passengers of the train slept soundly at this late hour. The train rumbled around a bend, throwing off Winston's gait, then straightened out as it crossed a bridge traversing the Ohio River. He pulled the door to enter the small portico that bookended each car. It allowed the passengers to be undisturbed by the noise of the outside as porters entered and left the car. Winston opened the next to last car and the wind scraped at him. The cacophony of the rush of air, the clangor of the engine, and the rattle along the tracks rose to a near physical assault. He clutched his cane as he leapt from car to car, latching on to the rail with his free hand. Once inside, it took a moment for his ears to adjust to the eerie silence once more. The engine room wasn't what he expected. He remembered the days of coal-shovelling engine jockeys crying black tears as soot mixed with perspiration around their goggles. This engine room gleamed with polished metal. Two figures struggled at the far end of the car. The swarthy man glanced at pressure gauges, flipping levers like a mad man as he turned a wayward crank; Lady Trystan, in a red silk dressing gown, held fast under one arm. His stomach bottomed out. His heart lurched, so desperately afraid she might be hurt or taken away.

'Unhand her, cur,' Winston shouted.

The man turned and revealed a weapon aimed at Lady Trystan – a pistol of some sort, with a glass sphere where the cylinder should be. Energy crackled in it like a miniature plasma ball. Winston has seen such weapons before and is cognizant of the charred remains they can reduce a body to.

'I have no wish to harm the young lady. However, my employer does wish her to be delivered to him. So while this train will make a detour so that we may depart, her condition upon arrival was not . . . specified.' The man yanked her, tightening his grip to drive home his point.

Leaning on his cane, Winston raised his left hand to show that he was unarmed and for the man to relax. He caught Lady Trystan's eye, counting on her intelligence and resourcefulness.

'You'll get no trouble out of me. I actually feel sorry for your client. Lady Trystan is a mouthful. A vexing woman prone to outbursts.'

He nodded.

Lady Trystan bit the man's arm. In a savage hurl, he flung her into the control panel and raised his weapon to take aim at her, but Winston drew a bead with his cane first. He squeezed the open mouth of his dragon-head handle and the cane discharged with a sharp report. A wisp of smoke tapered from the tip of Winston's cane, and the bullet pierced the man's heart. The man stared at him in mild disbelief. He staggered back one step, touching his vest, as if checking the measure of his wound and determining it as fatal. For a moment he seemed to waver, enough life in him to fire one shot of his weapon, but as Winston scampered to get between the man and Lady Trystan, the weapon fell from his fingertips, as if he'd decided it would be unsporting of him.

Winston offered his hand to help Lady Trystan from the ground, and she rose to her feet with an awkward dignity.

'I turn my back on you for a moment and you get into all manner of trouble.'

'I find I must ever seek to draw attention to myself to keep the men in my life entertained.'

'But it's not your job to keep your husband entertained.' Caught up in their droll banter, the ill-considered intimation of spousehood tripped from his tongue before he could stop it. Were he a man prone to blushing, he might have beamed a torrid crimson. As it were, he fumbled at his pocket to find a new cartridge to reload into the breach of his cane.

'Kiss me.' Lady Trystan leaned close to him, her voice lowered to a husky tone directly in his ear. She touched his shoulder.

'God save you. You're a complete romantic. People like me aren't meant to be with people like you. It isn't . . . proper. Our roles—'

'*Their* roles be damned. *Our* role is to love. There's not enough of it in our world, so when we find it, no matter how proper society finds it, we must embrace it.'

Winston kissed her tenderly.

The private car of Mr St Ives had a bench of crimson velvet with arms of mahogany, on which he sat within an array of cushions reading a book as he smoked a briar pipe. Music poured out of a small contraption with a gleaming carapace. At Winston's entry, St Ives leaned over to shut off the electro-transmitter device.

'Your agent failed.'

'An agent of an agent? I have no idea what you're talking about,' St Ives said. 'I will say this, the pursuit won't cease. Lady Trystan, as she calls herself, is still her father's daughter and, as such, ever the most visible pawn to move.'

'And if she should disappear?'

'It is a complicated world we live in. However, a pawn out of play is of no concern to me. Or my employer.'

Lady Trystan carried herself with the bearing of a woman prone to athletics. Dressing with a seductive modesty, her gown snug enough to reveal every curve of her voluptuous breasts and fitted to show off the flatness of her belly, all without exposing any skin. In stark contrast to his mannered fastidiousness, her eyes sparkled with an arcane fire, a vivaciousness that threatened to consume him. The curious curl of her lips added a certain coquettishness to her manner, a coy edge compounded in her posture. Something about her scent captivated him, rushing straight to his head like a fog settling on his brain. No one should radiate so much sexual energy simply by sitting down.

'I have an acquaintance in Indianapolis I was due to call upon after delivering you to your father,' Winston said.

'I do so wish the men in my world would quit discussing me as if I were a sack of potatoes being shipped somewhere.'

'After some careful consideration, a clear mind would determine that a fortnight of acquaintance is no basis for any claim of intimacy.'

'You're quite circumspect. I imagine it takes you hours to convey the cleverest of anecdotes.' Lady Trystan leaned closer, running her fingertips along his hand. He jumped, snatching his hand back as if bitten. She smiled. 'Do you wish me to go with you?'

'You delight in vexing me.'

'I delight in being me. Perhaps you are too easily vexed. Led by your nose from passion to passion, spending it recklessly on any passing fancy.'

Lord have mercy, the way that woman stared at him, Winston thought. His own eyes drank her in. Large, brown pupils danced in a pool that reflected only her. He attempted to not appear conspicuous, following the curve of her body, her dress barely contained. His mouth grew dry, his tongue a swollen useless thing that choked back any words his brain managed to string together. He couldn't imagine what to say, not to a woman like that: all woman, confident, unapologetically sexual and with a devouring seductiveness. Someone who knew the power of her sex and wielded it like an expert martial artist. Winston's hands laboured to remain fixed on his cane handle. Instead, he consulted his pocket watch, then blew on its pewter finish to polish it with a handkerchief, avoiding the power of her gaze. 'I thought perhaps it might be prudent for you to accompany me, away from the schemes of your father and his enemies, to be somewhere you could determine your own course.'

'With you?'

'It would honour me to accompany you.' Most women concerned themselves with the attentions and fortunes of available men and their standing in society. She was a woman of deep reflection. A woman of no discretion, as proud of it as she was difficult. A woman who preoccupied his thoughts.

'Would there be horses? I love to ride.'

'Surely we could find a horse for you to mount.' He donned his top hat, then tugged at the vest that covered his white shirt, left open at the neck.

'You carry on like a brooding old man.'

'I have enough vitality left in me to keep up with you.'

'Come on then.'

The Tejas Express slowed as it pulled into Indianapolis station. Its gears ground, creating a universal clangour; the rattletrap box of their car shook. Winston directed his soldiers to carry Lady Trystan's belongings from the train and gave his number two a message to give to Sir Anthony upon their arrival in Chicago. Lady Trystan also gave him a note to pass along, informing her father of her decision to go her own way, and that pursuit of her would only put her in further danger, though he shouldn't worry; she'd be in touch soon and, in the meantime, she was in perfectly safe hands.

Winston spied the father he'd stopped from beating his son. As they both disembarked at the same stop, he gestured that he would have his eye on him. Finally, he turned to Lady Trystan.

'Do you believe in love at first sight?' she asked.

'Only inasmuch as I believe in the tooth fairy and leprechauns. It is the domain of fanciful schoolgirls and bored housewives.'

'You are quite the romantic.' She crossed her arms and turned her head in a feigned pout.

'Indeed I am. I believe in love, deep and unbridled, not the turn of a pretty phrase, polite gestures and barely engaged feelings that pass for courtship. I believe in putting in the work for love rather than contenting myself with the dream of romance.'

'You still manage to turn the pretty phrase, nonetheless.'

'I have my moments.'

IRREMEDIABLE

Ella D'Arcy

A young man strolled along a country road one August evening after a long delicious day – a day of that blessed idleness the man of leisure never knows: one must be a bank clerk forty-nine weeks out of the fifty-two before one can really appreciate the exquisite enjoyment of doing nothing for twelve hours at a stretch. Willoughby had spent the morning lounging about a sunny rickyard; then, when the heat grew unbearable, he had retreated to an orchard where, lying on his back in the long cool grass, he had traced the pattern of the apple leaves diapered above him upon the summer sky; now that the heat of the day was over, he had come to roam whither sweet fancy led him, to lean over gates, view the prospect, and meditate upon the pleasures of a well-spent day.

Five such days had already passed over his head, fifteen more remained to him. Then farewell to freedom and clean country air! Back again to London and another year's toil.

He came to a gate on the right of the road. Behind it a foot-path meandered up over a grassy slope. The sheep nibbling on its summit cast long shadows down the hill, almost to his feet. Road and field path were equally new to him, but the latter offered greener attractions; he vaulted lightly over the gate and had so little idea he was taking thus the first step towards ruin that he began to whistle 'White Wings' from pure joy of life.

The sheep stopped feeding and raised their heads to stare at him from pale-lashed eyes; first one and then another broke into a startled run, until there was a sudden woolly stampede of the entire flock. When Willoughby gained the ridge from

which they had just scattered, he came in sight of a woman
sitting on a stile at the further end of the field. As he advanced
towards her he saw that she was young, and that she was not
what is called 'a lady'– of which he was glad: an earlier episode
in his career having indissolubly associated in his mind ideas of
feminine refinement with those of feminine treachery.

He thought it probable this girl would be willing to dispense
with the formalities of an introduction, and that he might
venture with her on some pleasant foolish chat.

As she made no movement to let him pass, he stood still
and, looking at her, began to smile.

She returned his gaze from unabashed dark eyes, and then
laughed, showing teeth white, sound, and smooth as split
hazelnuts.

'Do you wanter get over?' she remarked familiarly.

'I'm afraid I can't without disturbing you.'

'Dontcher think you're much better where you are?' said
the girl, on which Willoughby hazarded:

'You mean to say looking at you? Well, perhaps I am!'

The girl at this laughed again, but nevertheless dropped
herself down into the further field; then, leaning her arms upon
the crossbar, she informed the young man: 'No, I don't wanter
spoil your walk. You were goin' p'raps ter Beacon Point? It's
very pretty that wye.'

'I was going nowhere in particular,' he replied; 'just exploring, so to speak. I'm a stranger in these parts.'

'How funny! Imer stranger here too. I only come down larse
Friday to stye with a Naunter mine in Horton. Are you stying
in Horton?'

Willoughby told her he was not in Orton, but at Povey Cross
Farm, out in the other direction.

'Oh, Mrs Payne's, ain't it? I've heard aunt speak ovver. She
takes summer boarders, don' chee? I egspeck you come from
London, heh?'

'And I expect you come from London, too?' said Willoughby,
recognizing the familiar accent.

'You're as sharp as a needle,' cried the girl with her unre-
strained laugh; 'so I do. I'm here for a hollerday 'cos I was so
done up with the work and the hot weather. I don't look as

though I bin ill, do I? But I was, though, for it was just stiflin' hot up in our workrooms all larse month, an' tailorin's awful hard work at the bester times.'

Willoughby felt a sudden accession of interest in her. Like many intelligent young men, he had dabbled a little in Socialism, and at one time had wandered among the dispossessed; but since then, had caught up and held loosely the new doctrine – it is a good and fitting thing that woman also should earn her bread by the sweat of her brow. Always in reference to the woman who, fifteen months before, had treated him ill; he had said to himself that even the breaking of stones in the road should be considered a more feminine employment than the breaking of hearts.

He gave way therefore to a movement of friendliness for this working daughter of the people, and joined her on the other side of the stile in a token of his approval. She, twisting round to face him, leaned now with her back against the bar, and the sunset fires lent a fleeting glory to her face. Perhaps she guessed how becoming the light was, for she took off her hat and let it touch to gold the ends and fringes of her rough, abundant hair. Thus and at this moment she made an agreeable picture, to which stood as background all the beautiful, wooded Southshire view.

'You don't really mean to say you are a tailoress?' said Willoughby, with a sort of eager compassion.

'I do, though! An' I've bin one ever since I was fourteen. Look at my fingers if you don't b'lieve me.'

She put out her right hand and he took hold of it, as he was expected to do. The finger-ends were frayed and blackened by needle-pricks, but the hand itself was plump, moist and not unshapely. She, meanwhile, examined Willoughby's fingers enclosing hers.

'It's easy ter see you've never done no work!' she said, half admiring, half envious. 'I s'pose you're a tip-top swell, ain't you?'

'Oh, yes! I'm a tremendous swell indeed!' said Willoughby ironically. He thought of his £130 salary; and he mentioned his position in the British and Colonial Banking house, without shedding much illumination on her mind, for she insisted:

'Well, anyhow, you're a gentleman. I've often wished I was a lady. It must be so nice ter wear fine clo'es an' never have ter do any work all day long.'

Willoughby thought it innocent of the girl to say this; it reminded him of his own notion as a child, that kings and queens put on their crowns the first thing on rising in the morning. His cordiality rose another degree.

'If being a gentleman means having nothing to do,' said he, smiling, 'I can certainly lay no claim to the title. Life isn't all beer and skittles with me, any more than it is with you. Which is the better reason for enjoying the present moment, don't you think? Suppose, now, like a kind little girl, you were to show me the way to Beacon Point, which you say is so pretty?'

She required no further persuasion. As he walked beside her through the upland fields where the dusk was beginning to fall, and the white evening moths to emerge from their daytime hiding places, she asked him many personal questions, most of which he thought fit to parry. Taking no offence thereat, she told him, instead, much concerning herself and her family. Thus he learned her name was Esther Stables, that she and her people lived Whitechapel way; that her father was seldom sober, and her mother always ill; and that the aunt with whom she was staying kept the post office and general shop in Orton village. He learned, too, that Esther was discontented with life in general; that, though she hated being at home, she found the country dreadfully dull; and that, consequently, she was extremely glad to have made his acquaintance. But what he chiefly realized when they parted was that he had spent a couple of pleasant hours talking nonsense with a girl who was natural, simple-minded, and entirely free from that repellently protective atmosphere with which a woman of the 'classes' so carefully surrounds herself. He and Esther had made friends with the ease and rapidity of children before they have learned the dread meaning of 'etiquette', and they said good night, not without some talk of meeting each other again.

Obliged to breakfast at a quarter to eight in town, Willoughby was always luxuriously late when in the country, where he took his meals also in leisurely fashion, often reading from a book propped up on the table before him. But the morning after his meeting with Esther Stables found him less disposed to read than usual. Her image obtruded itself upon the printed page, and at length grew so importunate he came to the conclusion that the only way to lay it was to confront it with the girl herself.

Wanting some tobacco, he saw a good reason for going into Orton. Esther had told him he could get tobacco and everything else at her aunt's. He found the post office to be one of the first houses in the widely spaced village street. In front of the cottage was a small garden ablaze with old-fashioned flowers; and in a large garden at one side were apple trees, raspberry and currant bushes, and six thatched beehives on a bench. The bowed windows of the little shop were partly screened by sun blinds; nevertheless, the lower panes still displayed a heterogeneous collection of goods – lemons, hanks of yarn, white linen buttons upon blue cards, sugar cones, churchwarden pipes, and tobacco jars. A letter box opened its narrow mouth low down in one wall, and over the door swung the sign, 'Stamps and money-order office', in black letters on white enamelled iron.

The interior of the shop was cool and dark. A second glass door at the back permitted Willoughby to see into a small sitting room, and out again through a low and square-paned window to the sunny landscape beyond. Silhouetted against the light were the heads of two women; the rough young head of yesterday's Esther, the lean outline and bugled cap of Esther's aunt.

It was the latter who, at the jingling of the doorbell, rose from her work and came forward to serve the customer; but the girl, with much mute meaning in her eyes and a finger laid upon her smiling mouth, followed behind. Her aunt heard her footfall. 'What do you want here, Esther?' she said with thin disapproval. 'Get back to your sewing.'

Esther gave the young man a signal seen only by him and slipped out into the side garden, where he found her when his purchases were made. She leaned over the privet hedge to intercept him as he passed.

'Aunt's an awful ole maid,' she remarked apologetically. 'I b'lieve she'd never let me say a word to ennyone if she could help it.'

'So you got home all right last night?' Willoughby inquired. 'What did your aunt say to you?'

'Oh, she arst me where I'd been, and I tolder a lotter lies.' Then, with a woman's intuition, perceiving that this speech jarred, Esther made haste to add, 'She's so dreadful hard on me. I dursn't tell her I'd been with a gentleman or she'd never have let me out alone again.'

'And at present I suppose you'll be found somewhere about that same stile every evening?' said Willoughby foolishly, for he really did not much care whether he met her again or not. Now he was actually in her company, he was surprised at himself for having given her a whole morning's thought; yet the eagerness of her answer flattered him, too.

'Tonight I can't come, worse luck! It's Thursday, and the shops here close of a Thursday at five. I'll havter keep aunt company. But tomorrer? I can be there tomorrer. You'll come, say?'

'Esther!' cried a vexed voice, and the precise, right-minded aunt emerged through a row of raspberry bushes. 'Whatever are you thinking about, delayin' the gentleman in this fashion?' She was full of rustic and official civility for 'the gentleman', but indignant with her niece. 'I don't want none of your London manners down here,' Willoughby heard her say as she marched the girl off.

He himself was not sorry to be released from Esther's too friendly eyes, and he spent an agreeable evening over a book, and this time managed to forget her completely.

Though he remembered her first thing next morning, it was to smile wisely and determine he would not meet her again. Yet by dinner time the day seemed long; why, after all, should he not meet her? By tea time prudence triumphed anew – no, he would not go. Then he drank his tea hastily and set off for the stile.

Esther was waiting for him. Expectation had given an additional colour to her cheeks, and her red-brown hair showed here and there a beautiful glint of gold. He could not help admiring the vigorous way in which it waved and twisted, or the little curls which grew at the nape of her neck, tight and close as those of a young lamb's fleece. Her neck here was admirable, too, in its smooth creaminess; and when her eyes lit up with such evident pleasure at his coming, how could he avoid the conviction that she was a good and nice girl after all?

He proposed they should go down into the little copse on the right, where they would be less disturbed by the occasional passer-by. Here, seated on a felled tree trunk, Willoughby began that bantering, silly, meaningless form of conversation known among the 'classes' as flirting. He had but the wish to make himself agreeable, and to while away the time. Esther, however, misunderstood him.

Willoughby's hand lay palm downwards on his knee, and she, noticing a ring which he wore on his little finger, took hold of it.

'What a funny ring!' she said. 'Let's look?'

To disembarrass himself of her touch, he pulled the ring off and gave it her to examine.

'What's that ugly dark green stone?' she asked.

'It's called a sardonyx.'

'What's it for?' she said, turning it about.

'It's a signet ring, to seal letters with.'

'An' there's a sorter king's head scratched on it, an' some writin' too, only I carn't make it out?'

'It isn't the head of a king, although it wears a crown,' Willoughby explained, 'but the head and bust of a Saracen against whom my ancestor of many hundred years ago went to fight in the Holy Land. And the words cut round it are our motto, '*Vertue vauncet*', which means virtue prevails.'

Willoughby may have displayed some accession of dignity in giving this bit of family history, for Esther fell into uncontrolled laughter, at which he was much displeased. And when the girl made as though she would put the ring on her own finger, asking, 'Shall I keep it?' he coloured up with sudden annoyance. 'It was only my fun!' said Esther hastily, and gave him the ring back, but his cordiality was gone.

He felt no inclination to renew the idle word pastime, said it was time to go and, swinging his cane vexedly, struck off the heads of the flowers and weeds as he went. Esther walked by his side in complete silence, a phenomenon of which he presently became conscious. He felt rather ashamed of having shown temper.

'Well, here's your way home,' said he with an effort at friendliness. 'Goodbye; we've had a nice evening anyhow. It was pleasant down there in the woods, eh?'

He was astonished to see her eyes soften with tears, and to hear the real emotion in her voice as she answered, 'It was just heaven down there with you until you turned so funny-like. What had I done to make you cross? Say you forgive me, do!'

'Silly child!' said Willoughby, completely mollified, 'I'm not the least angry. There, goodbye!' and like a fool he kissed her.

He anathematized his folly in the white light of next morning and, remembering the kiss he had given her, repented it very sincerely. He had an uncomfortable suspicion she had not received it in the same spirit in which it had been bestowed, but, attaching more serious meaning to it would build expectations thereon, which must be left unfulfilled. It was best indeed not to meet her again; for he acknowledged to himself that, though he only half liked and even slightly feared her, there was a certain attraction about her – was it in her dark, unflinching eyes or in her very red lips? – which might lead him into greater follies still.

Thus it came about that for two successive evenings Esther waited for him in vain, and on the third evening he said to himself, with a grudging relief, that by this time she had probably transferred her affections to someone else.

It was Saturday, the second Saturday since he left town. He spent the day about the farm, contemplated the pigs, inspected the feeding of the stock, and assisted at the afternoon milking. Then at evening, with a refilled pipe, he went for a long lean over the west gate, while he traced fantastic pictures and wove romances in the glories of the sunset clouds.

He watched the colours glow from gold to scarlet, change to crimson, sink at last to sad purple reefs and isles, when the sudden consciousness of someone being near him made him turn round. There stood Esther, and her eyes were full of eagerness and anger.

'Why have you never been to the stile again?' she asked him. 'You promised to come faithful, and you never came. Why have you not kep' your promise? Why? Why?' she persisted, stamping her foot because Willoughby remained silent.

What could he say? Tell her she had no business to follow him like this; or own what was unfortunately the truth, that he was just a little glad to see her?

'P'raps you don't care for me any more?' she said. 'Well, why did you kiss me, then?'

Why, indeed! thought Willoughby, marvelling at his own idiocy, and yet – such is the inconsistency of man – not wholly without the desire to kiss her again. And while he looked at her she suddenly flung herself down on the hedge-bank at his feet and burst into tears. She did not cover up her face, but simply pressed one cheek down upon the grass while the water poured from her eyes with astonishing abundance. Willoughby saw the dry earth turn dark and moist as it drank the tears in. This, his first experience of Esther's powers of weeping, distressed him horribly; never in his life before had he seen anyone weep like that, he should not have believed such a thing possible; he was alarmed, too, lest she should be noticed from the house. He opened the gate. 'Esther,' he begged, 'don't cry. Come out here like a dear girl and let us talk sensibly.'

Because she stumbled, unable to see her way through wet eyes, he gave her his hand, and they found themselves in a field of corn, walking along the narrow grass path that skirted it, in the shadow of the hedgerow.

'What is there to cry about because you have not seen me for two days?' he began. 'Why, Esther, we are only strangers, after all. When we have been at home a week or two we shall scarcely remember each other's names.'

Esther sobbed at intervals, but her tears had ceased. 'It's fine for you to talk of home,' she said to this. 'You've got something that is a home, I s'pose? But me! My home's like hell, with nothing but quarrellin' and cursin', and a father who beats us whether sober or drunk. Yes,' she repeated shrewdly, seeing the lively disgust on Willoughby's face, 'he beat me, all ill as I was, jus' before I come away. I could show you the bruises on my arms still. And now to go back there after knowin' you! It'll be worse than ever. I can't endure it, and I won't! I'll put an end to it or myself somehow, I swear!'

'But my poor Esther, how can I help it? What can I do?' said Willoughby. He was greatly moved, full of wrath with her father, with all the world which makes women suffer. He had suffered himself at the hands of a woman, and severely, but this, instead of hardening his heart, had only rendered it the more supple. And yet he had a vivid perception of the peril in which he stood. An interior voice urged him to break away, to seek safety in flight, even at the cost of appearing cruel or ridiculous; so, coming to a point in the field where an elm hole jutted out across the path, he saw with relief that he could now withdraw his hand from the girl's, since they must walk singly to skirt round it.

Esther took a step in advance, stopped and suddenly turned to face him; she held out her two hands and her face was very near his own. 'Don't you care for me one little bit?' she said wistfully, and surely sudden madness fell upon him. For he kissed her again, he kissed her many times, he took her in his arms and pushed all thoughts of the consequences far from him.

But when, an hour later, he and Esther stood by the last gate on the road to Orton, some of these consequences were already calling loudly to him.

'You know I have only a hundred and thirty pounds a year?' he told her. 'It's no very brilliant prospect for you to marry me on that.' For he had actually offered her marriage, although to the mediocre man such a proceeding must appear incredible, uncalled for. But to Willoughby, overwhelmed with sadness and remorse, it seemed the only atonement possible.

Sudden exultation leaped at Esther's heart.

'Oh, I'm used to managing,' she told him confidently, and mentally resolved to buy herself, so soon as she was married, a black feather boa, such as she had coveted last winter.

Willoughby spent the remaining days of his holiday in thinking out and planning with Esther the details of his return to London and her own, the secrecy to be observed, the necessary legal steps to be taken, and the quiet suburb in which they would set up housekeeping.

And so successfully did he carry out his arrangements that, within five weeks from the day on which he had first met

Esther Stables, he and she came out one morning from a church in Highbury, husband and wife. It was a mellow September day, the streets were filled with sunshine, and Willoughby, in reckless high spirits, imagined he saw a reflection of his own gaiety on the indifferent faces of the passers-by. There being no one else to perform the office, he congratulated himself very warmly, and Esther's frequent laughter filled in the pauses of the day.

Three months later, Willoughby was dining with a friend, and the hour hand of the clock nearing ten, the host no longer resisted the guest's growing anxiety to be gone. He arose and exchanged with him good wishes and goodbyes.

'Marriage is evidently a most successful institution,' said he, half jesting, half sincere. 'You almost make me inclined to go and get married myself. Confess now, your thoughts have been at home the whole evening.'

Willoughby, thus addressed, turned red to the roots of his hair, but did not deny it.

The other laughed. 'And very commendable they should be,' he continued, 'since you are scarcely, so to speak, out of your honeymoon.'

With a social smile on his lips, Willoughby calculated a moment before replying, 'I have been married exactly three months and three days.' Then, after a few words respecting their next meeting, the two shook hands and parted – the young host to finish the evening with books and a pipe, the young husband to set out on a twenty minutes' walk to his home.

It was a cold, clear December night following a day of rain. A touch of frost in the air had dried the pavements, and Willoughby's footfall ringing upon the stones re-echoed down the empty suburban street. Above his head was a dark, remote sky, thickly powdered with stars, and as he turned westward, Alpherat hung for a moment '*comme le point sur un i*', over the slender spire of St John's. But he was insensible to the worlds about him; he was absorbed in his own thoughts, and these, as his friend had surmised, were entirely with his wife. For Esther's face was always before his eyes, her voice was always in his ears, she filled the universe for him; yet only four months ago he had never seen her, had never heard her name. This was the curious part of it – here, in December he found himself the husband of a girl who was completely dependent upon him, not only for food, clothes and lodging, but for her present happiness, her whole future life; and yet last July he had been scarcely more than a boy himself, with no greater care on his mind than the pleasant difficulty of deciding where he should spend his annual three weeks' holiday.

But it is events, not months or years, which age. Willoughby, who was only twenty-six, remembered his youth as a sometime companion irrevocably lost to him; its vague, delightful hopes were now crystallized into definite ties, and its happy irresponsibilities displaced by a sense of care inseparable perhaps from the most fortunate of marriages.

As he reached the street in which he lodged, his pace involuntarily slackened. While still some distance off, his eye sought out and distinguished the windows of the room in which Esther awaited him. Through the broken slats of the Venetian blinds he could see the yellow gaslight within. The parlour beneath was in darkness; his landlady had evidently gone to bed, there being no light over the hall door either. In some apprehension, he consulted his watch under the last street lamp he passed, to find comfort in assuring himself it was only ten minutes after ten. He let himself in with his latch key, hung up his hat and overcoat by the sense of touch, and, groping his way upstairs, opened the door of the first-floor sitting room.

At the table in the centre of the room sat his wife, leaning upon her elbows, her two hands thrust up into her ruffled hair; spread out before her was a crumpled yesterday's newspaper, and so interested was she to all appearance in its contents that she neither spoke nor looked up as Willoughby entered. Around her were the still uncleared tokens of her last meal: tea slops, breadcrumbs and an egg-shell crushed to fragments upon a plate, which was one of those trifles that set Willoughby's teeth on edge – whenever his wife ate an egg, she persisted in turning the egg cup upside down upon the tablecloth, and pounding the shell to pieces in her plate with her spoon.

The room was repulsive in its disorder. The one lighted burner of the gaselier, turned too high, hissed up into a long tongue of flame. The fire smoked feebly under a newly admin-istered shovelful of 'slack', and a heap of ashes and cinders littered the grate. A pair of walking boots, caked in dry mud, lay on the hearthrug just where they had been thrown off. On the mantelpiece, amidst a dozen other articles which had no business there, was a bedroom candlestick; and every single article of furniture stood crookedly out of its place.

Willoughby took in the whole intolerable picture, and yet spoke with kindliness. 'Well, Esther, I'm not so late, after all. I hope you did not find the time dull by yourself?' Then he explained the reason of his absence. He had met a friend he had not seen for a couple of years, who had insisted on taking him home to dine.

His wife gave no sign of having heard him; she kept her eyes riveted on the paper before her.

'You received my wire, of course,' Willoughby went on, 'and did not wait?'

Now she crushed the newspaper up with a passionate movement and threw it from her. She raised her head, showing cheeks blazing with anger, and dark, sullen, unflinching eyes.

'I did wyte then!' she cried. 'I wyted till near eight before I got your old telegraph! I s'pose that's what you call the manners of a 'gentleman', to keep your wife mewed up here, while you go gallivantin' off with your fine friends?'

Whenever Esther was angry, which was often, she taunted Willoughby with being 'a gentleman', although this was the precise point about him which, at other times, found most favour in her eyes. But tonight she was envenomed by the idea he had been enjoying himself without her, stung by fear lest he should have been in company with some other woman.

Willoughby, hearing the taunt, resigned himself to the inevi-table. Nothing that he could do now might avert the breaking storm; all his words would only be twisted into fresh griefs. But sad experience had taught him that to take refuge in silence was more fatal still. When Esther was in such a mood as this it was best to supply the fire with fuel that, through the very violence of the conflagration, it might the sooner burn itself out.

So he said what soothing things he could, and Esther caught them up, disfigured them and flung them back at him with scorn. She reproached him with no longer caring for her; she vituperated the conduct of his family in never taking the smallest notice of her marriage; and she detailed the insolence of the landlady who had told her that morning she pitied 'poor Mr Willoughby', and had refused to go out and buy herrings for Esther's early dinner.

Every affront or grievance, real or imaginary, since the day she and Willoughby had first met, she poured forth with a fluency due to frequent repetition, for, with the exception of today's added injuries, Willoughby had heard the whole litany many times before.

While she raged and he looked at her, he remembered he had once thought her pretty. He had seen beauty in her rough brown hair, her strong colouring, her full red mouth. He fell into musing . . . a woman may lack beauty, he told himself, and yet be loved . . .

Meanwhile, Esther reached white heats of passion, and the strain could no longer be sustained. She broke into sobs and began to shed tears with the facility peculiar to her. In a moment her face was all wet, with the big drops which rolled down her cheeks faster and faster, and fell with audible splashes on to the table, on to her lap, on to the floor. To this tearful abundance, formerly a surprising spectacle, Willoughby was now acclimatized; but the remnant of chivalrous feeling not yet extinguished in his bosom forbade him to sit stolidly by while a woman wept, without seeking to console her. As on previous occasions, his peace overtures were eventually accepted. Esther's tears gradually ceased to flow, she began to exhibit a sort of compunction. She wished to be forgiven, and, with the kiss of reconciliation, passed into a phase of demonstrative affection perhaps more trying to Willoughby's patience than all that had preceded it.

'You don't love me?' she questioned. 'I'm sure you don't love me?' she reiterated, and he asseverated that he loved her until he despised himself. Then at last, only half satisfied, but wearied out with vexation – possibly, too, with a movement of pity at the sight of his haggard face – she consented to leave him.

Only, what was he going to do? she asked suspiciously; write those rubbishing stories of his? Well, he must promise not to stay up more than half an hour at the latest – only until he had smoked one pipe.

Willoughby promised, as he would have promised anything on earth to secure to himself a half-hour's peace and solitude. Esther groped for her slippers, which were kicked off under the table; scratched four or five matches along the box and threw them away before she succeeded in lighting her candle; set it down again to contemplate her tear-swollen reflection in the chimney-glass and burst out laughing.

'What a fright I do look, to be sure!' she remarked complacently, and again thrust her two hands up through her disordered curls. Then, holding the candle at such an angle that the grease ran over on to the carpet, she gave Willoughby another vehement kiss and trailed out of the room with an ineffectual attempt to close the door behind her.

Willoughby got up to shut it himself, and wondered why it was that Esther never did any one mortal thing efficiently or well. Good God! How irritable he felt. It was impossible to write. He must find an outlet for his impatience, rend or mend something. He began to straighten the room, but a wave of disgust came over him before the task was fairly commenced. What was the use? Tomorrow all would be bad as before. What was the use of doing anything? He sat down by the table and leaned his head upon his hands.

The past came back to him in pictures: his boyhood past first of all. He saw again the old home, every inch of which was as familiar to him as his own name; he reconstructed in his thought all the old well-known furniture, and replaced it precisely as it had stood long ago. He passed again a childish finger over the rough surface of the faded Utrecht velvet chairs, and smelled again the strong fragrance of the white lilac tree, blowing in through the open parlour window. He savoured anew the pleasant mental atmosphere produced by the dainty neatness of cultured women, the companionship of a few good pictures, of a few good books. Yet this home had been broken up years ago, the dear familiar things had been scattered far and wide, never to find themselves under the same roof again; and from those near relatives who still remained to him he lived now hopelessly estranged.

Then came the past of his first love-dream, when he had worshipped at the feet of Nora Beresford, and, with the whole-heartedness of the true fanatic, clothed his idol with every imaginable attribute of virtue and tenderness. To this day there remained a secret shrine in his heart wherein the lady of his young ideal was still enthroned, although it was long since he had come to perceive she had nothing whatever in common with the Nora of reality. For the real Nora he had no longer any sentiment, she had passed altogether out of his life and thoughts; and yet, so permanent is all influence, whether good or evil, that the effect she wrought upon his character remained. He recognized tonight that her treatment of him in the past did not count for nothing among the various factors which had determined his fate.

Now the past of only last year returned and, strangely enough, this seemed farther removed from him than all the rest. He had been particularly strong, well and happy this time last year. Nora was dismissed from his mind, and he had thrown all his energies into his work. His tastes were sane and simple, and his dingy, furnished rooms had become, through habit, very pleasant to him. In being his own, they were invested with a greater charm than another man's castle. Here he had smoked and studied, here he had made many a glorious voyage into the land of books. Many a homecoming, too, rose up before him out of the dark ungenial streets, to a clear blazing fire, a neatly laid cloth, an evening of ideal enjoyment; many a summer twilight when he mused at the open window, plunging his gaze deep into the recesses of his neighbour's lime tree, where the unseen sparrows chattered with such unflagging gaiety.

He had always been given to much daydreaming, and it was in the silence of his rooms of an evening that he turned his phantasmal adventures into stories for the magazines; here had come to him many an editorial refusal, but here, too, he had received the news of his first unexpected success. All his happiest memories were embalmed in those shabby, badly furnished rooms.

Now all was changed. Now might there be no longer any soft indulgence of the hour's mood. His rooms and everything he owned belonged now to Esther, too. She had objected to most of his photographs, and had removed them. She hated books, and were he ever so ill-advised as to open one in her presence, she immediately began to talk, no matter how silent or how sullen her previous mood had been. If he read aloud to her she either yawned despairingly or was tickled into laughter where there was no reasonable cause. At first Willoughby had tried to educate her, and had gone hopefully to the task. It is so natural to think you may make what you will of the woman who loves you. But Esther had no wish to improve. She evinced all the self-satisfaction of an illiterate mind. To her husband's gentle admonitions she replied with brevity that she thought her way quite as good as his; or, if he didn't approve of her pronunciation, he might do the other thing. She was too old to go to school again. He gave up the attempt and, with humiliation at his previous fatuity, perceived that it was folly to expect that a few weeks of his companionship could alter or pull up the impressions of years, or rather of generations.

Yet here he paused to admit a curious thing: it was not only Esther's bad habits that vexed him, but habits quite unblameworthy in themselves, which he never would have noticed in another, irritated him in her. He disliked her manner of standing, of walking, of sitting in a chair, of folding her hands. Like a lover, he was conscious of her proximity without seeing her. Like a lover, too, his eyes followed her every movement, his ear noted every change in her voice. But then, instead of being charmed by everything as the lover is, everything jarred upon him.

What was the meaning of this? Tonight the anomaly pressed upon him: he reviewed his position. Here was he, quite a young man, just twenty-six years of age, married to Esther, and bound to live with her so long as life should last – twenty, forty, perhaps fifty years more. Every day of those years to be spent in her society; he and she face to face, soul to soul; they two alone amid all the whirling, busy, indifferent world. So near together in semblance; in truth, so far apart as regards all that makes life dear.

Willoughby groaned. From the woman he did not love, whom he had never loved, he might not again go free; so much he recognized. The feeling he had once entertained for Esther, a strange compound of mistaken chivalry and flattered vanity, was long since extinct; but what, then, was the sentiment with which she inspired him? For he was not indifferent to her – no, never for one instant could he persuade himself he was indifferent, never for one instant could he banish her from his thoughts. His mind's eye followed her during his hours of absence as pertinaciously as his bodily eye dwelt upon her actual presence. She was the principal object of the universe to him, the centre around which his wheel of life revolved with an appalling fidelity.

What did it mean? What could it mean? He asked himself with anguish. And the sweat broke out upon his forehead and his hands grew cold, for on a sudden the truth lay there like a written word upon the tablecloth before him. This woman, whom he had taken to himself for better, for worse, inspired him with a passion, intense indeed, all-masterful, soul-subduing as Love itself . . . But when he understood the terror of his Hatred, he laid his head upon his arms and wept, not facile tears like Esther's, but tears wrung out from his agonizing, unavailing regret.

ITEM 317: HORN FRAGMENT, W/ILLUS

E. Catherine Tobler

I am a shadow, slipp'd.

Those poor, poor women, sliced apart, carried to God knows where. Me, seemingly whole, though life still taken from my body, warm and crying, never seen by these black eyes. A pale thread of skin across my throat, easily concealed; the rest of me wrapped in black and tucked away in a place no one would have to look, until I am swallowed by the blessed forgetfulness of time.

Under the flickering light of the gas lamp struggling to illuminate the apothecary's back room, the horn fragment looked oily, as though one could lay a finger to it, and come away with a black stream running down said finger. I did not touch the horn, only looked at it for a long moment before pushing the small, black wood case to the side, where it sat for another week before I eyed its unmarked sides again and drew it close.

A cork-capped glass jar encased the horn fragment, a four-folded slip of paper curling between jar and packing straw. I pulled the paper free and unfolded it, a bull's magnificent head rearing from the page. Grey horns swept upwards against the yellowing paper, an address in Greece neatly printed in one corner.

My uncle's voice, when it came, was filled with something I had not heard before. For the first time in my occupancy with him, he sounded genuinely worried. Emotion from him, directed at me, was unusual to say the least. 'Where did you find that?'

I looked from the illustration to my uncle, frowning at his tone. 'It was among the other cases, though unmarked,' I began, but said no more, for he tugged the page from my fingers and folded it in half, and in half again. He slipped the page under the jar and closed the case's lid before giving me a smile one might give an infant.

'Nothing to worry yourself about.' He nodded his greying head towards the other similar cases that lined the counter, as if to direct my attention towards them, but my attention didn't waver from my uncle and the case beneath his arm. I watched as he carried it out of the room and down the long, door-lined corridor that led to a narrow, shadowed staircase. I heard his quick steps move upward, toward the living quarters.

Nothing to worry myself about, perhaps, but I couldn't stop considering image and artefact even so. Each time I asked about the horn fragment, my uncle attempted to brush it off as something random, something that had not been intended for his shop at all, but had been included by clear mistake. He would return it at once. The case wasn't even marked with a number as the others had been. It belonged nowhere, much like myself.

When asked again, my uncle hedged, and allowed that horns *did* have certain properties that certain patrons of the shop might find pleasing, but that was not why *he* was in possession of the thing. Certain properties and certain patrons, indeed. His denials only made me believe otherwise: that my uncle, one of London's most respected apothecaries, knew precisely what he was doing with the item and was ashamed I had discovered it.

Still, the following day, the small wood case sat in my workspace, as though waiting for me. I lifted the lid and peered inside, finding all as it had been, jar nestled in packing straw with illustration and horn. I looked to the outer room of the shop, seeing my uncle and Missus Baker beyond the dark fall of the velvet curtain in the doorway. Beyond them a black-cloaked figure, gloved fingers slipping through the bundled herbs, and a suited gentleman, taking an interest in the tobacco.

'And Stella is here *now*?' Missus Baker murmured. My uncle's head bobbed and Missus Baker exhaled, shaking her own head. 'My Oscar is to wed in *three* weeks, Raymond!'

My uncle hushed her and drew her far enough away that I could no longer hear the conversation, but what more did I need overhear? I drew the curtain closed.

The wooden stool caught me as I sank to sit, and I contemplated the thing before me, the small unmarked case. I drew my notebook close and opened it to the ribbon-marked page, adding a line for the box. The box was unnumbered, but I had turned up no item 317 in the lot my uncle had received. Thus, it became 'Item 317: horn fragment, w/illus.'.

Item 316 was a small vial of dried Egyptian locusts, resting in a small bundle like brown, papery cigars, and item 318 was a bottle of what seemed to be water, but the enclosed documentation assured it was liquefied hail collected from Egypt during a fierce storm. The inclusion of the horn near these Egyptian items seemed to indicate that it, too, originated from that dusty land, but the illustration noted an address in Greece, which made more sense, all things considered.

'Leave it be,' my uncle told me over supper that night, setting his knife upon the table top with undue force after cutting a slice of roast. 'I was wrong to take the thing from you. I appreciate your willingness to catalogue what we have obtained at all, niece, for surely there are more than nine hundred cases total, and I would not have the time . . .'

I stopped paying attention to my uncle's spoken words, and watched instead his eyes, how they flit from knife to roast and back again to knife.

Razor-thin blade drawing under my throat, the heated rush of blood after.

The candle between us illuminated my uncle's dark eyes and made them seem like oil. Restless, that gaze, moving everywhere except to me as he made his denials.

Spill of gaslight down the street and then only dark in the alley – dark, damp, bruised and screams . . . no one came.

My head came up sharply as the building around us groaned. My uncle fell silent at that, listening to this terrible sound that seemed to rise up through every timber to shake the roof shingles. I imagined I could feel the rumbling through the soles of my shoes.

'Restless spirits, mm?'

My uncle returned to his roast. I pressed my shoes hard to the now-still floor, my hands tight in my skirts. My appetite had fled like . . . *Dark coat-tails moving away, heels sharp on stone, bright crimson across my chest and thighs* . . .

Restless. Every building in this city had a tale of someone being buried in the foundations to appease the spirits of the land as the city rose from what had once been nothing, and while these buildings did make noise from time to time, I had never imagined it as a spirit until now.

A fresh crack of thunder made me jump in my chair. I came to my feet and tossed my napkin atop my uneaten meal, sliding away from the table. My uncle looked up, eyebrows arched. Surprise on that worn face.

'I think . . .' I sucked in a breath and resisted the desire to lift a hand to the black lace that covered my throat and the mark of my attack. 'I'll do a little more work.'

I stepped out of the room to the sound of my uncle's soft laughter; how like him I was, even at twenty, he murmured, finding solace in work through the long hours of the night.

I wasn't certain it was solace that my workspace contained, so much as a focus. I lit the lamp and watched its light spread across the collection of boxes. There were too many and yet, not enough. If cataloguing new arrivals at the apothecary were to be my life, how might I make these cases last for ever?

My eyes were drawn back to the unmarked box, the one I listed as 317. The box sat close to my left hand, its lid askew. I could not remember leaving it such and meant only to nudge the lid back into its place, but I found myself lifting the box, looking again at the horn.

What had my uncle been trying to hide?

I traced a finger down the jar and the building seemed to give another low shudder around me. With my finger still pressed to the glass, I looked up, imagining that I saw dust sift down from the ceiling boards, over the tops of the boxes piled before me like faint snow. It was then the gaslight stuttered before going out entirely. My breath caught in my throat and I strained to hear anything in the darkness.

Surely there were footsteps behind me, why didn't I hear them?

There was only a low moan, as if the very building were in pain. And then another rumble of thunder, before a steady thrum of rain on the roof above.

The lid of the case slid easily into place and I stood, gathering the other two boxes already logged. With these held close to my chest, I made my way down the dark and yet familiar hallway, toward the third door on the left, one of many rooms my uncle claimed for storage.

Old dust on brass made the doorknob slippery beneath my fingers, but the door was silent as it moved inward. My first step inside, however, was my last; strangely there was no floor as there should have been and I was falling, small wooden boxes flying from my grip as I plummeted downward.

I seemed to fall for ever, weightless, which was folly, for all too soon the ground rushed up to meet me. The boxes hit first, wood and glass falling to pieces, then my own hands, striking cold, damp stone and glass. Glass pierced my palms, bright pain, and far above, the sound of a latching door.

A footstep, there must have been, why didn't I hear . . .

My head snapped towards that distant sound, but there was nothing to see, not even my own injured hand in front of my face, so absolute was the dark. I passed a hand across my face, thinking that perhaps the lace at my throat blinded me, but there was nothing. Even that lace was gone.

'Uncle!' My voice did not echo in the space; I somehow expected it to, believing this darkness without end. I willed my vision to clear, for my legs to cease their shaking. Neither happened.

I pushed myself up from the damp stone floor and reached out. My injured hands touched the same damp stone on either side, fingers discovering individual stones wedged together with mortar. A man-made thing, then, and narrow enough that I could reach both sides with arms spread. I turned to my left and reached again, but there was no stone, nor any to the right.

I pictured a hallway, but could not make myself move down it. I stood convinced that the floor would vanish if I took a step in either dark direction, and so sank back down into this strange nothingness around me. This little square of stone beneath my shoes; how easy to imagine the rest of the world fallen away, the whole of it dwindled to this small darkness.

'Uncle!'

Again, there came no reply and no echo. Whatever this place was, he could not hear me, or could hear and simply didn't care. How easy for him if I *did* vanish. I tried to stop myself from shaking, but couldn't, and it was this motion that eventually began to calm me. It was familiar.

My trembling skirts brushed something papery, and I recalled the boxes and reached into the darkness for whatever remained of them. My fingers passed over dried locusts, and a chill that seemed darker than even the space already around me – bits of broken glass and wood and scattered straw, but not the curled horn. Its loss felt like a knife in my heart.

'Item three sixteen.' My whisper sounded impossibly small in the space. I counted out nine locusts and set them to the side. 'Item three seventeen . . . presently unaccounted for. Item three eighteen, likely spilled when the bottle broke.' I exhaled, exhaustion starting to curl around my shoulders, as though it longed to pull me into a different kind of darkness. 'No.'

The refusal was not enough, for I slept. I slumped on to the cool, damp stone, one hand covered in blood, still reaching for the dried locusts.

When I woke, it was the curled horn I saw before me. The jar was gone, likely shattered with the others, but the horn fragment lay close to hand, gleaming in . . .

I blinked, trying to clear my vision. Gleaming. Could a thing gleam without light? I looked up to a curious warm glow that radiated beyond the rising curve of darkness before me.

'Uncle?'

Had the door opened? Had I only tripped over my skirts as a child might and hit my head?

I tried to sit up, but my body protested, bruised from the fall. I frowned at the curve of darkness, amazed I could see anything at all. One's vision might adjust to any circumstance if given time, as would hearing, but—

A breath that was not my own sounded in the small space. I reached a hand out, meaning to grab the bit of horn and go, get up and run and run and—

The darkness shifted and with it the horn. The curve of black moved, and for a moment wholly obliterated the golden light beyond it. *Shadow – no, body.* A different kind of gold made itself known then, one that was rimmed in ink and focused on *me.* Wide eyes, watching.

An immense head lifted and the golden light ran like liquid down twin horns that spiralled from the skull, down wide black shoulders and equally black arms. Gold dipped between and over naked breasts and belly, washing down thighs as the creature rose upon its unshod hoofs with a strange kind of grace. If starlight were gold, this black body was the whole of the sky, stretching to encompass the entire world.

I screamed. Like that night long ago in the alley, I screamed. Instinct made me bolt upright, heedless of where I was; I sought only to get away. *There must have been a footstep . . . from this I would have run.* I turned, but quickly realized I was within an enclosed space, one fire providing heat and light, one arched doorway just beyond the creature.

'No locked doors in my house.'

The voice startled me into stillness. The voice was as dark as the outlying world around us, as dark as the creature itself, but yet gilded in gold. I curled my shaking hands into my skirts and watched the creature as it – as *she* – stood straight and spread her hands, as if welcoming me to a banquet.

'Many courtyards, many hearths.'

Those black hands swept towards the fire, which seemed blinding when compared to what I had known, but my attention moved past the fire to the doorway. The arch was filled with darkness and I knew not where the corridors might lead.

I knew only that I wanted to be there, wanted out and away. And yet . . .

My gaze returned to the creature, horrible and fascinating all at once. Tightly curled and glossy black hair covered her scalp and a piece of fabric looped the base of one horn, its colour lost to the firelight. Those horns – how like the fragment.

'Three seventeen,' I whispered.

'You are injured. Come.'

The hands beckoned me forwards to the fire, where I noticed a bucket filled with water. Still convinced the floor would evaporate beneath my feet, I moved slowly, eyes on the beast as it turned and curled hands around the bucket's handle. She placed the bucket before me.

That I was dreaming was the simplest explanation, but the cold water against my injured hands felt real enough, each cut screaming pain as I washed the dried blood away.

'Dreaming.' I had fallen asleep in my workspace, that was all, and the storm dragged me down into strange dreams.

'Countless dreams,' the creature said.

I looked up at this thing my memory had likely drawn from a half-remembered book. It was less frightening when viewed through a dream's spectacles.

'Asterion?' I asked.

The golden eyes blinked, as if in surprise. The big black head shook once. 'Asteria,' she said, and offered me a length of clean, old cloth.

I took the fabric, finding it warm from the fire, and wrapped my hands to both warm and dry them. Asteria. The creature had a name and was female. Trapped in darkness – no locked doors she had said, but did doors matter in a place such as this?

'Such a dream.' I closed my hands into loose, aching fists and lowered my head, thinking to only sleep for a moment more. I could no longer hear the storm, perhaps dawn had come and my uncle would soon be laughing at me when he found me slumped over the counter.

When I opened my eyes however, it was the same stone room I found myself in, the fire dwindled down to embers. The creature from before was gone. This did not relieve me as much as it should have, for I felt more alone than I did even when supping with my uncle. The doorway stood across from me, unguarded.

No locked doors, she had said, and countless dreams. Which dream was this? I did not know as I stood and crossed to the archway. I unwrapped my hands when I got there and peered out, dark corridor leading in either direction. I had no idea which branch to take, but then I had no idea where I meant to *go*, either.

I dropped the end of the old fabric in the doorway and stepped into the hall. Letting the fabric fall behind me as I walked, I trailed a hand over the stone wall to my left, too, hearing nothing but my own breath as I went. This place was as a womb, dark and unfamiliar, though the further I walked, the more recognizable it grew. The path I walked curved inward and came to an abrupt end, before seeming to curve back in on itself, and back yet again.

These curving paths seemed endless, and the longer I walked them, the more frightened I became. I kept trying to fit this place into the world I knew; the world above, as I came to think of it. My logic didn't work, for this labyrinth seemed old. These stones were not new; they were worn against my hands and beneath my shoes, as though many people had known these corridors for years and years. If this place were so old, then it had always been here, beneath the apothecary, and the apothecary had always been in my family, thus . . .

It was a train of thought I did not like. I recalled the groans of the building above, the strange scents that often filled the rooms, and wondered if this underground labyrinth – and its monster – were the cause. How long had Asteria been here, and how had she come to this place at all?

The darkness rushed up on me, cold and so black. I shivered and pressed myself against a wall, willing myself to vanish. I could not see, could only navigate with my hands outstretched to either wall. The fabric had long since run out, but I needed no trail to find my way back, for this corridor was not a maze. It seemed to have but one path.

I slept again, and on waking found myself wedged against a warm, black body. My hand was splayed across Asteria's belly; I could feel the rise and fall with each breath. She smelled like warm soil and her skin was smooth like rose petals as I drew my hand back – but here, my fingers discovered a scar marring her ebony flesh.

This closeness should have alarmed me more than it did, but in the dark, Asteria's even breathing was a comfort, something to hold on to, proof that I wasn't alone. Which was worse? Being alone in the dark or being in the dark with a monster? Whichever, I gravitated towards her, curling deeper against her body and closing my eyes to sleep once more.

There seemed to be no time in these dark corridors. When I woke, Asteria threaded her fingers through mine and guided me through the corridor, towards another courtyard of sorts, this one with pools of water and fire. Asteria bid me drink, and I did, greedily.

What is this place, I wanted to ask, and how did you come here, but the sight of Asteria in the firelight stole my voice. She was ink given shape, held together by sorrow. I could see that much in her eyes. This place might be home for her now, but it had not always been such. She was not of this damp country, nor maybe even of this time.

'You are also marked,' she said. Her hoofs seemed to cause the stone floor to vibrate as she moved, and I imagined this vibration moving upwards, through the very timbers of the apothecary far above us. Asteria stepped from the doorway towards the pool of water, where she dipped her magnificent head and drank.

'Marked?'

I asked the question, but then I knew, and lifted a hand to cover my bare throat. My cravat was lost, which exposed the thin bright scar against my skin. I drew in an uneasy breath and nodded.

'A man, in an alley.'

There must've been a footstep . . .

Asteria lifted her head, water gleaming down her chin and drew her fingers low across her belly. The scar I had felt earlier was plain, very pale against the rest of her.

'A man, on a ship,' she said.

She was close enough to touch then, and I found myself lifting a hand to do just that. My wet fingers felt cool against her dark cheek. She flinched but did not draw away, and I kept my touch slow and gentle, the way one might with a horse. I moved my fingers up to the bit of cloth around her horn. It was my cravat.

My hand stilled and I looked into those strange gold eyes, wondering. 'You're tangled,' I said, though the knot in the fabric was quite deliberate.

A small snarl escaped Asteria, but she allowed me to loosen the knot and pull the lace free.

Beneath the lace, I saw the deep mark in her horn, a carved number. The number six. Her eyes closed and her ears flicked, the latter just a whisper between us.

I swept my thumb over the marking upon her horn. It felt as old as these stone halls; smooth, as if she had tried to worry it away. She turned into my touch, cautious, eyes still closed.

Who marked her wasn't important right then to me. The number, though, made me think of the cases I was meant to catalogue, each item with its own number. A thing labelled and placed in darkness so that no one would have to see it, unless they came looking for such a terrible thing from the kindly apothecary.

Thoughtful, I slid my fingers upwards along the curve of Asteria's horns, finding no place where the fragment may have come from. Another minotaur then, I thought, and wondered if my uncle had requested a sample from such a creature, one who lived far from these city streets. A male perhaps, I allowed myself to imagine, though not meant to keep Asteria company precisely.

'Will you show me your house?' I tied the lace back around her horn, to cover her marking once more.

'It is like no other,' Asteria said and she rose, offering me a hand, for I would be blind again when we left the fire's gold glow.

As we walked, I knew not what I meant to do. Every hall was like the one before it, twisting back on itself time and again, until I grew weary of counting. Thirteen, fourteen – Asteria took me past pools of water, one showing me my face like a mirror, others coloured gold from tiles or blue and green from algae; there were pits of crimson fire, and small, soot-smudged temples built to gods who were no longer honoured above ground. No doors, no furniture, but when I grew hungry, a small rat caught and cleaned by Asteria's hands, cooked to a crisp over one of these fires, so that my stomach might cease its complaints. I grew accustomed to the sound of Asteria's hoof falls beside me as we went, to the left and the right and back again, comforted by the feel of her steady hand in my own.

These winding halls might lead us to Rome, for it felt that we covered this much ground, but the place it did lead us to was special in its own right, and even after all we had seen, just as staggering to me.

This courtyard was different than those we had visited before. Four small bowls of fire were clustered around a damp central slab of stone that was strewn with debris. I squinted as we came into the room, the fire so bright, and peered at what was on the slab: small bones, bits of paper, a coin or two, a cufflink. I couldn't understand the significance of any piece, be they looked at collectively or apart, until I thought of my own work above ground, and the many numbered boxes. But even then I was unsure, for what did Asteria need with a cufflink? A glance at her revealed no answer, so I moved deeper into the room, to the edge of the stone slab, where I saw the hole.

Into the ceiling, a hole had been carved. Large enough for a person to fit inside, the hole reached upward through the stone and ended in a small metal grate, which allowed watery daylight to leak in. I circled the stone slab until I found a rusted set of rungs on one side of the hole, water trickling down its interior to drop on to the slab.

It was a way out and the idea made my throat tighten. I looked at Asteria and she bowed her head – she knew she could leave but she never had. She had kept herself in this dark, cold place, for how long, with a way out right—

'No locked doors in my house,' she said, and lifted one long leg to step on to the stone slab. A bone crunched beneath the step as she gave me a hand up.

Asteria boosted me up towards the rungs, for I could not reach them without her. I clung to them, shaking, and looked down at her, not thinking then of all the things that must keep her here, of all the ways the world had locked the doors for her.

'Come with me,' I said and reached a hand down for her, silently begging. Where she would go in such a world, I couldn't say. Nor could she. She shook her head and stepped back, allowing me to climb. I only did so slowly.

At the top of the ladder, I looked down, seeing no sign of Asteria below. The stone slab seemed to flicker in the firelight, but all else was still. The grate above me dripped water, and though the metal was rusted and sharp, I took hold of it and pushed it up, which allowed me to climb into a dark alley.

As upon my arrival in Asteria's house, I crouched there, too afraid to move, though this world was more familiar to me. I closed my eyes a moment and then heard the fall of a footstep. My throat tightened in reflex and I ran blindly down this alley and that, until I had to stop and catch my breath and press a hand to the stitch in my side.

Beyond the alley was the world I knew and there, strangely, the entrance to the apothecary. A couple perched upon the steps, laughing softly. Oscar Baker, my heart whispered, once mine but no longer, for how could he claim the wretch this world made of me? I stepped deeper into the alley shadows, and slept there till morning light tried to pry its way between the high stone walls and the mourning doves began to coo to one another.

In the night someone had spread a cloak over me. It smelled of smoke and sweat, but the morning was cold and I drew the fabric around me. The apothecary stood closed, the street quiet yet, so I waited and watched the door. Watched my uncle come and open the drapes, watched him unlock and open the door to test it as he did; watched as he turned the sign to open and dipped his head to a passing merchant.

My shoes made nearly no sound when eventually I crossed the street, the apothecary doorknob cold when I last took hold of it. How strange to come to this place now, I thought, for Asteria's corridors seemed more familiar. The bell above the door chimed at my entry and I immediately sought my uncle's face in the room, his head bowed as he listened to a customer describing this ailment or that. I thought he would look up, but he did not.

Even as I crossed the floor, even as my fingers whispered across the bundled herbs, my uncle took no notice of me. Nor did the customer, a sturdy-looking man, who gestured to his nose and then his throat. Once his eyes met mine, his a watery green, and though I know he saw me, I also knew he did not. It was then I understood.

I moved like a ghost through the shop, meaning to reach my workspace when the items in the main counter drew my interest. There, behind the glass display, were nine bundled locusts. Another jar claimed to be liquefied hail from Egypt. I blinked and looked at the last item.

'Item 317: horn fragment, w/illus.'

It was my own handwriting there upon the slip, a new jar cradling the horn and its illustration. I looked up once, to my uncle and his customer, but they did not see me. They did not see me round the counter and slide open the case, nor reach my hand inward to take the horn and its drawing. They paid me no mind as I left the apothecary and took to the street, the bell chiming once more overhead. I slipped as easily as a shadow between the people who passed in the street, lost in their conversations about the Season, about marriages and breads and the tremendous thing the Queen had done last Tuesday. I moved among them, but not with them, and when at last I reached the alley, I did not look back.

Though I had run in a blind panic the night before, my feet seemed to know the way. This turn and then that. A left and then two rights. Past the slumbering drunk, unseen by the thief trying to pick a lock. I let my shoe fall with more weight as I passed, and the thief jumped, leaping away. *Surely there must have been a footstep.*

I found the metal grate and kneeled beside it, to pry it upward and peer down at the slab of firelit stone. I smiled softly to see the shadowed outline of two curling horns against that stone and then slipped into the narrow passage, pulling the grate into place before I stepped down, rung by rusted rung.

JANE

Sarah Prineas

Miss Jane Bigg-Wither reached her twenty-first year and, as a single woman must do upon attaining such an advanced age, resigned herself to spinsterhood. That is to say, she embraced it wholeheartedly.

Jane was not ugly; she was not without family connections; she was in possession of a comfortable inheritance. Really, she had hardly any reason to remain unmarried. Yet in the face of proposals and the occasional not-very-subtle hint from her uncle, Sir Percival Bigg-Wither, she did, in fact, remain Miss Bigg-Wither and not Mrs Somebody or Lady Something or Countess Whatsername.

Instead of marrying, then, Jane lived as quietly as possible, under the circumstances, in the country with her uncle, who was fascinated with all things to do with the magical element, though he had no practical ability himself.

'My dear Jane,' said Sir Percival over toast and tea one afternoon, 'I've just received the most wonderful news.' He held up a letter as proof.

Jane looked up from her book. The post brought wonderful news nearly every day. 'What is it, Uncle Percy?'

'Well, it's the Thameside College of Magic and Technology. It seems they want to name a new building after me! Isn't that lovely?'

'Oh, indeed.' Jane sighed, closed her book and prepared to listen.

Sir Percival beamed. 'You know I gave them a little money last year. A trifle, really, nothing much.'

'I remember it well, sir,' Jane replied, smiling briefly at the thought of calling fifteen thousand pounds a 'trifle'.

'And by way of saying thank-you, they want to name the new building after me. The Sir Percival Bigg-Wither Laboratories. It sounds rather good, does it not?' He glanced down at the letter. 'The deans of the college wish me to attend a dedication ceremony in a fortnight. Would you like to come along, Jane?'

'Oh, not again,' Jane muttered.

'I beg your pardon, my dear?'

Jane sighed. How could she say no? But visiting the Thameside College of Magic and Technology meant encountering . . .

. . . Wizards. Ugh. Jane shuddered, thinking back to her last experience with those practitioners of elemental magic.

The previous year Sir Percival had invited several newly qualified wizards to Wither Castle, and every single one of the young men had proposed to Jane. The worst suitor had been Viscount Sanditon. He had followed her around the estate; he had challenged one of his fellow suitors to a duel over who got to escort her into dinner; he had taken every opportunity to accidentally-on-purpose brush up against her or take her hand. Poor Sir Percival had been devastated when Jane had turned down every proposal, including Sanditon's, for he would have been delighted to call a wizard his nephew-in-law. But Jane was adamant: absolutely no wizards. And so she remained a spinster.

'You will come, won't you, my dear?' her uncle asked.

Jane composed herself. 'Yes, of course I will, Uncle Percy.'

Sir Percival gave a satisfied nod. 'Very good.' He cocked his head and gave her a sly wink. 'I believe the Viscount Sanditon will be in attendance.'

'That's what I'm afraid of,' Jane murmured.

'I beg your pardon?'

'I am quite sure he will be, Uncle Percy.'

Sir Percival patted her hand. 'Then it's all settled. Thameside College a fortnight from today. Lovely!'

As Jane had expected, the dedication ceremony consisted of one tedious speech followed by another, which were in turn followed by a tedious celebratory tea held in the Dean's gardens overlooking the river. Jane kept an eye on her Uncle Percy – as the centre of attention, his round face grew pink with happiness and sherry. Jane, of course, was besieged by admirers, wizards-in-training and several professors of magic. At the earliest opportunity she pleaded indisposition and escaped with a cup of tea to a quiet, shaded pergola.

She was not alone for long.

A lean figure wearing a fashionable high-collared black cape, an embroidered waistcoat and a quizzing glass hanging from a ribbon around his neck approached: Sanditon. He was rich, handsome, dashing, titled, everything a spinster might desire.

Jane raised the teacup before her face and shrank into the shadows, but it was too late; she had been spotted. 'Oh dear,' she murmured.

As the viscount spied her he gave an elegant bow. 'My dear Miss Bigg-Wither!'

In response to his unctuous smile Jane lifted the corners of her mouth and showed her teeth.

'Alas,' he said, seating himself with a flourish on the bench beside her and seizing her hand, 'that the fairest flower should hide herself away to bloom unseen.'

Jane remained silent; she could hardly agree or disagree with such a statement and she refused to waste a simper on this particular suitor. Instead she sipped her tea.

'I have been speaking with your uncle,' Sanditon said.

Jane looked up, alarmed. 'Upon what subject, sir?'

Sanditon stroked her hand. When he spoke, Jane thought she could see tiny blue sparks – the lingering presence of the magical element – winking from his teeth. 'We spoke, Miss Bigg-Wither, about Wither Castle. I overheard your uncle mention to the Dean that his estate is somewhat... troubled.'

Troubled wasn't the half of it, Jane thought. Despite Uncle Percy's inability to practice magic, the Bigg-Wither estate was strangely fraught with elemental storms and the odd occurrences that accompanied them. The castle's west tower had been rebuilt repeatedly after being transformed by elemental bolts into ice and, on one memorable occasion, butter. The knot garden was infested with homunculi. The ha-ha had migrated from one field to another, and sheep continually stumbled into it, the stupid creatures, and never came out again. The maze was dangerous; nobody knew any longer what lurked at its centre, and the gardeners refused outright to enter it.

'In order to explain all the odd phenomena,' Sanditon was saying, 'Sir Percy and the Dean of the college have requested that I, as their most capable recent graduate, pay you a visit to investigate.' He gave Jane's hand a lingering kiss. 'As a wizard, I was most delighted to agree; as a man, I am even more delighted. I shall join you at Wither Castle in five days' time.'

'Oh,' said Jane. 'How nice.' He'd made a mistake. By giving advance warning, she could make arrangements to go on a shopping trip to London or a visit to friends; one way or another, she'd not be at Wither castle when Lord Sanditon arrived.

Later, after Jane had managed to scrape Sanditon off, she entered the Dean's house in search of her uncle. She'd had enough tea and had fended off several more unwanted advances by young wizards; it was time to return home.

As she padded down one long, carpeted hallway, she heard raised voices coming from a room at the end. Jane continued more quietly, and peered through a crack in the door into the Dean's study. The Dean himself was seated behind a wide, polished desk. Standing on the patterned carpet, his back to Jane, was another man. The first thing about him that Jane noticed was his height, which was exceptional; the second thing was his anger, for it was evident in the set of his shoulders and the clenched fists at his sides.

'Absolutely not,' the man was saying.

The Dean leaned back in his chair and laced his fingers over the waistcoat stretched across his belly. 'You haven't any choice, Day. To begin with, someone must go along to keep an eye on Sanditon – you know about his . . . er . . . condition. Second, I shouldn't have to remind you that you still owe the tuition from last semester, and you shan't be granted a diploma until it is paid.'

'I realize that,' Day replied. He sounded as if he were speaking through gritted teeth. 'So now I've got to drop everything to trot out to some nobleman's estate to find out why his damned sheep are behaving strangely?'

The Dean nodded. 'Better that, Day, than reading the *Political Register* and fraternizing with Cobbett and his lot.'

'On the contrary,' the man replied. 'The efforts of the Luddites are far more important than the Bigg-Wither shrubbery. Elemental magic must never be used to run machines that take work away from honest craftsmen. We will stop it any way we can.'

'Machine breaking, you mean,' the Dean said, shaking his head. 'Diploma or not, Day, you're the finest wizard the college has ever produced, and you're wasting your talent on radical activities that will only land you in prison.'

The tall man shrugged. His coat, Jane noticed, was rather shabby, and his dark hair needed cutting; this, she felt sure, was no fine gentleman. His next words confirmed her suspicion. 'Then I'll go to prison,' he said. 'But at least—' Suddenly he broke off and straightened, his head cocked as if listening to something. Jane was certain she hadn't made a noise, but somehow he'd sensed her presence. Slowly, he turned to face the door.

As his eyes met hers, Jane caught her breath, as if his angry gaze were penetrating the door, the silken folds of her tea gown and her skin to the very core of her self, to a secret place where no one had ever been before. What did he see there, she wondered, and why did it make him look so fierce? She broke the gaze, looking down to compose herself. After taking a deep, calming breath, she smoothed her dress and opened the door wider.

As she entered the room, the tall man's frown grew deeper. 'You've been eavesdropping!'

'You have a very loud voice,' Jane replied and, retreating into politeness, held out her hand. 'I am Jane Bigg-Wither. I believe you have been invited with Viscount Sanditon to investigate the odd things that have been happening at my uncle's estate.'

The man named Day continued to stare, stepping closer, as

if drawn against his will, to take her hand. 'You're Jane Bigg-Wither.'

'As I said, that is my name.'

His eyes narrowed. 'I've heard about you.'

Jane cursed inwardly and gave him a tight smile. From Sanditon, she had no doubt. What on earth had the viscount told this man? 'How very interesting.'

He nodded. Still gripping her hand, he moved closer, peering down at her. His eyes were grey, she noted, and his nose was rather long. 'What they say is true,' he said. 'How do you do it?'

'Do what, sir?' she asked.

He opened his mouth to speak, then gave himself a little shake and released her hand. 'My name is William Day.'

'I am pleased to make your acquaintance, Mr Day,' Jane said. 'You will be arriving at Wither Castle in five days?'

'I don't seem to have any choice.'

Jane smiled and he blinked. 'Good.' She nodded at the Dean, who bobbed a hasty bow in return and left the room.

In the hallway, Jane leaned against a wall, her knees weak. Mr William Day was a wizard like all the others, but she'd never encountered anyone like him, anyone who made her feel so . . . exposed. And he was odd in a way that all the others were not, from his radical politics to his anger to his unusual height. Perhaps she would be at Wither Castle after all in five days' time.

If Miss Jane Bigg-Wither took extra care with her dress and coiffure on the fifth day hence one might argue that she did so at the behest of her uncle, who wanted her to appear at her loveliest for the visiting wizards.

Those two gentlemen arrived in Viscount Sanditon's private carriage, followed by another carriage packed full of baggage and the nobleman's valet, hairdresser and bootblack. The carriages rattled over the cobblestoned courtyard and came to a halt before the castle, which loomed in all its moated, turreted majesty before them. Jane and her uncle came out of the keep's great double doors to meet their visitors. The afternoon was cold and blustery and Jane's skirts blew against her legs while tendrils of her hair loosed themselves from their pins. The air felt prickly, the way it did before the advent of elemental storms.

'My dear Viscount!' Sir Percival cried, beaming and clapping a hand to his old-fashioned wig, which threatened to fly away in the wind. 'And Mr Day. Welcome, indeed!'

'See to the baggage, Day,' Sanditon ordered. Tossing a fold of his cape over his shoulder he bowed, then advanced upon Jane and took her hand. 'You are a most gracious host, Sir Percival. And your niece! As always, a delight. Miss Bigg-Wither, I greet you.' He bent to kiss her hand. Jane let it lie limp in his grasp.

William Day, who wore a muffler around his neck and the same shabby coat he'd worn the last time they'd met, turned from where he had been unloading a crate from the second carriage and greeted her uncle with a brief bow. To Jane he gave a nod and a look of suspicion. Then he turned back to the baggage.

Sir Percival was intrigued. 'Mr Day! What is that you've got there?' He pattered down the steps and out into the courtyard. 'Did you bring . . . equipment and, perhaps . . . instruments?'

William Day nudged one wooden crate with his foot. 'This is a portable Tuppence device.'

Leaving Sanditon at the front door to instruct his servants, Jane followed her uncle, noticing that William Day edged away from her to stand behind another pile of crates.

'Portable! Really! And this one?' Sir Percy asked, pointing to a cloth-covered dome.

'Good afternoon, Mr Day,' Jane said.

Ignoring her outstretched hand, William Day muttered a greeting and turned to her uncle. 'This, sir,' he said, 'is a bellweather.'

Despite herself, Jane was curious. A bellweather was a creature that was completely somnolent unless in the presence of magic. It was used for predicting the onset of elemental storms; when a storm was coming, it awoke and became active.

'A bellweather!' Sir Percival stooped towards the dome. 'Is it a bird? Might I have a look?' Before William Day could answer, Jane's uncle had swept the cover from what proved to be a domed cage. The animal within, a small, brown mouse, lifted its nose at the disturbance, twitched its tail and settled again into a furry ball. 'It stirred!' Sir Percival said, squatting down to peer into the cage.

William Day crouched beside him, frowning. 'Yes, it did. As far as I know, no elemental storms are forecast for this area. It's very odd.'

As he stood up, Sir Percival laid a sly finger alongside his nose. 'Ah ha, Mr Day!'

William Day got to his feet. Without seeming to realize it, he had moved to stand close beside Jane. 'Ah ha, Sir Percival?'

Jane answered. 'He means, Mr Day, that elemental storms do not behave as predicted around Wither Castle. We have many rather unexpected manifestations of magic, in fact. That is part of the problem.'

William Day frowned down at her. 'Only part of it, though.' He gave himself a shake, as he had in the Dean's office, and stepped away from her.

At that moment, Sanditon minced down the steps from the front door of the castle. As he stepped towards them, he sucked a few minuscule sparks of magical element from his fingertips, which he wiped with great fastidiousness on a handkerchief. 'Be sure the device is handled carefully, Day.' He seized Jane's arm. 'And, my dear Miss Bigg-Wither, we must immediately get you in out of this nasty wind.'

Later, after the visitors had seen to their baggage and been shown their rooms, they gathered in the drawing room for conversation, to be followed by tea. Jane tried to ignore Sanditon, who had squeezed in beside her on the sofa and kept pressing his thigh against hers, even while nibbling sparks from his fingertips. Her uncle sat opposite her in a comfortable armchair, and William Day stood with an elbow on the mantel, glaring at the fire.

After an exchange of pleasantries, Jane's uncle introduced his favourite subject. 'My dear Viscount, now that you're unpacked, have you had an opportunity to consult your etherometer?'

Sanditon gave an elegant shrug. 'You must ask Day, Sir Percival. I leave all of the . . . er . . . more instructive tasks to him, as he has not yet taken his degree. It is good practice for him, you see.'

William Day continued to frown at the fire. 'You were right, Sir Percival; the glass is falling, which means a storm is approaching. The bellweather is agitated enough that I think it will arrive by tonight.'

Uncle Percy beamed. 'Then we will certainly see some magical transformations.'

'Indeed,' said Sanditon, reaching beneath the tea table to place a hand on Jane's knee. 'The storm will offer a perfect opportunity for me to conduct a few experiments.' He caught Jane's eye and gave her a glinting smile. 'I like experiments, Miss Bigg-Wither, don't you?'

Jane responded by reaching down to push his hand off her knee.

Sanditon continued, unfazed. 'Now that you have a true expert on hand, Sir Percival, I will have the odd occurrences explained in a trice, I assure you.'

'I do hope so,' said Uncle Percy. He went on to describe in detail some of the major and minor transformations wreaked upon his estate by elemental storms during the past ten years. 'We have', he concluded, 'had some very odd chicks hatching from the eggs laid on the home farm. The pullets are not fit for eating, of course.'

After this comment, a brief silence fell. William Day stirred at his post by the hearth. 'What about you, Miss Bigg-Wither? Have you an interest in elemental magic?'

Jane blinked, surprised at being brought so suddenly into the conversation. 'Yes I do, Mr Day,' she replied. 'I have long wished to commence a course of study, in fact, in order to educate myself.'

William Day nodded. 'You should begin with the Ferrys' treatise on minor transformations. Professor Borneman's book is very good, too, though it contains a number of esoteric equations.'

'I plan to read Sally Tuppence's work,' Jane said. 'I've always thought it would be interesting to replicate some of her experiments. Uncle Percy, did she not attend Thameside College?'

'Well, yes, my dear Miss Bigg-Wither,' Sanditon interrupted. He gave Jane a benevolent smile and returned his hand to her knee. 'But a lady such as you are ought not pursue such studies. Those sorts of things are better left to men.'

At the hearth, William Day straightened. 'How can you say that, Sanditon? Tuppence was a genius, the greatest scientist we've ever known. Without her work, we'd know almost nothing about the operations of the magical element.'

Sanditon gave a dismissive sniff. 'Day, we all know that Mistress Tuppence was a very great scientist, but she carried out her research sixty years ago, and the world was a very different place then. Our age is more refined, more polite. We would never think of training up members of the gentler sex to be scientists or, worse, practitioners of magic. In any case, Day, you are not a suitable advisor to a young lady of Miss Bigg-Wither's class.'

Scowling down at the carpet, his hands thrust into his pockets, Day replied, 'I don't see why Miss Bigg-Wither shouldn't study magic if she wants to.'

Jane opened her mouth to state her enthusiastic agreement when she was interrupted by her uncle: 'Viscount Sanditon is quite right, Jane. Magic is for men. And now, my dear, you may ring for tea.'

Jane bit her lip to hold back her comment. She had always hoped to learn more about magic, to engage in readings that might explain why wizards behaved so strangely around her. But her uncle had always forbidden it, and his gentle commands were to be obeyed. With a sigh, Jane rose from the sofa and crossed to the bell pull, where she rang for the maid. William Day returned to his morose contemplation of the flames.

As the tea tray was brought in, Jane reseated herself by the tea table and poured, offering sugar and lemon and cucumber sandwiches. 'Sugar, Mr Day?' Jane asked, holding up his teacup. 'Lemon?'

'No.' He looked up, hesitating before crossing the room to her. As she held out his tea, their hands met and his jerked back; the cup and saucer fell to the floor between, them making a mess of delicate shards and tea on the patterned carpet.

'Oh, damn,' Jane cursed quietly. William Day looked up, his expression shifting from dismay to amused surprise.

'I beg your pardon, my dear?' her uncle asked from his armchair.

Jane picked up a napkin and bent to dab at the tea, which had stained the hem of her skirt. 'I said, "Oh bother," Uncle Percy. I've broken the cup.'

'You could never be so clumsy, Miss Bigg-Wither,' Sanditon interjected with his glinting smile. 'It was clearly Day's fault.'

'No matter, my dear,' Sir Percival said. 'Ring for the abigail; she will clean it up.'

'My lord Viscount, would you be so kind?' Jane asked.

Sanditon agreed, rising from the sofa to cross to the bell pull. As he stood, William Day knelt down beside Jane and began picking up pieces of broken china, his bent head very close to hers. The frayed collar of his coat, Jane noted, was turned up at the back, untidy. She restrained the urge to reach out to smooth the collar, instead leaning closer to whisper, 'I wish to speak privately with you, sir.'

William Day placed a handful of shards on to the tea tray. 'Why?'

'Hmm. You might give me a reading list.' She straightened and put down the napkin.

William Day remained on his knees beside her. 'Really.'

'Yes,' Jane whispered.

'Really?' he repeated, leaning towards her.

'Well, no, sir.' What excuse might she give? 'As my uncle indicated, something very strange is going on here.'

'I am very well aware of that.'

Having rung for the maid and explained the accident, Sanditon was returning to his place on the sofa.

Jane let out an exasperated breath. 'Quickly, sir. Might we meet later?'

'All right.'

Jane gave a relieved nod. 'Good. The library, then, in one hour.'

As evening fell, the storm predicted by the bellweather and etherometer was advancing. Though she was not a wizard,

Jane could feel a kind of tingling excitement in the air as she entered the library. The room took up two storeys in the castle's south turret and consisted of tiers of shelves built into the curving walls, each shelf jammed with books on every subject. The shelves were interrupted here and there by tall windows, which had replaced the original arrow slits, and by a set of French doors that opened up on to a veranda, which in turn looked over the infested knot garden and the maze. Through the windows, Jane could see an elemental storm crouched over the distant hills, ready to pounce. Now and then a blue flash of magical element flickered on the under-belly of the grey-green clouds.

Moments after Jane arrived, William Day joined her, closing the door behind him. 'I wasn't sure you would be here,' he said, crossing the room to stand before her, frowning.

'Frankly, sir,' Jane replied, 'I thought the same thing of you.' He was standing rather close, and in the dim light he appeared very tall and dark. He is a radical and a wizard, Jane reminded herself. She took a step back.

'Oh, no,' he said, following. 'I came. I didn't want to, but I did.'

'You didn't want to, sir?' Jane repeated.

'No.' With a visible wrench, he turned away from her and, as if seeking protection, went to stand behind a reading table. 'I can't figure it out. You are the niece of an idle nobleman; I should hate you on principle.'

Jane thought about protesting, but it was true: Uncle Percy was, indeed, idle. And so was she, for that matter.

Day continued. 'Even so, I can't stay away from you.'

Jane nodded. 'You're just like all the rest.'

He looked up, and suddenly his face seemed alert and not quite as angry. 'Just like all the rest? What do you mean?'

'Wizards.' She shuddered.

'What do you mean, wizards?'

'Whenever I meet a wizard he ...' Jane paused, embar-rassed, then told herself to be practical. 'He attempts to take liberties with my person.'

William Day raised his eyebrows. 'You mean you were not encouraging Sanditon? He is not your lover?'

'Certainly not! He simply will not leave me alone.'

'That is very interesting.' He looked around the room. 'Go and stand over there, Jane, by the window. And I will stand here, by the door.'

Jane went to stand by the window. The room darkened as, outside, the storm clouds advanced over the setting sun. 'We ought to light a candle,' she said.

'Just a minute. Stay over there.'

He really should address her as 'Miss Bigg-Wither'. Most ladies would not put up with such behaviour. 'You are not very polite,' she noted.

'No,' he agreed absently. He frowned down at the carpet for a long, silent minute, then looked up at her. 'There's definitely something. I can still feel it, but it's not too bad. I'm coming closer now. Stay where you are.' He took a few steps towards her, keeping the table between them and avoiding her eyes. 'All right.' He swallowed. 'Don't be alarmed, Jane. I'm coming right up to you.' He did so.

Jane closed her eyes, but she felt his presence very near. When she opened her eyes, he was standing before her, arms folded, as if restraining himself, again staring at the floor. 'What is the matter, Mr Day?'

'It's stronger here.' He drew a shaky breath. 'I'd better go back to the door.' He retreated, leaning against the door, clinging to the knob as if to anchor himself. 'There's only one explanation for it.' He fell silent, gnawing his lip.

'What explanation, sir?'

He did not answer.

'Tell me at once or I shall come closer!' she threatened.

He looked up, alarmed. 'No,' he said hastily. 'Don't do that.' He looked around the room. 'Sit down in that chair next to you. I'll sit down here and we'll be safe.'

She sat down next to the window. 'Now tell me.'

'All right.' Without seeming to realize what he was doing, he stood up and began pacing across his side of the room. 'We know of three types of magical creatures. The first are the reservoirs, which draw the element within themselves and store it. Then bellweathers, like the mouse I brought.' As he lectured, his pacing continued, but with each pass he was drawn closer to her side of the room. 'Bellweathers are some-what common, and reservoirs come along perhaps once in a generation.' He halted and stood before her chair, looking down at her, his eyes alight. 'But you, Jane, are almost unique.'

Jane slowly rose to face him. The room had grown very dark. From the windows came, at frequent intervals, flashes of elemental lightning; growls of thunder could be heard, even through the thick stone walls of the turret. Jane saw elemental sparks twinkling from the ends of William Day's hair, and then she saw nothing but darkness, for he had bent down to seize and kiss her.

Jane expected to feel repelled, for in her experience wizards were repellent. For some reason, she did not. Instead, she returned the kiss with interest.

At that moment the elemental storm broke with a crashing roar over the castle and the library door flew open to reveal a lean, shadowy figure: Sanditon.

Jane and William Day drew apart, but it was too late: they'd been seen.

The Viscount advanced, his mouth asnarl and his black cape aswirl. 'I might have known!' he shrieked. 'Sneaking away, Day, to assault this innocent young maiden!'

Beside her, Jane thought she heard William Day mutter a comment on who was assaulting whom.

Sanditon circled the table and advanced. 'Fear not, Miss Bigg-Wither!' He paused and gave what sounded to Jane like a high-pitched cackle. 'I will avenge you! This blackguard will not live to rue the day he stole you away from me!' The storm punctuated his challenge with a ferocious strike of elemental magic. There goes the west turret again, Jane thought.

William Day took her hand and they backed away from the advancing viscount. 'What is the matter with him?' Jane whispered.

'He's addicted to the element,' Day replied. 'It makes him . . . well, you can see for yourself.'

As they watched, the magical element saturated Sanditon's body; he stood before them, lighting the room, cobalt sparks sizzling from his skin and the ends of his hair surrounding him like a scintillant aura. 'I challenge you, Day, to a duel!' he shouted.

William Day glanced at the window; the storm crashed and rolled outside, the sky flickering with elemental bolts. 'All right.' He shrugged. 'Name your weapon.'

Jane gave an exasperated shake of her head. 'Oh, this is stupid. You can't fight him, William.'

Ignoring Jane's comment, Sanditon sneered. 'Of course, you wouldn't know this, Day, as you are not a gentleman, but it is for you to name the weapon.'

'Fine,' William Day said. 'Magic.'

For a moment, Jane thought she saw Sanditon hesitate. But then he gave one of his shrieking laughs. Without waiting for Jane to get out of the way, he shouted out a spell, which emerged from his mouth as a roiling ball of element. After floating in the air for a second, as if orienting itself, the spell flew through the air towards them, shedding sparks as it came. Calmly, William Day stepped out of the way, pulling Jane with him, and the ball of element splattered into the French doors, which dissolved into a whirl of sawdust and sand.

Invited in, the storm blasted through the open door. Thunder shook the turret and bolts of elemental lightning ricocheted across the room, striking the shelves; each book hit by the element was transformed into a bewildered white dove, which floundered in the buffeting gusts. Sanditon was forced to his knees, the cape wrapped around his face.

Over the howl of the wind, William shouted, 'It's too dangerous in here, Jane! Go outside!'

'But the storm!' she shouted back.

He grasped Jane by the shoulders and bent to speak into her ear. 'It won't hurt you, Jane – it can't. The element' – he paused to glance over his shoulder at Sanditon, who was struggling to his feet – 'it loves you.' With that, he pushed her towards the veranda and turned to face Sanditon.

Jane stumbled outside. The storm had pounced upon the castle and was shaking it as a cat does a mouse. Playful, she thought, but with rather serious effects for the mouse.

Elemental bolts zinged through the air. Peering through the darkness, Jane saw the knot garden writhing under the gyrations of thousands of tiny, green-skinned, dancing homunculi. Beyond, a dark shadow loomed up out of the maze. Jane heard the sound of cracking branches and saw an ancient oak topple beneath the onslaught of wind and magic.

Yet not a single stray bolt threatened her; even the wind seemed to caress, rather than buffet her. William Day was right, she realized. The magical element loved her. She was not a wizard, so she could not use the element to transform the world. But if she called it might it come to her?

Jane stepped to the edge of the veranda and opened her arms, welcoming the element, not with words, but with every particle of her being. At once, the storm whirled into a vortex above her, sizzling and snapping with elemental lightning and blue-black clouds. Jane felt her skin tingling and saw sparks effervescing from her fingertips; a great bubble of joy expanded in her chest.

As the focus of such exaltation, Jane faltered for a moment, then composed herself. 'Very well,' she told the storm. 'I've very much enjoyed your visit, but you must leave now.'

From inside the library came a flash of sapphirine light and a crash of thunder as the element used by the duelling wizards rushed to obey Jane's request. The storm reluctantly drew off; Jane felt the element tingling in her bones, then fizzing slowly away. As the magical storm departed, the clouds opened and ordinary rain pelted down.

From the hole in the turret where the French doors had stood, Jane saw a tiny lizard-like creature emerge – it was all that was left of Viscount Sanditon. Peering through the curtain of rain, she saw it skitter across the veranda, down the steps and into the maze. The bushes there twitched, as if a large shape had shifted, and were still.

A few battered-looking white doves fluttered next from the opening, and then William Day appeared. He looked a bit ragged, but seemed otherwise unharmed.

He approached her cautiously. 'Are you all right, Jane?'

Jane smiled. She felt far beyond all right; she felt

transformed. From now on, even her uncle would not be able to determine her fate. She would study magic, if she liked; perhaps she'd even attend Thameside College and become a scientist, like Sally Tuppence. 'I am quite all right, thank you.'

William Day glanced at the storm, which was trundling off over the distant hills. 'Good,' he said, then he turned his full attention on her. 'Jane, I will leave you alone now, if that is what you want.'

'No, sir,' Jane said. 'I think . . .' She paused. The lingering elemental magic seemed to be sparking in her bones, making her want to rise up on her toes and do . . . something . . . to the man before her, but she restrained herself. 'In the library, earlier, sir, we were interrupted.'

William Day swiped the ragged fringe of hair from his eyes and paced in a tight circle. 'Right. Interrupted.'

Jane couldn't stop herself from smiling, thinking of the kiss Sanditon had broken up. 'You were about to tell me what kind of magical creature I am,' she prompted.

'Ah. Right. You are a lure, Jane.'

'A lure?'

'The lure attracts the element to itself, which is why you have so many storms here. You lure them, Jane. Wizards nearly always have a very low level of the element present in our bodies. Not enough to effect a spell . . .'

'But enough that you respond to the lure,' Jane noted.

'Yes. So it's just mechanical.'

'What is?'

'My attraction to you.'

'What a relief that must be,' Jane said. 'You can go away and never think about me again.'

'Yes,' William Day agreed.

Jane frowned. He'd answered just a bit too quickly. Well then, it was up to her. 'I suggest an experiment.'

He raised his eyebrows but did not speak.

'You must kiss me, sir, and I will kiss you, and we will determine whether the attraction is, as you say, mechanical, or whether it is, as I suspect, not.'

Without hesitation, William Day bent down and kissed her.

She, at the same time, kissed him. After a few minutes he stopped. 'Not,' he said.

'Not, sir?'

'No, Jane. Not.'

THE WIDE WIDE SEA

Barbara Roden

Blue sky and white clouds above, yellow and green plains below, stretching as far as the eye could see and brushed by the wind that never seemed to rest: no relief, no respite, no indication that either sky or plains had an end. Rolling hills tantalized with hints of what could be just over, just beyond them; false hints. Eliza, raising a weary, weathered hand to brush a limp strand of brown hair from her face, knew that if she were to make her way to the top of one of the hills, she would only see more of the same. The same sky, the same endless plains, perhaps a few trees or low bushes to indicate where water was to be found, a few brave wildflowers – harebells, anemones, prairie roses – striving to bring some colour to the landscape, but none of the landmarks with which she was familiar, that had marked her world in the small village in which she had spent all her life until a few short months ago. That had been a landscape defined by man, with roads and walls and fences, fields still called by the names of people who had lived generations earlier, houses and barns that had stood for hundreds of years and might stand for hundreds more. Here there was nothing old except the land itself, and it had no names, no landmarks to which someone might point, nothing to guide the unwary or the lost.

Peter was out there, breaking more of the land – their land, the 160 acres the government of Canada had promised to anyone who was prepared to come and start a new life in a new country. He had been mesmerized by the railway car, which had appeared at the country fair near Devizes two years earlier, garlanded with wheat sheafs and promises of land, opportunity and prosperity in a place that was, to Eliza, as remote as the mountains of the moon. Canada was a large mass of red on the map, which Mr Jenkins, the schoolmaster, had hung on the wall of the schoolhouse with his thin white hands, part of the great British Empire, on which the sun never set. When Eliza thought about Canada at all, which was seldom, she had a vague idea of mountains and snow; of trappers, hunters and explorers; of brave priests bringing the word of God to Red Indians. It had never occurred to her that people – ordinary people – might choose to live there, and when she saw the railway car she was unable to muster more than a cursory interest. She and Peter had only been officially walking out together for a few days, and she was anxious that they be seen and noted, and hopeful that Peter would comment on her new bonnet. Not that it was, strictly speaking, new – merely an old bonnet she had turned and adorned with fresh ribbon – but she had still hoped for a compliment, or a comment about how the blue of the ribbon set off her eyes.

Peter's own brown eyes, however, were fixed on the wagon. A cheerful agent, his ruddy complexion and clear eyes a testimony to the healthy Canadian air, his accent strikingly at odds with what Eliza was used to, was busy handing out leaflets to all who were interested. Peter stood, listening intently in a way that he had never managed in the schoolroom, where he had always seemed constrained and hemmed in, his clear eyes and strong body wanting to be outdoors, working and doing. He even overcame his habit of silence enough to ask the occasional question, referring often to the papers clutched in his hand. Eventually Eliza, bored, moved away towards the tea tent, where Peter found her a few minutes later.

'Look at this!' he exclaimed, holding up one of the leaflets. 'Free Land!' it cried, and 'Cash Bonuses!' Peter's eyes gleamed with an excitement Eliza had never seen before. 'It says here' – he fumbled open the slender leaflet with his large, rough farmer's hands and found the passage he wanted – 'that the government of Canada will give one hundred and sixty acres of land to any man as wants to claim it!' His face filled with wonder. 'Can you imagine that, Eliza? One hundred and sixty acres of land free for the taking?' He shook his head. 'And they say it's a grand land for growing; all you need is seed and a bit of water, and any man can have as fine a crop of wheat as you can imagine, and ready markets for it too. Look.' He shuffled through the assortment of papers until he found the one he wanted and held it out to Eliza, who hesitated a moment before stretching out one of her small, delicate-looking hands – of which she was inordinately proud – to take it. Emblazoned across the front were the words 'The Last Best West', and a hand-tinted image of a field of wheat, stretching out endlessly under a clear blue sky until both were halted by the white border around the picture.

She thought of that image now as she gazed out at the reality before her. It had looked so safe, so placid, neatly contained by the leaflet's cover: manageable, knowable. Eliza had been here for two months, but already she realized how wrong she had been. It had been presented to her as a Promised Land, but she saw now that it was more akin to Egypt under the Pharaohs, a place where fire and hail, drought and insects could wipe out the work of a summer, a year, a lifetime in an instant. She would never know this land, never feel content here the way Peter did. He did not feel the pressure of the sky bearing down upon him until he wanted to scream; he saw only the clear blue immensity of it, felt the life-giving sun. He did not feel as if he were drowning when he gazed out across the land, lost in its immensity; he only realized the opportunity it afforded, a rare chance for a man to make a new life. He did not hear the ever-present wind calling his name; he only raised his face to it, welcoming its cooling breath.

And he never saw Mrs Oleson.

Eliza turned sharply, suddenly, in a gesture that had become so habitual she scarcely noticed it any more, and looked back at the house that was her entire world. It stood alone and unprotected, its unweathered wood harsh against the backdrop of prairie. It might have fallen from the sky, dropped by some god's careless child who had tired of a plaything. For a moment a vision came to her of the low stone farmhouse in which she had spent her whole life; in which the lives of generations of her family had been spent, so that every room, every piece of furniture, even the stones themselves, were as familiar to her as her own name, were infused – or so it seemed to her now – with the unseen presences of many people, of births and deaths, the commonplace, the everyday, the normal. Here, in this alien landscape, there was nothing familiar, no landmarks, nothing to guide her, nowhere to hide.

She shivered, feeling exposed, naked. Nothing had prepared her for this. She had spent most of the long sea voyage in the tiny cabin she had shared with three other girls – strangers, all – and had seldom ventured up on deck. The first time she had done so the vastness of the ocean had made her hang back from the railings, afraid that she would fall into those endless depths and be lost for ever. A fragment of a poem that Mr Jenkins had read to them came unbidden, to her mind:

> Alone, alone, all, all alone,
> Alone on a wide wide sea!
> And never a saint took pity on
> My soul in agony.

She had almost hoped that she would be seasick, so that she would have an excuse to stay safely in her cabin, a reason for avoiding the deck; but her body was as robust as always, and she hadn't felt the slightest twinge of sickness. She knew that this was one of the reasons Peter had asked her to marry him; he had said as much on the evening of the country fair, when he had walked her home. It was their first chance to be alone and, while he had still said nothing about her bonnet, she had wondered if he would hold her hand, or at least take her arm when they skirted the field where Mr Miller's bull glared out at the world from angry eyes and pawed the ground in fierce jabs. But Peter had merely said, 'You aren't afraid of anything, are you, Eliza?' and she had tossed her head and said, 'Of course not. Why?'

Peter stopped and faced her. 'Because if I do this thing, I'll be needing a wife who isn't afraid. I'll be needing a wife who's strong, who won't turn away from a hard job; because it will be hard, I don't want to lie to you. But we'd be starting a new life, a better life than we could ever have here, in a place where there's room to breathe, room to grow, room for any man with fire in his belly and a good strong wife by his side.'

Eliza caught her breath. She tried to make some sense of what he had just said, but one fact stood out clear and firm, like lightning ripping through a dark sky.

'Are you asking me to marry you?'

'Yes.'

Eliza opened her mouth to speak, but no words came. She had thought, from the moment Peter had first asked her to walk out with him, that this day would come, but she had pictured it as something entirely different. He would not go down on bended knee – that, she suspected, only happened in romances – but it would be in her parents' front room, Peter dressed in his best, at some vague point in the far future, and Peter would stammer a little, as befitted a man asking a woman to marry him and unsure of her answer, even though Eliza knew that she would say yes, with one younger sister already married and the prospect of spinsterhood looming ever more strongly before her. She had never pictured it happening so soon, though, in a darkening lane, Peter's face glowing with a passion which – the thought came and went quickly, but was there nonetheless – had more to do with the wagon and the stranger than with her.

Her mind had now put his words into some kind of sense, and she realized with a shock the full implications of what he had said. He was asking her to marry him, yes, but he was also asking her to go with him to this vast new land, to leave behind everything and everyone she knew, and trust herself to a place about which she knew nothing, to join him in a grand project about which they had both been ignorant a few hours earlier, and which, she could see, was now consuming him like a flame. An answering flame of resentment flared up within her for a moment, an anger against this place which had, in so short a time, inspired in him an ardour she had imagined would be reserved for her.

Peter was looking at her anxiously, and Eliza realized that she needed to answer. There was no time for prevarication, for coyness, for protestations of how sudden this was, even if she had been inclined to indulge in such luxuries. She knew, as clearly as if Peter had shouted it to the heavens, that he was bent on doing this thing, and that he would only ask her once;

if she refused him now, or hesitated, then all would be lost, for he would see that she was not a woman who could be trusted to be strong, unhesitating, fearless. She allowed herself one quick moment of calculation, a survey of her bleak prospects should she demur; then she met his gaze firmly, strongly, and said, 'I will marry you,' and hoped that the flame that burned inside him would one day warm her too.

Now, almost two years later, she stood under the pitiless eye of the prairie sun, against which there was no defence, and which had turned her face, once so fair and fresh, first red and then brown.

They had not married immediately; Peter had no home of his own to take her to, and they had agreed, after due consideration and much discussion, that it would be best if they were married shortly before Peter left for Canada. He would go out alone to that new land. He did not expect Eliza to come until he had a home for her, and she had not argued, although when she said goodbye to him – her husband of three days – she had wondered, for a brief moment, if he had secretly hoped that she *would* argue with him, insist on going, on taking her place beside him, even though neither had any real idea of where that place would be or what it would look like. It had been too late then, even if he or Eliza had wanted it, and the last sight she'd had of him was his head looking at her from out the window of the train as it pulled away, and his arm waving, before his train vanished.

There began a curious, almost dream-like year in which Eliza felt as if she were two people living the same existence, each aware of the other but having little in common. She lived as she always had, performing her chores around the house and farm, walking to the village, sharing a room with her younger sister Jane, and there were times when she could almost feel that what had happened between her and Peter had been little more than a dream, a fancy spun out of her imagination. Then she would catch sight of the thin gold ring on her finger, and realize with a shock that she was now a married woman, her husband – the word sounded odd, almost nonsensical, like a child's made-up assortment of letters – far from her in a strange land. His occasional letters were a reminder of him, and she scanned them eagerly when they came, paying scant heed to the details of his new life, his new home – soon to be her home too – looking instead for anything more personal, more private, something of the man himself; but in this quest she was more often than not disappointed, and she would fold each new letter, once it had been read and remarked upon by her family, and place it with the others in the bottom of the large chest she was slowly filling with clothes and linens and her few personal possessions, realizing as she did so that when the chest was filled it would mark the end of all she had known of life until that point, and the beginning of another life, which she was not even sure would be her own.

Occasionally, as she passed through her day, she would notice some small detail to which she had never really paid heed before; something she had accepted as being a part of her life that would never change, and which, she now realized, would continue, unseen, without her. It seemed impossible, but she would look at the chestnut trees in bloom, their flowers white against the rich green leaves, or the bluebells carpeting the ground, or the redstarts and nightingales nesting in the hedgerows, and think for a moment, I shall not see this again, and the enormity of what she was about to do would well up inside her. Each detail she noticed marked the passage of time, every one reminding her inexorably that she had started down a road from which she could not turn back, and she would go back to the house and look at how full the chest now was, how little room there was in it, and realize how few were the days remaining to her in her old life.

A year after Peter departed, Eliza made her own voyage, by train to Liverpool to board the *Numidian*, accompanied by her father, who was nervous of the city in a way that Eliza would never have suspected, and who stood twisting a large white handkerchief in his hands as he waved goodbye to her from the dockside. Then the long trip across the endless ocean, and the first blessed sight of land, of Halifax, swelling up out of the water until it filled her sight. Another train journey, longer than she had thought possible, to Montreal and then Toronto, and then through country that at first inspired

Eliza with memories of home: there were towns and villages, farms ands fields, if not quite of the shape and design to which she was accustomed, then at least familiar, known, knowable. Then the train had swept north, around the great inland seas of which she had read, and slowly, inexorably, the traces of the world she had known at home, and half-glimpsed in this new land, vanished, and her only link with it was the iron rail under the wheels that bore her onward.

She gained her first glimpse of the prairie when they left Winnipeg, and she pressed her face to the glass of the carriage, first wiping away the dust that streaked the windows and coated everything else with a fine layer of grit. She had been unprepared for the vastness of it; another ocean, with an occasional town or farm doing nothing to make it seem any less implacable than the sea she had crossed. She began to have some dim sense of what she had taken on, and pulled back from the window with a small, stifled gasp.

Her destination was, she knew, a place called Moose Jaw. The name had seemed impossibly foreign, even faintly exotic, in a way that Halifax, Montreal and Toronto had not when she read of it in the Wiltshire countryside in a letter from Peter; now it sounded almost sinister, hinting at something on which she dared not let her thoughts dwell. As the train drew in to the dusty station, Eliza peered out the window into the harsh sun, looking for Peter, and for a moment did not see him. Her heart fluttered in something like panic. 'Let him be here. Please, let him be here,' she heard herself say in a low voice that almost did not tremble; and then she saw him, standing beside a curious-looking cart drawn by a pair of massive, ungainly, dirty brown oxen, and she was off the train and into his arms, heedless of the people watching and Peter's faint air of embarrassment, burying her face in his shirt so that she could block out, if only for a moment, the vast blankness that surrounded them and which seemed to be searching for a foothold within her, the relentless wind that she could feel pushing at her; the dry, dusty air that filled her nostrils.

They would not stop in the town, which seemed bustling and purposeful. Peter was anxious to be away, explaining that he wanted to arrive home before dark. 'But it's only noon! said

Eliza, puzzled. 'How far away is our home? Can't we walk from there to town?'

Peter stared at her. 'It's not far,' he said slowly, after a pause. 'Not here, at any rate.'

'What do you mean, "not here"?' Eliza said.

'Well . . .' There was another pause. 'Things are different here; bigger,' said Peter at last. 'You have to realize that. Places aren't so close together. I told you, in my letters, that we weren't in the town. You knew that.'

'Yes.' He had said that their house was outside town; not far, he had added, but she realized now that he had never been more precise than that, and she had pictured the town and their farm a short distance away, within an easy walk certainly; the town, or some of it, visible from where she was to live, full of the promise of life and noise and people. Memories of the land she had just passed through – of that wide ocean of grass and hills stretching away for ever, unbroken, untouched – made the bright day seem chill.

'How far?' she asked again in a low voice.

'About twenty miles,' replied Peter. She stood motionless, silent, taking in those three bare words. 'I tried to get land closer to town,' said Peter defensively, 'but it was all gone, and what was left wasn't worth having. It's a fine spot, where we are; there's water, and a few trees, and I'll plant more, soon as I have a chance, around the house to make a wind-break and some shade. It'll be the prettiest, snuggest spot you ever saw, Eliza, I promise.'

He was almost cajoling, now, as if she were a child who had turned away, disappointed, from a gift that was not to her liking, and Eliza felt ashamed. He had worked so hard – she could see that in his hands, his face, the lines of his body, all of which were harder than they had been – and she knew that she had to say something to take away the hurt from his voice, his eyes. She said faintly, 'Twenty miles; it's not so very far, is it?'

Peter smiled, relieved. 'Course it's not. That's my girl.' He hugged her clumsily, and Eliza hoped that he would say something else, add words of comfort, anything to chase away the thoughts that were prowling the corners of her mind. But he did not, and as he turned away and busied himself with her cases, she realized dully that there was nothing he could say. She watched as her entire life was loaded into the back of the ungainly wagon, then took a deep breath and climbed up beside Peter to start the final, and longest, stage of her journey.

The town was soon a distant blur behind them. Eliza kept turning to watch it, straining her eyes until it vanished altogether and they were alone on the prairie. She tried to make some note of where they had come from and where they were going, but there were no signposts or markers, nothing except the road itself, a dusty, hard-packed, rutted ribbon, and the occasional homestead with small, huddled houses, a few outbuildings, and perhaps a straggling row of young trees, full of the promise of future shade and shelter, but for the moment a reminder of how recently this old land had been settled. The high clouds overhead did little to distil the glare of the sun, and all looked harsh and brassy beneath its rays, with not even the green and gold of the prairie grasses, the dark brown earth, or the occasional flowers – what looked to her like buttercups and pale crocuses – able to soften this first impression, and utterly unable to provide the familiarity she suddenly craved.

Eventually they turned off the main road on to a dispirited track that wound southwards. The houses – although Eliza could hardly think of them as such – grew more sparse, and some struck her as odd, although they were far enough away that she could not say precisely why. As each one came into view she hoped Peter would announce that they were home, but the houses rose and then fell behind as the oxen plodded on. Just as she was beginning to think their journey was going to continue for ever, Peter coaxed the team of oxen from their straight line towards a small house – what Eliza thought of as one of the 'odd ones' – and she felt her spirits lift slightly. This, then, was their home, and she watched with some eagerness as they drew closer.

When Peter stopped the cart she sat gazing at the building, her expression puzzled; then she turned to him, eyes wide, trying to take in what she was seeing.

'It's made of dirt!'

Peter, who had jumped down from the cart, looked up at her. 'Sod,' he corrected. 'It's made of sod. They're called soddies. They're what folk build when they don't have enough money to buy lumber.'

'But . . .' She tried to find words. 'This is our house?' she said faintly. 'Made of dirt?'

'Our house?' Peter looked at her for a moment, puzzled, then laughed. 'No! Our house is a little piece on. I just thought we'd stop and pick up a few things while we were here. This was the Oleson's place; Oleson said I could take what I needed.'

A wave of tiredness swept over Eliza and suddenly she felt like crying. Nothing seemed to make sense in this land; everything was changed, all the markers and boundaries she had known all her life swept away in a place where twenty miles was considered no distance and houses were made of dirt and they could help themselves to another's possessions. There were so many things she wanted to say, so many questions, but all she said was, 'Why?'

'Why?' Peter looked puzzled, and Eliza had to stop herself from shouting at him.

'Why can we take what we want?'

'Oh.' Peter scratched his head. 'Oleson cleared out, went back to Sweden after his wife died. Couldn't stand being alone, he said, though I don't think he was cut out for this kind of life. Didn't know what he was getting himself into. He was having a rough time of it before his wife died. If she'd lived then he might have made a go of it, with her and all – she were the strong one, I reckon – but after what happened . . . well, he just sort of gave up, and soon as spring came and the roads were passable, he upped and left. Said I could take what I wanted.'

'What happened to her – to Mrs Oleson?'

Peter paused and looked at her, as if weighing his answer. 'It was in winter,' he said finally. 'You'd not think, to look at it now, what winter can be like here. The snow comes and it's like a curtain comes down, and you can't see a hand in front of your face, it's that fierce.'

They walked towards the house, and Peter gestured towards a small wooden outbuilding some thirty yards away. 'They had a cow and some chickens, in the barn there; they had enough wood for that, but not for the house. Oleson used to make a sort of joke of it, that they lived in a soddie, but the cow had a proper house.' He paused. 'Don't know what happened, exactly, but I reckon that Mrs Oleson went out to the barn and got lost in the storm. There was a fierce one, the day she died. I was glad enough to stay snug inside, myself.'

Eliza stared in disbelief. 'But . . . but it's no more than a few steps! How could someone get lost?'

Peter shrugged. 'You'll see, come winter,' he said, and though his tone was resolutely normal, as though he were discussing something of no more moment than the likelihood of another sunny day, Eliza felt a chill strike her. 'The wind comes up, and it's as if the snow was a living thing, trying to beat you down. I told Oleson he should put a line up between the house and the barn, as a guide, and he said he would, but he never got round to it. Near as I can figure, his wife went out and got turned round by the wind and the snow. She wouldn't have realized until she'd walked far enough to know she'd missed the barn, and then she would have turned herself round and tried to follow her footprints back, but . . . well, they'd have been filled in already, and she'd have been good as blind in all that snow, just wandering, hoping to stumble across the house. Oleson found her next day, half a mile away, frozen to death.'

Eliza stared, eyes wide, mouth open to frame words that she could not say. *What kind of land is this that you've brought me to? she wanted to scream. How can anyone live here, in dirt and snow, and freeze to death in sight of . . .*

Her thoughts broke off. In sight of what? In all the land around there was nothing to be seen save the dirt house and the tiny barn, and a few straggling trees in the distance that would afford no shelter, no warmth, no aid. It would be a simple matter to freeze to death here, she thought, within steps of safety.

Some of what she was thinking must have been visible in her face, for Peter said soothingly, 'Don't you fret, it won't happen. I'll string a line between our house and the barn nearer to winter; long as you keep hold of that you'll be right as rain.' He glanced up at the sky, to where the sun was gently dipping towards the horizon. 'Best get what we want, and then we'll be off. I expect you could be doing with a cup of tea after your trip, make you feel better.'

She looked at him for a moment, and then laughter rose up, unbidden, at the suggestion that a cup of tea would be sufficient to restore her. She saw Peter smile, and then as the laughter continued to spill out of her, she saw his face change into something wary, almost frightened, and she wondered for a moment what he could be frightened of, before she realized that it was her; or rather her laughter, which had a cracked, brittle sound even to her own ears. That look sobered her in an instant. She forced herself to stop and draw a few ragged breaths while the echo of her laughter was caught by the wind and whirled away to dance across the prairie.

'I'm sorry, Peter.' She did not know precisely what she was sorry for, but the words needed to be said, to erase that look from his face. 'I'm just tired, is all.' From some half-remembered place inside her she conjured up the ghost of a smile. 'A cup of tea', she said carefully, not fully trusting herself, 'would be lovely.'

He watched her for a moment, thoughtfully, and nodded. 'Right then. Best hurry along in that case.'

Eliza stood for a moment, drawing another deep breath. A sound behind her made her turn sharply, and her eyes swept the landscape. There was no one, nothing except the wind, sighing over the bright grass. Surely it was only her imagination that had conjured her name out of the sound, as if someone had called her. She shivered once, then turned and followed Peter into the dimness of the house.

Peter was proud of the fact that he could afford to build a house of wood during his first year, and Eliza had, at first, been reassured by it. The thought of living in a house made of dirt had appalled her; it was, she felt, something she simply could not have borne. When she followed Peter into the Oleson house she had felt like an animal creeping into a burrow, and had stood uncertainly near the door, her eyes sweeping around the interior, dim despite the blazing sunshine outside. They retrieved a few items – some cloth from which Eliza could make curtains; a few kitchen utensils; oddments of clothing left behind – the residue of a life begun in hope and ended in . . . but Eliza did not want to think of that.

Her days settled into a routine that was not unfamiliar to her from her past life; what she could not accustom herself to was the intense loneliness of it. Peter was gone for most of the day, breaking the land with the oxen, planting, maintaining the fire-break he had erected away from the house – 'Just in case,' he had tried to reassure her – and Eliza was busy around the house; there was so much to do, and no other pair of hands to do it. There were two cows in the barn – one had been the Olesons', Peter explained – and chickens, and a half-wild cat that stayed sleek on mice and rats but was rarely seen. Eliza had tried to coax it into the house, but the cat had glared at her with feral eyes and scorned her attempts at friendship. There was the house to tend, and the vegetable garden to hoe and plant and weed, water to be drawn and carried and wood to be chopped and carried and stacked, and always something to cook, clean, mend or make. She did not mind the hard work – she was accustomed to that – but she could not rid herself of an ache, a hunger for the company of someone or something. Even a dog would have been some comfort, but a dog was not a necessity, not yet, and in this land, anything that was not a necessity was relegated to some future day. Even the sight of another house on the horizon would have been enough, she told herself, to provide reassurance that she was not completely alone and unprotected, but no such reassurance was forthcoming.

Increasingly, she found herself stopping in the middle of what she was doing and listening, straining for the sound of something, anything, that would prove she was not alone. It wasn't long before she thought she heard someone calling her name, as on the first day at the Olesons', but it was the wind, she told herself, which never seemed to end, never rested. She could see it before she felt it, watch the grasses and the crops blowing before the gust swept over her, and if she was outside she would fight an urge to drop to the ground and try to dig her way in, like an animal seeking the safety of its den.

More and more she tried not to spend much time outside. The cry of the wind and the sigh of the wide sea of land stretching endlessly away, frightened her, and she kept her head down as much as possible, concentrating on the ground immediately beneath her feet, looking neither to left nor right. If she did not look up she could not see how alone she was.

Their closest neighbours lived two miles away, the house out of sight behind a fold of hill. Eliza walked over one day, not long after arriving, desperate for the sight of another person, another house, but she came away disappointed. Mrs Reilly, a hearty, red-faced matron, was glad enough to see her, but was largely preoccupied with her five children, who ranged in age from a girl of about ten to a babe in arms of indeterminate sex, who seemed to cry incessantly. The older children were scarcely less noisy, and the change from the silence of her own house made Eliza want to clap her hands to her ears. As it was, she emerged with a violent headache and a vague, dull pain.

She started the weary walk back to her house, but before she was halfway there she thought of the Olesons' soddie. The house was still unoccupied, and Eliza had a sudden urge to see it again, justifying her curiosity with the excuse that there might well be more items that would be of use to her and Peter. She turned her footsteps in the direction of the abandoned house, which looked no less forlorn than the first time she had seen it, when finally it came into view, alone on the prairie. Yet as she drew nearer, Eliza realized it seemed less of an intrusion on the land than their own home, of which Peter was so proud. The soddie was built from the land, the soil itself. It might even have grown up there, springing from the earth like the grass that surrounded it: part of the landscape, not an imposition upon it.

When she entered the soddie, Eliza was struck by how cool it was. She found their own house stifling, with the sun beating relentlessly upon the thin roof and walls; whereas the soddie was deliciously refreshing, a welcome respite from the heat. She ran a hand over one of the walls, feeling the roughness. The dirt was dark and wholesome; life-giving, she thought, not like the thin, dry dust against which she waged a ceaseless war in her own home.

She glanced around the interior of the soddie, noting how compact it was, how well ordered. A few pieces of roughly made furniture remained, and a large trunk was pushed against one wall, where it had obviously served as a makeshift table. Eliza gazed at it, idly wondering why it had been left behind. Perhaps it contained his wife's things, for which Mr Oleson presumably had no need after she died. What had they been like, this couple who now existed only as names? Peter had said that Mrs Oleson had been the strong one of the pair, better suited to the life here than her husband. Would she and Mrs Oleson have been friends? The answer darted through her mind, sharp and unwelcome, that they would not have been, and she brushed it away, wondering where Mr Oleson was now. Home, she supposed, wherever that was. She felt a sudden ache at the thought. A picture arose before her, so vivid she could almost touch and hear and smell it, of her home in England, and she closed her eyes to block out the vision and prevent the tears she could feel rising.

She felt rather than heard a movement behind her, and whirled round, visions of home forgotten. She was facing the door, which she'd left open. Framed in the glare of the sun was a figure: a woman, Eliza thought, although it was difficult to be sure. She squinted against the sunlight, trying to make out details, but the contrast between the dim interior of the soddie and the brightness outside made it impossible to register anything beyond a general impression of someone tall and pale, silent and watchful. She uttered a tremulous, 'Who is it? Who's there?' but there was no answer. Then, before Eliza could frame some faltering words of explanation or apology, there was nothing.

Eliza darted to the door and swept her gaze over the land in front of her. There was no one in sight, no sign that anyone was, or had been, there – no cart or wagon or horse, nothing to break the vastness, except the small barn, which stood thirty or so feet off to her left, impossible to reach in the short time it had taken her to leave the soddie.

Of course, if the woman had gone round the side of the house, she could even now be waiting, out of sight, for Eliza to follow. But that was ridiculous. What reason could anyone have for such an action? She had imagined the figure, that was all; the darkness within, the light without and her own loneliness had tricked her into thinking she had seen someone where there was no one. Her decision not to walk around the house was not inspired by fear, she told herself, she needed to start back to their house, as Peter would be back soon and there were chores to do.

She did not look back at the soddie, not even when the sound of her name was borne to her on the wind. There could not be anyone there.

Later that evening, she asked Peter what the Olesons had been like; particularly Mrs Oleson.

Peter scratched his head ruminatively.

'Quiet,' he said finally. 'Hard workers. Leastways, she was. They both had fair hair, like all them Swedes seem to, and she was tall; as tall as him, with rough hands, like a farmhand's, on account of her working in the fields alongside her husband. Oh, not that he didn't do his fair share, but she were the strong one, I reckon. I saw a bit of them, what with being so close and all, and I got the feeling that coming here were her idea more'n it was his; he'd have been content to stay where they were, but she wanted something else.' He stopped, and shook his head. 'That's why it struck so hard when she died. If she hadn't, well, then, they'd have made a go of it; she'd have seen to that. But the heart just seemed to go out of him after. Terrible thing, it was. He came staggering up to the house, more dead than alive, soon as the storm were over and he could get out. Don't know how he made it; he were half-froze when he got here, and it were all I could do to get the story from him. Well, soon as I heard it I knew what must have happened, and so did he, but he kept saying she were out there, waiting for him, that he could hear her calling. I never heard anything except the wind, but . . . well, I didn't have the heart to say that, not with him standing there, with a look on his face like he was in hell itself. The way I reckon it, he'd been in hell for a fair time, and this put the cap on it. Soon as spring came he couldn't get away fast enough. Left most of his things behind; said I could have what I wanted, that maybe they'd bring us better luck than he'd had.'

It was a long speech for Peter, who generally came back from his day's work so tired that he had scant energy left to waste on words, and Eliza had listened in horrified fascination. She could picture the scene: Peter, alone in the house, thankful that the storm had ended, and then the pounding at the door; Oleson's story, gasped out between sobbing breaths; the search for the missing woman, which could only end one way; the broken man, wanting nothing but to leave this hard land that had cost him so dear.

But he got to leave, came the thought, unbidden, to Eliza's mind; *he was lucky, because he got to go home again*. Her hand flew to her mouth, as if she had spoken the words aloud, and Peter stared at her, puzzled. 'What's wrong?' he asked.

'Nothing. I was . . . I was just thinking what a terrible thing to happen.'

'Aye.' Peter sighed. 'It's a hard land, no denying that. I don't blame Oleson for leaving She might have, though.'

'What do you mean?' asked Eliza, more sharply than she intended.

Peter shrugged. 'I mean that she weren't the kind to back down from a challenge. If it'd been the other way round – if anything had happened to her husband – I'd wager she'd have stayed on by herself, made a go out of it, just to show she couldn't be beat. A strong woman – just like the one I've got, eh, lass?' He grinned at her. 'A good, strong wife; that's what a man needs here. When I asked you to marry me and you said yes straight off, like, knowing what it meant without having to think about it: well, I knew then and there I'd made the right choice.'

'What would you have done if I'd not given you an answer when you asked?' said Eliza in a low voice.

'Why, I'd have said, "It's no good, my girl, I can't take a wife who doesn't know her own mind off to Canada with me!"' He laughed. 'But you've always known your own mind, no fear of that.' He yawned and stretched. 'Best think about getting off to bed. You, too, lass; you look a bit peaky. You're not sickening for something, are you, or . . . or anything else?'

'No,' she replied, 'I'm just a bit tired, is all. What else could there be?'

'Well,' Peter paused and looked suddenly shy. 'Sometimes women . . . that is . . . when they're going to . . . well, when someone else is on the way . . .' His voice trailed off and Eliza realized what he meant.

'No, Peter, I'm not going to have a baby; not yet, anyway.'

'Aye. Just thought that . . . Plenty of time, eh?' He rose from his chair. 'Are you coming?'

'In a few minutes, Peter; I have one or two things to do, then I'll be in.'

'Right. Don't be too long.'

'I won't, Peter.'

She continued sitting after he had disappeared into their tiny bedroom, closing the door behind him. She knew that he would be asleep within moments of his head touching the pillow, and she sat waiting patiently until she heard the creak of the bed. Then she stood up and moved to the door, opening it wide and passing through so that she could stand in front of the house and feel the wind upon her hot face. She didn't mind being outside at night – the darkness pressing down was every bit as merciless as the sun – but at night she couldn't see the vast landscape stretching away from her in all directions; could pretend that there would be houses, roads, signs of life visible, were it not for the blackness that shrouded these things and hid them from her sight. Peter did not feel this way. He exulted in the land, the space, in everything that made her shrink back and pull away. Mrs Oleson would not have felt the way Eliza did. She had been strong, Peter said; the land had not frightened her. Hearing the way her husband spoke about the dead woman, Eliza knew that she could never speak of the way she herself felt, never let him know the thoughts that chased around inside her head as she went about her daily routine.

She looked back at the house, silvery in the moonlight. How flimsy it was! She tried to picture the house in winter, buffeted by wind and snow, and wondered how they could hope to keep safe in so meagre a shelter. She knew that it was possible to freeze to death in a house here; and what of Mrs Oleson? She had frozen to death within sight of her own house, had got lost within a few feet of safety. She had never in her life imagined a place such as this, and no one had thought to warn her of it: not the smiling agent, who had been full of the promises of the new land and free with pictures that did nothing to show the reality of it, and not Peter, who had never once mentioned that they were so far from anyone, that days could pass when she would see no one but him, that a person could lose her way just a few steps from her own door, and wander the snowbound prairie alone, unheeded, until she froze to death.

Eliza felt a surge of anger, sudden and biting – at the land, at the agent, at Peter. She hated them, hated them all. They had all lied to her, or if not lied then failed to speak the truth, to tell her how alien this place was, how lonely she would be, how she would feel the sky and the land beating down on her until she felt she had to scream and hide and find a place of safety. She wanted to scream now, scream to the uncaring heavens, to the stars shining coldly. She actually felt a scream rising, and clenched her hands so tightly that her nails, blunt as they were, dug semi-circles into the flesh of her palms.

A thread of movement out of the corner of her eye made her turn her head, eyes scanning the darkness. Had Peter come outside? No; the movement had been in the direction of the barn, and Peter could not have walked there without Eliza seeing him. There was no one and nothing there that she could see.

The Eliza of two years ago, of the new hat and blue ribbons, would have strode to the barn to see what was there. Now, however, she began to shiver, and backed towards the house, not wanting to turn her back on the barn until she was within reach of safety. She stumbled over the door sill and almost fell, but had just enough presence of mind not to slam the door. She was glad the curtains were drawn over the windows; the thought of something looking in was unbearable.

Peter was sound asleep, as she had known he would be. Quietly, furtively, Eliza undressed and slipped into her night-gown, then lay down on the bed and pulled the sheet over her, despite the warmth of the night. She wanted to move closer to Peter, cling to him, but she did not want him to wake, so she lay rigid on her side of the narrow bed, eyes closed, mouth set firm, her hands at her sides, formed into fists. At some point she slept, and was mercifully untroubled by dreams.

She said nothing of this to Peter the next day. Her anger had passed, leaving her feeling weary to her very bones and unrefreshed by sleep. He was out all day, breaking land for next year's planting; every acre he broke now would mean a larger crop the following season. When he came home, tired yet satisfied, speaking confidently of what they were accomplishing, she found she could not talk to him of how she felt, could not tell him that the vastness of the land terrified her, that she felt as if someone were watching her always, that she was desperate for human contact, the sound of voices, the sight of people and places. The only voice she heard, other than Peter's, was the one that called her name across the fields, the one that she had at first thought was the wind. But now she knew better; she knew who was calling.

Mrs Oleson.

She knew it was Mrs Oleson because she had seen her again that day, standing once more by the barn, silent, watchful. She was tall and fair-haired, and Eliza knew that her hands, could she see them, would be rough and chapped from working in the fields alongside her husband. She had to, Eliza knew, because it was the only way in which all the work would get done, the only way in which her dreams and hopes would be realized. She did not see her directly; it was only out of the corner of her eye, and when she turned to look there was no one there. But she was conscious of the woman, even when she could not see her, and she found herself trying to get a closer look, pretending to ignore the figure and then turning her head with sudden swiftness in an attempt to catch it. It was no use; Mrs Oleson moved too swiftly for Eliza to see clearly.

Over the next few days Mrs Oleson was a constant presence every time Eliza went outside. She hurried about her chores as quickly as possible, seeking the solace of the inside of the house whenever she could, keeping the curtains drawn lest the face appear at the window. She wondered what she would do if the figure came into the house, then pushed the thought from her mind. That could not happen. The house was the only place left to her. If she was not safe in there . . . She let the thought trail off, as her thoughts did more and more often. Sometimes, when Peter was speaking to her, he had to repeat himself two, even three times before she took in what he was saying, and she often found that she had forgotten his words within minutes of his saying them. Sometimes she would look up and find Peter watching her, with a look in his eyes that worried her, although she could not say why.

One afternoon, when she had gone outside to tend to the garden, after putting it off for as long as possible, she had been conscious of Mrs Oleson standing by the barn, and had been trying without success to get a better look at her when Peter's voice broke the silence with a puzzled, 'What's wrong with you, Eliza?'

She jerked herself upright, suppressing the cry that rose to her lips and willing her heart to stop its frantic beating. 'Peter!' she said finally, when she could trust herself to speak. 'You . . . you startled me.'

'I'm sorry, lass. Thought you'd have heard me coming.' He glanced in the direction of the barn. 'What were you looking at?'

Eliza stopped herself following his gaze. Out of the corner of her eye she could still see the figure, tall and fair, beside the door, which Peter was looking straight at.

'I . . . I thought I saw someone at the barn.'

'Ah.' Peter looked from the barn to Eliza and back again. 'Your eyes must be playing tricks. Anyone had been there, I'd have seen them, too.'

'Yes.' She straightened slowly, like an old woman, and turned to face the barn. There was no figure to be seen; only the blank face of the building and the endless land stretching out behind it.

Now she stood under the blue sky, looking at the endless plains, feeling the sun blazing down upon her and wondering vaguely what she was doing there, so far from the shelter of the house, and why she felt so cold. The thought came to her, slowly, as from a great distance, that it was because of Mrs Oleson. That morning Eliza had seen her inside the house for the first time, standing motionless in the corner of the main room, and the sight of her had made Eliza drop the bucket of milk she had just carried in from the barn. She had not even tried to clean it up; her only thought had been that her sanctuary had been despoiled, and that she must leave quickly, without looking back. It was only when she had found herself 200 yards from the house that she had stopped, as if an invisible wall lay across her path. Ahead of her there was nothing but open plain; Peter was out there, somewhere, but she knew that she could not go to him, could not explain. The house was barred to her, now; she could not go back, could not face what was waiting patiently inside. She thought of the barn; that was possible. She might be safe there . . .

She turned to look at the structure, and cried out when she saw the figure of Mrs Oleson standing in front of the barn door, as if barring her way. It took a moment to register the fact that the woman had not disappeared when she'd looked full upon her, and when the realization hit her, she screamed once, a high, keening sound. The noise was picked up by the wind, which seemed to throw it back in her face, and she thought she could hear her own name amongst the rush of sound. She screamed again, trying to form the word 'No!', but it did not come, and the dancing wind seemed to mock and push at her, as if she were in a crowd of people, all jostling her, trying to force her in the direction of the barn and the woman in front of it.

She would not go there. Her feet turned, away from the house and barn, away from Peter across the grass, and she began to run, blindly, heedlessly, knowing only that she needed to get away from this pitiless land, from the emptiness that consumed her, within and without. She had no clear idea of where she was going, but stumbled on, her breath coming in choked sobs, refusing to turn and look behind her at what might be following.

She had no idea how long she ran; she knew only that she must keep moving. She stumbled often and fell more than once, but did not stop; and it was only when she saw the soddie looming up in front of her that she realized this was where she had to go. She would find safety inside the house of earth; she could hide herself away in the cool shadows, let the land shelter her from itself.

She reached the door, which was hanging open. She could not remember whether or not she had closed it behind her the last time she had been there. It did not matter. She plunged inside and stumbled over something on the floor, coming to rest against the far wall, where she huddled herself into a tight ball, trying to draw ragged gasps of breath. She felt the roughness of the dirt through her dress, and turned and dug her hands into it, clawing away clods of cool brown earth. Over the sound of her laboured breathing and the pounding of her heart, she heard a noise, faint as a whisper, from the door. She half-turned towards it, thinking she saw a movement outside, and knew that she had been followed. She was not safe. She would be found.

Her eyes darted wildly about the interior of the soddie, searching for somewhere more sheltered. Her world had shrunk to these four dark walls, and still it was not small enough. Hide. She needed to hide. Under something, behind something, inside something, where she could not be seen, where she could not see the figure at the door, darker now, more solid. It would see her in a moment. She had no time; she must be quick, no time for thought, no time . . .

Peter found her that evening, when the harshness had gone out of the sun and the land was bathed in a soft light that tipped the grasses with gold. He might not have seen her inside the dimness of the soddie's interior had it not been for the dirty fringe of blue dress hanging out from under the closed lid of the trunk which, when opened, revealed Eliza's body, curled up like a broken doll, discarded by a careless and uncaring child.

HER LAST APPEARANCE

Mary Braddon

Chapter 1 – Her Temptation

He is a scoundrel,' said the gentleman.

'He is my husband,' answered the lady.

Not much in either sentence, yet both came from bursting hearts and lips passion-pale.

'Is that your answer, Barbara?'

'The only answer God and man will suffer me to give you.'

'And he is to break your heart and squander your earnings on his low vices – keep you shut up in this shabby lodging, while all the town is raving about your beauty and your genius – and you are to have no redress, no escape?'

'Yes,' she answered, with a look that thrilled him, 'I shall escape him – in my coffin. My wrongs will have redress – at the day of judgement.'

'Barbara, he is killing you.'

'Don't you think that may be the greatest kindness he has ever shown me?'

The gentleman began to pace the room distractedly. The lady turned to the tall narrow glass over the chimney piece, with a curious look, half mournful, half scornful.

She was contemplating the beauty which was said to have set the town raving. What did that tarnished mirror show her? A small, pale face, wan and wasted by studious nights and a heavy burden of care, dark shadows about dark eyes. But such eyes! They seemed, in this cold light of day, too black and large and brilliant for the small white face, but at night, in the lamplit theatre, with a patch of rouge under them and the fire of genius burning in them, they were the most dazzling, soul-ensnaring eyes man had ever seen; or so the cognoscenti said, Horace Walpole among them; and Mrs Barbara Stowell was the last fashion at Covent Garden Theatre.

It was only her second season on those famous boards, and her beauty and talent still wore the bloom of novelty. The town had never seen her by daylight. She never drove in the Ring, or appeared at a fashionable auction, or mystified her admirers at a masquerade in the Pantheon, or drank whey in St James's Park – in a word, she went nowhere – and the town had invented twenty stories to account for this secluded existence. Yet no one had guessed the truth, which was sadder than the most dismal fiction that had floated down the idle stream of London gossip. Barbara Stowell kept aloof from the world for three reasons – first, because her husband was a tyrant and a ruffian, and left her without a sixpence; secondly, because her heart was broken; thirdly, because she was dying.

This last reason was only known to herself. No stethoscope had sounded that aching breast – no stately physician, with eye-glass and gold-headed cane, chariot and footman, had been called in to testify in scientific language to the progress of the destroyer; but Barbara Stowell knew very well that her days were numbered and that her span of life was of the briefest.

She was not in the first freshness of her youth. Three years ago she had been a country parson's daughter, leading the peacefullest, happiest, obscurest life in a Hertfordshire village, when, as ill luck would have it, she came to London to visit an aunt, who was in business there as a milliner, and at this lady's house had met Jack Stowell, an actor of small parts at Covent Garden – a cold-hearted rascal with a fine person, a kind of surface cleverness which had a vast effect upon simple people, and ineffable conceit. He had the usual idea of the unsuccess-ful actor: that his manager was his only enemy, and that the town was languishing to see him play Romeo and Douglas and a whole string of youthful heroes. His subordinate position soured him; and he sought consolation from drink and play, and was about as profligate a specimen of his particular genus as could be found in the purlieus of Bow Street. But he knew how to make himself agreeable in society, and passed for a 'mighty pretty fellow'. He had the art of being sentimental, too, on occasion, and could cast up his eyes to heaven and affect a mind all aglow with honour and manly feeling.

Upon this whitened sepulchre, Barbara wasted the freshness of her young life. He was caught by her somewhat singular beauty, which was rather that of an old Italian picture than of a rustic Englishwoman. Beauty so striking and peculiar would make its mark, he thought. With such a Juliet he could not fail as Romeo. He loved her as much as his staled and withered heart was capable of loving, and he foresaw his own advantage in marrying her. So, with a little persuasion, and a great many sweet speeches stolen from the British Drama, he broke down the barriers of duty, and wrung from the tearful, blushing girl a hasty consent to a Fleet marriage, which was solemnized before she had time to repent that weak moment of concession.

The milliner was angry, for she had believed Mr Stowell her own admirer, and although too wise to think of him as a husband, wished to retain him as a suitor. The Hertfordshire parson was furious, and told his daughter she had taken the first stage to everlasting destruction without his knowledge, and might go the rest of the way without his interference. She had a step-mother who was very well-disposed to widen the breach, and she saw little hope of reconciliation with a father, who had never erred on the side of fondness. So she began the world at twenty years of age, with Jack Stowell for her husband and only friend.

In the first flush and glamour of a girlish and romantic love, it seemed to her sweet to have only him, to have all her world of love and hope bound up in this one volume. This fond and foolish dream lasted less than a month. Before that moon which had shone a pale crescent in the summer sky of her wedding night had waxed and waned, Barbara knew that she was married to a drunkard and a gambler, a brute who was savage in his cups, a profligate who had lived amongst degraded women until he knew not what womanly purity meant, a wretch who existed only for self-gratification, and whose love for her had been little more than the fancy of an hour.

He lost no time in teaching her all he knew of his art. She had real genius, was fond of study, and soon discovered that he knew very little. She had her own ideas about all those heroines of which he only knew the merest conventionalities and traditions. She sat late into the night studying, while he was drinking and punting in some low tavern. Her sorrows, her disappointments, her disgusts drove her to the study of the drama for consolation and temporary forgetfulness. These heroines of tragedy, who were all miserable, seemed to sympathize with her own misery. She became passionately fond of her art before ever she had trodden the stage.

Jack Stowell took his wife to Rich, and asked for an engagement. Had Barbara been an ordinary woman, the manager would have given her a subordinate place in his troupe and a pittance of twenty shillings a week, but her exceptional beauty struck the managerial eye. He had half a dozen geniuses in his company, but their good looks were on the wane. This young face, these Italian eyes, might attract the town – and the town had been leaning a little towards the rival house lately.

'I'll tell you what, Stowell,' said the manager, 'I should like to give your wife a chance. But to take any hold upon the public she must appear in a leading part. I couldn't trust her till she has learnt the A B C of her profession. She must try her wings in the provinces.'

They were standing at noontide on the great stage at Covent Garden. The house was almost in darkness, and the vast circle of boxes shrouded in linen wrappings had a ghostly look that chilled Barbara's soul. What a little creature she seemed to herself in that mighty arena! Could she ever stand there and pour out her soul in the sorrows of Juliet or the Duchess of Malfi or Isabella, as she had done so often before the looking glass in her dingy lodging?

'Jack,' she said, as they were walking home – he had been unusually kind to her this morning – 'I can't tell you what an awful feeling that great, dark, cold theatre gave me. I felt as if I were standing in my tomb.'

'That shows what a little goose you are,' retorted Jack contemptuously. 'Do you think anybody is going to give you such a big tomb as that?'

Mrs Stowell appeared at the Theatre Royal, Bath, and tried her wings, as the manager called it, with marked success. There could be no doubt that she had the divine fire, a genius and bent so decided that her lack of experience went for nothing; and then she worked like a slave, and threw her soul, mind, heart – her whole being – into this new business of her life. She lived only to act. What else had she to live for, with a husband who came home tipsy three or four nights out of the seven, and whose infidelities were notorious?

She came to London the following winter and took the town by storm. Her genius, her beauty, her youth, her purity, were on every tongue. She received almost as many letters as a prime minister in that first season of success; but it was found out in due time that she was inaccessible to flattery, and the fops and fribbles of her day ceased their persecutions.

Among so many who admired her, and so many who were eager to pursue, there was only one who discovered her need of pity and pitied her. This was Sir Philip Hazlemere, a young man of fashion and fortune – neither fop nor fribble, but a man of cultivated mind and intense feeling.

He saw, admired and, ere long, adored the new actress, but he did not approach her, as the others did, with fulsome letters which insulted her understanding, or costly gifts which offended her honour. He held himself aloof and loved in silence – for the instinct of his heart told him that she was virtuous. But he was human, and his sense of honour could not altogether stifle hope. He found out where she lived, bought over the lodging-house keeper to his interest and contrived to learn a great deal more than the well-informed world knew about Barbara Stowell.

He was told that her husband was a wretch and ill-used her; that this brilliant beauty, who shone and sparkled by night like a star, was by daylight a wan and faded woman, haggard with sorrow and tears. If he had loved her before, when the history of her life was unknown to him, he loved her doubly now, and, taking hope from all that made her life hopeless, flung honour to the winds and determined to win her.

Could she be worse off, he asked himself, than she was now – the slave of a low-born profligate – the darling of an idle, gaping crowd, scorned and neglected at home, where a woman should be paramount? He was rich and his own master; there was all the bright, glad world before them. He would take her to Italy, and live and die there for her sake, content and happy in the blessing of her sweet companionship. He had never touched her hand, never spoken to her, but he had lived for the last six months only to see and hear her, and it seemed to him that he knew every thought of her mind, every impulse of her heart.

Had he not seen those lovely eyes answer his fond looks sometimes, as he hung over the stage box, and the business of the scene brought her near him, with a tender intelligence that told him he was understood?

If John Stowell should petition for a divorce, so much the better, thought Philip. He could then make his beloved Lady Hazlemere and let the world see the crowning glory of his life. He was so deeply in love that he thought it would be everlasting renown to have won Barbara. He would go down to posterity, famous as the husband of the loveliest woman of his time; like that Duke of Devonshire, of whom the world knows so little, except that he had a beautiful duchess.

One day, Sir Philip Hazlemere took courage – emboldened by some new tale of Jack Stowell's brutality – and got himself introduced to the presence of his beloved. She was shocked at first, and very angry; but his deep respect melted her wrath, and for the first time in her life Barbara learnt how reverential, how humble, real love is. It was no bold seducer who had forced himself into her presence, but a man who pitied and honoured her, and who would have deemed it a small thing to shed his blood for her sake.

He was no stranger to her, though she had never heard his voice till today. She had seen him in the theatre night after night, and had divined that it was some stronger feeling than love of the drama that held him riveted to the same spot, listening to the same play, however often it might be repeated in the shifting repertoire of those days. She knew that he loved her, and that earnest look of his had touched her deeply. What was it now for her, who had never known a good man's love, to hear him offer the devotion of a lifetime, and sue humbly for permission to carry her away from a life which was most abject misery!

Her heart thrilled as she heard him. Yes, this was true love – this was the glory and grace of life which she had missed. She could measure the greatness of her loss now that it was too late.

She saw what pitiful tinsel she had mistaken for purest gold. But, though every impulse of her heart drew her to this devoted lover, honour spoke louder than feeling, and made her marble. On one only point she yielded to her lover's pleading. She did not refuse him permission to see her again. He might come sometimes, but it must be seldom, and the hour in which he should forget the respect due to her as a true and loyal wife would be the hour that parted them for ever.

'My life is so lonely!' she said, self-excusingly, after having accorded this permission. 'It will be a comfort to me to see you now and then for a brief half-hour, and to know that there is someone in this great, busy world who pities and cares for me.'

She had one reason for granting Sir Philip's prayer, which would have well-nigh broken his heart could he have guessed it. This was her inward conviction that her life was near its close. There was hardly time for temptation between the present hour and the grave, and every day seemed to carry her further from the things and thoughts of earth. Her husband's cruelties stung less keenly than of old; his own degradation, which had been the heaviest part of her burden, seemed further away from her, as if he and she lived in different worlds. Her stage triumphs, which had once intoxicated her, now seemed as unreal as the pageant of a dream. Yes, the ties that bind this weak flesh to earthly joys and sufferings were gradually loosening. The fetters were slipping off this weary clay.

Chapter 2 – Her Avenger

Sir Philip showed himself not undeserving Barbara's confidence. He came to the sordid London lodging – a caravansera that had housed wandering tribes of shabby-genteel adventurers for the last twenty years, and whose dingy panelling seemed to exhale an odour of poverty. He brought his idol hothouse flowers and fruits; the weekly papers; those thin little leaflets which amused our ancestors; a new book now and then, and the latest news of the town – that floating gossip of the clubs, which Walpole was writing to Sir Horace Mann. He came and sat beside her, as she worked at her tambour frame, and cheered her by a tenderness too reverent to alarm. In a word, he made her happy.

If she were slowly fading out of life, he did not see the change, or guess that this fair flower was soon to wither. He saw her too frequently to perceive the gradual progress of decay. Her beauty was of an ethereal type, to which disease lent new charms.

One day he found her with an ugly bruise upon her forehead; she had tried to conceal it with the loose ringlets of her dark hair, but his quick eye saw the mark. When pressed hard by his solicitous questioning, she gave a somewhat lame account of the matter. She had been passing from the sitting room to her bedchamber last night when a gust of wind extinguished her candle, and she had fallen and wounded herself against the edge of the chest of drawers. She crimsoned and faltered as she tried to explain this accident.

'Barbara, you are deceiving me!' cried Sir Philip. 'It was a man's clenched fist left that mark. You shall not live with him another day.'

And then came impassioned pleading which shook her soul – fond offers of a sweet glad life in a foreign land; a divorce; a new marriage; honour; station.

'But dishonour first,' said Barbara. 'Can the path of shame ever lead to honour? No, Sir Philip, I will not do evil that good may come of it.'

No eloquence of her lover's could move her from this resolve. She was firm as the Bass Rock, he as passionate as the waves that beat against it. He left her at last, burning with indignation against her tyrant.

'God keep and comfort you,' he cried at parting. 'I will not see you again till you are free.'

These words startled her, and she pondered them, full of alarm. Did he mean any threat against her husband? Ought she to warn Jack Stowell of his danger?

Sir Philip Hazlemere and John Stowell had never yet crossed each other's path. The surest place in which not to find the husband was his home. But now Sir Philip was seized with a sudden fancy for making Mr Stowell's acquaintance, or at any rate for coming face to face with him in some of his favourite haunts. These were not difficult to discover. He played deep and he drank hard, and his chosen resort was a disreputable tavern in a narrow court out of Long Acre, where play and drink were the order of the night, and many a friendly festivity had ended in a bloody brawl.

Here on a December midnight, when the pavements about Covent Garden were greasy with a thaw, and the link boys were reaping their harvest in a thick brown fog, Sir Philip resorted directly the play was over, taking one Captain Montagu, a friend and confidant, with him. A useful man this Montagu, who knew the theatres and most of the actors, among them Jack Stowell.

'The best of fellows,' he assured Sir Philip, 'capital company.'

'That may be,' replied Sir Philip, 'but he beats his wife, and I mean to beat him.'

'What, Phil, are you going to turn Don Quixote and fight with windmills?'

'Never mind my business,' answered Philip; 'yours is to bring me and this Stowell together.'

They found Mr Stowell engaged at faro with his own particular friends in a private room – a small room at the back of the house, with a window opening on to the leads, which offered a handy exit if the night's enjoyment turned to peril. The mohawks of that day were almost as clever as cats at climbing a steep roof or hanging on to a gutter.

Captain Montagu sent in his card to Mr Stowell, asking permission to join him with a friend, a gentleman from the country. Jack knew that Montagu belonged to the hawk tribe, but scented a pigeon in the rural stranger, and received the pair with effusiveness. Sir Philip had disguised himself in a heavy fur-bordered coat and a flaxen periwig, but Mr Stowell scanned him somewhat suspiciously notwithstanding. His constant attendance in the stage box had made his face very familiar to the Covent Garden actors, and it was only the fumes of brandy punch that prevented Stowell's recognition of him.

The play was fast and furious. Sir Philip, in his character of country squire, ordered punch with profuse liberality, and lost his money with a noisy recklessness, vowing that he would have his revenge before the night was out. Montagu watched him curiously, wondering what it all meant.

So the night wore on, Sir Philip showing unmistakable signs of intoxication, under which influence his uproariousness degenerated by and by into a maudlin stupidity. He went on losing money with a sleepy placidity that threw Jack Stowell off his guard and tempted that adventurer into a free indulgence in certain manoeuvres which, under other circumstances, he would have considered dangerous to the last degree.

What was his astonishment when the country squire suddenly sprang to his feet and flung half a tumbler of punch in his face!

'Gentlemen,' cried Stowell, wiping the liquor from his disconcerted countenance, 'the man is drunk, as you must perceive. I have been grossly insulted, but am too much a gentleman to take advantage of the situation. You had better get your friend away, Captain Montagu, while his legs can carry him, if they are still capable of that exertion. We have had enough play for tonight.'

'Cheat! swindler!' cried Sir Philip. 'I call my friend to witness that you have been playing with marked cards for the last hour. I saw you change the pack.'

'It's a lie!' roared Jack.

'No, it isn't,' said Montagu, 'I've had my eye on you.'

'By God! Gentlemen, I'll have satisfaction for this,' cried Jack, drawing his sword a very little way out of its scabbard.

'You shall,' answered Sir Philip, 'and this instant. I shall be glad to see whether you are as good at defending your own cur's life as you are at beating your wife.'

'By heaven, I know you now!' cried Jack. 'You are the fellow that sits in the stage box night after night and hangs on my wife's looks.'

Sir Philip went to the door, locked it, and put the key in his pocket, then came back with his rapier drawn.

Montagu and the other men tried to prevent a fight, but Sir Philip was inexorably bent on settling all scores on the spot, and Stowell was savage in his cups and ready for anything. Preliminaries were hurried through, a table knocked over and a lot of glasses broken; but noise was a natural concomitant of pleasure in this tavern, and the riot awakened no curiosity in the sleepy drawer waiting below.

A space was cleared, and the two men stood opposite each other, ghastly with passion.

Sir Philip's assumed intoxication thrown off with his fur-bordered coat; John Stowell considerably the worse for liquor.

The actor was a skilled swordsman, but his first thrusts were too blindly savage to be effective. Sir Philip parried them easily, and stood looking at his antagonist with a scornful smile that goaded Stowell to madness.

'I'll wager my wife and you have got up this play between you,' he said. 'I ought to have known there was mischief afoot. She's too meek and pretty-spoken not to be a—

The word he meant to say never passed his lips, for a sudden thrust in tierce from Philip Hazlemere's sword pierced his left lung and silenced him for ever.

'When I saw the mark of your fist on your wife's forehead this morning, I swore to make her a widow tonight,' said Sir Philip, as the actor fell face downward on the sanded floor.

The tavern servants were knocking at the door presently. Jack Stowell's fall had startled even their equanimity. Tables and glasses might be smashed without remark – they only served to swell the reckoning – but the fall of a human body invited attention. Captain Montagu opened the window and hustled his friend out upon the slippery leads below it, and, after some peril to life and limb in the hurried descent, Sir Philip Hazlemere found himself in Long Acre, where the watchman was calling, 'Past four o'clock, and a rainy morning.'

Chapter 3 – Her Farewell

Before next evening the town knew that Jack Stowell the actor had been killed in a tavern brawl. Captain Montagu had bribed Mr Stowell's friends to keep a judicious silence. The man had been killed in fair fight, and no good could come of letting the police know the details of his end. So when the Bow Street magistrate came to hold his interrogatory, he could only extort a confused account of the fatal event. There had been a row at faro, and Stowell and another man, whose name nobody present knew, had drawn their swords and fought. Stowell had fallen, and the stranger had escaped by a window before the tavern people came to the rescue. The tavern people had seen the stranger enter the house, a man with flaxen hair and a dark green riding coat trimmed with grey fur, but they had not seen him leave. The magistrate drew the general conclusion that everybody had been drunk, and the examination concluded in a futile manner, which in these days would have offered a fine opening for indignation leaders in the daily papers, and letters signed, 'Fiat Justitia' or 'Peckham Rye', but which at that easy-going period provoked nobody's notice, or served at most to provide Walpole with a paragraph for one of his immortal epistles.

Sir Philip called at Mrs Stowell's and was told that she was ill and keeping to her room. There was a change of pieces announced at Covent Garden, and the favourite was not to appear 'until tomorrow se'nnight, in consequence of a domestic affliction'.

Sir Philip sent his customary offerings of hothouse fruits and flowers to Mrs Stowell's address, but a restraining delicacy made him keep aloof while the actor's corpse lay at his lodgings and the young widow was still oppressed with the horror of her husband's death. She might suspect his hand, perhaps, in that untimely end. Would she pity and pardon him, and understand that it was to redress her wrongs his sword had been drawn? Upon this point Sir Philip was hopeful. The future was full of fair promises. There was only a dreary interval of doubt and severance to be endured in the present.

The thought that Barbara was confined to her room by illness did not alarm him. It was natural that her husband's death should have agitated and overwhelmed her. The sense of her release from his tyranny would soon give her hope and comfort. In the meanwhile, Sir Philip counted the hours that must pass before her reappearance.

The appointed night came, and the play announced for representation was Webster's *Duchess of Malfi*, concluding with the fourth Act: 'the Duchess by Mrs Stowell'. They were fond of tragedies in those days, the gloomier the better. Covent Garden was a spacious charnel house for the exhibition of suicide and murder.

Sir Philip was in his box before the fiddlers began to play. The house was more than half empty, despite the favourite's reappearance after her temporary retirement, despite the factitious interest attached to her as the widow of a man who had met his death under somewhat mysterious circumstances a week ago. There was dire weather out of doors – a dense brown fog, some of which had crept in at the doors of Covent Garden Theatre, and hung like a pall over pit and boxes.

The fiddlers began the overture to Gluck's *Orpheus and Eurydice*. Philip Hazlemere's heart beat loud and fast. He longed for the rising of the curtain with an over-mastering impatience. It was more than a week since he had seen Barbara Stowell, and what a potent change in both their destinies had befallen since their last meeting! He could look at her now with triumphant delight. No fatal barrier rose between them. He had no doubt of her love, or of her glad consent to his prayer. In a little while – just a decent interval for the satisfaction of the world – she would be his wife. The town would see her no more under these garish lights of the theatre. She would shine as a star still, but only in the calm heaven of home.

The brightness of the picture dispelled those gloomy fancies, which the half-empty theatre and its dark mantle of fog had engendered. The curtain rose and at last he saw her. The lovely eyes were more brilliant than ever, and blinded him to the hollowness of the wan cheek. There was a thrilling tragedy in her every look, which seemed the very breath and fire of genius. The creature standing there, pouring out her story of suffering, was wronged, oppressed; the innocent, helpless victim of hard and bloody men. The strange story, the strange character, seemed natural as she interpreted it. Sir Philip listened with all his soul in his ears, as if he had never seen the gloomy play before, yet every line was familiar to him. The Duchess was one of Barbara's greatest creations.

He hung with rapt attention on every word, and devoured her pale loveliness with his eyes, yet was eager for the play to be over. He meant to lie in wait for her at the stage door, accompany her home to her lodgings and stay with her just long enough to speak of their happy future, and to win her promise to be his wife so soon as her weeds could be laid aside. He would respect even idle prejudice for her sake, and wait for her while she went through the ceremony of mourning the husband who had ill-used her.

The play dragged its slow length along to the awful fourth act, with its accumulated horrors – the wild masque of madmen, the tomb-maker, the bellman, the dirge, the execu-tioners with coffin and cords. Barbara looked pale and shadowy as a spirit, a creature already escaped from earthly bondage, for whom death could have no terrors. Thinly as the house was occupied, the curtain fell amidst a storm of applause. Sir Philip stood looking at the dark-green blank-ness, as if that dying look of hers had rooted him to the spot, while the audience hurried out of the theatre, uneasy as to the possibility of hackney coaches or protecting link boys to guide them through the gloom.

He turned suddenly at the sound of a sigh close behind him. – a faint and mournful sigh, which startled and chilled him.

Barbara was standing there, in the dress she had worn in that last scene – the shroud-like drapery that had so painfully reminded him of death. She stretched out her hands to him with a sad, appealing gesture. He leaned forward eagerly and tried to clasp them in his own, but she withdrew herself from him with a shiver, and stood, shadowlike, in the shadow of the doorway.

'Dearest!' he exclaimed, between surprise and delight, 'I was coming round to the stage door. I am most impatient to talk to you, to be assured of your love, now that you are free to make me the most blessed of men. My love, I have a world of sweet words to say to you. I may come, may I not? I may ride home with you in your coach?'

The lights went out suddenly while he was talking to her, breathless in his eagerness. She gave one more faint sigh, half pathetic, half tender, and left him. She had not blessed him with a word, but he took this gentle silence to mean consent.

He groped his way out of the dark theatre and went round to the stage door. He did not present himself at that entrance, but waited discreetly on the opposite side of the narrow street, till Barbara's coach should be called. He had watched for her thus, in a futile, aimless manner, on many a previous night, and was familiar with her habits.

There were a couple of hackney coaches waiting in the street under the curtain of fog. Presently a link boy came hurriedly along with his flaring torch, followed by a breathless gentleman in a brown coat and wig of the same colour. The link boy crossed the road, and the gentleman after him, and both vanished within the theatre. Sir Philip wondered idly what the breathless gentleman's business could be.

He waited a long time, as it appeared to his impatience, and still there was no call for Mrs Stowell's hackney coach. A group of actors came out and walked away on the opposite pavement, talking intently. The gentleman in brown came out again, and trotted off into the fog, still under guidance of the link boy. The stage doorkeeper appeared on the threshold, looked up and down the street, and seemed about to extinguish his dim oil lamp and close his door for the night. Sir Philip Hazlemere ran across the street just in time to stop him.

'Why are you shutting up?' he asked. 'Mrs Stowell has not left the theatre, has she?' It seemed just possible that he had missed her in the fog.

'No, poor thing, she won't go out till tomorrow, and then she'll be carried out feet foremost.'

'Great God! what do you mean?'

'It's a sad ending for such a pretty creature,' said the doorkeeper with a sigh, 'and it was that brute's ill usage was at the bottom of it. She's been sickening of a consumption for the last three months – we all of us knew it – and when she came in at this door tonight I said she looked fitter for her coffin than for the stage. And the curtain was no sooner down than she dropped all of a heap, with one narrow streak of dark blood oozing from her lips and trickling down her white gown. She was gone before they could carry her to her dressing room.

They sent for Dr Budd, of Henrietta Street, but it was too late; she didn't wait for the doctors to help her out of this world.'

Yes, at the moment when he had looked into that shadow face and seen those sad eyes looking into his with ineffable love and pity, Barbara's troubled soul had winged its flight skyward.

THE CORDWAINER'S DAINTIEST LASTS

Mae Empson

Thomas traced the stitching on the shoes that he had almost completed, counting a consistent forty-two stitches to the inch. He'd never made better. He resisted the temptation to light a candle and see how the shoes actually looked, stretched across Anna's lasts. Had he finally made shoes worthy of her? No, he couldn't know that. He hadn't made master yet. Without the masters' secrets, how could he judge if the shoes were worthy, even if he brought them into the light?

He undressed the lasts and felt along his workbench for the half-moon knife that he used for cutting leather. He sliced the shoes into strips thin enough to braid into another cat-o'-nine-tails, only nicking a finger once. He'd sliced leather to shreds in complete darkness so many times now that he only accidentally cut himself every third time or so. There'd be blood enough regardless. He'd carve the price of his failure and arrogance for even trying before he made master into his own back with a whip made from the imperfect shoes.

Thomas's back stung from numerous cuts by the time he let himself ease down on to his mattress, to try to catch a little sleep before opening the shop in the morning. Though it would have felt better sleeping on his stomach, he took an odd comfort from marrying the cuts on his back to the cuts on his mattress. He'd stashed every pound note that he could spare into the mattress, slicing the fabric and re-stitching the hole so that he would not be tempted to remove the note and spend it. The blood-flecked mattress had forty-three scars now, and he expected to be paid for two particularly fine pairs of boots tomorrow, for the younger son of an earl. Then he'd finally have enough money to pay the guild fee to be tested for master.

Thomas knew that the master cordwainers of London and Northampton each contributed one mystery to the hidden arts of their trade on the night of their initiation. One mystery and fifty pounds. Each new master recorded his discovery on the soles of a pair of lasts made in the shape of his own feet, which were stored in two locked chests in the guildhall of each city, the left lasts in Northampton and the right lasts in London. Once initiated, a new master gained access to all of his fellows' soles.

Thomas had spent years trying to find or replicate a mystery worthy of initiation. He had failed to make an awl so sharp that its puncture drew no blood, requisite to achieve the famed Northampton sixty-four stitches to the inch. He had failed to learn which of Lord Byron's feet caused his limp, and for what reason, though the great man himself had graced his shop once last year before leaving for the Mediterranean. He had failed to discover which bird's feathers had shafts so narrow that they could be threaded through the holes made by awls that could achieve the more standard thirty stitches to the inch. His tools were not carved from St Crispin's bones, much as he might have wished it. He had failed to lure elves to work his uncut leather, or to find a hairless goat whose endlessly regenerating skin required no preparation before tanning.

What he *had* found was Anna.

Since that discovery, almost two years ago, his shop had become one of the most prosperous in London. His flat-soled half boots, fashioned from kid leather and embellished with delicate embroidery and silk rosettes, could be glimpsed under the finest skirts at court and at Almack's Assembly Rooms.

Anna only visited him at night, and only while he worked the leather or shaped the lasts in complete darkness, training his fingers to see. In that darkness, he had whispered his need so many times, praying first to St Crispin, and then to anyone with the power to hear. And in that darkness, on a night almost two years ago now, when his fingers had bled white trying to make fine enough awls, he had finally heard her first whispers.

He was going about it all wrong, trying to make the finest shoes he could make, she whispered. He needed to make the finest *customers* he could make. Such clever whispers, like the rustle of silk on silk. He spent that night inventing customers. By the morning, he'd filled the shelves at the back of his shop with bespoke lasts, as if he had fifty customers wealthy enough to pay for custom shoes.

At the far end of the right wall, he displayed the daintiest lasts he had ever carved. Anna's lasts. These lasts he had made for his whispering muse. They were perceptibly slighter than any other pair, and arched exquisitely, based on the imagined shape of her perfect feet. He'd promised, in exchange for her advice and ongoing blessing of his shop, to make her the most perfect shoes when he at last made master and had all the mysteries within his grasp.

Anna's lasts seemed to cast a remarkable spell over his ever-increasing pool of customers. Women stole glances at them, and flushed with envy and sudden shame at the comparative largeness of their own feet, and then with pride that they shopped where that perfect woman shopped. Men wandered close to the daintiest lasts and stared, imagining flesh and ankle. Bolder men tried to caress the lasts, though Thomas threatened to never make them another pair of boots.

Thomas drifted off to sleep, sorry he had not heard Anna's whisper tonight, but sure that she would speak to him again when he made master.

Thomas' first scheduled appointment was with the earl for whom he'd made the fine boots, but there was another man waiting when he opened the shop.

Ignacio de la Rúa. The merchant who provided him with the finest cordovan leathers. 'I've come to settle our debt before my next sailing. Surely you have sold enough shoes by now, from the leathers I gave you.'

He had sold many shoes, but he had destroyed more than he could afford. In calculating which pound notes he could save, he had assumed that his debt to Ignacio would not be called until the end of the season, long after he'd made master and realized the additional profits from incorporating the masters' secrets.

'Not yet. But, I am close to making master. I will pay you what I owe, and another twenty per cent above it, if you will just let me wait and pay you at the end of the season.'

'You will settle at least half your debt before I leave your shop, or I will never sell you another scrap of leather, and I will tell my guild, and no one else will sell you a scrap either.'

Thomas could see no option but to raid his mattress, much as it pained him to realize that it would be months before he'd collect the guild fee at this rate. 'I . . . I will have to fetch the money from the bank.' He certainly couldn't let Ignacio know that he'd need time to carve it back out of the mattress. 'I will pay you half the debt before tea time. I must attend to some morning appointments, and then I'll run to the bank and meet you at your shop.'

'Agreed.'

Perhaps he could convince the Honorable Mr Compton to buy a third pair of boots, to help offset the losses. Thomas had made a very fine pair for another customer, who wasn't due for his appointment until the end of the week, and he knew their feet were so close in size that they could have been twins.

The earl's son arrived shortly after Ignacio departed, and Thomas explained to him that he wanted to show him an additional pair. Mr Compton seemed willing to at least consider it.

When Thomas returned from fetching the boots from the workroom, he found Mr Compton bent in front of Anna's lasts. As Thomas approached, he could see that Mr Compton's face resembled nothing so much as a vicar in prayer, eyes tilted up and lips moving in wordless supplication.

'Step back from those lasts, sir,' Thomas demanded. 'What will the fine ladies think?'

'My apologies, craftsman,' Mr Compton replied, but he did not move and his gloved hand inched closer to the lasts.

'Sir, I must insist.'

Mr Compton finally stood and turned to Thomas. 'You must tell me, who is the owner of these lovely lasts.'

'I cannot tell you. I must respect her privacy.' Damn, but the earl's son was persistent. He could not let him discover that there was no actual customer. 'Here are the boots I mentioned. Would you like to try them on?'

'Can you tell me when her next appointment is? Surely there is no harm in that. I would never break your confidence. I could pretend I recalled the time of my own appointment incorrectly. A happy accident.'

'Sir, I must respect her wishes in this.'

'And your loyalty does you credit, but I would make it worth your while, I assure you. I am the son of an earl.'

'Again, I must say no. Look at the polish on these Hessians. You would cut quite a figure in them.'

'Can you send a message to her from me?'

'Sir, it would be a presumption on my part to assume that she would welcome it. I must decline. May I draw your attention to the tassels?'

'Can you send a message to her asking permission to send a message from another customer? You could convey to her my station.'

'She could not correspond with a man to whom she has not been properly introduced. You must know that. You could have no expectation of a return letter.' Thomas felt his temper stirring. Anna was *his*. Mr Compton had no right to even think about her lasts. 'Look at the semi-pointed toe of these boots. Perfect for stirrups.'

Mr Compton's eyes narrowed. 'I cannot possibly want these new boots, or even the ones that you have already made, while my heart is pining for a woman who will never have a chance to see me in them.'

Not buy the boots he had already ordered? Thomas swallowed and paled, imagining how many more stitches he would have to open on the mattress if he could not conclude this sale. 'But I . . . I can't.'

'There is plenty that you can and will do. You will tell her simply that I wish to meet her, and tell her who I am. If she is the least inclined or curious, she will know how to finesse an introduction.'

Thomas nodded, attempting to school his features into the shape of reluctance when primarily he felt relief. 'That much, I suppose, I can do. You must not be angry with me if she chooses not to pursue you. I have no power in this.'

'Of course. The hope of contact is all that I ask.' Apparently satisfied, Mr Compton paid him for all three pairs of boots without even trying on the new pair.

Thomas calculated the dent the three pairs of boots would put in his debt to Ignacio. It was still not enough to cover the half of the debt due today. Not even close.

He sat on his mattress and picked open the stitching on several seams. He couldn't even imagine how many weeks it would take to recover the losses and refill the slashes.

At least Mr Compton had bought the boots. What kind of man had so much money that he could afford three pairs of new boots? He recalled that the ludicrously wealthy Mr Compton was rumoured to have raised a fortune at the card tables, on top of his money from his family. Ludicrously wealthy. And obsessed with Anna's lasts.

Think. Could Anna's lasts, and Mr Compton's apparent obsession with them, be his salvation? Could he perhaps hire an actress to play the part of a mysterious dainty footed woman, and see how many necklaces and other niceties she could wheedle out of Mr Compton before he lost interest, or caught on that she wasn't as gently born as he'd hoped? Who could she claim to be? A dispossessed French noblewoman having fled the recent unpleasantness as a child? He'd make back the debt to Ignacio so much faster.

Really, it would make Mr Compton happy. It was a kindness.

Now he just needed to find an actress with exceedingly small feet.

No, it would be harder than that. If Thomas knew anything, he knew feet. Feet gave so much away, and Mr Compton would surely want to touch them. He needed to find a woman who had taken exceptionally good care of her feet. A woman who had never developed callouses from walking barefoot, or working on her feet all day in common shoes. He needed a woman who'd been idle, or one who had worked in a position other than on her feet from childhood, and who had reason to be given the resources to take care of her skin.

He needed a very expensive courtesan.

The Worshipful Company of Fleshpeddlers, like the Worshipful Company of Parish Clerks and the Company of Watermen and Lightermen, had never applied for a grant of livery, and by ancient status and custom never planned to do so. They would never be listed on the order of precedence of livery companies on which the Worshipful Company of Cordwainers were a respectable twenty-seventh. But they were no less organized.

He would start with the master madam and see who she recommended. Their meticulous records would also assure that he did not select a woman who had ever been visited by the Honorable Mr Compton before – a critical precaution.

He needed a way to tell if her feet matched the shape of Anna's lasts. Easy enough. He'd make a pair of shoes from the lasts. Anna would understand that these weren't 'her' shoes. He wasn't a master yet. He'd be able to make 'her' shoes all the faster if this venture succeeded.

Thomas fetched some of his finest scarlet-dyed kid leather, stretched it across the daintiest lasts and began to stitch. Any woman with otherwise elegant feet who could fit into those shoes would definitely serve his purpose. Mr Compton would see the shoes, clearly made by Thomas, as further proof that the woman was a real customer.

When he had made the shoes, he closed his shop early and set out on his errands. He settled the debt with Ignacio, and then took the shoes and his request to three journeyman madams recommended by the master madam, and watched nineteen attractive but insufficiently small-footed whores attempt to shove their feet into the exquisite red half boots. He feared the shoes would never be quite the same.

He could find no one.

Perhaps it had been a foolish idea. He decided to head home. There was no hope for it. He'd have to make back the money one pair of shoes at a time.

Thomas opened the door to his shop.

Crispin's blood! The shop had been ransacked. The lasts had all been pulled down from the shelves and strewn about the floor. It would take hours to sort them all out again. Had he been robbed? He took quick stock of his finished shoes and boots and did not think any were missing. He thought of Anna's lasts. No! He sorted through the mingled lasts, found the pairs and again took stock. Gone. The only things that appeared to be missing were Anna's lasts.

His heart shuddered in his chest. What would happen to him, and to the shop, without those beautiful lasts to entice his customers? What would Anna say? Would she ever speak to him again? Had the earl's son returned, obsessed with the wooden lasts themselves, and determined to have them close to hand while he waited for contact from their owner?

Shaken, Thomas left the store closed. He considered contacting the guard, but the word of a craftsman against the son of an earl would be nearly useless. Perhaps if he'd already made master . . .

The guild! Could the person who'd ransacked the shop have thought to check his mattress? Perhaps it was someone who knew he planned to test for master soon and suspected that he had stockpiled money? Were all his remaining savings gone as well?

Thomas lit a taper and hurried up the stairs, increasingly afraid that his mattress would be gutted like a fish. He reached his bedchamber, and the light of the taper showed nothing out of the ordinary. No assailants waited in the shadows. The upper mattress, criss-crossed with stitched seams, remained intact, except for the places he had opened up himself that morning. The lower mattress, crammed with wool flocking, likewise remained balanced and undisturbed on the tight lattice of ropes that suspended it from the bedframe.

Thank the Creator. He couldn't quite catch his breath or calm his pounding heart. The loss of Anna's lasts remained a heavy blow. He could try to re-make them, of course, but truly, he thought there was some magic in the originals. He felt sure that the rapid growth of his customers after displaying Anna's lasts defied the limits of word of mouth, and the impact of an assumption that he had a larger and more refined base of customers than he initially did. He imagined how angry she would be that he could not keep better care of her lasts.

He decided to lie down for a bit to give this better thought. He removed his boots, his jacket, his vest and his cravat, and draped them over his dresser. The rest of his clothing could wait. He only needed to clear his head and catch his breath.

Thomas extinguished the taper and set it on the bedside dresser. He lay back on the stitch-scarred mattress and tried to distract his racing thoughts by tracing the seams. He closed his eyes, still gasping for air. He just couldn't believe that Anna's lasts were gone. Had he somehow missed them in the chaos below? Would he find them again in the morning, with better light? How could he possibly make back the lost money if his sales faltered because the lasts were missing?

Maybe he could still try to find a woman with small enough feet to beguile the earl's son. Maybe his existing base of customers was sufficiently large and well-born that his shop would prosper without Anna's lasts. All the other bespoke lasts on display now represented real paying customers.

The tension slowly drained out of his chest and shoulders. He was a clever man. He could sort this out.

Weight and pressure on the mattress jerked him from his slumber. Someone had slid into the bed beside him.

'Thomas.' A woman's voice? Like silk on silk.

'Anna?'

She nestled up against his back, and he could feel each contour of her body through the rough cloth of his shirt and buckskin breeches. She was so much more than a rustling voice. Could it truly be her?

'I'd been waiting for you to finish a pair of shoes on my lasts, so I could come to you as more than a voice.'

'Anna? Is that really you?'

'You gave my shoes to other women, Thomas. My shoes. I've waited two years for you to finish those shoes to give me sufficient life to come to you. You promised.'

The flesh pressed against his back was perfectly shaped and warm but had a certain hardness to it. He tentatively reached behind him and encountered the skin of her hip. Smooth. Warm. Wooden. He caressed the perfect curve of her hip in disbelief. Her whole body appeared to be made from the same supple wood as her lasts.

'Stop.' She pulled away from him. 'That is not what I want. I heard it all. I felt you give my shoes to whores. Huge-footed, sweating whores. Whore after whore.'

'The red shoes? Those weren't your shoes. I'm going to make you perfect shoes once I make master. I just have to re-make the money for the guild fee.'

'You made the shoes on *my* lasts, Thomas. They were my shoes.'

She pounded her fists against his back. Each blow landed hard as a hammer, igniting his whip welts.

He scrambled out of the bed, dragging the sheet with him and fumbled for the taper.

'I'm leaving, Thomas. You will never hear from me again.'

He heard a footstep on the other side of the bed.

He lit the taper. Nothing. No one.

He raced around to the other side. Anna's lasts were neatly positioned, side by side, on the floor beside the bed. He leaned down to pick them up, and the left last kicked him in the face. He reeled back, lost his balance and fell to the floor. Anna's lasts – the wooden shape of her bare feet and the only part of her apparently visible – turned to face him one last time, then walked out of his bedroom.

'Anna! Wait.'

He struggled to his feet and heard her walking down the stairs. By the time he'd reached the top of the stairs, there was no sign of her.

Though he had erased all evidence of the disruption to his shop, his customers looked around uncertainly the next day, as if they could still see the chaos from Anna's temper tantrum.

Some backed quickly out of his shop and others cancelled their appointments.

He needed his remaining savings, one opened seam at a time, to keep paying his bills in the wake of this bad fortune. He gave up all hope of applying to become a master. What did it matter now? Anna was gone. His Anna, who had proved to be so much more than a whisper.

He sat in the dark each night, working on new shoes, which in his mind displayed such exquisite craftsmanship that they would return his customers, but when he relit the taper, they looked like the work of a blind man. Had he ever been able to work in the dark like this? He had.

He knew he had. She was his muse. He needed her.

He gave up working in the dark and returned to simply whispering his need into the darkness, hoping that Anna would answer.

He tried answering for her, but his voice never sounded like rustling silk, try as he might to give himself good advice.

He remembered that he'd bled from testing the sizes of his awls the night he first heard her whisper, and he tried bleeding on to new leather, new thread and new lasts in the darkened workroom, but still he heard nothing but silence.

In the light, he made new lasts specifically for Anna, remembering how he'd imagined her perfect feet. He did not display them in his store. He kept them in his room, and made the most beautiful shoes he could imagine for them. These shoes alone approached the quality of his prior work, and he never showed them to another customer.

When he had only five stitches left to re-open in the mattress, he tore out all the remaining money. He found an earnest young journeyman with the resources to buy the shop, his tools and his remaining supplies. He kept only Anna's lasts and the three pairs of shoes he had made for her.

He wondered from town to town, living off the proceeds from the sale of his shop and occasional cobbler-work on people's old shoes, much as it shamed him. He begged for bread when he had to.

Thomas always stopped at each cordwainer's shop, be they apprentice, journeyman, or master, in order to examine their lasts and see if they had a pair dainty and perfect enough to suggest that the shop's owner might have finally replicated the mystery of summoning Anna.

If he could just find such a shop, he'd be content to sit outside the workroom window each night and listen for the rustling silk of her voice, and tell Anna, finally, that he'd made her shoes.

WAITING FOR HARRY

Caroline Stevermer

Timothy Ferrars knew not which he detested more, his aunt or his aunt's distinctive sniff. Ordinarily, he would have said his aunt, by a neck. Yet after an evening spent in her company, he was inclined to think he hated the sniff more. After all, it was possible, albeit barely, to imagine his aunt without her sniff. The sniff without the aunt – unthinkable. Hence, the sniff was worse.

'You have been playing patience ever since Edmond and Augusta left, Timmy. Won't you trouble yourself to play just one hand of piquet with Eleanor? It may take her mind off Harry.'

Timothy responded soothingly to the note of command in his aunt's piercing voice. His tone betrayed nothing of his annoyance. 'Dear Aunt Lucy, it would require more than my poor efforts to take Eleanor's mind off Harry. And she's lucky in love, so she mustn't play cards with anyone. It would be ruinous.'

Aunt Lucy sniffed.

That sniff, that voice, the antiquated family stories she told over and over, scarcely deviating by a single word from one telling to the next – Timothy winced and rubbed his forehead. He'd had a headache at dinner, a dreadful one, but it had gone as suddenly as it came. Remnants of the headache stirred slightly, however, whenever that dreadful sniff sounded.

On the other hand, Timothy admitted to himself, the sniff had never done him any harm, and his aunt had. It was his aunt's fault, really, that he was in these dire financial straits. If Aunt Lucy had never presented Uncle Henry with a son, the entire Ferrars estate would have gone to Timothy years ago. Instead, just as Timothy had grown old enough to understand he might someday inherit, she had put an end to that possibility. She had produced Harry. Ugly, cheerful, *rich* Harry.

Lucy Ferrars, foiled in her efforts to order her only nephew about, turned to easier prey. 'Come away from the window, child. Even if the fog lifts, you can't possibly see anything at this hour of the night.'

'I think it is growing worse,' said Eleanor. Obediently, she crossed the drawing room to return to her place at Lucy Ferrars' side. 'I can scarcely see the lights across the square now.'

The ormolu clock on the mantel struck midnight.

Timothy looked up from his cards.

Aunt Lucy sniffed. 'Sensible people have gone to bed. That may explain why some of the lights across the square are gone.' She regarded Timothy with lifted brows. 'Of course, some people are accustomed to very late hours.'

Eleanor stared into the fire. There was a slight pucker between her brows, and her wide-set brown eyes were worried. She toyed with a fold of her white gown, pleating and twisting the silk in her lap, without seeming to realize she did so.

Timothy smiled at her reassuringly. 'Don't worry. Harry's sure to be here soon. Probably just looked in at his club.'

That was a hum, of course. Timothy had a very shrewd idea what was keeping Harry. He'd arranged the matter himself.

Harry had asked Timothy to join his mother and his betrothed, who was staying with them, and assorted relatives for dinner promptly at eight o'clock. Unfashionably early hour, eight, but Harry could never see the error of his countrified ways.

Harry had not come home for dinner. The relatives arrived and were duly introduced to Eleanor, and the party made what they could of the evening without their host. Aunt Lucy had sniffed and put off ordering the tea tray in hopes of Harry's return. At last, the relatives made their farewells and departed. Timothy had stayed on, with an eye towards establishing an alibi.

After the long, awkward silence, in which the loudest sound in the room was the ticking of the ormolu clock, Aunt Lucy began to tell Eleanor tales of Harry's exploits as a small child. Timothy remembered hearing several of the stories at the dinner table that very evening, but Eleanor did not seem to notice the repetition. Perhaps she wasn't listening.

It was all Harry's fault, really. Had Harry only been a sickly child, there might still have been hope. But Harry had been horribly healthy, able to beat his older, more delicate cousin at almost any sport. From Eton to the army, Harry had excelled at everything. And from Eton to the army, Timothy had watched his cousin's sporting prowess with interest. After all, younger necks than Harry's had been broken in the hunting field.

Timothy's father died, leaving Timothy a paltry sum, little more than enough to settle his accounts in town. Timothy, of course, had not wasted the ready money on any such foolishness as paying his debts. Instead, he enjoyed an interesting run of luck at the gaming tables, ordered a new pair of Hessians and spent the rest on claret.

Uncle Henry died and Harry came into the Ferrars inheritance. But did Harry settle down in London to spend his fortune in decent comfort, as befitted a gentleman? No. Nothing would do but he must buy himself a pair of colours and hare off to fight the Frenchies.

Those had been happy days. When Harry joined the army, Timothy had felt sure he would inherit after all. The army offered many dangers, not merely those of battle, but of disease and privation of every sort. During the Peninsular Campaign, Timothy learned to search the casualty lists. Harry's name never appeared. The peace depressed Timothy, but like an answer to his prayers, Napoleon returned. Waterloo sent Timothy's spirits soaring. All too soon the news came, in a cheerful letter home, that during the course of that hard-fought day, the Frenchies had shot two perfectly good horses out from under him, but Harry went unscathed.

Harry sold out at last. That autumn, he came home a hero and invited Timothy to join him at his hunting box in Leicestershire. Although never keen to take part in any sport, Timothy had accepted, in the hope of touching his wealthy cousin for a loan. It was there, in the wilds of Leicestershire, that Harry had said, 'Wish me happy, Timmy. I'm going to be married.'

It was too much to bear. To be so close, no more than a squinting Frenchman's rifle sight from the Ferrars fortune, and then to have it all swept away by those little words: 'Wish me happy . . .'

Timothy had shaken Harry's hand and wished him happy. He had also wished him dead.

Aunt Lucy's penetrating voice wore its way into Timothy's thoughts. She had moved on to Harry's exploits at Eton. Eleanor was nodding attentively, but she still looked worried. If Aunt Lucy knew but half of Harry's schoolboy exploits, Timothy reflected, she would not look so well-pleased.

Timothy stifled a sigh as he examined the cards spread before him. He had reached the awkward stage of the game. He must either concede defeat and start over, or find a satisfactory way to cheat. Nothing too extreme. Just the nudge the deck needed to surmount the cards chance had dealt him. After much deliberation, he slid a bothersome knave out of the way behind a stranded ten.

Earlier in the evening, Aunt Lucy's elaborate dinner, of which his strained nerves made him eat far too much, had given him a headache that made it hard for him to see his plate. A quiet interlude with the port had restored him. He now felt able to wait out the night. Yet the delay made him squirm in his superbly cut evening clothes. London was a large city, rife with footpads. But were footpads so plentiful that an attack could go unremarked? Was London so large that it took hours to bring word to the victim's family? Timothy tugged discreetly at his oriental, exquisite but excruciating, and stifled another sigh. He gave up on the game, gathered the cards, and began to shuffle them with crisp efficiency.

Aunt Lucy cleared her throat and moved on to the circumstances in which she had been introduced to that paragon, Uncle Henry. Eleanor was no longer nodding attentively. She probably had a headache herself by now.

Had Harry done the thing properly, he would have chosen a beauty for his bride. After all, he could afford it, and the Ferrars looks could certainly use improvement. He and

Harry both had 'em: forehead too high, chin too heavy, ears too big, nose . . . well, Timothy had escaped the Ferrars nose, but Harry hadn't. A terrible burden for a baby, the Ferrars nose.

Instead of choosing a beauty, Harry had offered for Eleanor Sterling, who had a good name, a good temper and a face that would have been plain if not for £5,000 a year – £5,000 pounds a year rendered almost any face interesting. And it was just like Harry to find an heiress who doted upon him. Why, she had been Friday-faced all evening long, only because Harry hadn't come home when he'd promised her he would.

Even Aunt Lucy noticed the girl's anxiety. 'A poor hostess you must think me, Eleanor. I've kept you with me for hours. Go to bed, my dear. Harry will be home by the time you wake in the morning.'

'Oh, I can't,' Eleanor protested. 'I couldn't possibly sleep. It's so silly, but I can't help feeling that something's happened to him.'

Aunt Lucy sniffed. 'Don't let such fancies trouble you. If anything *serious* had happened, Mistress Eliza Ferrars would have been here by now.'

Timothy suppressed a shudder. He knew this one by heart. Sad Mistress Eliza Ferrars in her severe grey gown. To distract himself from the tale, Timothy laid out the cards for another game of patience.

Eleanor smiled politely and asked, 'Who is Miss Ferrars? Another cousin? I think I have not met her.'

'No, and I'm quite sure you won't meet her, not for many years,' Aunt Lucy replied. She dropped her voice to a conspiratorial murmur. 'You mustn't tell anyone, for we do not like to discuss the matter with outsiders, but Mistress Eliza Ferrars is our family ghost. She appears only to warn us of impending death.'

Startled out of her worry for a moment, Eleanor laughed aloud. 'Harry would say you are bamming me.'

Her soft laughter made Timothy look up from his cards with new interest. Eleanor's amusement gave her features animation that improved her looks enormously. Perhaps Harry was even luckier than he had supposed.

'Indeed, he would say no such thing. Harry knows that Mistress Eliza Ferrars is a valued part of our family history.'

'Then I am surprised he hasn't told me of her before,' said Eleanor, 'if only to give me the shivers.' Her dark eyes gleamed. 'Tell me more. Does she walk at midnight, clad all in white and weeping?'

Aunt Lucy sniffed disdainfully. 'No, she does *not*. Mistress Eliza Ferrars is a well-behaved ghost. She is pale, pale as death, and her hair is black as night. She wears a very severe grey gown and she looks sad. I can't forget how sad she looked.'

Eleanor's eyes widened. 'But surely – ma'am, you speak as though you had seen her yourself!'

Lucy Ferrars smiled a little at Eleanor's startled expression. 'I *have* seen her, though only once. She came into this very room the morning dear Henry died. I was sitting just where Timmy is now, trying to compose myself so that I could go to Henry's bedside, when from the corner of my eye, I saw someone cross the room towards me. I hadn't heard the door open, but I thought it must be a maid. I looked up and saw her. She seemed so sad, I nearly called out to her. She looked at me, directly at me.' She paused for a moment, gazing intently into the fire, as though she saw the past there, then cleared her throat and continued. 'In the next instant, she was gone. I was staring at empty air. And within a moment or two, Smith came in to tell me that my darling Henry was dead.'

Prompt work, Mistress Eliza, thought Timothy. He played his cards out languidly, trying to make the game last through the boring, genealogical part of the story.

'Has she always haunted this house?' Eleanor asked. Her eyes held no gleam of irreverent humour now. She was caught up in the old wives' tale, hanging almost breathlessly on Aunt Lucy's words.

'Only since Cromwell's day. Back then, when she was just sixteen years old, she was betrothed to a very promising young man, James Langworthy. But James's younger brother George was a wicked and devious fellow. He persuaded the authorities that James was loyal to the Crown, not the Commonwealth. George meant to inherit all James had, you see, and he did not like the idea of his older brother marrying Eliza and having children that would take the property away from him.'

'He betrayed his own brother?' Eleanor looked horrified.

Timothy smiled grimly to himself.

Aunt Lucy continued her tale with scarcely a pause. 'James tried to fly to France, but they caught him. He died of gaol fever before his case came to trial. Mistress Eliza's heart was broken. She went into a decline and died within the year.'

Eleanor frowned. 'And what became of brother George?'

'Oh, George did his treacherous work too well, and the Langworthy estates fell forfeit to the Commonwealth. George ended up in debtors' prison. On the whole, I think it was fortunate that our family never allied with theirs. Bad blood, don't you know.' Aunt Lucy sniffed.

Someone hammered at the front door.

It was not a polite sound, no small apologetic knock, mindful of the late hour. It was a series of thunderous blows, harbinger of disaster. With difficulty, Timothy schooled his expression and rose as the ladies did.

The instant he stood, his headache returned, severe enough to set off pinwheels at the perimeter of his vision. 'I'll go see what's wrong,' he said faintly, but Aunt Lucy had already brushed past him. Eleanor caught up her skirts and followed. Timothy hesitated, sat down again and pressed his fingertips hard against his temples.

A tangle of voices, reassuringly upset, floated from the entrance hall. Then Aunt Lucy's voice rose above the jumble, a shriek of horror. 'Harry!'

That piercing cry made Timothy's head throb even more, though his vision was clearing. He looked up as a young woman came through the door. She was very pale. Her black hair, parted in the centre and pulled back into ringlets, was dressed in a style that was a century or more out of fashion, and she wore a plain grey gown. She was handsome – she would have been beautiful, but for the Ferrars nose. She did not look sad. As Timothy stared at her, she returned his scrutiny with calm interest. He thought her dark eyes held a gleam that might have been amusement.

Timothy just had had time to think, The olds wives' tale is true, then, and, By, gad, I've done it! Then, with a shimmer like the pinwheels that had troubled his vision, she was gone.

He struggled to compose himself, to look concerned, anxious – anything but what he felt. For what he felt, after the first moment of disbelief, was triumph. The footpads he'd engaged had been as good as their word. His cousin was dead. The Ferrars fortune would be his. And there was nothing left for him to do but force the relief out of his expression and go to comfort his stricken aunt.

Timothy blinked at the empty doorway. In the next instant, it was full. Exclaiming loudly, Eleanor and Aunt Lucy entered first. They were followed by two servants, steadying a man between them. A large man, an ugly man, a struggling man. It was Harry, bloodstained but undeniably alive and remonstrating.

'Dash it, Mother, I don't need a doctor, I need a drink. Timmy, don't just sit there gaping. Get me some brandy. I've had the fright of my life. Eleanor, I'm all right, I promise you. I had a little bout of fisticuffs, that's all. Scrope-Davies heard me yell and came to help, bless him. They pinched my purse and latch key, but the two of us gave them something for their pains. I'm fine, Eleanor. It's only blood. Don't, love, you'll stain that frock. Oh, dash it. Well, Mama's bound to know some antique remedy to get it out. Timmy, have you gone deaf? Brandy!'

As Timothy rose to his feet, his headache returned, this time so savagely he cried out. His vision failed and his balance left him. He fell into darkness. And as the stroke felled him his hearing tricked him. He thought he heard his aunt's voice say, 'Bad blood, don't you know.'

Finally, unmistakably, the last thing Timothy Ferrars heard in life was his Aunt Lucy's distinctive sniff.

QUEEN VICTORIA'S BOOK OF SPELLS

Delia Sherman

I'm in Windsor Castle.

To be exact, I'm in the Round Tower, in the Reading Room of the Royal Archives. It's raining outside – not an astonishing occurrence given English springs. My feet are wet and will undoubtedly stay wet, because the Royal Archives are like a meat locker. The Royal Archivist has an electric fire under her desk and still looks cold.

On the table in front of me lies a stout folio volume, bound in red calf's leather, with 'Queen Victoria's Book of Spells' stamped on the cover in gold. Beside it lies a pair of acid-free white cotton gloves. As soon as I put them on, I will have begun what my sponsor, Sir Reginald Jolley, calls the Victoria Project.

It's a real plum. Reggie has told me so numerous times. 'There are wizards all over England,' he says, 'with bloodlines going back generations, dying to get their hands on Victoria's spell book. You should be grateful.'

And I might be. If I were a Victorianist. If the project were actually mine.

Slowly, I pull the clownish gloves over my hands and rest my cold fingers lightly on the cover. Through the thin cotton I feel a faint prickling, like a mild electrical charge. My excitement rises, as it does when I discover a new *oratio obscura*.

An *oratio obscura* (the phrase means 'hidden word') is a spell that obscures text. It's like a code, in that it can be used to hide sensitive information from prying eyes. There are three basic *orationes obscurae*, which, with their respective aperients ('revealers') are familiar to any bright schoolchild with access to a spell book. People with more important secrets to hide typically craft their own, personalized variations, giving out the aperients on a need-to-know basis, if at all. It's possible to create a new aperient for a custom *oratio obscura*, but not easy. They're hard to detect, hard to analyse, and hard to unravel.

I'm lucky. I have a talent for it.

I can't take credit for it, really – it's genetic. Both my parents are preternaturally good at finding things. Mom finds tumours in cancer patients. Dad finds oil deposits. I find encoded texts.

I open the book.

The text of Victoria's first diary entry hides nothing but the creamy linen paper it covers. It has been quoted often, but it's different seeing it in the fourteen-year-old princess's own hand:

7 June 1883
<u>Today</u> is my first lesson in <u>magic</u>. My tutor is Sir Thomas Basingstoke, of the <u>Royal College of Wizards</u>. He is a Professor of <u>Practical Magic</u>. Mamma says a <u>lesser</u> wizard would be sufficient to teach a <u>neophyte</u> her first spells, but <u>he</u> says it is an <u>honour</u> to teach the future <u>Queen of England</u>. He has given me this <u>book</u> for the <u>spells</u> I learn and the <u>theory</u> behind them, as well as any <u>exercises</u> he may give me to <u>strengthen</u> my <u>self-discipline</u>.

The lesson was <u>very odd</u>. He began by asking me to knock a <u>spillikin</u> from a table without touching it, which I did. And he asked me about my <u>dreams</u> and whether I was prone to <u>sleepwalking</u>. Mamma answered that I was not.

Next week we will begin to study magic in <u>earnest</u>, with a spell to <u>light a candle</u>.

I remember lighting my first candle. It was in seventh grade. The spell was in the book of basic spells I'd stolen from my mother's study. It worked the first time I tried it, although I almost set the house on fire. My parents sent me to the

Westaway Magic Academy in Amherst. I did well enough to earn a free ride to Harvard, where I majored in Thaumaturgy.

I discovered my sensitivity to text in junior year at Harvard. I was home for Thanksgiving break, hanging out in Dad's study, when I felt something odd in a letter on my father's desk. It was a business letter about oil rights, as I recall, from an associate of his, and it burned my fingers. On the off-chance this might mean something, I ran a decoding spell over the letter. It was from the business associate, all right, but it was a love letter. A torrid love letter that made it clear Dad had been living a double life for years.

That night, when Dad came home, I was waiting for him. Mom heard us arguing, came in to see what the fuss was about and, well, the cat was out of the bag. It wasn't pretty. Mom and Dad divorced. Dad moved to Amsterdam to be with his lover. I applied to the Master of Thaumaturgy programme at York University, which led to my current Junior Research Fellowship in the History of Magic at John Dee College, Cambridge University, under the direction of Sir Reginald Jolley, BT, MT, DThau.

Reggie is a jerk. The grants he gets for his fellows are generally more useful to him than they are to the fellows. My current project is a prime example.

Up until recently, Queen Victoria's spell book had caused everybody to assume that Victoria's magical education was limited to the candle-lighting and silk-sorting taught to all young women of noble blood. It is little more than a commonplace book of spells and potions copied down from other sources, of interest mostly to biographers and scholars of women's studies. Then Prince Philip, the only royal with a degree in scientific magic, ran his newly invented thaumatograph over it and discovered that the T-readings were off-the-charts high.

This fluttered the dovecotes of every department of thaumaturgical study in England. It is a tribute to Reggie's wheeling and dealing skills, as well as the purity of his pedigree (his father is the Earl of Avon), that the grant should come to John Dee. Not to mention the fact that he had a canary to check out the magical mines for him.

That would be me.

Which is why I'm stuck here in the Royal Archives, reading a teenager's exercise book. A royal teenager, granted, but I don't care about that.

Victoria had one two-hour magic lesson a week. With summers off for grand tours through England with her mother and her household, that works out to between thirty and forty entries a year, at a page or more a lesson. In order to get a feel for her personal *oratio obscura*, the way her mind works and the kind of spells she knew how to cast, I have to read them all. In order.

22 June 1833
(A Receipt for a Potion Against Carriage Sickness.)

Today's lesson was to be summoning a <u>breeze</u>, which is the first lesson in the <u>Mastery of Air</u>. However, as Mamma is planning another tour, I begged Sir T to teach me some small cantrip or spell against carriage sickness, from which I suffer <u>extremely</u>. He gave me the receipt I have writ down above. It is my <u>first potion</u>, and I am <u>eager</u> to try it.

Eager to make a mess, I suspect. I know I was, at that age, although my messes were more likely to explode than settle the stomach.

My hands are so cold they ache. I cast a very small warming spell. The Royal Archivist shakes her head warningly. I flash her my most charming smile. She does not seem to be charmed. Her eyes are slightly protuberant, very good for glaring.

Noon brings me to the end of 1833 and my endurance simultaneously. I find a pub, eat, and warm up. Then it's back to the Royal Icehouse for more schoolgirl exercises. I'm glad to see Victoria's potion seems to have relieved her motion sickness, although it didn't do a thing for the backaches brought on by hours in a jolting carriage. Improved carriage springs – and the smoother roads they ran on – were mechanical breakthroughs, not magical ones. And mechanics, like science, was a skill of the working classes. Magic, in those days, was the sole prerogative of the nobility.

Reggie frequently bemoans (humorously, of course) the passage of the Alchemical Act of 1914, which opened the study of English magic to foreigners and commoners. He seems to think that my American blood somehow makes me more foreign than if Mom were French or German. But what he really minds is my father, who may be as English as five o'clock tea, but is also descended from a long line of engineers and fabricators, as black-blooded (the idiom refers to coal) as Reggie is blue-blooded (the idiom refers to haemophilia).

The afternoon wears on. I'm cold and irritated and so impatient to reach the first *oratio obscura*, I almost miss the tell-tale tingle, like a cell phone vibrating deep in a briefcase. It's pretty faint, but then my hands are freezing. I huff on my fingers, rub them together like a safecracker, and check again. Yep. There it is.

My heart rate goes up. I close my eyes and search for the threads of the spell. It's a variant of the oldest of the basic *orationes obscurae* – simple, elegant and clearly not the work of a girl who has been studying magic for less than a year. Bit by bit, I feel my way into it, and the text relaxes under my hands like a Victorian lady released from her corset, revealing the second text lurking beneath it.

4 January 1834
(Text hidden under A Spell for Finding Lost Objects)

Today Sir T (who has a nose like a <u>parrot's beak</u> and smells most <u>pungently</u> of bay rum) taught me a <u>very special</u> spell. Its purpose is to keep anything I write <u>hidden</u> from all eyes save <u>my own</u>. I said I should <u>never</u> wish to write <u>anything</u> Mamma or dear Lehzen might not read. He said he did not doubt that, but that I might well <u>change my mind</u> as I grew <u>older</u>.

The spell is <u>extremely</u> advanced. I am a little anxious lest my casting be <u>clumsy</u>. Were Mamma to discover that I have tried to keep <u>secrets</u>, I shall be writing in my Book of Good Behaviour for <u>hours</u>.

Later: <u>TRIUMPH!</u> Both Sir T and Lehzen have read over my opening words without so much as a conscious <u>look</u>. Lehzen, of course, cannot penetrate the <u>flimsiest</u> illusion. But Sir T is a powerful Wizard – <u>much</u> more powerful than Mamma, who cannot levitate a <u>teacup</u> without slopping its contents into the saucer. In any case, as he did not react to my <u>uncivil</u> (though <u>accurate</u>) description of his nose, I am confident he <u>could not read it!</u>

I like my magic lessons <u>extremely</u>. I only wish I had one <u>every day</u>.

No sooner have I read the entry – the *true* entry – than the spell snaps back over it.

In the Reading Room of the Royal Archive, it's not the done thing to cheer or even cry 'Eureka!' The archivist would certainly object, and might even turf me out, permission from the Royal College of Wizards notwithstanding. I restrict myself to beaming goofily down at the page.

'Dr Ransome?'

I look up. The archivist is hovering at my elbow, looking stern.

'Yes?'

'The Reading Room closes at five thirty, Dr Ransome.'

'Oh, yes, of course. Listen, I've just found something interesting, I wonder if I might—'

'The book will still be here in the morning.'

Her round face is stern. I remind myself that it never pays to alienate the support staff. On my way out, I humbly request a table near an outlet for my computer, then retreat to the nearest pub for a celebratory pint.

The Windsor Knot is not my first choice for a watering hole. It's a Victorian theme park of a pub, all horse brasses, tartan carpet and men in Savile Row suits, but it's near the archive and they brew their own beer. I take my hoppy bitter to a table in a back corner and try to sort out my emotions.

I should be pleased. I *am* pleased. My first day of work and already I've cracked Victoria's code. From now on, it's just a matter of finding the coded entries and transcribing them. Easy. Mechanical. Boring. Victoria as a girl is rather charming, but I can't forget that she grew up to be the widow of Windsor, prim, pious, pig-headed, perennially unamused. After all the research I've done on her for this project, I'm forced to admit that she was a better ruler than her grandfather or either of her uncles, but that's hardly a ringing endorsement, given that George III was barking mad, George IV was a libertine, and William IV a royal wastrel. In addition, I profoundly disapprove of her support of the Crimean War, her expansionist policies, and her championship of the Alien Magic Act of 1862. You'd think she would have known better, given her ghastly childhood.

From the moment her father the Duke of Kent died, when Victoria was eight months old, to the moment she became Queen of England at eighteen, her mother and Sir John Conroy, her mother's treasurer and secretary, oversaw every aspect of her life. They developed something they called the Kensington System, after the palace King George IV had given them to live in, designed to keep the young princess safe from infection, accident, and making her own decisions.

Victoria was never to be alone. She spent her days with her governess, the Baroness Lehzen, and her nights in her mother's room. She could not go up or down the stairs without someone holding her hand. She had to record her transgressions in a Book of Good Behaviour and each day's events in a journal. Every word she wrote was read and approved by her mother.

Except, apparently, these.

Limited magical education, my sweet Aunt Sally. Clearly, there was more to our dear Queen than even the most revisionist historians have imagined. Reggie is going to be delighted. I just wish I didn't feel quite so much like a trained pig, hunting for truffles.

The next morning is clear and brisk. The Reading Room is as cold as a tomb. The Royal Archivist, looking like a tiny Michelin man in a puffy down vest, is up on a ladder with a clipboard. She descends when she sees me and shows me to a table by a narrow window. Icy drafts seep under the wooden frame, but there's a grounded double outlet in easy reach. I wrap my muffler around my neck, set up my computer and get to work.

At first, Victoria is sparing in her use of the *oratio obscura*. In early July, she encodes a quarrel with her mother; two weeks later, a small trick played on Conroy's daughter Victoria. Then comes something Reggie will love.

12 March 1834
(Text hidden under a receipt for sorting embroidery silks)

C <u>particularly</u> horrid today. I am <u>astonished</u> that Mamma allows herself to be ruled by such a <u>monster</u>. I have heard the Duke of Wellington say they are <u>lovers</u>, presuming, perhaps that I would not understand his meaning. Well, I <u>do</u> understand, and I think that he is <u>wrong</u>. <u>Primus</u>, I have often heard Mamma remark upon the <u>foulness</u> of C's breath, which does not sound lover-like; <u>secundus</u>, Mamma retires to bed with me, even when C sleeps at Kensington; <u>tertius</u>, C is <u>Irish</u> and <u>base born</u> and Mamma is a <u>princess</u> and <u>very</u> proud.

If it weren't for the fact that Sir John Conroy was, by all accounts, vain, controlling, and cruel, I might have some sympathy for him. I've had my own difficulties infiltrating the sacred company of English wizards. Admittedly, I'm also hampered by my politics, which have inspired Reggie to call me a Communist. He has also, at different times, called me a boor (for coming to work in jeans), and an uncultured, bourgeois Yank (pretty much constantly). If I weren't a kind of magical sniffer dog, he'd have found a way to get rid of me by now. As it is, I'm useful. And John Dee College does have the most prestigious Department of Thaumaturgy in the country.

As I turn the page, I wonder just what Victoria understood about lovers and how she came by her information. Frustratingly, she doesn't say.

★　★　★

Days pass. Outside, it's either raining or about to rain – or, occasionally, to sleet: in other words, a typical English spring. The archivist huddles over her electric fire; I take to wearing thermal underwear. I'm becoming a regular at the Windsor Knot.

Page by hidden page, I watch Victoria learn the basic principles of elemental magic. In early 1835, she begins using a new *oratio obscura*. It's simpler than the old one, but it takes me much longer to find my way into it. When I do, I find that she has invented it herself. She uses it to complain about her mother and fantasize about what she'd do to Sir John, if Sir Thomas would only consent to teach her some curses. She's surprisingly inventive, and more than once the archivist is forced to request that I refrain from laughing.

3 July 1835
(Text Hidden Under a Spell to Make Dolls Dance.)

Today, I asked Sir T if I might not learn a spell that would allow Dash to walk upon his <u>hind legs</u> and <u>speak sensibly</u>. Sir T looked grave. 'There is a cost to such spells, your Highness,' he said. 'A dog's legs and back are not designed by nature to bear him upright, nor his mind for human discourse. He would pay a price of <u>pain</u>, <u>confusion</u> and possible <u>madness</u>.'

When I heard this, I caught my <u>dearest</u> Dashie in my arms and promised, sobbing, that I would <u>never, never</u> cause him as much as a <u>moment's</u> pain. When I was calm again, Sir T taught me a spell to animate my <u>dolls</u>, which amused me extremely. Lehzen, however, finds their wooden capers so <u>distasteful</u> I am determined <u>never</u> to cast it when she is present.

Most wizards wouldn't think twice about turning a spaniel into a miniature courtier if they knew the spell. Power is heady stuff. I know. Once you've had a little, you want more. I've never met a wizard who didn't have control issues. Look at Reggie. After all, what is magic but the exercise of control over the essentially uncontrollable: nature, physics, logic, free will? A wizard who doesn't, on some level, want to abuse the power magic gives him (or her) isn't a very good wizard.

Victoria, apparently, was a very good wizard – with a conscience, which is a lot rarer. And nobody's wooden dancing doll.

10 July 1835
(Text Hidden Under a Passage on Spells of Influence and Coercion, from On Political Magic *by Viscount Mortimer)*

I have been wondering whether C might not have cast a <u>spell of coercion</u> on Mamma. There is something about the way she <u>never</u>, <u>ever</u> disagrees with him, even when he is <u>wrong</u>. As he himself could not <u>be</u> a wizard, he must have <u>hired</u> a wizard to cast it – a <u>Foreign</u> wizard, for I <u>will not</u> believe an <u>English</u> wizard would so <u>debase</u> himself. I cannot but <u>wonder</u> why he has not had one cast upon <u>me</u>.

I have heard that my uncle, the King, when he was Regent, used spells of coercion upon <u>respectable</u> ladies to make them fall in love with him. I find this <u>extremely</u> shocking. I would <u>never</u>, upon <u>any provocation whatso-ever</u>, use such a spell. It is <u>wrong</u> to tamper with the free will of <u>any human soul</u>.

I've been wondering myself when Victoria would work out that particular equation. She's bright, but not terribly imaginative. Also a terrible snob. I note, without surprise, that she is incapable of believing that a base-born Irishman would be able to enchant a royal duchess. Commoners don't learn magic, therefore commoners can't learn magic. QED.

A year of dealing with Reggie has persuaded me that, the law and all evidence to the contrary, deep down he believes the same thing. Which is probably why he felt free to cast a coercion spell on me.

It was not long after I'd turned down a flattering offer of an off-campus fling. Not because he's a man, mind you – I've never seen the point of limiting myself to one gender when it comes to lovers. I do, however, limit myself to people I actually fancy. Which is what I told Reggie, with perhaps more force than diplomacy. The episode was unpleasant, but I thought the subject closed.

Until I found myself in Reggie's office, unbuttoning my shirt and wondering how I'd failed to notice before how utterly hot he was. If he'd just sat still, I'd probably have been another notch on his bedpost before I knew what was happening. But because he couldn't wait to get his hands on me, because he stood up, leering and eager, the spell broke.

I left his office even more abruptly than I'd entered, went to the loo and was sick. Then I washed my face in cold water and got back to work.

Of course, I thought about turning him in, but what would that have got me? Humiliated, unemployed, with a cloud over my head that would make employment at a first-class institution all but impossible.

It has crossed my mind that this project is Reggie's idea of a fitting punishment for escaping his clutches. If I don't turn up anything useful, so sad, too bad, not all scholars can make the grade, and I'm out on my ear, scrambling for a job teaching survey courses. If I do, he gets lots of lovely data for his next book.

15 August 1835

<u>Hateful</u> touring. <u>Hateful</u>, <u>hateful</u> carriages and crowds and having to smile when my head aches and Mamma <u>refusing</u> to believe that I feel unwell, even when I am <u>fainting</u> from weariness. Yet even this <u>endless</u> travel is preferable to Kensington, with C <u>insisting</u> I appoint him my private secretary when I am queen and Mamma <u>insisting</u> I dismiss <u>dearest</u> Lehzen.

I refused. Lehzen is the <u>only</u> person in the whole of England who loves me for myself alone. And I would rather have an <u>adder</u> or a <u>rat</u> for my secretary than C. He has turned Mamma into a <u>mindless automaton</u>, who smiles when he threatens me and agrees that I am stupid, childish, undutiful, <u>unfit</u> to be Queen. With Lehzen's help, I stand my ground, but I do not scruple to confess that I <u>fear</u> John Conroy as much as I <u>loathe</u> him.

I think about the Duchess of Kent, smiling and nodding while Conroy does his methodical best to break her daughter's spirit. It's not exactly news – there are accounts in all the standard biographies of the lengths Conroy went to while trying to make himself defacto King of England – but seeing it in her own hand makes it more real, more immediate.

The next entry, written during Victoria's convalescence from a bad case of typhoid in September of 1835, is even more infuriating.

15 November 1835
(Text Hidden under a Spell to Change the Colour of Silk Ribbons)

I <u>hate</u> Sir John Conroy. I know this is a <u>sin</u>, but so is it a sin to <u>persecute</u> the <u>sick</u>. While I lay ill, almost to the point of <u>death</u>, he read me a letter he had prepared in which I declared myself too young to be Queen and appointed Mamma my Regent and himself my private secretary and personal treasurer until I am <u>twenty-five years of age!</u> Then he <u>thrust</u> a pen between my fingers and <u>commanded</u> me to sign it.

I held <u>firm</u> in my refusal, despite his <u>bullying</u> and Mamma's <u>tears</u> and <u>recriminations</u>. My <u>anger</u> strengthened me wonderfully, while <u>Lehzen,</u> with her <u>kind looks</u>, reminded me that I need only <u>endure</u> a little while longer, until my <u>eighteenth</u> birthday frees me from the threat of a <u>regency</u>.

Sometimes, I hate <u>Mamma</u> hardly less than C. Surely a mother's duty is to <u>comfort</u> and <u>protect</u> her child, not stand by while a monster <u>savages</u> her. I try to remind myself that she is unable to help herself. Still, it is <u>hard</u> to forgive her.

Poor kid, I think. Poor isolated, beleaguered, abused kid.

Who, I remind myself, will be crowned Queen of England before she turns nineteen. Who will banish Conroy back into obscurity, move Mamma's apartments as far from her own as the endless corridors of Buckingham Palace will allow, marry the love of her life and live happily – if not for ever after, at least for the next twenty years.

Still. She didn't know that when she wrote in her Book of Spells.

I'm lucky. My parents are proud of me. 'You're like me,' Mom says. 'Total dedication to your career!' 'Ruthless,' Dad says. 'A scholar has to be ruthless to get ahead.'

I would be delighted to be ruthless. All I need is an opportunity.

The Archivist is beside me. I get the impression she's been there for a while. 'Last call,' she says.

13 May 1836
We are <u>over-run</u> with princes! In March, there was Prince August of Saxe-Coburg-Kohary and his brother Ferdinand; in April, the Princes of <u>Orange</u>. Augustus is <u>good-looking</u> and <u>quite</u> clever, although not so handsome as Ferdinand, who is <u>worldly</u>, <u>dances beautifully</u> and <u>kissed</u> my cheek <u>very near my lips</u>. I love him <u>extremely</u>, but he is to marry the Queen of Portugal. The Oranges <u>will not do</u>. In fact, I wonder at <u>anyone</u> thinking that they <u>might</u>. They <u>look</u> like frogs, they <u>dance</u> like frogs and their hands are <u>damp</u>, even through their gloves.

Uncle Leopold makes no secret of intending me to marry his <u>nephew</u>. He writes so frequently of Dear Albert's <u>beauty</u>, <u>purity</u>, <u>cleverness</u>, and <u>kindness</u> that I am quite <u>sick</u> of the subject. I shall do my <u>duty</u>, however, and <u>strive</u> to like him – better than the <u>Orange frogs</u>, in any case. I do hope he <u>dances</u>, because there is to be a <u>ball</u> for my 17th birthday, and I intend to be as <u>dissipated</u> as possible.

Reggie's more like a bull than a frog, although he does have damp hands. The thought of him getting the inside scoop on Victoria and Albert's love story is more than a little distasteful. Maybe I won't tell him about it. Maybe I'll just throw in the towel altogether and get a job on a freighter. There's lots of time to read at sea.

30 May 1836

What can Uncle Leopold be <u>thinking</u>? Albert is <u>impossible</u>. I suppose he is good-looking enough, or will be when he grows out of his spots and into his whiskers. His <u>eyes</u> are quite beautiful, but he is <u>stiff</u> and <u>brusque</u>, <u>blushes</u> when I speak, <u>looks grave</u> when I am merry, turns faint after <u>two dances</u> and retires at <u>eight</u>. I would a <u>thousand</u> times rather marry his elder brother Ernest, who is <u>much</u> handsomer and more <u>charming</u> – though Uncle Leopold warns me that Ernest is <u>very</u> like Uncle King, and likely to prove a <u>sad husband</u>.

In truth, I do not wish to marry <u>at all</u>. Yet it seems I will be compelled to do so. Lord Melbourne believes it <u>unnatural</u> for a woman to reign <u>alone</u>, and indeed, I have recently made some <u>very serious</u> errors of judgement that have cost me dearly. Albert is <u>steady</u> and <u>thoughtful</u>, as I am not. And I have so <u>few</u> other choices. I have written Uncle Leopold what he wishes to hear, and have promised Albert that I will answer any <u>letters</u> he may please to write me. But I am very <u>unhappy</u>. What is the use of being <u>Queen</u> when I may not please <u>myself</u>?

That doesn't sound much like the romance of the century. I wonder what happened. I wonder if she's going to write about it.

I've been here nearly two weeks. The archivist has relented to the extent of giving me my own electric fire. My greatest disappointment is that Victoria rants about how much she hates Conroy, her mother and her life rather than talk about Albert, who she hardly mentions.

On 26 May, she celebrates achieving her majority by inventing a new and more sophisticated *oratio obscura*; it takes me a full day to unravel. 'My BIRTHDAY celebration was <u>one in the eye</u> for Mamma and C,' she writes, 'who were hard-put to pay me the most <u>commonplace</u> compliments of the day.' She was now an adult, legally able to rule England in her own right. Unfortunately, it did not make her life significantly easier.

15 June 1837
(Text Hidden Under a Spell for Prolonging the Life of Cut Flowers)

Word comes from Windsor that Uncle William is almost certainly on the point of death. Mamma and C have redoubled their efforts to bully me into signing away my rightful authority. I am very, very weary. When I am Queen, I shall be able to speak my mind without fear. Or will I? Is it possible that my crown will prove but another, heavier chain upon my soul? My life here in Kensington is insupportable. Will my life in Buckingham Palace be less so? I do not know, I cannot tell and I am very afraid.

I comfort myself with the certainty that I shall, at last, have a room of my own and need not show my journal to anyone if I do not wish to. I shall no longer be forced to hide my true thoughts in my Book of Spells. And yet I find I cannot contemplate abandoning it, any more than I can abandon Dash or Lehzen or my dolls.

This book holds the heart of a princess. Surely it may hold the heart of a QUEEN.

Victoria was young, so very young. Smarter than she thought she was, arrogant and insecure, with a strong sense of duty and a trusting nature scabbed over by repeated betrayals. I haven't changed my opinion about hereditary monarchs, but nobody can say Victoria didn't try to be a good one.

The next entry is dated 11 October 1839. I check to see if pages have been torn out. They haven't. Apparently, Victoria overstated her devotion to her spell book, if not to her spaniel or her governess. It's interesting, though, that she should return to it the day after Albert comes to visit her for the second time.

(Text Hidden Under a Spell to Settle a Nervous Stomach.)

I cannot think what is wrong with me. When I am with HIM, I feel quite clumsy. When by chance HIS hand brushes mine, my heart <u>pounds</u> so I am almost <u>suffocated</u>. Last night, I was visited by <u>dreams</u> that confused me <u>extremely</u>, and yet, upon waking, I <u>longed</u> to dream again. He is <u>very</u> beautiful, with his eyes like limpid pools and his mouth so grave and sweet, and his strong, broad shoulders. I <u>love</u> him so <u>extremely</u> that it quite <u>frightens</u> me.

But what if <u>HE</u> does not love <u>me</u>? He is so <u>calm</u>, so <u>moderate</u>! And I am so <u>passionate</u>, so <u>headstrong</u>! I yearn to <u>kiss</u> him, to feel his arms around my body, but dare not. He <u>says</u> he loves me, but I fear lest the <u>violence</u> of <u>my</u> love <u>frighten</u> and <u>disgust</u> him.

I know he will be a good and conformable husband to me, for he is very <u>dutiful</u>. Is it wrong of me to desire his <u>love</u> as well? I am Queen of England, but it will mean <u>nothing</u> if I cannot be Queen of <u>ALBERT'S heart</u>.

At this point, I am much less surprised by Victoria's passion than she is. She's always had it in her – all her heavy underlines; her violent hates and her no less violent enthusiasms; her sensual delight in music and dancing and food, indicate that she's more like her Uncle King George IV than she knows. And yet there's something there that's more than lust, something that reads very much like real love.

I've never felt like that. Oh, I have had affairs, but love scares me. Mom and Dad loved each other, and they made each other miserable. Dad couldn't bear being tied down; Mom couldn't bear secrets and silences. The battleground of their marriage has left me with a fear of commitment and a perfect horror of manipulation and power games.

Victoria, who had even more pressing reasons to fear love than I do, clearly overcame them. Knowing the story has a happy ending, at least for her, I give an indulgent chuckle and turn the page.

The 13 of October is a very short entry, hidden under a simple spell to keep domestic animals off the furniture: 'He <u>must</u> love me. He <u>shall</u> love me. My plans are laid. I will go <u>tonight</u>.'

And then, nothing.

Well, nothing I can read, anyway. When I touch the entry dated 15 October, I can feel the resonance of the *oratio obscura* clear to my teeth. But the obscuring knot is denser and more complex than anything I've ever seen before. I can't even tell which spell it's based on.

My first reaction is pure, unadulterated fury. Things were going along so smoothly: Victoria would come up with a new variation on her familiar theme, and I'd unravel it. We were growing more sophisticated together. Why would she spring something like this on me?

In the back of my mind, my internalized Reggie Jolley chuckles nastily. 'Because you're a muck-common Yankee with ideas above your station and Victoria was Queen of England, that's why.'

'Shut up, Reggie,' I mutter.

The archivist looks up from her work, startled. 'Sorry? Did you say something?'

'I'm going to lunch.'

At the Windsor Knot, I order a pint of bitter and a packet of crisps. I don't usually drink at lunch, but this is an emergency.

Oddly enough, I'm not mad at Victoria, who was just preserving her privacy, and very effectively, too. If I've learned nothing else in the past two weeks, I've learned that she was a first-rate practical wizard.

Well, I'm not a bad practical wizard myself. And the thoroughness with which she's locked this entry has got to mean that the mysterious plans mentioned on 13 October are very startling indeed.

I *must* decode this entry. I *will* decode this entry.

I go back to the Royal Archives, exchange nods with the archivist and set to work.

Day after chill, dreary day, I commune with Victoria's spell, analysing, tweaking, picking at its component threads. Lunch is a sandwich in the cloakroom. Sleep is a luxury I can't afford. I've never seen a working like this before: seven separately structured spells, cast at intervals, woven into an all-but-impenetrable barrier. I haven't had so much fun since I unravelled my first personalized *oratio obscura*.

Sunday night, after I hang up after talking to Dad, my cell phone rings. It's Reggie. There's no use ignoring it. I'm going to have to talk to him sooner or later.

'Hello, Reggie.'

'Ransome,' he says, all hearty bonhomie. 'How's it coming?'

'Fine.'

'Why haven't you checked in? It's been a fortnight.'

'I've been busy. There's a lot of material to get through.'

'Good,' he says. 'I look forward to getting your preliminary report. Shall we say Tuesday?'

'Are you still there?' I say. 'Sorry. I seem to have lost you.'

After that, I leave my mobile off.

It takes me seven solid days to untangle the spell. By the time I come up with an aperient that looks as if it should work, I'm almost too tired to cast it. But I can't possibly wait until tomorrow to find out. I suck back a cup of tarry tea in the staff canteen, come back upstairs and cast the spell before I lose my nerve.

The long, dull treatise on the permissible uses of magic in diplomacy falls away, revealing a heavily underlined scrawl.

Victoria always underlines a great deal when she's upset.

13 October 1839

I am <u>inexpressibly</u> weary. Today, I have broken the <u>law</u>. I have betrayed <u>everything</u> <u>dear, dear</u> Lehzen and <u>dear</u> Sir T have taught me. Though I value truth <u>extremely</u>, I have lied and lied.

The first lie was a <u>small</u> one: I informed Lord Melbourne I desired to learn about the <u>poorer boroughs</u> of London. He said that only <u>very low</u> folk lived there, and I told him, quite in <u>Mamma's</u> own manner, that I hoped I was <u>their</u> Queen as well. Which is not <u>precisely</u> a lie, for I <u>do</u> concern myself with the welfare of even the <u>most wretched</u> of my subjects, among whom the cunning folk of <u>Graymalkin Lane</u> and its environs must certainly be numbered.

I <u>blush</u> to remember the lies I told so that I might go to London. Suffice it to say that by a ½ after 11, I was in a common <u>hansom</u>, disguised in a plain cloak. <u>Alone</u>, although for once I did not wish to be, for I possess no <u>friend</u> – not even Lehzen – that I would trust not to betray me. Trust, no less than Truth, is a <u>luxury</u> a <u>Queen</u> cannot often <u>afford</u>.

Graymalkin Lane is a <u>horrid</u> place, <u>narrow</u> and <u>foul</u>, haunted with <u>shadows</u> that cough and spit and <u>jeer</u>. Having seen it with my own eyes, I shall never again be able to read Mr Dickens's <u>Witch Lane</u> with pleasure – although it did teach me the sign I must look for: a <u>card</u>, marked with a <u>heart</u> and a <u>dagger</u>.

After <u>much</u> anxious searching, I saw such a card stuck up in a window. The name on the card was 'Madame Rusalka'.

The lady who answered my ring was as foreign as her <u>nom de magie</u>, with high, flat cheeks and a bright shawl embroidered with flowers. She led me into a small, shabby parlour, and once I had made her understand what I sought, left me, returning with a <u>phial</u> made of polished stone. 'I sell this only because I am <u>poor</u>,' she said in strangely accented English. 'Please to remember, should you <u>regret</u> what you do.' Struck by the <u>intensity</u> of her manner, I wept and assured her that I <u>would</u> remember. Then I begged her to fetch me a hansom (for I was still <u>sadly distressed</u>), and reached Buckingham Palace just before dawn.

The cost of the philter was <u>30 shillings</u>.

Today, I am <u>extremely</u> weary. When I am rested, I shall return to Windsor and <u>take tea</u> with my <u>dearest</u> Albert. Then I shall ask him to <u>marry me</u>.

The page ends with a note, dated ten years later: 'I have devised a <u>sevenfold</u> *oratio obscura*. <u>Heaven grant</u> it will keep my words safe from all eyes but mine.'

The spell snaps shut as I reach the last line. If it weren't for the cold sweat prickling my armpits and the pounding in my ears, I'd think I'd fallen asleep and dreamed it. But I didn't. Victoria, twenty years old, popularly supposed to be sheltered, truthful and as emotionally naïve as her spaniel, had slipped Prince Albert a love mickey.

Reggie's going to bust his buttons over this. He might even decide to let bygones be bygones and allow me to get back to my beloved Elizabethans.

It's great material, after all. The articles will write themselves: 'Queen Victoria's Secret Journals: A Study in Domestic Tyranny'; 'The Seven-Fold *Oratio Obscura*: Queen Victoria's Super-Spell.'

There's only one more entry left in the Book of Spells, also locked seven-fold. It's dated 20 May 1841, some six months after the birth of the Princess Royal. The covering text is a receipt for an ointment to soothe teething pains.

I have come to realize that I have made a <u>TERRIBLE MISTAKE</u>. <u>Whoever</u> or <u>whatever</u> Albert might have been without my intervention, I will <u>never know</u>. Dearly as I love him, I see him <u>very</u> seldom, for it is only when I am <u>not</u> present that he can be his own <u>dear self</u>. In my presence, he becomes the creature of <u>Madame Rusalka's spell</u>, without a thought in his head but how he may <u>please</u> me. What a <u>fool</u> I was to think I would <u>like</u> a husband who always <u>agreed</u> with me. The reality is <u>terrifying</u>. And how can I <u>trust</u> a love that springs . . .

I try to turn the page, but there's nothing to turn. I've reached the end of the book.

'Damn!'

'Shhhh,' the archivist hisses.

I look around the Reading Room. She and I are alone. 'Why are you bloody shushing me?' I demand. 'I'm the only person bloody here.'

Her round face flushes. 'I am here as well, and I am not accustomed to being sworn at.'

I get a grip on my temper. None of this is her fault. In fact, she's been very helpful, hunting up magic texts for me to consult. 'Sorry. I've had a bit of a shock. The book of spells breaks off in the middle of a very interesting sentence. Is there another volume?'

'There was,' she says primly. 'At least, we think there must have been. But either Princess Beatrice burned it with the rest of Victoria's original journals, or it's been misplaced somewhere. I'm sorry.'

I shut my teeth against all the things I'd like to say, but shouldn't. After a long pause, I settle for, 'Oh. Oh, dear.'

She looks amused. 'Quite. I do, however, seem to remember a folder that no one's sure where to file. It has some loose sheets in it, written in the Queen's hand. Would you be interested in seeing it?'

Hope springs, painful and shaky, in my heart. 'I very well might.'

A very long half-hour later, she drops an acid-free file folder in front of me, hesitates, then goes back to her desk.

Hands shaking, I go through the papers carefully. The one that sears my fingers is, of course, on the bottom, by which time I'm so exhausted I can hardly cast the aperient.

. . . from <u>Magic</u> and not from the <u>Heart</u>? I <u>cannot</u> bear it. I cannot bear <u>myself</u>. I have deliberately <u>enslaved</u> Albert – I, who strove so <u>passionately</u> against Conroy's attempts to enslave me. Truly, I am <u>well punished</u>. For in <u>forcing</u> my darling to love me, I have not only robbed <u>him</u> of <u>himself</u>, but <u>myself</u> of his <u>unbiased</u> advice. Reading his <u>dear</u> letters, written in the years of our separation, I am struck anew by his <u>wisdom</u>, his <u>deep knowledge</u> of history. All <u>lost</u> to me through my own <u>great folly</u>!

I have resolved to make what <u>reparation</u> I may. First, I will bend <u>all my energies</u> to the discovery of a spell or potion to counteract Madam Rusalka's <u>cursed</u> brew. I will give my darling <u>responsibilities</u> in which I have no part. I shall encourage him to voice his <u>true opinions</u>, and <u>defer</u> to him, as a good wife <u>ought</u>, subduing my own <u>unhappy</u> nature. It is my <u>greatest fear</u> that, left <u>unchecked</u>, I shall grow to be a Monster <u>of self-regard</u>, like Conroy – without <u>compassion</u>, without <u>humility</u>, without <u>grace</u>.

Should I succeed in breaking the chains with which I have imprisoned my <u>darling</u>, I may again find some measure of <u>happiness</u> in the company of one who will always be as an <u>Angel</u> to me.

As I read, my excitement gives way to nausea.

It's like uncovering Dad's letter all over again, only worse. Much worse. That only blew up three private lives. This is going to cause a complete re-evaluation of Victoria and her reign. These entries add a whole new dimension to Victoria's character, and throw every biography of her into instant obsolescence. She's going to be called a slut, a hypocrite, the biggest fraud to dishonour the English throne since Charles II.

I have to tell Reggie. I can't tell Reggie.

He'll call a press conference; give Lady Antonia Fraser a run for her money. He'll publish articles and books and go on TV. He'll take poor Victoria's dirty laundry and wave it around in public, pointing out the significance of each ugly stain.

And if I don't tell him? Well, I won't perish, though my academic career is likely to. Reggie will find some way of cutting my fellowship short that will make it impossible for me to get another. On the other hand, I'll never wake up in the middle of the night worrying that I was turning into Reggie. And I won't feel as if I were nineteen again, watching my mother cry because I couldn't keep my nose out of other people's business. I might even feel as if, this time, I've done the decent thing.

Over the three weeks it has taken me to read, decode and transcribe Victoria's book of spells, I've grown fond of her. Not because I identify with her – Good Lord, no. I'm not sentimental over animals, and Italian opera bores me almost as much as politics and paperwork – and not because I feel sorry for her, either. I haven't lost sight of the fact that she was pig-headed, self-righteous, arrogant and made a number of very bad decisions, the consequences of which England is still suffering. But she did try to be good, she really did. God knows she didn't succeed, but at least she tried. And when she failed, she tried to fix it.

I bury my head in my hands. After a moment, I hear footsteps and feel a feather-light touch on my shoulder. 'I say. Are you all right?'

I give what I mean to be a sardonic laugh, but it comes out as more of a sob. 'No. I'm not all right.'

'Did you not find what you were looking for?'

I sit up and look at the Royal Archivist. Her face is a plump oval, her nose long and straight, her brows narrow and knitted with concern. 'No, I found the missing page – and thank you, by the way, for remembering that file. It's just . . .' I shrug helplessly.

She bites her lip. 'Look here. It's nearly five, and you look like you could use a drink. Come to the pub and I'll tell you nasty stories about Reggie.'

'You know *Reggie*?'

'My brother knew him at Harrow. He calls him the Jolly Roger.'

I snort.

She grins like a mischievous schoolgirl. 'Come on then.'

Her name, oddly enough, is Victoria. The Honourable Victoria Pendennis. She's a specialist in restorative magic and stasis spells. She's also a thoroughly nice woman. I tell her everything.

When I've finished, she goes to get another round. When she comes back with my pint and her single malt, she says, 'The situation is not as dire as you think it is, you know.'

'Isn't it?'

'No. There's no reason not to give Reggie the early entries. They're new material and they're genuinely useful.'

I shake my head. 'Reggie's never going to believe there's nothing hidden under the last two entries. They're too obviously place-holders.'

'Tell him you can't make them out, then. He'll get to feel superior and you'll have a chance to work on something more to your taste. You can always go back and publish them later, if you change your mind.'

'Why would I do that?'

Victoria smiles. It's a slightly wistful smile, but that could just be the way her mouth is shaped – a true Cupid's bow, with a full lower lip. 'Because you'll realize that, sooner or later, somebody's going to publish them. And it should be someone who really loves and understands her.'

I have no answer to that, so we finish our drinks in silence. As we leave the pub, I ask Victoria if she's hungry. She says she is and asks if I like curry. I say I do.

It's one of those April nights that feels more like late May. Even though it's half-past seven, the sky is still light. Victoria tucks her hand into my arm as we walk past a drift of daffodils blooming in an iron-fenced square. I unzip my leather jacket. Spring is really here.

LAMIA VICTORIANA

Tansy Rayner Roberts

The poet's sister has teeth as white as new lace. When she speaks, which is rarely, I feel a shiver down my skin.

I am not here for this. I am here to persuade my own sister Mary that she has made a terrible mistake, that eloping, as she has, with this poet who cannot marry her, will not only be her own ruin, but that of our family, too.

My tongue stumbles on the words, and every indignant speech I practiced on my way here has melted into nothing. The poet looks at me with his calm, beautiful eyes, and Mary sits scandalously close to him, determined to continue in her path of debauchery and wickedness. I cannot take my eyes from the poet's sister.

She is pale all over, silver like moonlight. The light twigged lawn of her day dress makes her skin seem milky and soft. I have never seen such a creature as her.

'If you are so worried about my reputation, Fanny, then come with us,' urges Mary. 'Be my companion. I know you have always longed to see the Continent. We are to Paris, and later Florence.'

Her deflowering has rendered her more confident than I have ever seen her. She glows with happiness and self-satisfaction.

'You may have relinquished society's good opinion, but I cannot countenance such a thought,' I say.

The poet's sister arches her neck and says, 'Come,' and I am lost.

Within a week, it becomes obvious that they are not human. The poet and his sister enter rooms so silently it is as if their footsteps are swallowed by the very air. When we leave hotels, one of them speaks softly to the owner, and we leave without any money or promissory notes changing hands.

Mary is immersed in her poet. At mealtimes, she gazes fiercely at his hands, the way that his fingers toy with the silverware or hold a wine glass. She sighs about hunger or thirst, but does little to assuage such desires.

I eat, but the food tastes like ashes, such is my fear. I should not have followed my sister. Her fate should not be my own. I tell myself that I chose this path because of my terror at what Father would do to me if I returned without Mary, but the truth is, I came with them because the poet's sister asked me to.

On the ninth day, she kisses me. I am distracted by my latest letter from home, the paper clutched tight in my fist, and my first concern is passing by the poet's sister in the passageway without our skirts getting tangled together, or my hip pressing unduly against hers. Unexpectedly, she turns to me so that our bodies are aligned in that narrow space and gasps her mouth against my own.

I drink her in, for a moment of perfumed air and warmth, and then she is gone, her laughter spilling against the walls as she moves, so fast, so fast.

Gone.

Mary cups her hands over the slight swell of her belly, admiring her new curves in the mirror. 'I am greater than I was, Fanny,' she tells me. 'The world is greater than it was.'

'You are foolish in love,' I tell her, snipping off the end of my embroidery thread. Love. Is that the fluttering feeling in my bones and stays when the poet's sister looks at me? Am I as foolish as my sister?

'Admit it,' says Mary, tugging the silk of her dress out so that she can imagine how she will look when she is more months round. 'Paris is beautiful.'

Paris. Paris is chocolate and pastries that we do not drink or eat, though it sits prettily before us at mealtimes in perfect china vessels. Paris is expensive frocks that my sister and her poet cannot afford, persuaded from fancy shops with quiet, forceful words.

Language is his coin, and he buys every trinket with a pearl from his tongue. I wonder, is someone, somewhere keeping track of the cost of this life of ours?

Mary buys me a travelling dress of sturdy linen and wool, with a jaunty hat. The colours are violet and black, as is proper for a widow rather than an unmarried chaperone. I wonder whom it is that I am supposed to be mourning, but I rather like the way that I look in the costume.

On the train to Florence, I stand at the window, gazing at the winding ribbon of Italian countryside. This, this is the world. I am finally away from the dust and the smallness of Father's house and our street in London. I feel as if I could fly.

The poet's sister brushes against me in the narrow cabin, and then again, so that I can tell it was not done by accident. Her fingertips linger on my waist as she steadies herself against the bunk. 'Shall we join Mary and my brother in the dining carriage?' she asks.

I shake my head, not willing to say aloud that I cannot bear another meal of artifice and elegance at which nothing is eaten. They all seem to enjoy the ritual, but it only serves to remind me of what we have lost and what we have left behind. It unsettles me that such a vital human need has been lost to us.

Hungry. I am so very hungry, and yet I cannot swallow even a crumb.

'Well then,' she says, and tugs down the stiff blind that shuts out the light. 'We are alone.'

The travelling dress comes apart so easily, as if it were designed for this. A button, a lace, and I am unpeeled. Her hands are cold against the heat of my skin, and her mouth fits against my neck perfectly.

My mind is overwhelmed with her fingers, her palms, the soft mound beneath her thumb, and the whisper of my chemise as it gives way to her. I do not notice the bite until she is so deep inside me that there is no return, no escape, just heat and taste and the rocking pulse of the train through every inch of my skin.

For the first time in days, in weeks, I am sated. Finally, I understand what I was hungering for: to be food.

Later, much later, there is a whistle. The train has stopped. I am lying dizzy in the lower bunk, my body wrapped in the languid arms of the poet's sister.

'We're here,' she says, and slides over my inert body to dress herself. I watch as her white skin is swallowed by layers of fabric, stockings, stays and damask. When she is her outer self again, she turns her attentions to me, drawing me to my feet and dressing me, as if I am a doll. She even combs my hair, playing the lady's maid.

When I speak, it is only to say, 'So quiet.' Where is the bustle of the other passengers, the calls and urgent conversations, the mutterings as they embark or depart?

'All the time in the world,' she says softly, and powders my face with a silken touch.

Every compartment on the train is empty as we pass. But no, not empty. If I look too closely, I can see a hand here, a foot there, a fallen lock of hair.

She catches me looking. 'My brother was hungry, too,' is her only explanation.

We meet Mary and the poet on the platform. They are bright with colour, delighted with themselves. Several porters come forth to carry our trunks, but they all have a dazed look about their eyes that proves the poet has already paid them with his dulcet words.

'I know we shall love it here in Florence,' says Mary.

'It is a most accommodating city,' agrees the poet, with a satisfied smile.

We have been in Florence only three days when someone tries to kill us. He is a most unassuming-looking gentleman. The poet's sister and I are wandering the city markets, choosing furnishings and flowers that will look splendid in the new house that her brother is buying for us.

He spends his days going from place to place, searching for the perfect villa, while Mary plans the garden where her children will play.

He lunges out of the shadows, a rope knotted in his hands, and wraps it around my lover's throat. She is caught unawares, but he does not expect me to savage him with the fine brass door-knocker I had been admiring on a nearby stall.

Blood pours from the wound on his head as I hurl the knotted rope away, cooing over the ugly bruises on her throat.

'Do not concern yourself, Fanny,' she says in a beautiful rasp. 'No one shall destroy us.'

'You are not one of them,' the man gasps, holding his sleeve to the wound. 'Do not let the lamia take your will and your life from you, Frances Wolstonecraft.'

I shiver that he knows my name. Or perhaps it is that other word – lamia. I do not know what it means.

'Come near us again', says the poet's sister, 'and my brother will kill you.' She takes my hand and we run away together, through the market.

'Who is that man?' I ask at the supper table that night. The poet, his sister and Mary all look at each other, as if I have said something unpleasant, a truth not to be named aloud. 'Why does he hate us?' I persist. Am I the only one not to know the secrets of this new family we have formed?

'He is an old enemy of my kind,' the poet says finally, shifting his wine glass one precise inch to the left, so that the candlelight makes a prettier pattern of ruby shapes on the tablecloth. 'He hates us for being, that is all. His name is Julius. He is not important.'

'He was so strong.' I can still remember that look in his eyes, as if my lady were some kind of monster.

'We are stronger,' says the poet's sister, and squeezes my fingers with her own.

From Florence, we travel to Switzerland, determined that our plan to live together in all happiness and beauty shall not be spoiled by the horrid man, Julius.

I wonder sometimes if he was sent by our father, if the poet only wished to spare Mary and I from that awful truth: that our own family would rather see us dead than happy.

We have our house of dreams, finally, in the midst of such green splendour, and a good distance outside the town, where prying eyes might seek to spoil our circle. The poet and Mary visit the town often, to buy pretty trinkets and to slake their thirst. When they are gone, it is as if the house is ours, only ours, and the poet's sister and I can finally love each other as we long to.

She needs no drink but what she takes from me, in sweet drugging kisses that make me feel alive.

Mary's child is born, a perfect silver nub of a creature with bright eyes. It is hungry, so very hungry, and nuzzles her constantly, sucking, biting, clawing at her for food. She hires a nursemaid from the town, and then another, but the babe's thirst is too great, and for a while it is as if we are constantly digging graves for the scraps left behind.

Left unsaid is our belief that she will not survive.

We will have to move again, and soon. We have been so happy here that it pains us to speak of leaving the garden, the egg-shell drawing room, the balcony that looks out over the valley.

We stay too long.

I am awoken from a deep befogged sleep against the body of my beloved when I hear a scream in the night. The baby makes so much noise that I am content at first to ignore the interruption, but then there is another, and the shattering of glass.

The poet's sister sits up in bed, shining and glorious in her white nightgown. 'Him,' is all she says, then she is up on her feet, hair streaming behind her, teeth gleaming in the darkness.

He has come for us.

The downstairs parlour is alight as we come down the stairs: flames crackle up the curtains and blacken the wooden walls. My beloved gasps as she finds the body of her brother in a pool of silver blood, his body pierced through the heart and his head lying some distance from his neck.

'Fanny!' Mary screams, and bursts through the flaming doorway like an angel, bearing her child wrapped in a sage-green blanket trimmed with ivory lace. 'Take her,' she begs, placing the wailing bundle in my arms.

I stand there, immobile as Mary and my beloved turn back to the smoke and the flames, ready to avenge the death of the poet.

He – Julius, slayer of lamia – walks through the wall of flames with his sword held high.

It is a short sword, and bronzed rather than steel. How odd, the things you notice at such moments.

My sister bares her teeth, as sharp as those of my beloved, and they swarm him. I do not want to watch. I flee through the kitchen, where I grab the only weapon I can find, a kitchen knife, and spare cloths for the baby. Then I run out of the house, my niece crying in my arms, down the hill and away from the beautiful house.

I feel it minutes later, the death of my beloved. It is a blossoming pain in my chest, as if someone has carved out my heart. I do not feel Mary die – we have no such connection – but my tears fall for them both.

I run and hide, but the baby is hungry and she will not stop crying. Finally I press her mouth again my upper arm and she suckles deeply, her teeth finding the vein and drinking in great gulping swallows. I shall have to wind her afterwards, and the thought is almost enough to make me burst with laughter.

Too late. I should have silenced her minutes ago. He is upon us. I can hear him treading the crisp grass nearby, and the rasp of his smoke-filled lungs.

'Frances,' he says, as if he still thinks he has an ally in me. 'Give me the child.'

The baby's feed is not as delicious as that of my beloved. It hurts, though there is still a satisfaction in it, in knowing that I am food, that I am needed. Little Mary. Mine now.

'No,' I say, quite calmly, though he is standing not far from me and he has a sword. I do not think he will hurt me. For some reason, he does not believe I am one of the monsters. I keep the knife hidden in my skirts, so that he shall not see that I can defend myself.

'Listen to me, Frances. I have tracked these creatures for years. They were the last, the three up there in the house.'

My family. Tears rush anew down my cheeks, and I cannot wipe them away without disturbing the babe.

'There is only that one,' he continues. 'When it is gone, the world will be safe. One less monster to ravage families, to destroy the lives of innocents such as yourselves. Lamia who are born rather than made are the most powerful, the most dangerous. I have worked for centuries to weaken them, and if this one lives to make more of its kind, it may be centuries more before they are wiped from the face of the earth.'

The baby releases me with a gasp and leans against my breast, breathing deeply. She is asleep. My niece, the perfect silver child. My daughter, now. He cannot even acknowledge that she is a 'she'.

'No,' I say again.

'You can go home, Frances,' he says in a soothing voice. 'Home to your father, to your old life . . .'

The thought of it makes me shudder. 'No!' I scream and run at him with the knife.

He does not expect it, even now. He thinks I am food, a docile milk cow, with no reason to defy him now that my lover and sister are dead. I catch him in the neck, and he twists badly, falling down the hillside on to his sword.

I do not think he survived. How could he, a blow like that? After months of sitting to one side as my sister and the poet killed for food, I have become a murderer myself.

Perhaps the murderer of thousands, by keeping my little Mary alive. I know that the blood of my body will not sustain her for ever, but I have learned that the lamia power of persuasive words is mine to share, if I hold the baby close to my skin, and that has been enough to get us from train to train and country to country.

We will travel as far as we can, to a land so distant that another Julius can never find us. She will grow, my darling daughter, and she will feed. Some day, perhaps, she shall make me another lover to replace what I lost. We shall be a family, all together.

She shall live, my little Mary, long after I have gone, and live, and live.

I am not sorry for it.

THE EFFLUENT ENGINE

N. K. Jemisin

New Orleans stank to the heavens. This was either the water, which did not have the decency to confine itself to the river, but instead puddled along every street, or the streets themselves, which seemed to have been cobbled with bricks of fired excrement. Or it may have come from the people, who jostled and trotted along the narrow avenues, working and lounging and cursing and shouting and sweating, emitting a massed reek of unwashed resentment and perhaps a bit of hangover.

As Jessaline strolled beneath the colonnaded balconies of Royal Street, she fought the urge to give up, put the whole fumid pile to her back and catch the next dirigible out of town.

Then someone jostled her. 'Pardon me, miss,' said a voice at her elbow, and Jessaline was forced to stop, because the earnest-looking young man who stood there was white. He smiled, which did not surprise her, and doffed his hat, which did.

'Monsieur,' Jessaline replied, in what she hoped was the correct mix of reserve and deference.

'A fine day, is it not?' The man's grin widened, so sincere that Jessaline could not help a small smile in response. 'I must admit, though; I have yet to adjust to this abysmal heat. How are you handling it?'

'Quite well, monsieur,' she replied, thinking, *What is it that you want from me?* 'I am acclimated to it.'

'Ah, yes, certainly. A fine negress like yourself would naturally deal better with such things. I am afraid my own ancestors derive from chillier climes, and we adapt poorly.' He paused abruptly, a stricken look crossing his face. He was the florid kind, red-haired and freckled, with skin so pale that it revealed his every thought – in point of which he paled further. 'Oh, dear. My sister warned me about this. You aren't Creole, are you? I understand they take it an insult to be called, er . . . by certain terms.'

With some effort Jessaline managed not to snap, *Do I look like one of them*? But people on the street were beginning to stare, so instead she said, 'No, monsieur. And it's clear to me you aren't from these parts, or you would never ask such a thing.'

'Ah, yes.' The man looked sheepish. 'You have caught me out, miss; I am from New York. Is it so obvious?'

Jessaline smiled carefully. 'Only in your politeness, monsieur.' She reached up to adjust her hat, lifting it for a moment as a badly needed cooling breeze wafted past.

'Are you perhaps . . .' The man paused, staring at her head. 'My word! You've naught but a scrim of hair!'

'I have sufficient to keep myself from drafts on cold days,' she replied and, as she'd hoped, he laughed.

'You're a most charming ne— woman, my dear, and I feel honoured to make your acquaintance.' He stepped back and bowed, full and proper. 'My name is Raymond Forstall.'

'Jessaline Dumonde,' she said, offering her lace-gloved hand, though she had no expectation that he would take it. To her surprise he did, bowing again over it.

'My apologies for gawking. I simply don't meet many of the coloured on a typical day, and I must say . . .' He hesitated, darted a look about, and at least had the grace to drop his voice. 'You're remarkably lovely, even with no hair.'

In spite of herself, Jessaline laughed. 'Thank you, monsieur.' After an appropriate and slightly awkward pause, she inclined her head. 'Well, then, good day to you.'

'Good day indeed,' he said in a tone of such pleasure that Jessaline hoped no one had heard it, for his sake. The folk of this town were particular about matters of propriety, as any society which relied so firmly upon class differences. While there were many ways in which a white gentleman could appropriately express his admiration for a woman of colour – the existence of the *gens de couleur libres* was testimony to that – all of those ways were simply *not done* in public.

Forstall donned his hat, and Jessaline inclined her head in return before heading away.

Another convenient breeze gusted by, and she took advantage of it to adjust her hat once more, in the process sliding her stiletto back into its hiding place amid the silk flowers.

This was the dance of things, the *cric-crac* as the storytellers said in Jessaline's land. Everyone needed something from someone. Glorious France needed money, to recover from the unlamented Napoleon's endless wars. Upstart Haiti had money from the sweet gold of its sugarcane fields, but needed guns – for all the world, it seemed, wanted the newborn country strangled in its crib. The United States had guns but craved sugar, as its fortunes were dependent upon the acquisition thereof. It alone was willing to treat with Haiti, though Haiti was the stuff of American nightmare: a nation of black slaves who had killed off their white masters. Yet Haitian sugar was no less sweet for its coating of blood, and so everyone got what they wanted, trading 'round and 'round, a graceful waltz – only occasionally devolving into a knife-fight.

It had been simplicity itself for Jessaline to slip into New Orleans. Dirigible travel in the Caribbean was inexpensive, and so many travellers regularly moved between the island nations and the great American port city that hardly any deception had been necessary. She was indentured, she told the captain, and he had waved her aboard without so much as a glance at her papers (which were false anyhow). She was a wealthy white man's mistress, she told the other passengers, and between her fine clothes, regal carriage and beauty – despite her skin being purest sable in colour – they believed her and were alternately awed and offended. She was a slave, she told the dockmaster on the levee; a trusted one, lettered and loyal, promised freedom should she continue to serve to her fullest. He had smirked at this, as if the notion of anyone freeing such an obviously valuable slave was ludicrous. Yet he, too, had let her pass unchallenged, without even charging her the disembarcation fee.

It had then taken two full months for Jessaline to make enquiries and sufficient contacts to arrange a meeting with the esteemed Monsieur Norbert Rillieux. The Creoles of New Orleans were a closed and prickly bunch, most likely because they had to be – only by the rigid maintenance of caste and privilege could they hope to retain freedom in a land that loved to throw anyone darker than tan into chains. Thus, more than a few of them had refused to speak to Jessaline on sight. Yet there were many who had not forgotten that there but for the grace of God went their own fortune, so from these she had been able to glean crucial information and finally an introduction by letter. As she had mentioned the right names and observed the right etiquette, Norbert Rillieux had at last invited her to afternoon tea.

That day had come, and . . .

And Rillieux, Jessaline was finally forced to concede, was an idiot.

'Monsieur,' she said again, after drawing a breath to calm herself, 'as I explained in my letter, I have no interest in sugar-cane processing. It is true that your contributions to this field have been much appreciated by the interests I represent; your improved refining methods have saved both money and lives, which could both be reinvested in other places. What we require assistance with is a wholly different matter, albeit related.'

'Oh,' said Rillieux, blinking. He was a savagely thin-lipped man, with a hard stare that might have been compelling on a man who knew how to use it. Rillieux did not. 'Your pardon, mademoiselle. But, er, who did you say you represented, again?'

'I did not say, monsieur. And if you will forgive me, I would prefer not to say for the time being.' She fixed him with her own hard stare. 'You will understand, I hope, that not all parties can be trusted when matters scientific turn to matters commercial.'

At that, Rillieux's expression turned shrewd at last; he understood just fine. The year before, Jessaline's superiors had informed her, the plan Rillieux had proposed to the city – an ingenious means of draining its endless, pestilent swamps, for the health and betterment of all – had been turned down. Six months later, a coalition of city engineers had submitted virtually the same plan and been heaped with praise and the funds to bring it about. The men of the coalition were white, of course. Jessaline marvelled that Rillieux even bothered being upset about it.

'I see,' Rillieux said. 'Then please forgive me, but I do not know what it is you want.'

Jessaline stood and went to her brocaded bag, which sat on a side table across Rillieux's elegantly apportioned salon. In it was a small, rubber-stopped, peculiarly shaped jar of the sort utilized by chemists, complete with engraved markings on its surface to indicate measurement of the liquid within. At the bottom of this jar swirled a scrim of dark-brown, foul-looking paste and liquid. Jessaline brought it over to Rillieux and offered the jar to his nose, waiting until he nodded before she unstoppered it.

At the scent that wafted out, he stumbled back, gasping, his eyes all a-water. 'By all that's holy! Woman, what is that putrescence?'

'That, Monsieur Rillieux, is effluent,' Jessaline said, neatly stoppering the flask. 'Waste, in other words, of a very particular kind. Do you drink rum?' She knew the answer already. On one side of the parlour was a beautifully made side table holding an impressive array of bottles.

'Of course.' Rillieux was still rubbing his eyes and looking affronted. 'I'm fond of a glass or two on hot afternoons; it opens the pores, or so I'm told. But what does that—'

'Producing rum is a simple process with a messy result: this effluent, namely, and the gas it emits, which until lately was regarded as simply the unavoidable price to be paid for your pleasant afternoons. Whole swaths of countryside are afflicted with this smell now as a result. Not only is the stench offensive to man and beast, we have also found it to be as powerful as any tincture or laudanum; over time it causes anything exposed to suffocate and die. Yet there are scientific papers coming from Europe which laud this gas's potential as a fuel source.

Captured properly, purified and burned, it can power turbines, cook food and more.' Jessaline turned and set the flask on Rillieux's beverage stand, deliberately close to the square bottle of dark rum she had seen there. 'We wish you to develop a process by which the usable gas – methane – may be extracted from the miasma you just smelled.'

Rillieux stared at her for a moment, then at the flask. She could tell that he was intrigued, which meant that half her mission had been achieved already. Her superiors had spent a profligate amount of money requisitioning a set of those flasks from the German chemist who'd recently invented them, precisely with an eye towards impressing men like Rillieux, who looked down upon any science that did not show European roots.

Yet as Rillieux gazed at the flask, Jessaline was dismayed to see a look of consternation, then irritation, cross his face.

'I am an engineer, mademoiselle,' he said at last, 'not a chemist.'

'We have already worked out the chemical means by which it might be done,' Jessaline said quickly, her belly clenching in tension. 'We would be happy to share that with you—'

'And then what?' He scowled at her. 'Who will put the patent on this process, hmm? And who will profit?' He turned away, beginning to pace and Jessaline could see, to her horror, that he was working up a good head of steam. 'You have a comely face, Mademoiselle Dumonde, and it does not escape me that dusky women such as yourself once seduced my forefathers into the most base acts, for which those men atoned by at least raising their half-breed children honourably. If I were a white man hoping to once more profit from the labour of an honest Creole like myself – one already proven gullible – I would send a woman just like you to do the tempting. To them, all of us are alike, even though I have the purest of French blood in my veins, and you might as well have come straight from the jungles of Africa!'

He rounded on her at this, very nearly shouting, and if Jessaline had been one of the pampered, cowed women of this land, she might have stepped back in fear of unpleasantness. As it was, she did take a step – but to the side, closer to her brocade bag, within which was tucked a neat little derringer, whose handle she could see from where she stood. Her mission had been to use Rillieux, not kill him, but she had no qualms about giving a man a flesh wound to remind him of the value of chivalry.

Before matters could come to a head, however, the parlour door opened, making both Jessaline and Norbert Rillieux jump. The young woman who came in was clearly some kin of Rillieux's; she had the same ocherine skin and loose-curled hair, the latter tucked into a graceful split chignon atop her head. Her eyes were softer, however, though that might have been an effect of the wire-rimmed spectacles perched atop her nose. She wore a simple grey dress, which had the unfortunate effect of emphasizing her natural pallor, and making her look rather plain.

'Your pardon, Brother,' she said, confirming Jessaline's guess. 'I thought perhaps you and your guest might like refreshment?' In her hands was a silver tray of crisp square beignets dusted in sugar, sliced merliton, with what looked like some sort of remoulade sauce, and tiny wedges of pecan penuche.

At the sight of this girl, Norbert blanched and looked properly abashed. 'Ah – er, yes, you're right, thank you.' He glanced at Jessaline, his earlier irritation clearly warring with his ingrained desire to be a good host; manners won, and he quickly composed himself. 'Forgive me. Will you take refreshment, before you leave?' The last part of that sentence came out harder than the rest. Jessaline got the message.

'Thank you, yes,' she said, immediately moving to assist the young woman. As she moved her brocade bag, she noticed the young woman's eyes, which were locked on the bag with a hint of alarm. Jessaline was struck at once with unease – had she noticed the derringer handle? Impossible to tell, since the young woman made no outcry of alarm, but that could have been just caution on her part. That one meeting of eyes had triggered an instant, instinctual assessment on Jessaline's part; *this* Rillieux, at least, was nowhere near as myopic or bombastic as her brother.

Indeed, as the young woman lifted her gaze after setting down the tray, Jessaline thought she saw a hint of challenge lurking behind those little round glasses and above that perfectly pleasant smile.

'Brother,' said the young woman, 'won't you introduce me? It's so rare for you to have lady guests.'

Norbert Rillieux went from blanching to blushing, and for an instant Jessaline feared he would progress all the way to bluster. Fortunately, he mastered the urge and, a little stiffly, said, 'Mademoiselle Jessaline Dumonde, may I present to you my younger sister, Eugenie?'

Jessaline bobbed a curtsy, which Mademoiselle Rillieux returned. 'I'm pleased to meet you,' Jessaline said, meaning it, *because I might have enjoyed shooting your brother to an unseemly degree, otherwise.*

It seemed Mademoiselle Rillieux's thoughts ran in the same direction, because she smiled at Jessaline and said, 'I hope my brother hasn't been treating you to a display of his famous temper, Mademoiselle Dumonde. He deals better with his gadgets and vacuum tubes than people, I'm afraid.'

Rillieux blustered at this. 'Eugenie, that's hardly—'

'Not at all,' Jessaline interjected smoothly. 'We were discussing the finer points of chemistry, and your brother, being such a learned man, just made his point rather emphatically.'

'Chemistry? Why, I adore chemistry!' At this, Mademoiselle Rillieux immediately brightened, speaking faster and breathlessly. 'What matter, if I may ask? Please, may I sit in?'

In that instant, Jessaline was struck by how lovely her eyes were, despite their uncertain colouring of browny green. She had never preferred the looks of half-white folk, having grown up in a land where, thanks to the Revolution, darkness of skin was a point of pride. But as Mademoiselle Rillieux spoke of chemistry, something in her manner made her peculiar eyes sparkle, and Jessaline was forced to reassess her initial estimate of the girl's looks. She was handsome, perhaps, rather than plain.

'Eugenie is the only other member of my family to share my interest in the sciences,' Rillieux said, pride warming his voice. 'She could not study in Paris as I did – the schools there do not admit women – but I made certain to send her all my books as I finished with them, and she critiques all my prototypes. It's probably for the best that they would not admit her; I daresay she could give my old masters at the École Centrale a run for their money!'

Jessaline blinked in surprise at this. Then it came to her; she had lost Rillieux's trust, but perhaps . . .

Turning to the beverage stand, she picked up the flask of effluent. 'I'm afraid I won't be able to stay, Mademoiselle Rillieux, but before I go, perhaps you could give me your opinion of this?' She offered the flask.

Norbert Rillieux, guessing her intent, scowled. But Eugenie took the flask before he could muster a protest, unstoppering it deftly and wafting the fumes towards her face rather than sniffing outright. 'Faugh,' she said, grimacing. 'Definitely hydrogen sulfide, and probably a number of other gases too, if this is the product of some form of decay.' She stoppered the flask and examined the sludge in its bottom with a critical eye. 'Interesting – I thought it was dirt, but this seems to be some more uniform substance. Something *made* this? What process could generate something so noxious?'

'Rum distillation,' Jessaline said, stifling the urge to smile when the Eugenie looked scandalized.

'No wonder,' Eugenie said darkly, 'given what the end product does to men's souls.' She handed the flask back to Jessaline. 'What of it?'

Jessaline was obliged to explain again, and as she did, a curious thing happened; Eugenie's eyes grew a bit glazed. She nodded, 'mmm-hmming' now and again. 'And as I mentioned to your brother,' Jessaline concluded, 'we have already worked out the formula— '

'The formula is child's play,' Eugenie said, flicking her fingers absently. 'And the extraction would be simple enough, if methane weren't dangerously flammable. Explosive even, under certain conditions, which most attempts at extraction would inevitably create. Obviously, any mechanical method would need to concern itself primarily with *stabilizing* the end products, not merely separating them. Freezing, perhaps, or . . .' She brightened. 'Brother, perhaps we could try a refinement of the vacuum-distillation process you developed for—'

'Yes, yes,' said Norbert, who had spent the past ten minutes looking from Jessaline to Eugenie and back in visibly increasing consternation. 'I'll consider it. In the meantime, Mademoiselle Dumonde was actually leaving; I'm afraid we delay her.' He glared at Jessaline as Eugenie made a moue of dismay.

'Quite right,' said Jessaline, smiling graciously at him; she put away the flask and tucked the bag over her arm, retrieving her hat from the back of the chair. She could afford to be gracious now, even though Norbert Rillieux had proved intractable. Better indeed to leave, and pursue the matter from an entirely different angle.

As Norbert escorted her to the parlour door with a hand rather too firm upon her elbow, Jessaline glanced back and smiled at Eugenie, who returned the smile with charming ruefulness and a shy little wave.

Not just handsome, pretty, Jessaline decided at last. And that meant this new angle would be most enjoyable to pursue.

There were, however, complications.

Jessaline, pleased that she had succeeded in making contact with *a* Rillieux, if not the one she'd come for, treated herself to an evening out in the Vieux Carré. It was not the done thing for a lady of gentle breeding – as she was emulating – to stop in at any of the rollicking music halls she could hear down side streets, though she was intrigued. She could, however, sit in on one of the new-fangled vaudevilles at the Playhouse, which she quite enjoyed, though it was difficult to see the stage well from the rear balcony. Then, as nightfall finally brought a breath of cool relief from the day's sweltering humidity, she returned to her room at the inn.

From time spent on the harder streets of Port-au-Prince, it was Jessaline's long-time habit to stand to one side of a door while she unlocked it, so that her shadow under the door would not alert anyone inside. This proved wise, as pushing open the door she found herself facing a startled male figure, which froze in silhouette before the room's picture window, near her travelling chest. They stared at one another for a breath, then

Jessaline's wits returned; at once she dropped to one knee, and in a single smooth sweep of her hand, brushed up her booted leg to palm a throwing knife.

In the same instant the figure bolted, darting towards the open balcony window. Jessaline hissed out a curse in her own Kreyòl tongue, running into the room as he lunged through the window with an acrobat's nimbleness, rolling to his feet and fetching up against the elaborately ironworked railing. Fearing to lose him, Jessaline flung the knife from within the room as she ran, praying it would strike, and heard the thunk as it hit flesh. The figure on her balcony stumbled, crying out, but she could not have hit a vital area, for he grasped the railing and pulled himself over it, dropping the short distance to the ground and out of sight.

Jessaline scrambled through the window as best she could, hampered by her bustle and skirts. Just as she reached the railing, the figure finished picking himself up from the ground and turned to run. Jessaline got one good look at him in the moonlight, as he turned back to see if she pursued: a pinch-faced youth, clearly pale beneath the bootblack he'd smeared on his face and straw-coloured hair to help himself hide in the dark. Then he was gone, running into the night, though he ran oddly and kept one of his hands clapped to his right buttock.

Furious, Jessaline pounded the railing, though she knew better than to make an outcry. No one in this town would care that some black woman had been robbed, and the constable would as likely arrest her for disturbing the peace.

Going back into her room, she lit the lanterns and surveyed the damage. At once a chill passed down her spine. The chest held a number of valuables that any sensible thief would've taken: fine dresses; a cameo pendant with a face of carved obsidian; the brass gyroscope that an old lover, a dirigible-navigator, had given her; a pearl-beaded purse containing twenty dollars. These, however, had all been shoved rudely aside, and to Jessaline's horror, the chest's false bottom had been lifted, revealing the compartment beneath. There was nothing here but a bundle of clothing and a larger pouch, containing a far more substantial sum – but that had not been taken either.

Jessaline knew what *would* have been in there, if she had not taken them with her to see Rillieux: the scrolls that held the chemical formula for the methane-extraction process, and the rudimentary designs for the mechanism to do so – the best her government's scientists had been able to cobble together. Even now these were at the bottom of her brocade bag.

The bootblack-boy had been no thief. Someone in this foul city knew who and what she was, and sought to thwart her mission.

Carefully Jessaline replaced everything in the trunk, including the false bottom and money. She went downstairs and paid her bill, then hired a porter to carry her trunk to an inn two blocks over, where she rented a room without windows. She slept lightly that night, waking with every creak and thump, and took comfort only from the solid security of the stiletto in her hand.

The lovely thing about a town full of slaves, vagabonds, beggars and blackguards was that it was blessedly easy to send a message in secret.

Having waited a few days so as to let Norbert Rillieux's anger cool – just in case – Jessaline hired a child who was one of the innkeepers' slaves. She purchased fresh fruit at the market and offered the child an apple to memorize her message. When he repeated it back to her word for word, she showed him a bunch of big blue-black grapes, and his eyes went wide. 'Get word to Mademoiselle Eugenie without her brother knowing, and these are yours,' she said. 'You'll have to make sure to spit the seeds in the fire, though, or Master will know you've had a treat.'

The boy grinned, and Jessaline saw that the warning had not been necessary. 'Just you hold on to those, Miss Jessaline,' he replied, pointing with his chin at the grapes. 'I'll have 'em in a minute or three.'

And indeed, within an hour's time he returned, carrying a small folded square of cloth. 'Miss Eugenie agrees to meet,' he said, 'and sends this as a surety of her good faith.' He pronounced this last carefully, perfectly emulating the Creole woman's tone.

Pleased, Jessaline took the cloth and unfolded it to find a handkerchief of fine imported French linen, embroidered in one corner with a tiny perfect 'R'. She held it to her nose and smelled a perfume like magnolia blossoms; the same scent had been about Eugenie the other day. She could not help smiling at the memory. The boy grinned, too, and ate a handful of the grapes at once, pocketing the seeds with a wink.

'Gonna plant these near the city dump,' he said. 'Maybe I'll bring you wine one day!' And he ran off.

So Jessaline found herself on another bright sweltering day at the convent of the Ursulines, where two gentlewomen might walk and exchange thoughts in peace without being seen or interrupted by curious others.

'I have to admit,' said Eugenie, smiling sidelong at Jessaline as they strolled amid the nuns' garden, 'I was of two minds about whether to meet you.'

'I suppose your brother must've given you an earful after I left.'

'You might say so,' Eugenie said, in a dry tone that made Jessaline laugh. (One of the old nuns glowered at them over a bed of herbs. Jessaline covered her mouth and waved apology.) 'But that wasn't what gave me pause. My brother has his ways, Mademoiselle Jessaline, and I do not always agree with him. He's fond of forming opinions without full information, then proceeding as if they are proven fact.' She shrugged. 'I, on the other hand, prefer to seek as much information as I can. I have made enquiries about you, you see.'

'Oh? And what did you find?'

'That you do not exist, as far as anyone in this town knows.' She spoke lightly, Jessaline noticed, but there was an edge to her words, too. Unease, perhaps. 'You aren't one of us, that much anyone can see; but you aren't a freed woman either, though the people at your old inn and the market seemed to think so.'

At this, Jessaline blinked with a surprise and unease of her own. She had not thought the girl would dig *that* deeply. 'What makes you say that?'

'For one, that pistol in your bag.'

Jessaline froze for a pace before remembering to keep walking. 'A lady alone in a strange, rough city would be wise to look to her own protection, don't you think?'

'True,' said Eugenie, 'but I checked at the courthouse, and there are no records of a woman meeting your description having bought her way free anytime in the past thirty years, and I doubt you're far past that age. For another, you hide it well, but your French has an odd sort of lilt; not at all like that of folk hereabouts. And thirdly, this is a small town at heart, Mademoiselle Dumonde, despite its size. Every time some fortunate soul buys free, as they say, it's the talk of the town. To put it bluntly, there's no gossip about you, and there should have been.'

They had reached a massive old willow tree, which partially overhung the garden path. There was no way around it; the tree's draping branches had made a proper curtain of things, nearly obscuring from sight the area about the trunk.

The sensible thing to do would have been to turn around and walk back the way they'd come, but as Jessaline turned to meet Eugenie's eyes, she suffered another of those curious epiphanies. Eugenie was smiling sweetly, but despite this there was a hard look in her eyes, which reminded Jessaline fleetingly of Norbert. It was clear that she meant to have the truth from Jessaline, or Jessaline's efforts to employ her would get short shrift.

On impulse Jessaline grabbed Eugenie's hand and pulled her into the willow-fall. Eugenie yelped in surprise, then giggled as they came through into the space beyond, green-shrouded and encircling, like a hurricane of leaves.

'What on earth—? Mademoiselle Dumonde—'

'It isn't Dumonde,' Jessaline said, dropping her voice to a near-whisper. 'My name is Jessaline Cleré. That is the name of the family that raised me, at least, but I should have had a different name, after the man who was my true father. His name was L'Overture. Do you know it?'

At that, Eugenie drew a sharp breath. 'Toussaint the Rebel?' she asked. 'The man who led the Revolution in Haiti? *He* was your father?'

'So my mother says, though she was only his mistress; I am natural-born. But I do not begrudge her, because her status spared me. When the French betrayed Toussaint, they took him and his wife and legitimate children and carried them across the sea to torture to death.'

Eugenie put her hands to her mouth at this, which Jessaline had to admit was a bit much for a gently raised woman to bear. Yet it was the truth, for Jessaline felt uncomfortable dissembling with Eugenie, for reasons she could not quite name.

'I see,' Eugenie said at last, recovering. 'Then, these interests you represent. You are with the Haitians.'

'I am. If you build a methane extraction mechanism for us, Mademoiselle, you will have helped a nation of free folk *stay* free, for I swear that France is hell-bent upon re-enslaving us all. They would have done it already, if one of our number had not thought to use our torment to our advantage.'

Eugenie nodded slowly. 'The sugarcane,' she said. 'The papers say your people use the steam and gases from the distilleries to make hot-air balloons and blimps.'

'Which helped us bomb the French ships most effectively during the Revolution, and also secured our position as the foremost manufacturers of dirigibles in the Americas,' Jessaline said with some pride. 'We were saved by a mad idea and a contraption that should have killed its first user. So we value cleverness now, Mademoiselle, which is why I came here in search of your brother.'

'Then,' Eugenie frowned, 'the methane, it is to power your dirigibles?'

'Partly. The French have begun using them, too, you see. Our only hope is to enhance the manoeuvrability and speed of our craft, which can be done with gas-powered engines. We have also crafted powerful artillery, which use this engine design, whose range and accuracy is unsurpassed. The prototypes work magnificently, but the price of the oil and coal we must currently use to power them is too dear. We would bankrupt ourselves buying it from the very nations that hope to destroy us. Rum effluent is our only abundant, inexpensive resource – our only hope.'

Eugenie had begun to shake her head, looking taken aback. 'Artillery? *Guns*, you mean?' she said. 'I am a Christian woman, Mademoiselle—'

'Jessaline.'

'Very well; Jessaline.' That look was on her face again, Jessaline noted; that air of determination and fierceness that made her beautiful at the oddest times. 'I do not care for the idea of my skills being put to use in taking lives. That's simply unacceptable.'

Jessaline stared at her, and for an instant fury blotted out thought. How dare this girl, with her privilege, wealth and coddled life . . . Jessaline set her jaw.

'In the Revolution,' she said in a low, tight voice, 'the last French commander, Rochambeau, decided to teach my people a lesson for daring to revolt against our betters. Do you know what he did? He took slaves – including those who had not even fought – and broke them on the wheel, raising them on a post afterwards, so the birds could eat them alive. He also buried prisoners of war alive in pits of insects, and boiled some of them in vats of molasses. Such acts, he deemed, were necessary to put fear and subservience back into our hearts, since we had been tainted by a year of freedom.'

Eugenie, who had gone quite pale, stared at Jessaline in purest horror, her mouth open.

Jessaline smiled a hard, angry smile. 'Such atrocities will happen again, Mademoiselle Rillieux, if you do not help us. Except this time we have been free for two generations. Imagine how much fear and subservience these *Christian* men will instill in us now?'

Eugenie shook her head slowly. 'I . . . I had not heard . . . I did not consider . . .' She fell mute.

Jessaline stepped closer and laid one lace-gloved finger on the divot between Eugenie's collarbones. 'You had best consider such things, my dear. Do you forget? There are those in this land who would like to do the same to you and all your kin.'

Eugenie stared at her. Then, startling Jessaline, she dropped to the ground, sitting down so hard that her bustle made an aggrieved creaking sound.

'I did not know,' she said at last. 'I did not know these things.'

Jessaline beheld the honest shock on her face and felt some guilt for having troubled her so. It was clear the girl's brother had worked hard to protect her from the world's harshness. Sitting beside Eugenie on the soft dry grass, she let out a weary sigh.

'In my land,' she said, 'men and women of *all* shades are free. I will not pretend that this makes us perfect – I have gone hungry many times in my life – yet there, a woman such as yourself may be more than the coddled sister of a prominent scientist, or the mistress of a white man.'

Eugenie threw her a guilty look, but Jessaline smiled to reassure her. The women of Eugenie's class had few options in life, and Jessaline saw no point in condemning them for this.

'So many men died in the Revolution that women fill the ranks now as dirigible pilots and gunners. We run factories and farms, too, and are highly placed in government. Even the bokors are mostly women now – you have vodoun here, too, yes? So we are important.' She leaned close, her shoulder brushing Eugenie's in a teasing way, and grinned. 'Some of us might even become spies. Who knows?'

Eugenie's cheeks flamed pink and she ducked her head to smile. Jessaline could see, however, that her words were having some effect; Eugenie had that oddly absent look again. Perhaps she was imagining all the things she could do in a land where the happenstances of sex and caste did not forbid her from using her mind to its fullest? A shame – Jessaline would have loved to take her there, but she had seen the luxury of the Rillieux household; why would any woman give that up?

This close, shoulder to shoulder and secluded within the willow tree's green canopy, Jessaline found herself staring at Eugenie, more aware than ever of the scent of her perfume, the nearby softness of her skin and the way the curls of her hair framed her long slender neck. At least she did not cover her hair, like so many women of this land, convinced that its natural state was inherently ugly. She could not help her circumstances, but it seemed to Jessaline that she had taken what pride in her heritage she could.

So taken was Jessaline by this notion, and by the silence and strangeness of the moment, that she found herself saying, 'And in my land it is not uncommon for a woman to head a family with another woman, and even raise children if they so wish.'

Eugenie started, and to Jessaline's delight, her blush deepened. She darted a half-scandalized, half-entranced look at Jessaline, then away, which Jessaline found deliciously fetching. 'Live with . . . another woman? Do you mean . . . ?' Of course she knew what Jessaline meant. 'How can that be?'

'The necessities of security and shared labour. The priests look the other way.'

Eugenie looked up then, and Jessaline was surprised to see a peculiar daring enter her expression, though her flush lingered. 'And . . .' She licked her lips and swallowed. 'Do such women, ah, behave as a family in . . . *all* matters?'

A slow grin spread across Jessaline's face. Not so sheltered in her thoughts at least, this one! 'Oh, certainly. All matters – legal, financial, domestic . . .' Then, as a hint of uncertainty flickered in Eugenie's expression, Jessaline got tired of teasing. It was not proper, she knew; it was not within the bounds of her mission, but – just this once – perhaps . . .

She shifted just a little, from brushing shoulders to pressing rather more suggestively close, and leaned near, her eyes fixed on Eugenie's lips. 'And conjugal,' she added.

Eugenie stared at her, eyes huge behind her spectacles. 'C– conjugal?' she asked, rather breathlessly.

'Oh, indeed. Perhaps a demonstration . . .'

But just as Jessaline leaned in to offer one, she was startled by the voice of one of the nuns, apparently calling to another in French. From far too near the willow tree, a third voice rose to shush the first two; it was the prying old biddy who'd given Jessaline the eye before.

Eugenie jumped, her face red as plums, and quickly shifted away from Jessaline. Privately cursing, Jessaline did the same, and an awkward silence fell.

'W–well,' said Eugenie, 'I had best be getting back. I told my brother I would be at the seamstress's, and that doesn't take long.'

'Yes,' Jessaline said, realizing with some consternation that she'd completely forgotten why she'd asked for a meeting in the first place. 'Well. Ah. I have something I'd like to offer you, but I would advise you to keep these out of sight, even at home where servants might see – for your own safety.' She reached into the brocade bag and handed Eugenie the small cylindrical leather container that held the formula and plans for the methane extractor. 'This is what we have come up with thus far, but the design is incomplete. If you can offer any assistance— '

'Yes, of course,' Eugenie said, taking the case with an avid look that heartened Jessaline at once. She tucked the leather case into her purse. 'Allow me a few days to consider the problem. How may I contact you, though, once I've devised a solution?'

'I will contact you in one week. Do not look for me.' She got to her feet and offered her hand to help Eugenie up. Then, speaking loudly enough to be heard outside the willow at last, she giggled. 'Before your brother learns we've been swapping tales about him!'

Eugenie looked blank for a moment, then grinned and opened her mouth in an 'o' of understanding. 'Oh, his ego could use a bit of flattening, I think. In any case, fare you well, Mademoiselle Dumonde. I must be on my way.' And with that, she hurried off, holding her hat as she passed through the willow branches.

Jessaline waited for ten breaths, then stepped out herself, sparing a hard look for the old nun who, sure enough, had moved quite a bit closer to the tree. 'A good afternoon to you, Sister,' she said.

'And to you,' the woman said in a low voice, 'though you had best be more careful from now on, *estipid*.'

Startled to hear her own tongue on the old woman's lips, she stiffened. Then, carefully, she said in the same language, 'And what would you know of it?'

'I know you have a dangerous enemy,' the nun replied, getting to her feet and dusting dirt off her habit. Now that Jessaline could see her better, it was clear from her features that she had a dollop or two of African in her. 'I am sent by your superiors to warn you. We have word that the Order of the White Camelia is active in the city.'

Jessaline caught her breath. The bootblack man! 'I may have encountered them already,' she said.

The old woman nodded grimly. 'Word had it they broke apart after that scandal we arranged for them up in Baton Rouge,' she said, 'but in truth they've just become more subtle. We don't know what they're after, but obviously they don't just want to *kill* you, or you would be dead by now.'

'I am not so easily removed, madame,' Jessaline said, drawing herself up in affront.

The old woman rolled her eyes. 'Just take care,' she snapped. 'And by all means, if you want that girl dead, continue playing silly lovers' games with her where any fool can suspect.' And with that, the old woman picked up her spade and shears and briskly walked away.

Jessaline did the same, her cheeks burning. But back in her room, ostensibly safe, she leaned against the door and closed her eyes, wondering why her heart still fluttered so fast now that Eugenie was long gone, and why she was suddenly so afraid.

The Order of the White Camelia changed everything. Jessaline had heard tales of them for years, of course – a secret society of wealthy professionals and intellectuals dedicated to the preservation of 'American ideals', such as the superiority of the white race. They had been responsible for the exposure – and deaths, in some cases – of many of Jessaline's fellow spies over the years. America was built on slavery, so naturally the White Camelias would oppose a nation built on slavery's overthrow.

Consequently, Jessaline decided on new tactics. She shifted her attire from that of a well-to-do freed woman to the plainer garb of a woman of less means. This elicited no attention as there were plenty such women in the city, though she was obliged to move to yet another inn that would suit her appearance. This drew her into the less-respectable area of the city, where not a few of the patrons took rooms by the hour or the half day.

Here she laid low for the next few days, trying to determine whether she was being watched, though she spotted no suspicious characters – or at least, no one suspicious for the area. Which, of course, was why she'd chosen it. White men frequented the inn, but a white face that lingered or appeared repeatedly would be remarked upon and easy to spot.

When a week had passed and Jessaline felt safe, she radically transformed herself using the bundle that had been hidden beneath her chest's false bottom. First, she hid her close-cropped hair beneath a lumpy calico headwrap and donned an ill-fitting dress of worn, stained gingham, patched here and there with burlap. A few small pillows rendered her effectively shapeless – a necessity, since in this disguise it was dangerous to be attractive in any way. As she slipped out in the small hours of the morning, carrying her belongings in a satchel and shuffling to make herself look much older, no one paid her any heed – not the drowsy old men sitting guard at the stables, nor the city constables chatting up a gaudily dressed woman under a gas lamp, nor the young toughs still dicing on the corner. She was, for all intents and purposes, invisible.

First she milled among the morning-market crowds at the waterfront awhile, keeping an eye out for observers. When she was certain she hadn't been followed, she made her way to the dirigible docks, where four of the great machines hovered above a cluster of cargo vessels like huge, sausage-shaped guardian angels. A massive brick fence screened the docks themselves from view, though this had a secondary purpose: the docks were the sovereign territory of the Haitian Republic, housing its embassy as well. No American-born slave was permitted to step upon even this proxy version of Haitian soil, since by the laws of Haiti they would then be free.

Yet practicality did not stop men and women from dreaming, and near the massive ironwork gate of the facility there was, as usual, a small crowd of slaves gathered, gazing in enviously at the shouting dirigible crews and their smartly dressed officers. Jessaline slipped in among these and edged her way to the front, then waited.

Presently, a young runner detached herself from the nearby rope crew and ran over to the fence. Several of the slaves pushed envelopes through the fence, commissioning travel and shipping on behalf of their owners, and the girl collected these. The whole operation was conducted in utter silence, and an American soldier hovered all too near the gate, ready to report any slave who talked. It was not illegal to talk, but any slave who did so would likely suffer for it.

Yet Jessaline noted that the runner met the eyes of every person she could, nodding to each solemnly, touching more hands than was strictly necessary for the sake of her work. A small taste of respect for those who needed it so badly, so that they might come to crave it and eventually seek it for themselves.

Jessaline met the runner's eyes, too, as she pushed through a plain, wrinkled envelope, but her gaze held none of the desperate hope of the others. The runner's eyes widened a bit, but she moved on at once after taking Jessaline's envelope. When she trotted away to deliver the commissions, Jessaline saw her shuffle the pile to put the wrinkled envelope on top.

That done, Jessaline headed to the Rillieux house. At the back gate, she shifted her satchel from her shoulder to her hands, re-tying it so as to make it square-shaped. To the servant who then answered her knock – freeborn; the Rillieuxs did not go in for the practice of owning slaves themselves – she said in coarse French, 'Package for Mademoiselle Rillieux. I was told to deliver it to her personal.'

The servant, a cleanly dressed fellow who could barely conceal his distaste at Jessaline's appearance, frowned further. '*English*, woman, only high-class folk talk French here.' But when Jessaline deliberately spoke in butchered English, rendered barely comprehensible by an exaggerated French accent, the man finally rolled his eyes and stood aside. 'She's in the garden house. Back there. There!' And he pointed the way.

Thus did Jessaline come to the overlarge shed that sat amid the house's vast garden. It had clearly been meant to serve as a hothouse at some point, having a glass ceiling, but when Jessaline stepped inside she was assailed by sounds most unnatural: clanks and squealing and the rattling hiss of a steam boiler. These came from the equipment and incomprehensible machinery that lined every wall and hung from the ceiling, pipes and clockwork big enough to crush a man, all of it churning merrily away.

At the centre of this chaos stood several high worktables, each bearing equipment in various states of construction or dismantlement, save the last. At this table, which sat in a shaft of gathering sunlight, sat a sleeping Eugenie Rillieux.

At the sight of her, Jessaline stopped, momentarily overcome by a most uncharacteristic anxiety. Eugenie's head rested on her folded arms, atop a sheaf of large, irregular sheets of parchment that were practically covered with pen scribbles and diagrams. Her hair was amuss, her glasses askew, and she had drooled a bit on to one of her pale, ink-stained hands.

Beautiful, Jessaline thought, and marvelled at herself. Her tastes had never leaned towards women like Eugenie, pampered and sheltered and shy. She generally preferred women like herself, who could be counted upon to know what they wanted and take decisive steps to get it. Yet in that moment, gazing upon this awkward, brilliant creature, Jessaline wanted nothing more than to be holding flowers instead of a fake package, and to have come for courting rather than her own selfish motives.

Perhaps Eugenie felt the weight of her longing, for after a moment she wrinkled her nose and sat up. 'Oh,' she said blearily, seeing Jessaline. 'What is it, a delivery? Put it on the table there, please; I'll fetch you a tip.' She got up, and Jessaline was amused to see that her bustle was askew.

'Eugenie,' she said, and Eugenie whirled back as she recognized Jessaline's voice. Her eyes flew wide.

'What in heaven's name—'

'I haven't much time,' she said, hastening forward. She took Eugenie's hands in quick greeting, and resisted the urge to kiss her as well. 'Have you been able to refine the plans?'

'Oh – yes, yes, I think.' Eugenie pushed her glasses straight and gestured towards the papers that had served as her pillow. 'This design should work, at least in theory. I was right; the vacuum-distillation mechanism was the key! Of course, I haven't finished the prototype, because the damned glassmaker is trying to charge pirates' rates—'

Jessaline squeezed her hands, exhilarated. 'Marvellous! Don't worry; we shall test the design thoroughly before we put it into use. But now I must have the plans. Men are searching for me; I dare not stay in town much longer.'

Eugenie nodded absently, then blinked again as her head cleared. She narrowed her eyes at Jessaline in sudden suspicion. 'Wait,' she said. 'You're leaving town?'

'Yes, of course,' Jessaline said, surprised. 'This is what I came for, after all. I can't just put something so important on the next dirigible packet—'

The look of hurt that came over Eugenie's face sent a needle straight into Jessaline's heart. She realized, belatedly and with guilty dismay, what Eugenie must have been imagining all this time.

'But . . . I thought . . .' Eugenie looked away suddenly and bit her lower lip. 'You might stay.'

'Eugenie,' Jessaline began uncomfortably. 'I . . . could never have remained here. This place . . . the way you live here . . .'

'Yes, I know.' At once Eugenie's voice hardened; she glared at Jessaline. 'In your perfect, wonderful land, everyone is free to live as they please. It is the rest of us, then, the poor wretched folk you scorn and pity, who have no choice but to endure it. Perhaps we should never bother to love at all, then! That way, at least, when we are used and cast aside, it will be for material gain!' And with that, she slapped Jessaline smartly and walked out. Stunned, Jessaline put a hand to her cheek and stared after her.

'Trouble in paradise?' said a voice behind her in a syrupy drawl.

Jessaline whirled round to find herself facing a six-shooter. And holding it, his face free of bootblack this time, was the young man who had invaded her quarters nearly two weeks earlier.

'I heard you Haitians were unnatural,' he said, coming into the light, 'but this? Not at all what I was expecting.'

Not me, Jessaline realized, too late. *They were watching Rillieux, not me!* 'Natural is in the eye of the beholder, as is beauty,' she snapped.

'True. Speaking of beauty, though, you looked a damn sight finer before. What's all this?' He sidled forward, poking with the gun at the padding around Jessaline's middle. 'So that's it! But . . .' To Jessaline's fury, he raised the gun and poked at her breasts none-too-gently.

'Ah, no padding here. Yes, I do remember you rightly.' He scowled. 'I still can't sit down thanks to you, woman. Maybe I ought to repay you that.'

Jessaline raised her hands slowly, pulling off her lumpy headwrap so he could see her more clearly. 'That's ungentlemanly of you, I would say.'

'Gentlemen need gentle*women*,' he said. 'Your kind are hardly that, being good for only one thing. Well – that and lynching, I suppose. But we'll save both for later, won't we? After you've met my superior and told us everything that's in your nappy little head. He's partial to your variety. I, however, feel that if I must lower myself to baseness, better to do it with one bearing the fair blood of the French.'

It took Jessaline a moment to understand his meaning through all his airs. But then she did, and shivered in purest rage. 'You will not lay a finger upon Eugenie. I'll snap them all off fir—'

But before she could finish her threat, there was a scream and commotion from the house. The scream, amid all the chaos of shouting and running servants, she recognized at once: Eugenie.

The noise startled the bootblack man as well. Fortunately he did not pull the trigger, though he did start badly, half turning to point the gun in the direction of Eugenie's scream. Which was all the opening Jessaline needed, as she drew her derringer from the wadded cloth of her headwrap and shot the man point-blank. He cried out, clutching his chest as he fell to the ground.

The derringer was spent; it carried only a single bullet. Snatching up the bootblack man's six-gun instead, Jessaline turned to sprint towards the Rillieux house – then froze for an instant in terrible indecision. Behind her, on Eugenie's table, sat the plans for which she had spent the past three months of her life striving, stealing and sneaking. The methane extractor could be the salvation of her nation, the start of its brightest future.

And in the house . . .

Eugenie, she thought, and started running.

* * *

In the parlour, Norbert Rillieux was frozen, paler than usual and trembling. Before him, holding Eugenie about the throat and with a gun to her head, was a white man whose face was so floridly familiar that Jessaline gasped. 'Raymond Forstall?'

He started badly as Jessaline rounded the door, and she froze as well, fearing to cause Eugenie's death. Very slowly, she set the six-gun on a nearby sideboard, pushed it so that it slid out of easy reach and raised her hands to show that she was no threat. At this, Forstall relaxed.

'So we meet again, my beauteous negress,' he said, though there was anger in his smile. 'I had hoped to make your acquaintance under more favourable circumstances. Alas.'

'*You* are with the White Camelia?' He had seemed so gormless that day on Royal Street; not at all the sort Jessaline would associate with a murderous secret society.

'I am indeed,' he said. 'And you would have met the rest of us if my assistant had not clearly failed in his goal of taking you captive. Nevertheless, I too have a goal, and I ask again, sir, *where are the plans?*'

Jessaline realized belatedly that this was directed at Norbert Rillieux, and he, too frightened to bluster, just shook his head. 'I told you, I have built no such device! Ask this woman – she wanted it and I refused her!'

The methane extractor, Jessaline realized. Of course – they had known, probably via their own spies, that she was after it. Forstall had been tailing her the day he'd bumped into her, probably all the way to Rillieux's house. She cursed herself for a fool for not realizing. But the White Camelias were mostly philosophers, bankers and lawyers, not the trained, proficient spies she'd been expecting to deal with. It had never occurred to her that an enemy would be so clumsy as to jostle and converse with his target in the course of surveillance.

'It's true,' Jessaline said, stalling desperately in hope that some solution would present itself to her. 'This man refused my request to build the device.'

'Then why did you come back here?' Forstall asked, tightening his grip on Eugenie so that she gasped. 'We had men watching the house servants, too. We intercepted orders for metal parts and rubber tubing, and I paid the glassmaker to delay an order for custom vacuum pipes.'

'*You* did that?' To Jessaline's horror, Eugenie stiffened in Forstall's grasp, trying to turn and glare at him in her affront. 'I argued with that old fool for an hour!'

'Eugenie, be still!' cried Norbert, which raised him high in Jessaline's estimation, since she had wanted to shout the same thing.

'I will not—' Eugenie began to struggle, plainly furious. As Forstall cursed and tried to restrain her, Jessaline heard Eugenie's protests continue. ' . . . interference with my work . . . very idea . . .'

Please, Holy Mother, Jessaline thought, taking a very careful step closer to the gun on the sideboard, *don't let him shoot her to shut her up*.

When Forstall finally thrust Eugenie aside – she fell against the bottle-strewn side table, nearly toppling it – and raised the gun to shoot her, Jessaline blurted, 'Wait!'

Both Forstall and Eugenie froze, now separated and facing each other, though Forstall's gun was still pointed at Eugenie's chest. 'The plans are complete,' Jessaline said to him. 'They are in the workshop out back.' With a hint of pride, she looked at Eugenie and added, 'Eugenie has made it work.'

'What?' said Rillieux, looking thunderstruck.

'What?' Forstall stared at her, then Eugenie, and then anger filled his expression. 'Clever indeed! And while I go out back to check if your story is true, you will make your escape with the plans already tucked into your clothes.'

'I am not lying in this instance,' she said, 'but if you like, we can all proceed to the garden and see. Or, since I'm the one you seem to fear most . . .' She waggled her empty hands in mockery, hoping this would make him too angry to notice how much closer she was to the gun on the sideboard. His face reddened further with fury. 'You could leave Eugenie and her brother here, and take me alone.'

Eugenie caught her breath. 'Jessaline, are you mad?'

'Yes,' Jessaline said, and smiled, letting her heart live in her face for a moment. Eugenie's mouth fell open, then softened into a small smile. Her glasses were still askew, Jessaline saw with a rush of fondness.

Forstall rolled his eyes, but smiled. 'A capital suggestion, I think. Then I can shoot you—'

He got no further, for in the next instant Eugenie struck him in the head with a rum bottle. The bottle shattered on impact. Forstall cried out, half-stunned by the blow and the sting of rum in his eyes, but he managed to keep his grip on the gun, keeping it trained more or less on Eugenie. Jessaline thought she saw the muscles in his forearm flex to pull the trigger – and then the six-gun was in her hand, its wooden grip warm and almost comforting as she blew a hole in Raymond Forstall's rum-drenched head. Forstall uttered a horrid gurgling sound and fell to the floor.

Before his body stopped twitching, Jessaline caught Eugenie's hand. 'Hurry!' She dragged the other woman out of the parlour. Norbert, again to his credit, started out of shock and trotted after them, for once silent as they moved through the house's corridors towards the garden. The house was nearly deserted now, the servants having fled or found some place to hide that was safe from gunshots and madmen.

'You must tell me which of the papers on your desk I can take,' Jessaline said as they trotted along, 'and then you must make a decision.'

'Wh–what decision?' Eugenie still sounded shaken.

'Whether you will stay here – or come with me to Haiti.'

'*Haiti*?' Norbert cried.

'Haiti?' Eugenie asked in wonder.

'Haiti,' said Jessaline, and as they passed through the rear door and into the garden, she stopped and turned to Eugenie. 'With me.'

Eugenie stared at her in such dawning amazement that Jessaline could no longer help herself. She caught Eugenie about the waist, pulled her near and kissed her most soundly and improperly, right there in front of her brother. It was the sweetest, wildest kiss she had ever known in her life.

When she pulled back, Norbert was standing at the edge of her vision with his mouth open and Eugenie looked a bit faint.

'Well,' Eugenie said and fell silent, the whole affair having been a bit much for her.

Jessaline grinned and let her go, then hurried forward to enter the workshop – and froze, horror shattering her good mood.

The bootblack man was gone. Where his body had been lay Jessaline's derringer and copious blood, trailing away . . . to Eugenie's worktable, where the plans had been and were no longer. The trail then led through the workshop's rear door.

'No,' she whispered, her fists clenching at her sides. 'No, by God!' Everything she had worked for, gone. She had failed, both her mission and her people.

'Very well,' Eugenie said after a moment. 'Then I shall simply have to come with you.'

The words penetrated Jessaline's despair slowly. 'What?'

She touched Jessaline's hand. 'I will come with you. To Haiti. And I will build an even more efficient methane extractor for you there.'

Jessaline turned to stare at her and found that she could not, for her eyes had filled with tears.

'Wait!' Norbert caught his breath as understanding dawned. 'Go to Haiti? Are you mad? I forbid—'

'You had better come too, brother,' Eugenie said, turning to him, and Jessaline was struck breathless once more by the cool determination in her eyes. 'The police will take their time about it, but they will come eventually, and a white man lies dead in our house. It doesn't really matter whether you shot him or not; you know full well what they'll decide.'

Norbert stiffened, for he did indeed know – probably better than Eugenie, Jessaline suspected – what his fate would be.

Eugenie turned to Jessaline. 'He *can* come, can't he?' Jessaline knew this was a condition, not an option.

'Of course he can,' she said at once. 'I wouldn't leave a dog to these people's justice. But it will not be the life you're used to, either of you. Are you certain?'

Eugenie smiled, and before Jessaline realized what was imminent, she had been pulled rather roughly into another kiss. Eugenie had been eating penuche again, she realized dimly, and then for a long perfect moment she thought of nothing but pecans and sweetness.

When it was done, Eugenie searched Jessaline's face, then smiled in satisfaction. 'Perhaps we should go, Jessaline,' she said gently.

'Ah. Yes. We should, yes.' Jessaline fought to compose herself; she glanced at Norbert and took a deep breath. 'Fetch us a hansom cab while you still can, Monsieur Rillieux, and we'll go down to the docks and take the next dirigible southbound.'

The daze cleared from Norbert's eyes as well; he nodded mutely and trotted off.

In the silence that fell, Eugenie turned to Jessaline.

'Marriage,' she said, 'and a house together. I believe you mentioned that?'

'Er,' said Jessaline, blinking. 'Well, yes, I suppose, but I rather thought that first we would—'

'Good,' Eugenie replied, 'because I'm not fond of you keeping up this dangerous line of work. My inventions should certainly earn enough for the both of us, don't you think?'

'Um,' said Jessaline.

'Yes. So there's no reason for you to work when I can keep you in comfort for the rest of your days.' Taking Jessaline's hands, she stepped closer, her eyes softening again. 'And I am so very much looking forward to those days.'

'Yes,' said Jessaline, who had been wondering just which of her many sins had earned her this mad fortune. But as Eugenie's warm breast pressed against hers, and the thick perfume of the magnolia trees wafted around them, and some clockwork contraption within the workshop ticked in time with her heart, Jessaline stopped worrying. And she wondered why she had ever bothered with plans and papers and gadgetry, because it was clear she had just stolen the greatest prize of all.

A KISS IN THE RAIN

O. M. Grey

He still felt the kiss from that rainy London night, but the magic it promised had become his nightmare. They had each forgotten their umbrellas, quite a foolish thing, so they had stood under an awning and got to talking while waiting for the storm to pass. The grey cobblestones shone like silver, and all he had heard was the clip-clop of horses hooves, the patter of the drops hitting the awning and his breath coming quicker with each passing moment, as he stood there next to that remarkable lady. The rain sprinkled down between the cracks of one building and the next, the only thing that had separated them on that fateful night. No chaperones were about, quite scandalous all around.

Her beauty and obvious grace had infused him with wonder. Watching her talk sent waves of joy through his soul. The sound of her voice, as melodic as the finest symphony. The way she smiled as she spoke, lighting his world. The way her lips formed the words and the way her passionate hands punctuated her story. Her green eyes twinkled as she spoke about her writing, and it had sparked something deep inside him, an immediate connection, such as he had never known. As he had watched her mouth move, talking about the inspiration behind her poetry, he could think of nothing else but wanting to kiss her, wanting to feel those lips on his own. After gaining the courage to reveal his desire, he had stammered and stumbled over his words when he said he wanted to kiss her.

She did not say a word, just smiled and tilted her head down, hiding the blush that had risen in her cheeks. Then, to his great surprise, she leaned towards him, and the raindrops decorated her black hair with little points of light when she crossed the watery barrier, mesmerizing him. He had met her halfway, and he recalled the softness of her lips and the excitement that had coursed through him as she parted them, inviting him deeper. Their tongues had brushed together, just for the briefest moment, and it stirred something at the core of his heart.

He remembered their first kiss, as if that magical night had passed mere moments ago. Then he sighed a piteous sigh as he remembered the last one.

'Professor,' said a man from the audience, and it snapped Eliot out of his bittersweet memory. With horror, he realized that he had actually stopped talking this time. He had done this demonstration so often he could do it by heart, thinking about anything and just letting his mouth form the familiar words. But not today. She consumed his thoughts, as she always did, but since she rested so close to this ancient church, sentimentality overwhelmed him. A useless emotion, but nonetheless . . .

'Forgive me, dear sir. Where was I?' Eliot looked down at the table full of his experiments and tried to remember where he had left off. The tiny purple lightning bolts still reached their electric arms from one coil to the other, but Eliot could not remember the last thing he had said aloud. His notes lay open beside the electric mechanisms, scribbled in his own hand, but he had no idea how to continue. Focus, Eliot, he chided himself, but still she haunted his thoughts. As the room of well-dressed people looked up at him with eyes full of expectation, Eliot pulled a handkerchief out of the tailcoat's breast pocket and mopped the nervous sweat from his brow.

As his thoughts scrambled to find his place, the utter silence in the back room of the stone church increased his mental pressure. Tall and thin, most would say lanky, he became all arms, knocking over one of the coils and breaking its electric connection. He shrunk, standing before them on the stage, scrutinized by all those waiting faces. Some began to fidget in impatience; others checked their time pieces as he set his experiment back to rights. Then a solitary giggle made everything much worse. Hot under the collar with his embarrassment, he looked up, mortified to think that someone had actually laughed at his folly. The chortle had come from his wife in the back corner, chatting with her lady friends. Gossiping and talking through his demonstration again, and now she had the audacity to snicker during this unending moment of utmost humiliation. There was something wrong there. A lack of respect, to say the least. Quite rude, actually. Certainly she had heard the lecture many times, as he did have a tendency to prattle on about his experiments, but she was his wife after all. She rested her hand on her distended belly, carrying his unborn child, but he felt no love for her in that moment, only resentment.

'Professor?' the same man said, this time with an annoyed clearing of the throat before he said the word with an impatient harshness. Others in the audience began to talk amongst themselves. The ladies in the back giggled again. Eliot swallowed hard, cleared his throat and started speaking.

'Yes, of course. Electricity', Eliot began again, 'is the future, ladies and gentlemen.' He ignored the frustrated grumblings of his audience and continued with his presentation from the beginning, his face a deeper shade of red than the fine tapestry hanging on the far wall. His forehead hotter than the fire that burned in the hearth beneath it.

The audience before him flickered in the gas lamps lighting the dark room, and his confidence returned as he watched their eyes shine with the purple glow of his demonstration. For he could control electricity. Just with the sound of his voice, those purple bolts would dance with the cadence of his speech. He could marvel the haughtiest of London's high society with his knowledge of this new, exciting science. If only he could keep his mind in the moment.

Another giggle came from the back of the room, and Eliot just closed his eyes and concentrated on his presentation.

The rain drenched the felt of his top hat, making it weigh heavy on his head, but Eliot couldn't bear to go back inside the dingy old church full of people. He had nothing more to say to them, especially in his shame. He had done his part of the gala. However humiliating it had been, he had got through it with a mere shred of dignity. Now this was his time, even if it was just a few stolen moments to himself. Here, alone, he could be with her at long last.

She lay in this very graveyard, and his memories of her smile and her voice assaulted his mind, but he didn't shake them away this time. His new wife, still inside with the others, chatted away. She was a fine woman, really, but she wasn't Deirdre. No one compared to Deirdre. The tragedy of her loss only served to strengthen his love for her, but it was an impossible love. The worst and most wondrous kind. Chloe, his new wife, tried her best, but he couldn't give himself to her in the way he knew he should. It wasn't for lack of trying, but their souls didn't connect in the way his would always be connected to Deirdre. It had been two years since her death. Childbirth had left him a new father and a widower all at once.

Chloe was a good mother to Hope, who looked more and more like Deirdre with every passing day, and now Chloe, too, was pregnant with their very own child, due within the month, but he could not find the joy a man should feel with a pending arrival. Everything since Deirdre's passing had been grey, as grey as the dark rain clouds covering the moon. He caught the barest glimpse of it now and again, when it would peek out from behind the clouds, gracing the sad night with its hopeful light. Full tonight, just like the night she had left him alone in this darkness of life. Just like the night of their first kiss in the rain.

The pain of her loss hit his heart and he gasped for breath, exhaling a fine mist into the darkness. He had held her as she took her last breath, covered in blood from the waist down. Hope had wailed as the midwife tried to soothe her, as if she knew her mother lay dying. As if she somehow knew it was her fault just for being born. And Eliot had held Deirdre, her blood on his hands and tears of regret filling his vision. 'Care for her,' Deirdre had said, and Eliot blinked the tears away. Just four more words escaped her lips: 'Kiss me, my love.'

And he did. He kissed her with all the life and love inside him, willing it to be enough to save her, but she exhaled her last breath between his lips. She went limp in his arms, and he cried out in that dank room, scaring his new daughter into momentary silence. Those few seconds of quiet, after his wail faded and before Hope cried anew, haunted him. For Deirdre's heart lie still beneath her breast. Her breath came no more. That awful second of silence filled every moment from that one to this.

'Just one more kiss,' he whispered into the rain. 'I would give my life just to hold her one last time, to kiss her one last time.' His voice was barely audible between the wind and the rain and the din wafting out from the church, but he said the words again, as if by repeating them he could will it to be so.

He turned his collar up to the wind and shoved his hands in his pockets. Just a quick visit, he thought as he moved towards the marble headstones stretched out behind the church. The heavy fog suspended near the ground swirled around his ankles as he walked. He needn't look at the engraved names, for he could find her grave blindfolded.

His shoes squished in the mud as he approached the over-grown grave, sinking into the earth with each step. The quiet night screamed in his ears, reminding him of that horrible night two years ago. From here, he could no longer hear the din of the gala back at the church. Only the hollow sound of raindrops on the rim of his top hat filled the void as he knelt down on to the soft earth. He didn't care about getting his fine suit dirty, not now. He wept there, in silence at first, taking his hat into his hands and lifting his face up to the grey night. The cool rain mixed with the hot tears on his cheek, masking his grief, but no one saw. He cried to God. He cried to the stars, their light hidden by the grey clouds just as the dank earth hid her light, took her light away from him and the world.

He put his hat down on her tombstone and kneeled before it, pushing his hands into the soft earth covering her grave, as if he could reach down and pull her back into his life. He so longed to be with her, even if it meant his own death.

'Will this torment never end?' he asked the night. Even after so much time and another wife, the pain of her loss tore at his shattered heart. He longed to be unconscious. Sleep offered the only reprieve from memories, regret and the endless questions of what could've been if he had only done something differently. If only they had not made love on that particular night, she would not have got pregnant, then Hope would never have been born. But then he wouldn't have Hope, but he would still have her. How could he lament even one night with her? Every time they had made love, it had been pure magic, full of joy, desire and ecstasy. A true union of heart and body and soul. How could so much joy turn into unending pain?

'Please help me,' he whispered down to her grave. 'Please save me from this empty life. Please release me from this chasm of regret.'

He covered his face with his muddied hands and wept. His suit, soaked through with rain, began to chill him, but he did not budge from that spot so near to her. Here, he felt close to her, and that, at least, provided some comfort. He wept.

'Eliot?'

Eliot sat up, eyes wide. He looked around, but saw no one. 'I'm going mad,' he said, running his muddied hands through his salt-and-pepper hair. He must be quite a sight out there, wet and smeared with mud. How would he explain any of this to the party? How could he return in this state, especially after his humiliating performance that evening. He'd be the laughing stock of the scientific community. A true mad scientist. No, he would just go home and send the coach back for Chloe with a message that he had fallen ill, for he had been gone far too long already. They must be wondering where he had got to, and he could not explain his state.

The voice came again. 'Eliot, I'm here.'

It was her voice. Deirdre. He'd know it anywhere, but that was impossible.

'Now look here!' Eliot demanded, standing up and wiping his tears away with fierce, angry hands. His mud-soaked trousers stuck to his knees as he looked around, but still, he saw no one, though the scent of her perfume permeated his nostrils.

'I am truly mad! But, no. A madman doesn't know he's mad. Surely that is worth something. I will be all right. I just need to get out of this cemetery . . . and stop talking to myself!'

The mist at his feet began to swirl in a most unnatural way. First just near the ground, but then it twisted around his legs and up his torso. Eliot caught his breath as he watched the fog rise around him.

'Eliot. I'm here, my love.'

'Who's there!' Eliot spun around, first to the left, then the right. The mist continued to rise around him until it started taking a definite human shape. Although not a religious man, Eliot crossed himself and backed away from the grave. He turned to go, wanting to run, but Deirdre stood there, blocking his way. Transparent at first, but as he gaped at her in wonder, the vision became opaque.

'Dear God!'

'Do not be afraid, my love,' she said, reaching out to him. He recoiled from the thing's touch, but the pained look on her face at his reaction warmed his heart. It was his Deirdre after all, and in that moment, he didn't care how or why or anything. She stood before him once again and nothing else mattered.

'Deirdre?' Caution permeated his whisper, not out of fear that she truly stood before him, but out of fear that she did not.

'Yes, love. Oh! How I've missed you.'

The night seemed to brighten around her. The pale figure caught the moonlight, and she almost glowed. Perhaps his love for her shone in the night, and she reflected his love like the full moon reflected the sun. She was as beautiful as he remembered. No, actually, her beauty exceeded even that of his memory.

She moved closer to him, and this time he did not recoil. Reaching out, she touched his cheek and he tilted his head into her hand. Cold, but solid. The night air caught the tears on his cheeks, stinging. Not wasting another moment, he grabbed her around the waist and pulled her tightly against him, kissing her again in the rain. Her cold, hard lips softened as his love warmed them, and she melted against him. He breathed her in, her scent so familiar even after all this time.

'Oh, my love,' he whispered into her mouth. 'How is this possible?'

'Does it matter?'

'Not in the slightest.' He forced himself to stop smiling so he could kiss her again. Their arms surrounded one another, each desperate in their embrace.

She withdrew and slipped her hands beneath the silk lapels of his coat, running her hands along his chest, up to his shoulders, pushing the tails off. He let go of her for a second, just enough to let his black dinner jacket fall into the mud, and then encircled her waist again with renewed passion. She pressed her hips into his, and his eagerness met hers, pushing his erection against her soft stomach.

'How can this be real?'

'Shhhhh. Just be here with me now. Don't worry about the future. We're here together now, and we're in love and it's beautiful.'

He devoured her mouth anew, kissing her with more passion then he ever had before. Grasping her thin frame with the desperation of someone who knew it would be over too soon, for it always was. Her breasts pressed against his chest and he hardened further. So long the memories of their love had haunted him, and now, despite all impossibilities, he held her in his arms once more. He knew that he must be dreaming, but it was so lucid, so very real he did not care. He never wanted to wake up. He just wanted to stay in this moment for ever, locked in this kiss in the rain.

Passion like he hadn't felt since before she died, since their last embrace, filled him from head to toe. His entire body sang with desire for her, and all his senses heightened to his surroundings. He heard the leaves rustle in the wind. He heard the drops of rain hit the tops of the granite gravestones in repeated dull thuds – Pit. Pat. Pit. Pat. Pit. Pat. He heard the birds in the trees, tweeting the glory of his love for her, and hers for him, in the darkness of this night.

Then everything else fell away – every sound, every smell, every sight – until nothing remained but the two of them together. His breath warmed her cheek, her neck, her arm, as he worked his kisses down her body, slipping the white satin nightgown off her shoulder. She gasped, breathless, and his hungry mouth found her full breast. Its nipple hardened beneath his encircling tongue.

'Oh, Eliot,' she breathed. 'How I've missed you, love.'

He cupped and caressed her other breast as his tongue continued to stimulate the first. She arched her back into him as his warm tongue swirled and sucked and nibbled, enticing her yearning for him.

He slid the nightgown down further, past her fleshy belly, a perfect, shallow hill that rose and fell between her slender hips. His kisses continued exploring down her torso, and he let the nightgown fall into a puddle of satiny moonlight at her feet, freeing his hands to caress the soft skin of her back as his kisses bathed her in love. He looked up at her, and her smile lit up his insides, as if she had infused him with his own electric experiments. Those purple lightning bolts reached from where he saw her through his very own eyes and sparked down his entire body, stimulating every part of him. Although naked on this cold, autumn London night, she didn't shiver. Her flesh did not show a trace of chill. Rather it was sweet and soft and smooth and supple and beautiful and pale, silvery in the light of the moon.

He crouched down and licked the inside of her knees, making her giggle, then traced his tongue up her inner thigh. She spread her legs, eager to be tasted. As he reached her wet lips, she angled her hips forward, allowing him easier access, and he licked, tasting her again, finally. He had given up all hope of ever tasting her sweet nectar again, for how could he have? But that delicious flavour once again delighted his tongue. Circling, circling, circling around her clitoris until her elation caused her to cry out, frightening away the birds in the nearby tree. Their wings flapping against the wind; their fear of the sudden sound taking them far away.

He continued in his task and brought her again, her juices drenching his chin. The ambrosia slid down his throat, his cheeks, his neck, and he revelled in the heaven of her savour.

Her hands putting gentle pressure on his shoulders urged him to stand. He kissed her again, full on the lips, pulling her nakedness into him.

She tasted herself on his tongue, and she moaned, the sound muffled by his mouth, by the envelopment of his kisses.

'I need you,' she whispered.

He pulled back from her just enough to unbutton his shirt as she worked on his trousers. His eyes never left hers, and he didn't even blink. He drank in every curve, every pore, every glorious muted colour of her in that grey night. Pure joy filled his soul as he gazed at the miracle before him. Never again did he think he would feel such elation, such love, for all that had died with her, but here they were: together.

She slipped each button of his trousers through its hole with one hand while the other caressed his erection beneath, screaming for release. With a quick slide of her hands around his sides, she pushed the trousers over his hips, and they fell down past his knees, exposing his engorged shaft to the cool night air. He stepped out of his crumpled pants, knowing he would be buried deep inside her just moments from now. But instead, she knelt in the mud, eager to return his gift. There in the rain, as it baptized both of them anew in their love, she took his hardness full into her hands and squeezed. Her touch, unlike any other before or since, occupied his every sense on this magical night.

He had indeed been given a gift. Although the questions of how and why would pop into his head, he'd just push them away because he didn't care. This was his reality, right now in this moment, and he would not miss a second of it.

She licked along the length of his erection and swirled her tongue around the tip, wetting it. Then, taking him completely in her mouth, his eyes rolled back in his delight. Feeling her lips encircle him almost proved more than he could bear after so long, but he waited and held back. She plunged to the base of him and then slowly withdrew, flicking her tongue back and forth along the underside, driving him wild with her skill. With her hand, she followed close behind her mouth, so as not to leave an inch of him unloved, she squeezed him and then slid him into her mouth again. Up and down and up and down and up and down.

He grabbed on to the headstone and braced himself, focusing on the moment, on the cold granite biting into his hand, willing himself not to come. Not yet. Still so much more to enjoy. So much more in this moment. In this beautiful moment of love and desire. But as she sucked and twirled and plunged, even the rough granite could not keep him at bay much longer. Placing his hands on her shoulders, he pushed her away.

'Now, my love. Let me have you now.' Fire burned in his eyes as he lifted her up to him.

'Always,' she said.

She kissed him gently, tenderly, before laying back on her own grave, legs spread and ready for him. He knelt before his goddess and positioned himself between her supple thighs. Priming her, he rubbed the tip of himself up and down her wetness. Up and down her swollen lips, so ready for him. Then, with one determined push, he slid inside her, and she gasped as he filled her with his love. Once again.

After all these years, they were one again. Laying on top of her, he enveloped her lips in a deep kiss as he thrust into her. Sliding together. She angled her hips up into him, meeting every thrust. And they moved together. And they moved faster. And they moved in their love. And they moved in their ecstasy. Crashing into her again and again. Her warmth surrounding him. Her body writhing beneath him. Her lips devouring his. And he crashed and he moved and he ground into her.

She clutched his back in her fervour, pushing herself into him, remembering that mounting feeling of the flesh. Knowing that she would soon climax right there in the dark graveyard. And he didn't stop. He ground into her and thrust deeper, pulling his knees up to gain more leverage. She pressed herself against his thrusting pubis and the pressure grew inside her. The pleasure spread through her belly and over her breasts. The ecstasy building as it rose and filled her entire body, until her frame could hold no more pleasure, and it burst forth out of her throat in a cry of jubilation. Loud and explosive bliss filled the dank cemetery. And he still didn't stop until she cried out again and again, then with a shudder that rippled through his entire body, exploded inside her. His vocalized delight mingling with hers in the dark night.

Then they lay in each other's arms, spent. He looked into those beautiful green eyes as she smiled up at him. Those eyes contained his very soul.

'Deirdre, I love you.'

He rested his head against her breast and held her close to him. She kissed the top of his head and said, 'My sweet Eliot. I love you, too.' Then, still inside her, perfectly content, he started to drift off to sleep. Naked, with his world in his arms on her grave. Impossible, but true.

Then in his dream – for this all must be a dream – she began to sink back into the earth. But the fear of losing her again did not distress him, for he would not lose her again. He would never let her go. Instead, he held on tight and descended into the dank earth with her. He would not let her go into the night alone, not this time. If she were to return to death, so would he.

'Eliot!' Chloe's voice shouted, echoed by the others', over and over as they called out into the darkness in the wee morning hours, the moon their only source of light. The rain had stopped and the bright orb peeked out from behind the black clouds above them, lighting the edges in a silver outline.

'Eliot? Where are you?'

'Where could he have gone?' She turned to the priest, grabbing his arm in desperation.

'Worry not, dear lady. We shall find him.'

The search party of about twenty men spread out over the dark cemetery, searching for her lost husband. Certainly he did not just leave with nary a word. How rude! She feared the worst. She knew that being so close to her grave – that woman; his obsession with that woman . . . then when he stumbled in his presentation . . . Plus he had been so melancholy of late. Yes, she feared the worst.

Father Charleston patted her hand on his arm, attempting to comfort her in her desperation.

'It will be all right, dear lady,' he repeated. 'We shall find him.'

'Thank you, Father.' But her fear remained. The baby moved inside her and she stopped short, grabbing her large belly and taking several deep breaths.

'Are you ill, my child?'

'No. It's all right, Father. Just the baby moving. It happens when I feel distress.'

'Over here!' A man's voice came from their left, deep in the graveyard, and they all rushed over to where he stood.

'Oh, my heavens!' Chloe cried and then turned into the waiting embrace of the priest, burying her face in his chest and cradling her full belly with both her arms, protecting it from this horror.

'What happened to his clothes?' one man said, looking

down at Eliot's nude, still figure. He stooped down and felt for a pulse on Eliot's wrist, his arms situated as if they were around someone, though no one lay beside him. 'Dead.'

Chloe wailed anew and held on tighter to her belly. The priest pulled her closer to him before turning and leading her away from the tragic scene, whispering words of support and comfort.

The others walked away mumbling about how they must get the police to come, and how they suspected foul play. For what other explanation could there be for leaving Eliot there on her grave, curled as if in a lover's embrace, smiling.